MESSY ROOTS

A Graphic Memoir of a Wuhanese American

LAURA GAO

with color and art assistance by Weiwei Xu

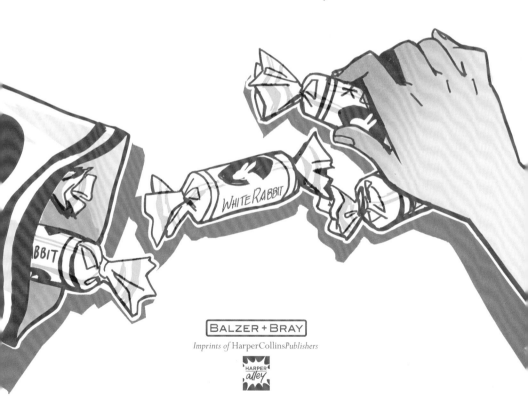

BALZER + BRAY

Imprints of HarperCollinsPublishers

HARPER
alley

This is a work of nonfiction.
Some names have been changed to protect the privacy of the individuals involved.

Balzer + Bray is an imprint of HarperCollins Publishers.

Messy Roots: A Graphic Memoir of a Wuhanese American

www.epicreads.com

Library of Congress Control Number: 2021939649
ISBN 978-0-06-306777-6 (trade bdg.) — ISBN 978-0-06-306776-9 (pbk.)

Typography by Andrea Miller and Catherine Lee
21 22 23 24 25 RTLO 10 9 8 7 6 5 4 3 2 1
❖
First Edition

To my greatest inspiration and mentor,
Ms. Alexander, for teaching me how to dream.

To Jerry, for keeping my ego in check while reviewing
this book like a true little brother.

And finally, to my parents, whom I'll always love.
I hope one day you'll read this and understand everything.

PROLOGUE

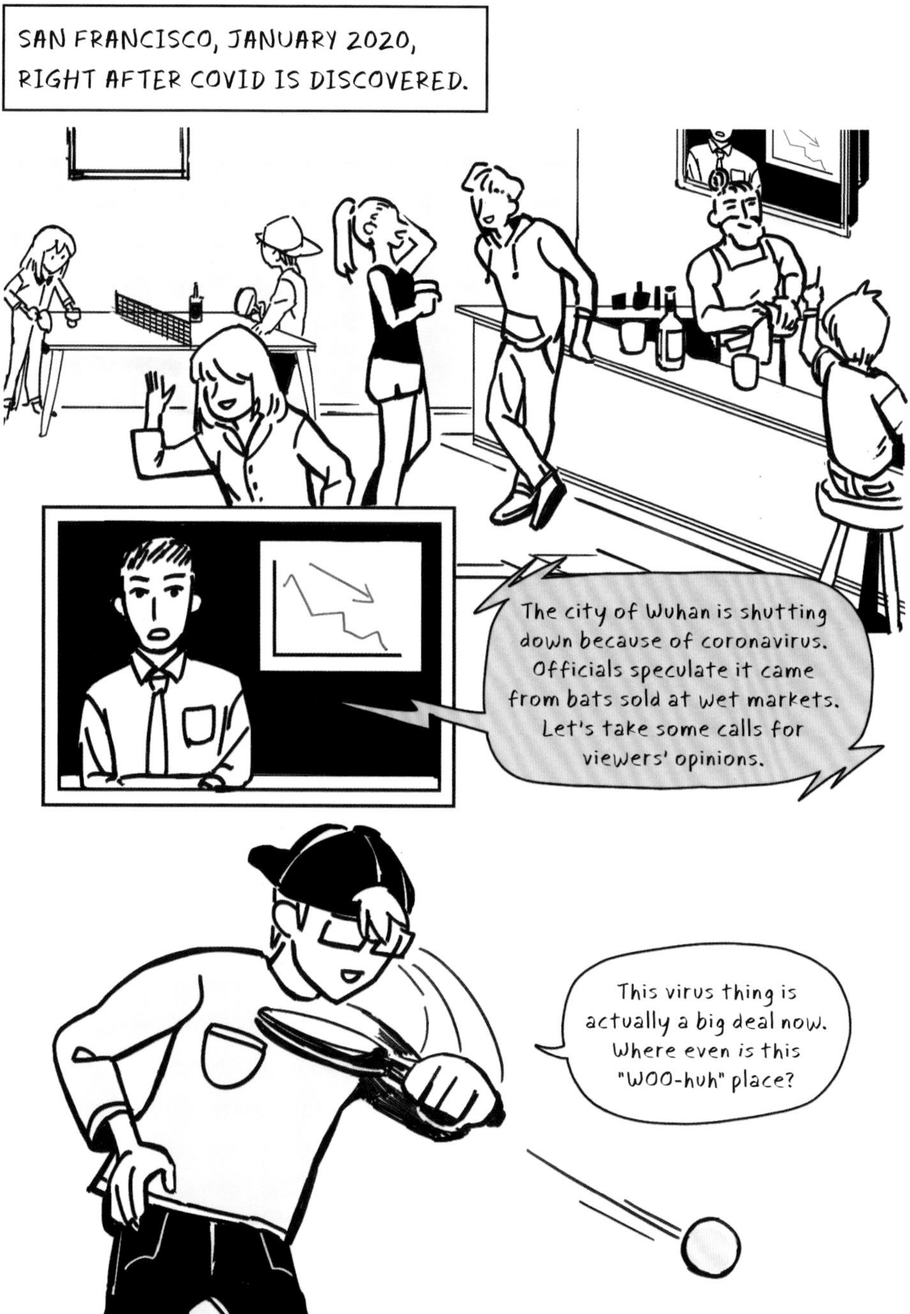

SAN FRANCISCO, JANUARY 2020, RIGHT AFTER COVID IS DISCOVERED.
The city of Wuhan is shutting down because of coronavirus. Officials speculate it came from bats sold at wet markets. Let's take some calls for viewers' opinions.
This virus thing is actually a big deal now. Where even is this "WOO-huh" place?

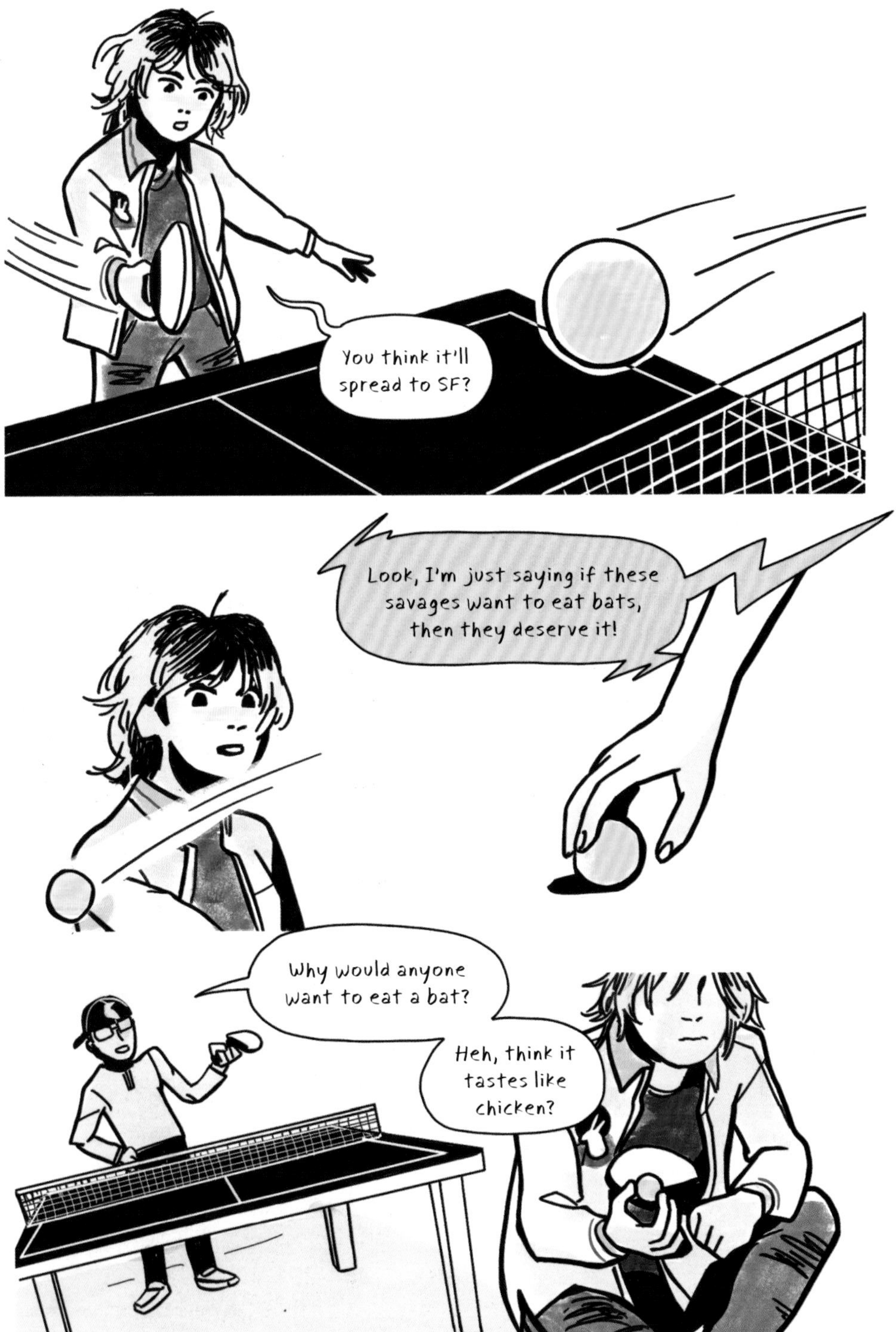
You think it'll spread to SF?
Look, I'm just saying if these savages want to eat bats, then they deserve it!
Why would anyone want to eat a bat?
Heh, think it tastes like chicken?

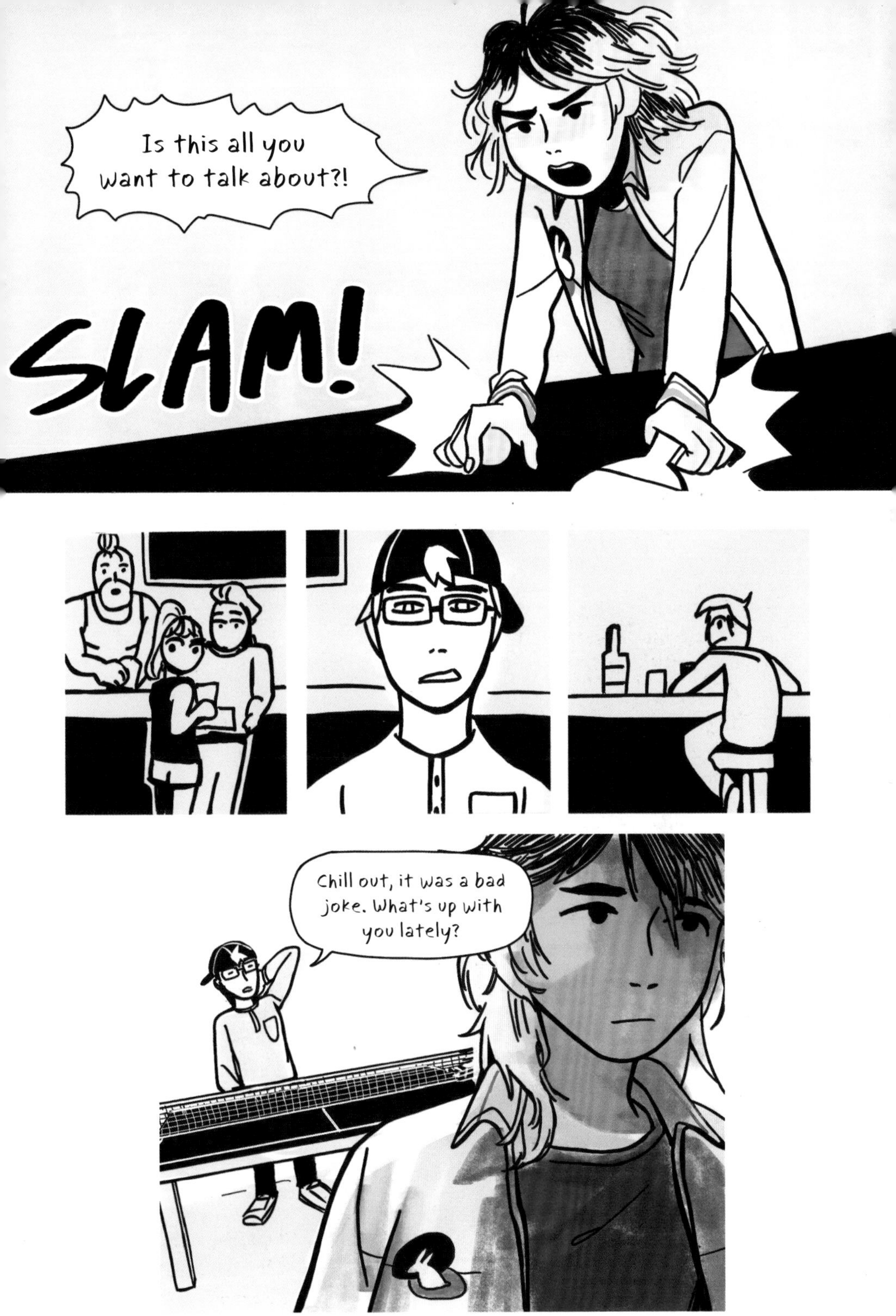
Is this all you want to talk about?!
SLAM!
Chill out, it was a bad joke. What's up with you lately?

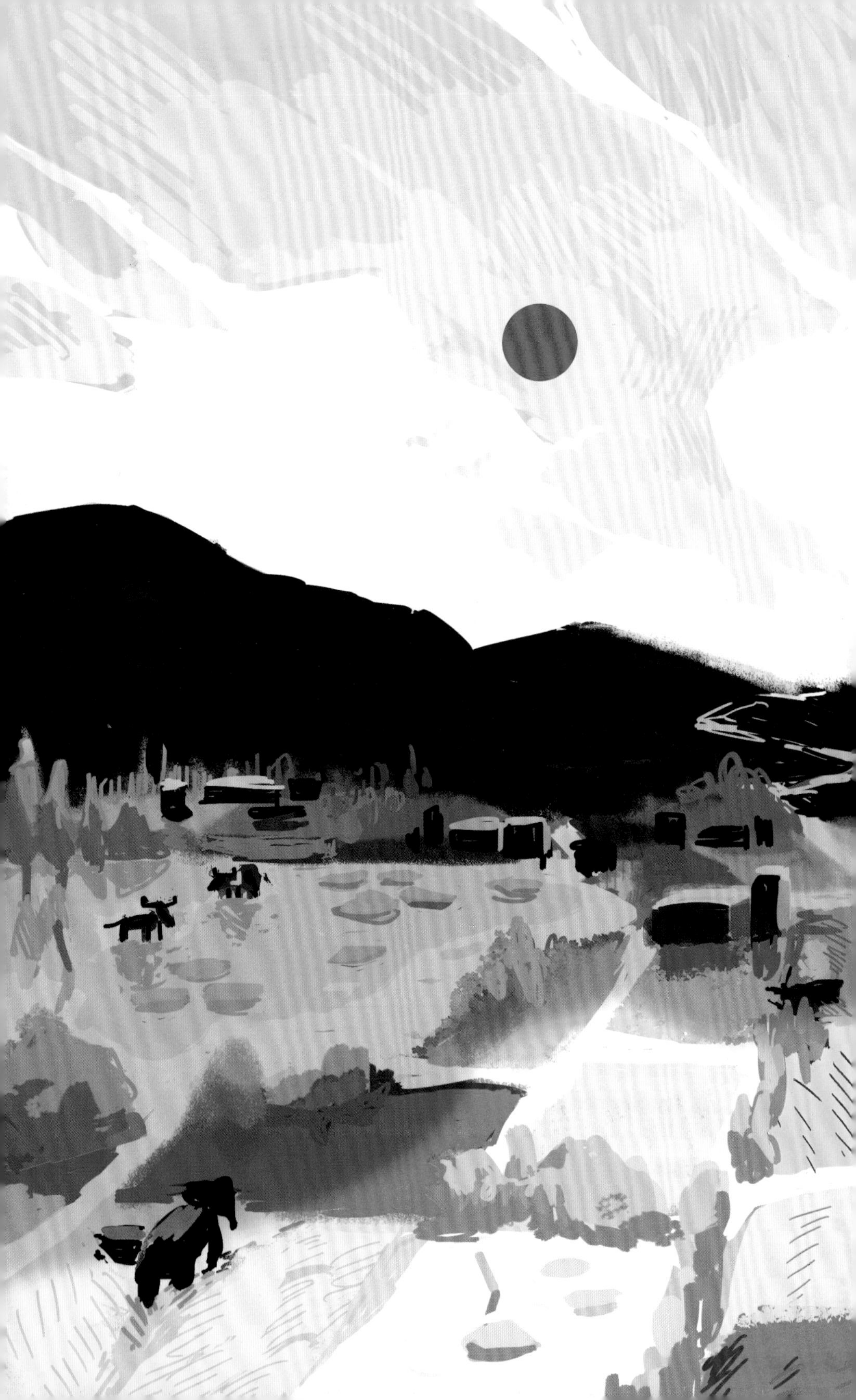

CHAPTER 1

The Wuhan I Knew

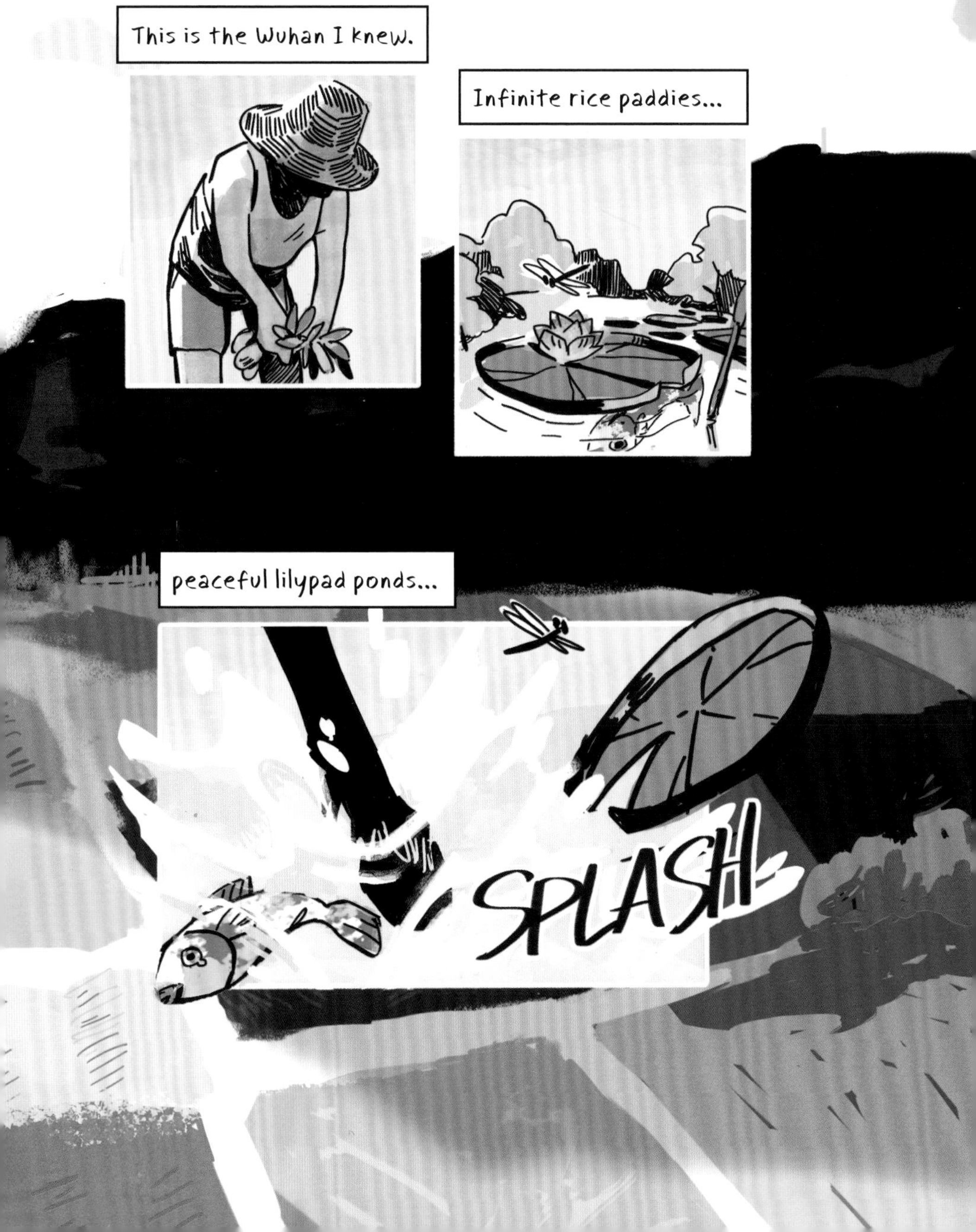
This is the Wuhan I knew.
Infinite rice paddies...
peaceful lilypad ponds...
SPLASH

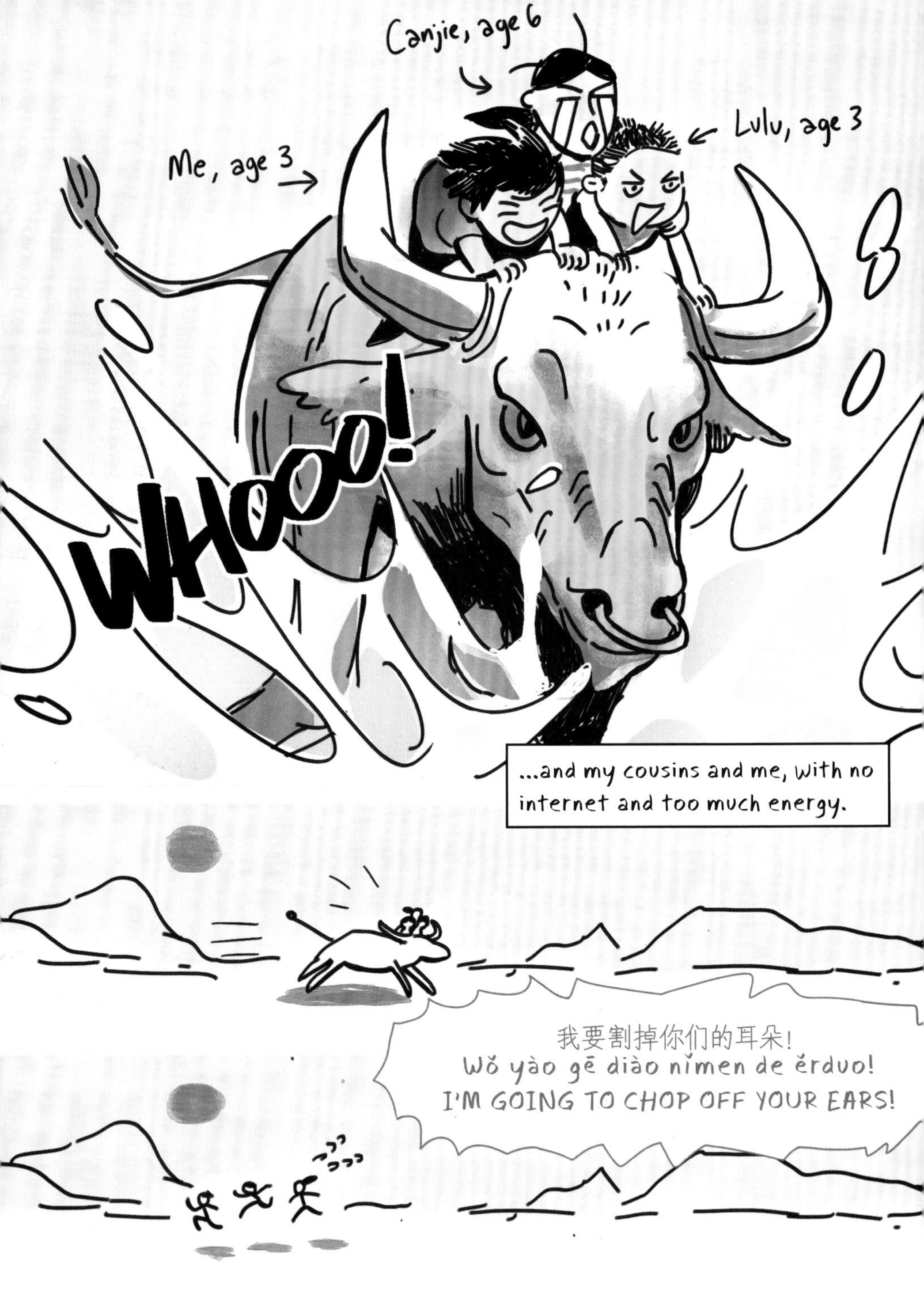
Canjie, age 6
Me, age 3
Lulu, age 3
WHOOOO!
...and my cousins and me, with no internet and too much energy.
我要割掉你们的耳朵!
Wǒ yào gē diào nǐmen de ěrduo!
I'M GOING TO CHOP OFF YOUR EARS!

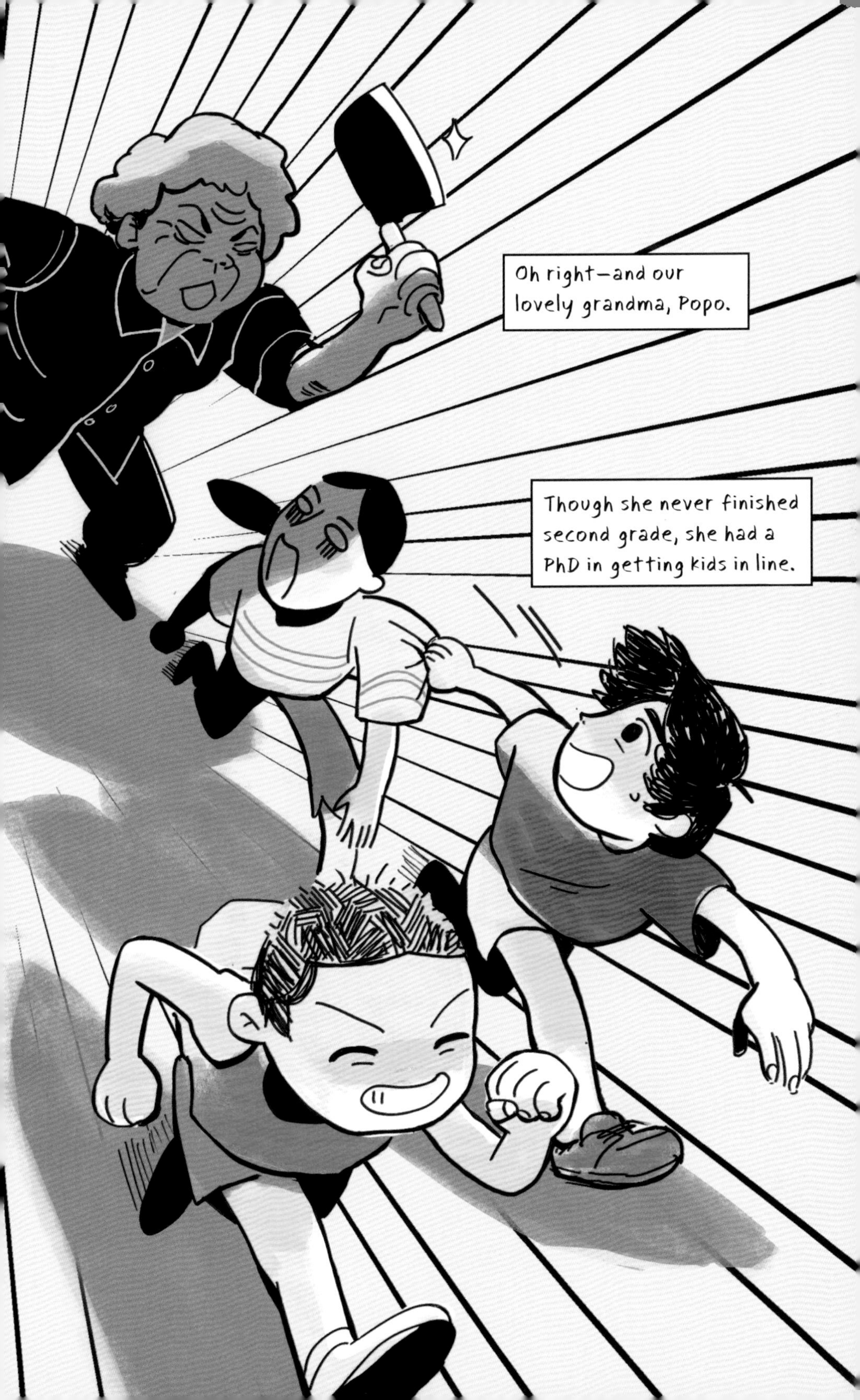
Oh right—and our lovely grandma, Popo.
Though she never finished second grade, she had a PhD in getting kids in line.

Our grandpa, Dede, toiled in the fields during the day and enjoyed a round of mahjong with a side of báijiǔ* at night.

*báijiǔ: potent Chinese liquor that puts vodka to shame

Who knew girls could be more trouble than boys?

Our ringleader was Lulu, who, despite being the youngest, had mastered the art of mischief.

Canjie, however, always tried (and failed) to be our babysitter.

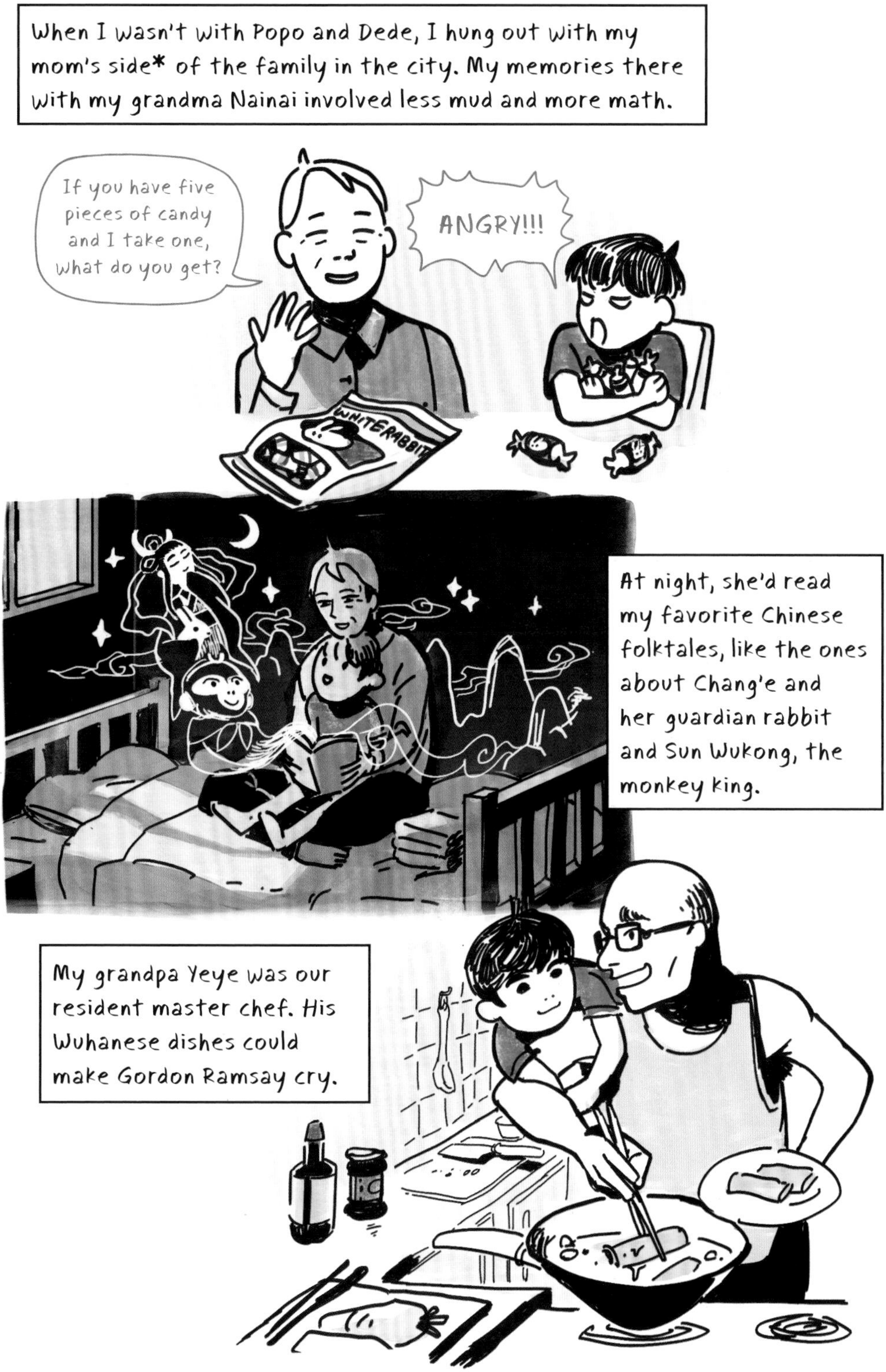
When I wasn't with Popo and Dede, I hung out with my mom's side* of the family in the city. My memories there with my grandma Nainai involved less mud and more math.
If you have five pieces of candy and I take one, what do you get?
ANGRY!!!
WHITE RABBIT
At night, she'd read my favorite Chinese folktales, like the ones about Chang'e and her guardian rabbit and Sun Wukong, the monkey king.
My grandpa Yeye was our resident master chef. His Wuhanese dishes could make Gordon Ramsay cry.

*Typically "Yeye" and "Nainai" are names for paternal grandparents, but I mixed them up early!

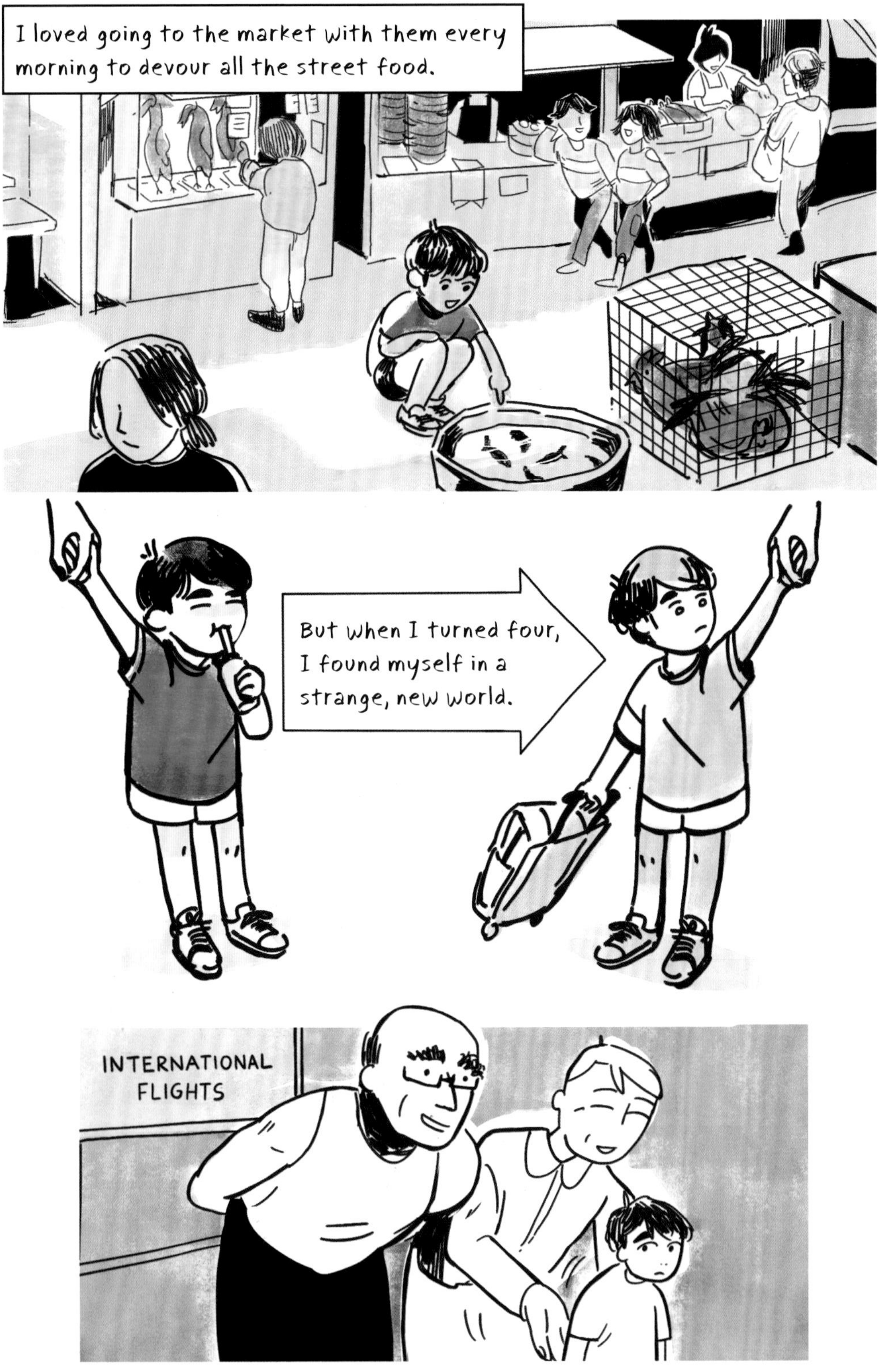
I loved going to the market with them every morning to devour all the street food.
But when I turned four, I found myself in a strange, new world.
INTERNATIONAL FLIGHTS

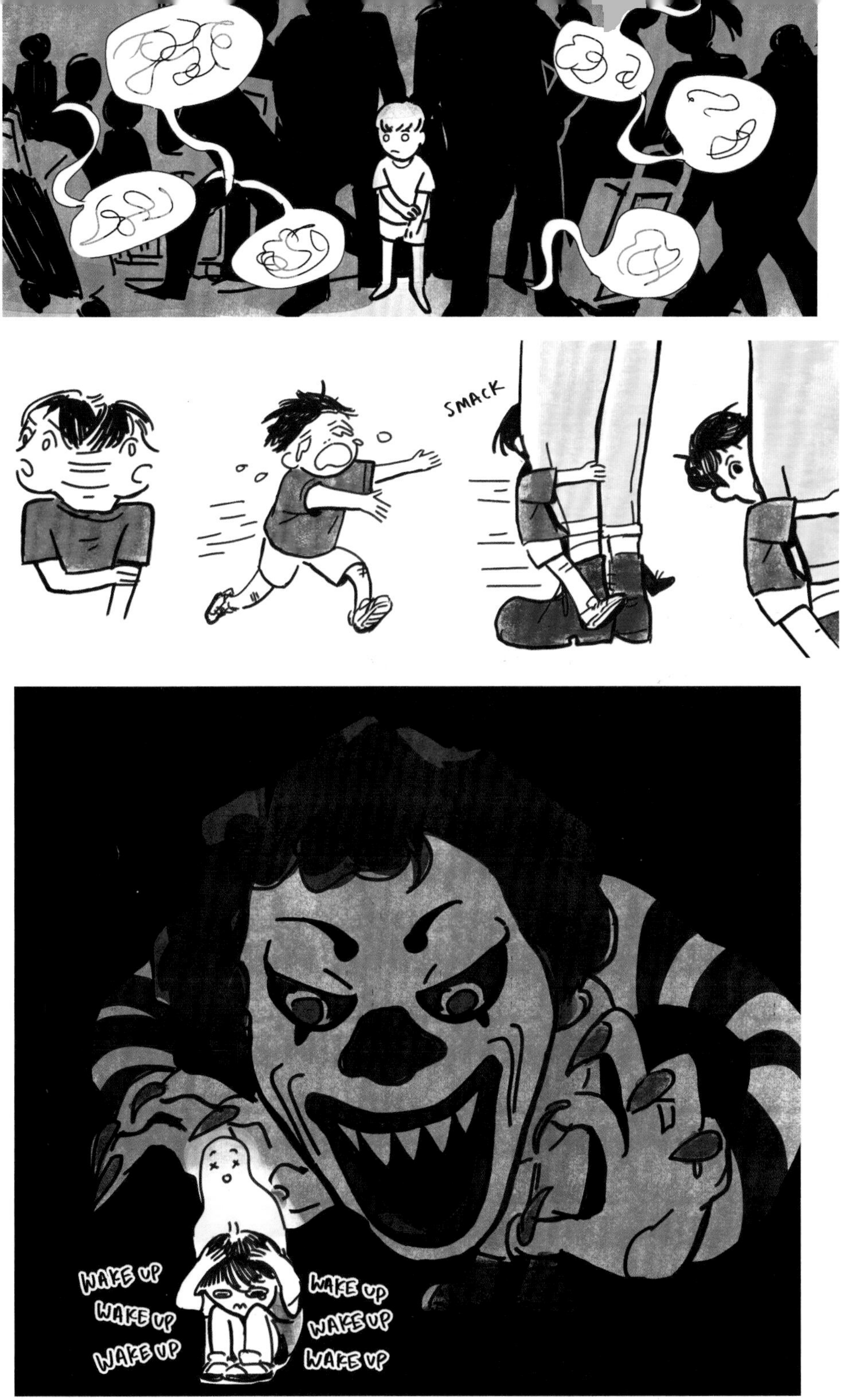
SMACK
WAKE UP
WAKE UP
WAKE UP
WAKE UP
WAKE UP
WAKE UP

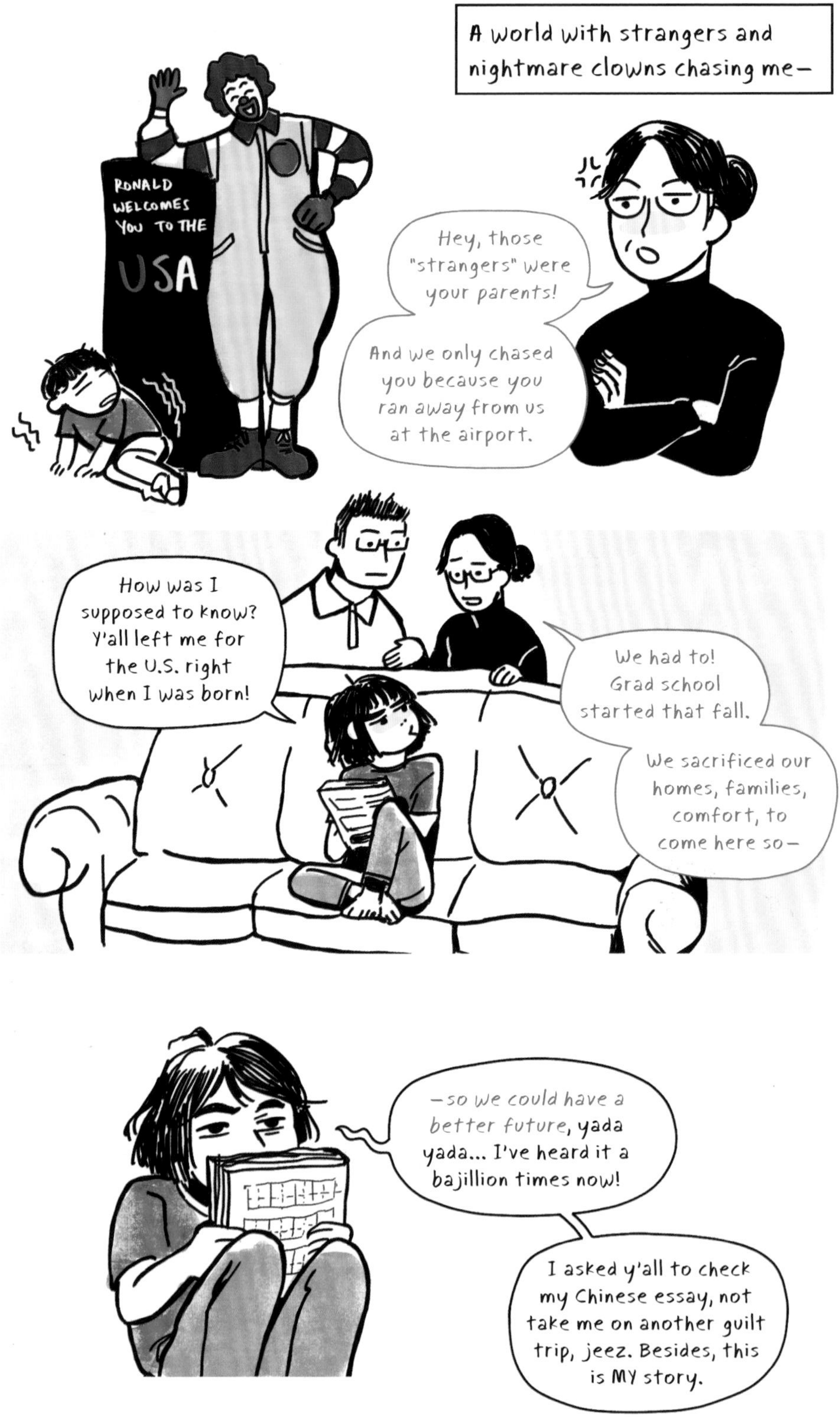
A world with strangers and nightmare clowns chasing me—
RONALD WELCOMES YOU TO THE USA
Hey, those "strangers" were your parents!
And we only chased you because you ran away from us at the airport.
How was I supposed to know? Y'all left me for the U.S. right when I was born!
We had to! Grad school started that fall.
We sacrificed our homes, families, comfort, to come here so—
—so we could have a better future, yada yada... I've heard it a bajillion times now!
I asked y'all to check my Chinese essay, not take me on another guilt trip, jeez. Besides, this is MY story.

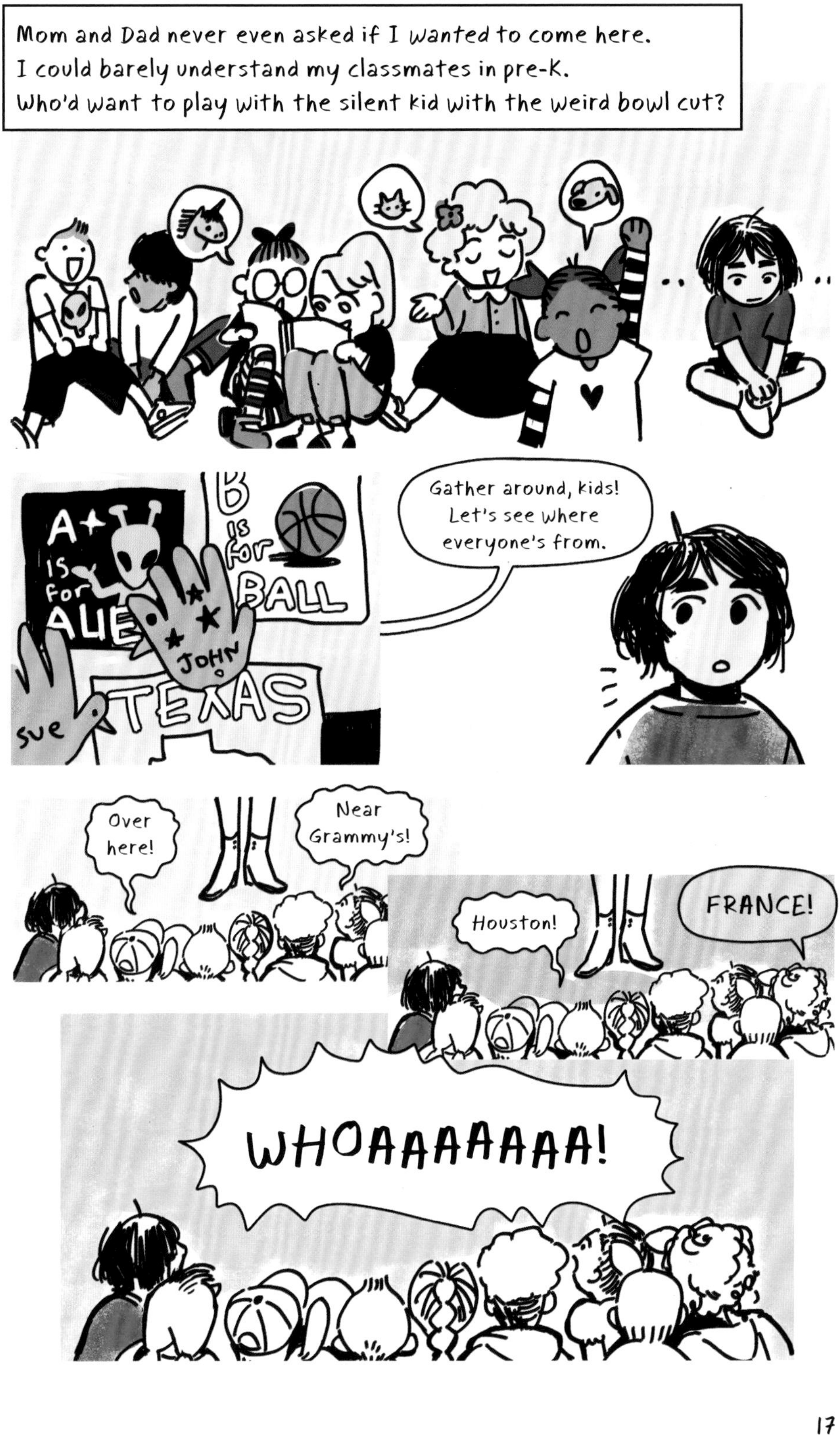
Mom and Dad never even asked if I wanted to come here.
I could barely understand my classmates in pre-K.
Who'd want to play with the silent kid with the weird bowl cut?
B is for BALL
JOHN
TEXAS
SUE
Gather around, kids! Let's see where everyone's from.
Over here!
Near Grammy's!
Houston!
FRANCE!
WHOAAAAAAAA!

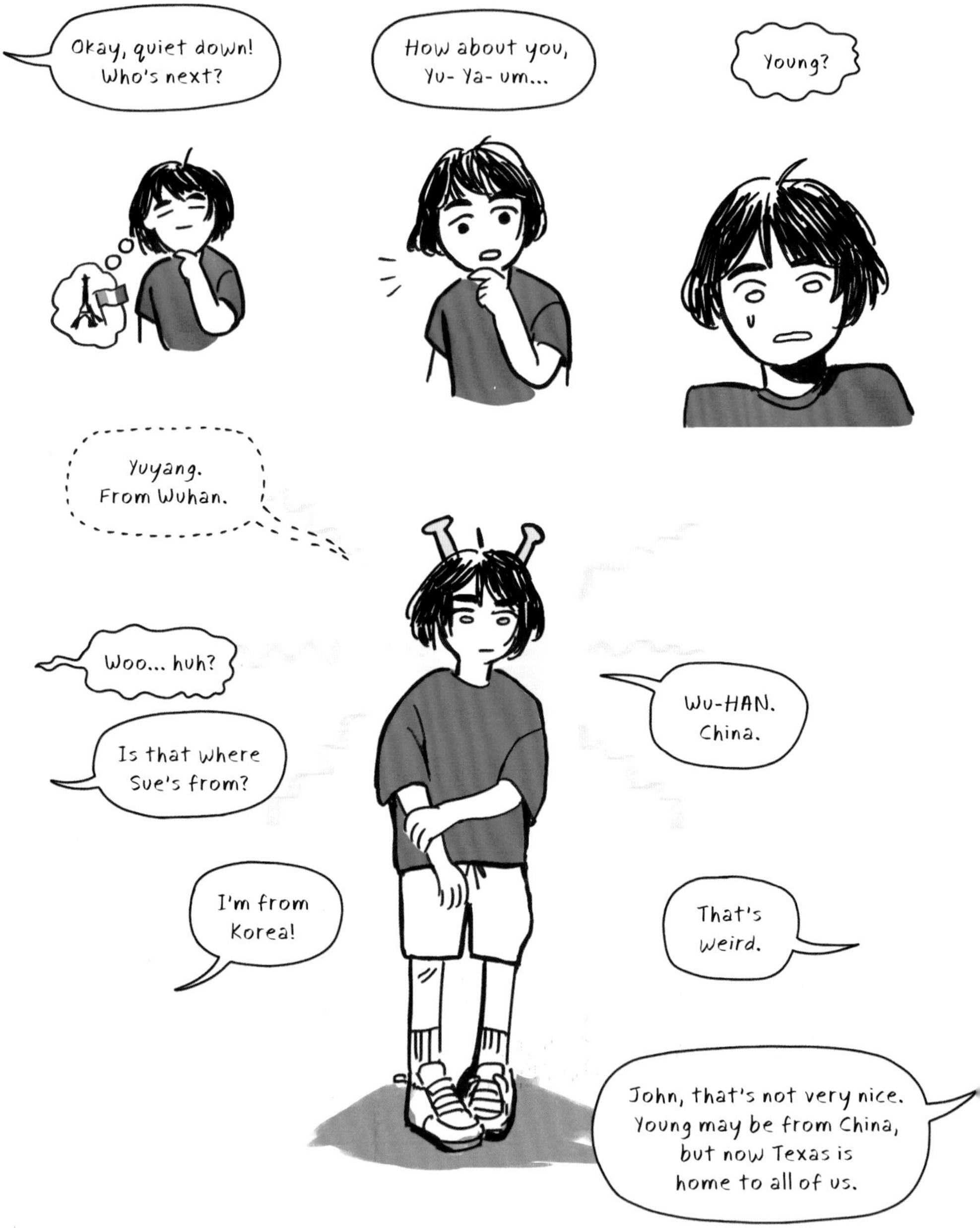
Okay, quiet down! Who's next?
How about you, Yu- Ya- um...
Young?
Yuyang. From Wuhan.
Woo... huh?
Wu-HAN. China.
Is that where Sue's from?
I'm from Korea!
That's weird.
John, that's not very nice. Young may be from China, but now Texas is home to all of us.

I barely knew how to pronounce "Texas," let alone call it my home. Wuhan was more foreign than Mars here. I wished we'd never moved so that I wouldn't have to explain myself.

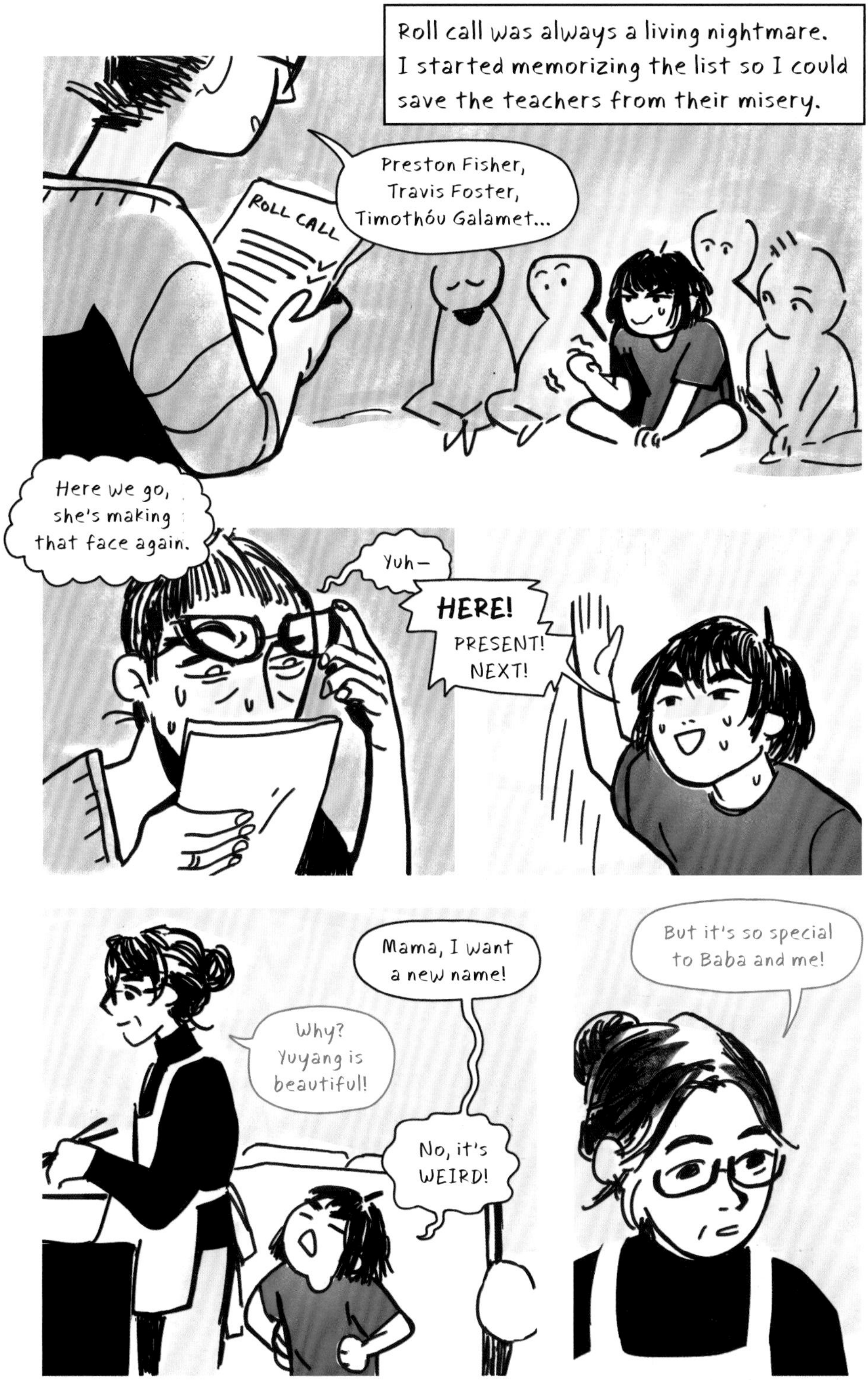
Roll call was always a living nightmare. I started memorizing the list so I could save the teachers from their misery.
ROLL CALL
Preston Fisher, Travis Foster, Timothóu Galamet...
Here we go, she's making that face again.
Yuh—
HERE!
PRESENT! NEXT!
Mama, I want a new name!
Why? Yuyang is beautiful!
No, it's WEIRD!
But it's so special to Baba and me!

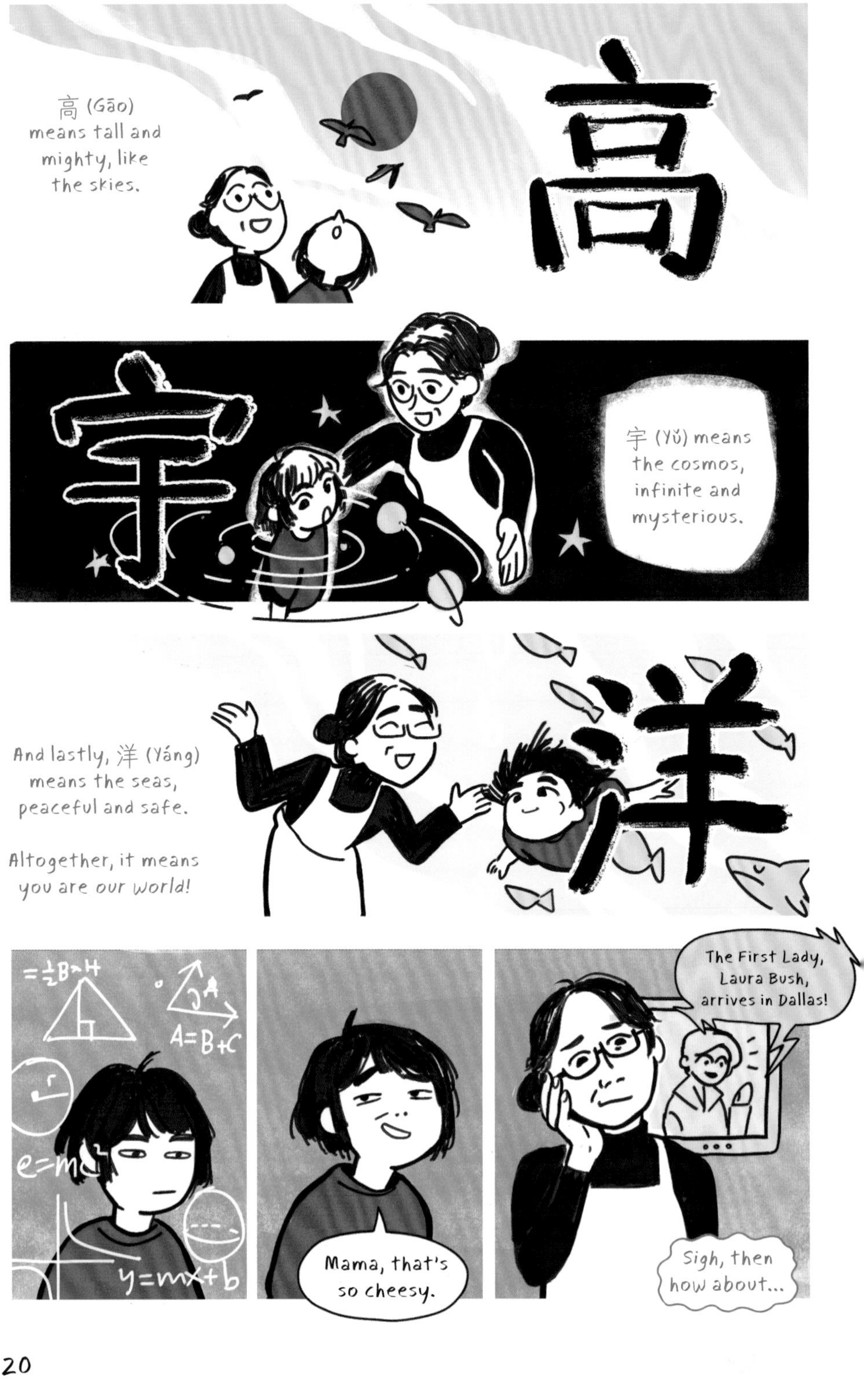

高 (Gāo) means tall and mighty, like the skies.
高
宇
宇 (Yǔ) means the cosmos, infinite and mysterious.
And lastly, 洋 (Yáng) means the seas, peaceful and safe.
Altogether, it means you are our world!
洋
= ½B×H
A=B+C
e=mc²
y=mx+b
Mama, that's so cheesy.
The First Lady, Laura Bush, arrives in Dallas!
Sigh, then how about...

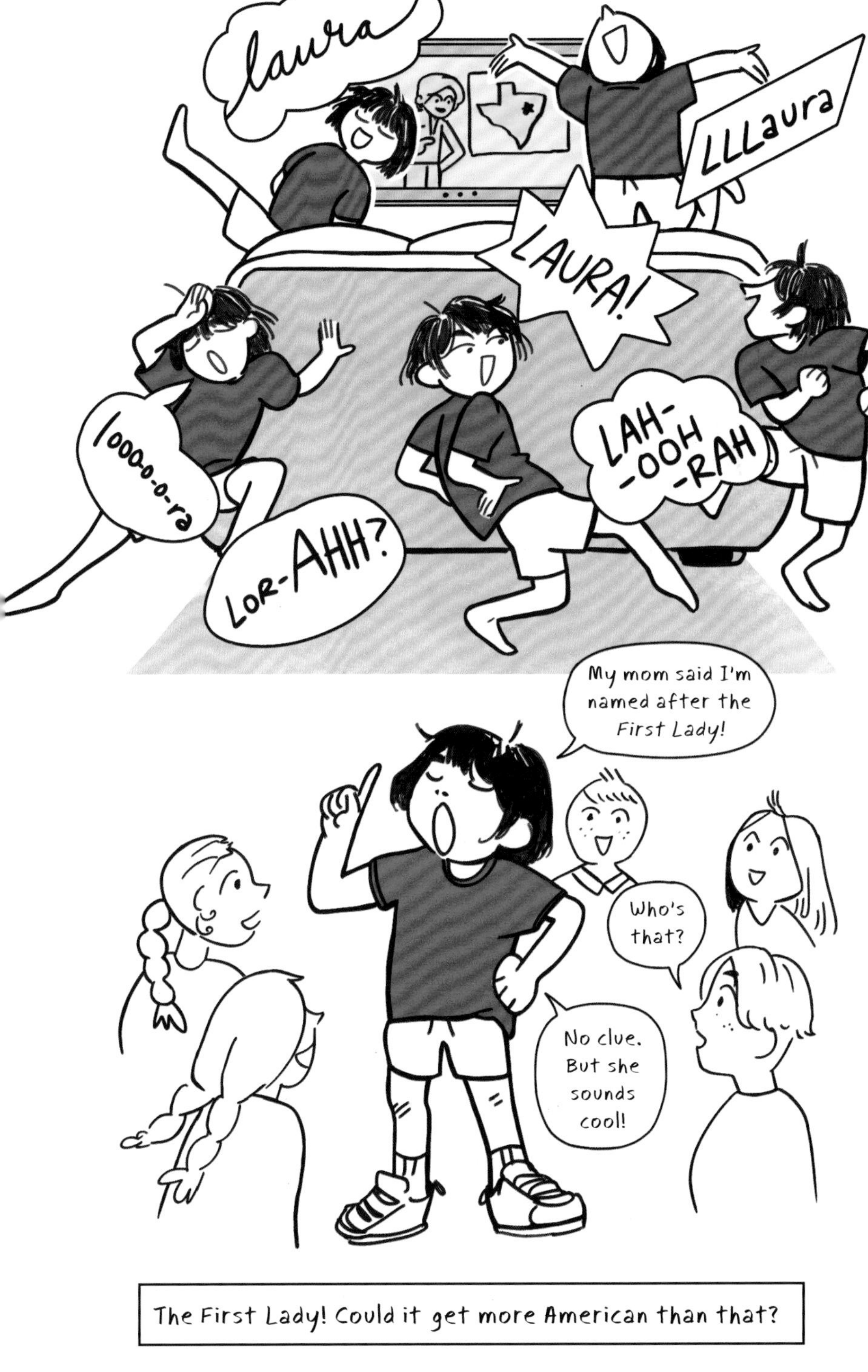
laura
LLLaura
LAURA!
looo-o-o-ra
LOR-AHH?
LAH-OOH-RAH
My mom said I'm named after the First Lady!
Who's that?
No clue. But she sounds cool!
The First Lady! Could it get more American than that?

CHAPTER 2
DISS (Deception for Immigrant Sibling Solidarity)

Rule #1:

If one of us hides something from our parents, we both hide it with our lives!

Rule #2

If one of us finds out something our parents are hiding, we must share it!

Rule #3
Snitches get stitches!

Sign here to mark your blood oath:

LAURA   JERRY

CRANBERRY JUICE

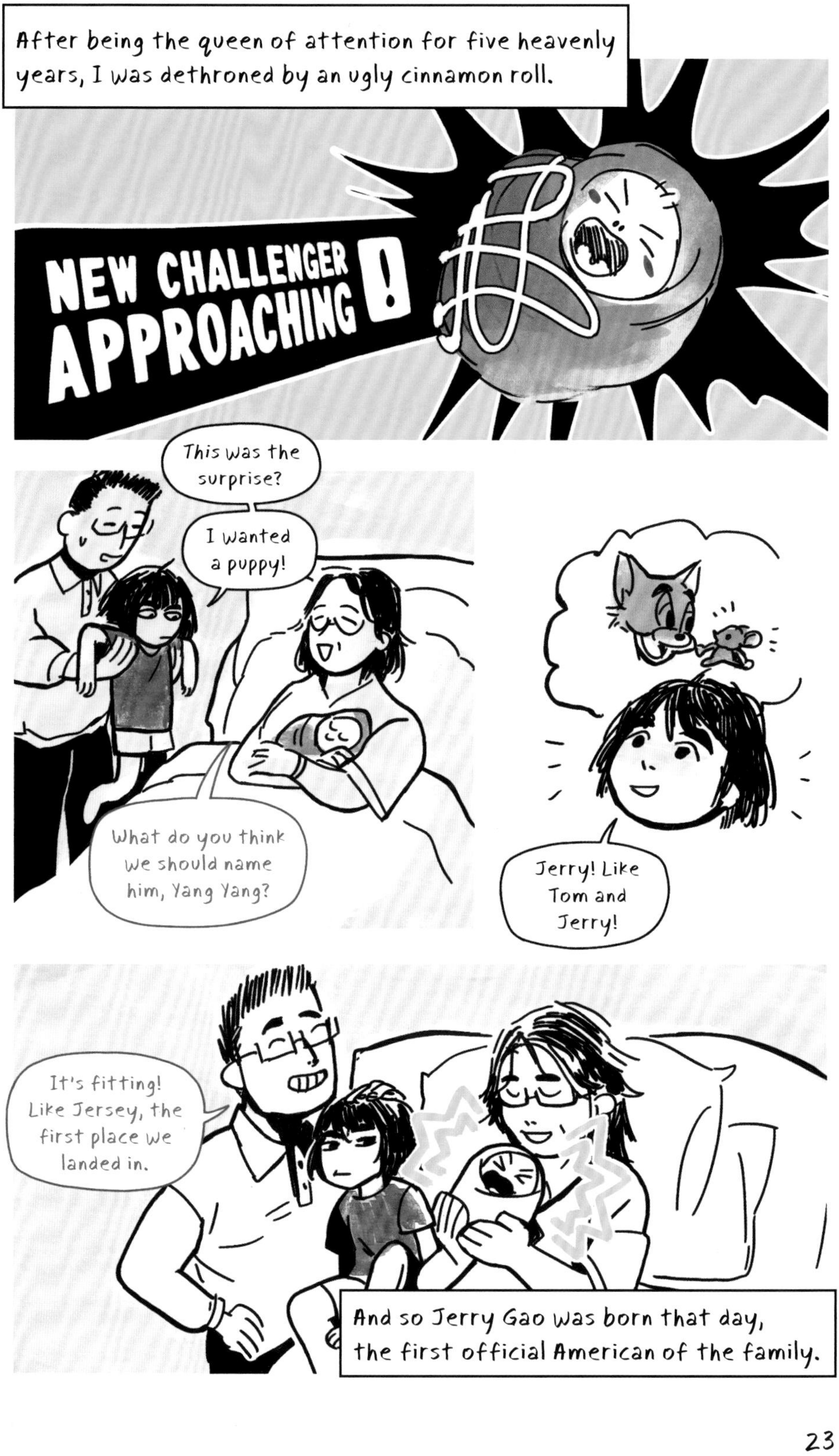
After being the queen of attention for five heavenly years, I was dethroned by an ugly cinnamon roll.
NEW CHALLENGER APPROACHING!
This was the surprise?
I wanted a puppy!
What do you think we should name him, Yang Yang?
Jerry! Like Tom and Jerry!
It's fitting! Like Jersey, the first place we landed in.
And so Jerry Gao was born that day, the first official American of the family.

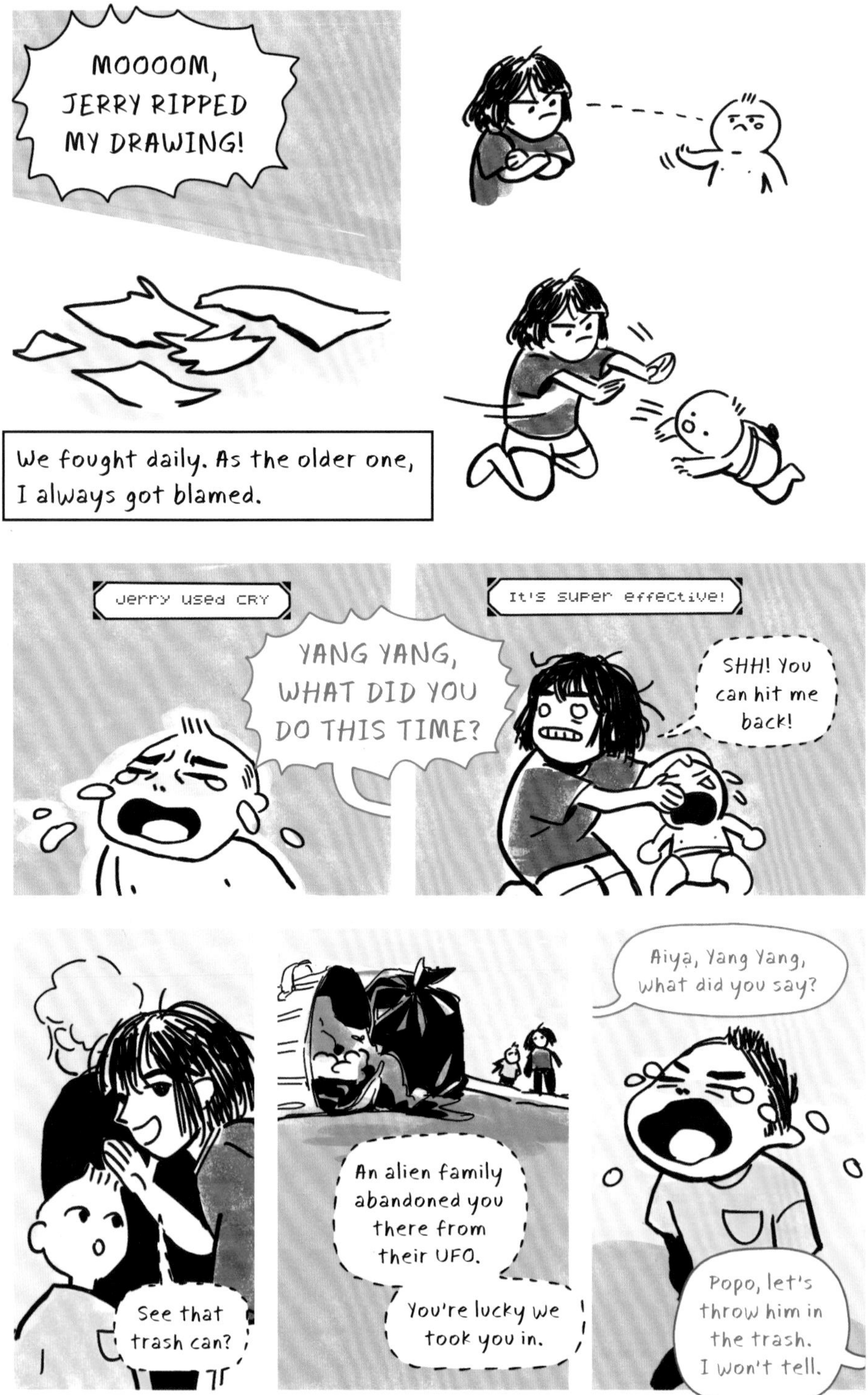

MOOOOM, JERRY RIPPED MY DRAWING!
We fought daily. As the older one, I always got blamed.
Jerry used CRY
YANG YANG, WHAT DID YOU DO THIS TIME?
It's super effective!
SHH! You can hit me back!
See that trash can?
An alien family abandoned you there from their UFO.
You're lucky we took you in.
Aiyạ, Yang Yang, what did you say?
Popo, let's throw him in the trash. I won't tell.

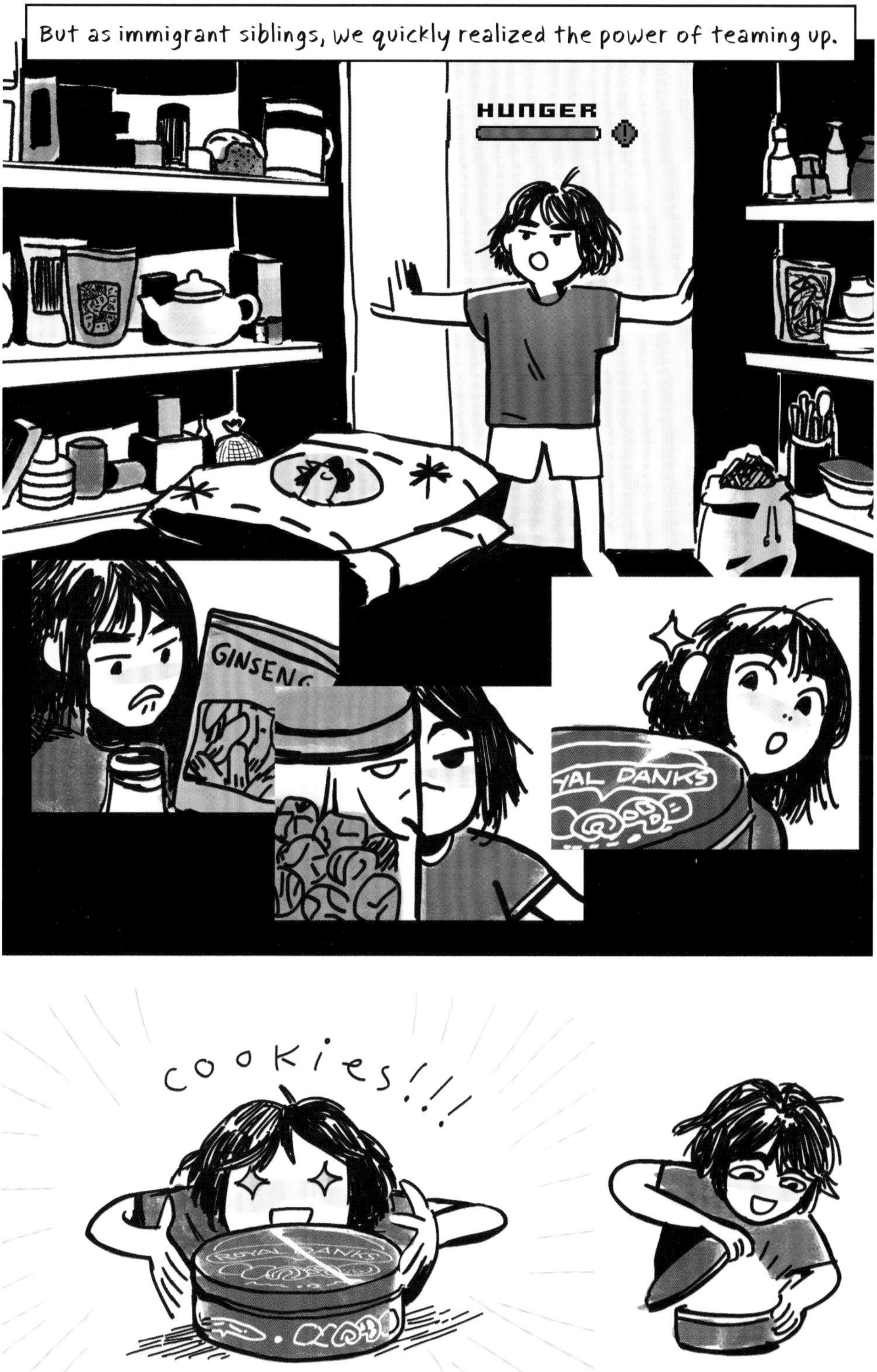
But as immigrant siblings, we quickly realized the power of teaming up.
HUNGER
GINSEN
YAL DANKS
cookies!!!

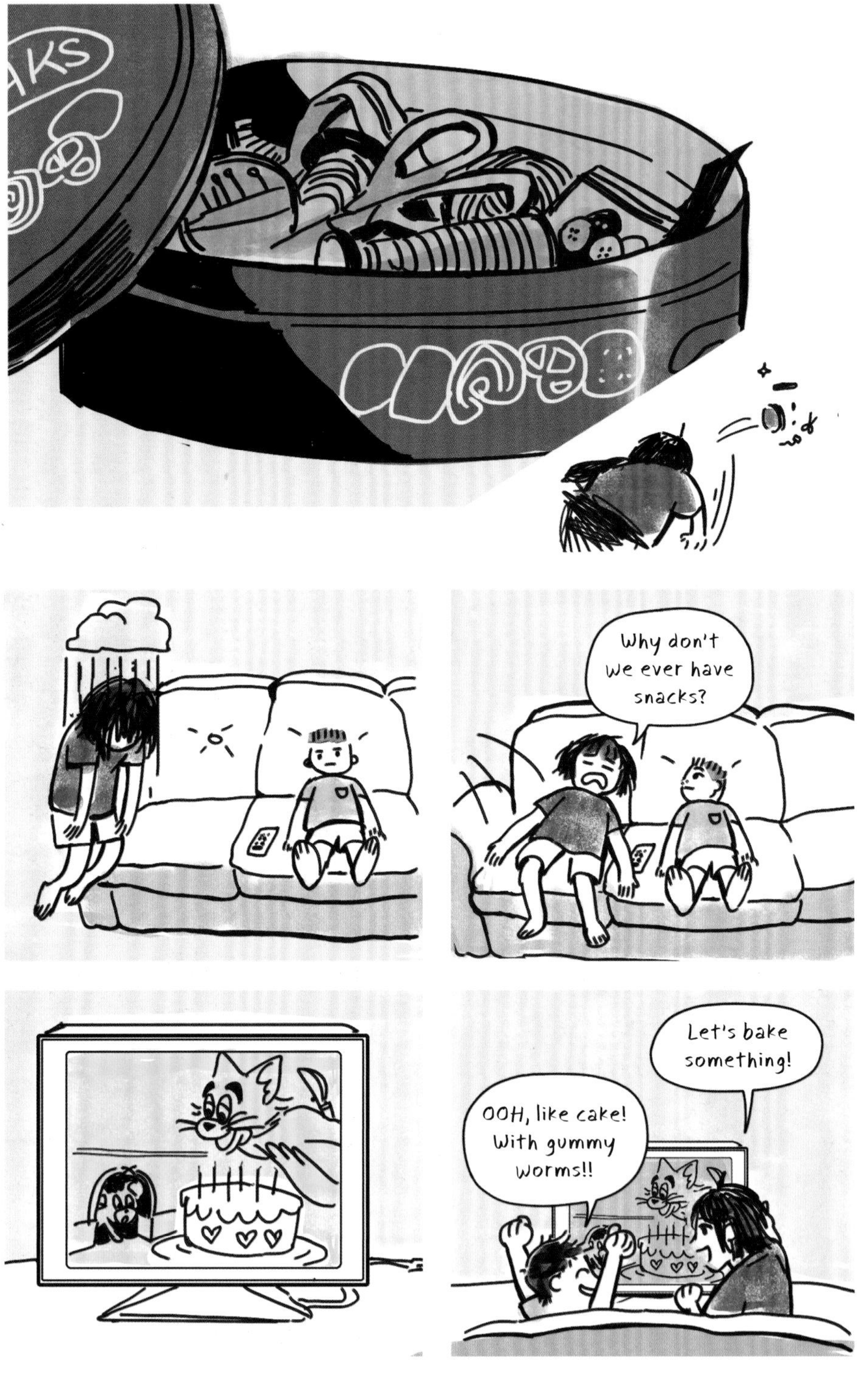
Why don't we ever have snacks?
Let's bake something!
OOH, like cake! With gummy worms!!

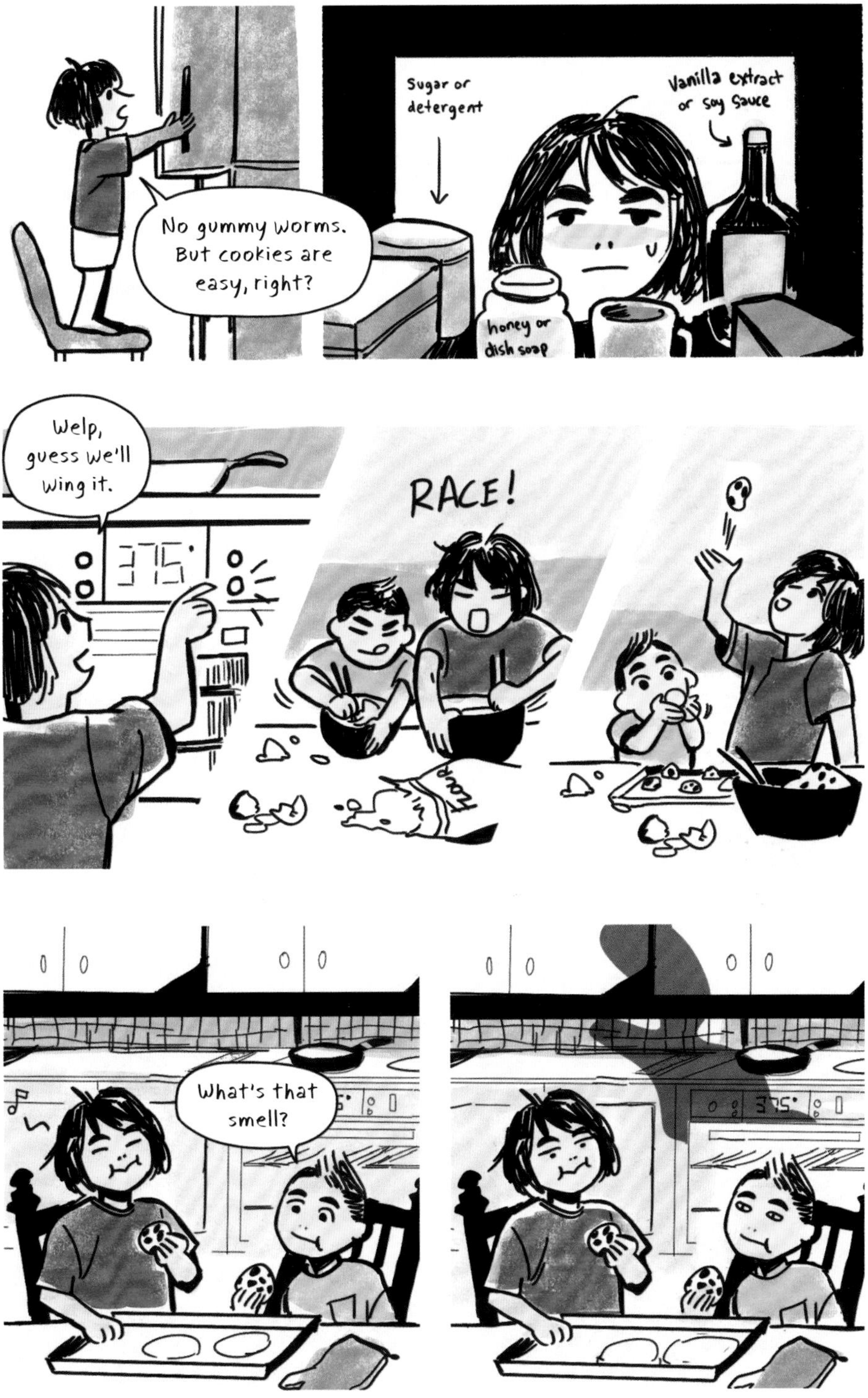
No gummy worms. But cookies are easy, right?
Sugar or detergent
Vanilla extract or soy sauce
honey or dish soap
Welp, guess we'll wing it.
375°
RACE!
What's that smell?

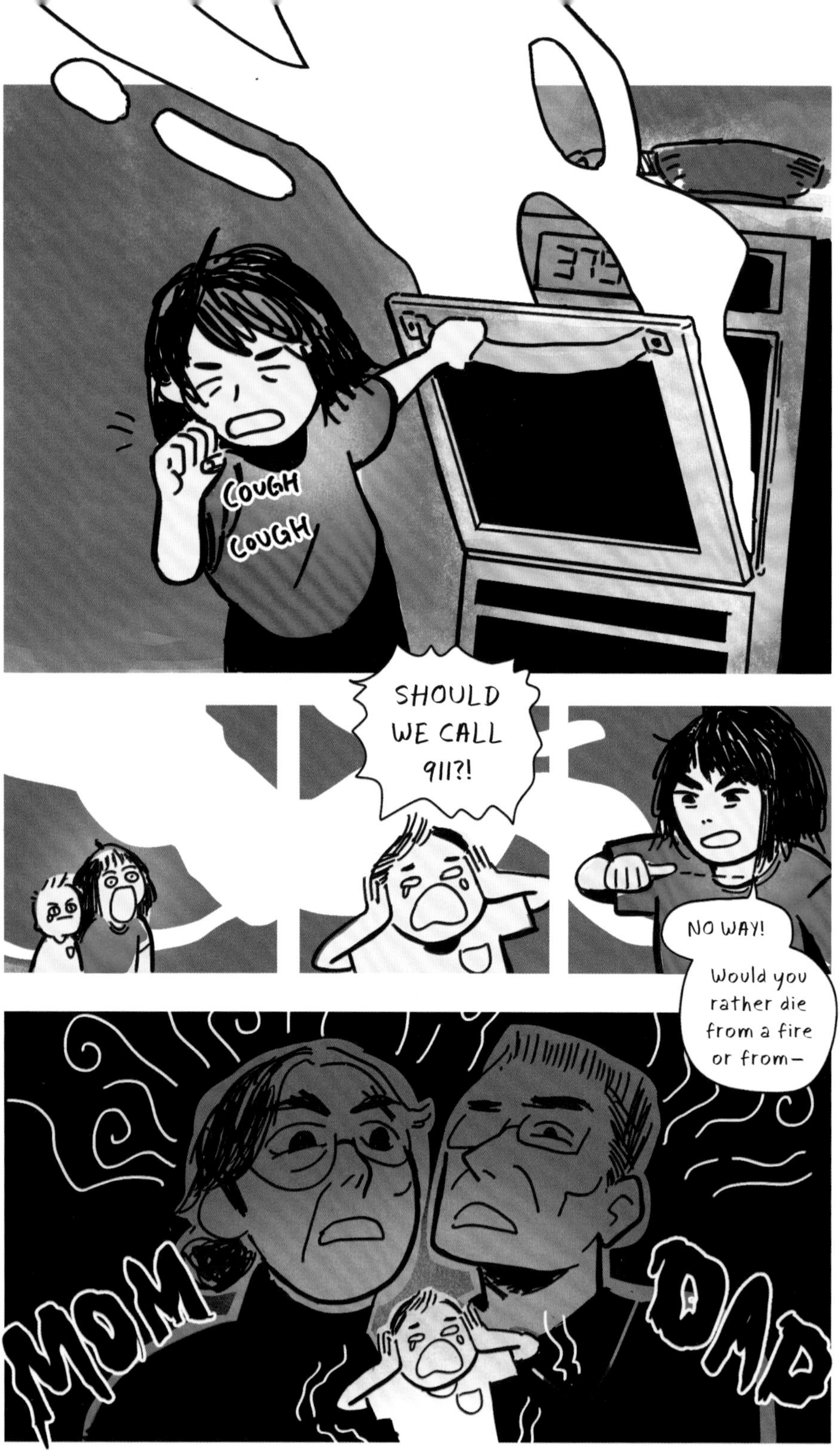
COUGH
COUGH
SHOULD WE CALL 911?!
NO WAY!
Would you rather die from a fire or from—
MOM
DAD

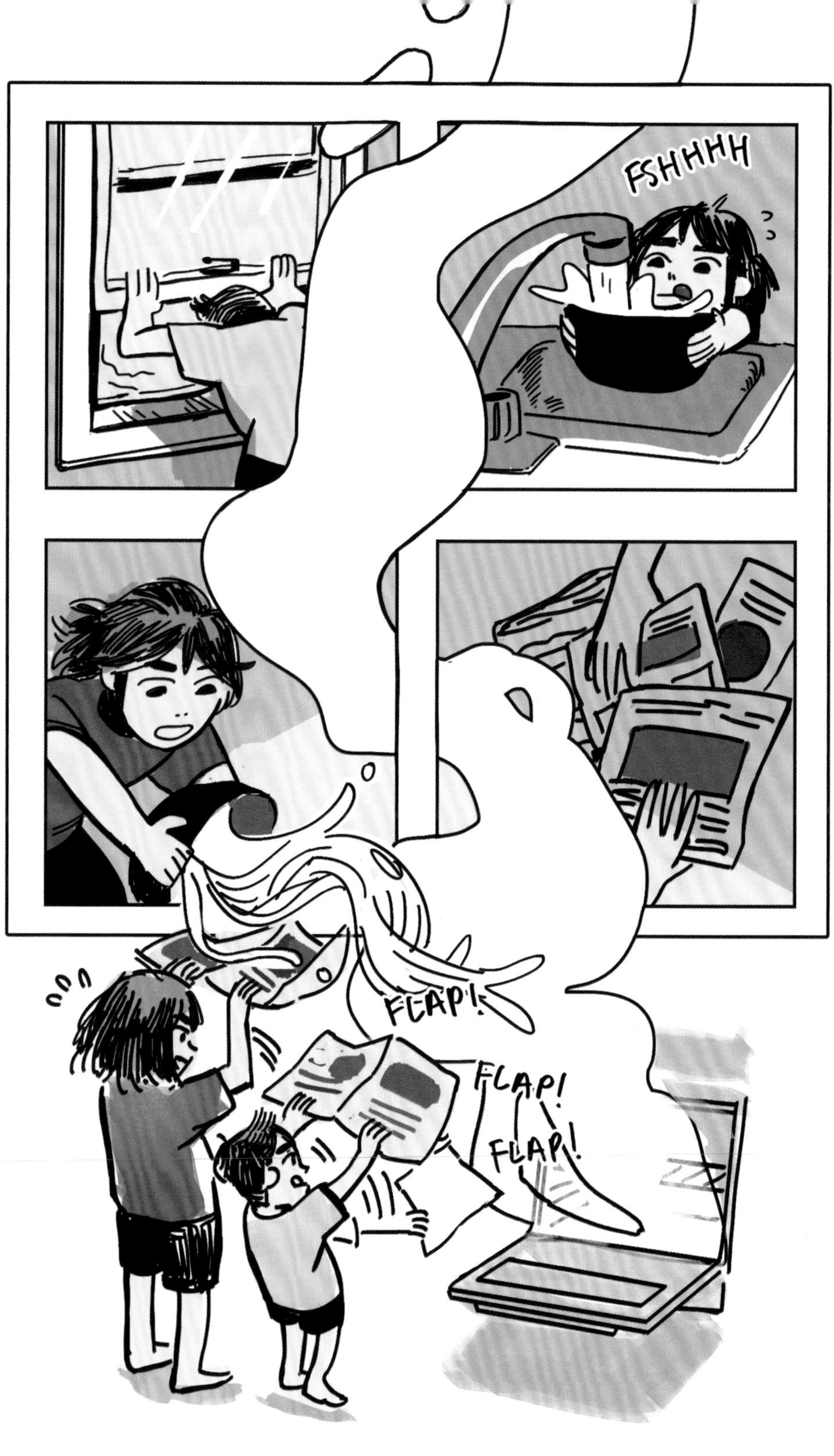
FSHHHH
FLAP!
FLAP!
FLAP!

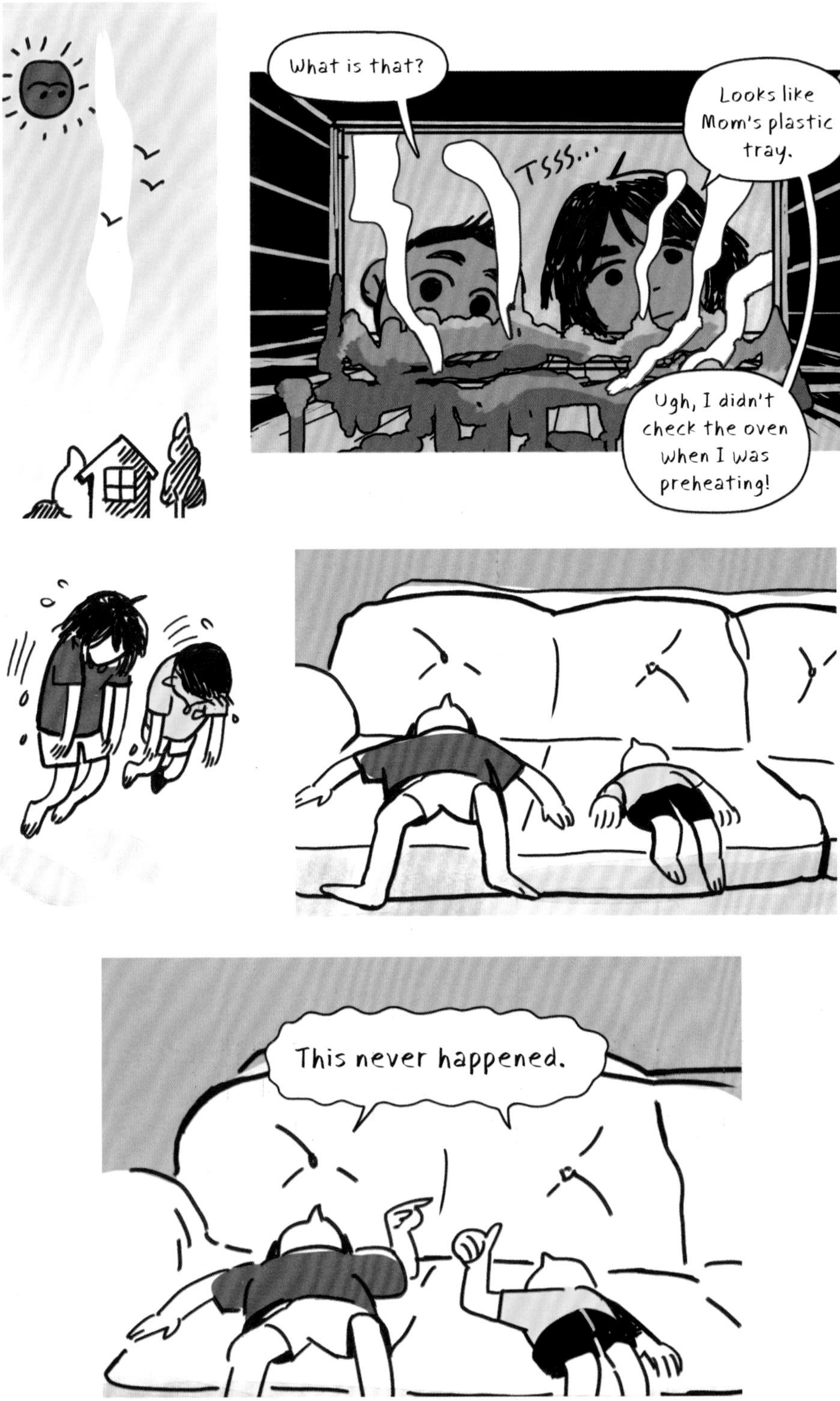
What is that?
TSSS...
Looks like Mom's plastic tray.
Ugh, I didn't check the oven when I was preheating!
This never happened.

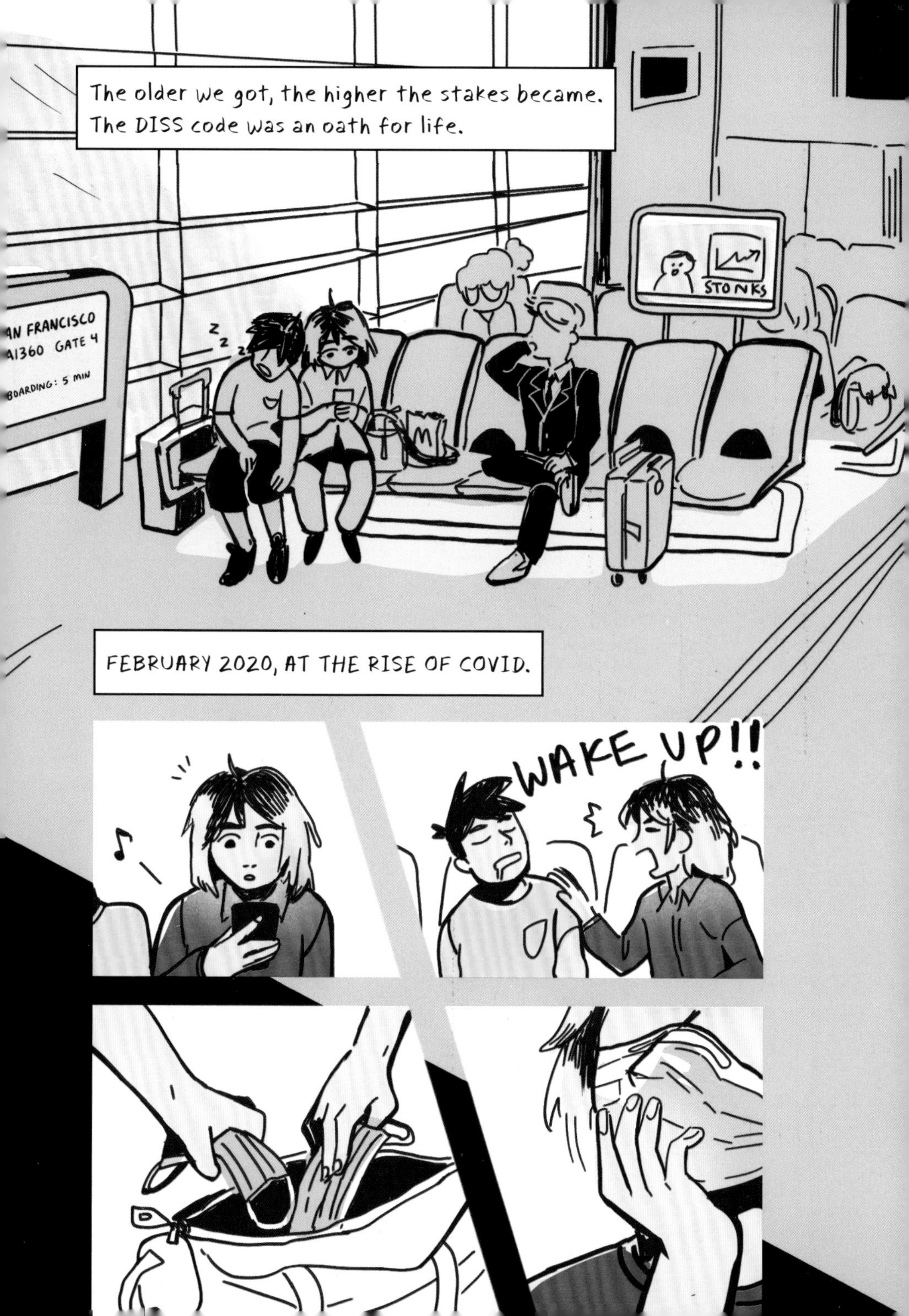

The older we got, the higher the stakes became. The DISS code was an oath for life.
AN FRANCISCO
A1360 GATE 4
BOARDING: 5 MIN
STONKS
FEBRUARY 2020, AT THE RISE OF COVID.
WAKE UP!!

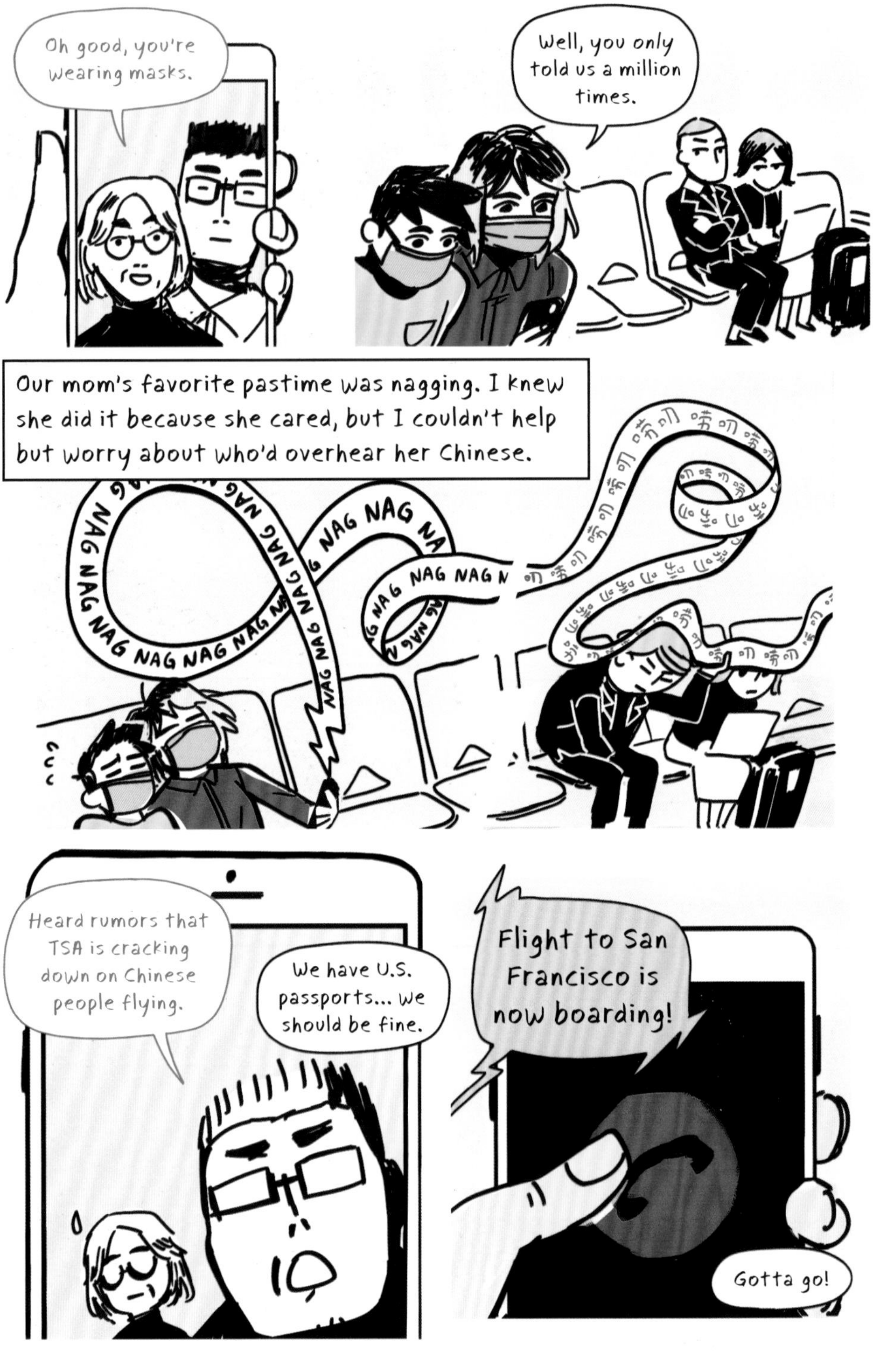
Oh good, you're wearing masks.
Well, you only told us a million times.
Our mom's favorite pastime was nagging. I knew she did it because she cared, but I couldn't help but worry about who'd overhear her Chinese.
NAG NAG NAG NAG NAG NAG NAG NAG
唠叨 唠叨 唠叨 唠叨
Heard rumors that TSA is cracking down on Chinese people flying.
We have U.S. passports... we should be fine.
Flight to San Francisco is now boarding!
Gotta go!

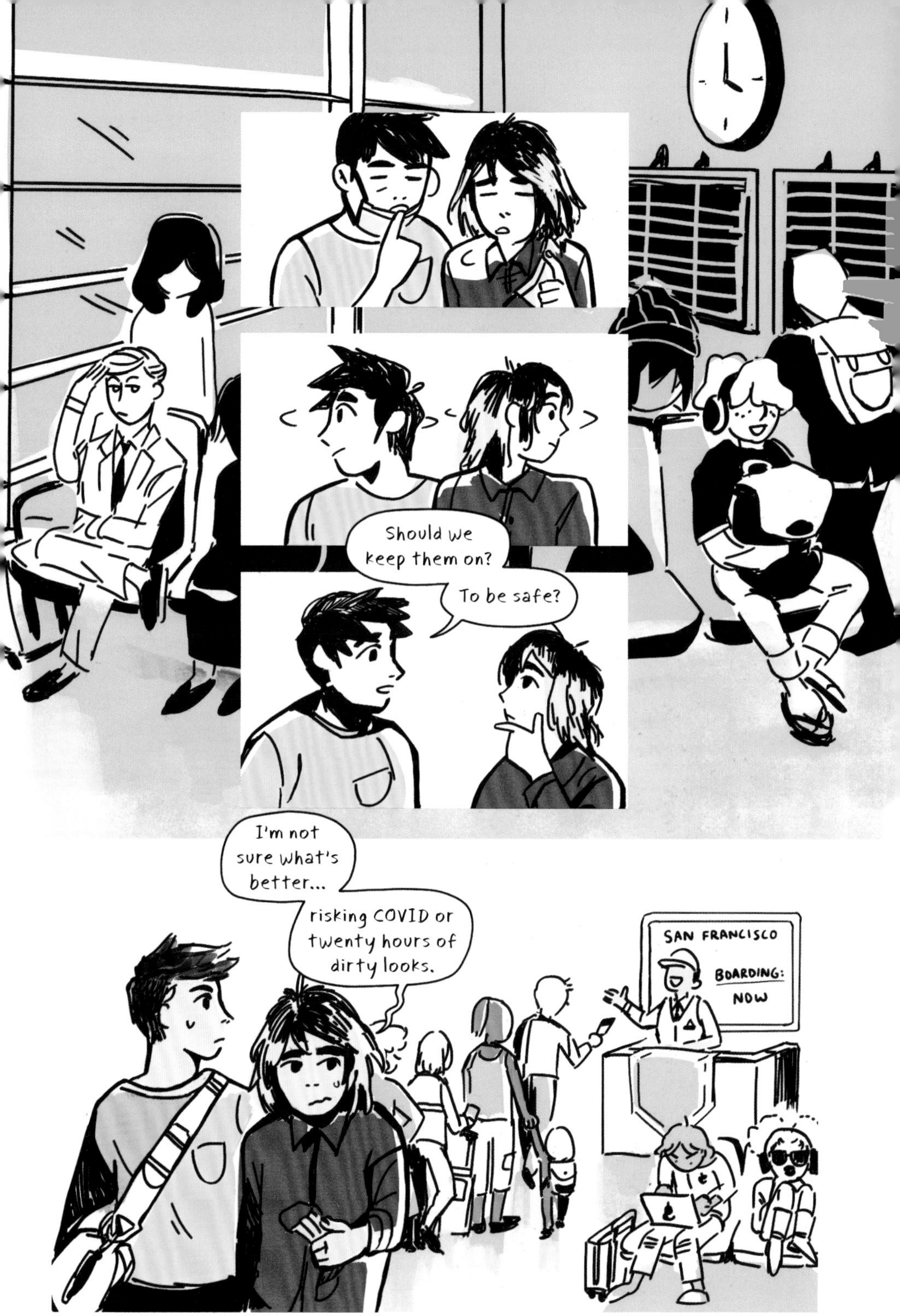
Should we keep them on?
To be safe?
I'm not sure what's better...
risking COVID or twenty hours of dirty looks.
SAN FRANCISCO
BOARDING: NOW

CHAPTER 3
Mathlete to Athlete

Growing up, I moved to a new school every year. Once I picked up some English, making friends as the new kid in elementary school was as easy as liking the same Pokémon.

First grade

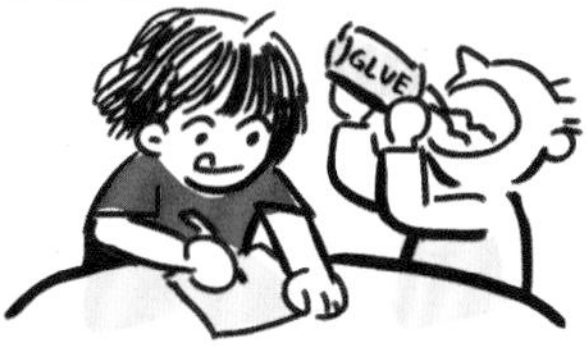
GLUE

Second grade

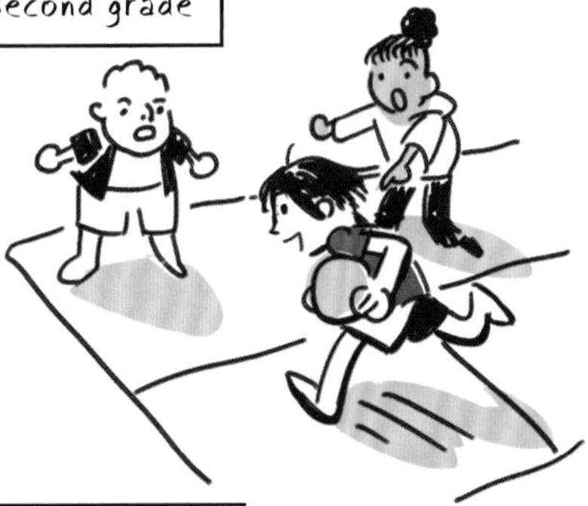

Third grade

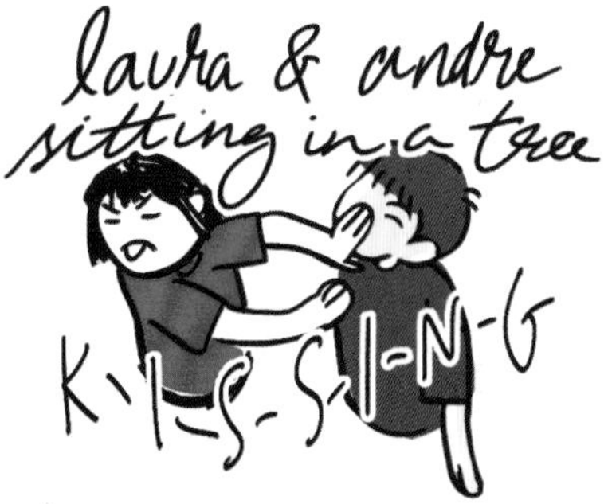
laura & andre
sitting in a tree
K-I-S-S-I-N-G

Fourth grade

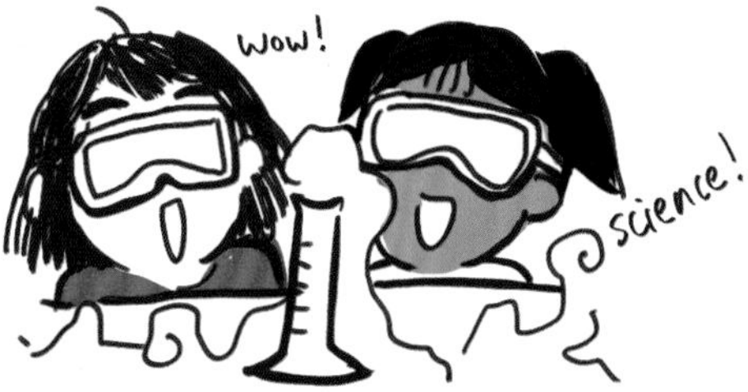
Wow!
science!

McCoy Elementary was where I felt most at home. My classmates were from all different backgrounds with unique passions. Together, we competed on the mathletes team and I got first place!

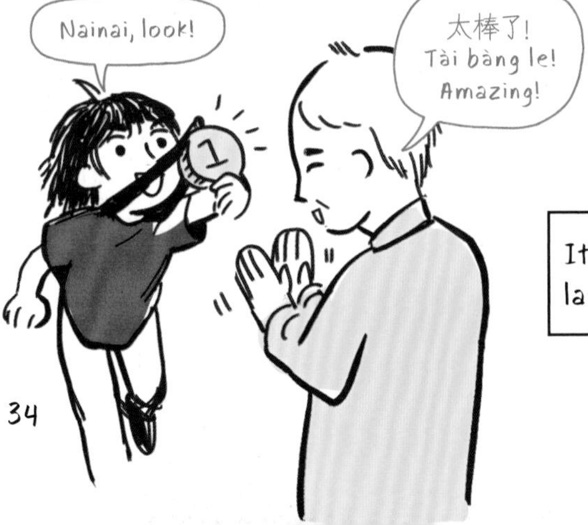
Nainai, look!
1
太棒了!
Tài bàng le!
Amazing!

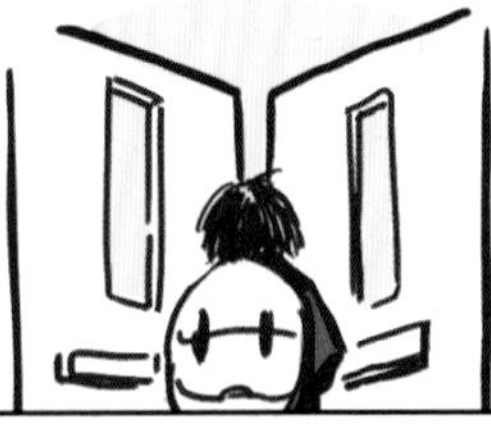

It was short-lived. I moved one last time for middle school.

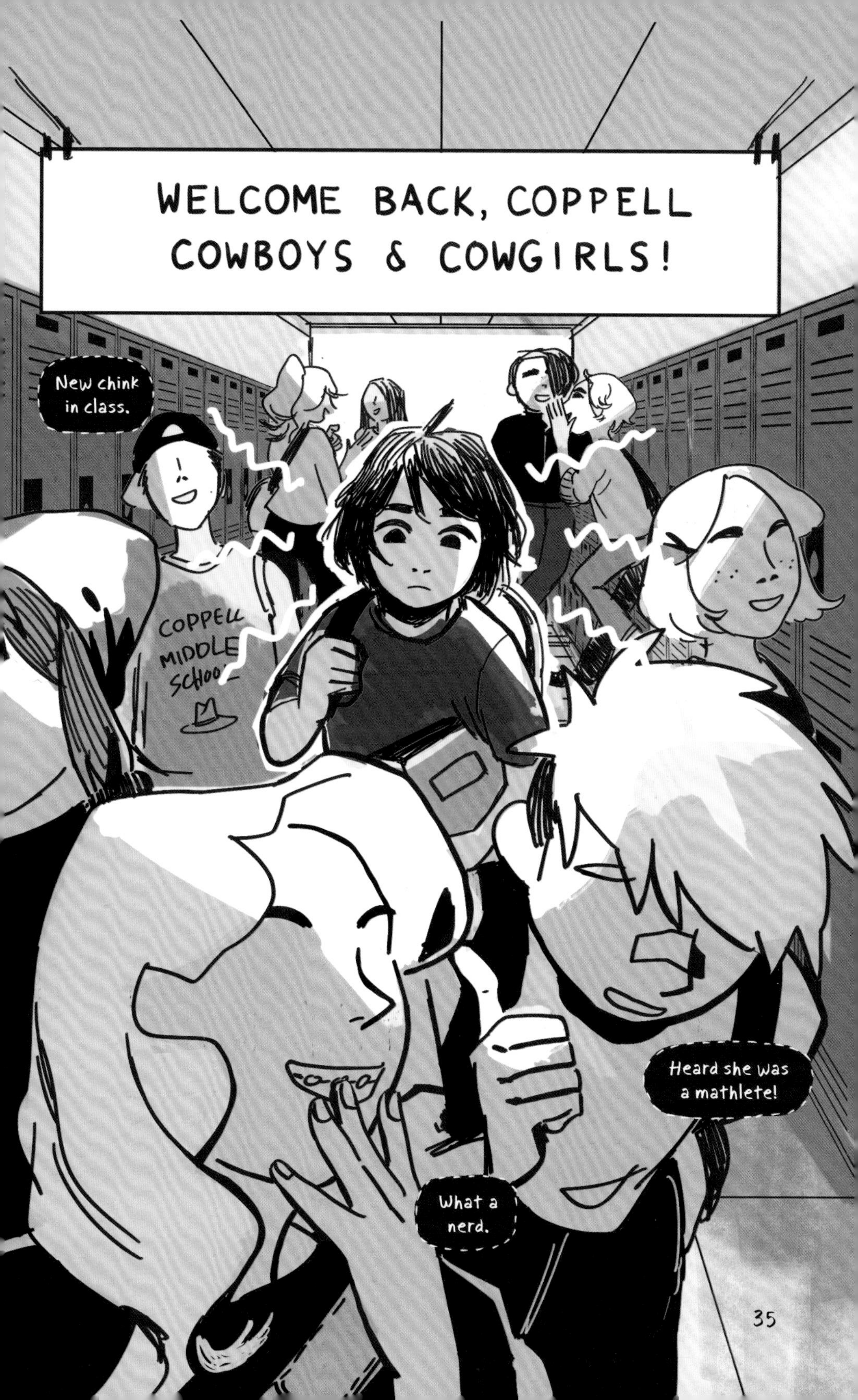
WELCOME BACK, COPPELL COWBOYS & COWGIRLS!
New chink in class.
COPPELL MIDDLE
Heard she was a mathlete!
What a nerd.

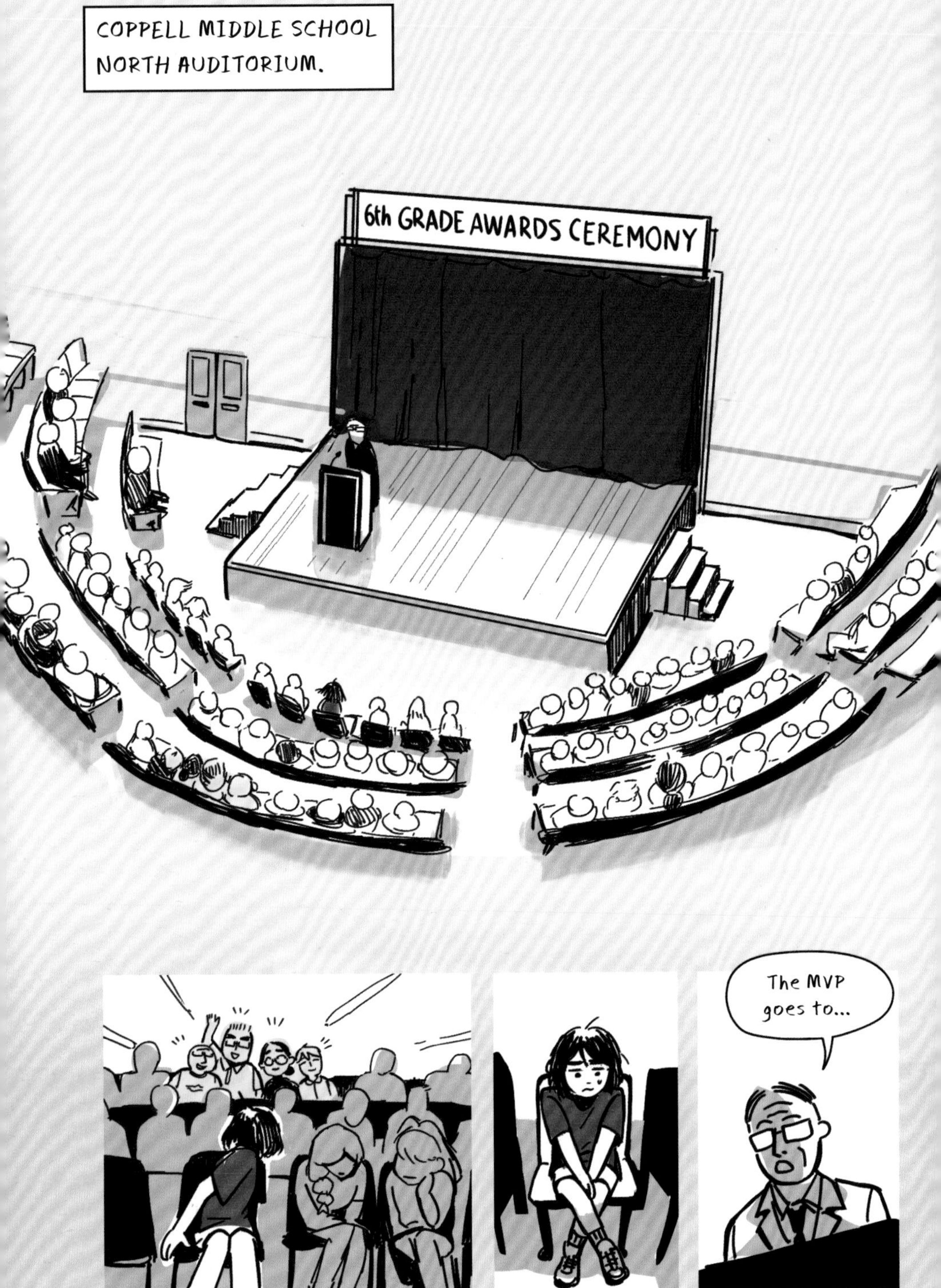
COPPELL MIDDLE SCHOOL
NORTH AUDITORIUM.
6th GRADE AWARDS CEREMONY
The MVP
goes to...

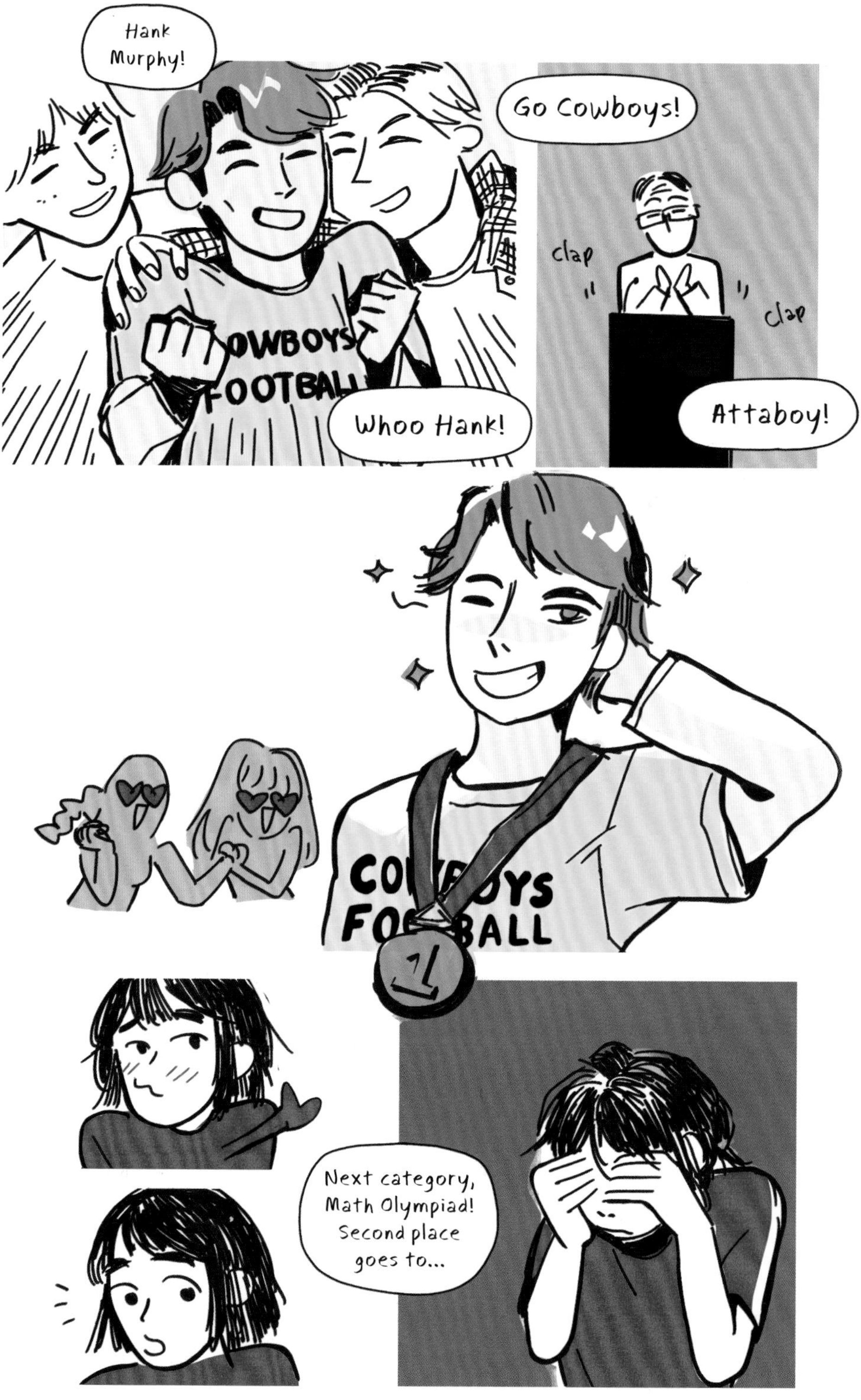
Hank Murphy!
COWBOYS FOOTBALL
Whoo Hank!
Go Cowboys!
clap
clap
Attaboy!
COWBOYS FOOTBALL
Next category, Math Olympiad! Second place goes to...

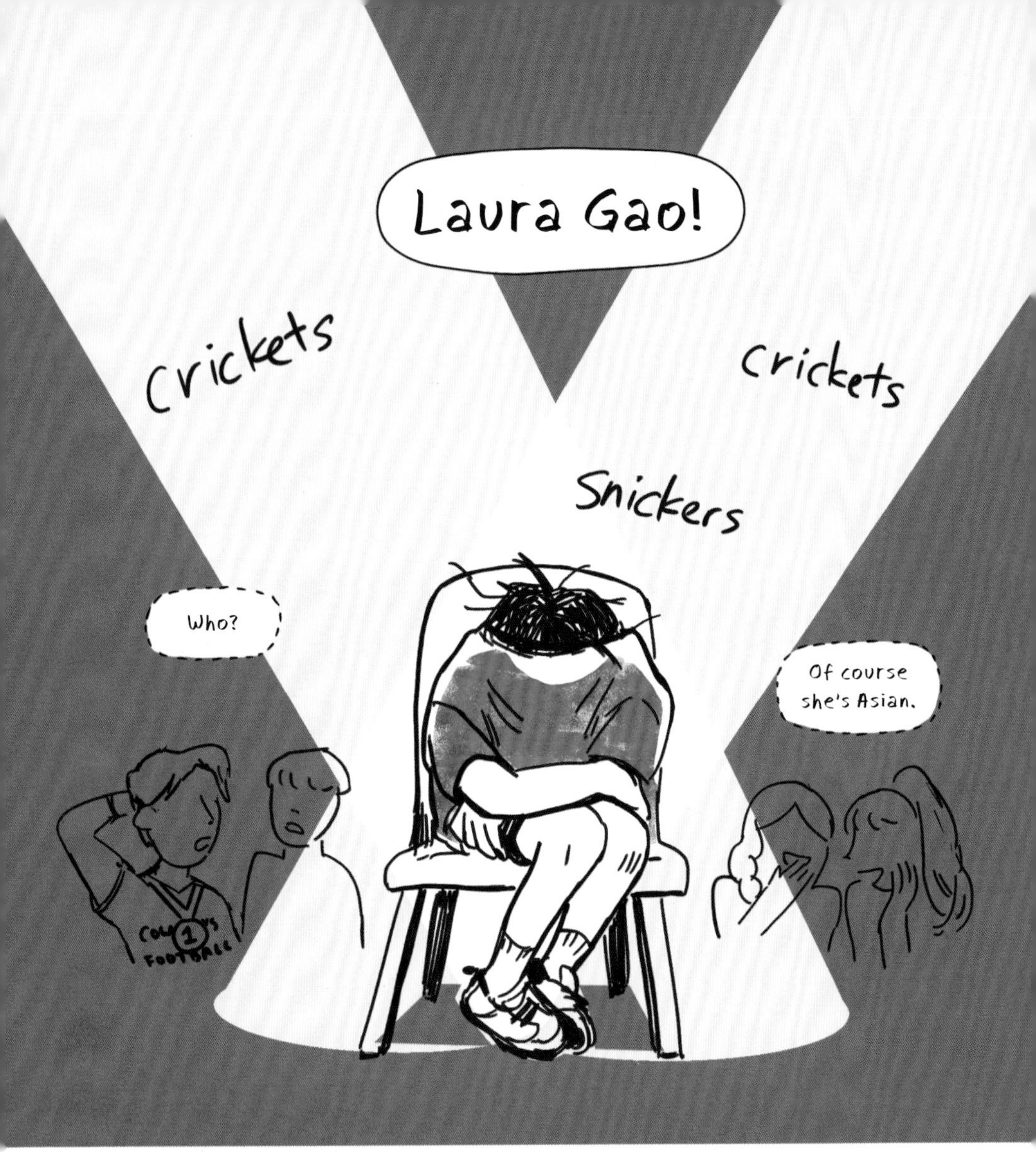
Laura Gao!
Crickets
Crickets
Snickers
Who?
Of course she's Asian.
COL 1 YS FOOTBALL

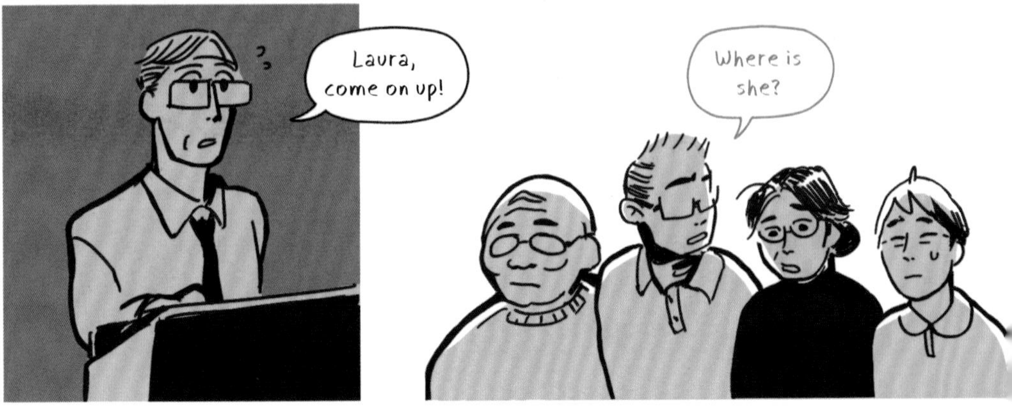
Laura, come on up!
Where is she?

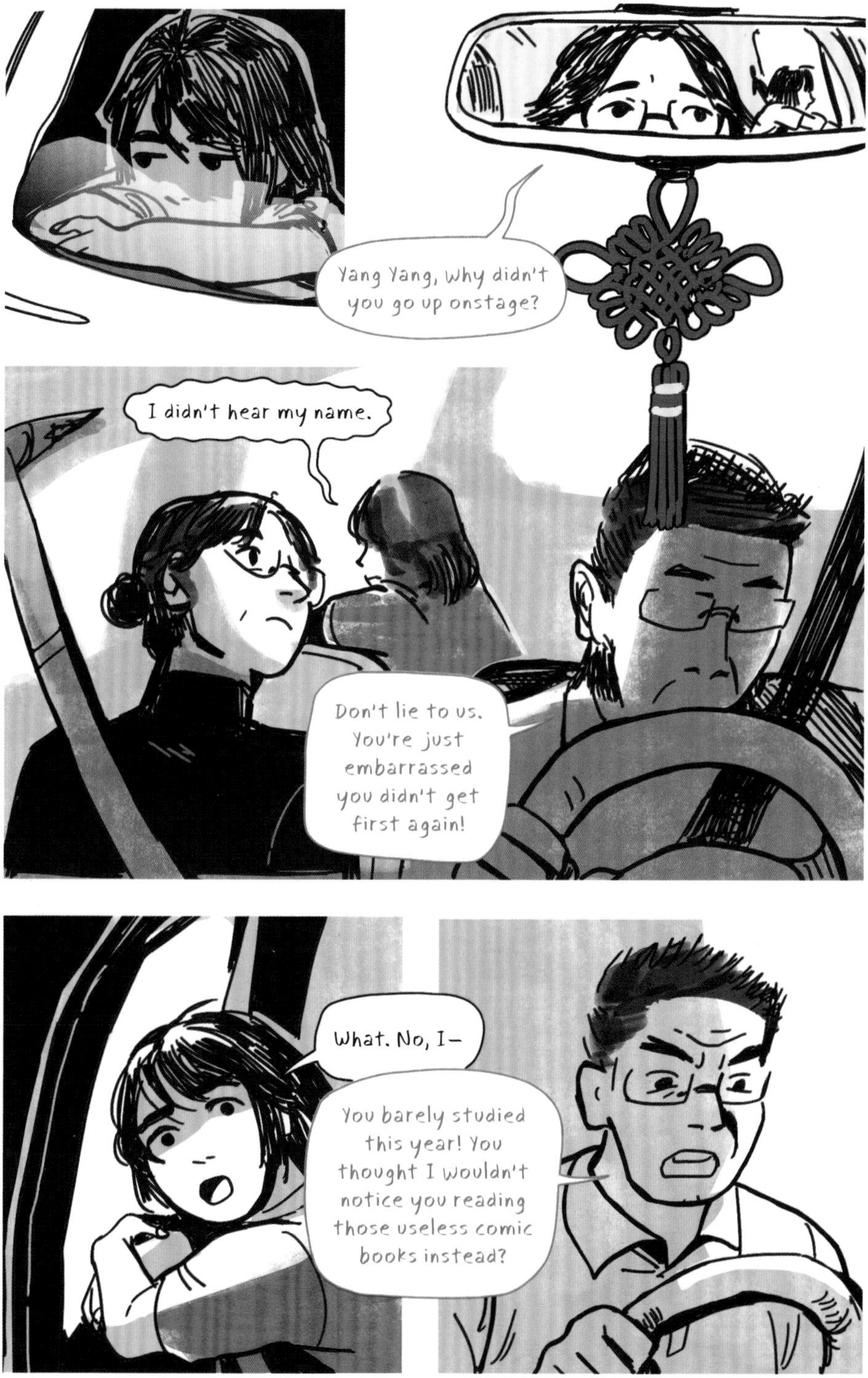

Yang Yang, why didn't you go up onstage?
I didn't hear my name.
Don't lie to us. You're just embarrassed you didn't get first again!
What. No, I–
You barely studied this year! You thought I wouldn't notice you reading those useless comic books instead?

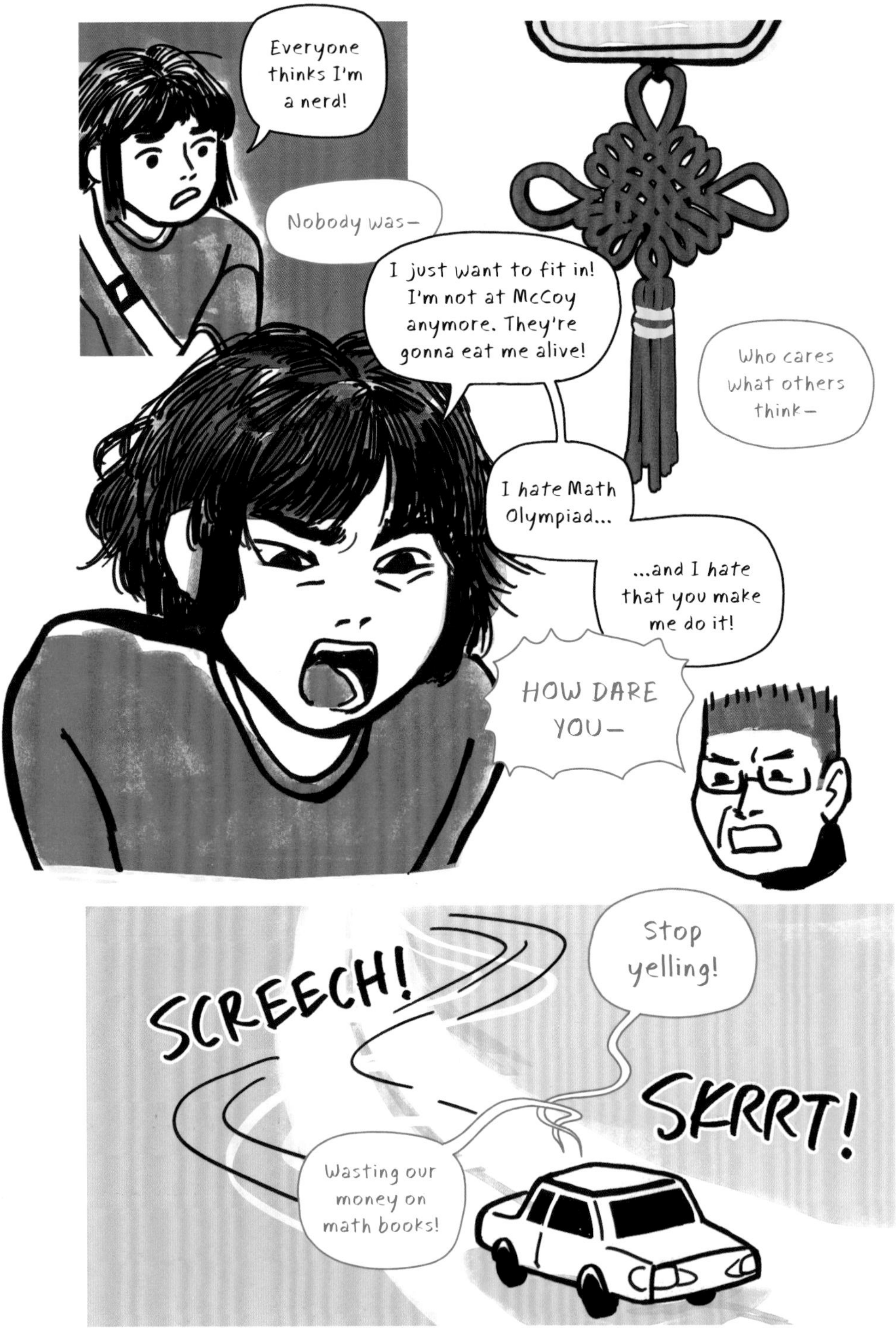
Everyone thinks I'm a nerd!
Nobody was—
I just want to fit in! I'm not at McCoy anymore. They're gonna eat me alive!
Who cares what others think—
I hate Math Olympiad...
...and I hate that you make me do it!
HOW DARE YOU—
SCREECH!
Stop yelling!
SKRRT!
Wasting our money on math books!

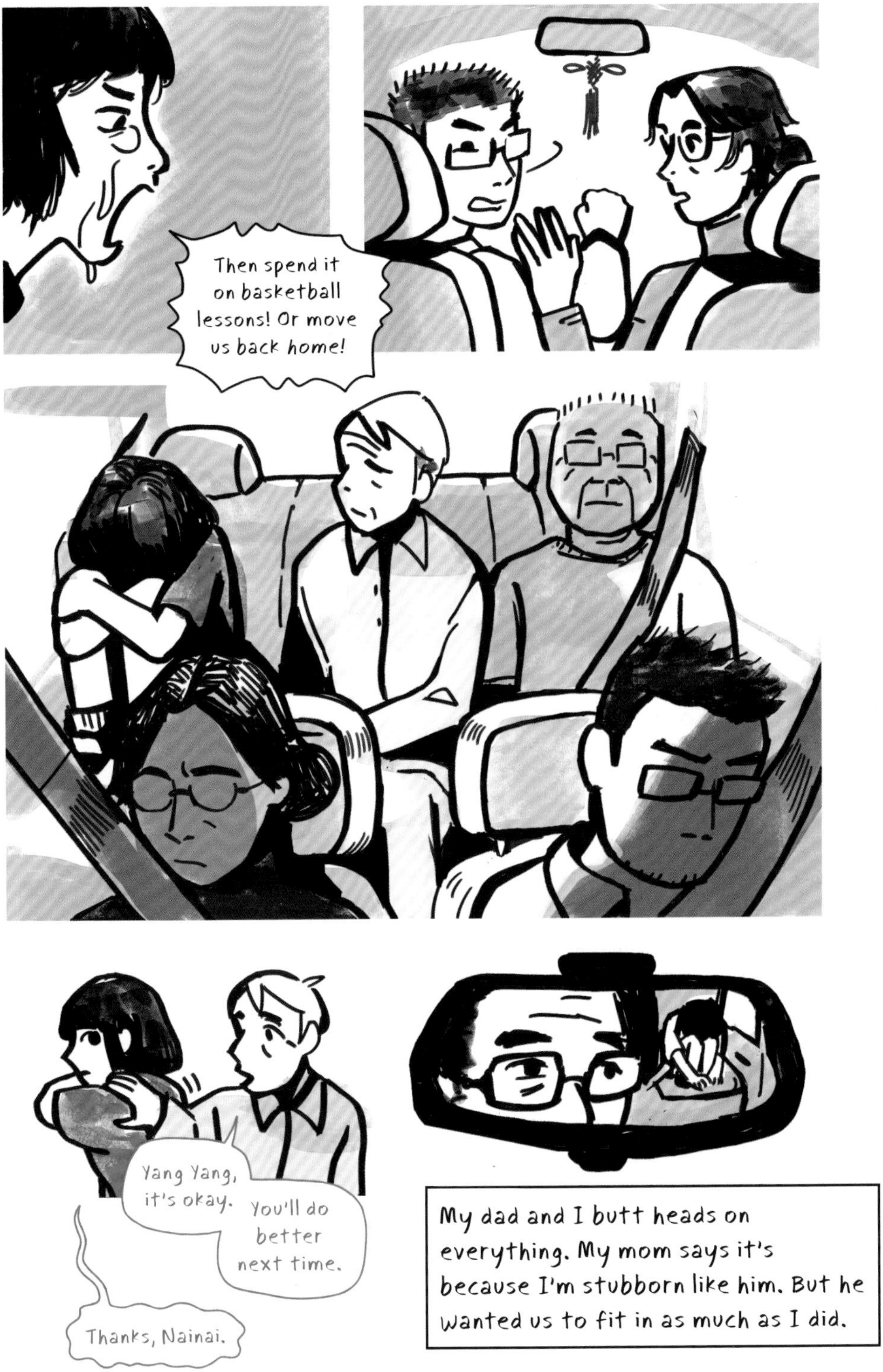
Then spend it on basketball lessons! Or move us back home!
Yang Yang, it's okay.
You'll do better next time.
Thanks, Nainai.
My dad and I butt heads on everything. My mom says it's because I'm stubborn like him. But he wanted us to fit in as much as I did.

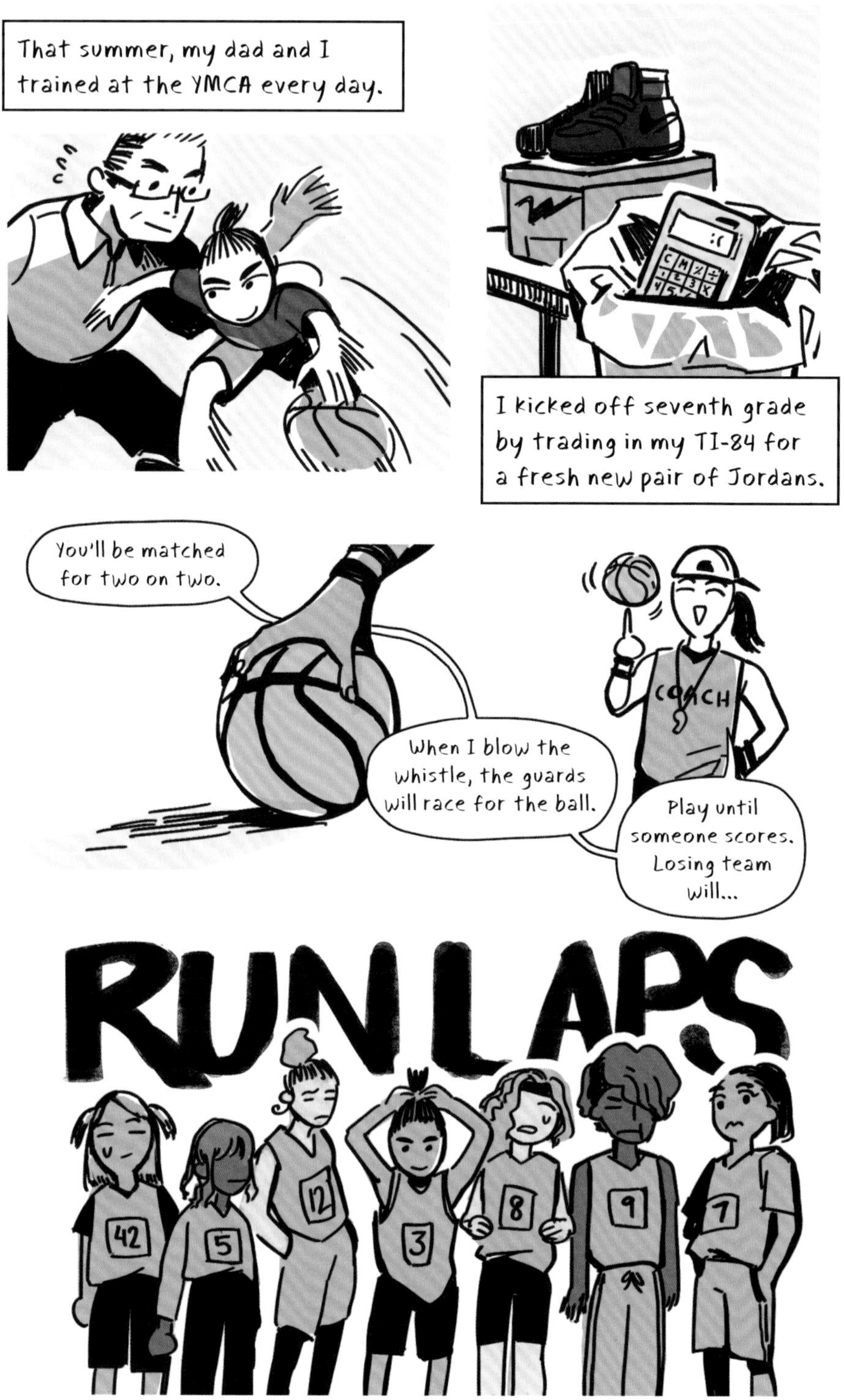
That summer, my dad and I trained at the YMCA every day.
I kicked off seventh grade by trading in my TI-84 for a fresh new pair of Jordans.
You'll be matched for two on two.
COACH
When I blow the whistle, the guards will race for the ball.
Play until someone scores. Losing team will...
RUN LAPS

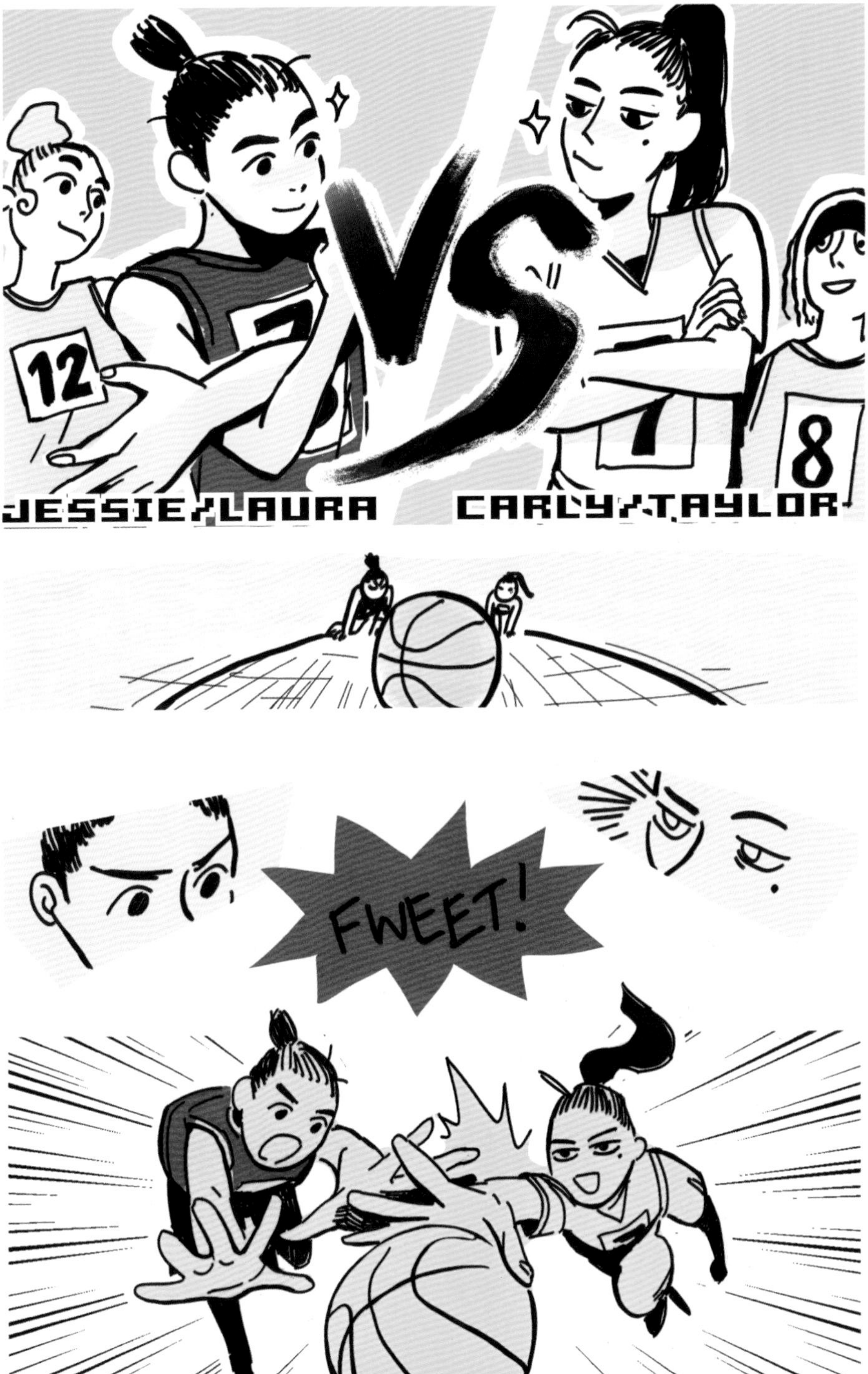
12
8
JESSIE/LAURA
CARLY/TAYLOR
FWEET!

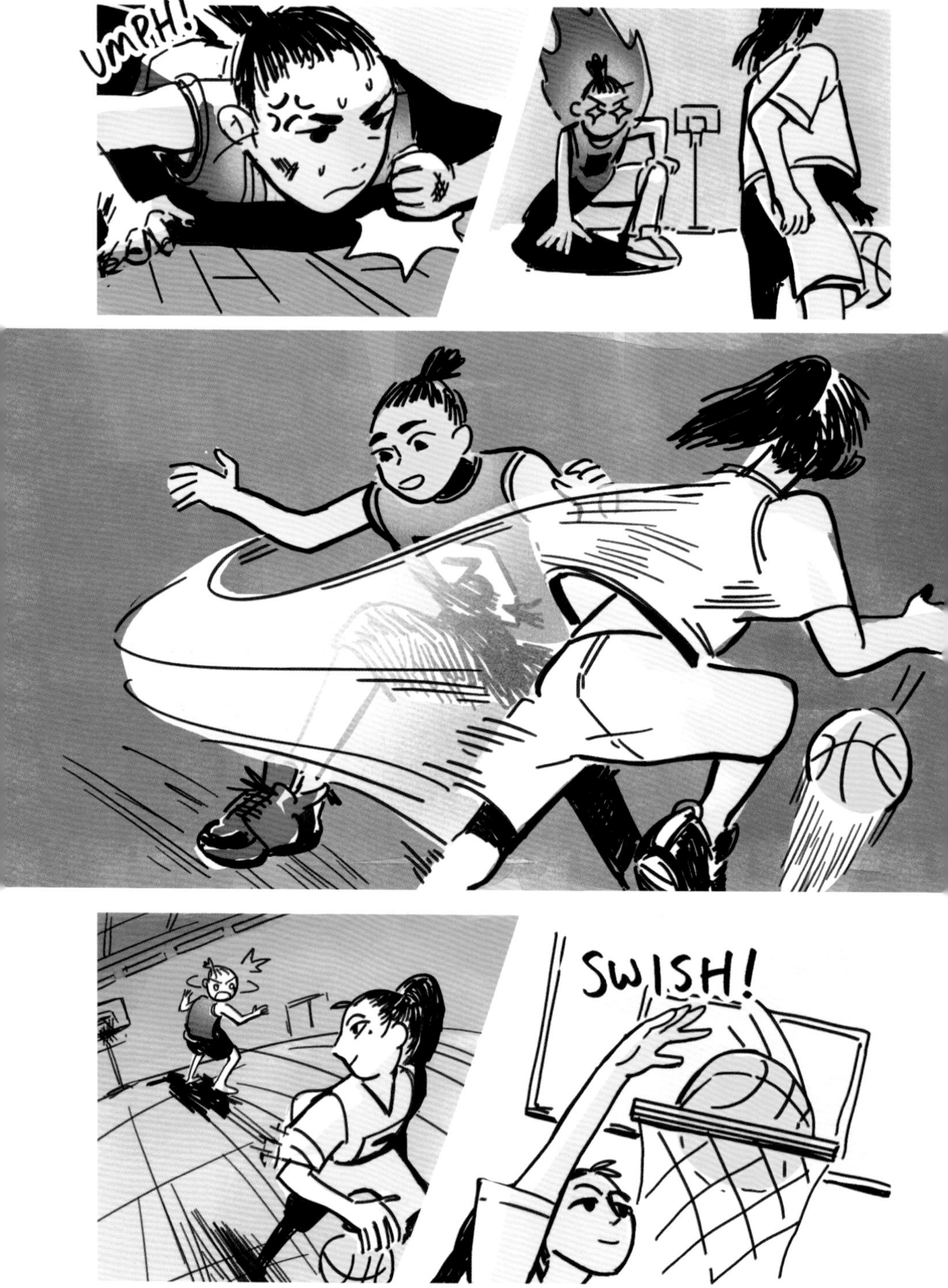
UMPH!
SWISH!

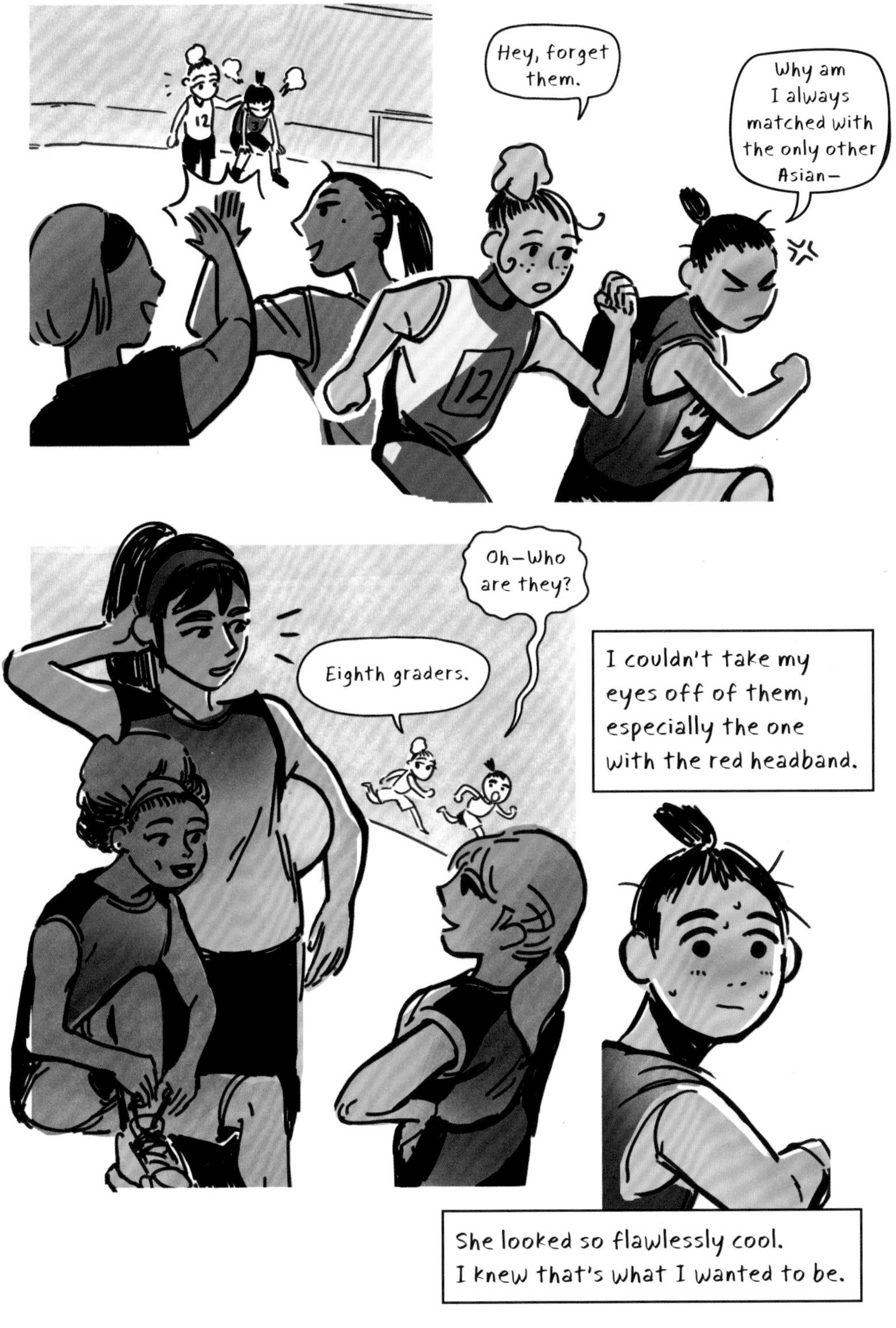
Hey, forget them.
Why am I always matched with the only other Asian—
Oh—Who are they?
Eighth graders.
I couldn't take my eyes off of them, especially the one with the red headband.
She looked so flawlessly cool. I knew that's what I wanted to be.

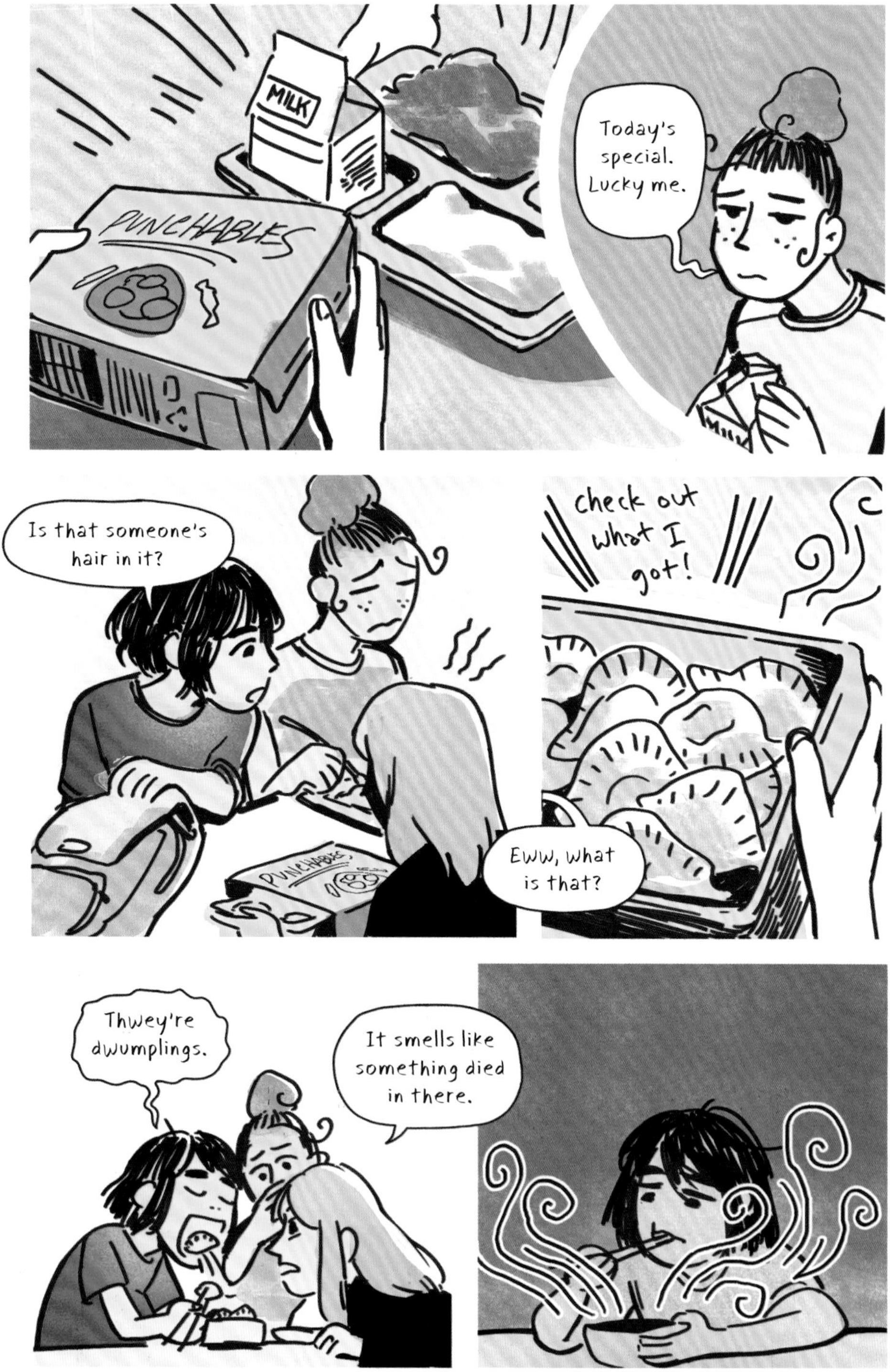
MILK
PUNCHABLES
Today's special. Lucky me.
MILK
Is that someone's hair in it?
PUNCHABLES
check out what I got!
Eww, what is that?
Thwey're dwumplings.
It smells like something died in there.

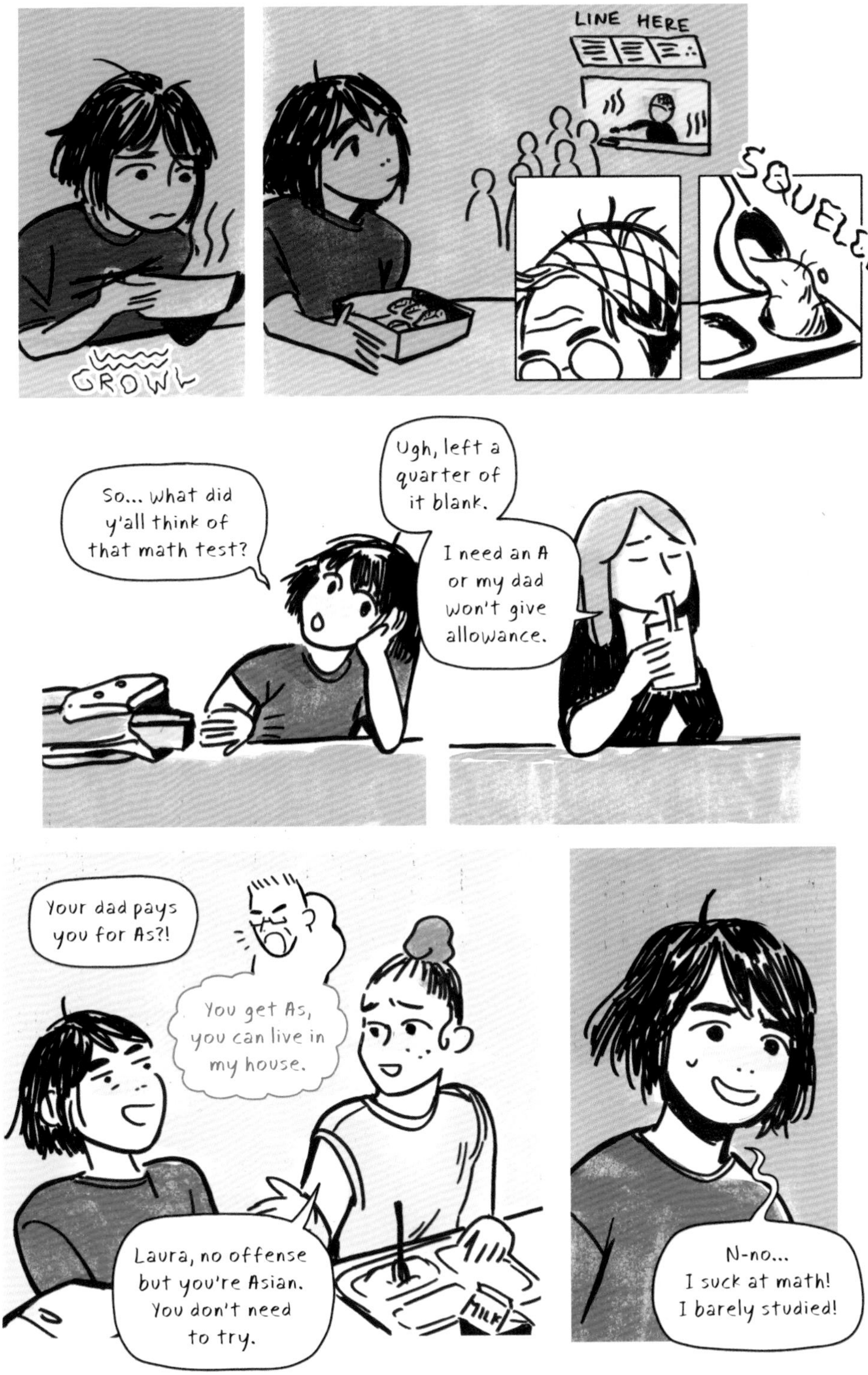
GROWL
LINE HERE
SQUELCH
So... what did y'all think of that math test?
Ugh, left a quarter of it blank.
I need an A or my dad won't give allowance.
Your dad pays you for As?!
You get As, you can live in my house.
Laura, no offense but you're Asian. You don't need to try.
N-no... I suck at math! I barely studied!

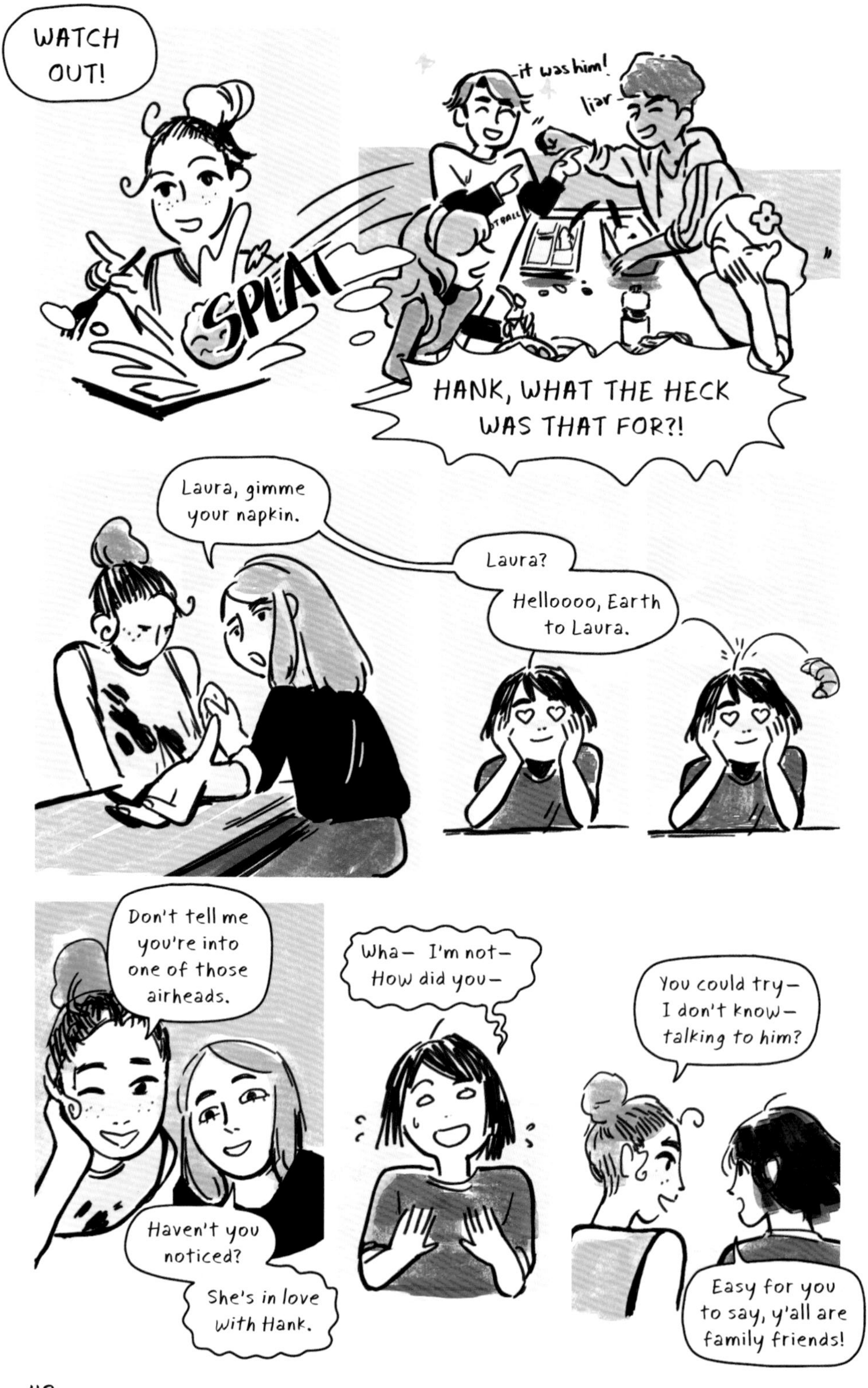
WATCH OUT!
SPLAT
-it was him!
liar-
HANK, WHAT THE HECK WAS THAT FOR?!
Laura, gimme your napkin.
Laura?
Helloooo, Earth to Laura.
Don't tell me you're into one of those airheads.
Haven't you noticed?
She's in love with Hank.
Wha- I'm not- How did you-
You could try- I don't know- talking to him?
Easy for you to say, y'all are family friends!

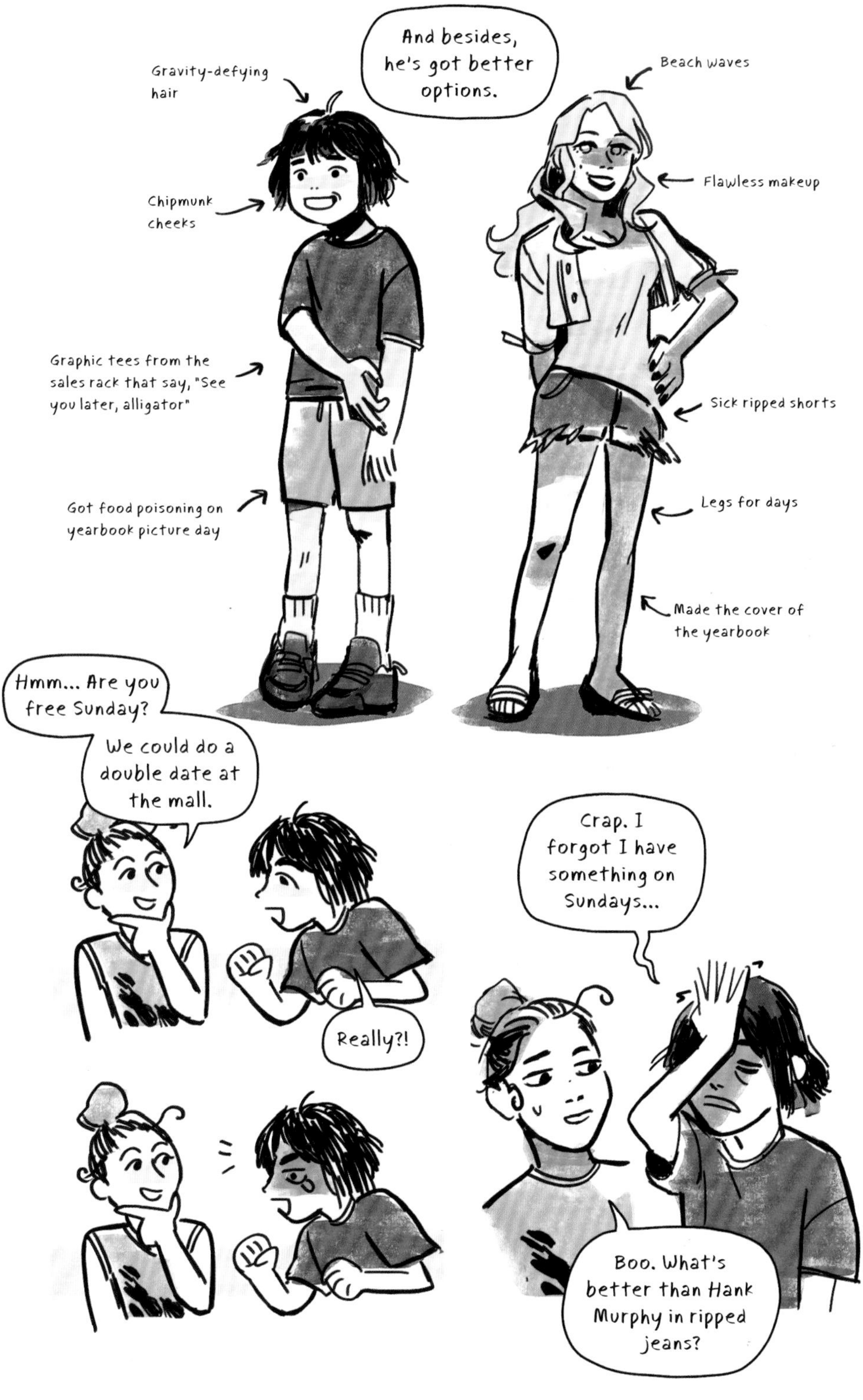

Gravity-defying hair
And besides, he's got better options.
Beach waves
Chipmunk cheeks
Flawless makeup
Graphic tees from the sales rack that say, "See you later, alligator"
Sick ripped shorts
Got food poisoning on yearbook picture day
Legs for days
Made the cover of the yearbook
Hmm... Are you free Sunday?
We could do a double date at the mall.
Really?!
Crap. I forgot I have something on Sundays...
Boo. What's better than Hank Murphy in ripped jeans?

CHAPTER 4
Messy Roots and Ripped Genes

Every Sunday, I went to Chinese school to pay my heritage dues.

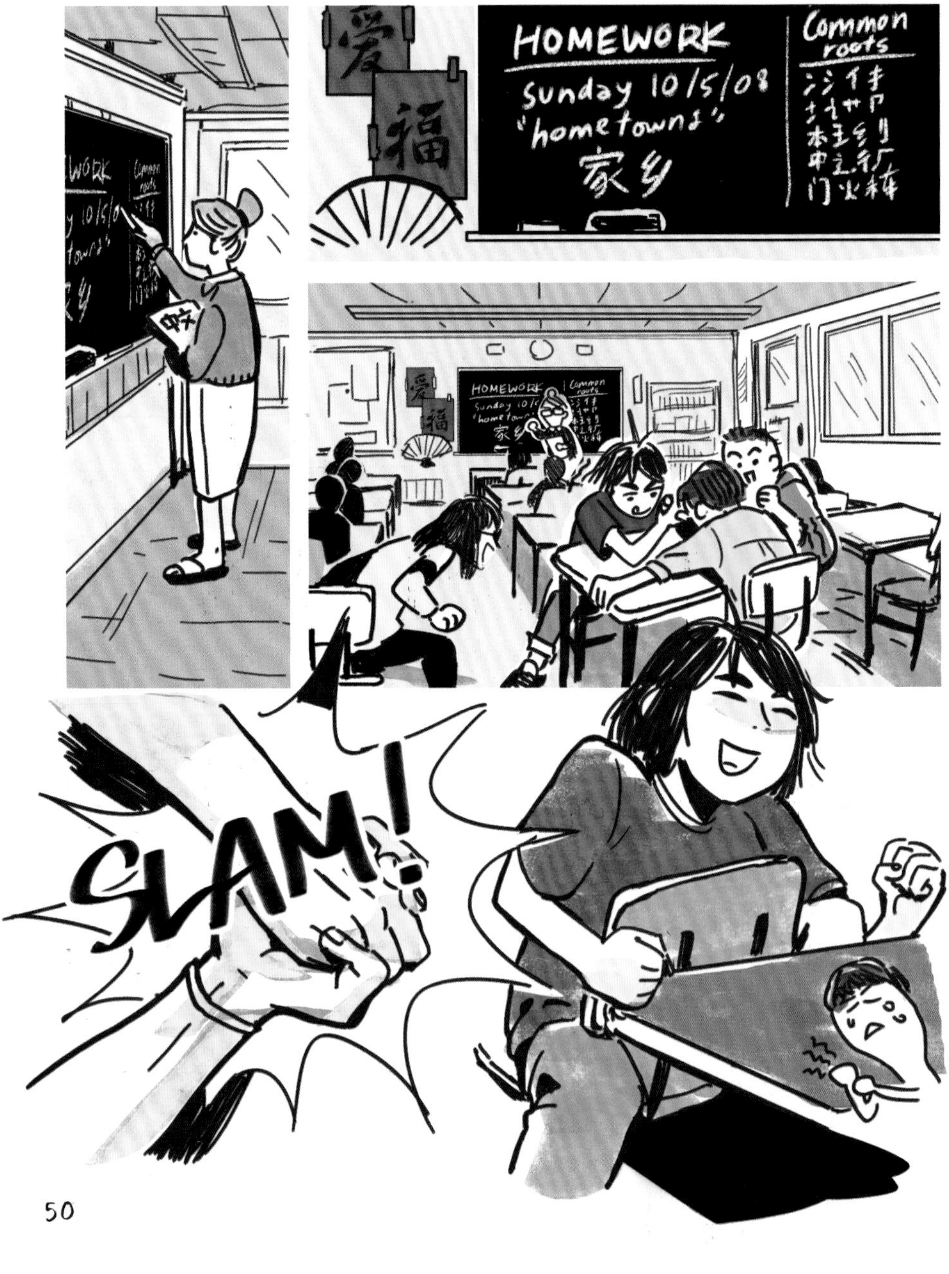

爱
福
HOMEWORK
Sunday 10/5/08
"hometowns"
家乡
Common roots
SLAM!

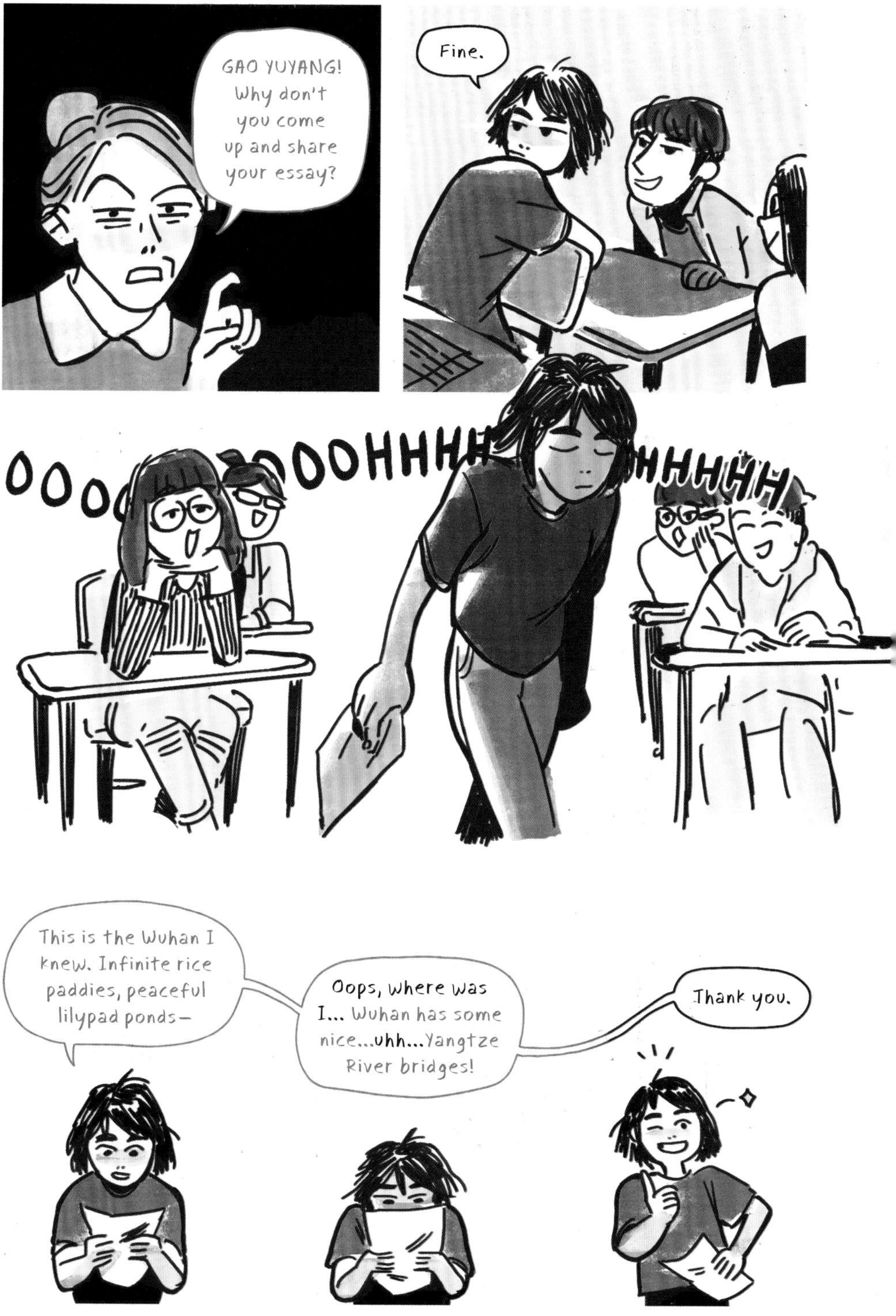
GAO YUYANG! Why don't you come up and share your essay?
Fine.
OOOOOOOHHHHHHHHHHH
This is the Wuhan I knew. Infinite rice paddies, peaceful lilypad ponds—
Oops, where was I... Wuhan has some nice...uhh...Yangtze River bridges!
Thank you.

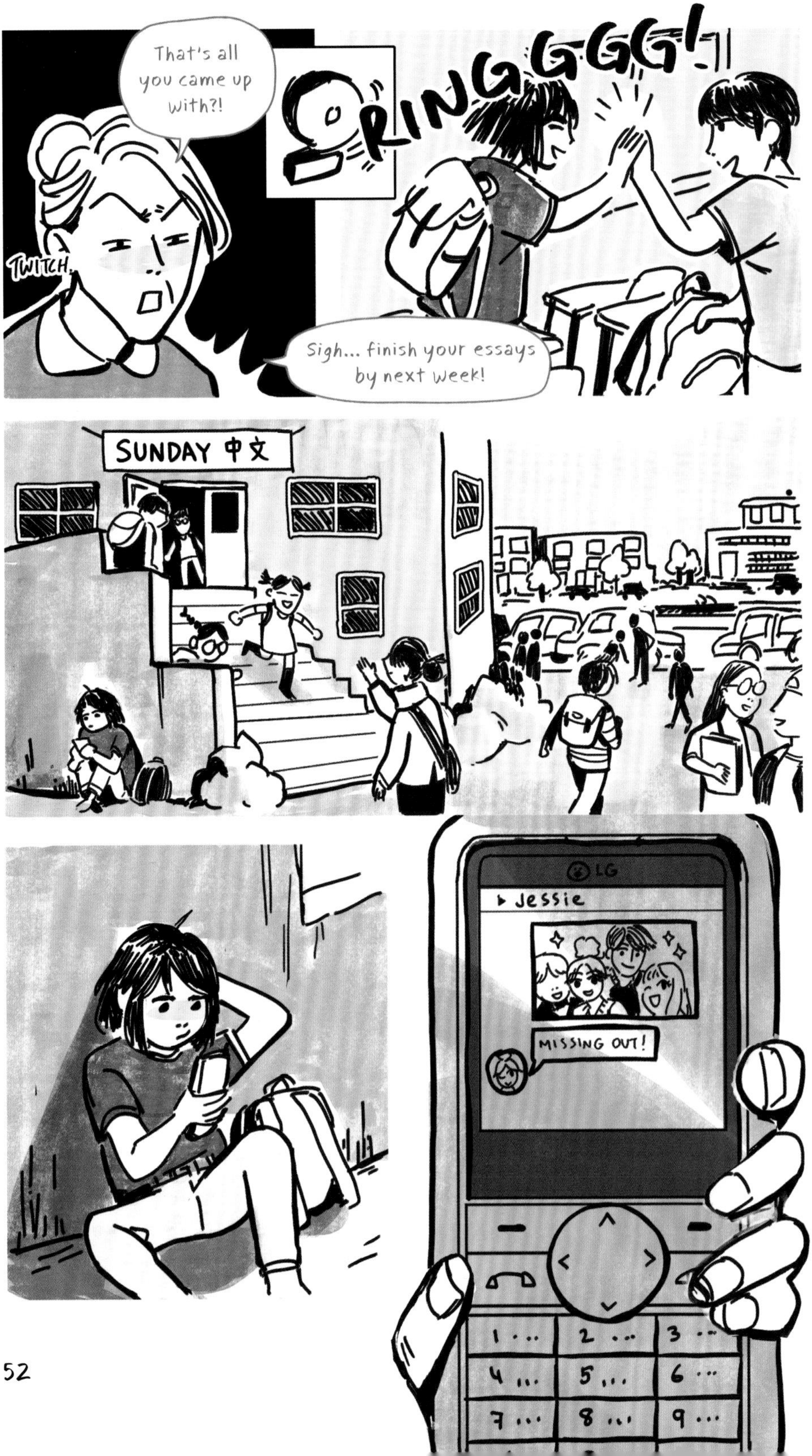

That's all you came up with?!
TWITCH
RINGGGG!
Sigh... finish your essays by next week!
SUNDAY 中文
LG
Jessie
MISSING OUT!

Everyone spoke English. Why did I have to learn one of the hardest languages in the world? Mandarin had everything from complex roots to characters that looked like chicken scratch.

I liked to imagine each word as a drawing.

Ai = love

A roof hiding lovers from their nosy parents.

Tears of laughter

A warm embrace

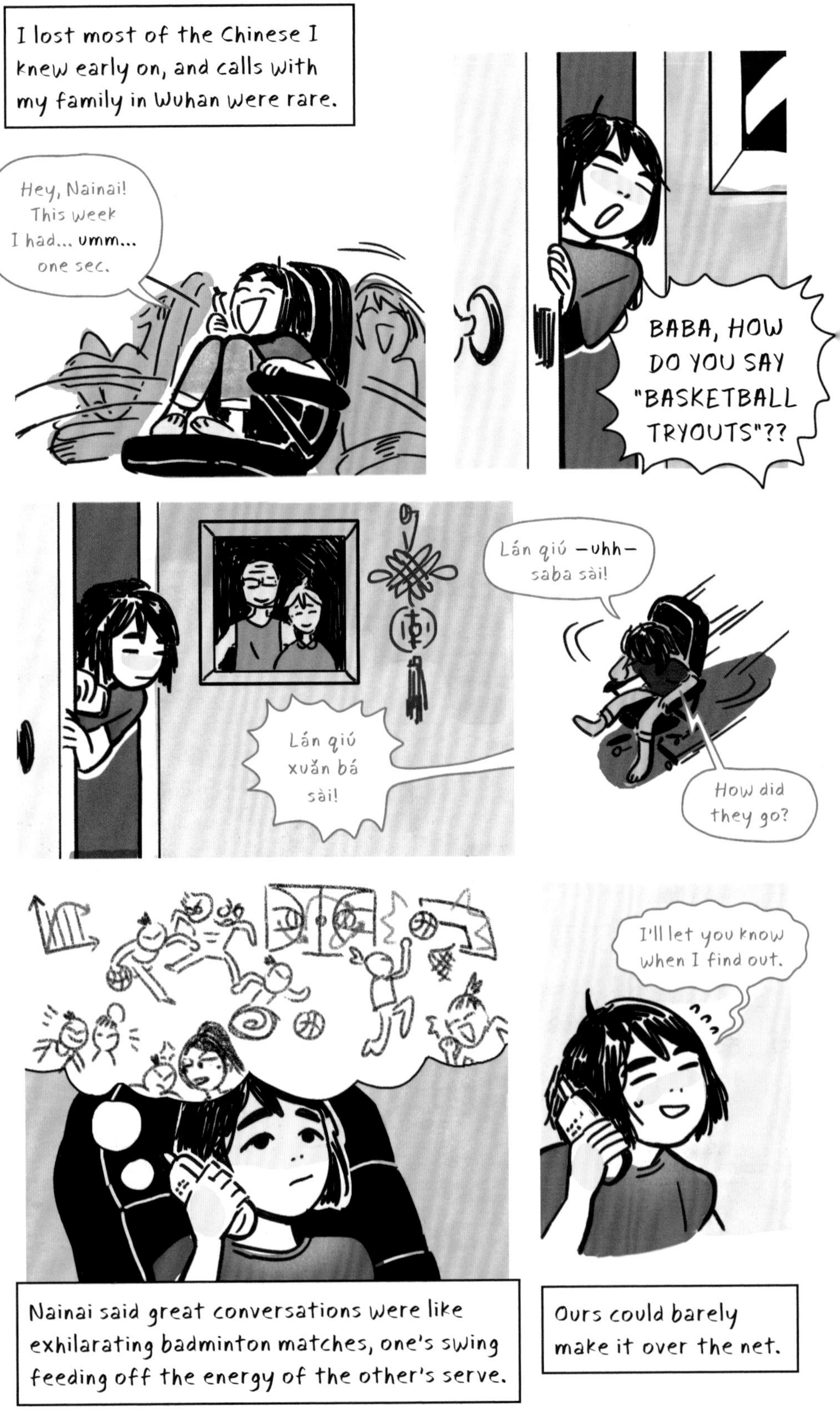
I lost most of the Chinese I knew early on, and calls with my family in Wuhan were rare.
Hey, Nainai! This week I had... umm... one sec.
BABA, HOW DO YOU SAY "BASKETBALL TRYOUTS"??
Lán qiú xuǎn bá sài!
Lán qiú —uhh— saba sài!
How did they go?
Nainai said great conversations were like exhilarating badminton matches, one's swing feeding off the energy of the other's serve.
I'll let you know when I find out.
Ours could barely make it over the net.

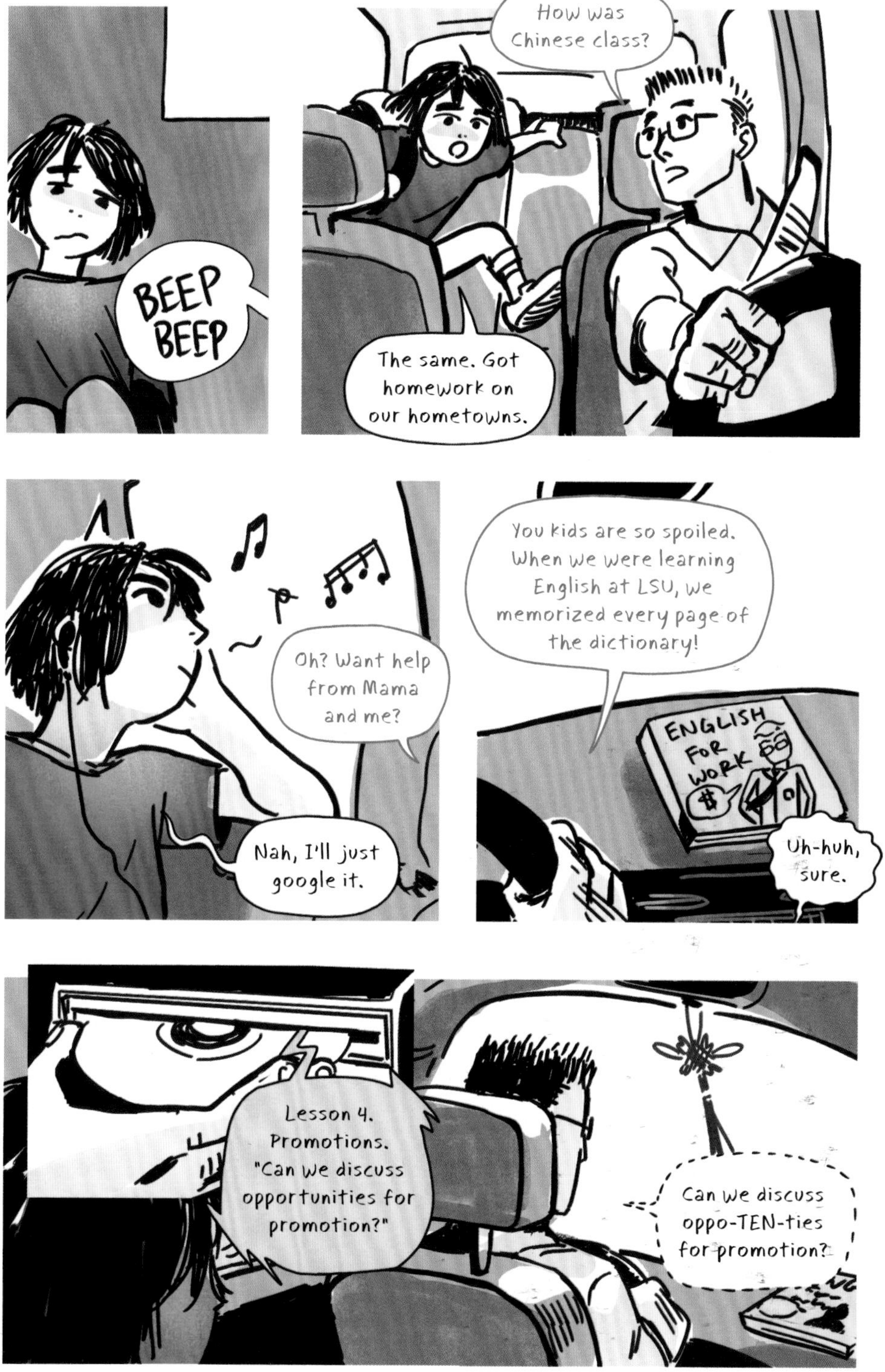
BEEP BEEP
How was Chinese class?
The same. Got homework on our hometowns.
Oh? Want help from Mama and me?
Nah, I'll just google it.
You kids are so spoiled. When we were learning English at LSU, we memorized every page of the dictionary!
ENGLISH FOR WORK
Uh-huh, sure.
Lesson 4. Promotions. "Can we discuss opportunities for promotion?"
Can we discuss oppo-TEN-ties for promotion?

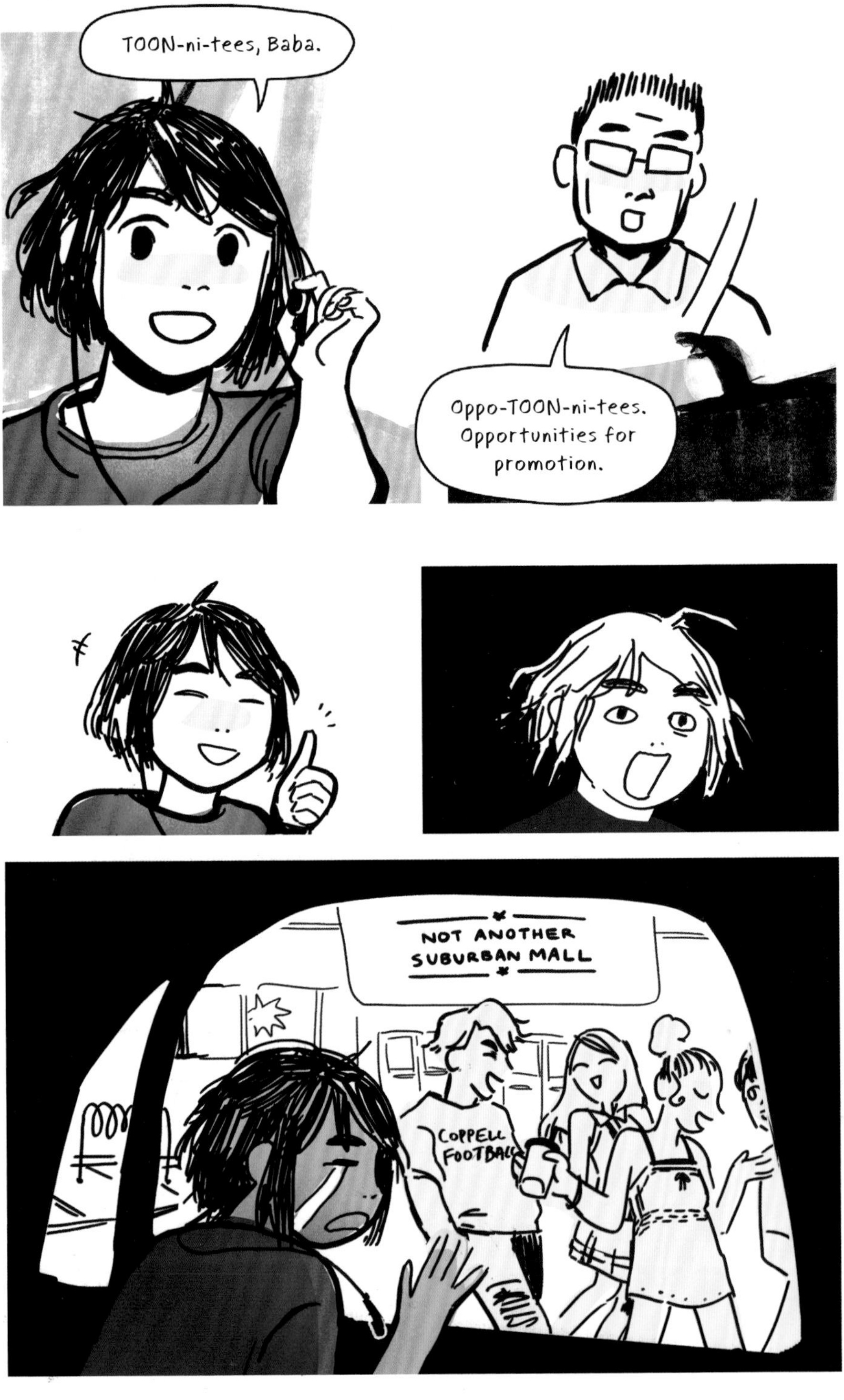
TOON-ni-tees, Baba.
Oppo-TOON-ni-tees. Opportunities for promotion.
NOT ANOTHER SUBURBAN MALL
COPPELL

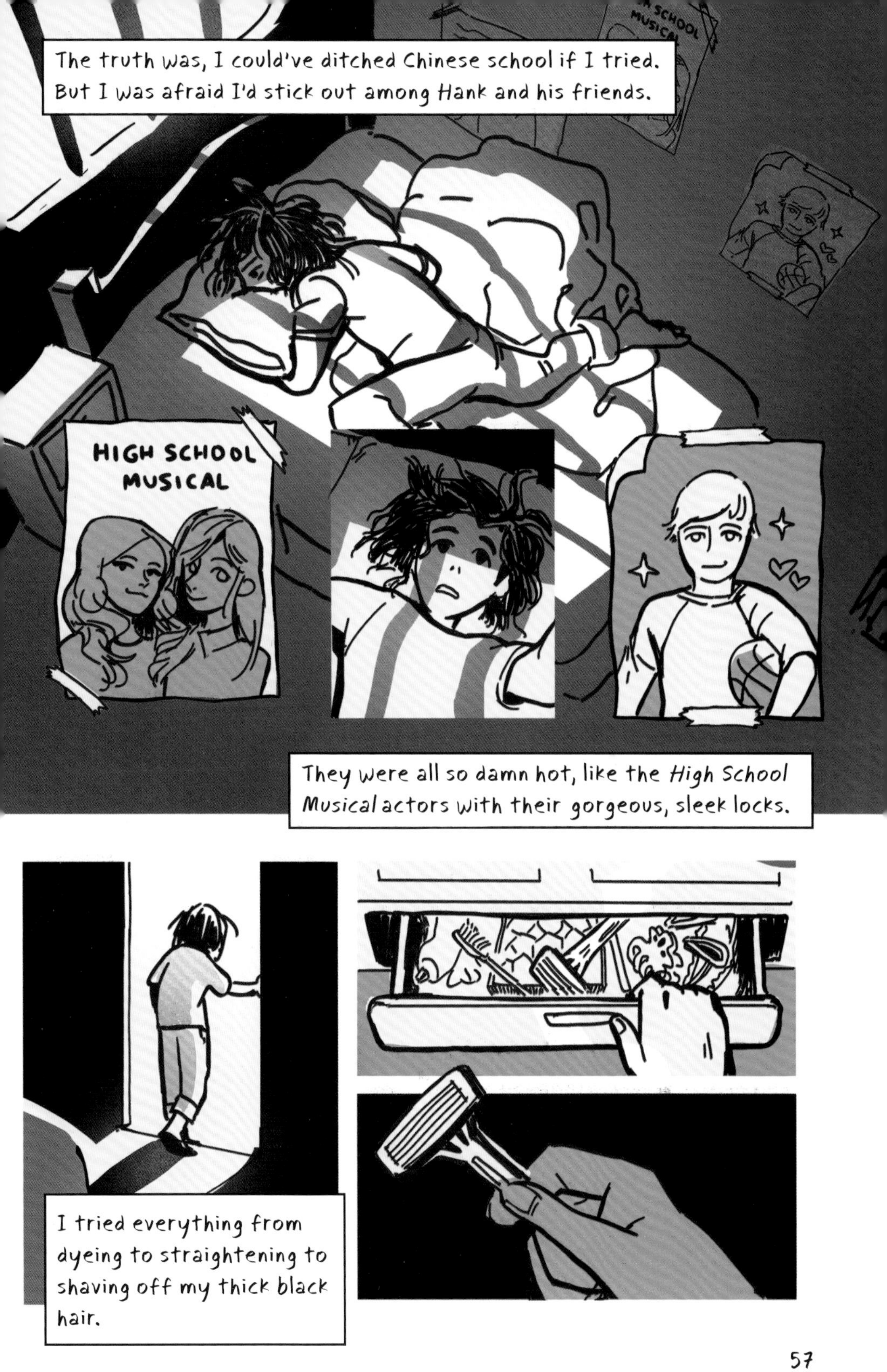
The truth was, I could've ditched Chinese school if I tried. But I was afraid I'd stick out among Hank and his friends.
HIGH SCHOOL MUSICAL
They were all so damn hot, like the *High School Musical* actors with their gorgeous, sleek locks.
I tried everything from dyeing to straightening to shaving off my thick black hair.

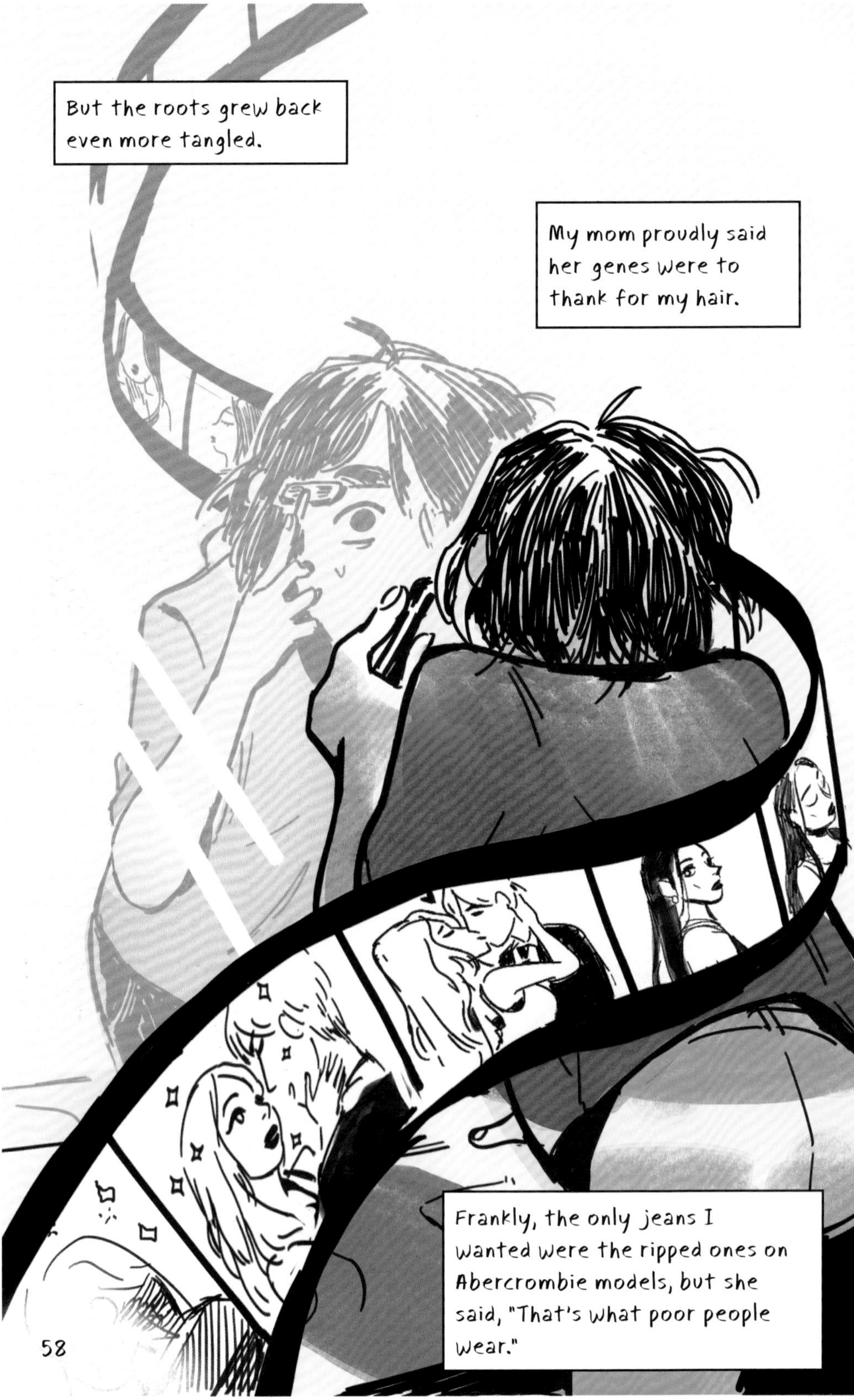
But the roots grew back even more tangled.
My mom proudly said her genes were to thank for my hair.
Frankly, the only jeans I wanted were the ripped ones on Abercrombie models, but she said, "That's what poor people wear."

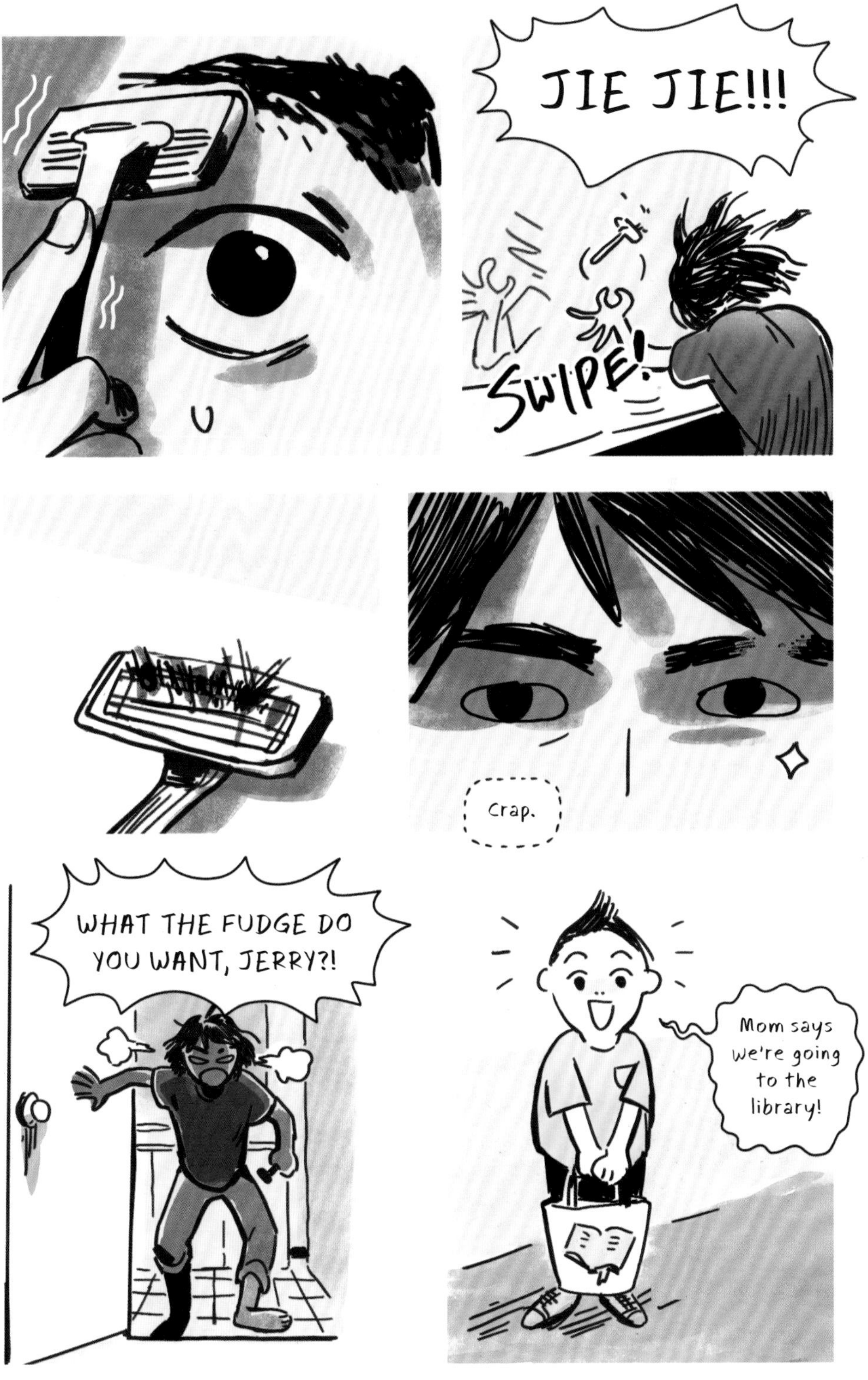
JIE JIE!!!
SWIPE!
Crap.
WHAT THE FUDGE DO YOU WANT, JERRY?!
Mom says we're going to the library!

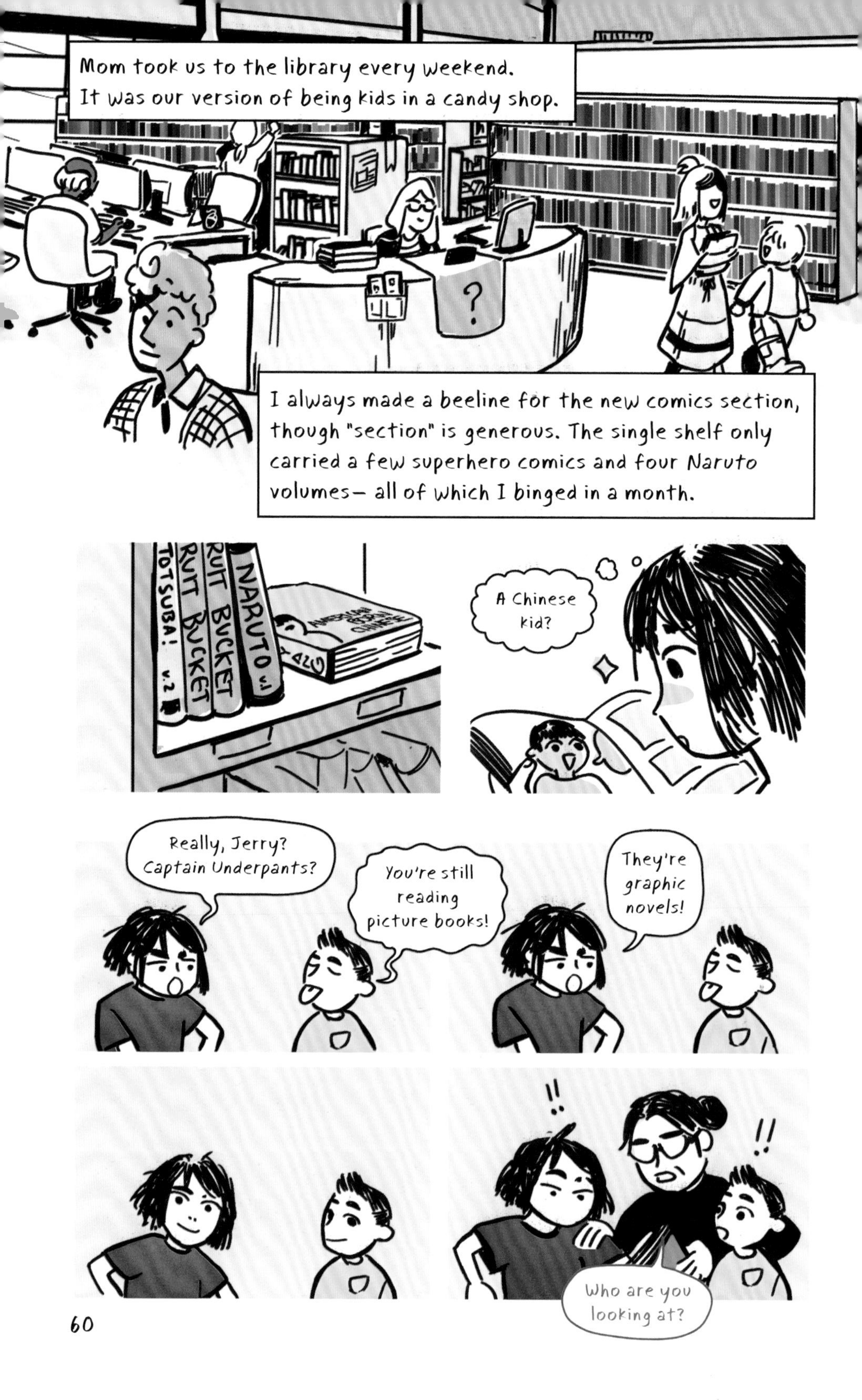

Mom took us to the library every weekend. It was our version of being kids in a candy shop.
?
I always made a beeline for the new comics section, though "section" is generous. The single shelf only carried a few superhero comics and four Naruto volumes— all of which I binged in a month.
NARUTO v.1
RUIT BUCKET
RUIT BUCKET
TOTSUBA! v.2
A Chinese kid?
Really, Jerry? Captain Underpants?
You're still reading picture books!
They're graphic novels!
!!
!!
Who are you looking at?

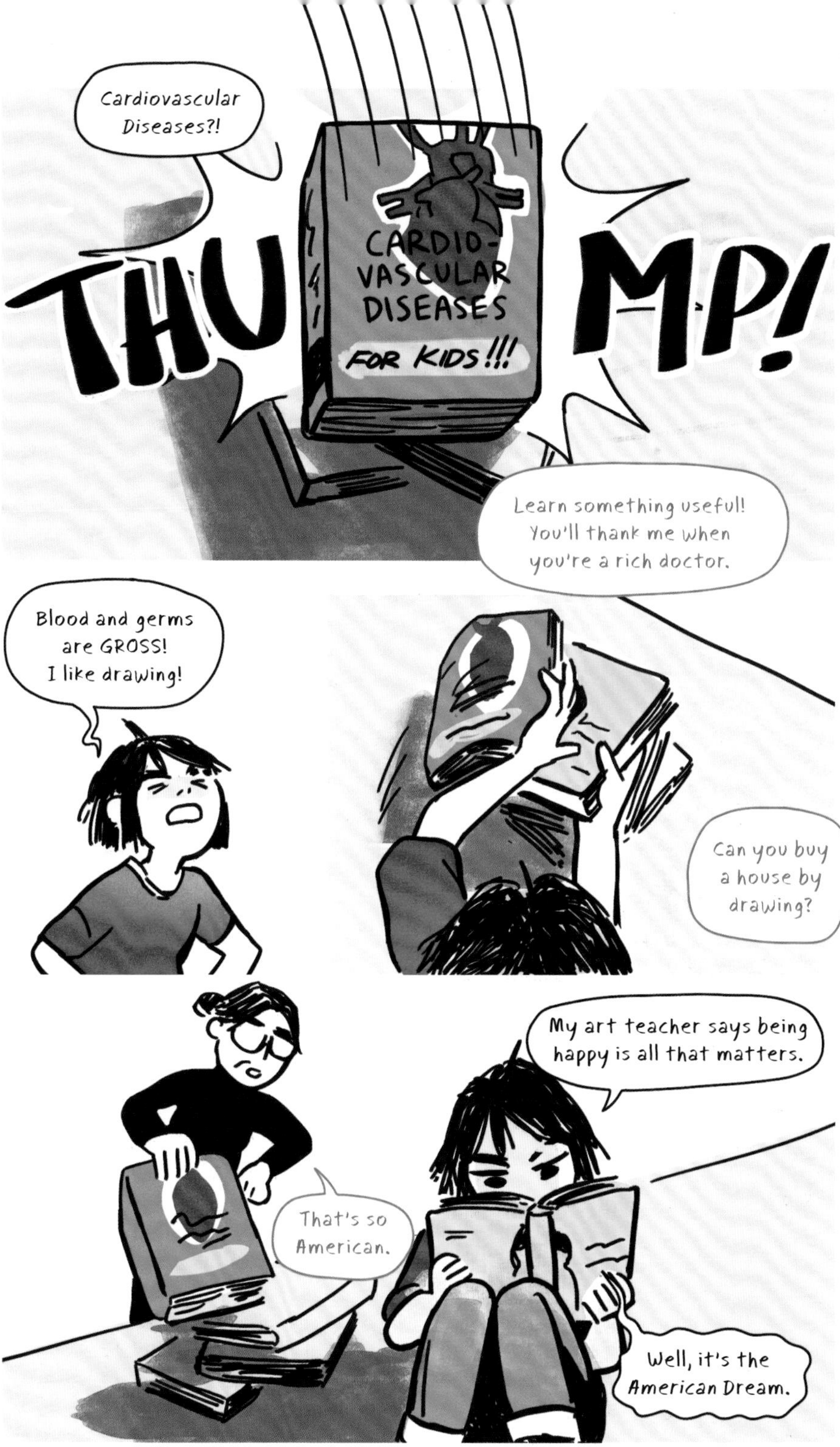
Cardiovascular Diseases?!
THUMP!
CARDIO-VASCULAR DISEASES FOR KIDS!!!
Learn something useful! You'll thank me when you're a rich doctor.
Blood and germs are GROSS! I like drawing!
Can you buy a house by drawing?
My art teacher says being happy is all that matters.
That's so American.
Well, it's the American Dream.

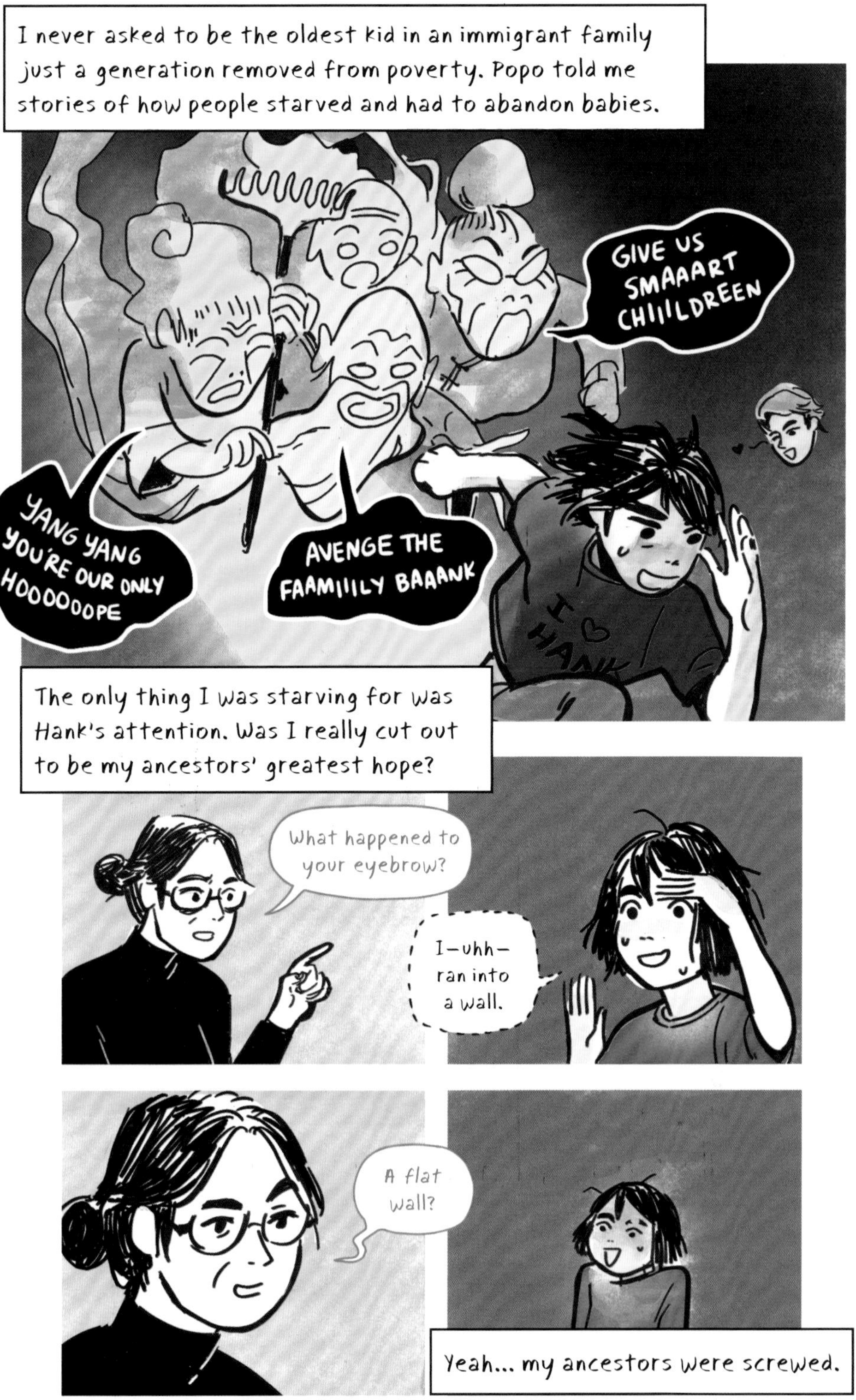
I never asked to be the oldest kid in an immigrant family just a generation removed from poverty. Popo told me stories of how people starved and had to abandon babies.
GIVE US SMAAART CHIIILDREEN
YANG YANG YOU'RE OUR ONLY HOOOOOOPE
AVENGE THE FAAMIIILY BAAANK
I ♡ HANK
The only thing I was starving for was Hank's attention. Was I really cut out to be my ancestors' greatest hope?
What happened to your eyebrow?
I—uhh— ran into a wall.
A flat wall?
Yeah... my ancestors were screwed.

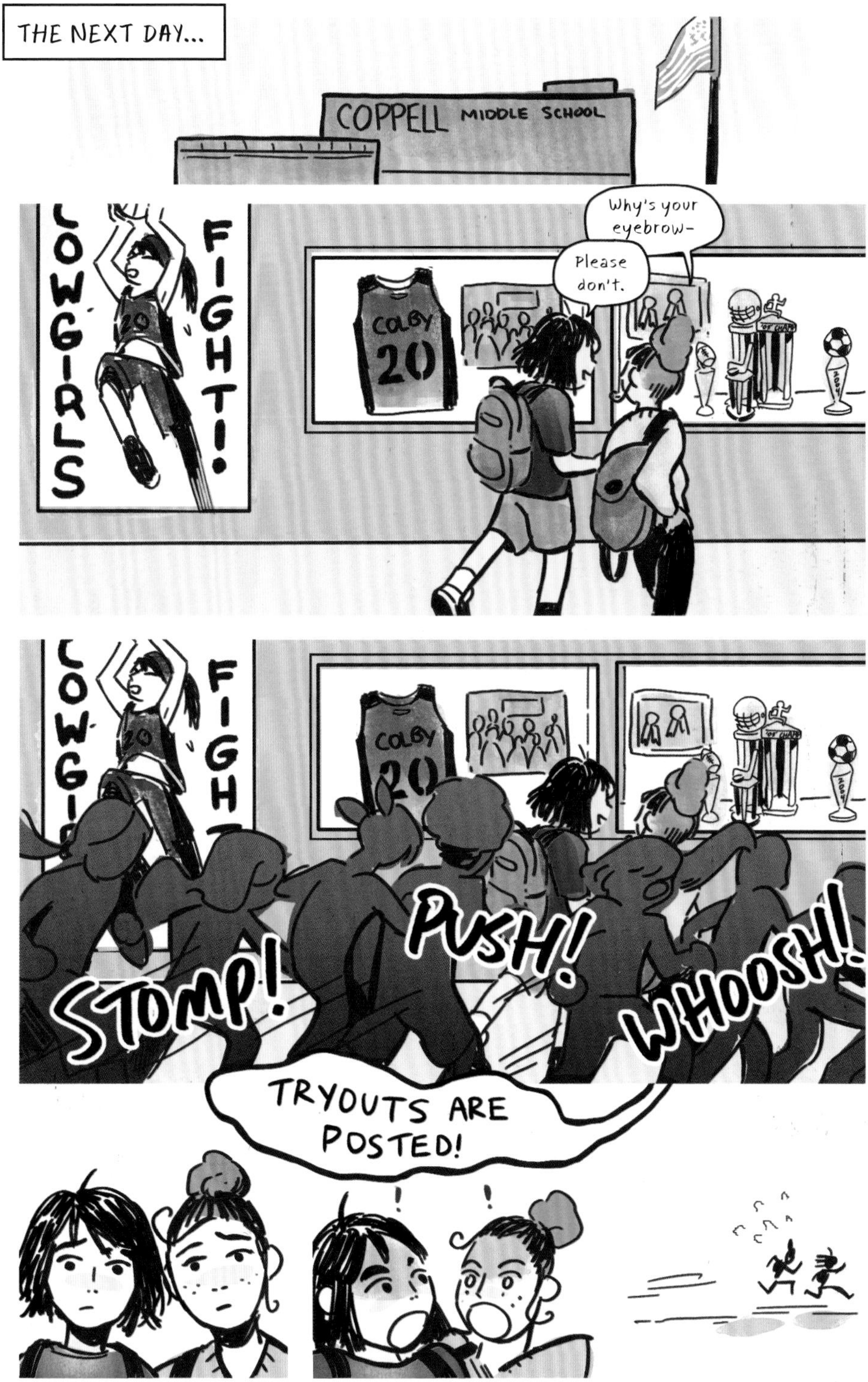
THE NEXT DAY...
COPPELL MIDDLE SCHOOL
COWGIRLS FIGHT!
COLBY 20
Why's your eyebrow-
Please don't.
STOMP!
PUSH!
WHOOSH!
TRYOUTS ARE POSTED!
!
!

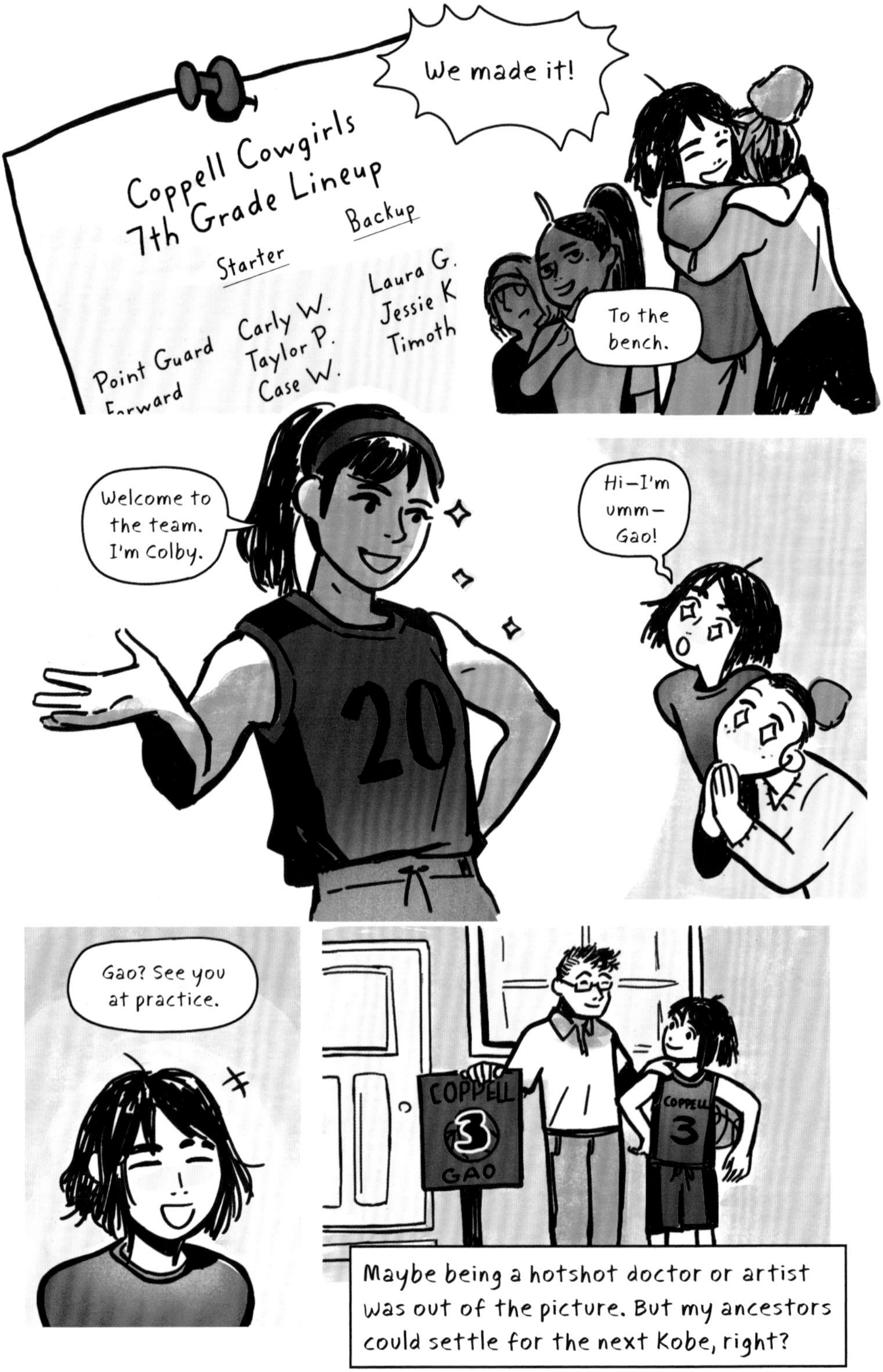
Coppell Cowgirls
7th Grade Lineup
Starter
Backup
Point Guard
Forward
Carly W.
Taylor P.
Case W.
Laura G.
Jessie K
Timoth
We made it!
To the bench.
Welcome to the team. I'm Colby.
20
Hi—I'm umm—Gao!
Gao? See you at practice.
COPPELL
3
GAO
COPPELL
3
Maybe being a hotshot doctor or artist was out of the picture. But my ancestors could settle for the next Kobe, right?

CHAPTER 5
Merry Jerry Christmas

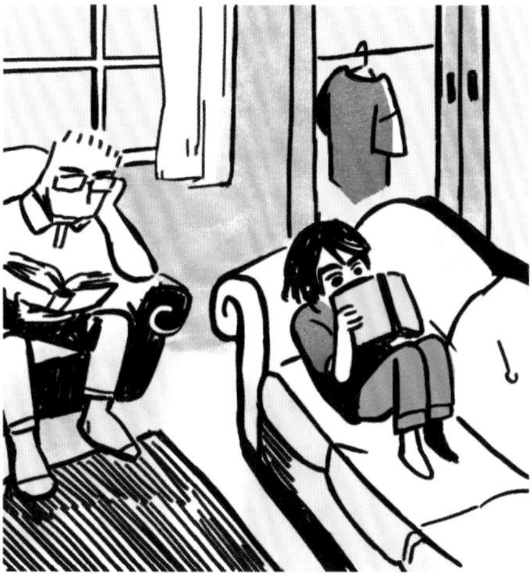

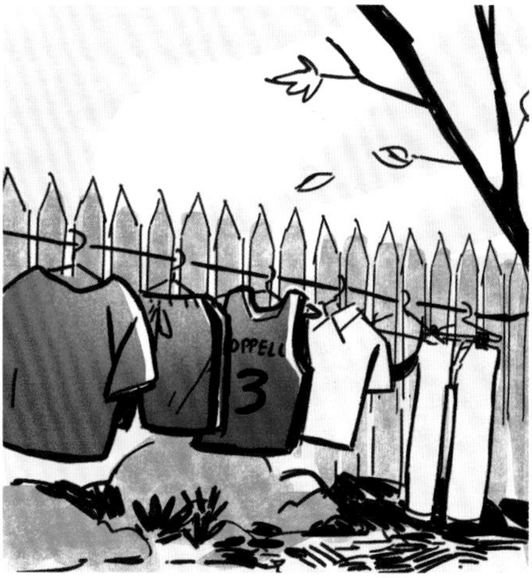

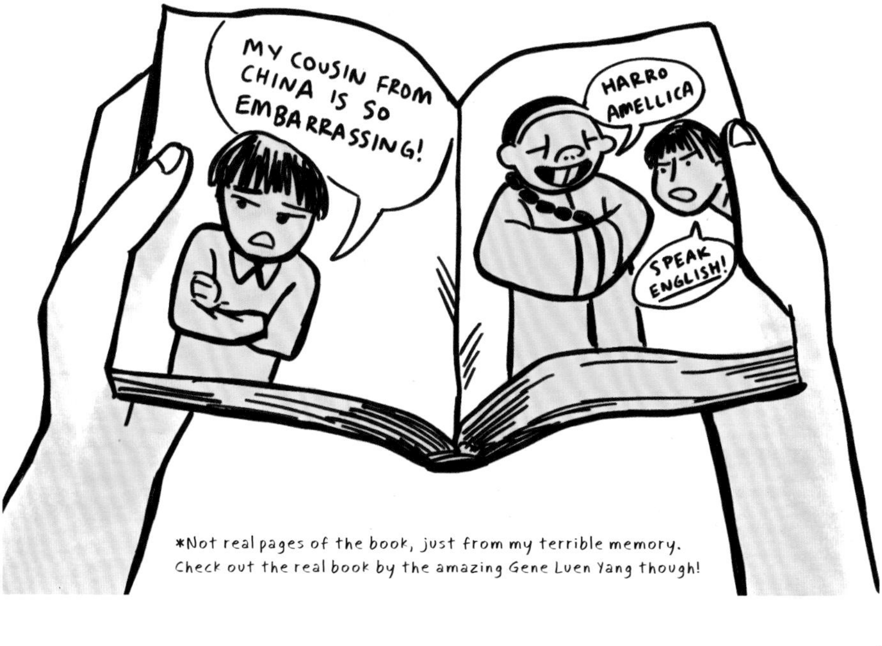
MY COUSIN FROM CHINA IS SO EMBARRASSING!
HARRO AMELLICA
SPEAK ENGLISH!
*Not real pages of the book, just from my terrible memory.
Check out the real book by the amazing Gene Luen Yang though!

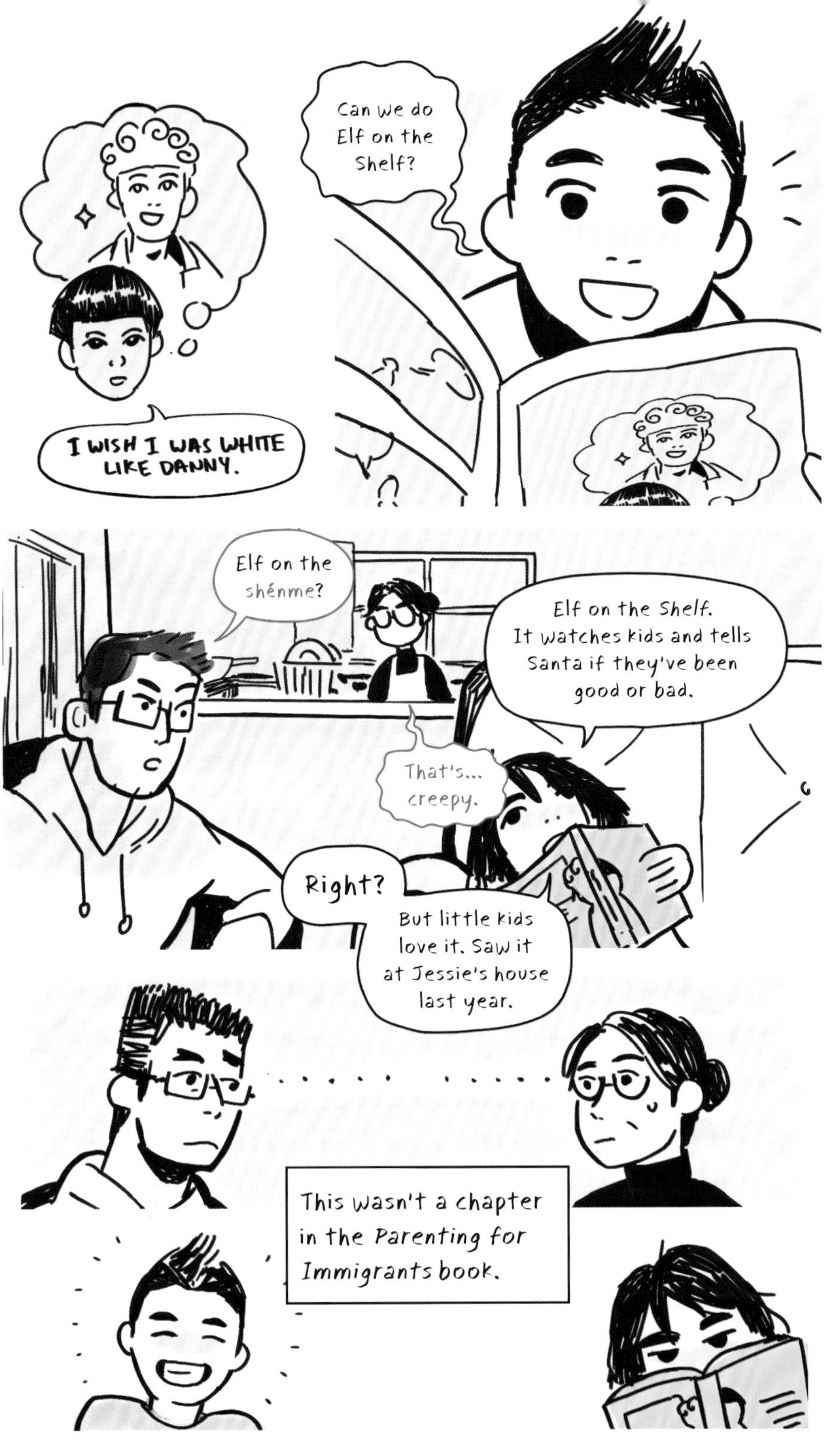
I WISH I WAS WHITE LIKE DANNY.
Can we do Elf on the Shelf?
Elf on the shénme?
Elf on the Shelf. It watches kids and tells Santa if they've been good or bad.
That's... creepy.
Right?
But little kids love it. Saw it at Jessie's house last year.
This wasn't a chapter in the Parenting for Immigrants book.

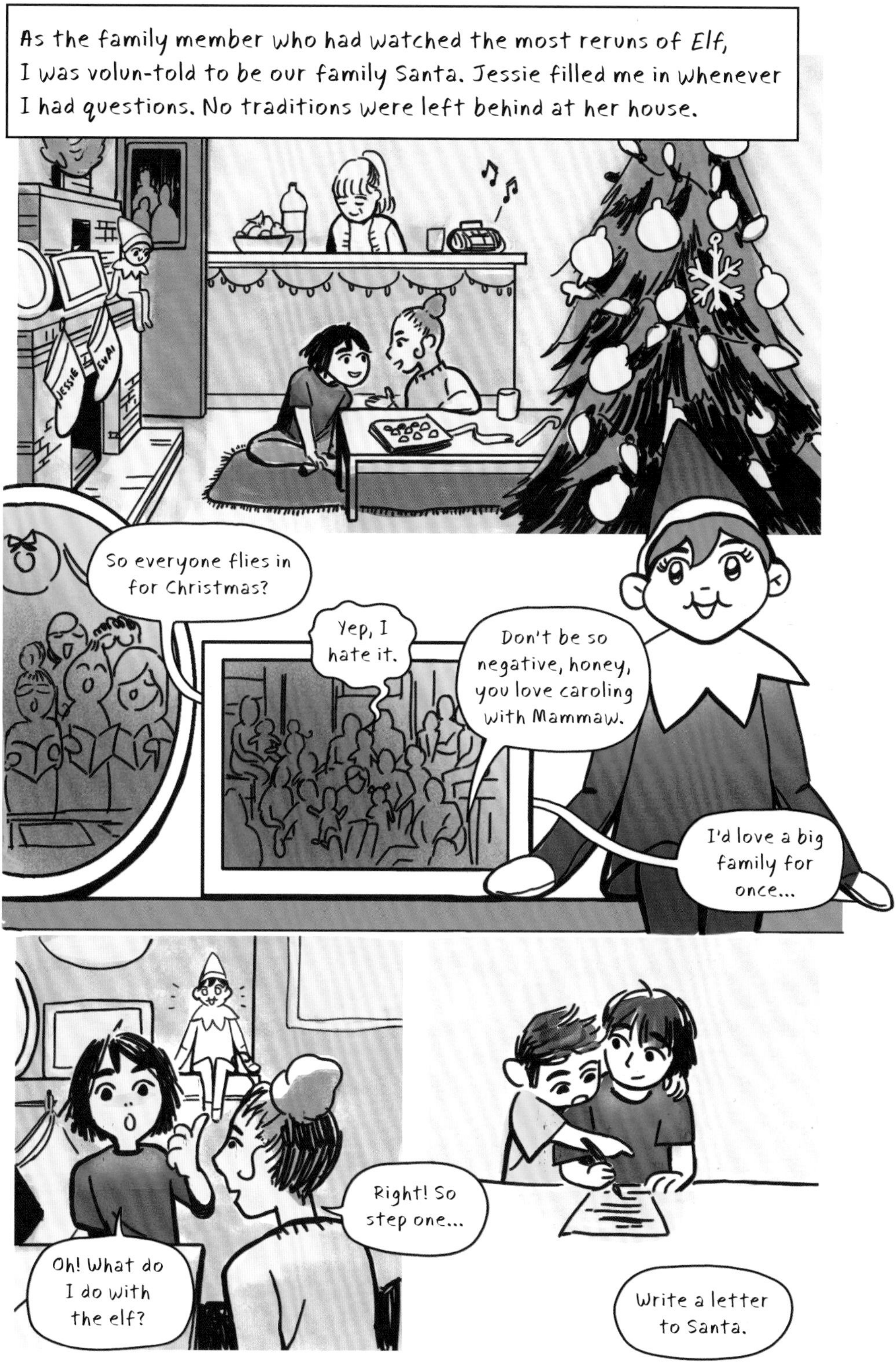
As the family member who had watched the most reruns of *Elf*, I was volun-told to be our family Santa. Jessie filled me in whenever I had questions. No traditions were left behind at her house.
JESSIE
So everyone flies in for Christmas?
Yep, I hate it.
Don't be so negative, honey, you love caroling with Mammaw.
I'd love a big family for once...
Oh! What do I do with the elf?
Right! So step one...
Write a letter to Santa.

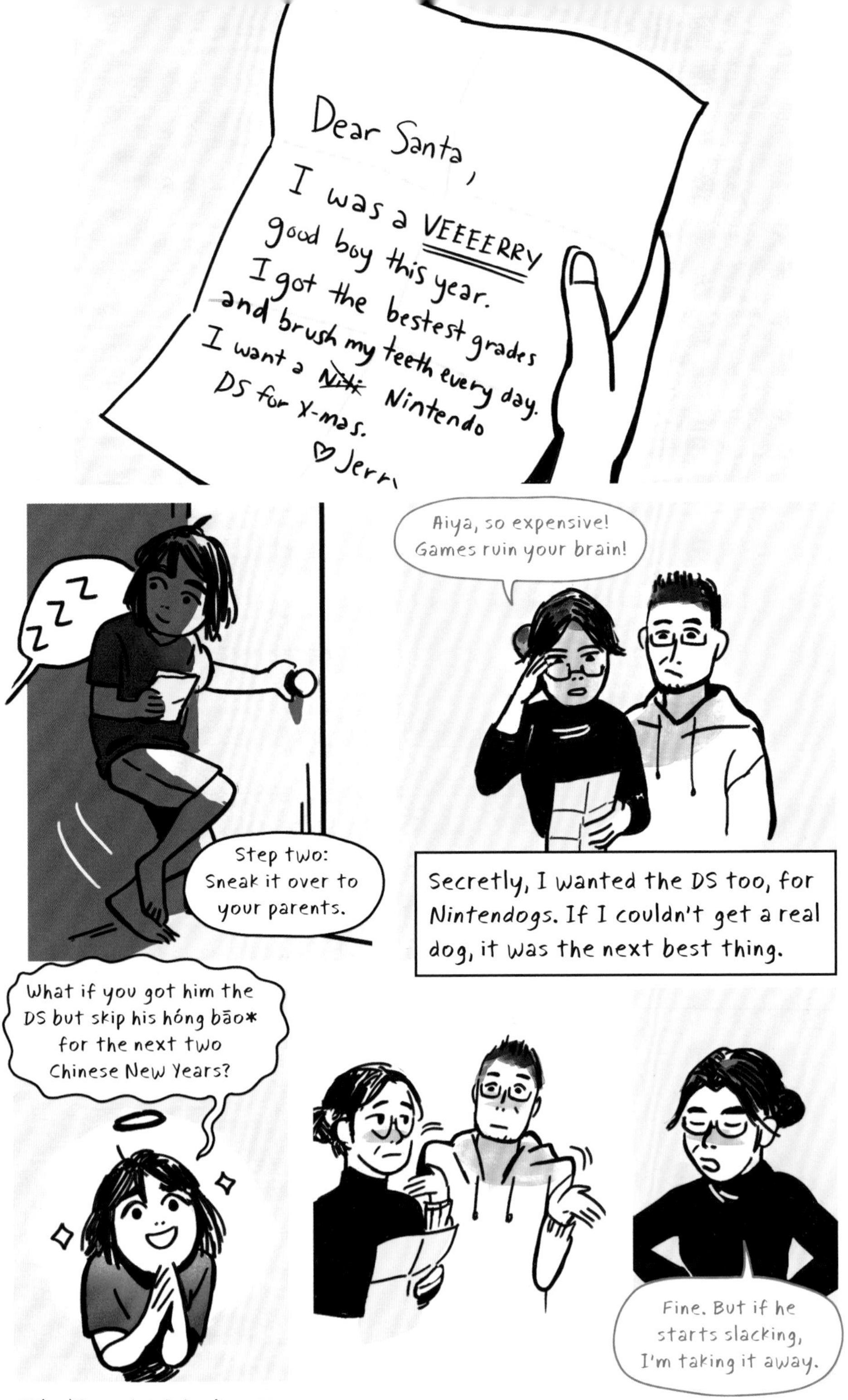
Dear Santa,
I was a VEEEERRY good boy this year.
I got the bestest grades and brush my teeth every day.
I want a ~~Nit~~ Nintendo DS for X-mas.
♡Jerr
ZZZ
Step two: Sneak it over to your parents.
Aiya, so expensive! Games ruin your brain!
Secretly, I wanted the DS too, for Nintendogs. If I couldn't get a real dog, it was the next best thing.
What if you got him the DS but skip his hóng bāo* for the next two Chinese New Years?
Fine. But if he starts slacking, I'm taking it away.

*hóng bāo = red packets of money given to kids for Chinese New Year

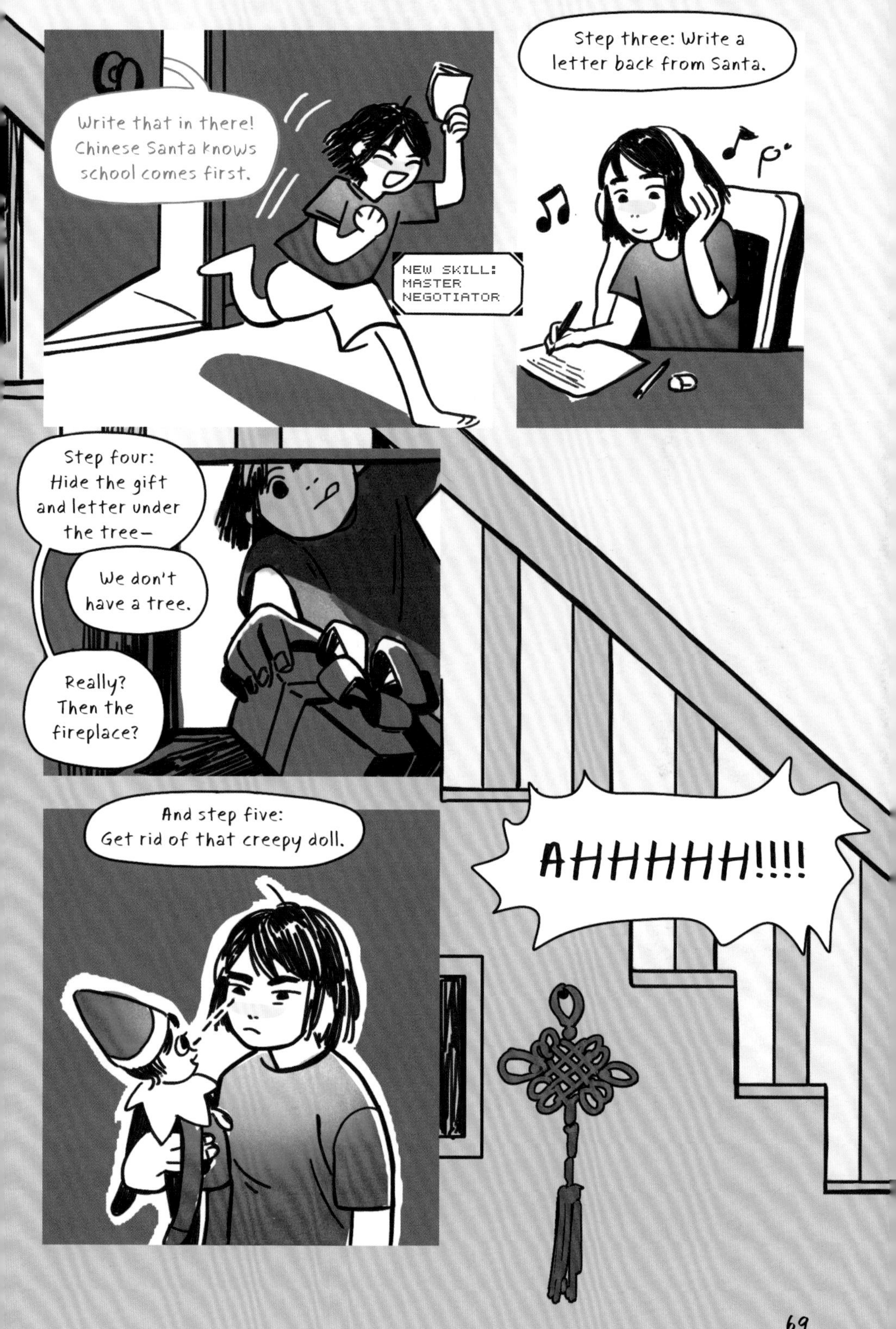
Write that in there! Chinese Santa knows school comes first.
NEW SKILL: MASTER NEGOTIATOR
Step three: Write a letter back from Santa.
Step four: Hide the gift and letter under the tree—
We don't have a tree.
Really? Then the fireplace?
And step five: Get rid of that creepy doll.
AHHHHHH!!!!!

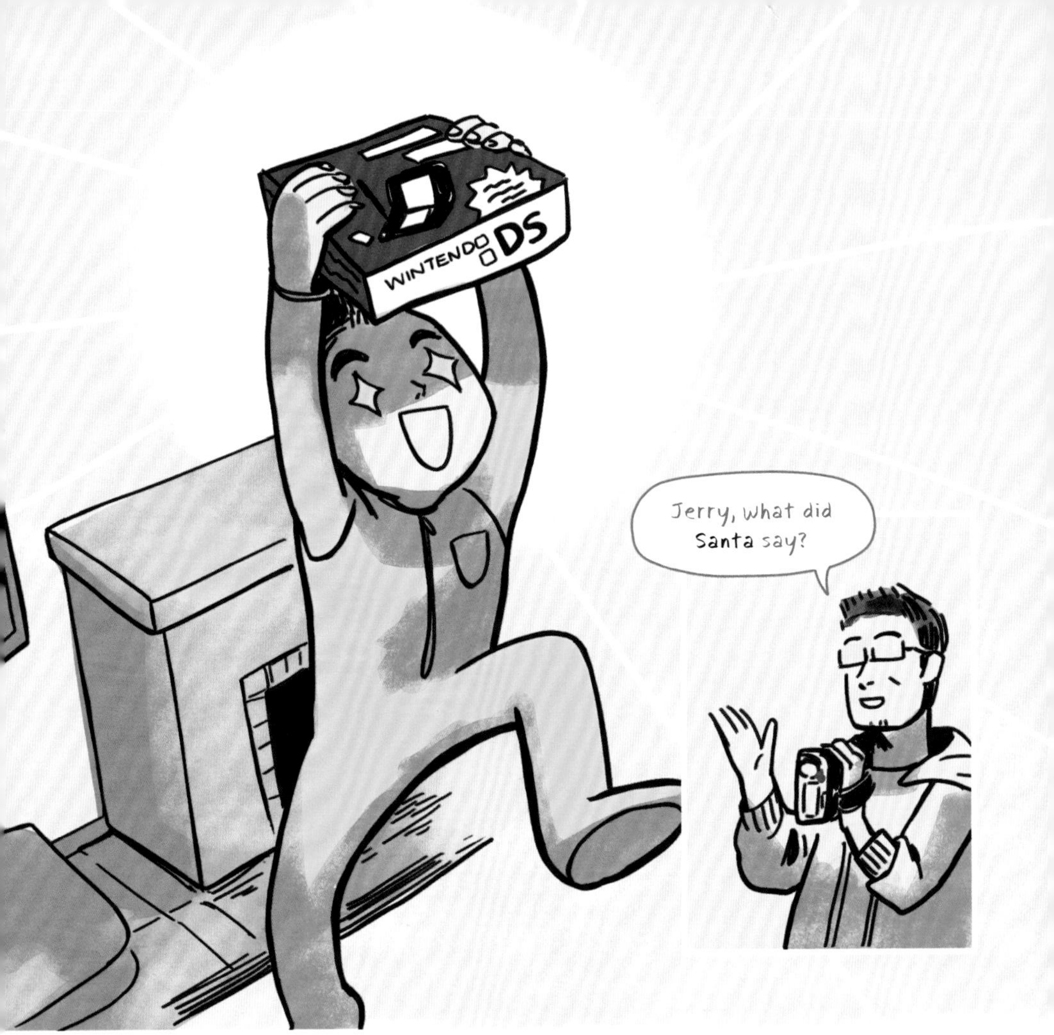
WINTENDO DS
Jerry, what did Santa say?

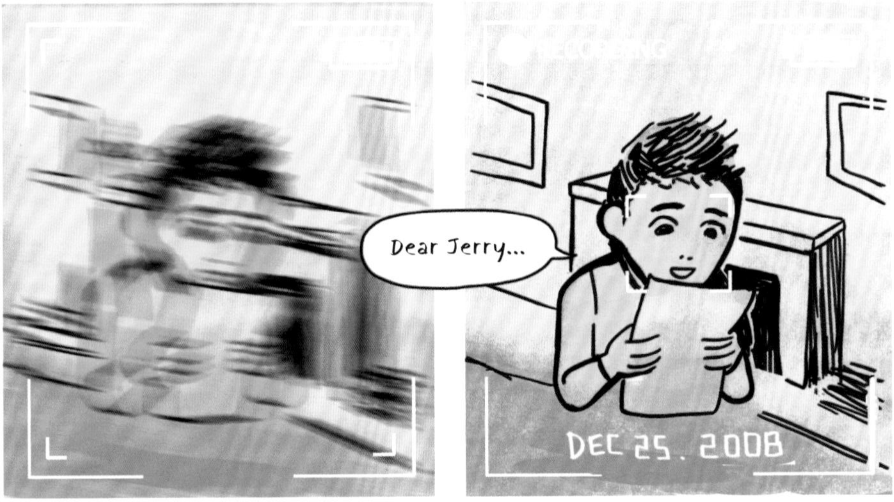
Dear Jerry...
DEC 25. 2008

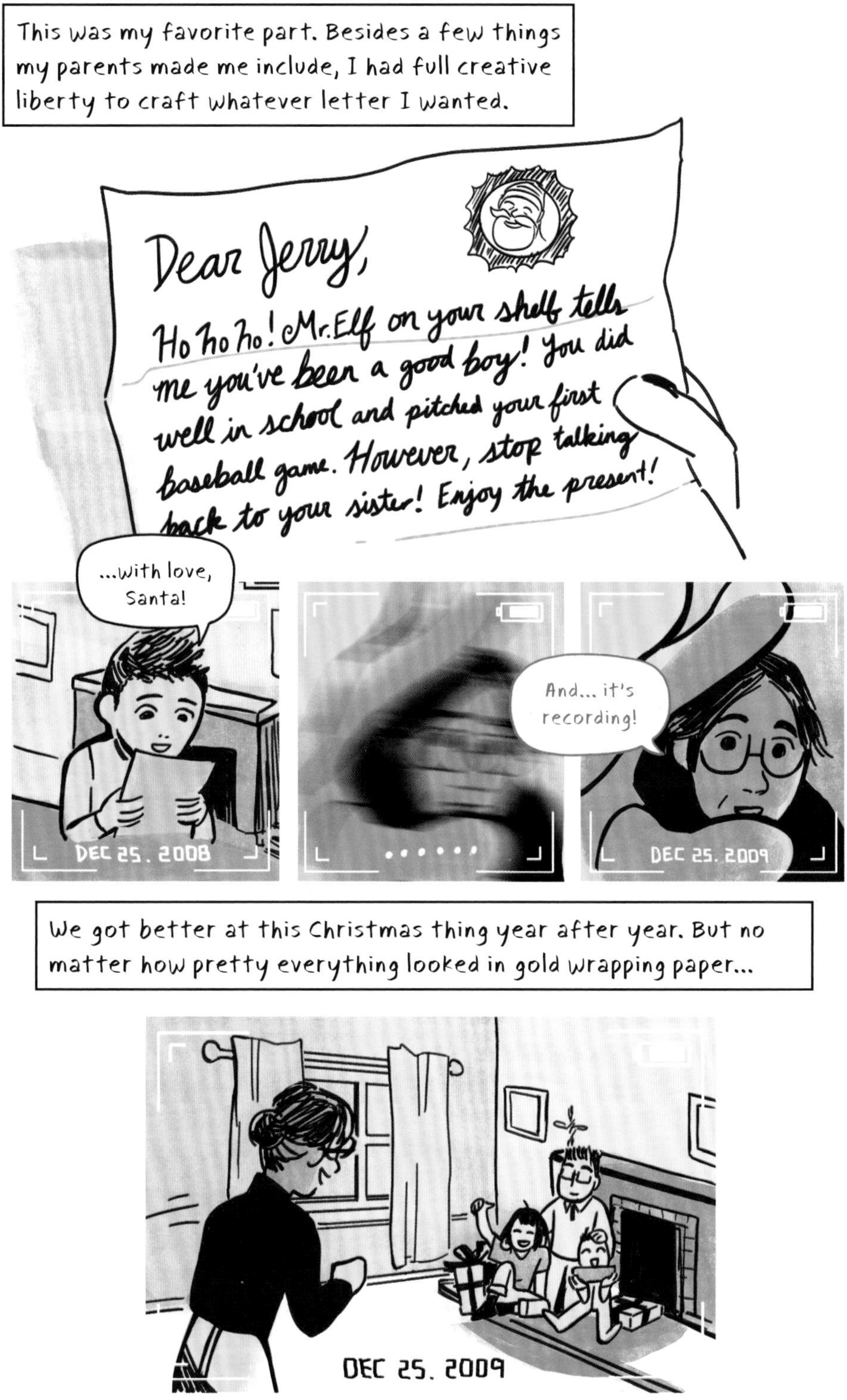
This was my favorite part. Besides a few things my parents made me include, I had full creative liberty to craft whatever letter I wanted.
Dear Jerry,
Ho ho ho! Mr. Elf on your shelf tells me you've been a good boy! You did well in school and pitched your first baseball game. However, stop talking back to your sister! Enjoy the present!
...with love, Santa!
DEC 25. 2008
And... it's recording!
DEC 25. 2009
We got better at this Christmas thing year after year. But no matter how pretty everything looked in gold wrapping paper...
DEC 25. 2009

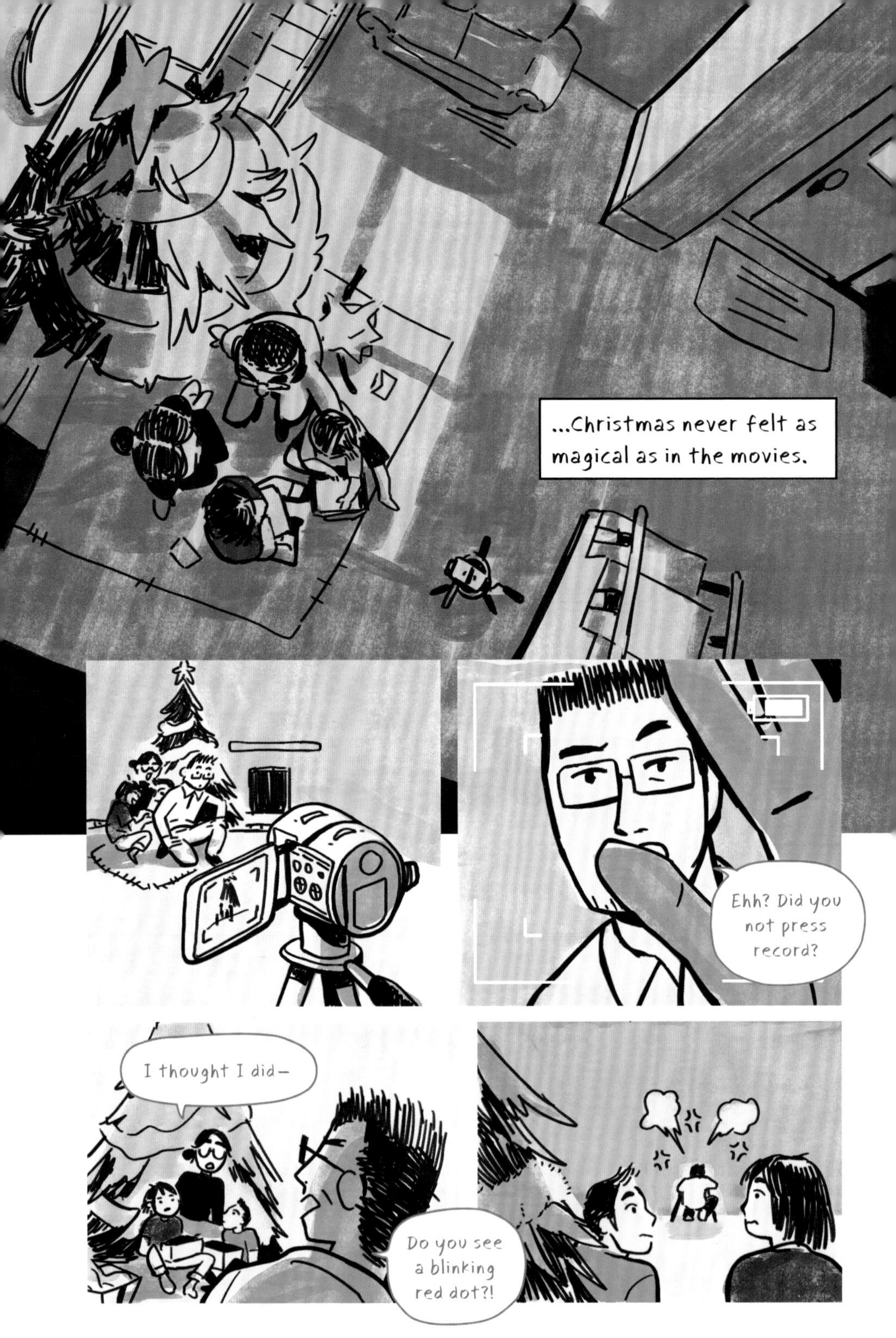
...Christmas never felt as magical as in the movies.
Ehh? Did you not press record?
I thought I did—
Do you see a blinking red dot?!

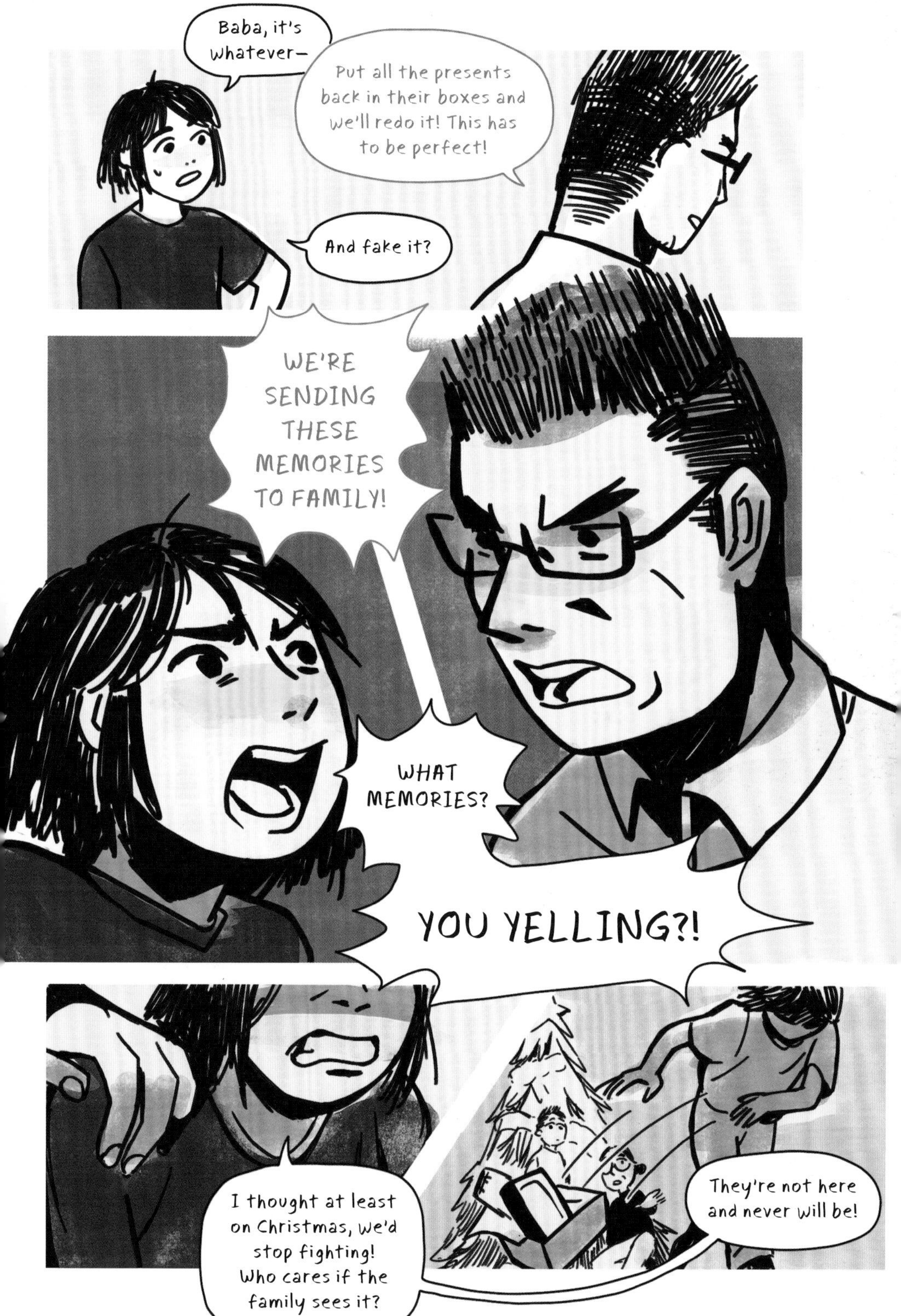

Baba, it's whatever—
Put all the presents back in their boxes and we'll redo it! This has to be perfect!
And fake it?
WE'RE SENDING THESE MEMORIES TO FAMILY!
WHAT MEMORIES?
YOU YELLING?!
I thought at least on Christmas, we'd stop fighting! Who cares if the family sees it?
They're not here and never will be!

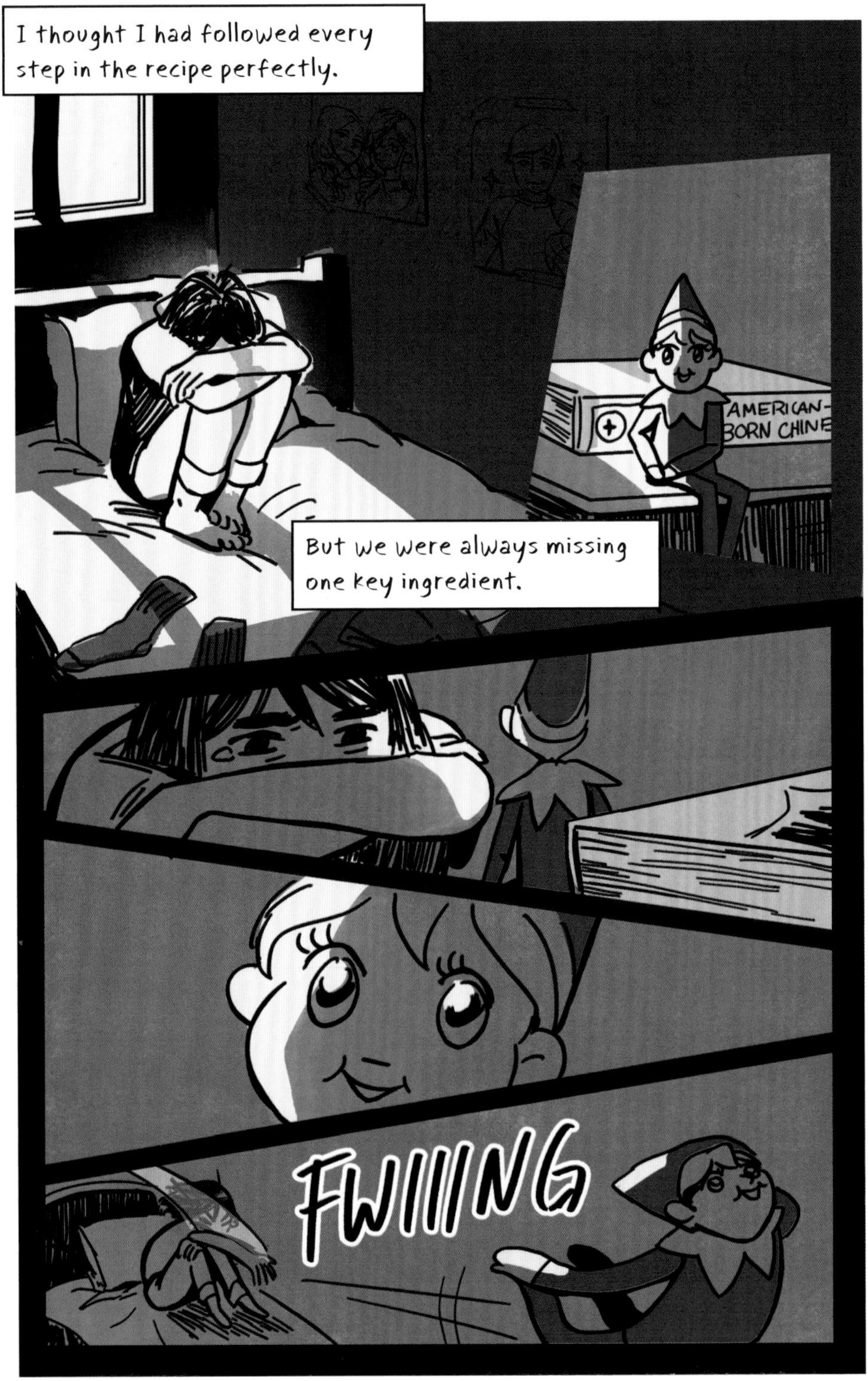
I thought I had followed every step in the recipe perfectly.
AMERICAN-BORN CHINE
But we were always missing one key ingredient.
FWIIING

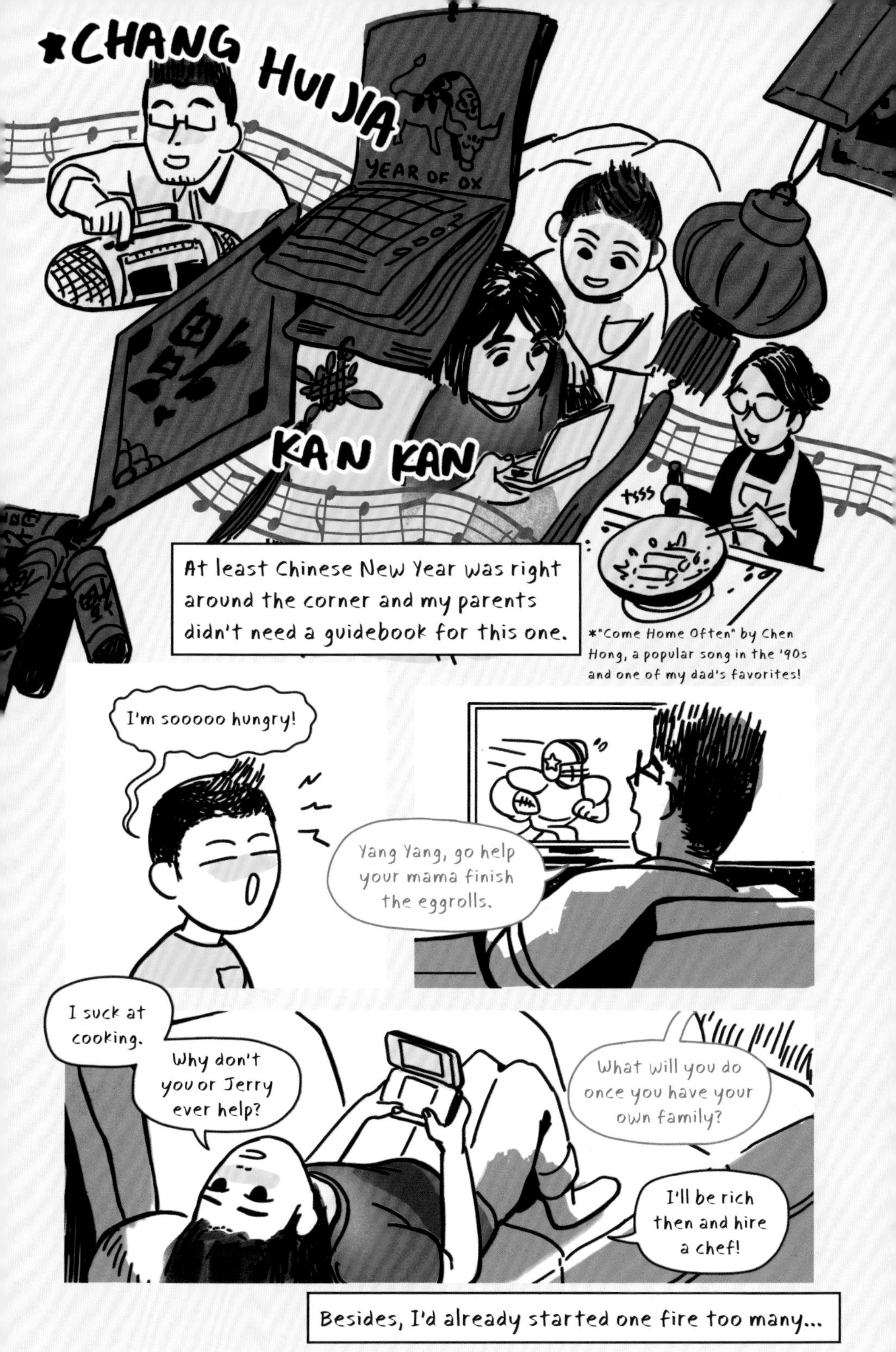
*CHANG HUI JIA
YEAR OF OX
2009
KAN KAN
TSSS
At least Chinese New Year was right around the corner and my parents didn't need a guidebook for this one.
*"Come Home Often" by Chen Hong, a popular song in the '90s and one of my dad's favorites!
I'm sooooo hungry!
Yang Yang, go help your mama finish the eggrolls.
I suck at cooking.
Why don't you or Jerry ever help?
What will you do once you have your own family?
I'll be rich then and hire a chef!
Besides, I'd already started one fire too many...

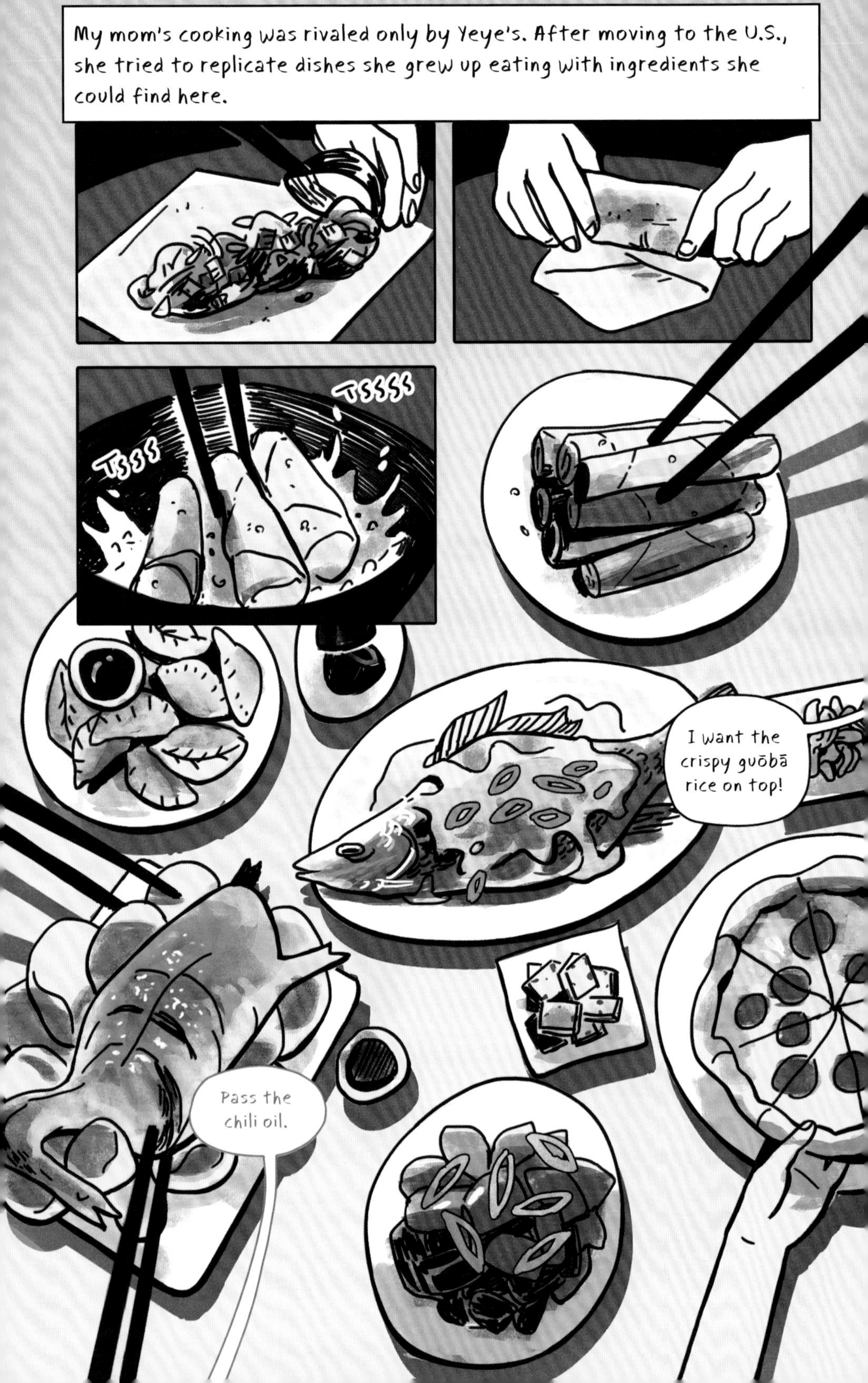
My mom's cooking was rivaled only by Yeye's. After moving to the U.S., she tried to replicate dishes she grew up eating with ingredients she could find here.
TSSSS
TSSS
I want the crispy guōbā rice on top!
Pass the chili oil.

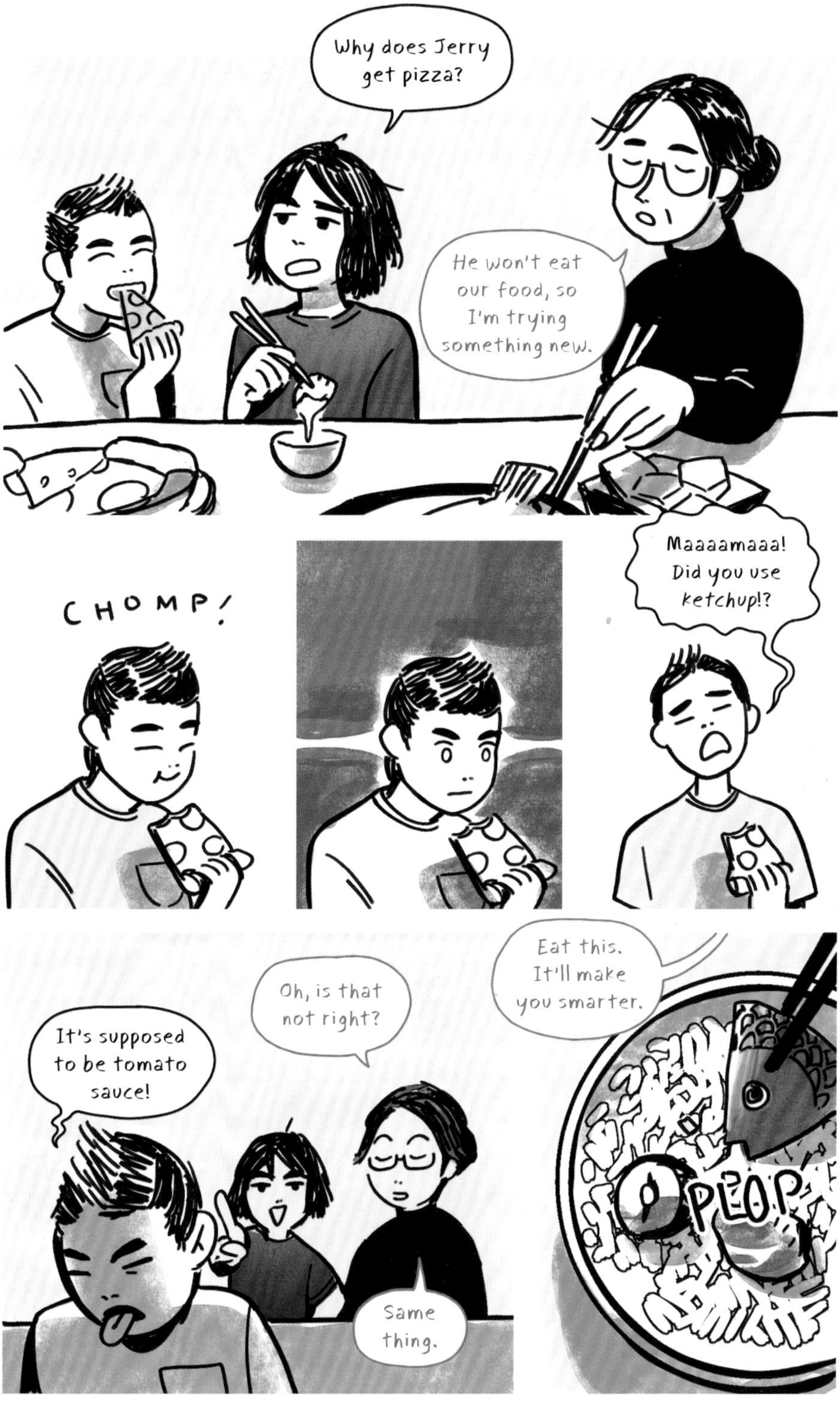
Why does Jerry get pizza?
He won't eat our food, so I'm trying something new.
CHOMP!
Maaaamaaa! Did you use ketchup!?
It's supposed to be tomato sauce!
Oh, is that not right?
Same thing.
Eat this. It'll make you smarter.
PLOP

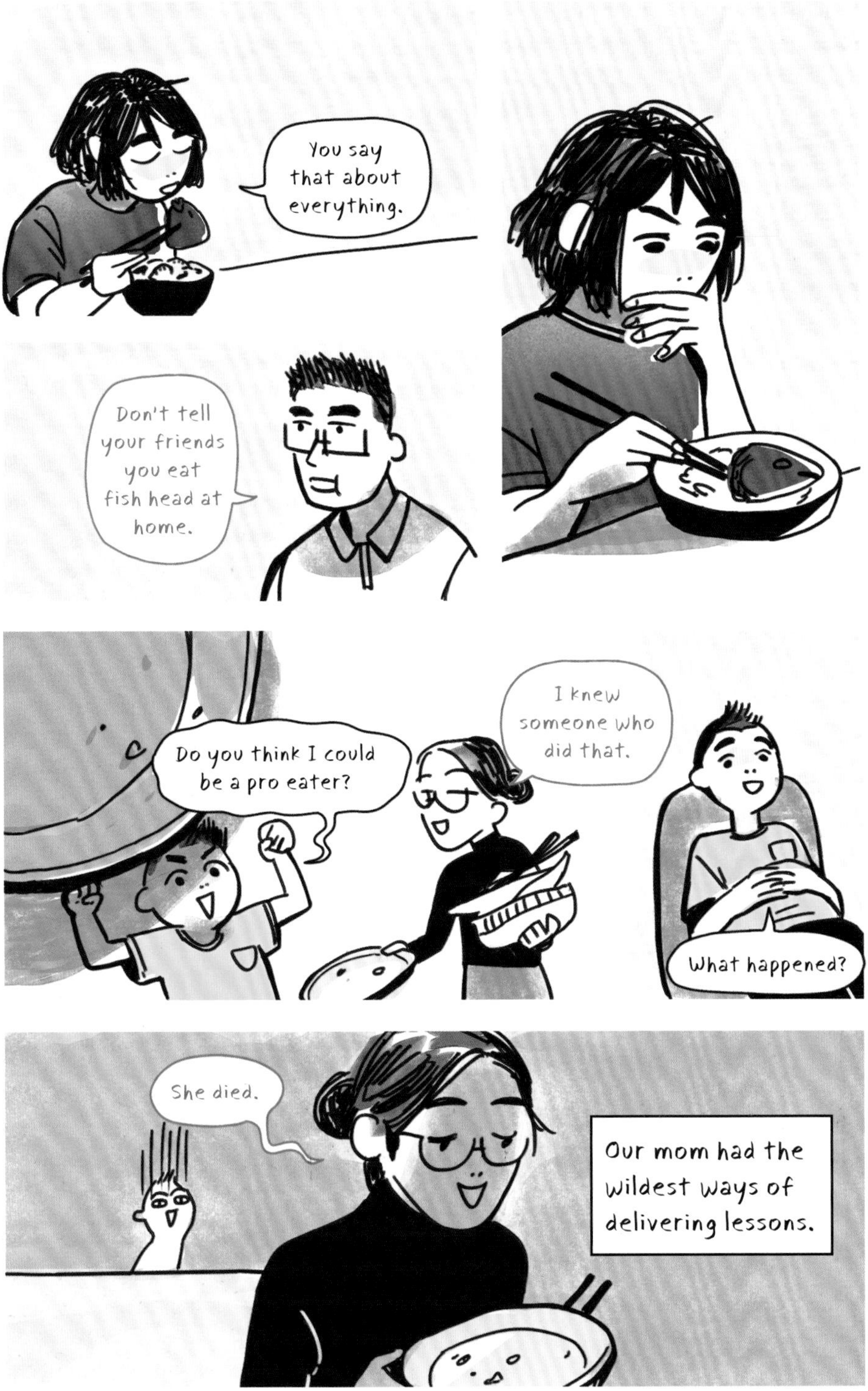

You say that about everything.
Don't tell your friends you eat fish head at home.
Do you think I could be a pro eater?
I knew someone who did that.
What happened?
She died.
Our mom had the wildest ways of delivering lessons.

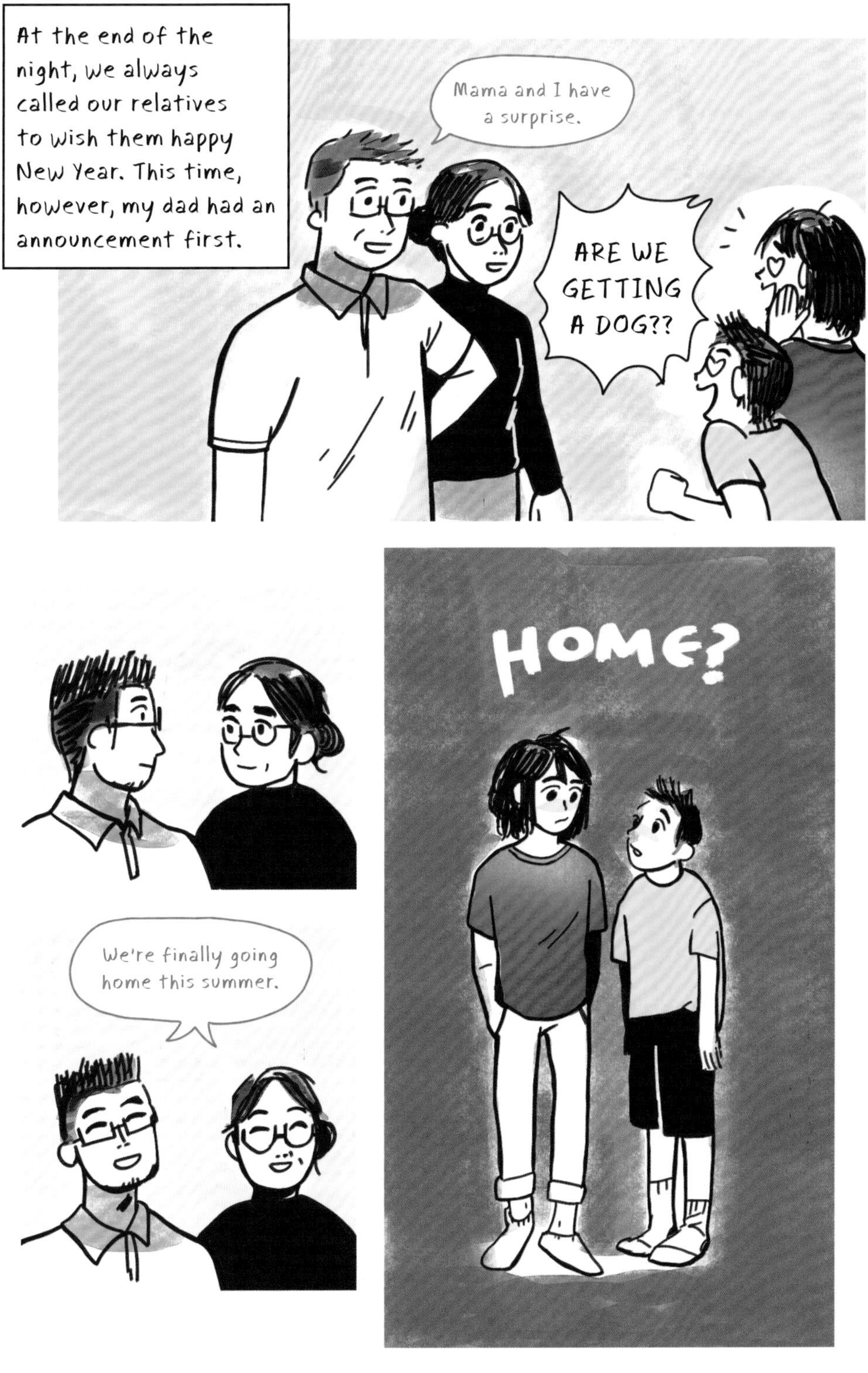
At the end of the night, we always called our relatives to wish them happy New Year. This time, however, my dad had an announcement first.
Mama and I have a surprise.
ARE WE GETTING A DOG??
We're finally going home this summer.
HOME?

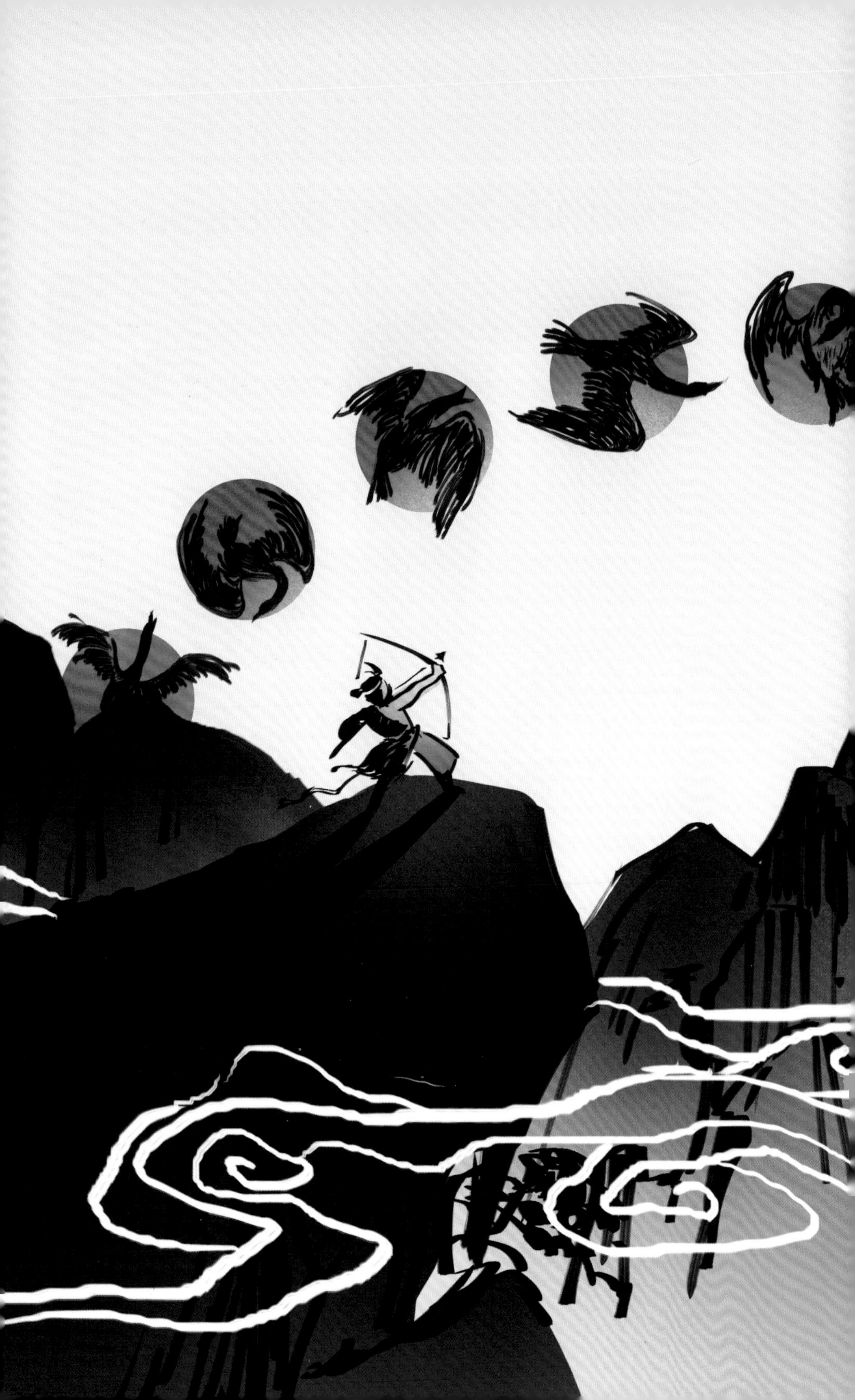

CHAPTER 6
The Wuhan I Knew?

My favorite Chinese folktale is Chang'e and her guardian rabbit on the moon.

Chang'e once lived on Earth with her lover, Houyi, an archer who saved humanity from burning up by shooting down nine sun spirits. For his deed, the gods gifted Houyi the elixir of immortality.

Honey, did you see that?
No, but have you seen this cat painting?

One day, to stop someone from stealing the elixir, Chang'e sacrificed herself and drank it, causing her body to fly up into the heavens. To stay close to her love, she decided to land on the moon.

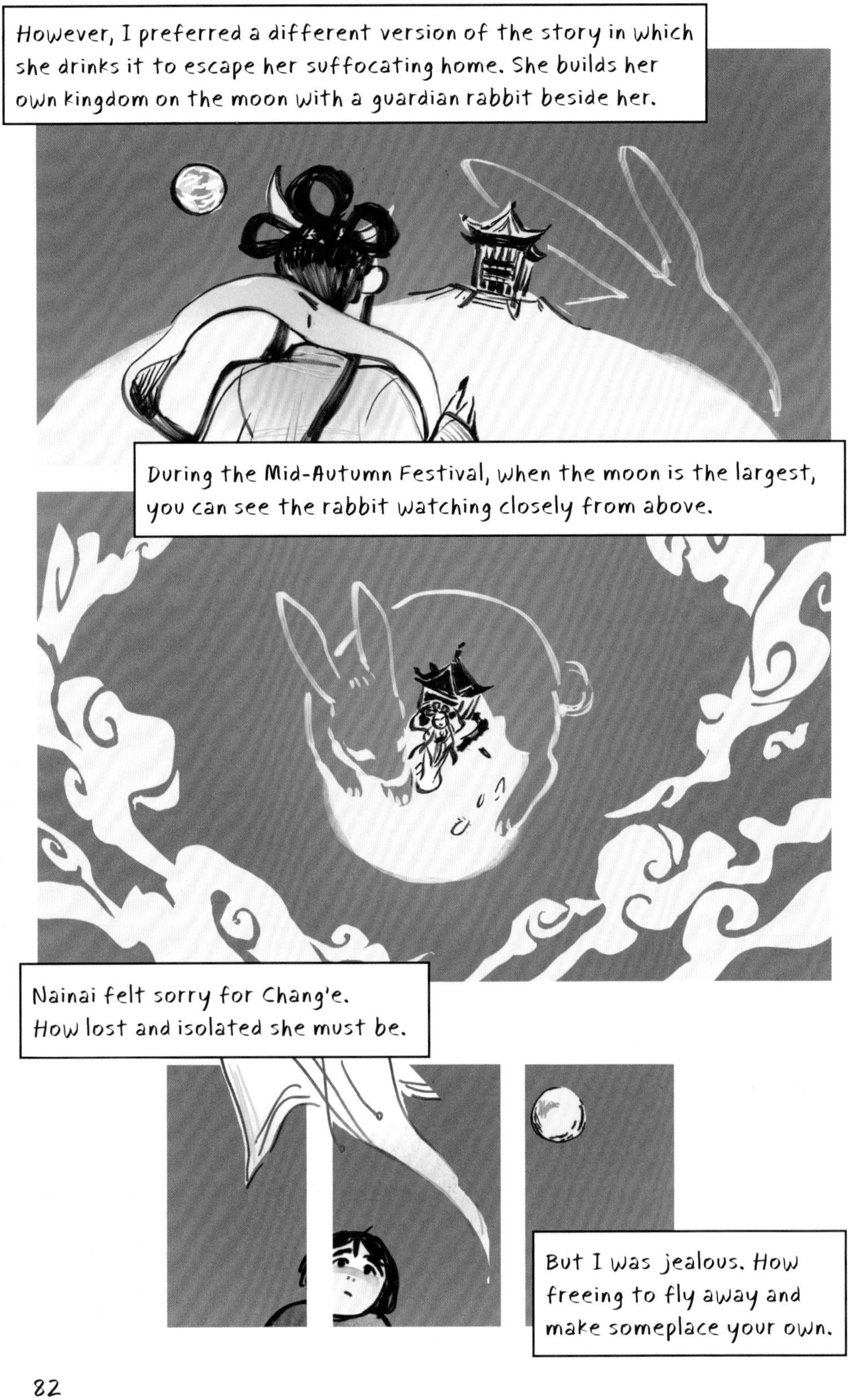
However, I preferred a different version of the story in which she drinks it to escape her suffocating home. She builds her own kingdom on the moon with a guardian rabbit beside her.
During the Mid-Autumn Festival, when the moon is the largest, you can see the rabbit watching closely from above.
Nainai felt sorry for Chang'e. How lost and isolated she must be.
But I was jealous. How freeing to fly away and make someplace your own.

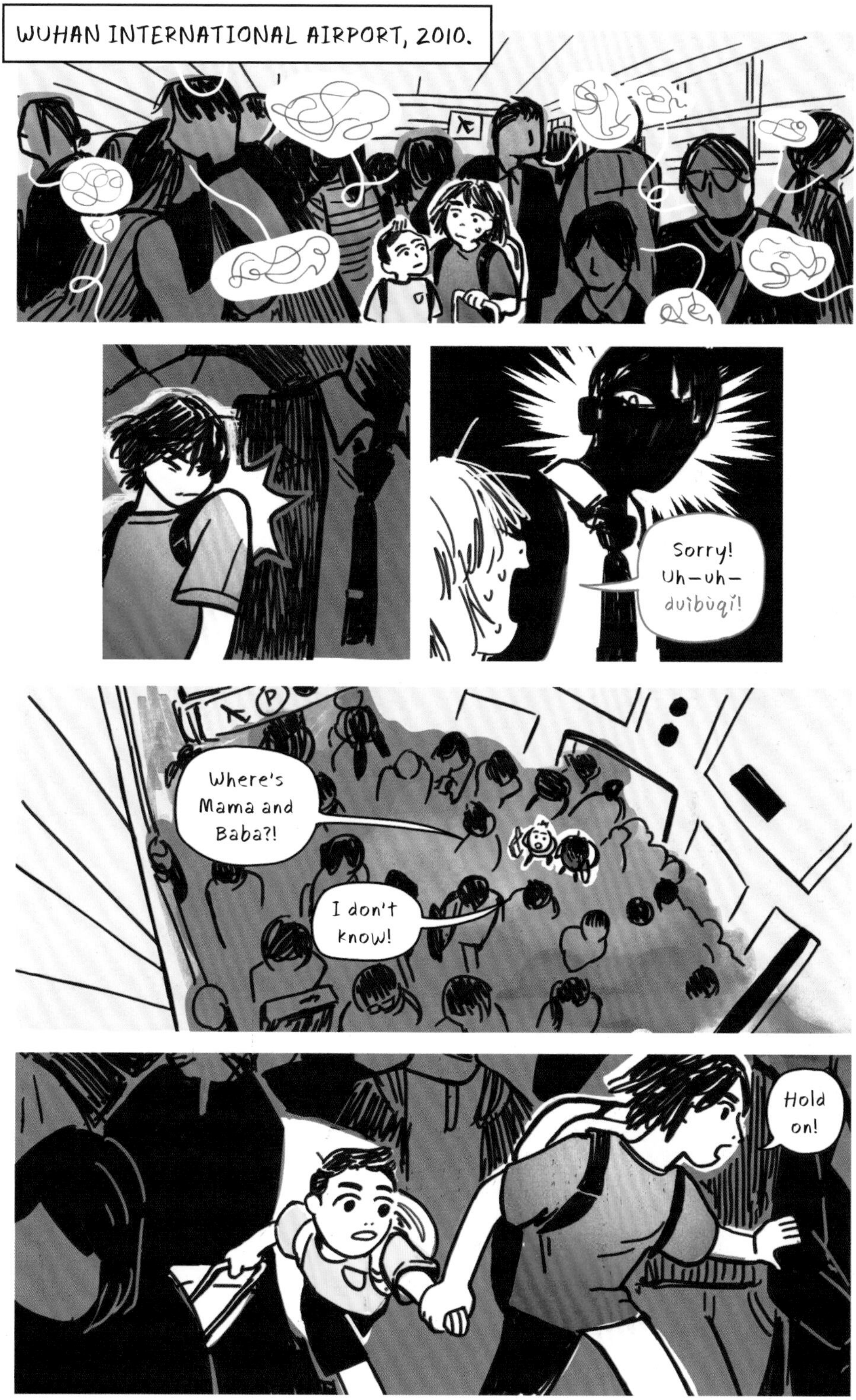
WUHAN INTERNATIONAL AIRPORT, 2010.
Sorry! Uh-uh- duìbùqǐ!
Where's Mama and Baba?!
I don't know!
Hold on!

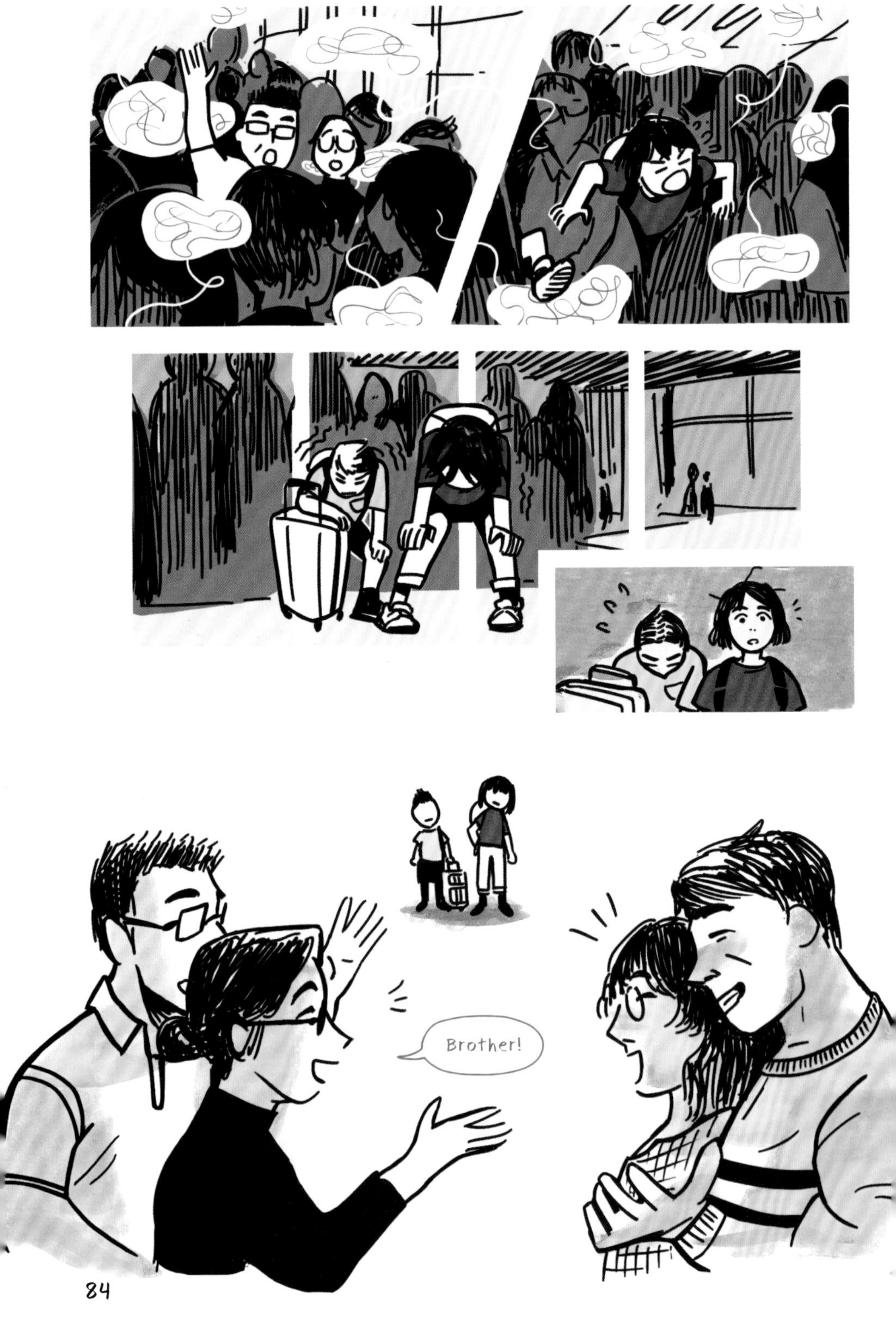
Brother!

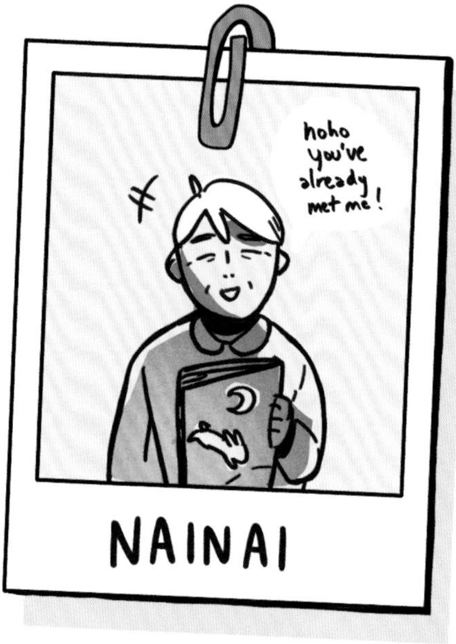
hoho you've already met me!
NAINAI

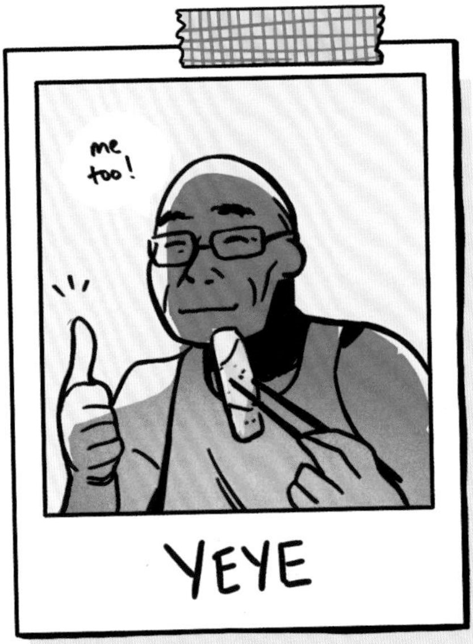
me too!
YEYE

MEET MOM'S SIDE

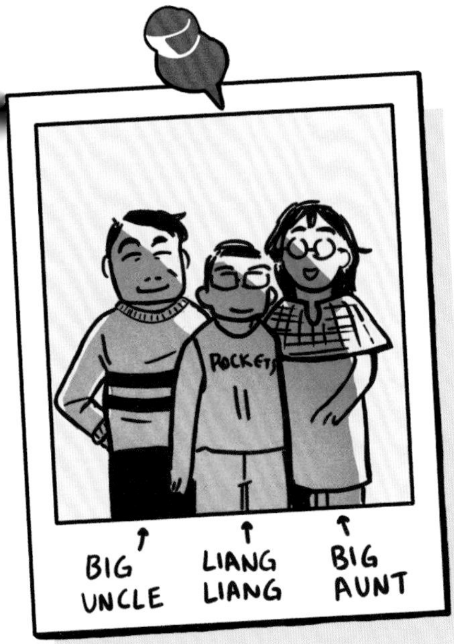
ROCKETS
11
BIG UNCLE
LIANG LIANG
BIG AUNT

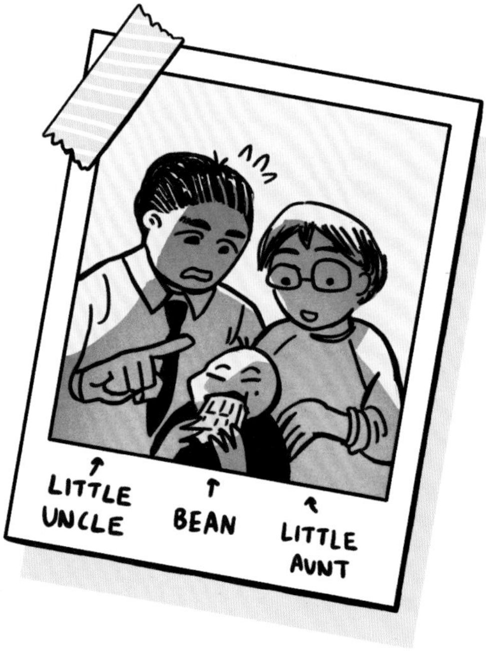
LITTLE UNCLE
BEAN
LITTLE AUNT

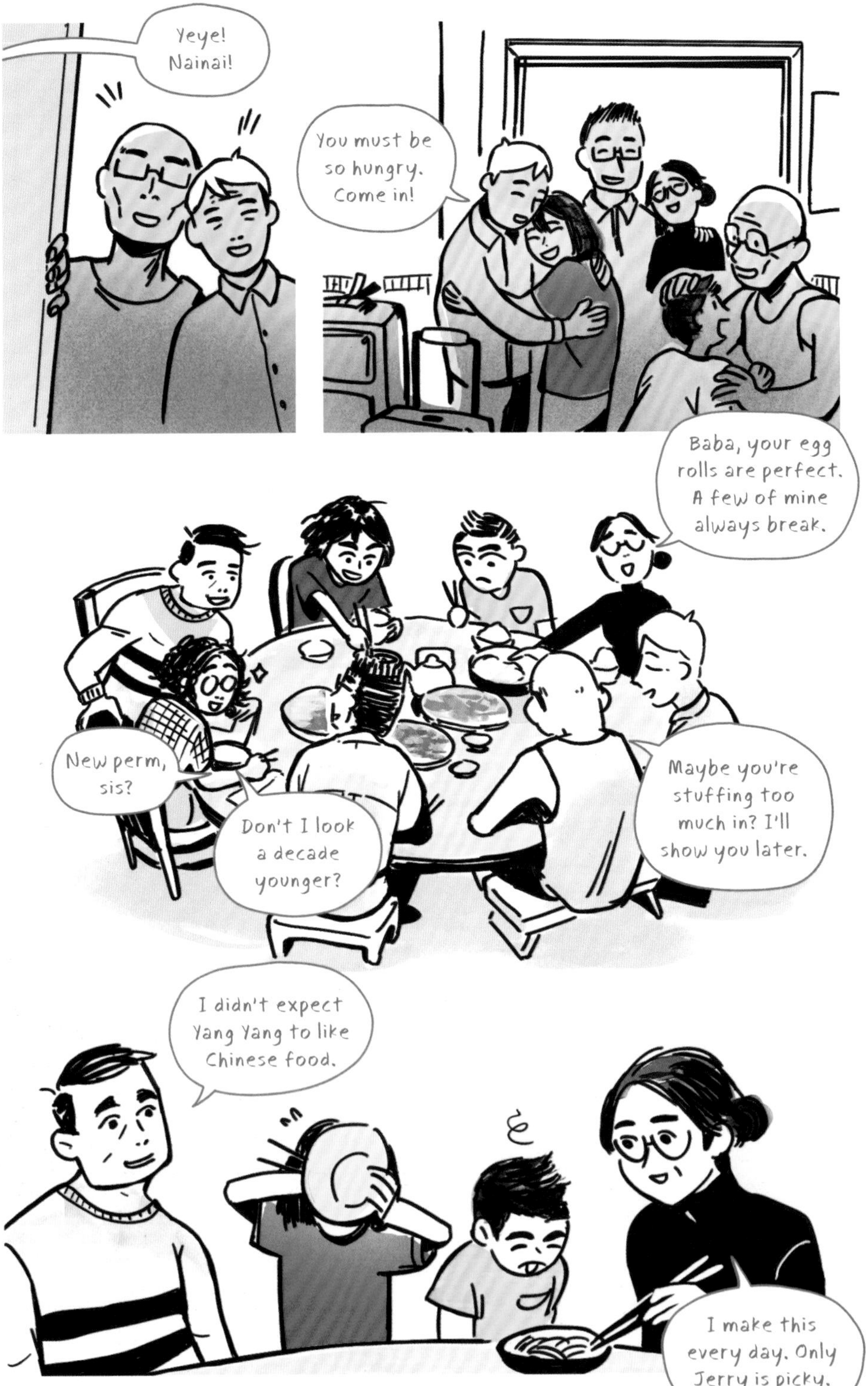
Yeye! Nainai!
You must be so hungry. Come in!
Baba, your egg rolls are perfect. A few of mine always break.
New perm, sis?
Don't I look a decade younger?
Maybe you're stuffing too much in? I'll show you later.
I didn't expect Yang Yang to like Chinese food.
I make this every day. Only Jerry is picky.

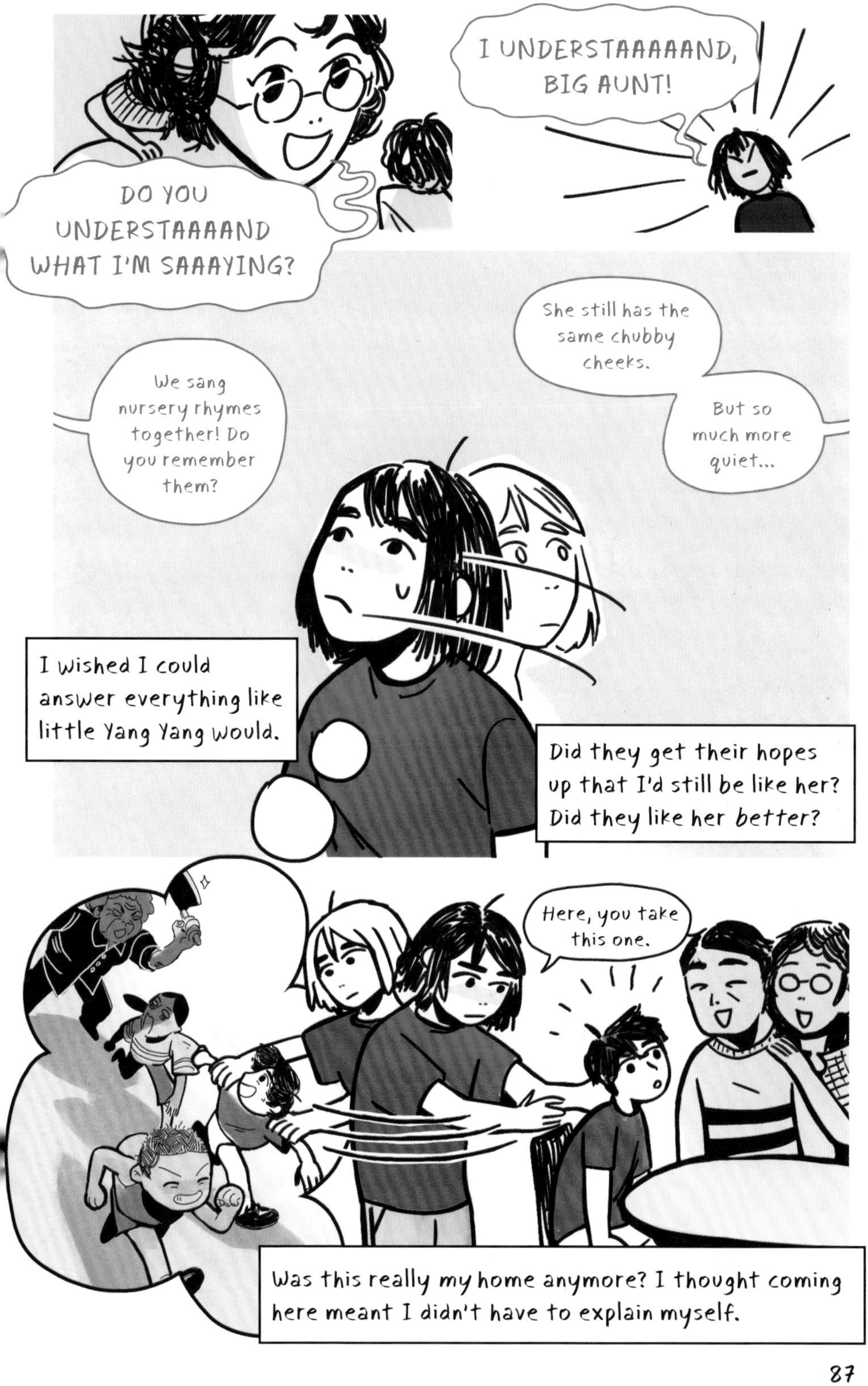
DO YOU UNDERSTAAAAND WHAT I'M SAAAYING?
I UNDERSTAAAAAND, BIG AUNT!
We sang nursery rhymes together! Do you remember them?
She still has the same chubby cheeks.
But so much more quiet...
I wished I could answer everything like little Yang Yang would.
Did they get their hopes up that I'd still be like her? Did they like her better?
Here, you take this one.
Was this really my home anymore? I thought coming here meant I didn't have to explain myself.

There was at least one thing that didn't need explaining: breakfast! In Wuhan, breakfast is an Olympic sport. There's even a unique verb for it in the Wuhanese dialect: 过早 guò zǎo! Little Uncle's family took us kids out on a street food tour.

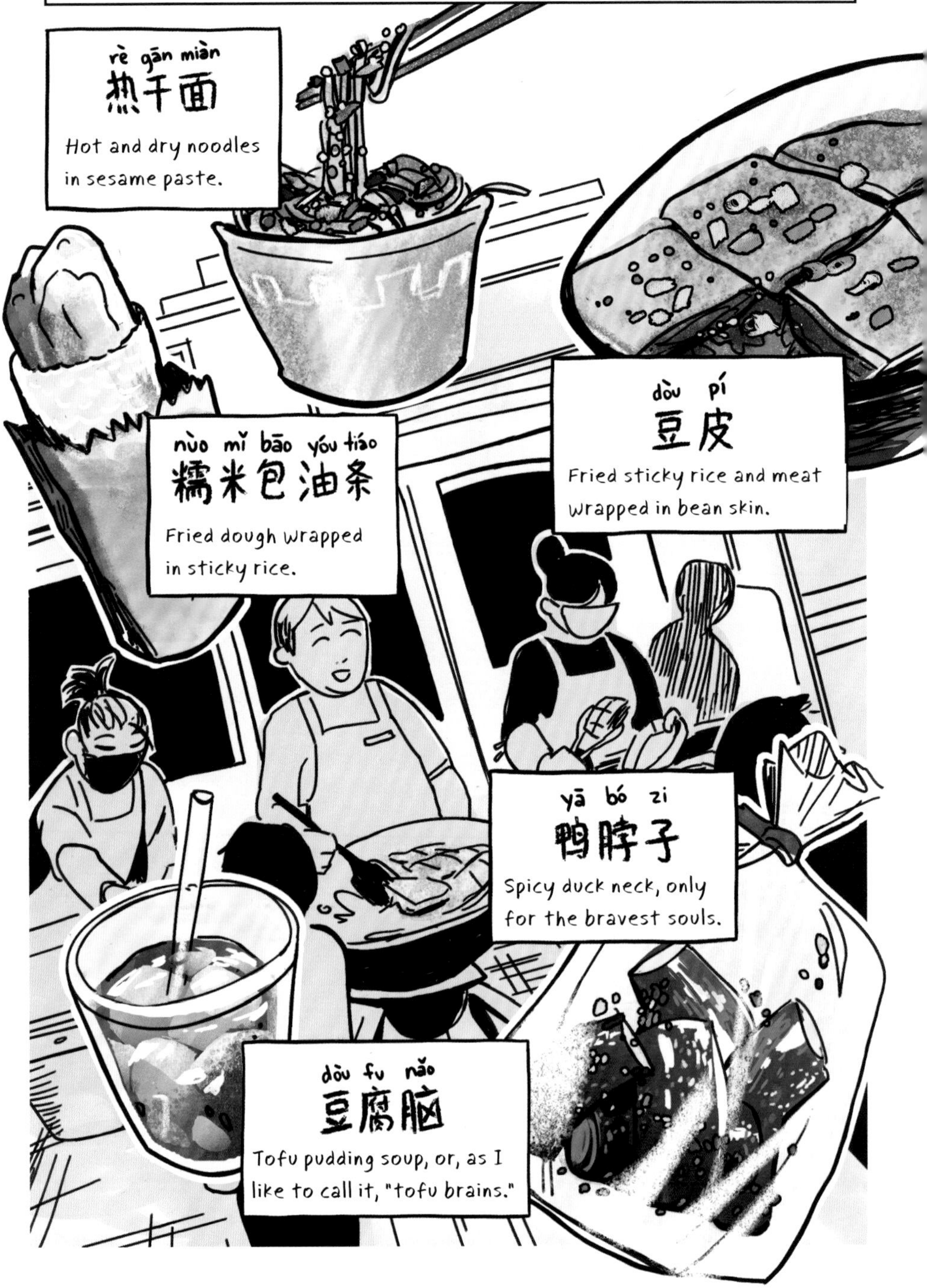

rè gān miàn
热干面
Hot and dry noodles in sesame paste.
dòu pí
豆皮
Fried sticky rice and meat wrapped in bean skin.
nùo mǐ bāo yóu tiáo
糯米包油条
Fried dough wrapped in sticky rice.
yā bó zi
鸭脖子
Spicy duck neck, only for the bravest souls.
dòu fu nǎo
豆腐脑
Tofu pudding soup, or, as I like to call it, "tofu brains."

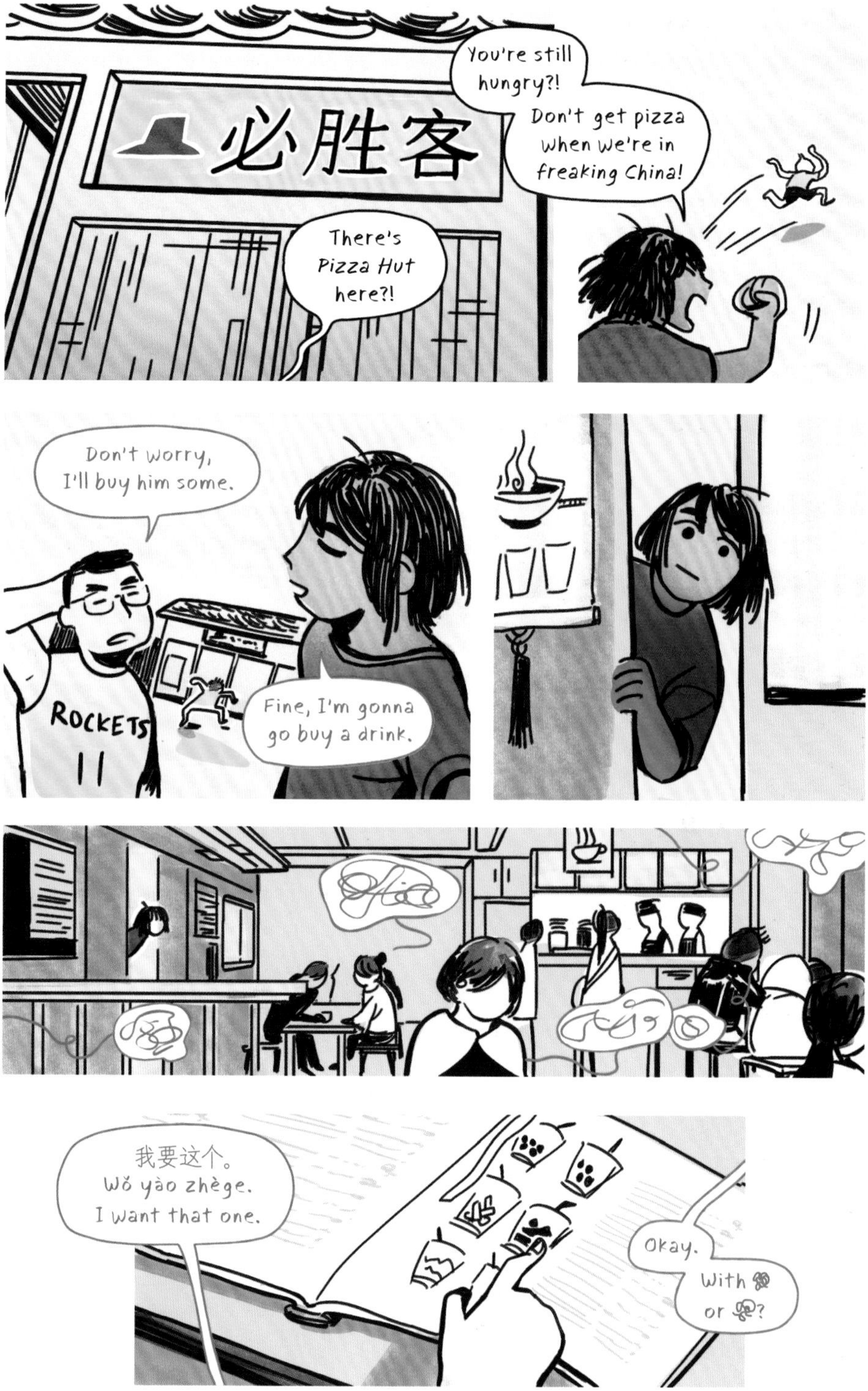
必胜客
There's Pizza Hut here?!
You're still hungry?!
Don't get pizza when we're in freaking China!
Don't worry, I'll buy him some.
ROCKETS 11
Fine, I'm gonna go buy a drink.
我要这个。
Wǒ yào zhège.
I want that one.
Okay.
With or ?

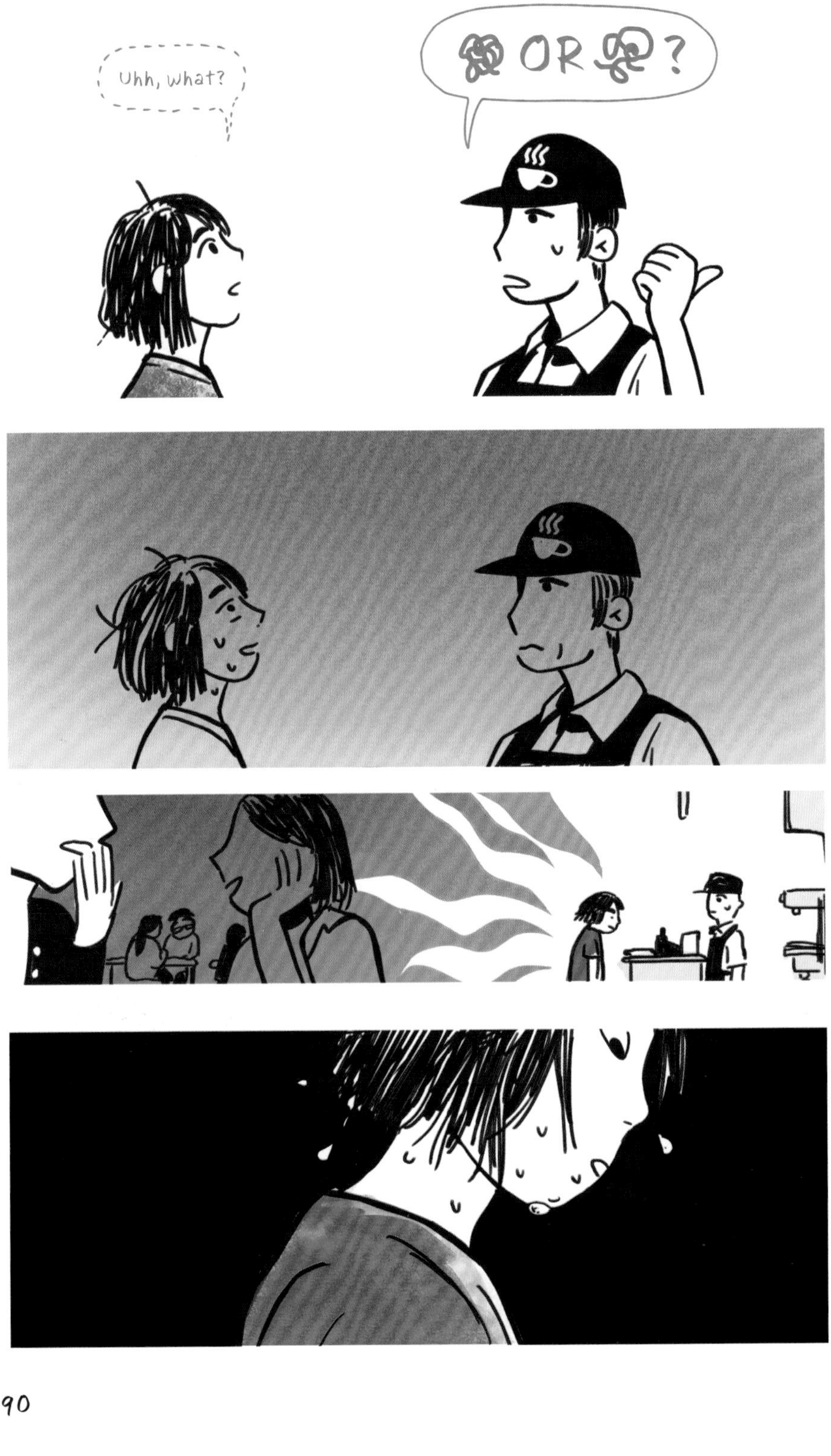
Uhh, what?
OR ?

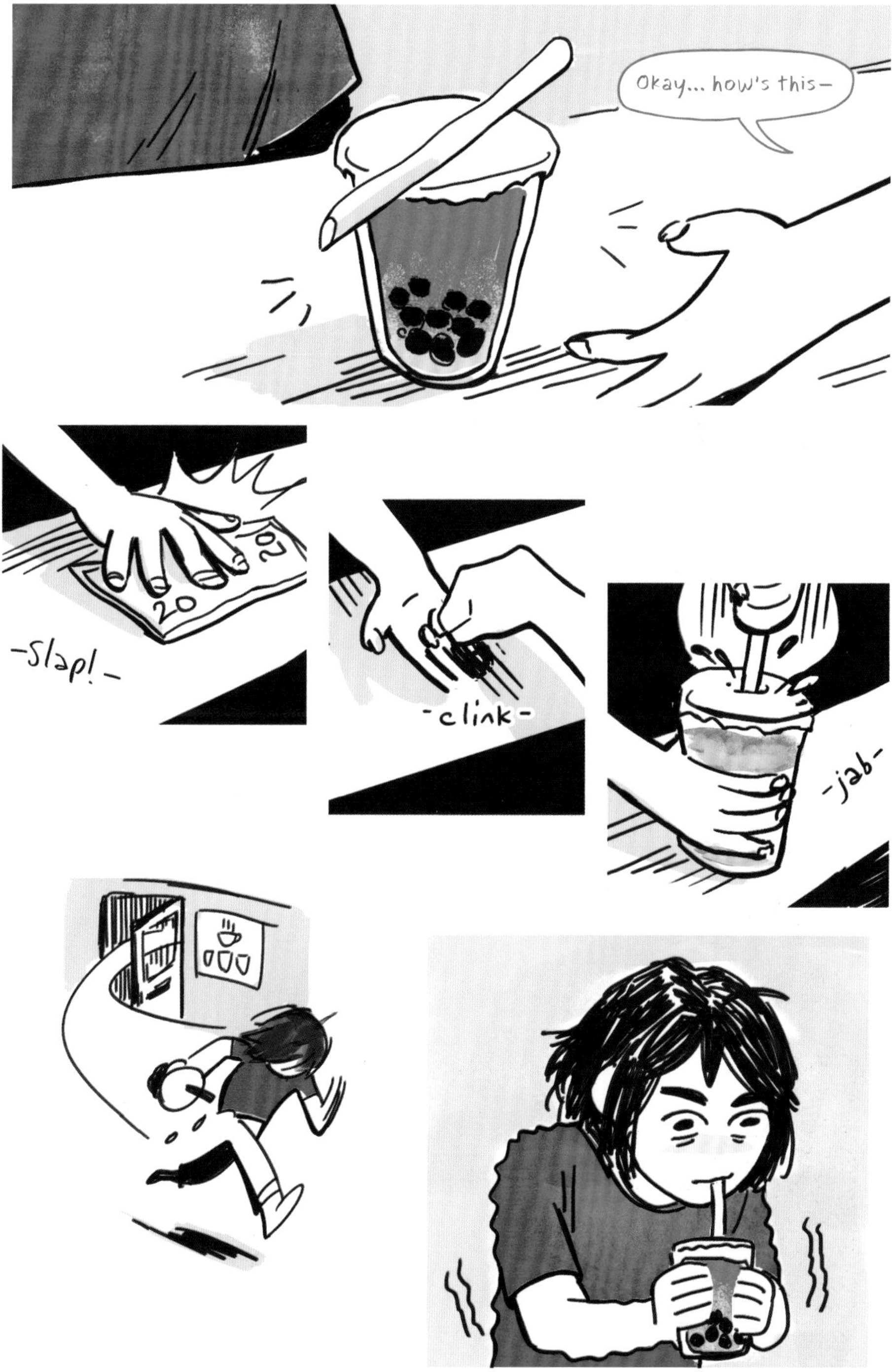
Okay... how's this—
20
20
-Slap!-
-clink-
-jab-

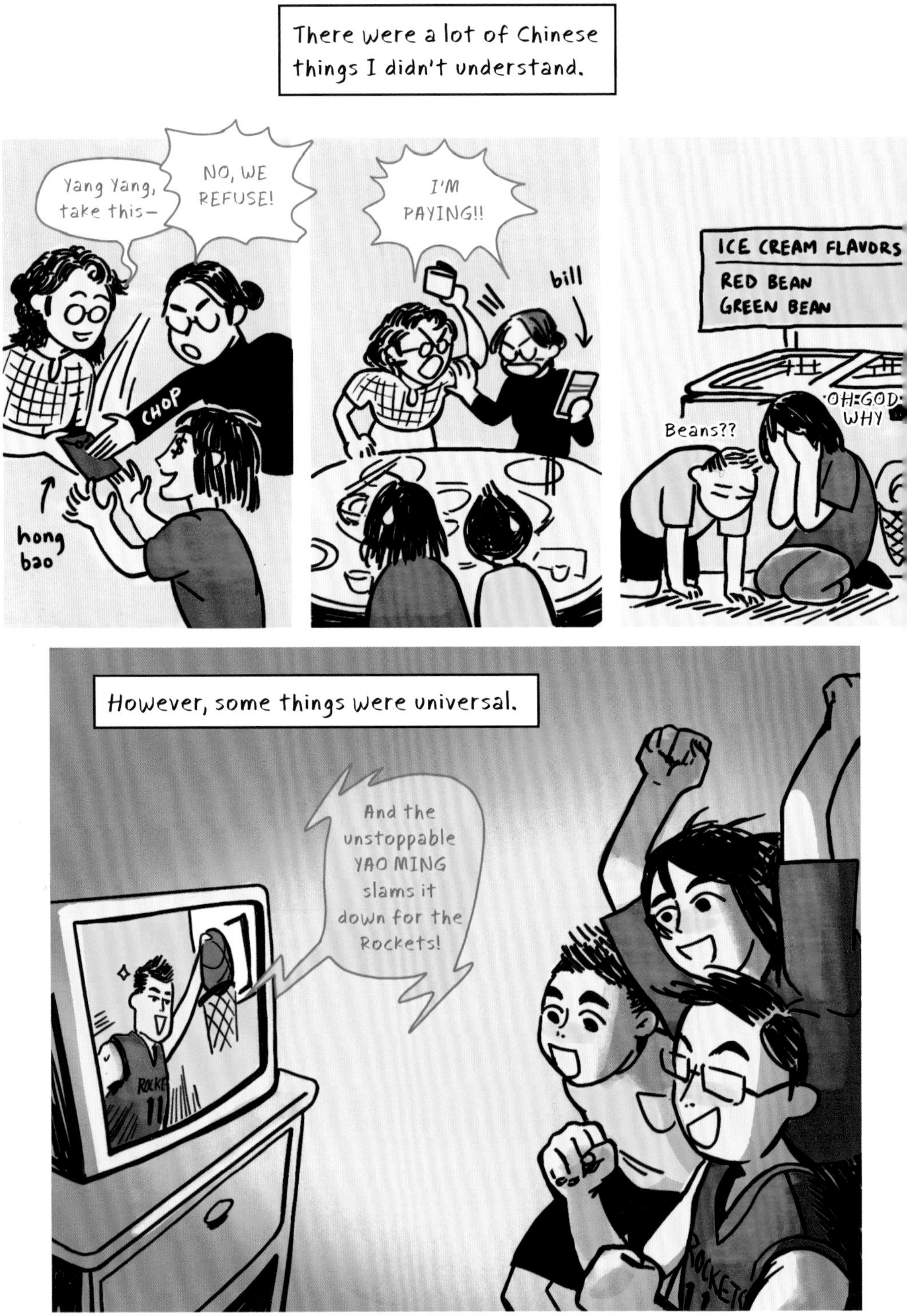
There were a lot of Chinese things I didn't understand.
Yang Yang, take this—
NO, WE REFUSE!
CHOP
hong bao
I'M PAYING!!
bill
ICE CREAM FLAVORS
RED BEAN
GREEN BEAN
Beans??
OH GOD WHY
However, some things were universal.
And the unstoppable YAO MING slams it down for the Rockets!
ROCKETS

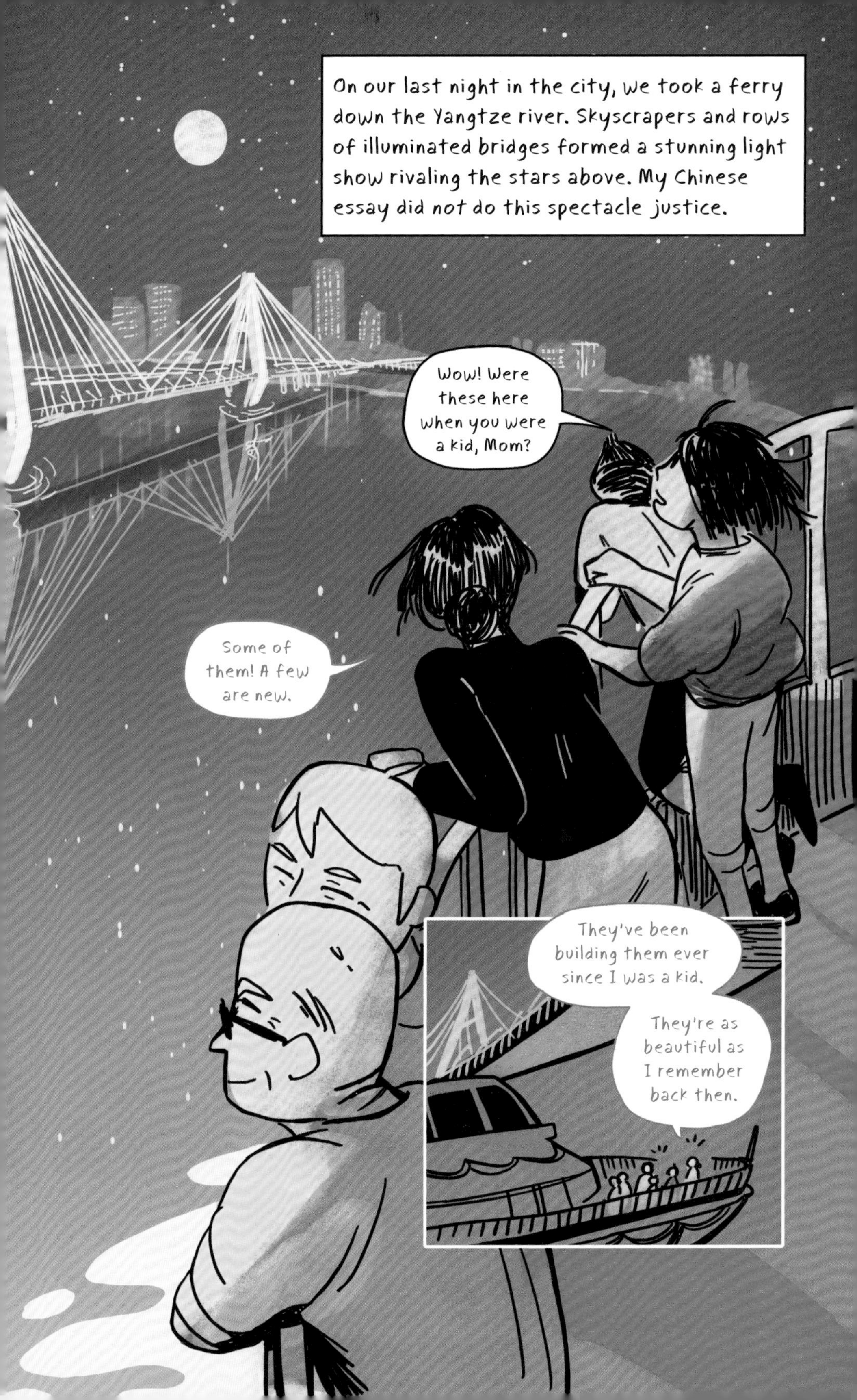
On our last night in the city, we took a ferry down the Yangtze river. Skyscrapers and rows of illuminated bridges formed a stunning light show rivaling the stars above. My Chinese essay did *not* do this spectacle justice.
Wow! Were these here when you were a kid, Mom?
Some of them! A few are new.
They've been building them ever since I was a kid.
They're as beautiful as I remember back then.

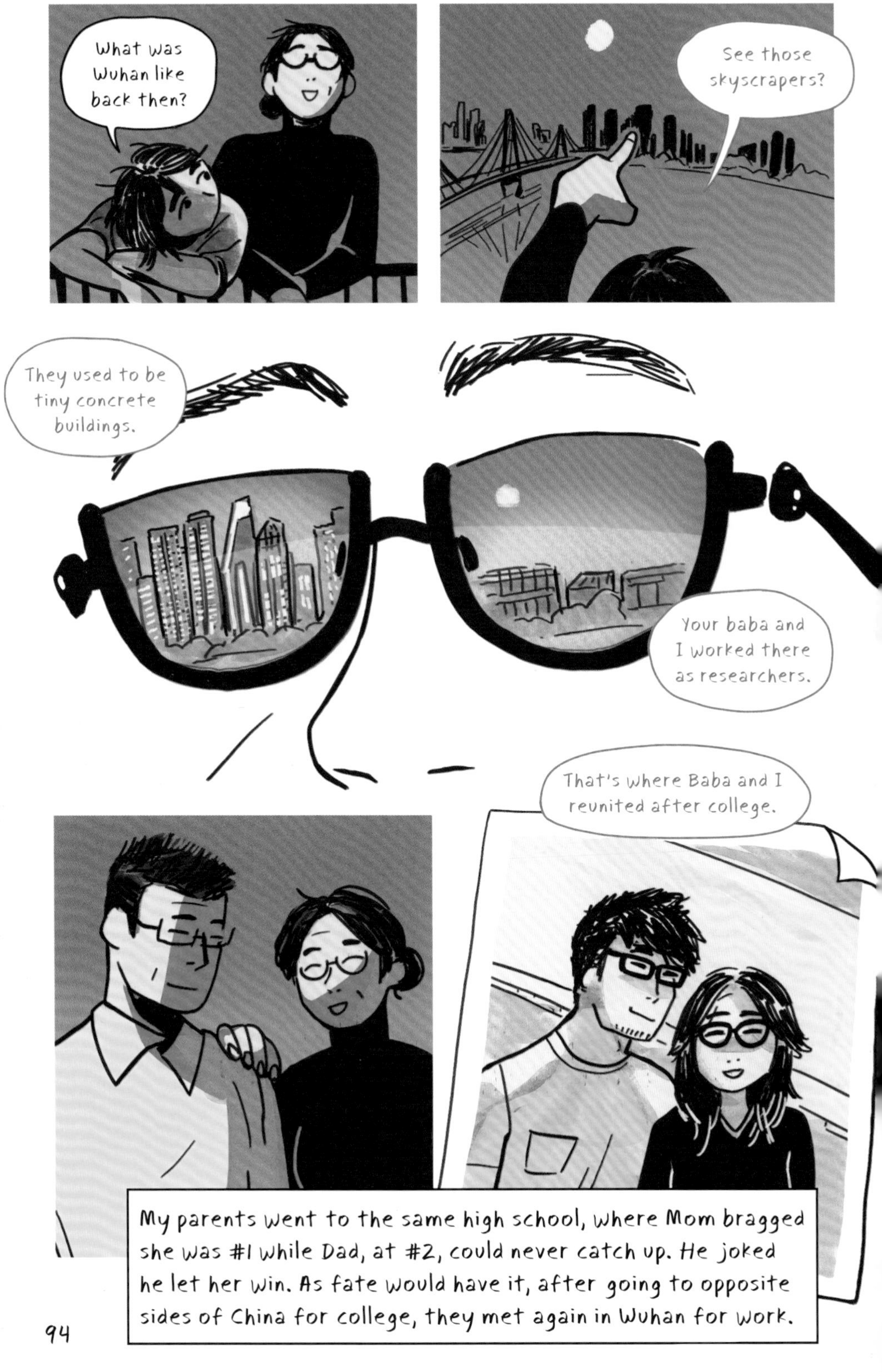
What was Wuhan like back then?
See those skyscrapers?
They used to be tiny concrete buildings.
Your baba and I worked there as researchers.
That's where Baba and I reunited after college.
My parents went to the same high school, where Mom bragged she was #1 while Dad, at #2, could never catch up. He joked he let her win. As fate would have it, after going to opposite sides of China for college, they met again in Wuhan for work.

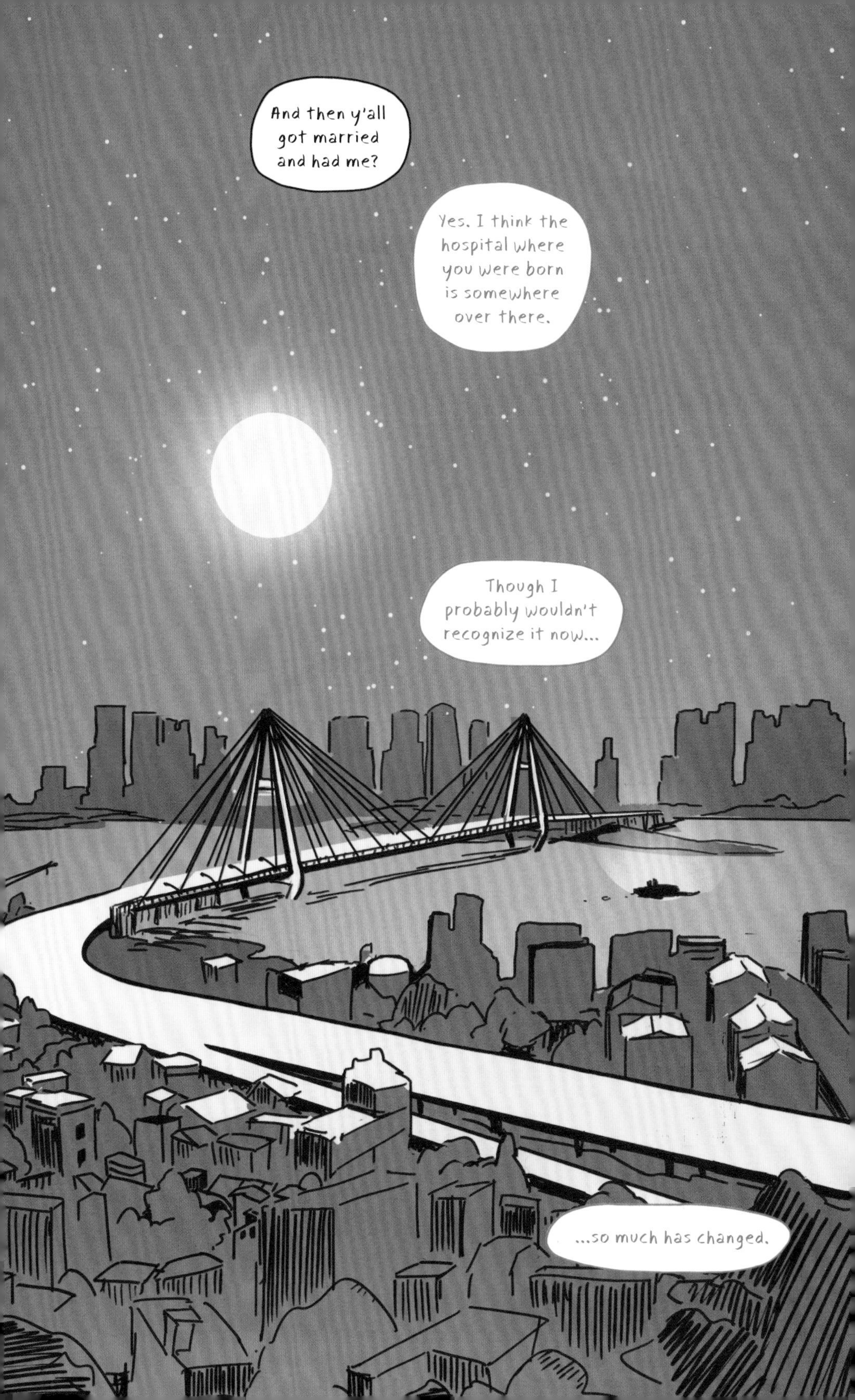
And then y'all got married and had me?
Yes. I think the hospital where you were born is somewhere over there.
Though I probably wouldn't recognize it now...
...so much has changed.

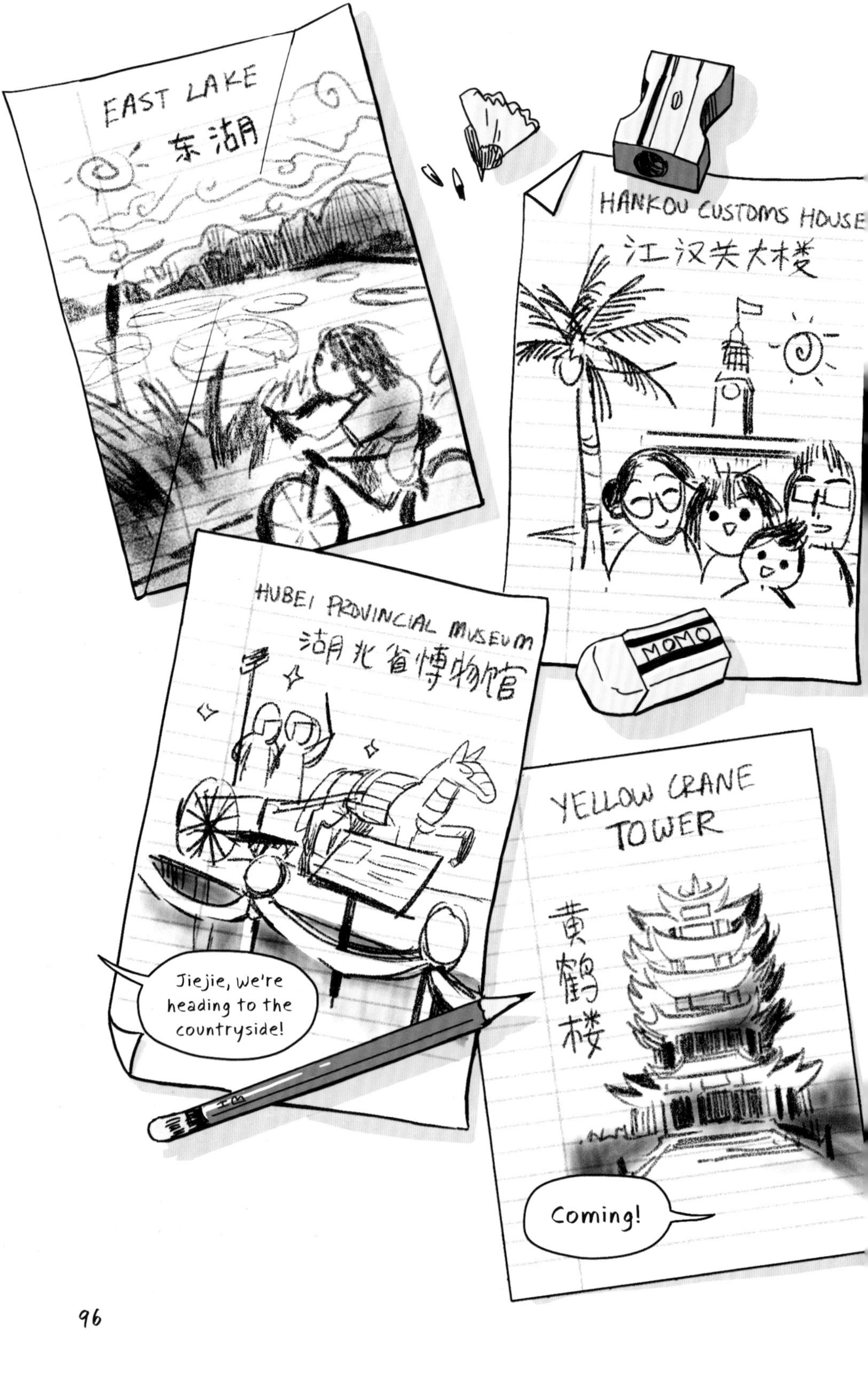
EAST LAKE
东湖
HANKOU CUSTOMS HOUSE
江汉关大楼
MOMO
HUBEI PROVINCIAL MUSEUM
湖北省博物馆
YELLOW CRANE TOWER
黄鹤楼
Jiejie, we're heading to the countryside!
Coming!

CHAPTER 7
Take Me Home, Country Roads

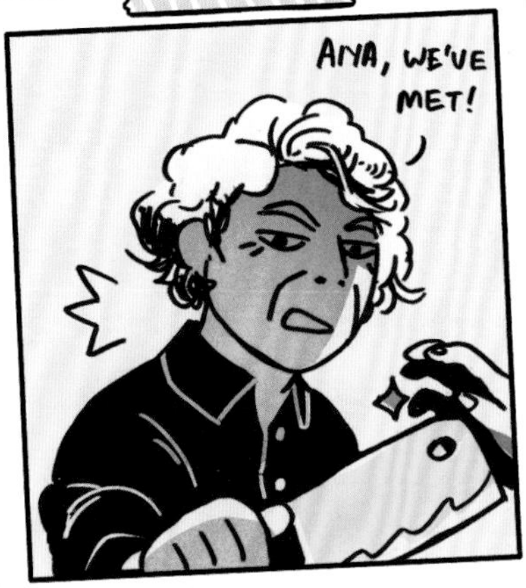
AIYA, WE'VE MET!

POPO

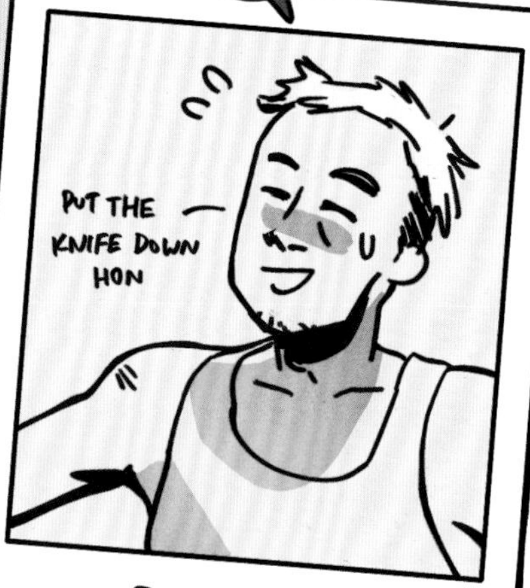
PUT THE KNIFE DOWN HON

DEDE

MEET DAD'S SIDE

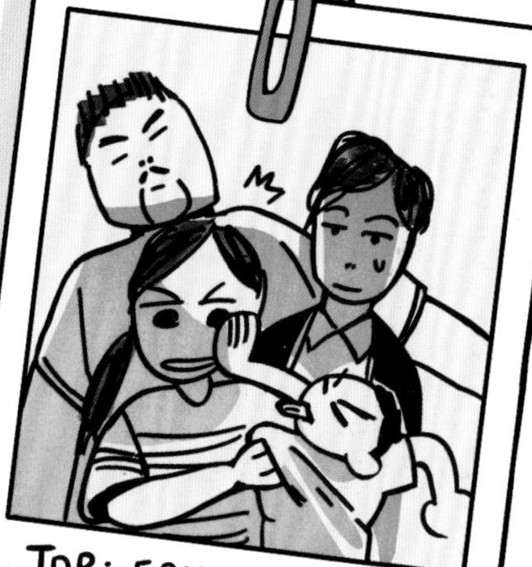

TOP: ERYE & ERMA
BOT: CANJIE & WENJIAN

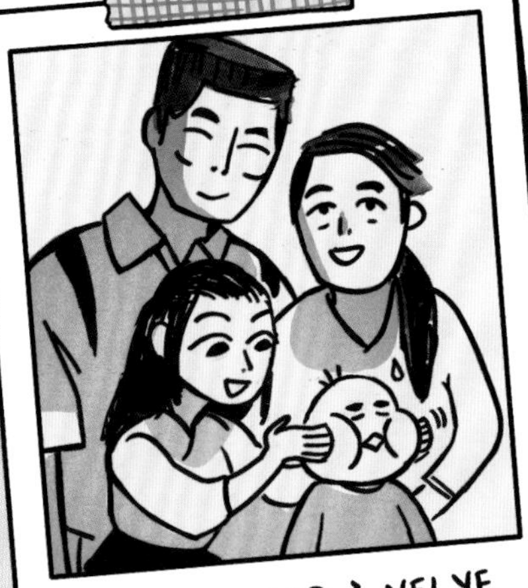

TOP: GANGAR & YELYE
BOT: LULU & TIAN

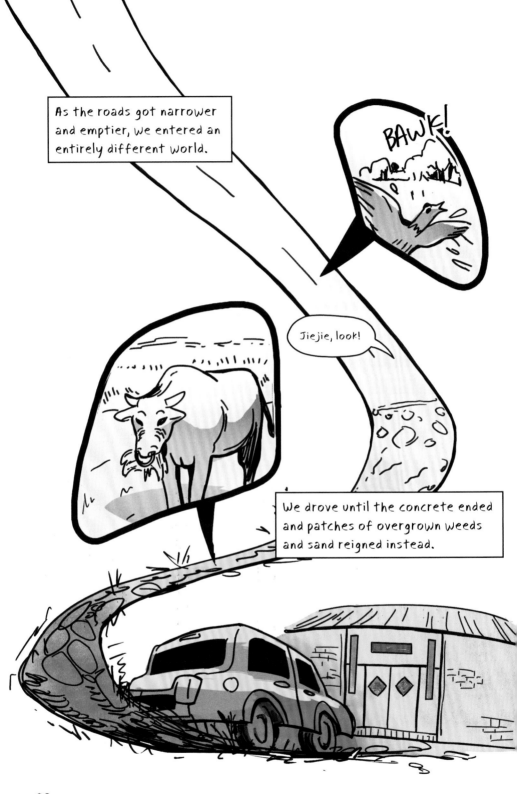

As the roads got narrower and emptier, we entered an entirely different world.

BAWK!

Jiejie, look!

We drove until the concrete ended and patches of overgrown weeds and sand reigned instead.

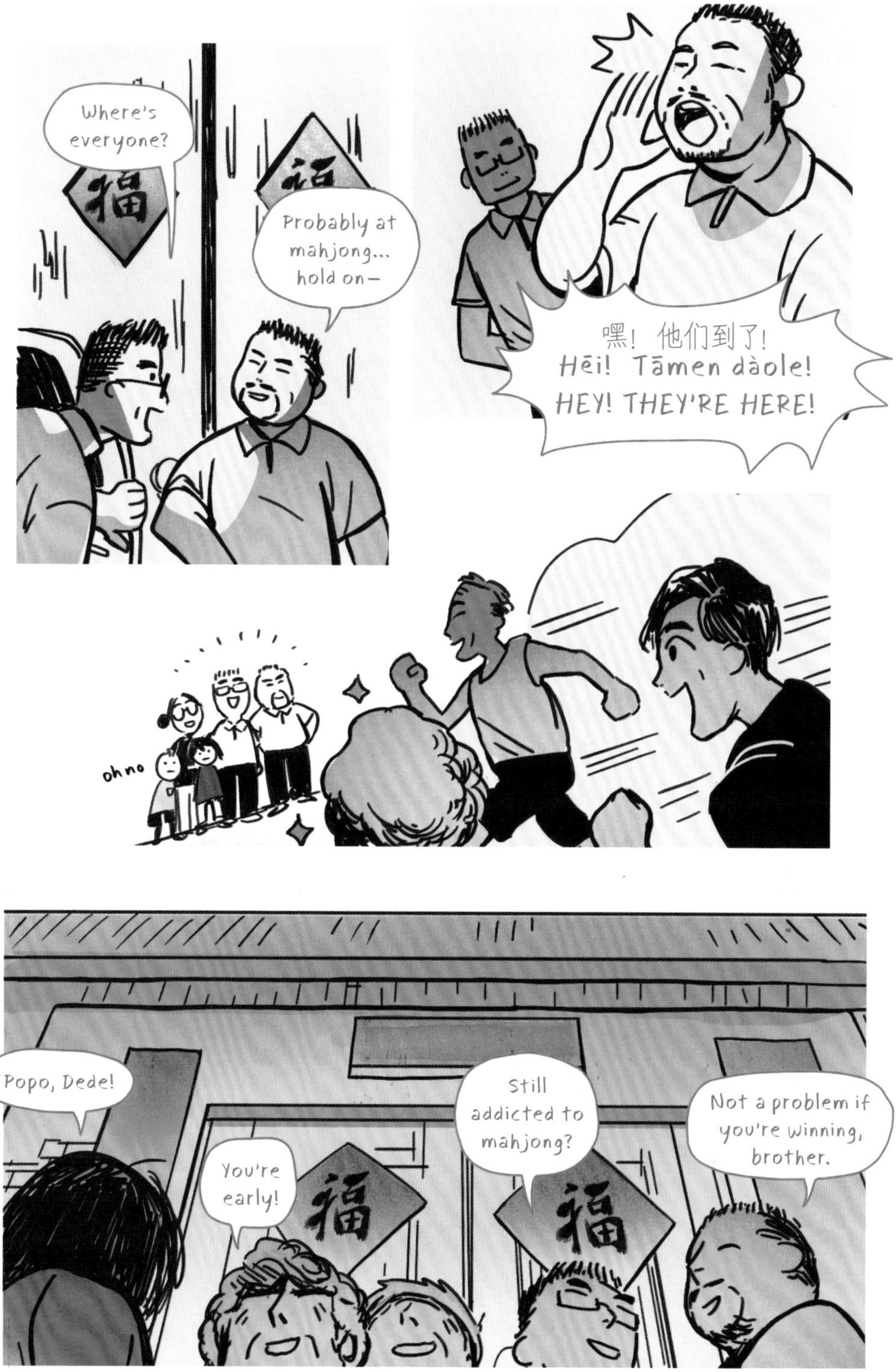
Where's everyone?
Probably at mahjong... hold on—
嘿！ 他们到了！
Hēi! Tāmen dàole!
HEY! THEY'RE HERE!
oh no
Popo, Dede!
You're early!
Still addicted to mahjong?
Not a problem if you're winning, brother.

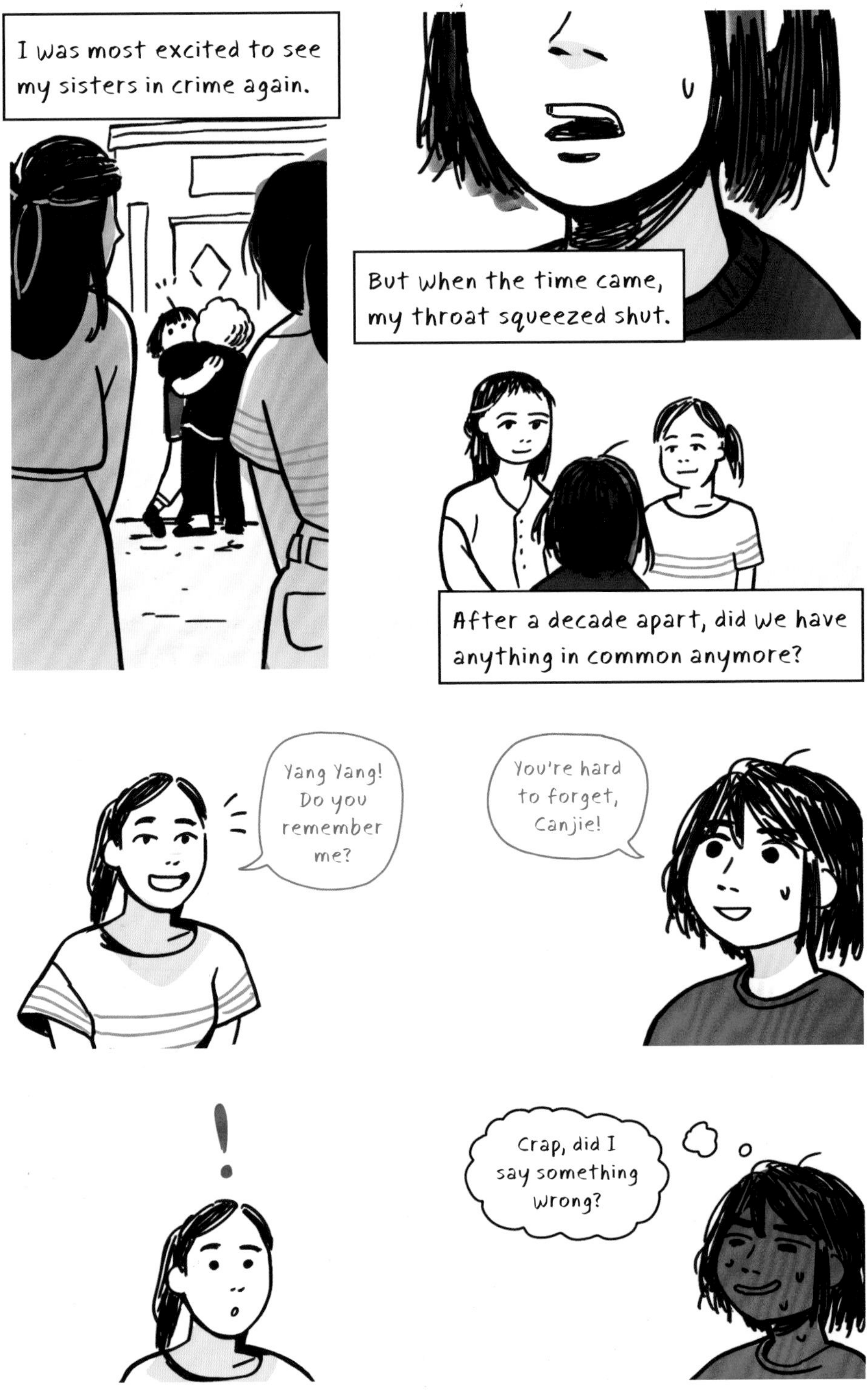

I was most excited to see my sisters in crime again.
But when the time came, my throat squeezed shut.
After a decade apart, did we have anything in common anymore?
Yang Yang! Do you remember me?
You're hard to forget, Canjie!
!
Crap, did I say something wrong?

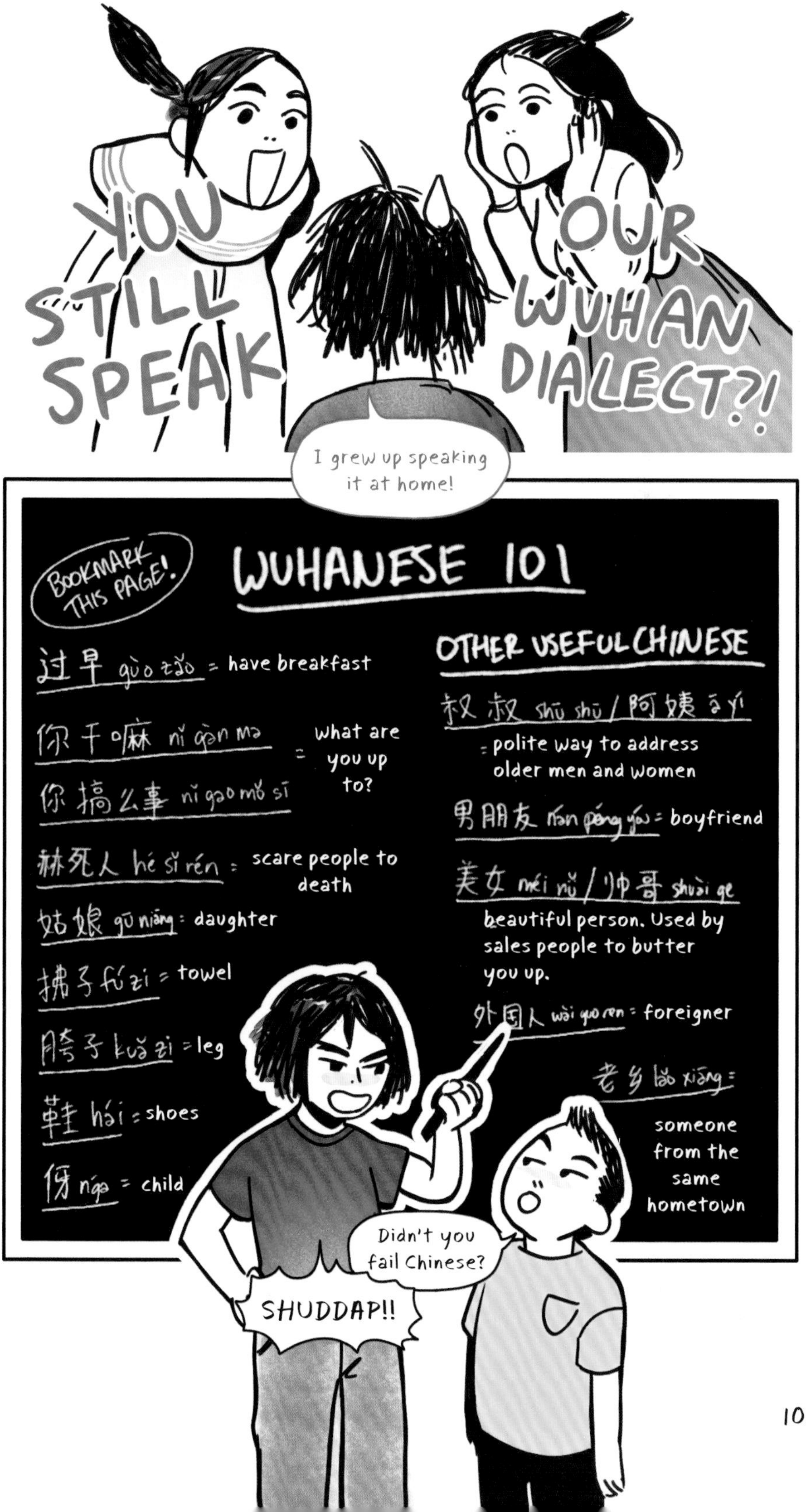

YOU STILL SPEAK
OUR WUHAN DIALECT?!
I grew up speaking it at home!
BOOKMARK THIS PAGE!
WUHANESE 101
过早 gùo zǎo = have breakfast
你干嘛 nǐ gàn ma
你搞么事 nǐ gao mǒ sī
= what are you up to?
赫死人 hé sǐ rén = scare people to death
姑娘 gū niāng = daughter
拂子 fú zi = towel
胯子 kuǎ zi = leg
鞋 hái = shoes
伢 ngá = child
OTHER USEFUL CHINESE
叔叔 shū shū / 阿姨 ā yí
= polite way to address older men and women
男朋友 nán péng yǒu = boyfriend
美女 méi nǚ / 帅哥 shuài ge
beautiful person. Used by sales people to butter you up.
外国人 wài guo ren = foreigner
老乡 lǎo xiāng =
someone from the same hometown
Didn't you fail Chinese?
SHUDDAP!!

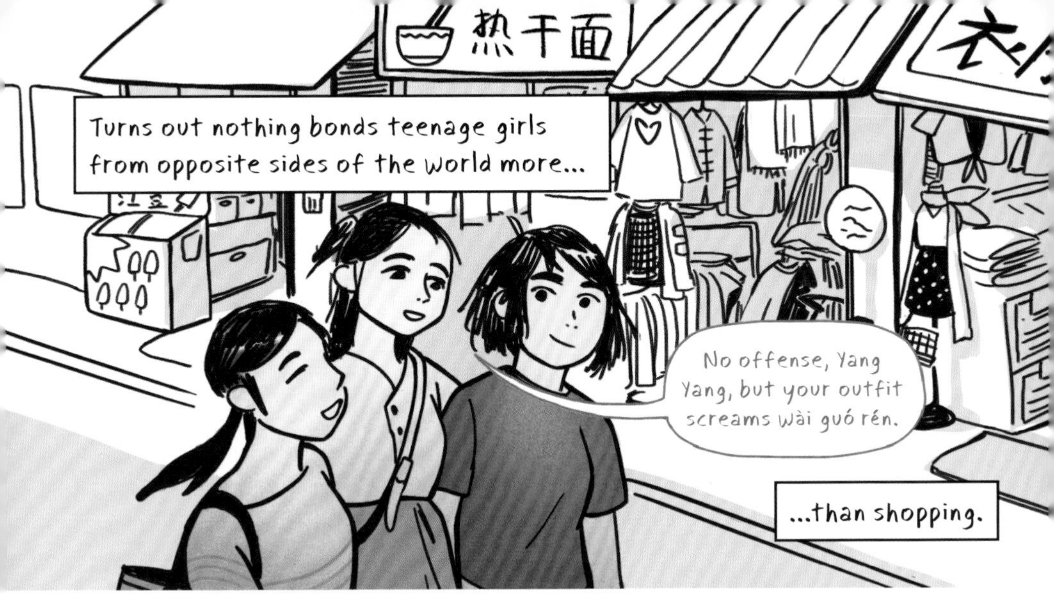
热干面
Turns out nothing bonds teenage girls from opposite sides of the world more...
No offense, Yang Yang, but your outfit screams wài guó rén.
...than shopping.

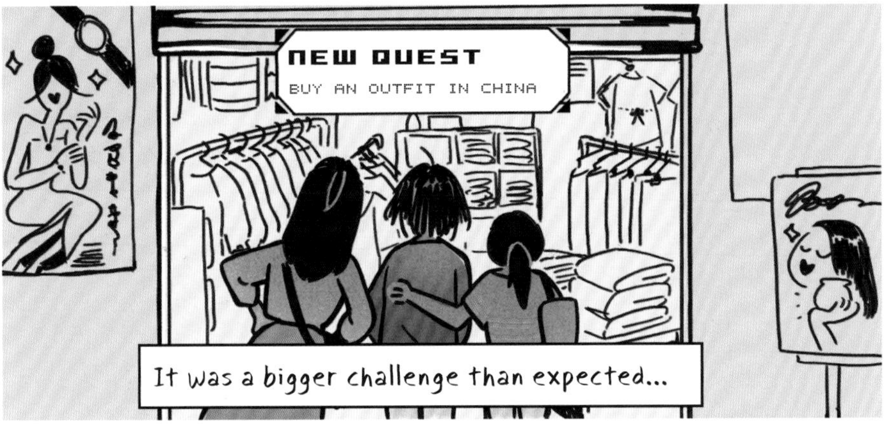
NEW QUEST
BUY AN OUTFIT IN CHINA
It was a bigger challenge than expected...

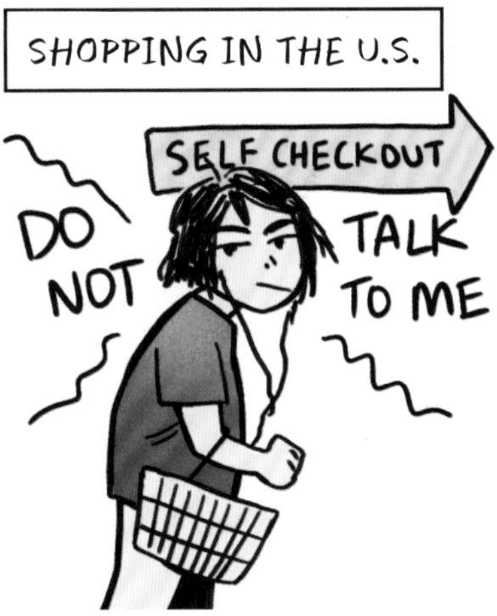
SHOPPING IN THE U.S.
SELF CHECKOUT
DO NOT TALK TO ME

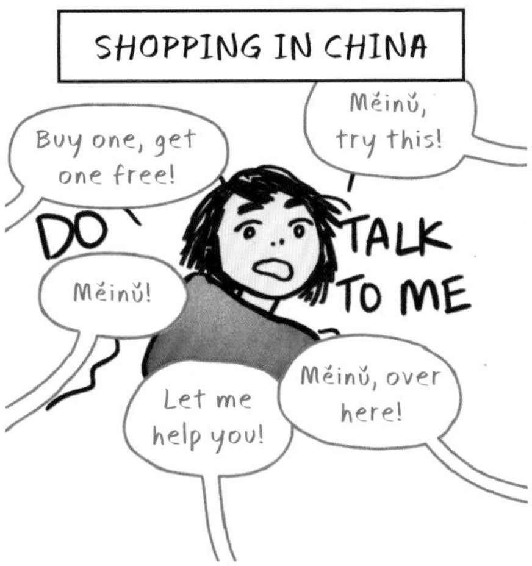
SHOPPING IN CHINA
Buy one, get one free!
Měinǚ, try this!
DO
TALK TO ME
Měinǚ!
Let me help you!
Měinǚ, over here!

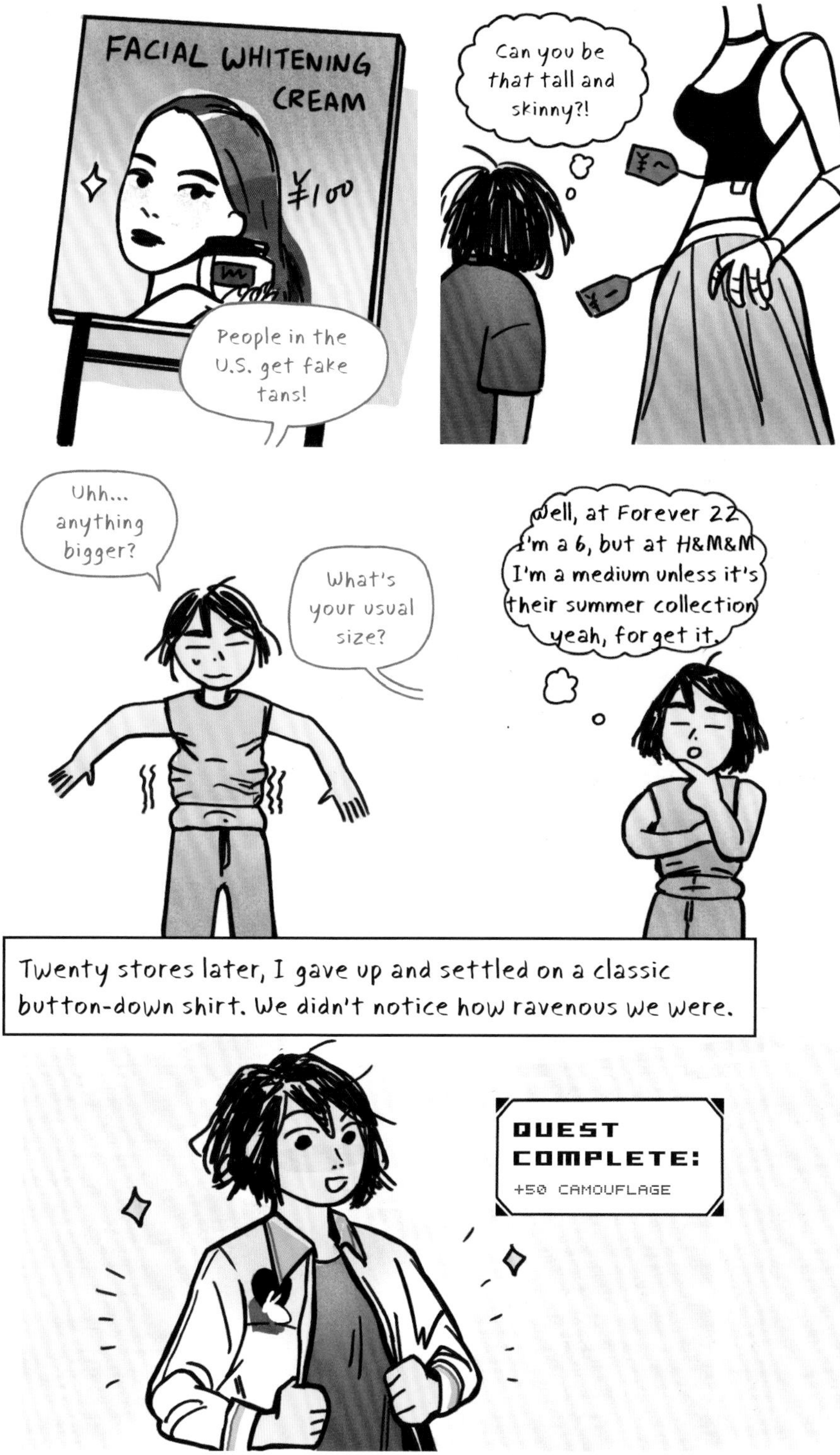
FACIAL WHITENING CREAM
¥100
People in the U.S. get fake tans!
Can you be that tall and skinny?!
Uhh... anything bigger?
What's your usual size?
Well, at Forever 22 I'm a 6, but at H&M&M I'm a medium unless it's their summer collection yeah, forget it.
Twenty stores later, I gave up and settled on a classic button-down shirt. We didn't notice how ravenous we were.
QUEST COMPLETE:
+50 CAMOUFLAGE

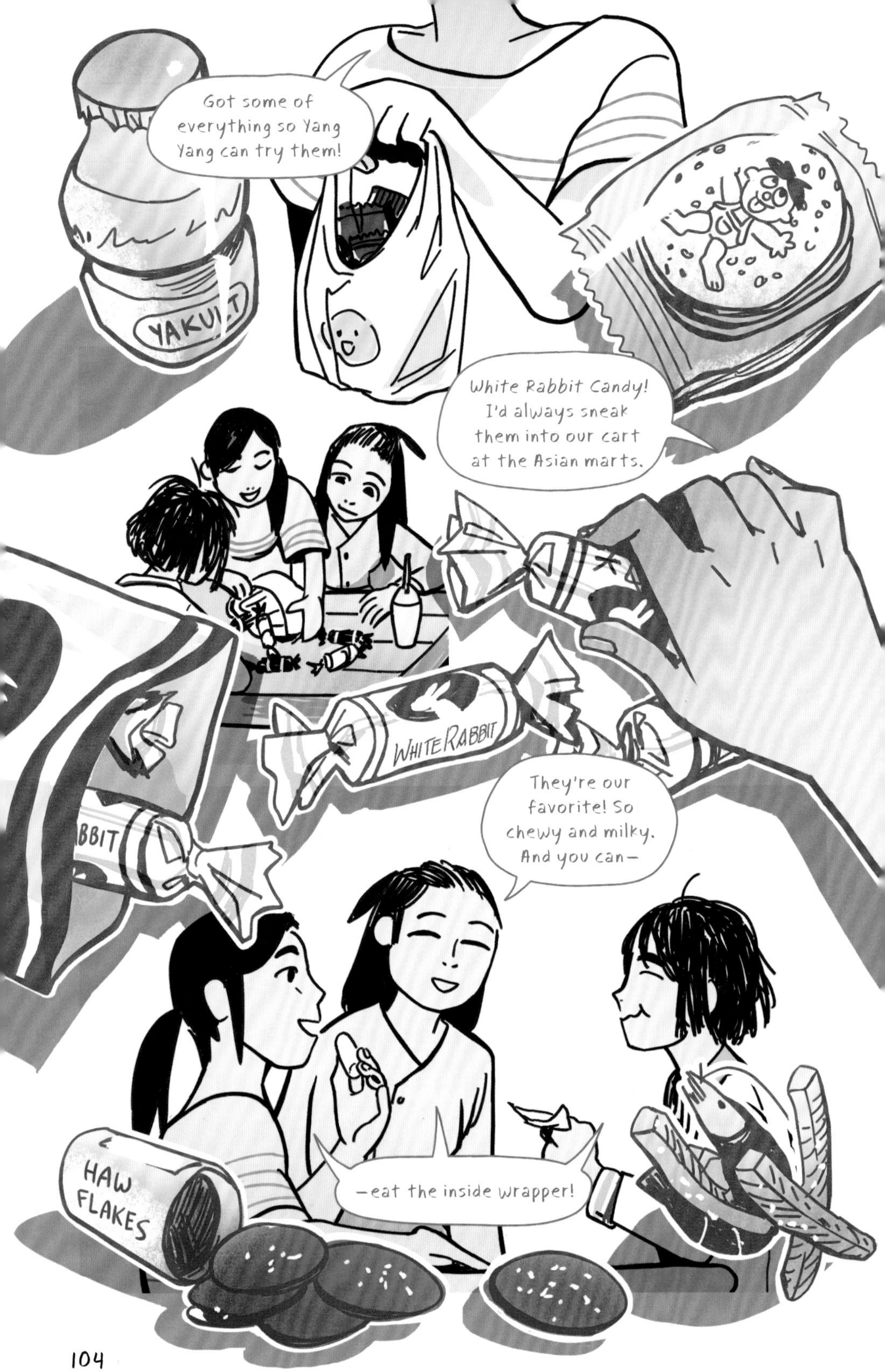
Got some of everything so Yang Yang can try them!
YAKULT
White Rabbit Candy! I'd always sneak them into our cart at the Asian marts.
WHITE RABBIT
They're our favorite! So chewy and milky. And you can—
—eat the inside wrapper!
HAW FLAKES

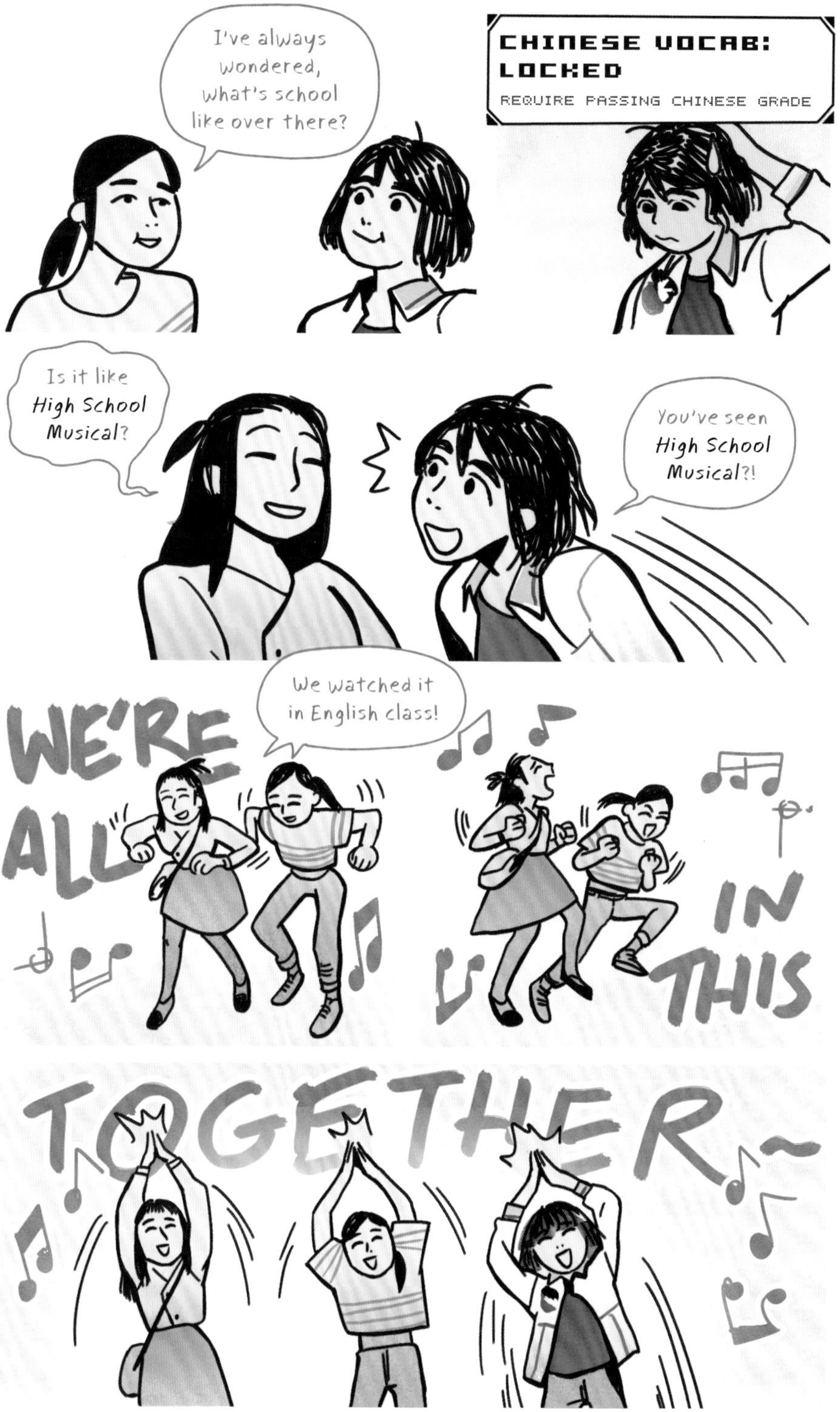
I've always wondered, what's school like over there?
CHINESE VOCAB: LOCKED
REQUIRE PASSING CHINESE GRADE
Is it like High School Musical?
You've seen High School Musical?!
We watched it in English class!
WE'RE ALL IN THIS
TOGETHER~

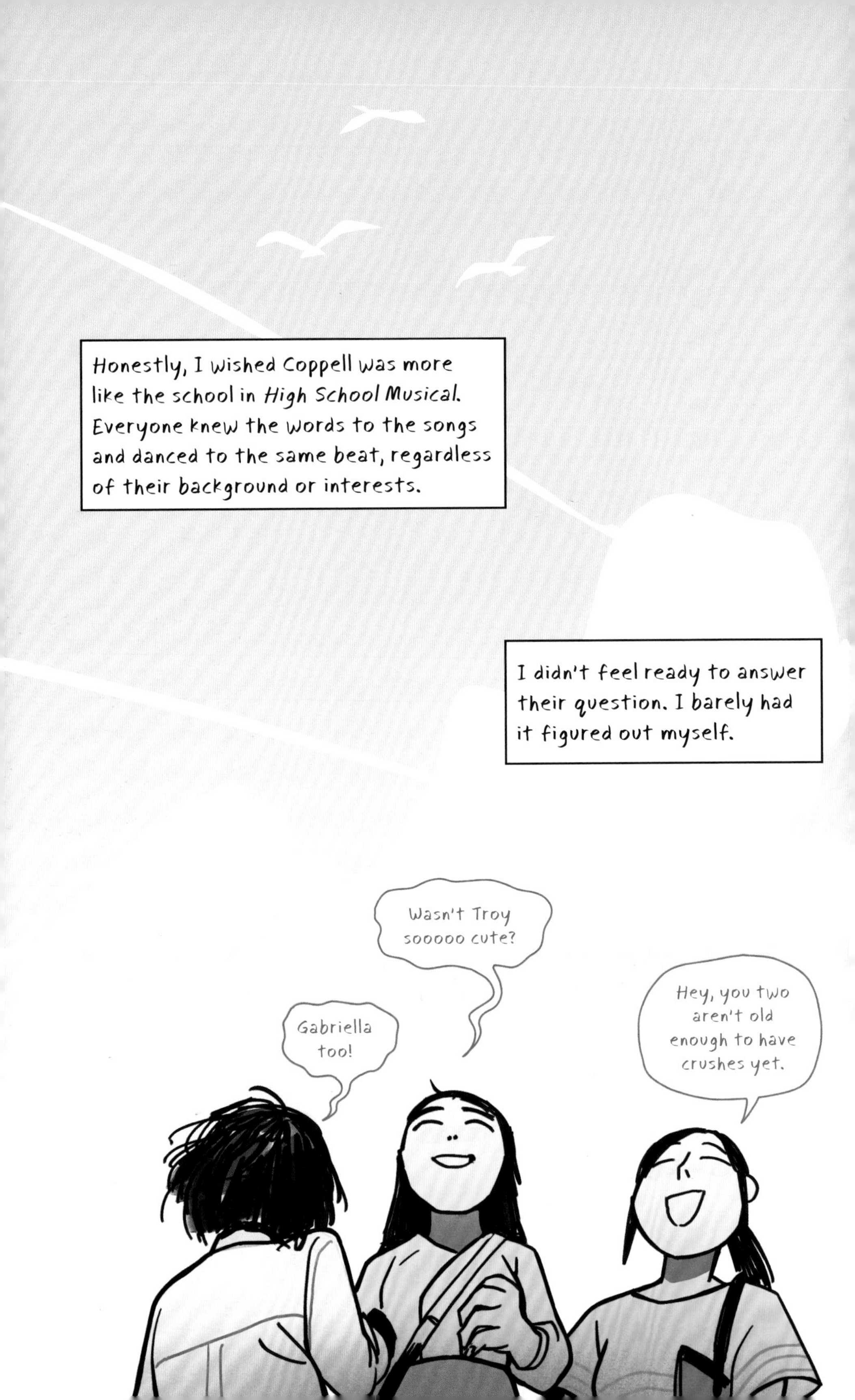
Honestly, I wished Coppell was more like the school in *High School Musical*. Everyone knew the words to the songs and danced to the same beat, regardless of their background or interests.
I didn't feel ready to answer their question. I barely had it figured out myself.
Gabriella too!
Wasn't Troy sooooo cute?
Hey, you two aren't old enough to have crushes yet.

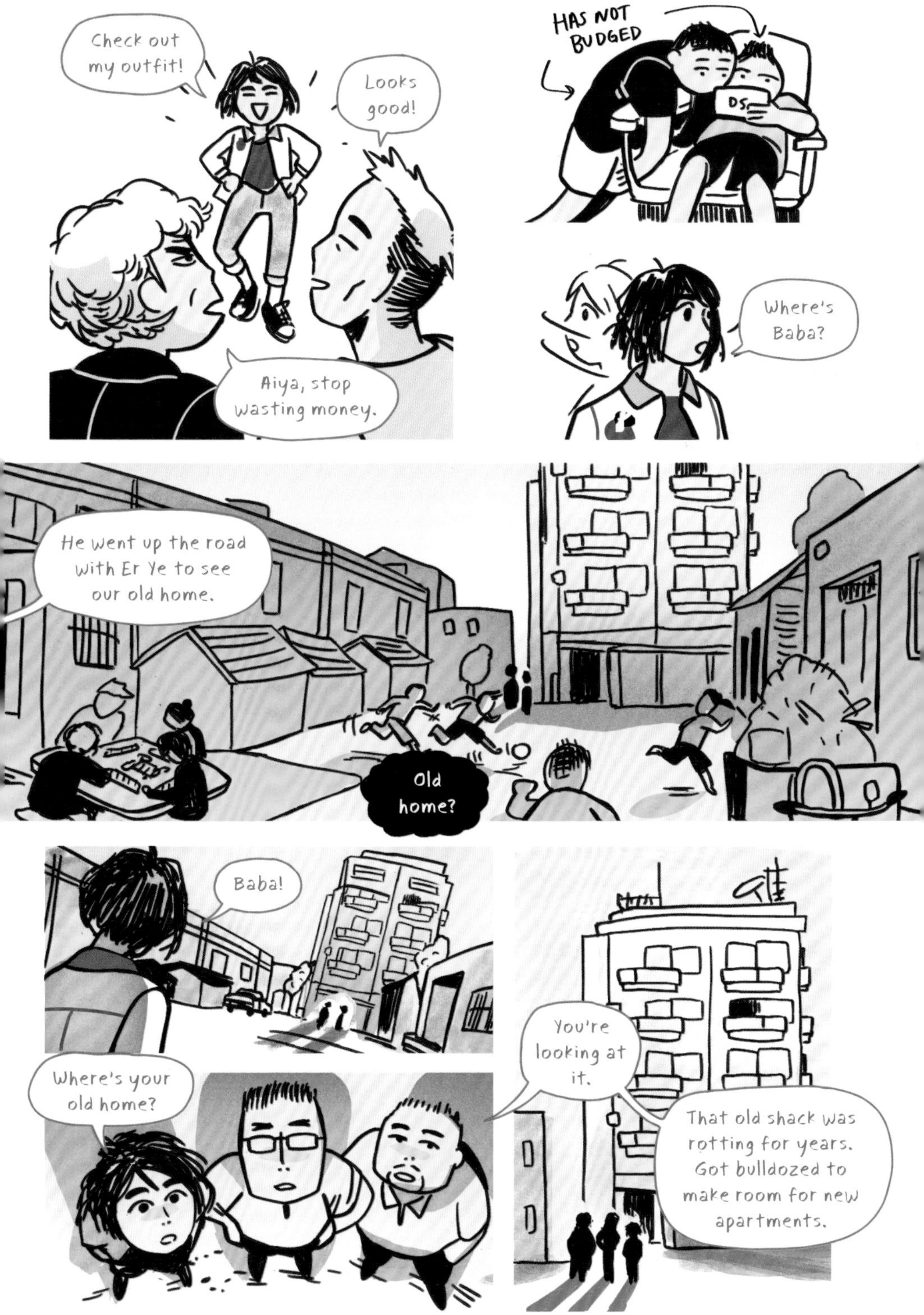

Check out my outfit!
Looks good!
Aiya, stop wasting money.
HAS NOT BUDGED
DS
Where's Baba?
He went up the road with Er Ye to see our old home.
Old home?
Baba!
Where's your old home?
You're looking at it.
That old shack was rotting for years. Got bulldozed to make room for new apartments.

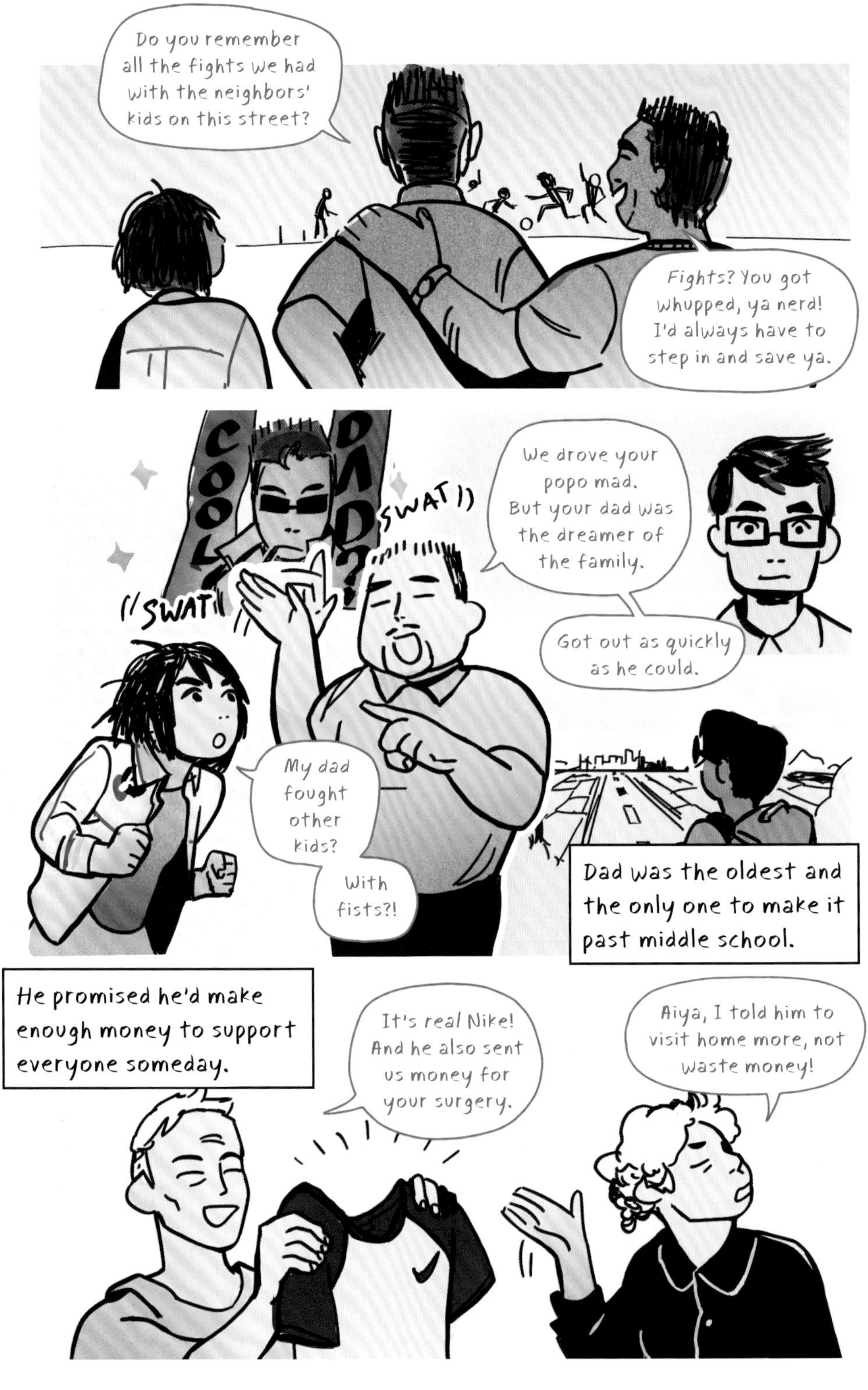
Do you remember all the fights we had with the neighbors' kids on this street?
Fights? You got whupped, ya nerd! I'd always have to step in and save ya.
COOL DAD?
SWAT
SWAT
We drove your popo mad. But your dad was the dreamer of the family.
Got out as quickly as he could.
My dad fought other kids?
With fists?!
Dad was the oldest and the only one to make it past middle school.
He promised he'd make enough money to support everyone someday.
It's *real* Nike! And he also sent us money for your surgery.
Aiya, I told him to visit home more, not waste money!

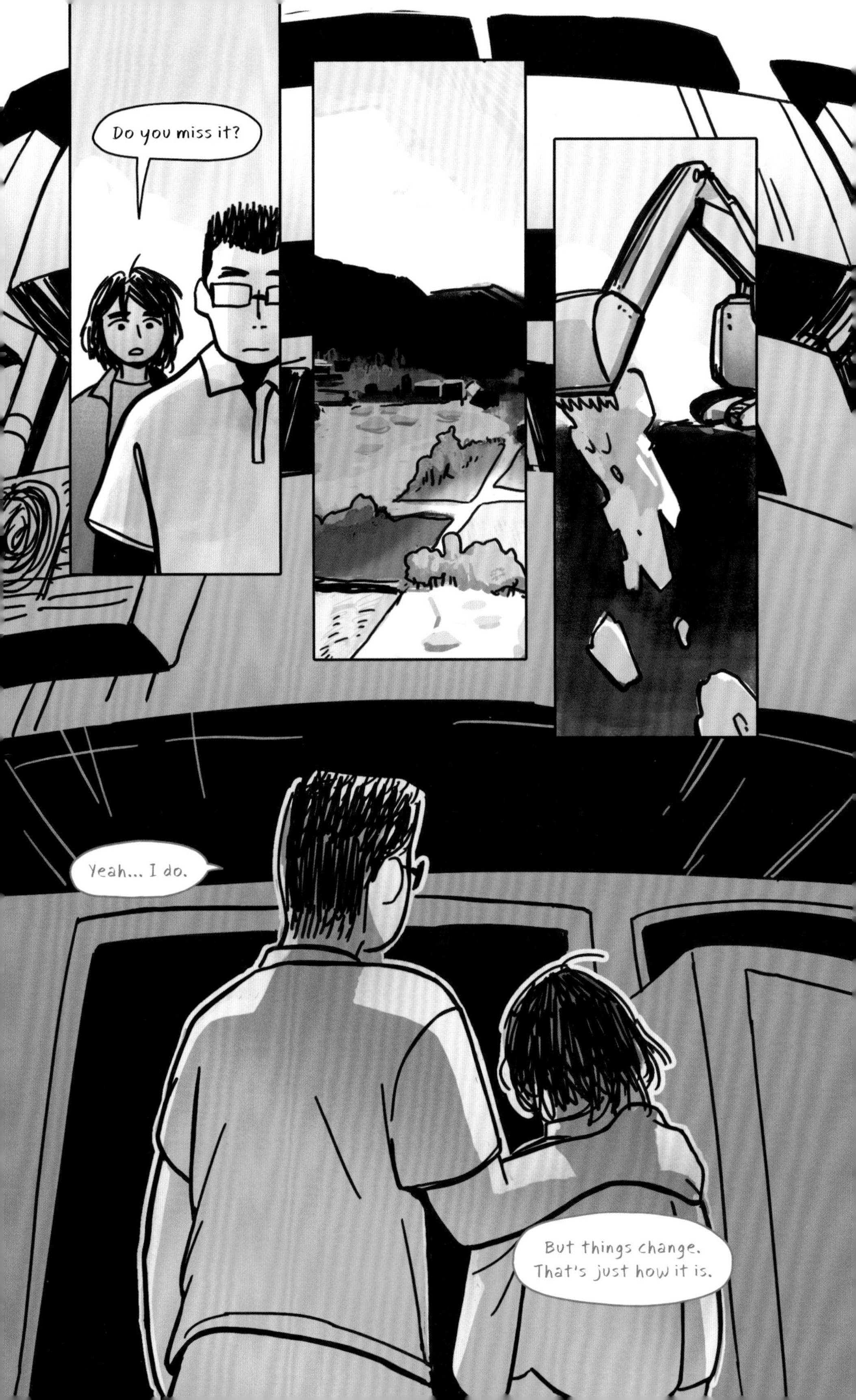
Do you miss it?
Yeah... I do.
But things change.
That's just how it is.

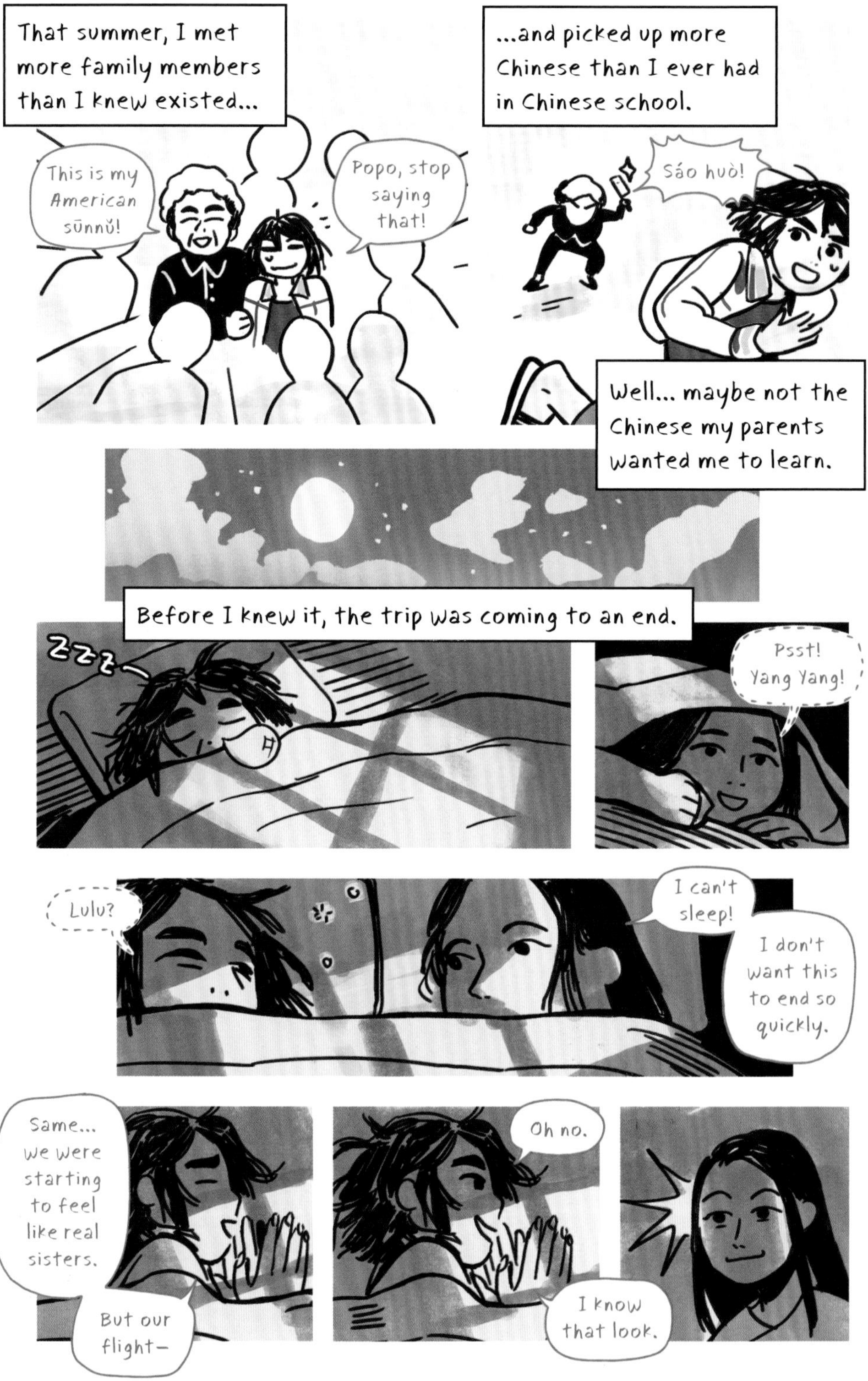
That summer, I met more family members than I knew existed...
This is my American sūnnǚ!
Popo, stop saying that!
...and picked up more Chinese than I ever had in Chinese school.
Sáo huò!
Well... maybe not the Chinese my parents wanted me to learn.
Before I knew it, the trip was coming to an end.
ZZZ
Psst! Yang Yang!
Lulu?
I can't sleep!
I don't want this to end so quickly.
Same... we were starting to feel like real sisters.
But our flight—
Oh no.
I know that look.

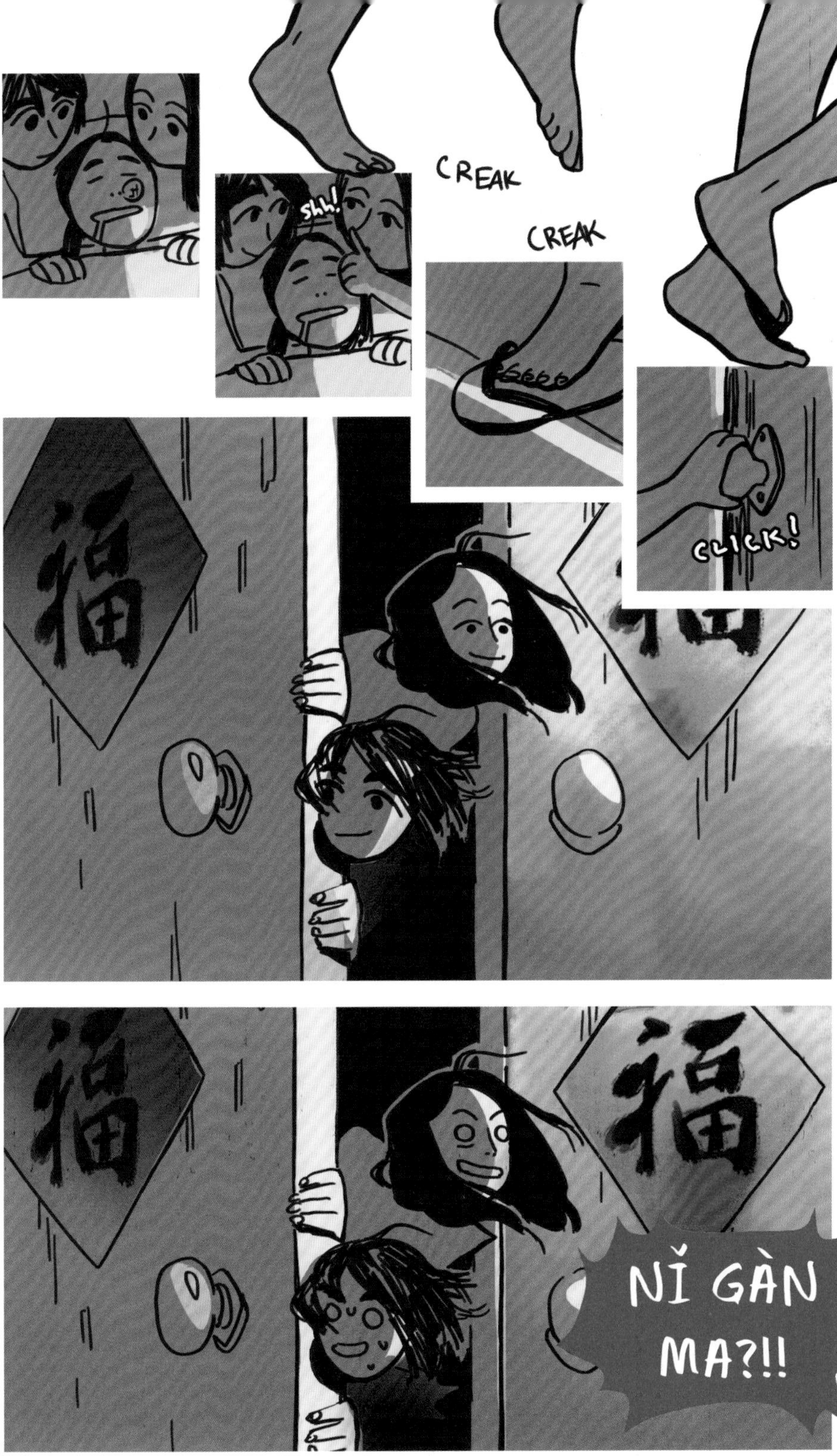
Shh!
CREAK
CREAK
CLICK!
福
福
福
NǏ GÀN
MA?!!

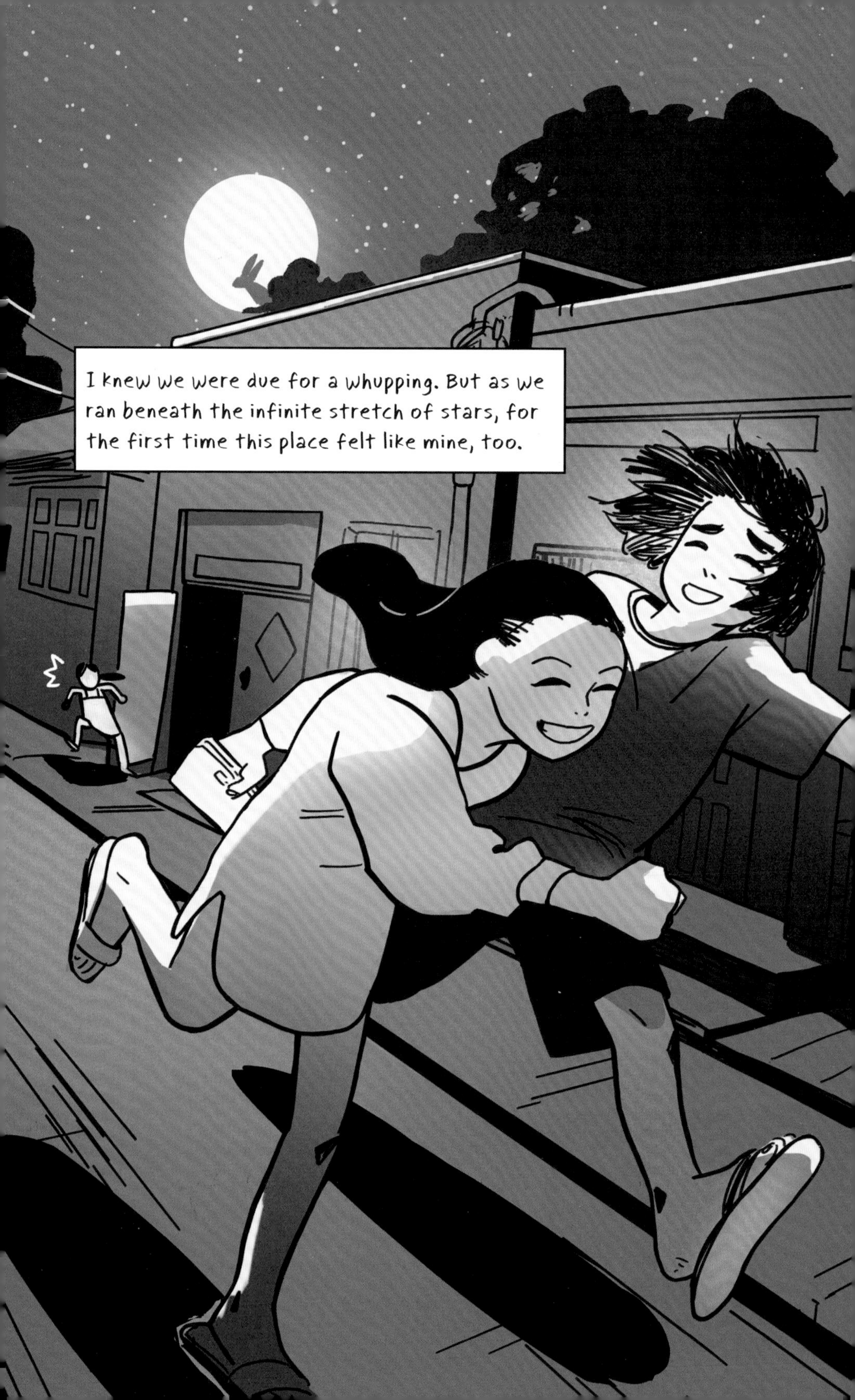
I knew we were due for a whupping. But as we ran beneath the infinite stretch of stars, for the first time this place felt like mine, too.

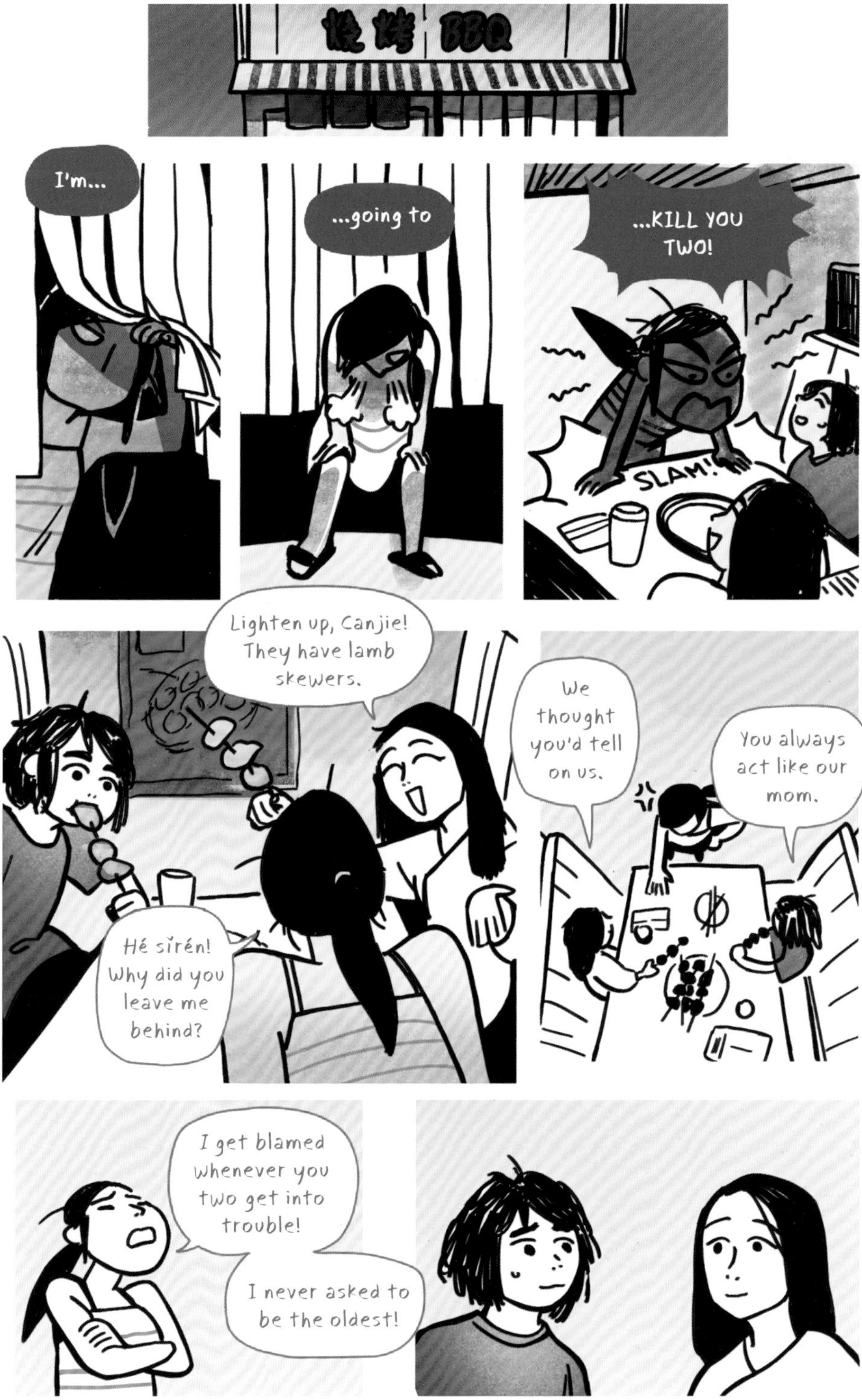
燒烤 BBQ
I'm...
...going to
...KILL YOU TWO!
SLAM!
Lighten up, Canjie! They have lamb skewers.
Hé sǐrén! Why did you leave me behind?
We thought you'd tell on us.
You always act like our mom.
I get blamed whenever you two get into trouble!
I never asked to be the oldest!

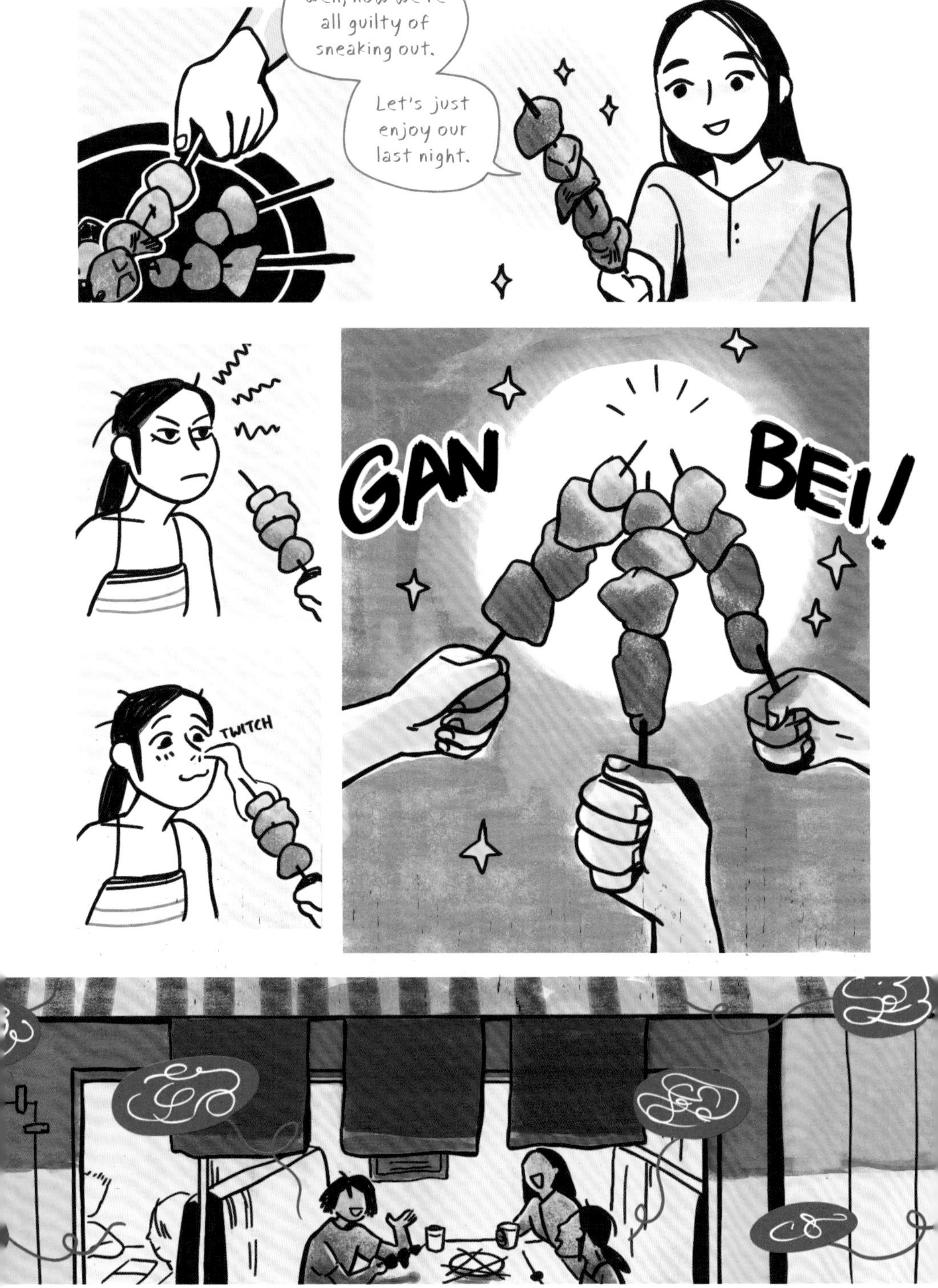
Well, now we're all guilty of sneaking out.
Let's just enjoy our last night.
TWITCH
GAN BEI!

CHAPTER 8
High School Woo-sical

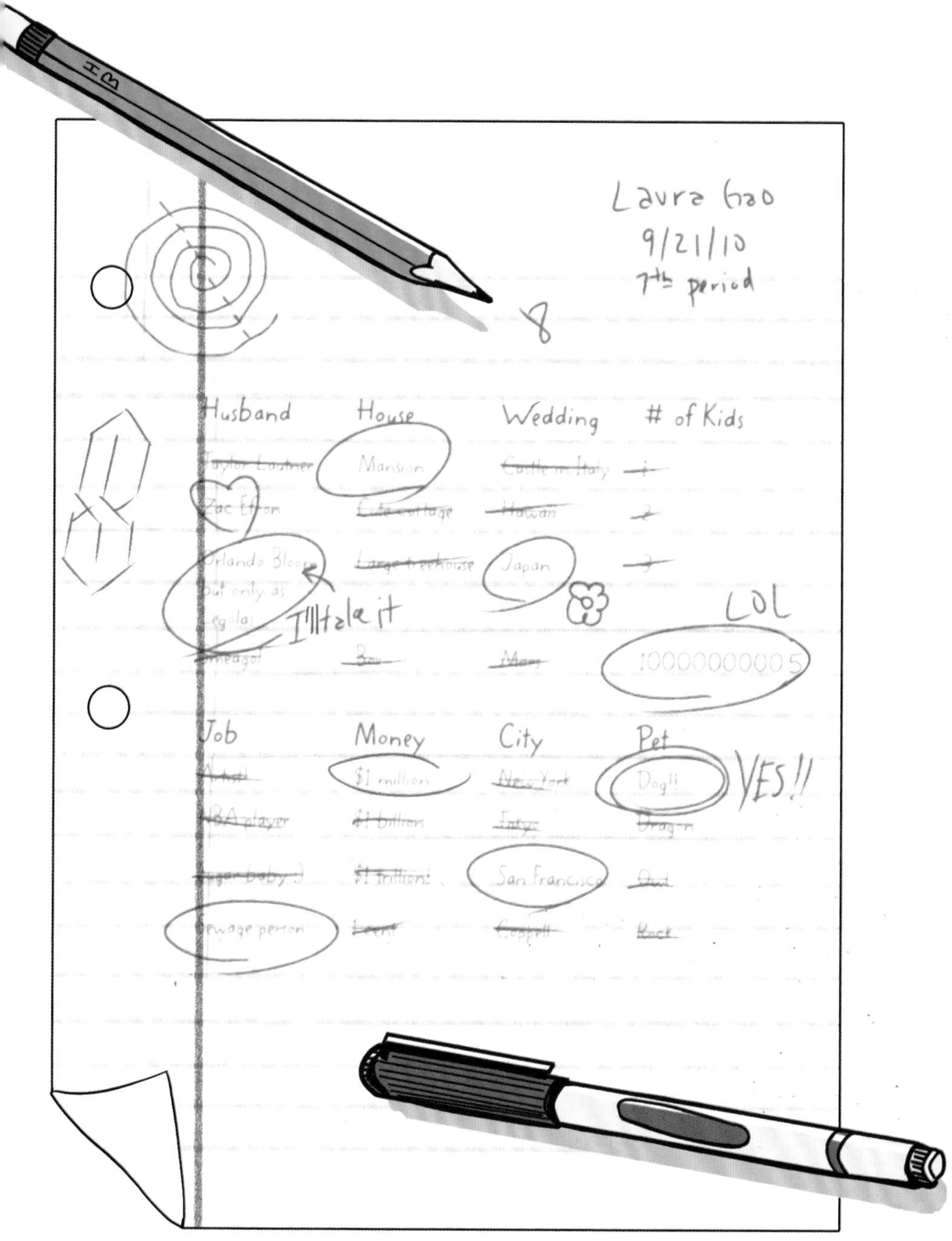

Laura Gao
9/21/10
7th period
8
Husband
House
Wedding
# of Kids
Taylor Lautner
Mansion
Castle in Italy
1
Zac Efron
Cute cottage
Hawaii
2
Orlando Bloom
but only as
Legolas
Large treehouse
Japan
3
I'll take it
LOL
Smeagol
100000000005
Job
Money
City
Pet
$1 million
New York
Dog!!
YES!!
NBA player
$1 billion
Dragon
$1 trillion!
San Francisco
Sewage person
Coppell

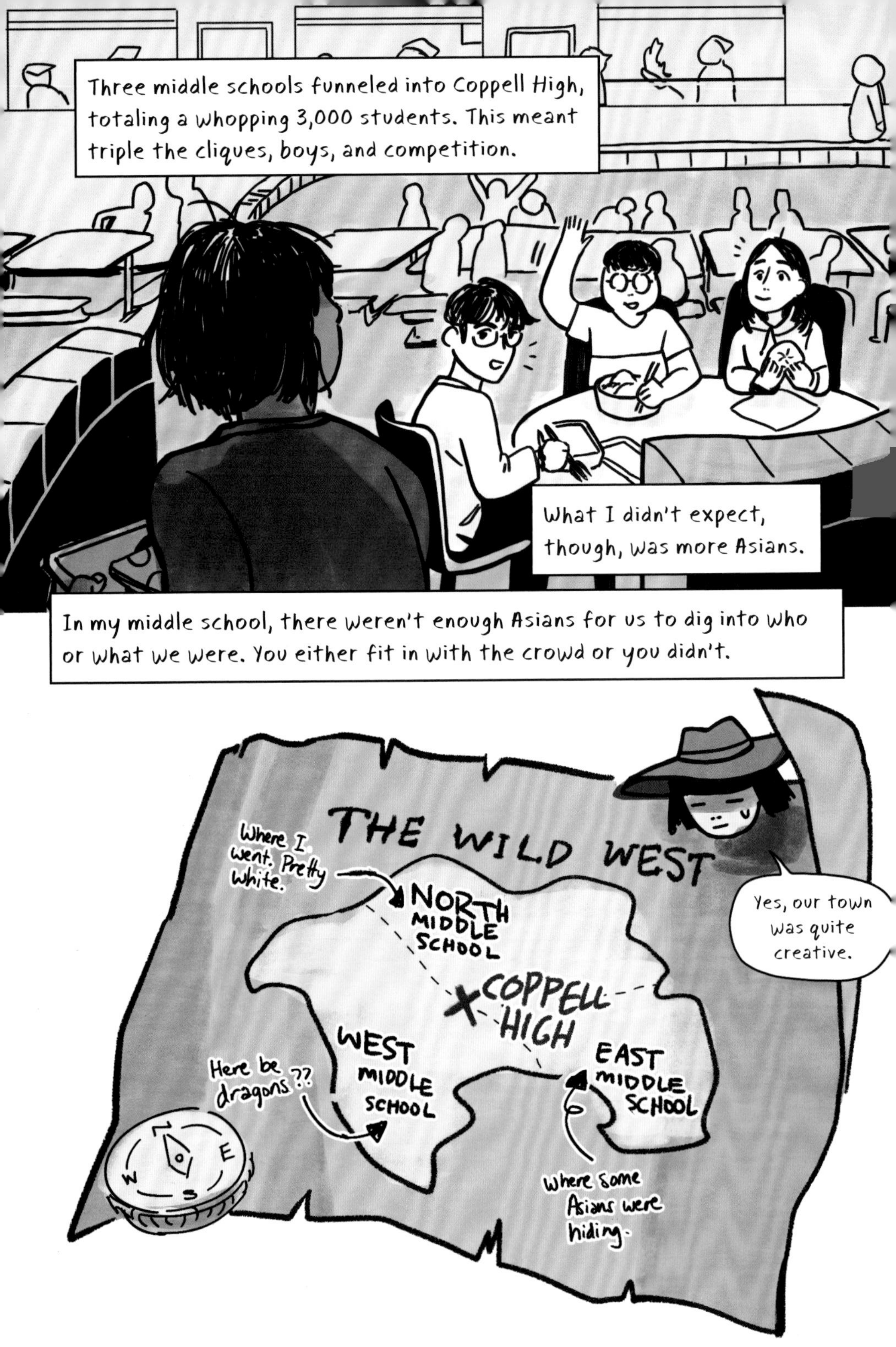
Three middle schools funneled into Coppell High, totaling a whopping 3,000 students. This meant triple the cliques, boys, and competition.
What I didn't expect, though, was more Asians.
In my middle school, there weren't enough Asians for us to dig into who or what we were. You either fit in with the crowd or you didn't.
THE WILD WEST
Where I went. Pretty white.
NORTH MIDDLE SCHOOL
COPPELL HIGH
WEST MIDDLE SCHOOL
EAST MIDDLE SCHOOL
Here be dragons ??
Where some Asians were hiding.
Yes, our town was quite creative.
N
E
W
S

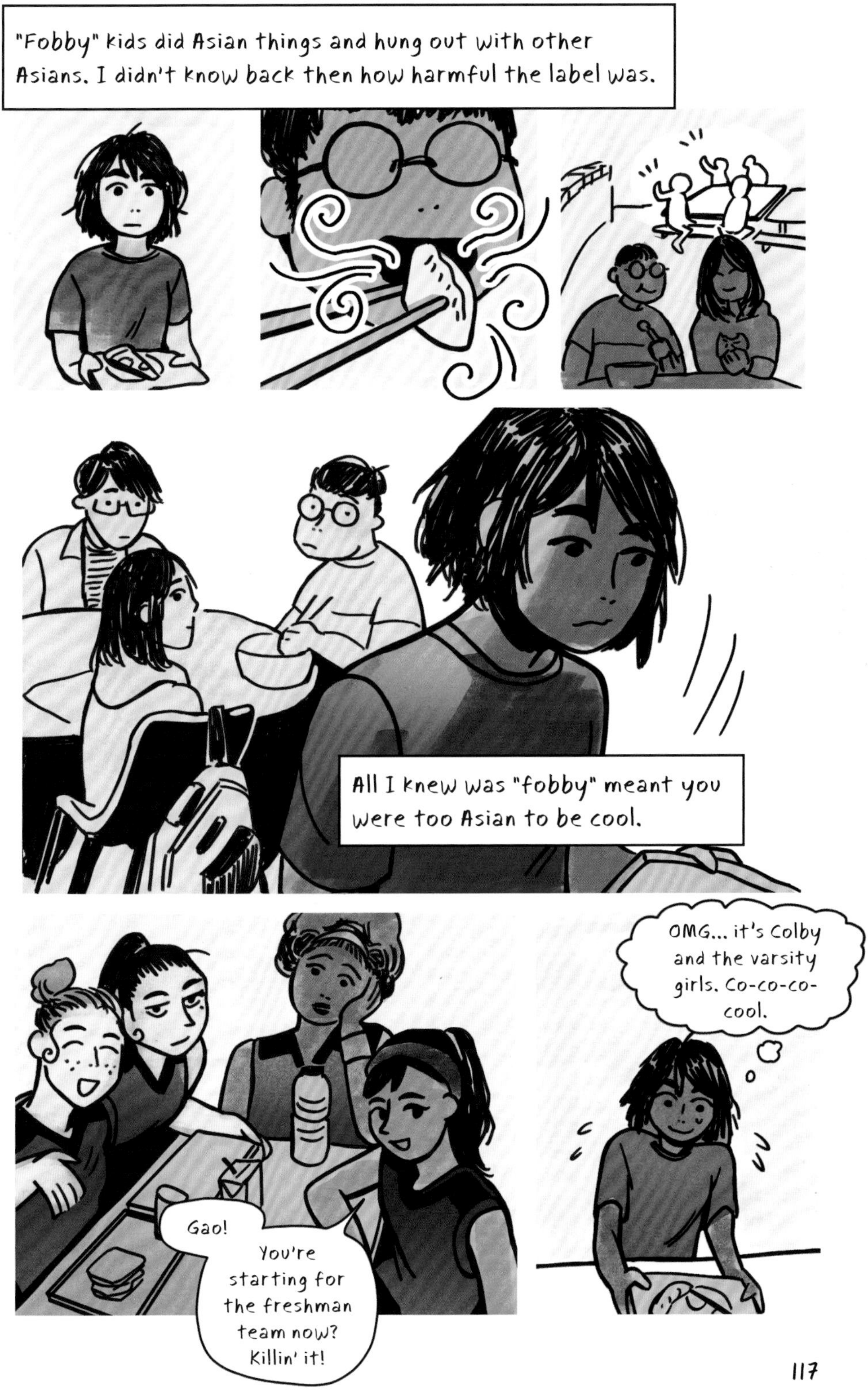
"Fobby" kids did Asian things and hung out with other Asians. I didn't know back then how harmful the label was.
All I knew was "fobby" meant you were too Asian to be cool.
Gao! You're starting for the freshman team now? Killin' it!
OMG... it's Colby and the varsity girls. Co-co-co-cool.

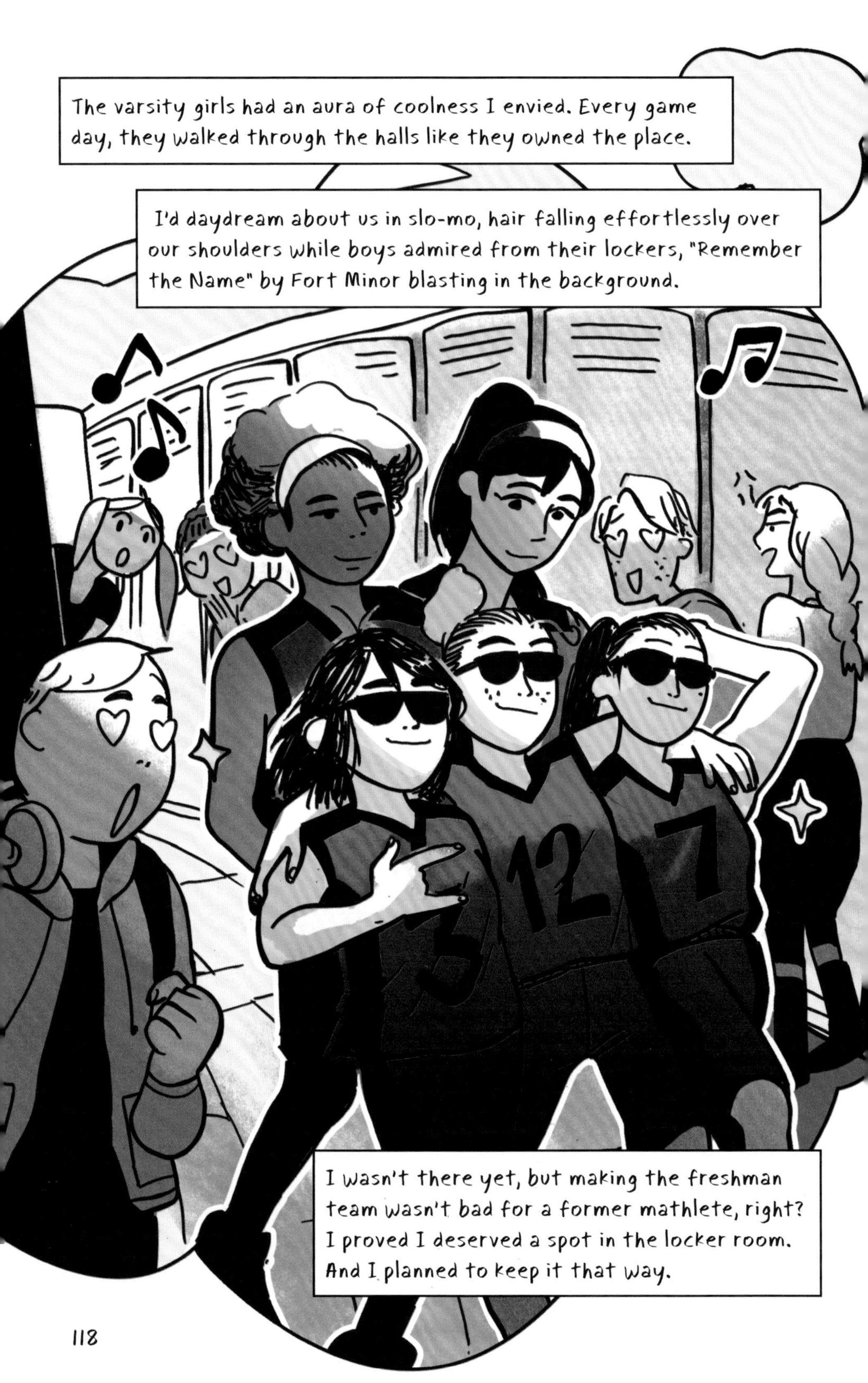
The varsity girls had an aura of coolness I envied. Every game day, they walked through the halls like they owned the place.
I'd daydream about us in slo-mo, hair falling effortlessly over our shoulders while boys admired from their lockers, "Remember the Name" by Fort Minor blasting in the background.
3
12
7
I wasn't there yet, but making the freshman team wasn't bad for a former mathlete, right? I proved I deserved a spot in the locker room. And I planned to keep it that way.

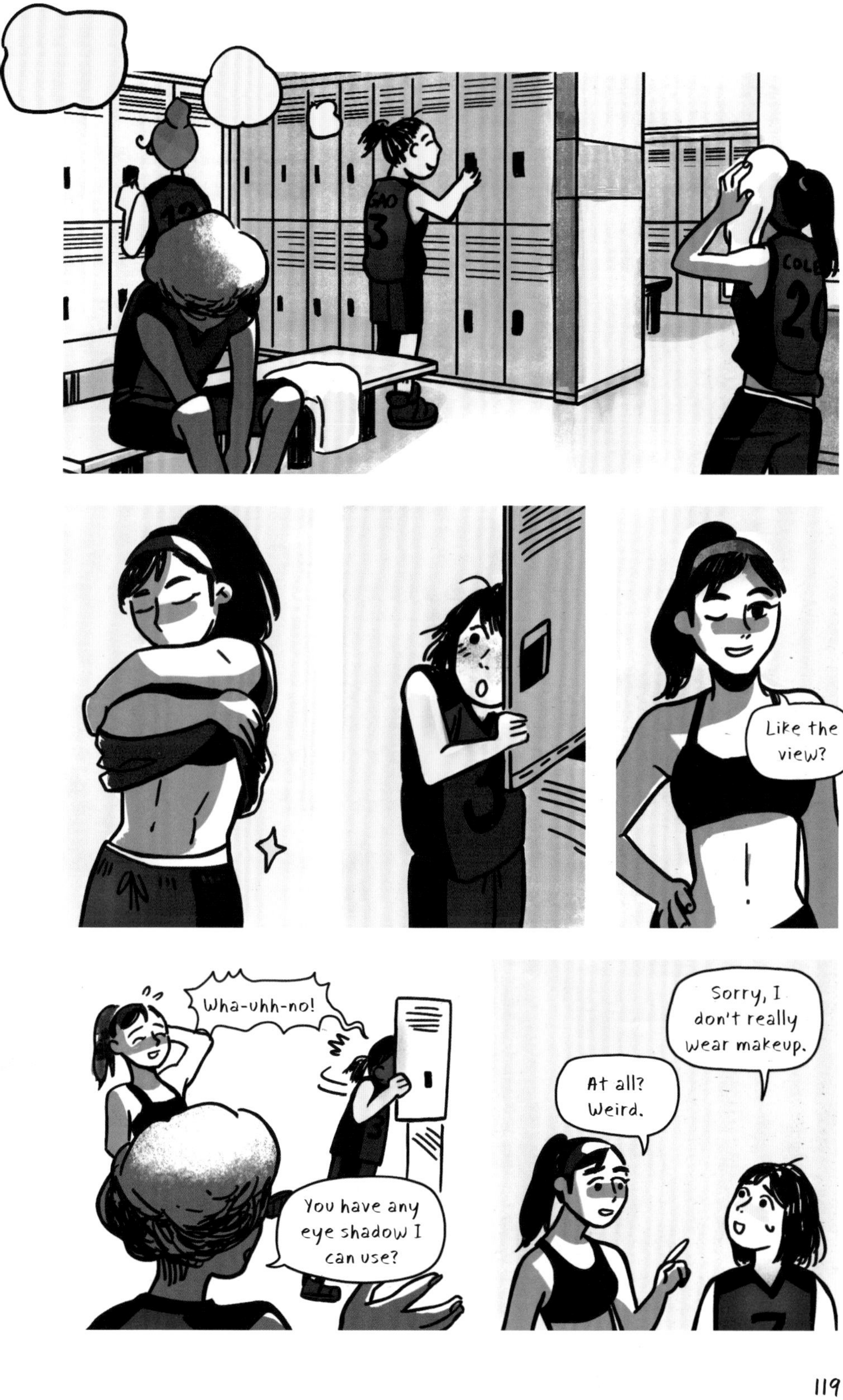
Like the view?
Wha-uhh-no!
You have any eye shadow I can use?
Sorry, I don't really wear makeup.
At all? Weird.

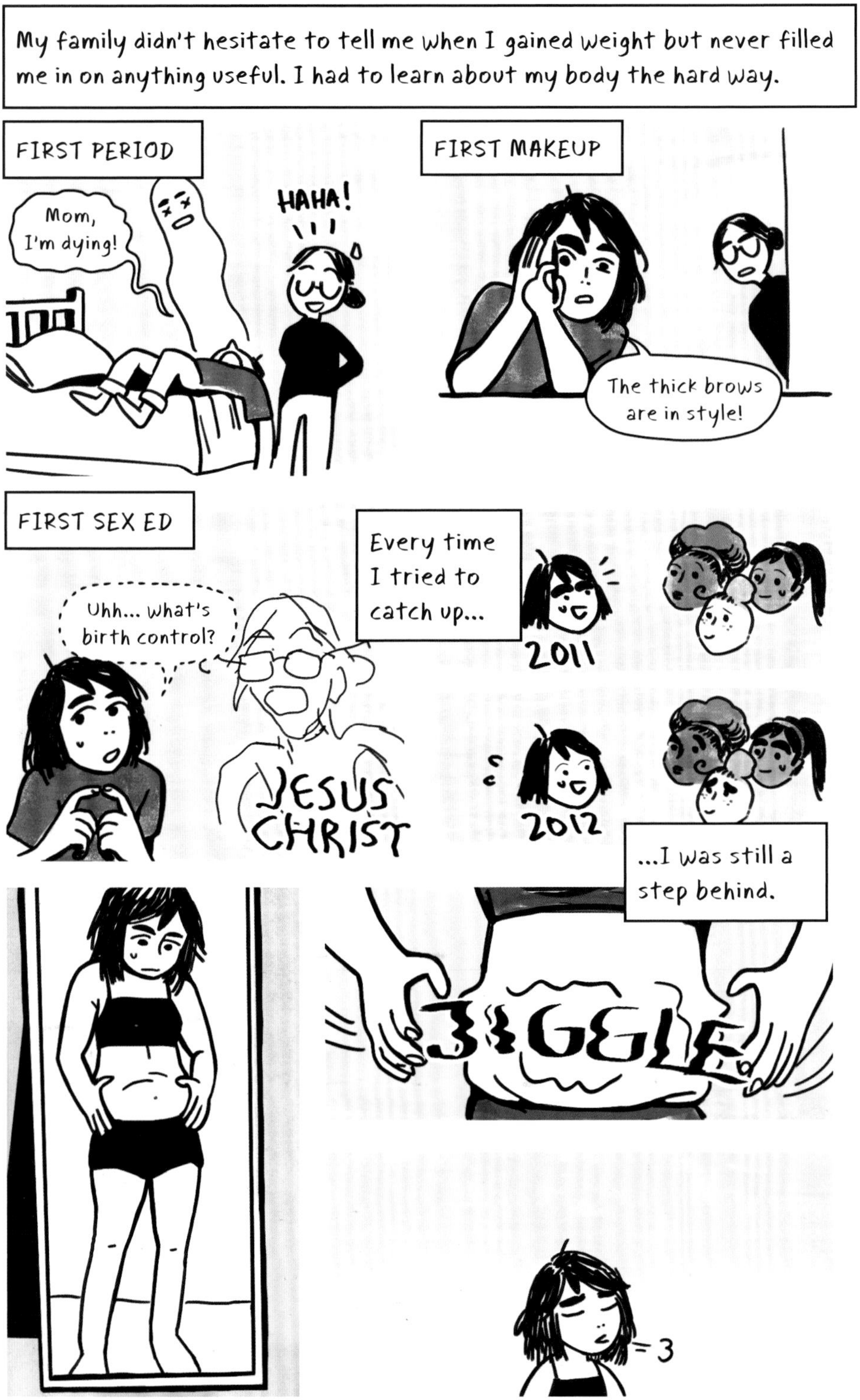

My family didn't hesitate to tell me when I gained weight but never filled me in on anything useful. I had to learn about my body the hard way.
FIRST PERIOD
Mom, I'm dying!
HAHA!
FIRST MAKEUP
The thick brows are in style!
FIRST SEX ED
Uhh... what's birth control?
JESUS CHRIST
Every time I tried to catch up...
2011
2012
...I was still a step behind.
JIGGLE
=3

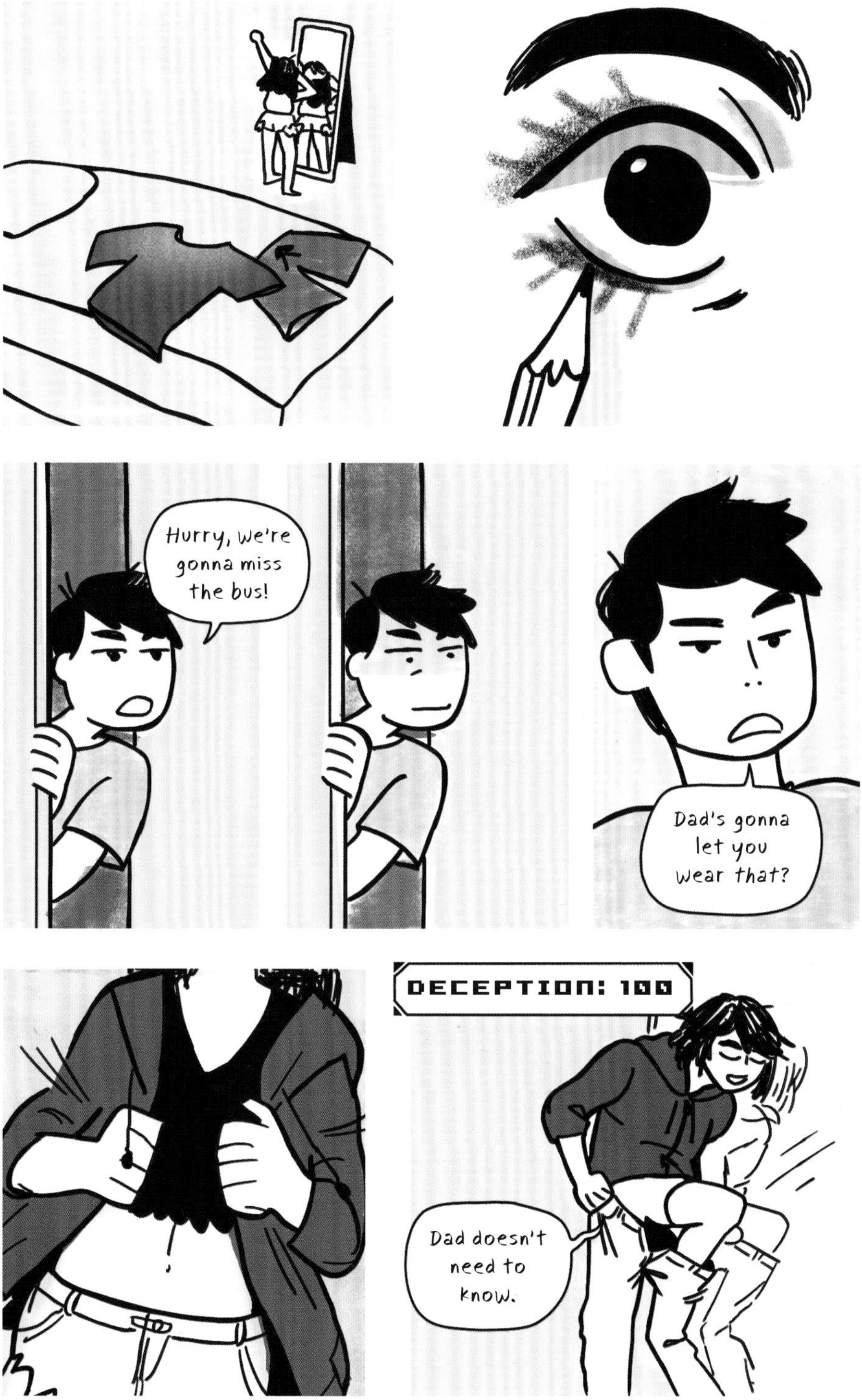
Hurry, we're gonna miss the bus!
Dad's gonna let you wear that?
DECEPTION: 100
Dad doesn't need to know.

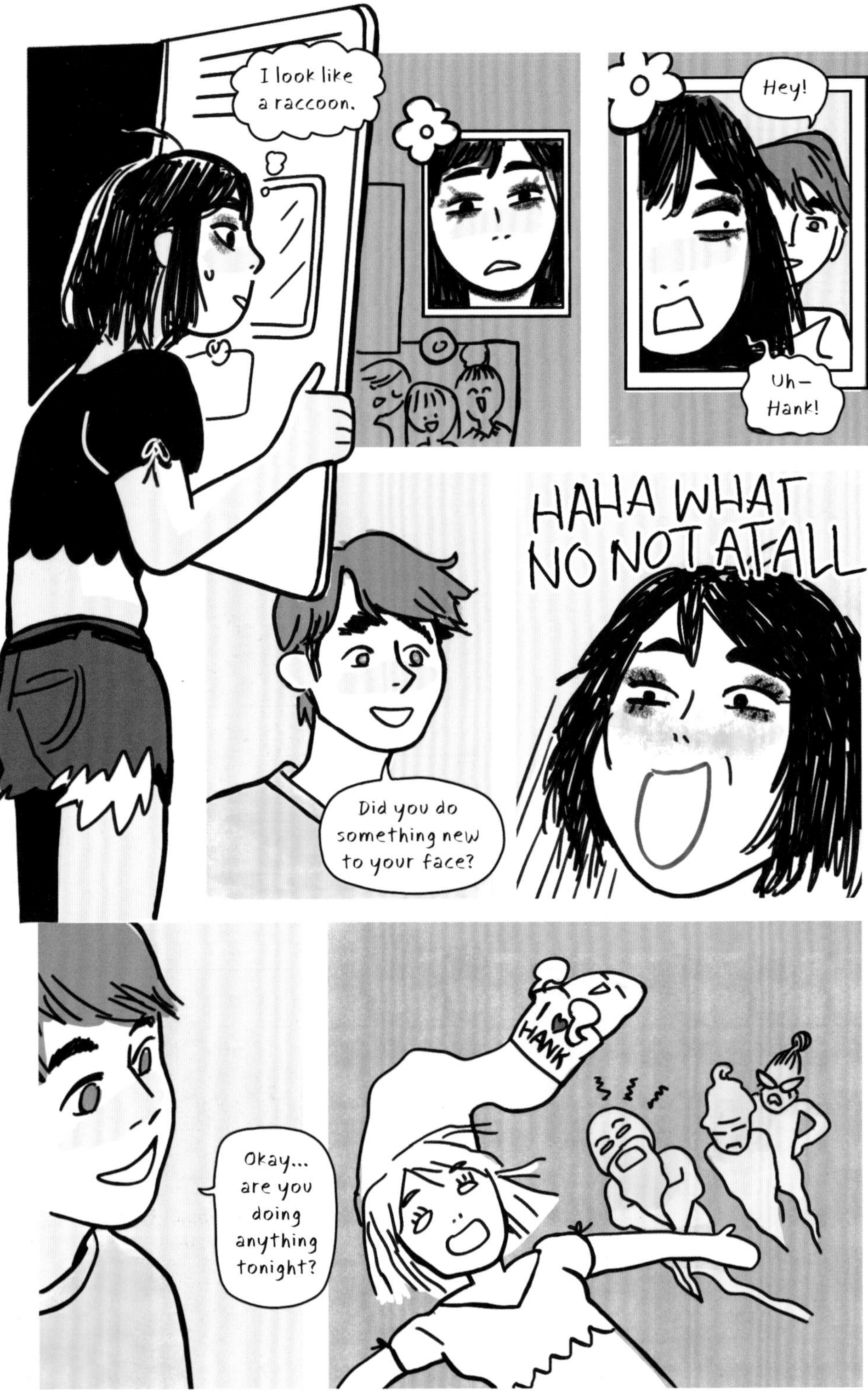

I look like a raccoon.
Hey!
Uh— Hank!
Did you do something new to your face?
HAHA WHAT NO NOT AT ALL
Okay... are you doing anything tonight?
I ♥ HANK

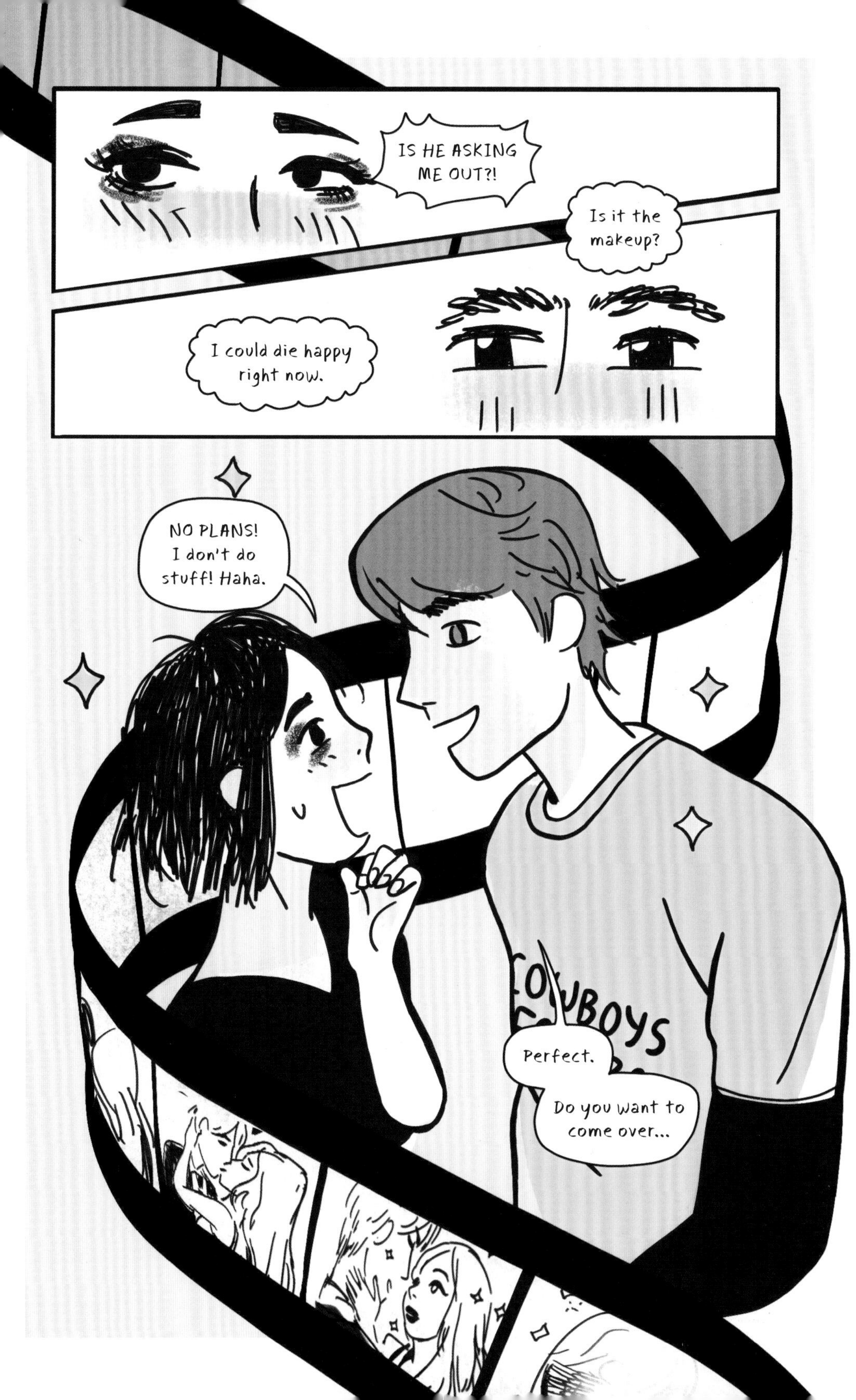
IS HE ASKING ME OUT?!
Is it the makeup?
I could die happy right now.
NO PLANS! I don't do stuff! Haha.
COWBOYS
Perfect.
Do you want to come over...

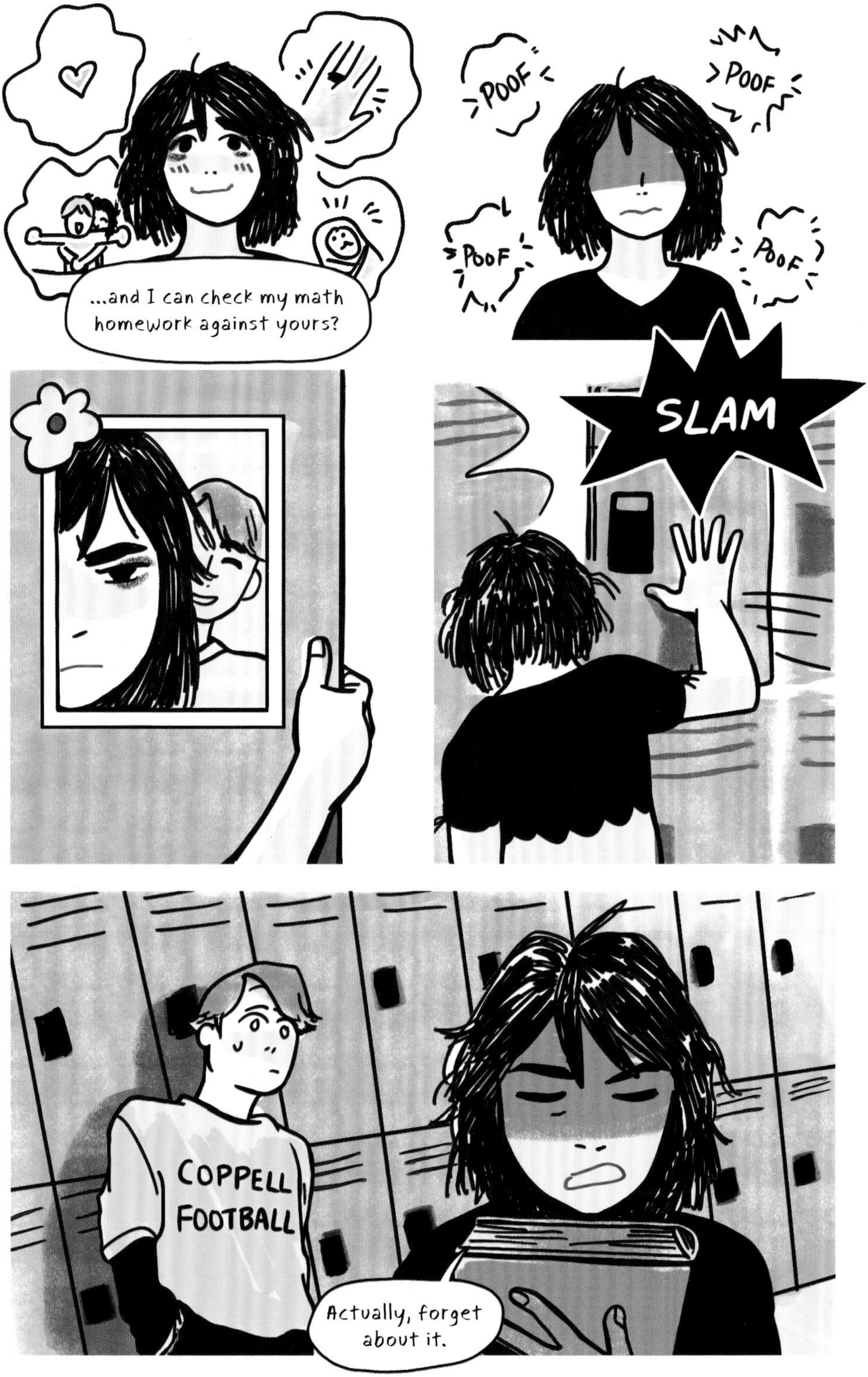
...and I can check my math homework against yours?
POOF
POOF
POOF
POOF
SLAM
COPPELL FOOTBALL
Actually, forget about it.

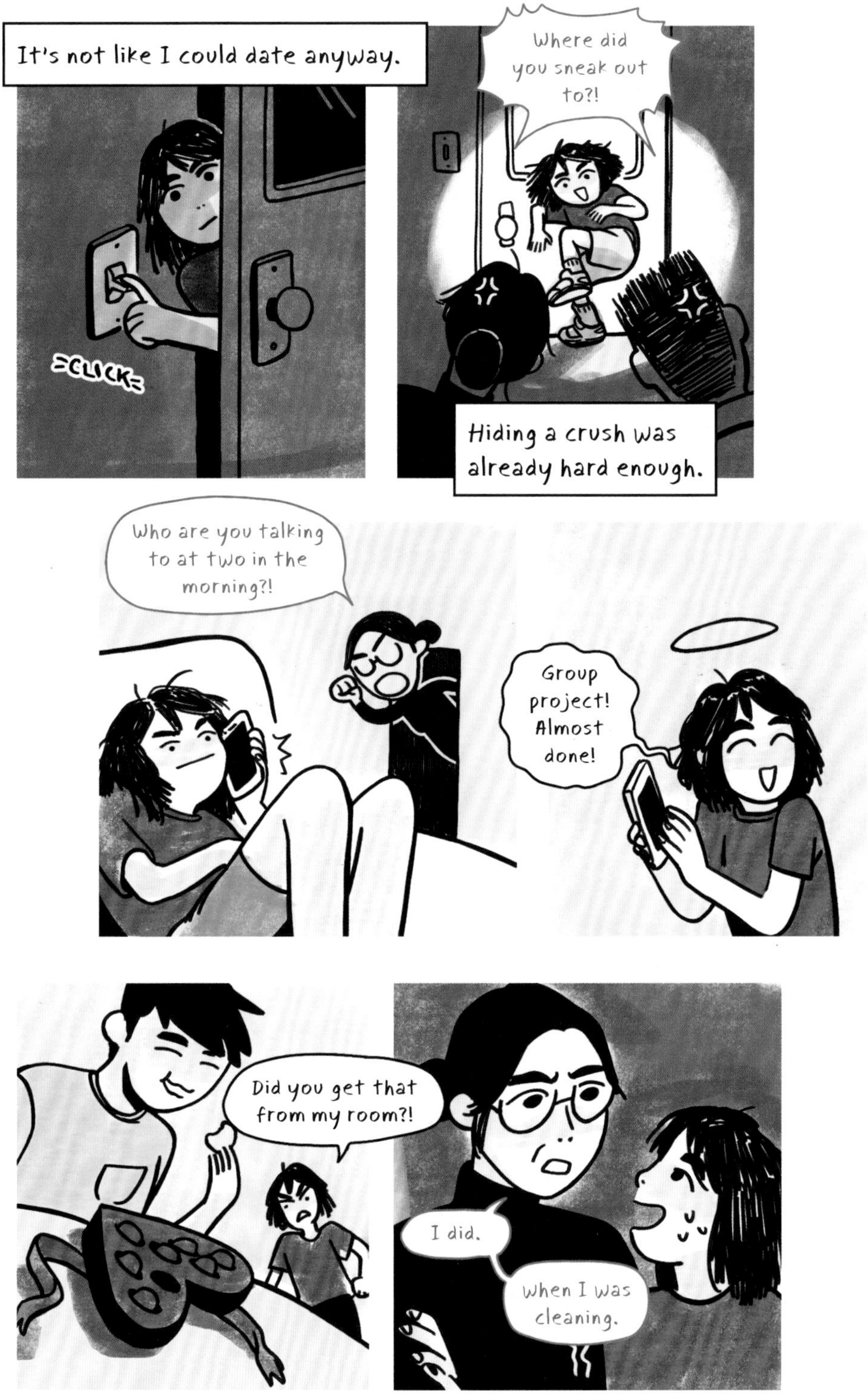
It's not like I could date anyway.
=CLICK=
Where did you sneak out to?!
Hiding a crush was already hard enough.
Who are you talking to at two in the morning?!
Group project! Almost done!
Did you get that from my room?!
I did.
When I was cleaning.

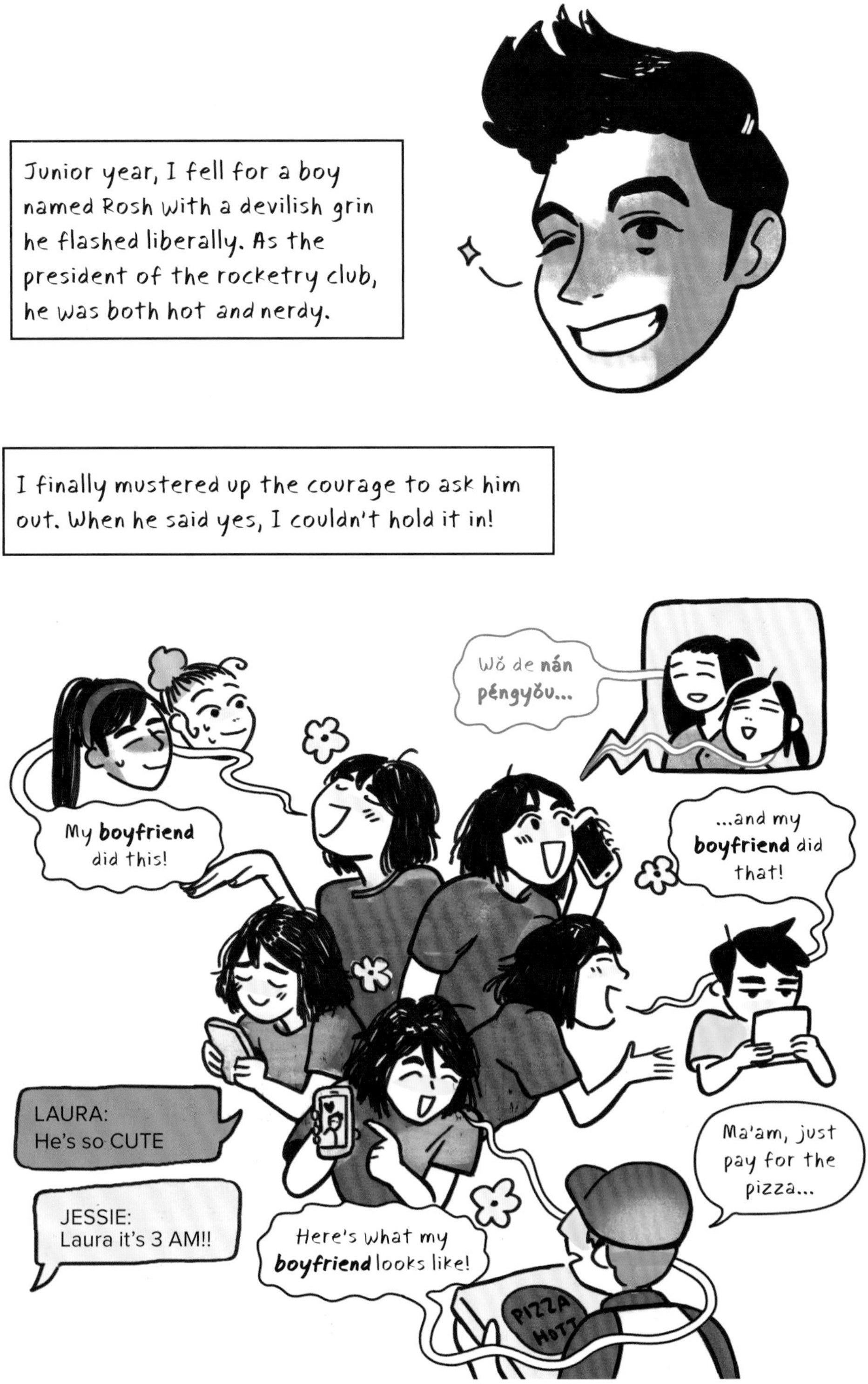
Junior year, I fell for a boy named Rosh with a devilish grin he flashed liberally. As the president of the rocketry club, he was both hot and nerdy.
I finally mustered up the courage to ask him out. When he said yes, I couldn't hold it in!
My **boyfriend** did this!
Wǒ de **nán péngyǒu**...
...and my **boyfriend** did that!
LAURA: He's so CUTE
JESSIE: Laura it's 3 AM!!
Here's what my **boyfriend** looks like!
Ma'am, just pay for the pizza...
PIZZA HOTT

Though he was no doctor, I figured a rocket scientist was a close second, right?

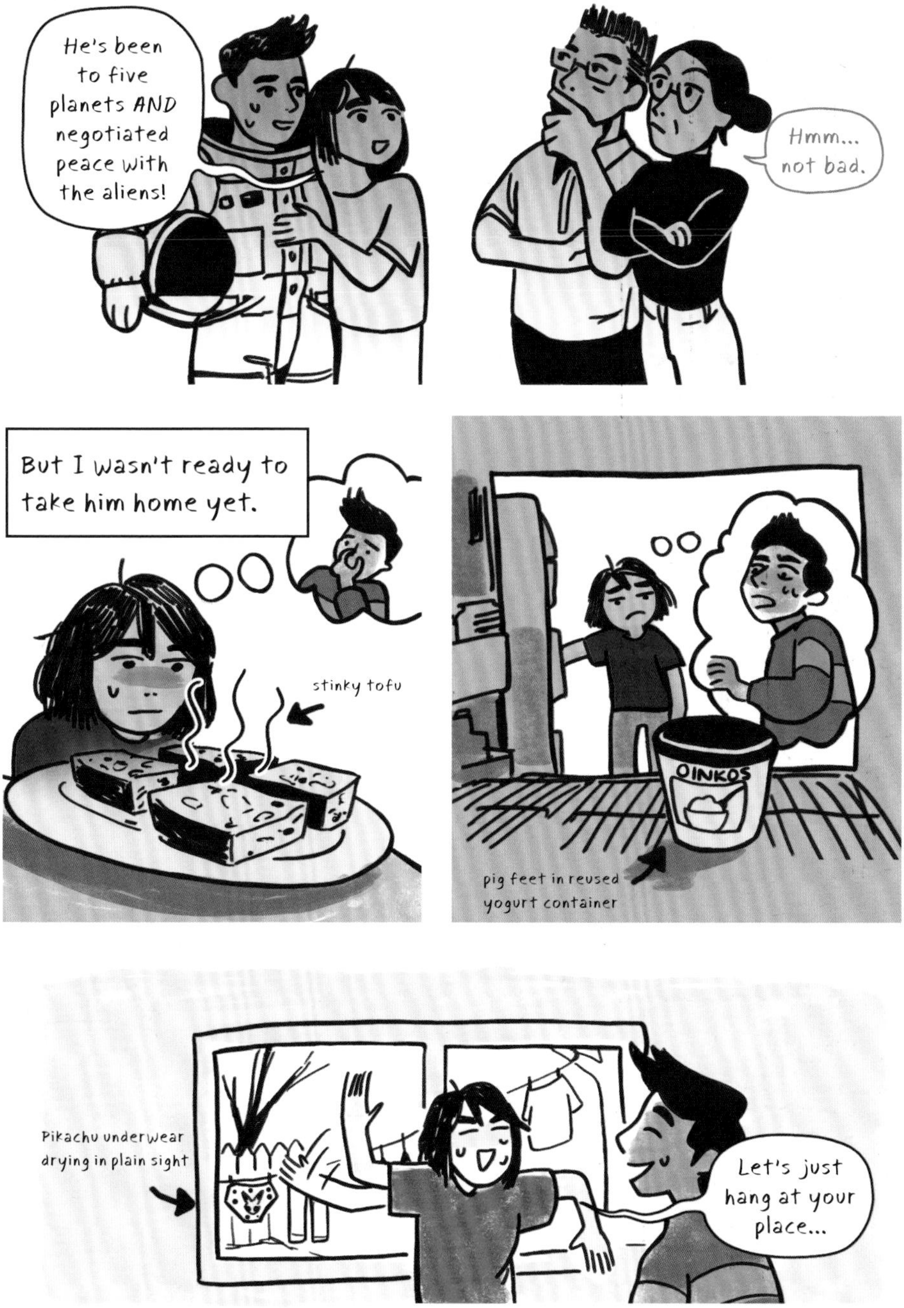
He's been to five planets AND negotiated peace with the aliens!
Hmm... not bad.
But I wasn't ready to take him home yet.
stinky tofu
pig feet in reused yogurt container
OINKOS
Pikachu underwear drying in plain sight
Let's just hang at your place...

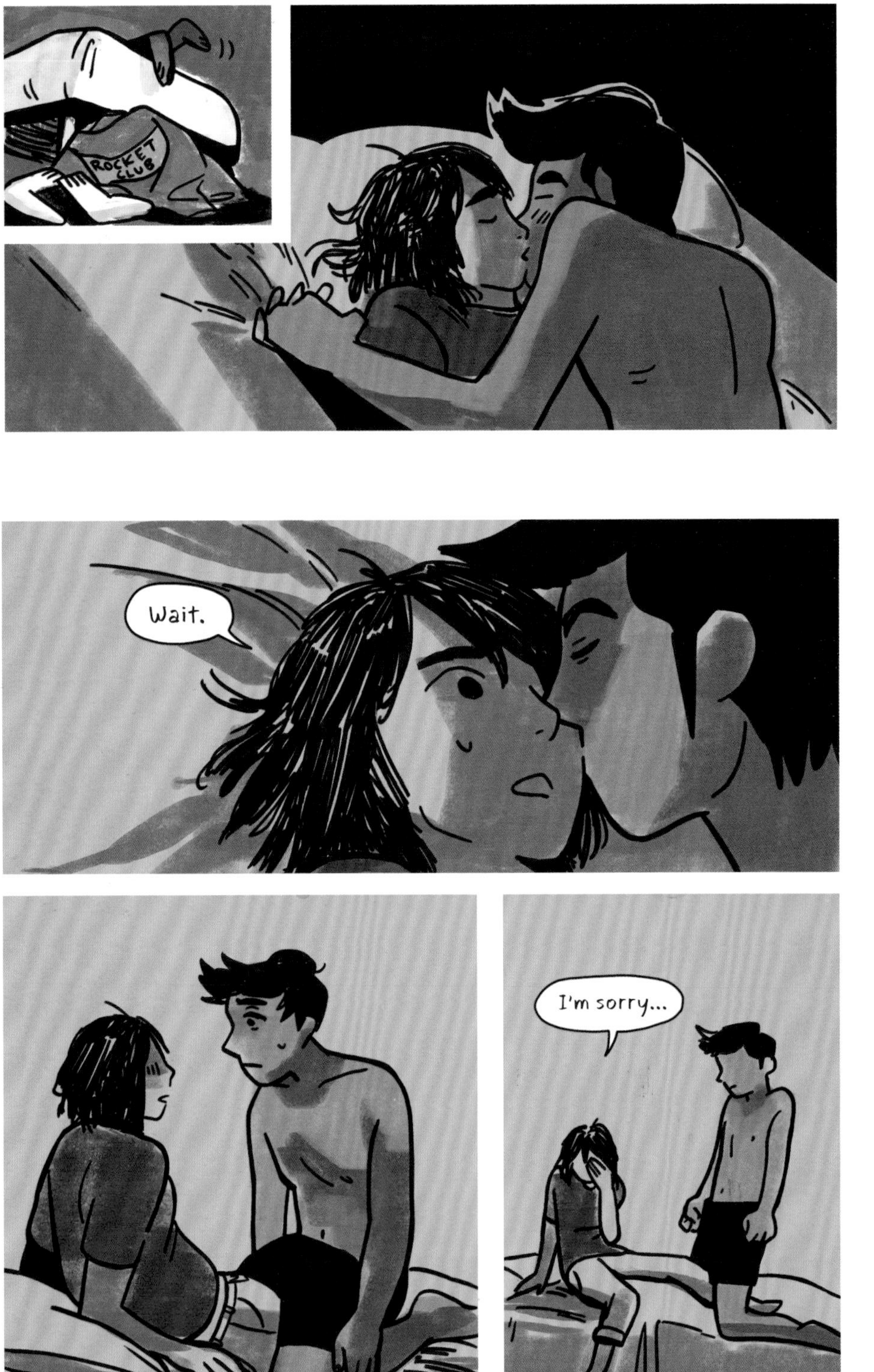
ROCKET CLUB
Wait.
I'm sorry...
It went downhill after that.

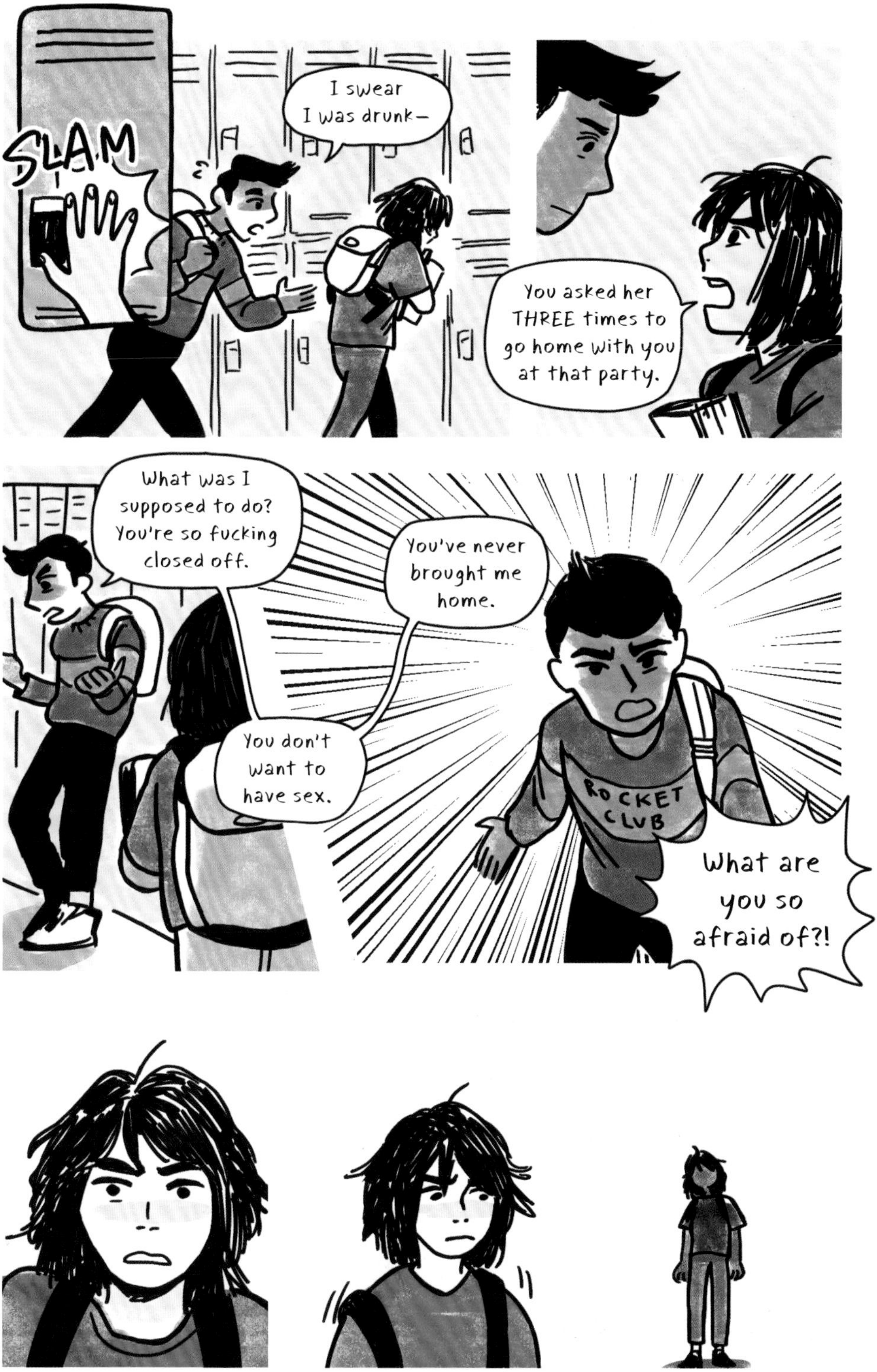
SLAM
I swear I was drunk—
You asked her THREE times to go home with you at that party.
What was I supposed to do? You're so fucking closed off.
You've never brought me home.
You don't want to have sex.
ROCKET CLUB
What are you so afraid of?!

CHAPTER 9
Benched

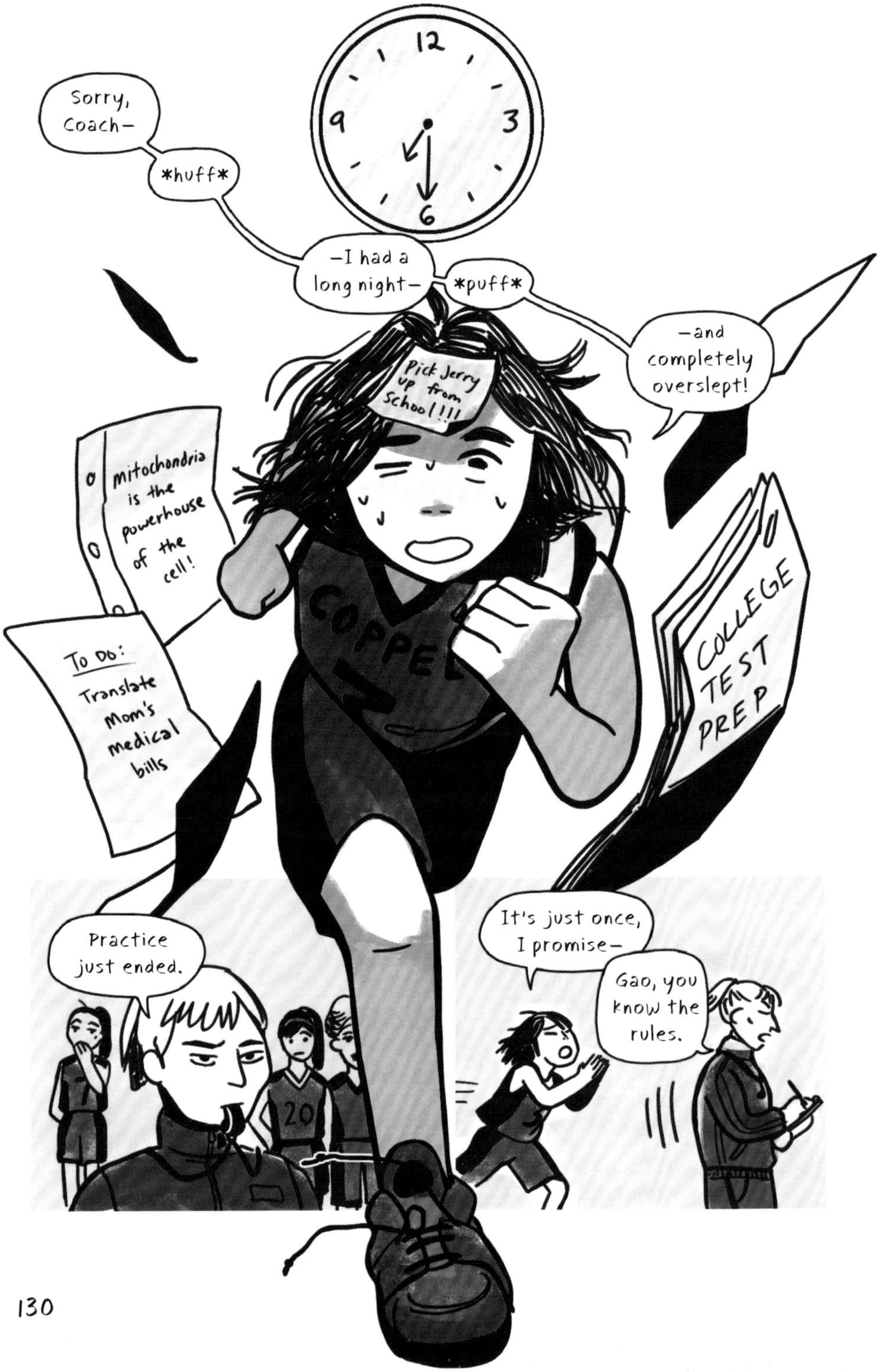

12
9
3
6
Sorry, Coach–
huff
–I had a long night–
puff
–and completely overslept!
Pick Jerry up from School!!!!
mitochondria is the powerhouse of the cell!
To Do: Translate Mom's medical bills
COPPEL
COLLEGE TEST PREP
Practice just ended.
20
It's just once, I promise–
Gao, you know the rules.

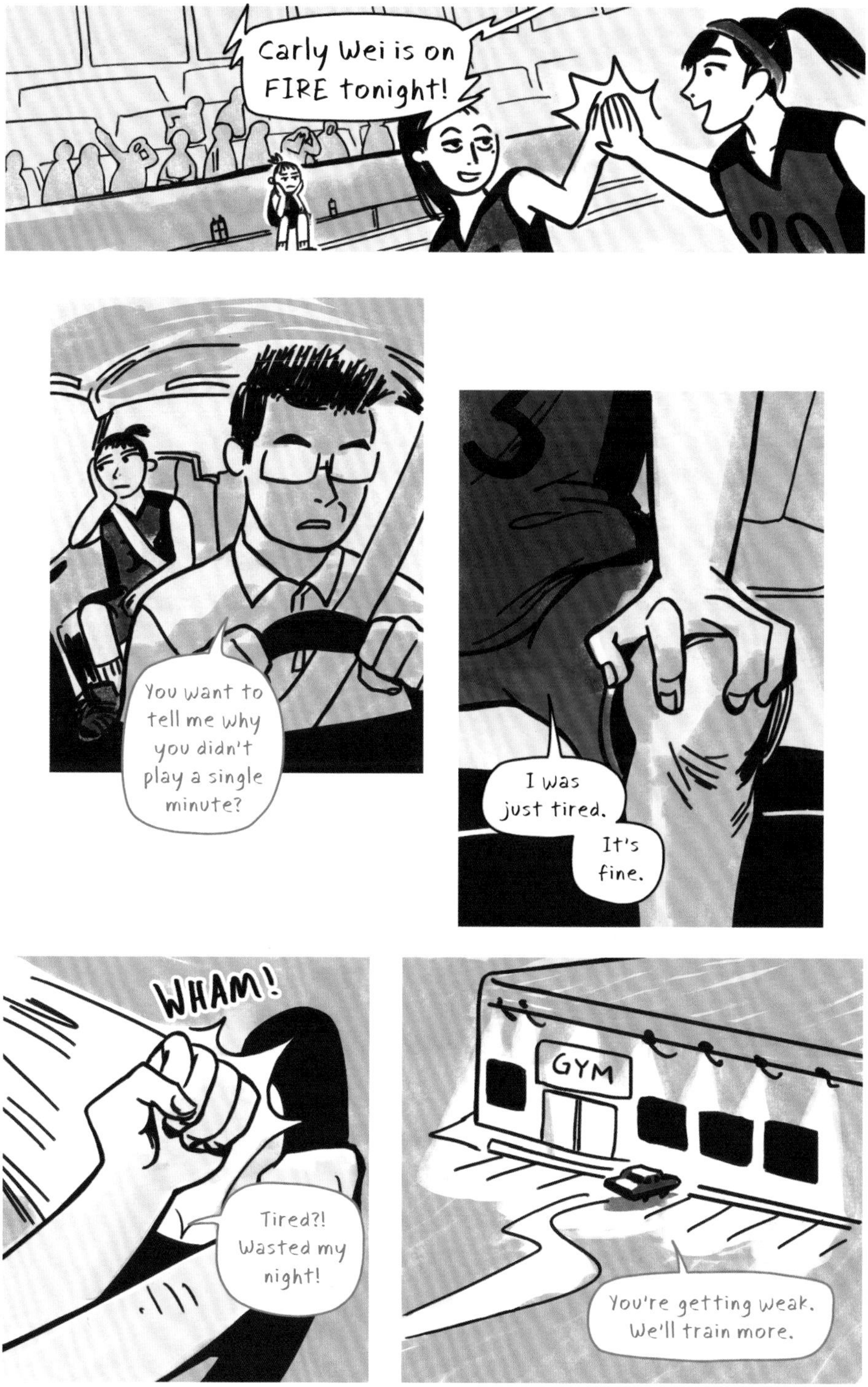
Carly Wei is on FIRE tonight!
You want to tell me why you didn't play a single minute?
I was just tired.
It's fine.
WHAM!
Tired?! Wasted my night!
GYM
You're getting weak. We'll train more.

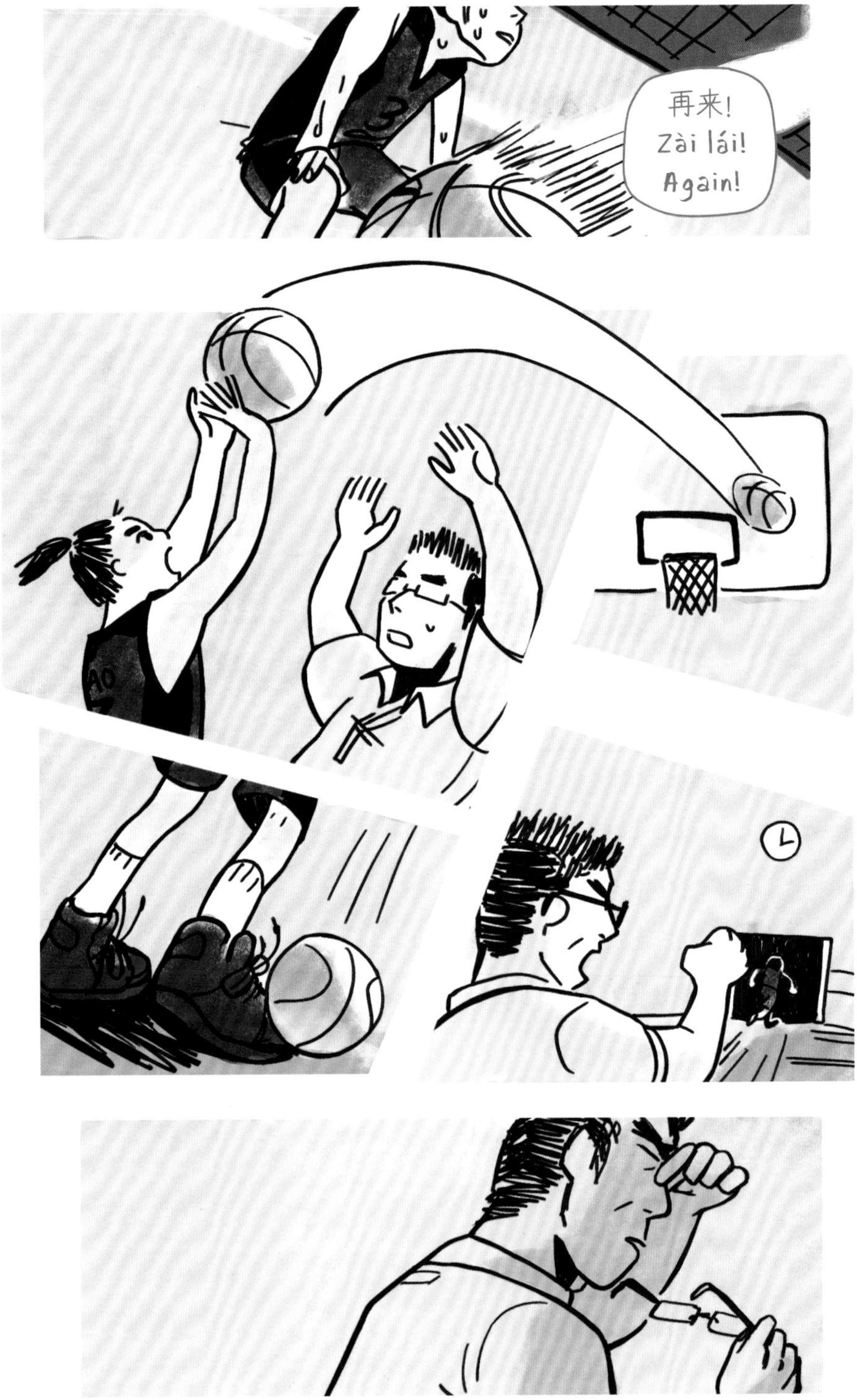
再来!
Zài lái!
Again!

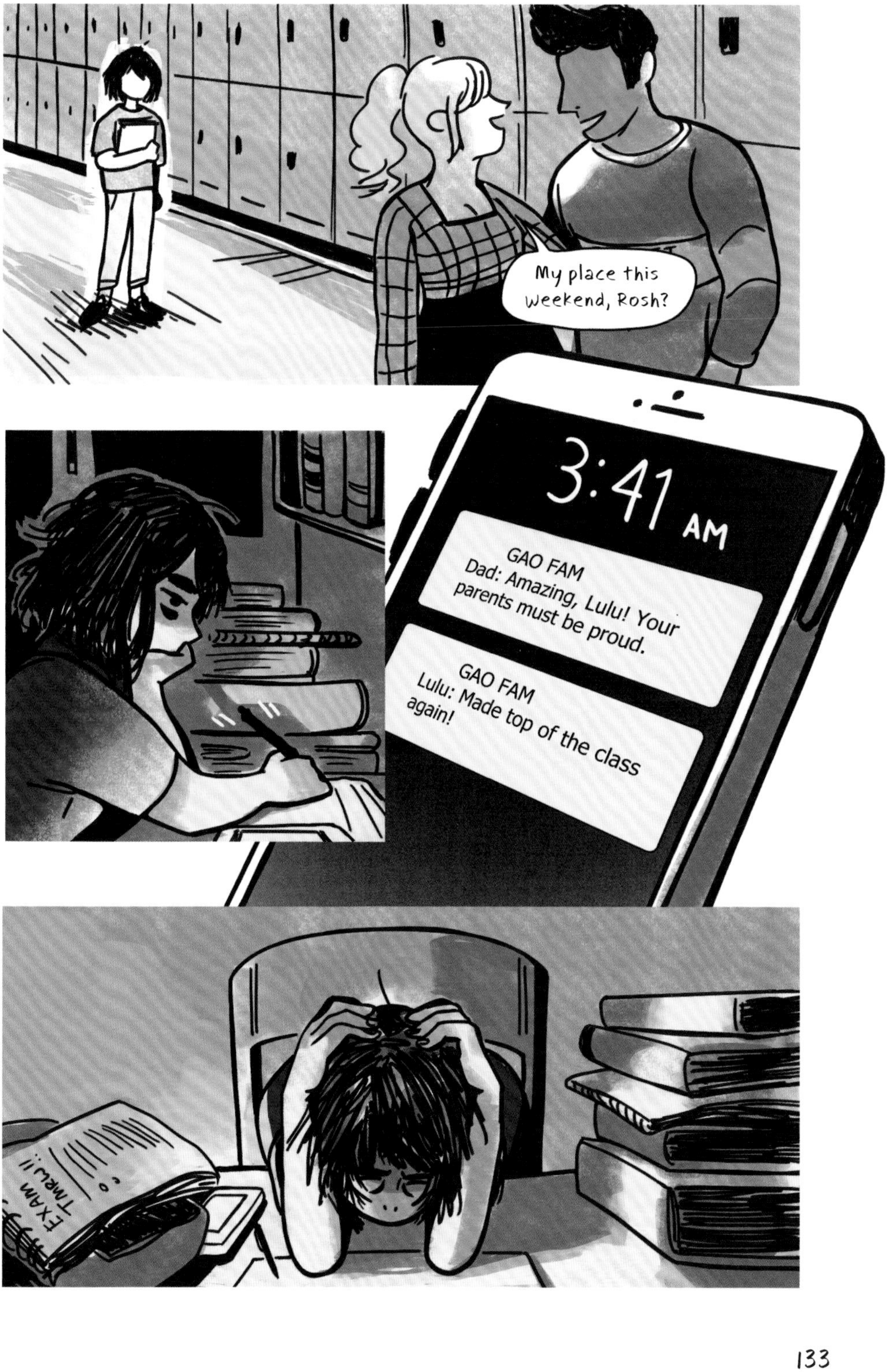
My place this weekend, Rosh?
3:41 AM
GAO FAM
Dad: Amazing, Lulu! Your parents must be proud.
GAO FAM
Lulu: Made top of the class again!
EXAM TMRW!!

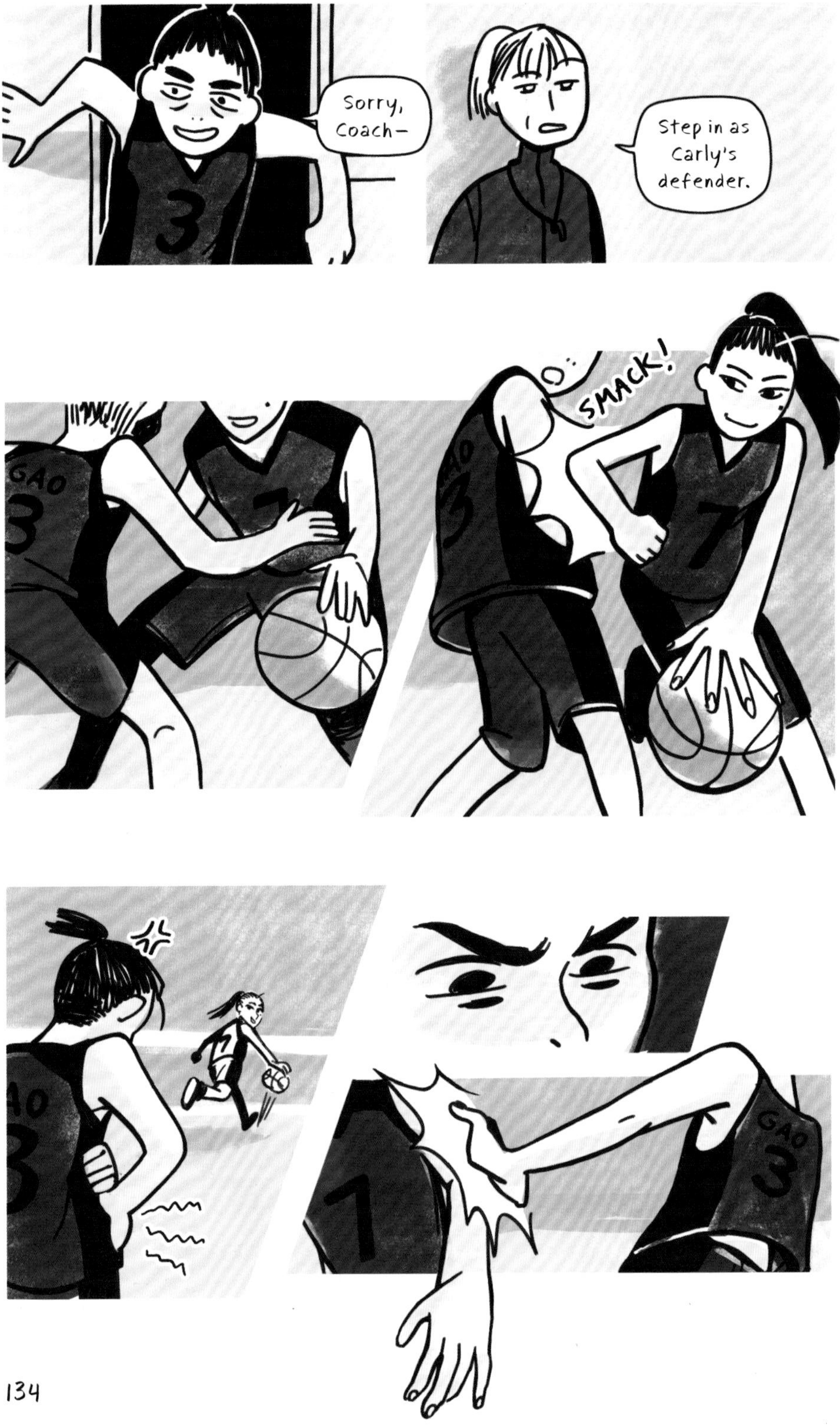
Sorry, Coach—
Step in as Carly's defender.
SMACK!
GAO
3
7
GAO
3
GAO
3
7

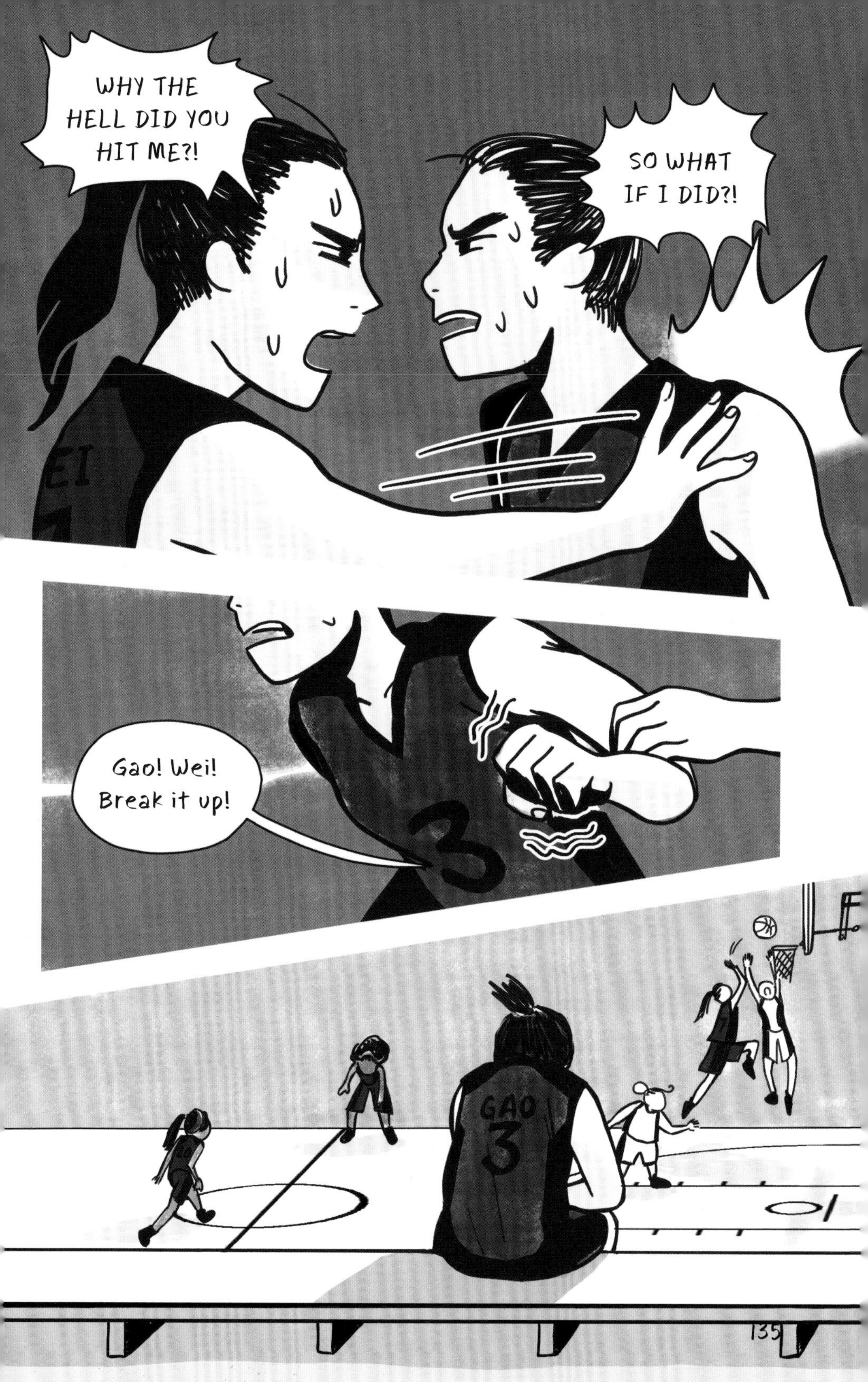
WHY THE HELL DID YOU HIT ME?!
SO WHAT IF I DID?!
Gao! Wei! Break it up!
GAO
3

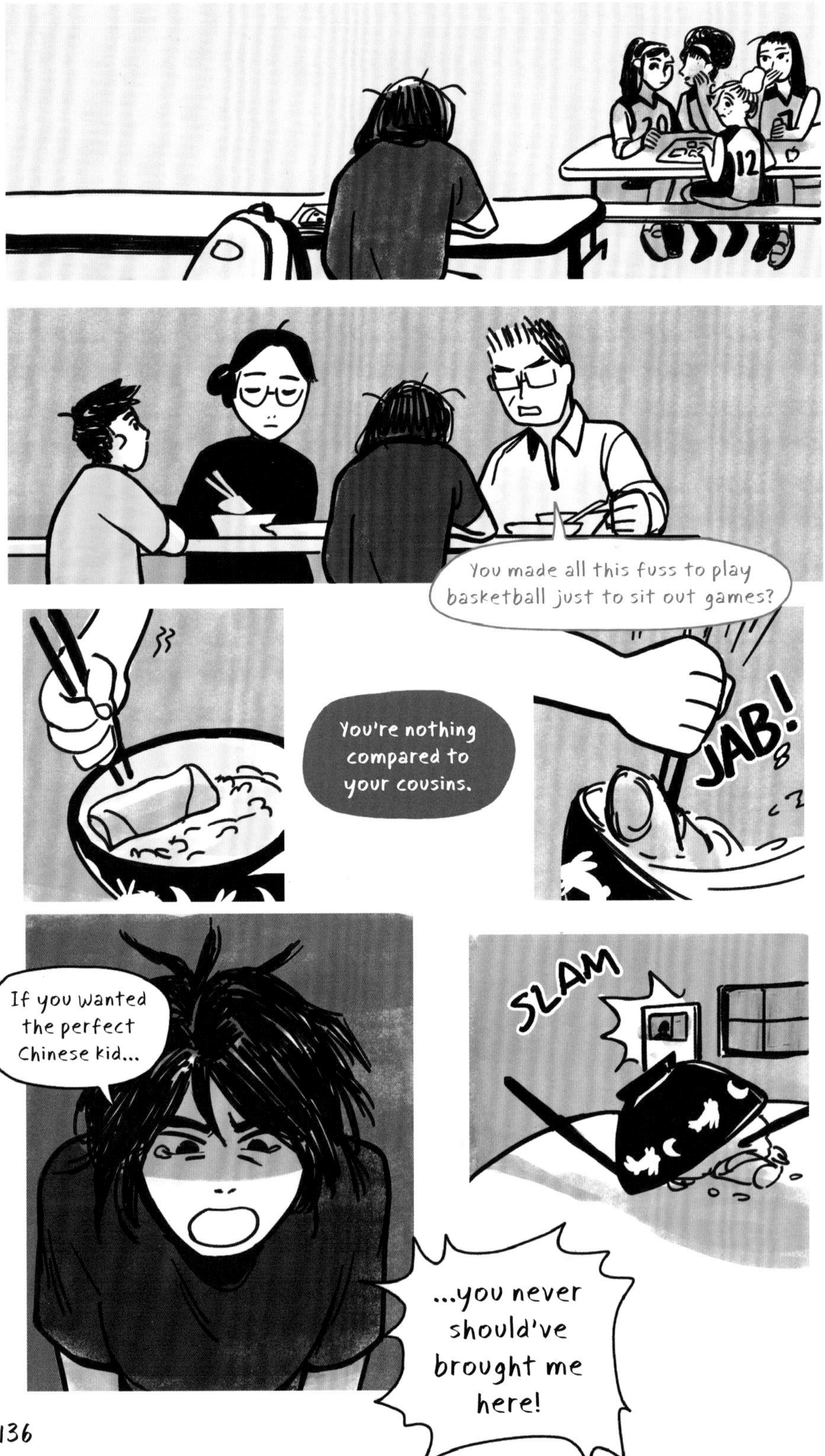
You made all this fuss to play basketball just to sit out games?
You're nothing compared to your cousins.
JAB!
SLAM
If you wanted the perfect Chinese kid...
...you never should've brought me here!

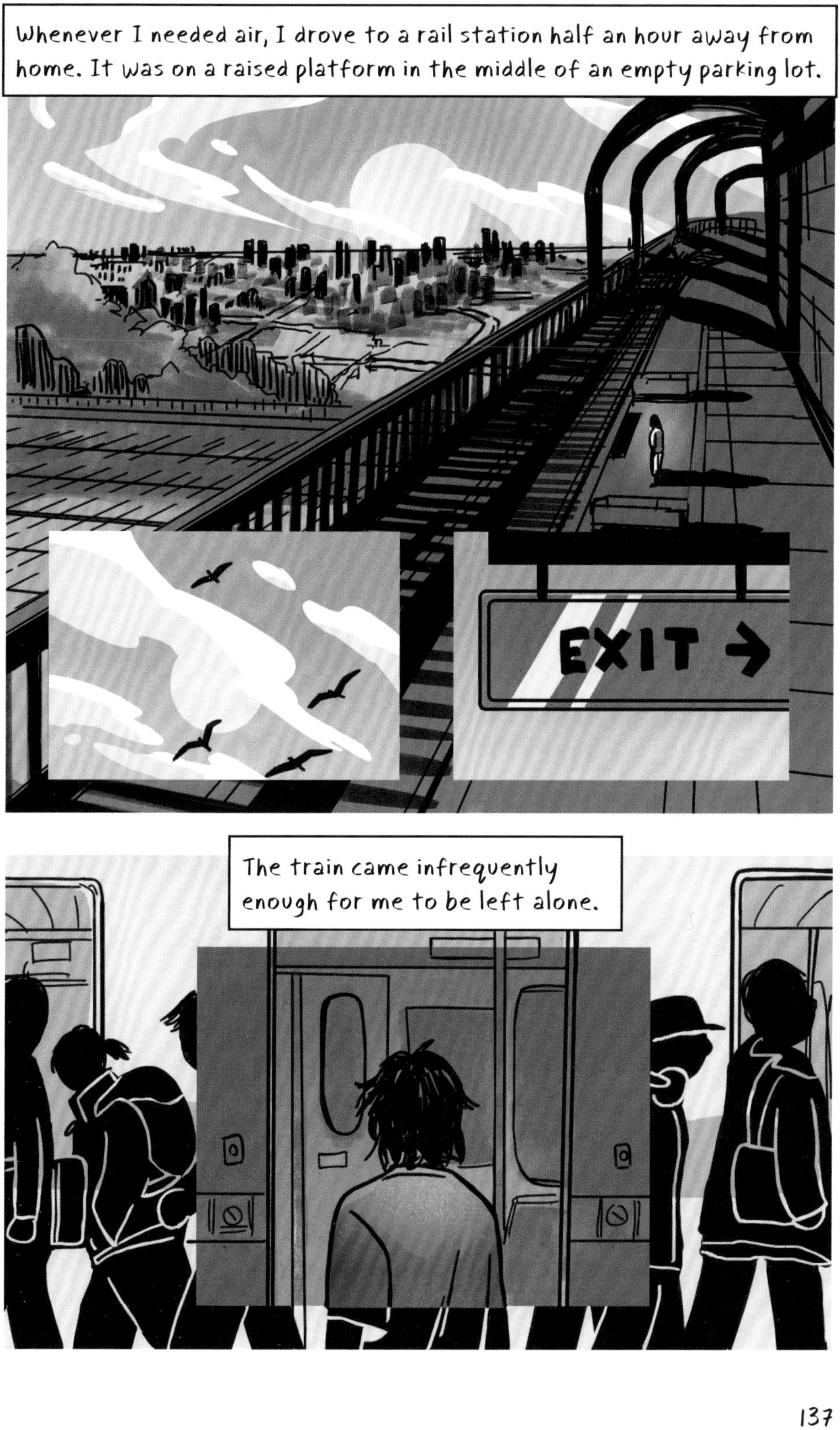
Whenever I needed air, I drove to a rail station half an hour away from home. It was on a raised platform in the middle of an empty parking lot.
EXIT →
The train came infrequently enough for me to be left alone.

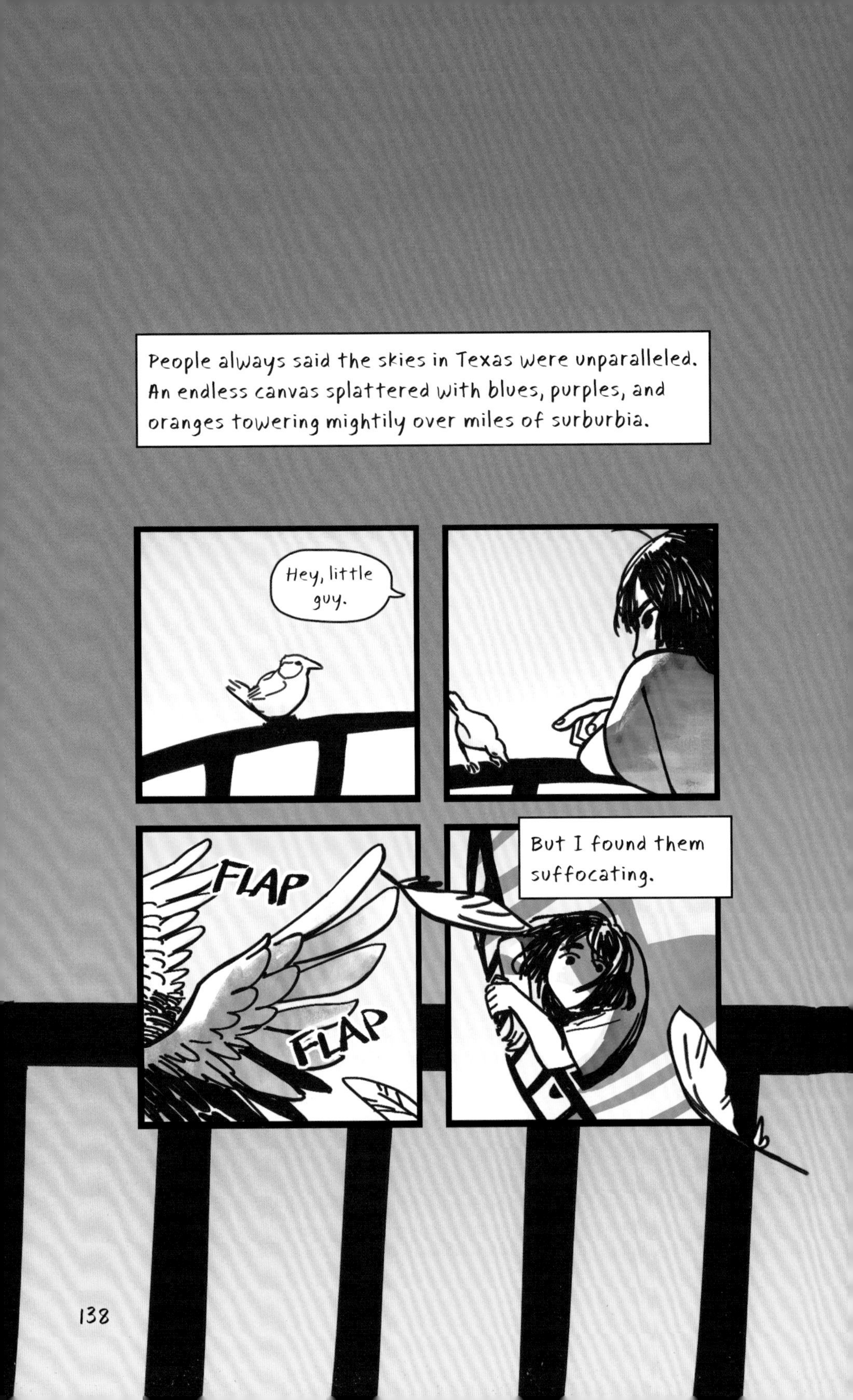
People always said the skies in Texas were unparalleled. An endless canvas splattered with blues, purples, and oranges towering mightily over miles of surburbia.
Hey, little guy.
FLAP
FLAP
But I found them suffocating.

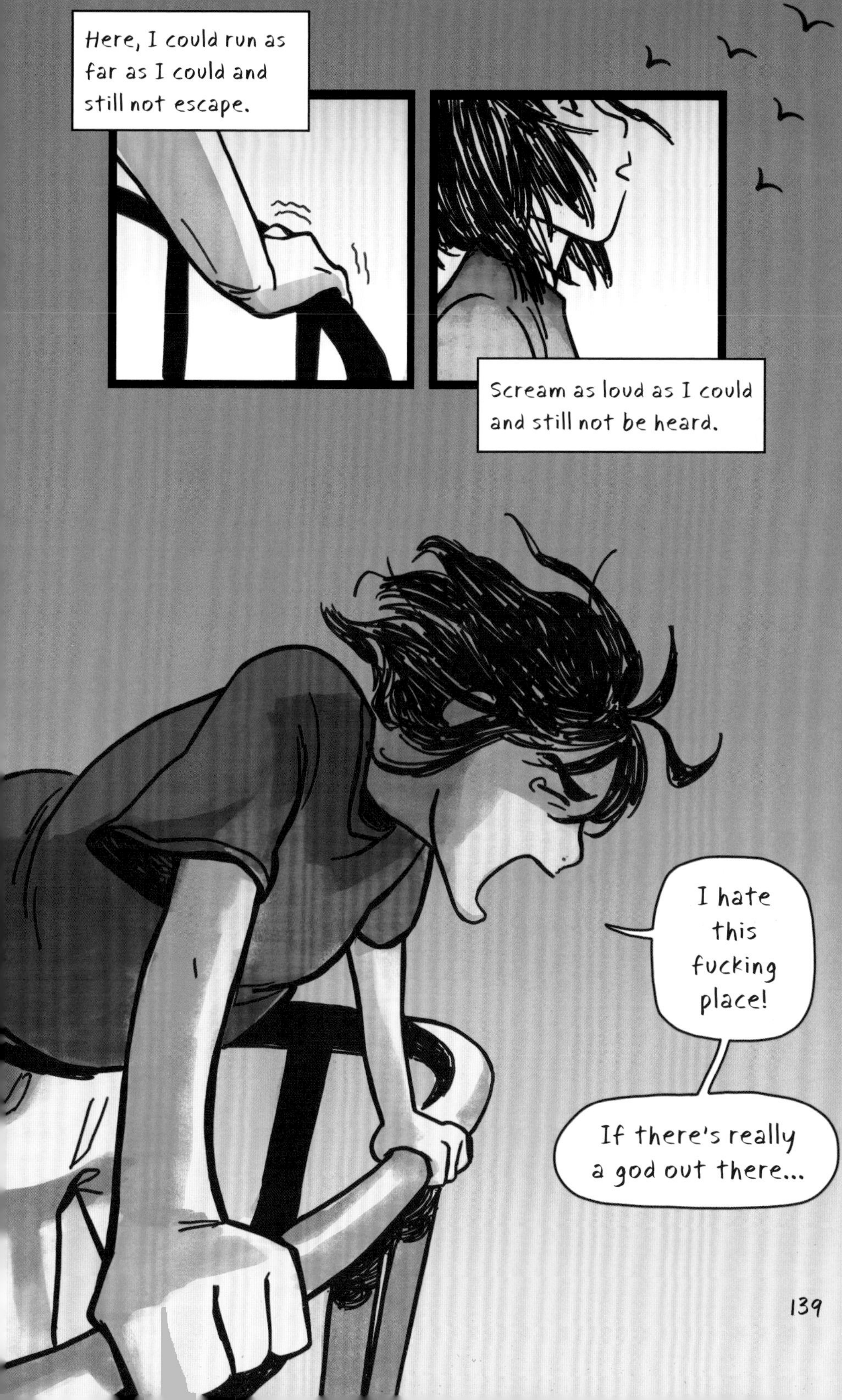
Here, I could run as far as I could and still not escape.
Scream as loud as I could and still not be heard.
I hate this fucking place!
If there's really a god out there...

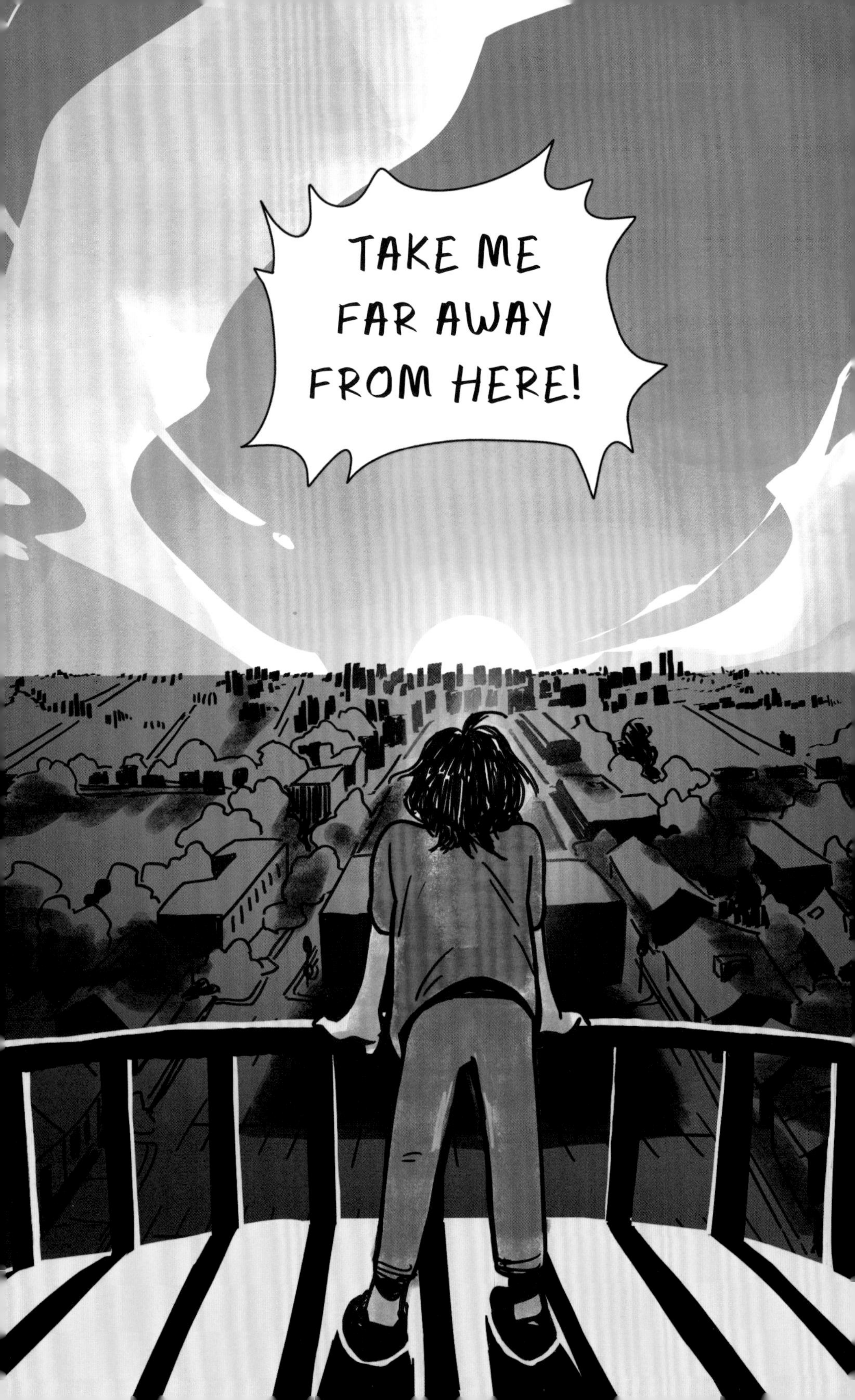
TAKE ME FAR AWAY FROM HERE!

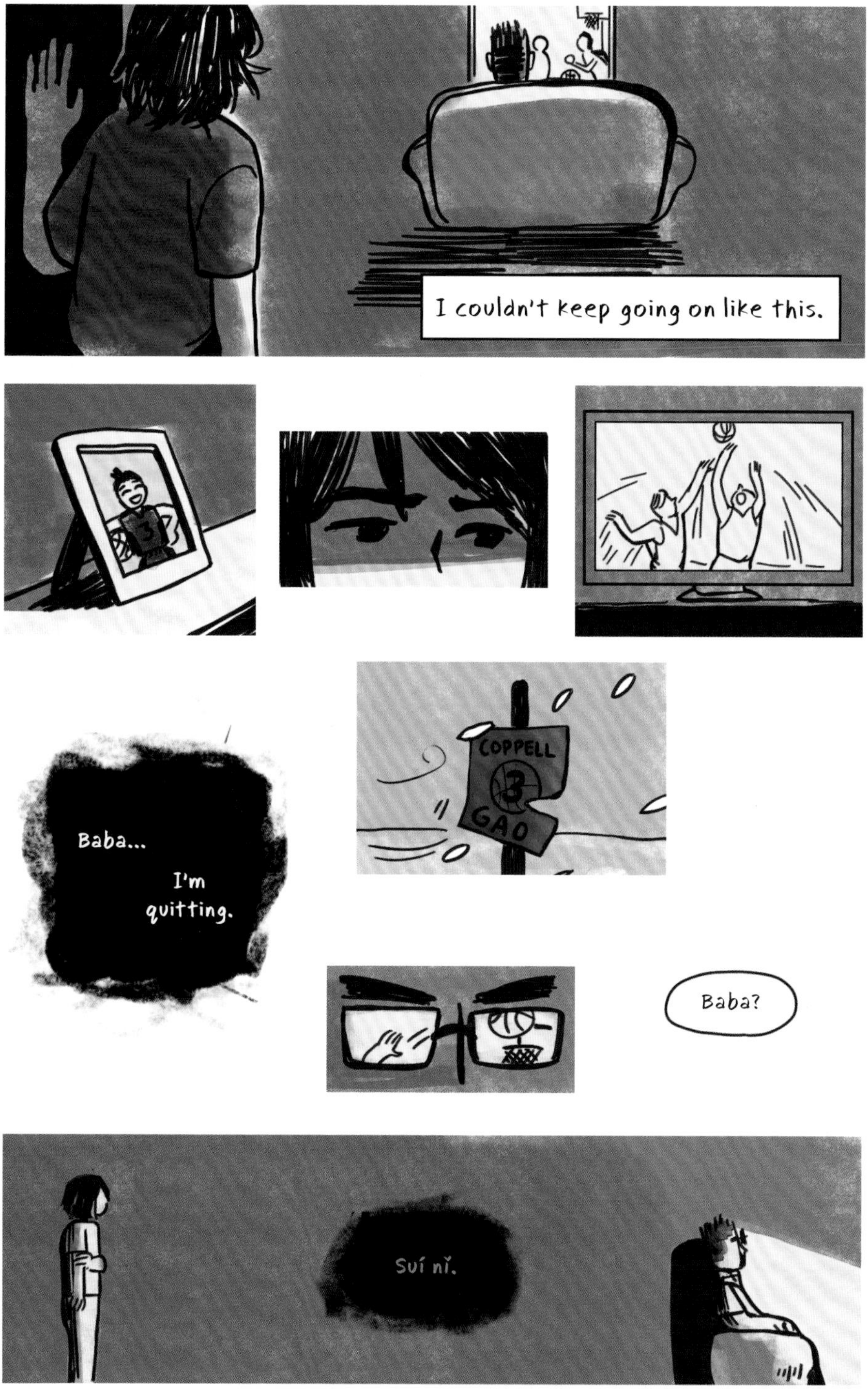
I couldn't keep going on like this.
COPPELL
3
GAO
Baba...
I'm quitting.
Baba?
Suí nǐ.

CHAPTER 10
Home Is Where the Art Is

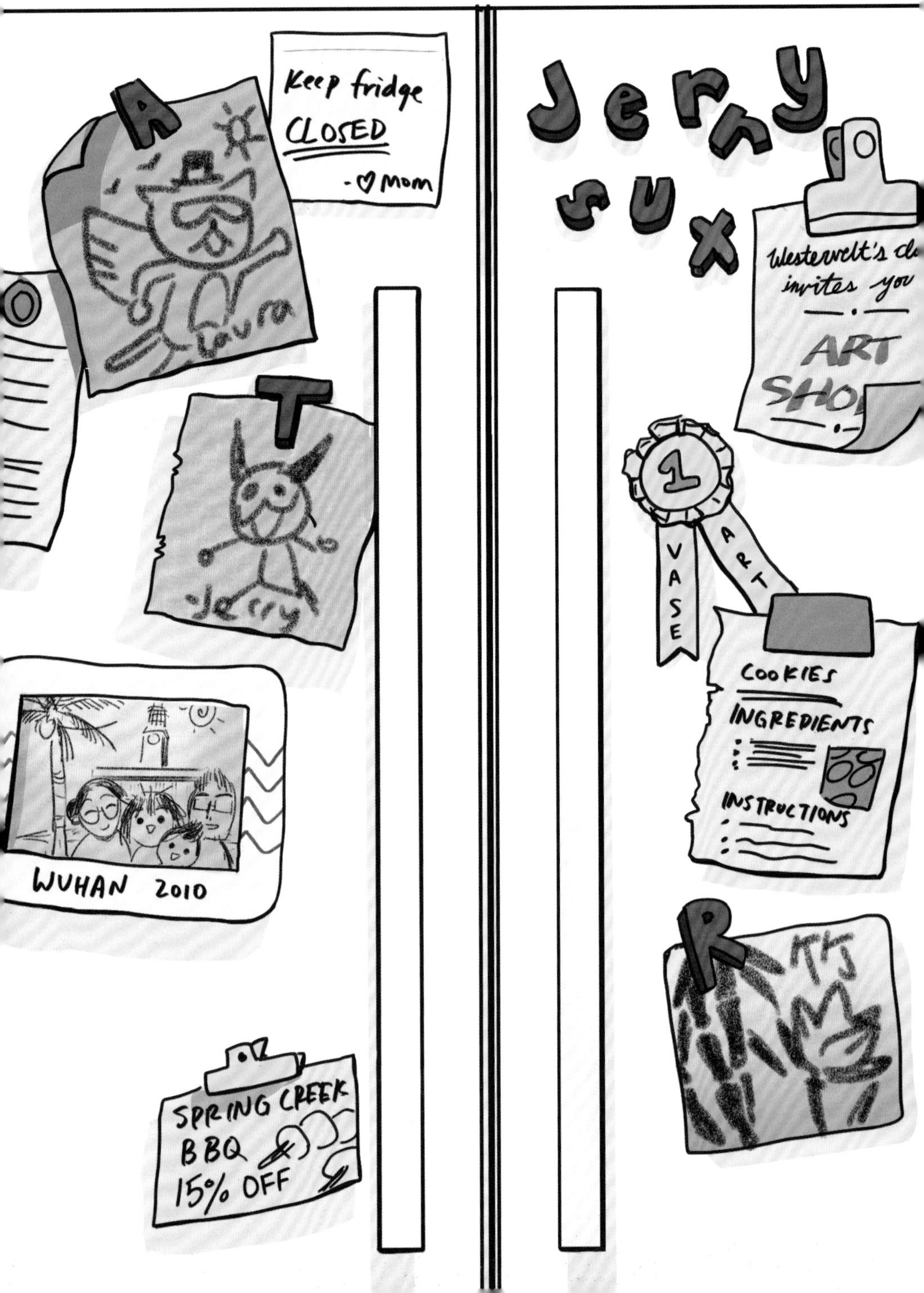
Keep fridge CLOSED
-♡ Mom
Laura
Jerry
WUHAN 2010
SPRING CREEK BBQ 15% OFF
Jerry sux
Westervelt's
invites you
ART SHO
1
VASE
ART
COOKIES
INGREDIENTS
INSTRUCTIONS
TKJ

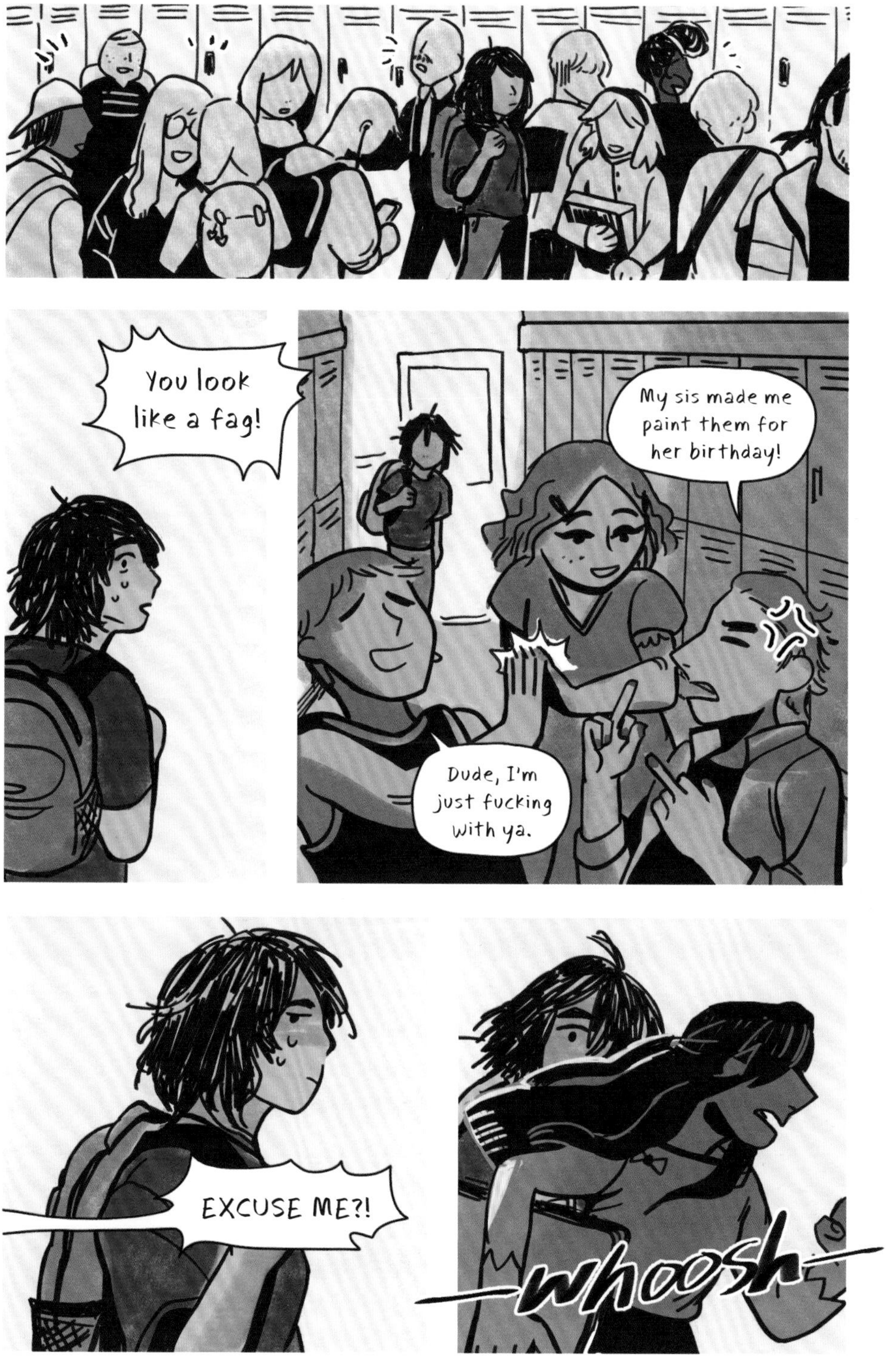
You look like a fag!
My sis made me paint them for her birthday!
Dude, I'm just fucking with ya.
EXCUSE ME?!
whoosh

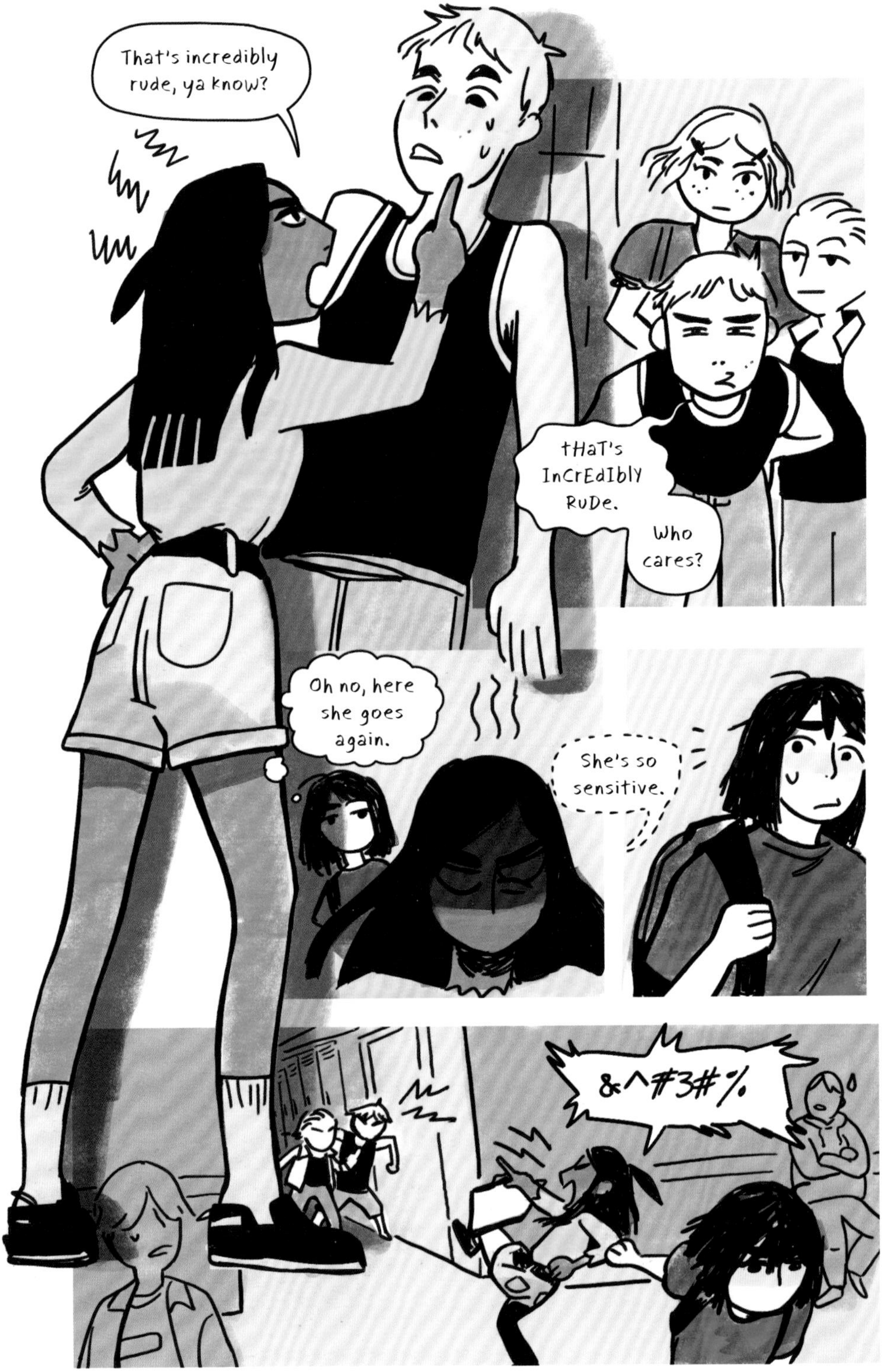
That's incredibly rude, ya know?
tHaT's InCrEdIblY RuDe.
Who cares?
Oh no, here she goes again.
She's so sensitive.
&^#3#%

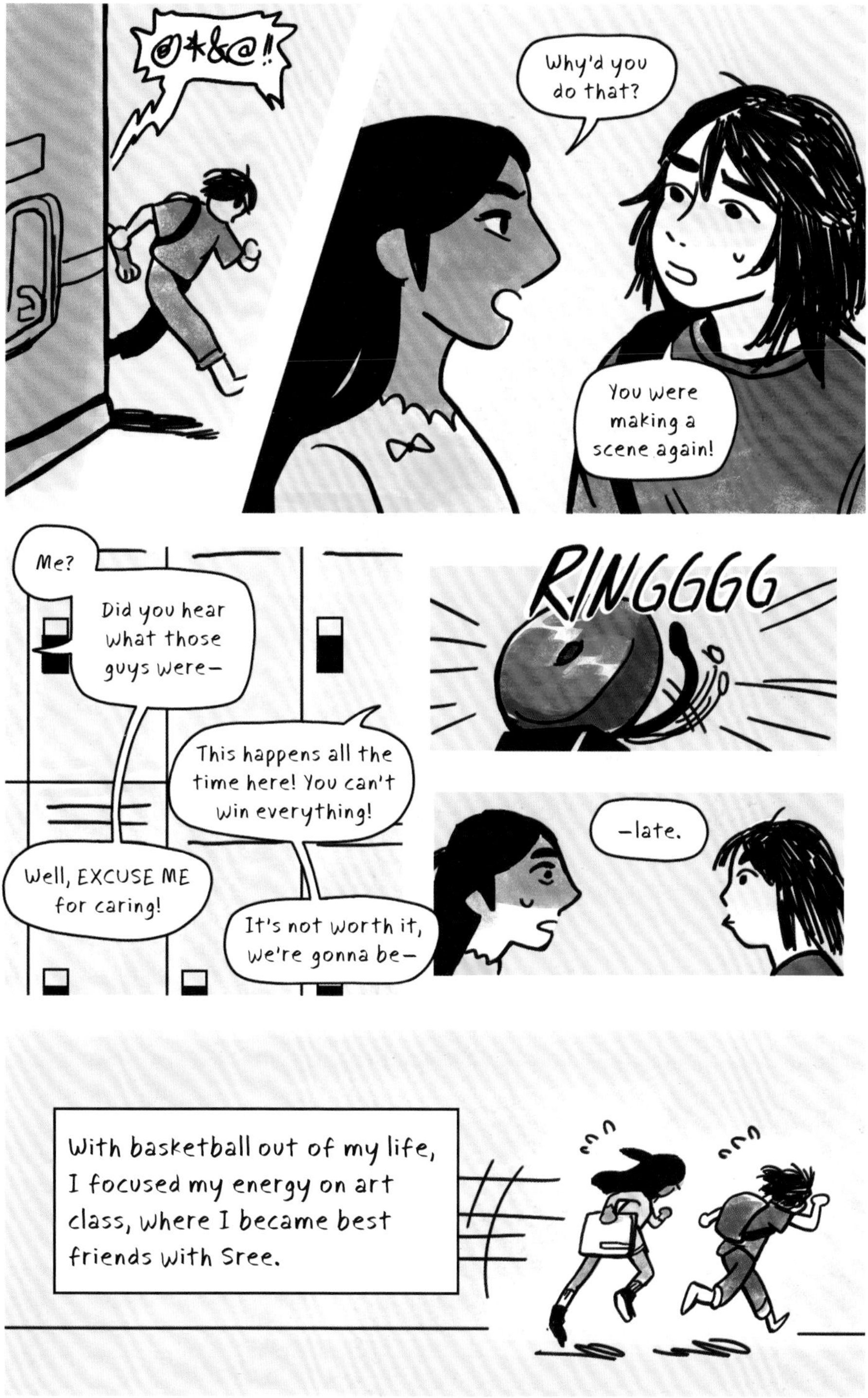
@*&@!!
Why'd you do that?
You were making a scene again!
Me?
Did you hear what those guys were—
This happens all the time here! You can't win everything!
Well, EXCUSE ME for caring!
It's not worth it, we're gonna be—
RINGGGG
—late.
With basketball out of my life, I focused my energy on art class, where I became best friends with Sree.

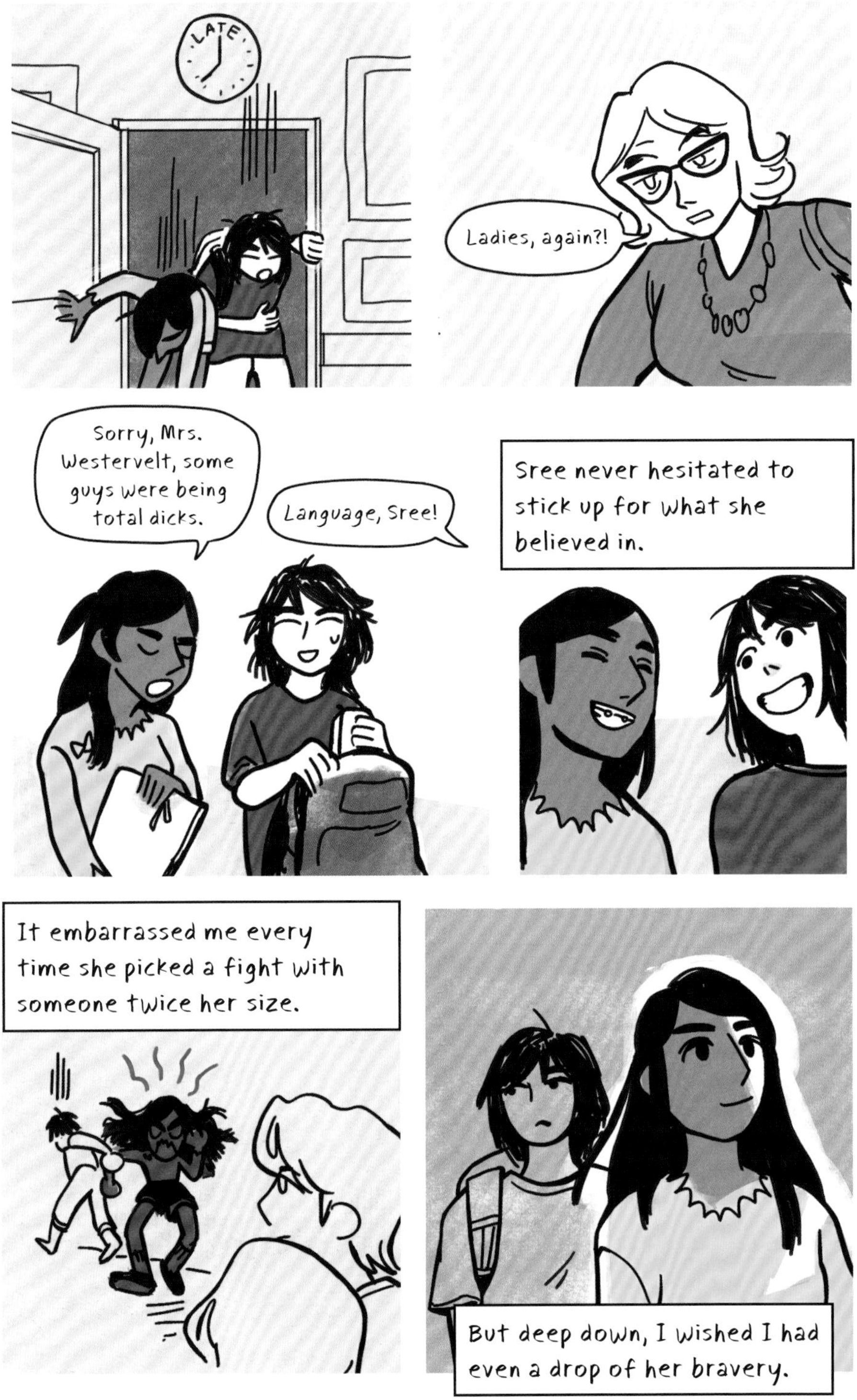
Ladies, again?!
Sorry, Mrs. Westervelt, some guys were being total dicks.
Language, Sree!
Sree never hesitated to stick up for what she believed in.
It embarrassed me every time she picked a fight with someone twice her size.
But deep down, I wished I had even a drop of her bravery.

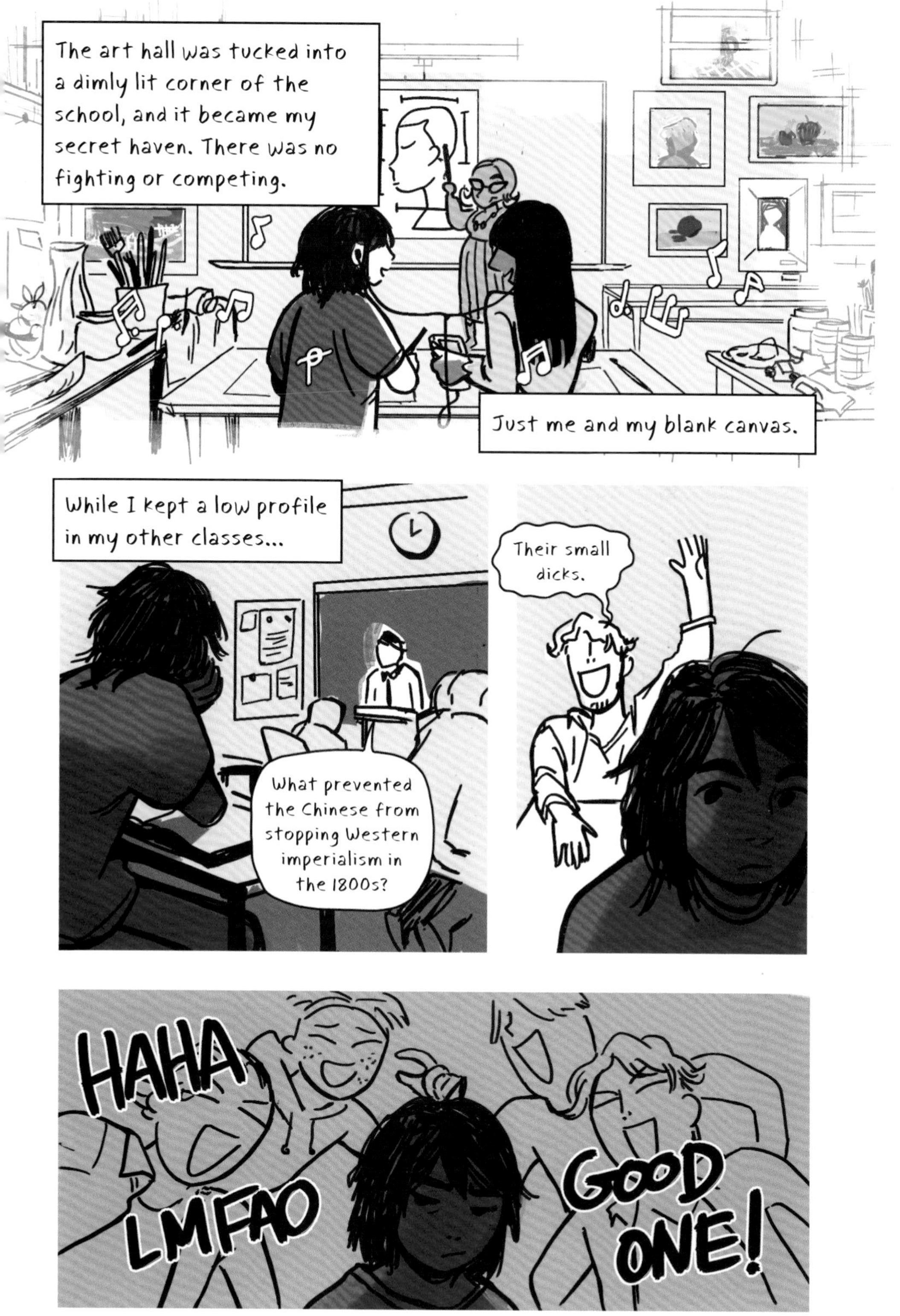
The art hall was tucked into a dimly lit corner of the school, and it became my secret haven. There was no fighting or competing.
Just me and my blank canvas.
While I kept a low profile in my other classes...
What prevented the Chinese from stopping Western imperialism in the 1800s?
Their small dicks.
HAHA
LMFAO
GOOD ONE!

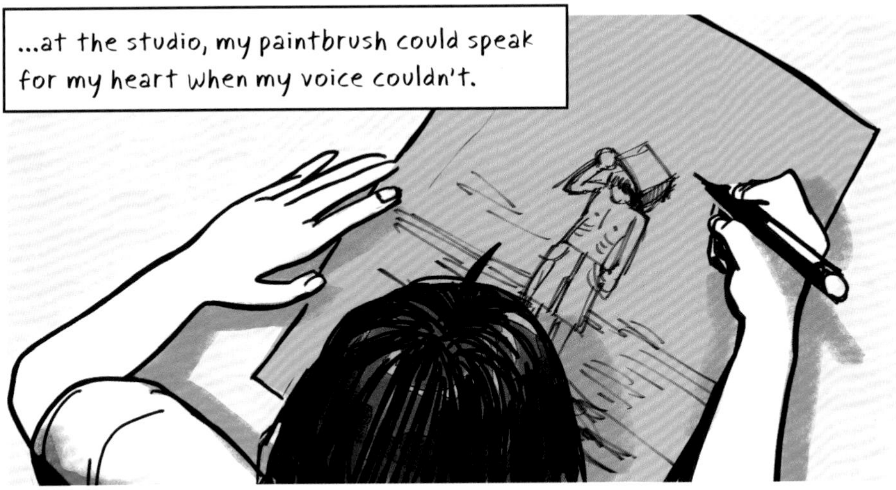
...at the studio, my paintbrush could speak for my heart when my voice couldn't.

Sree and I shared everything—earbuds, pep talks, and our best strategies for dealing with our immigrant parents.

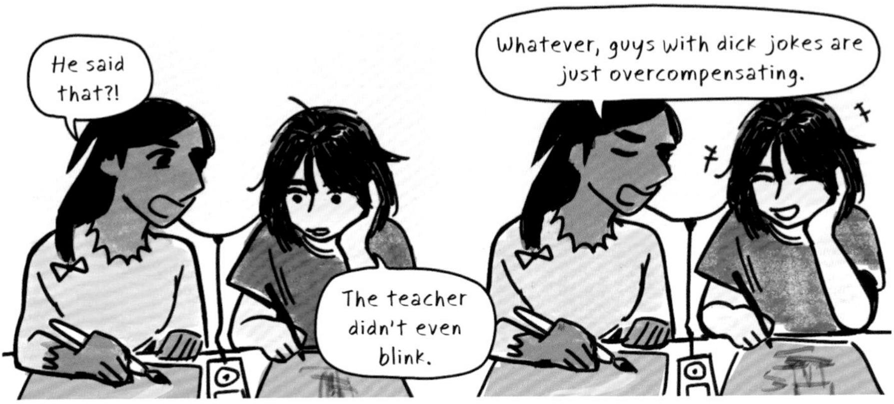
He said that?!
The teacher didn't even blink.
Whatever, guys with dick jokes are just overcompensating.

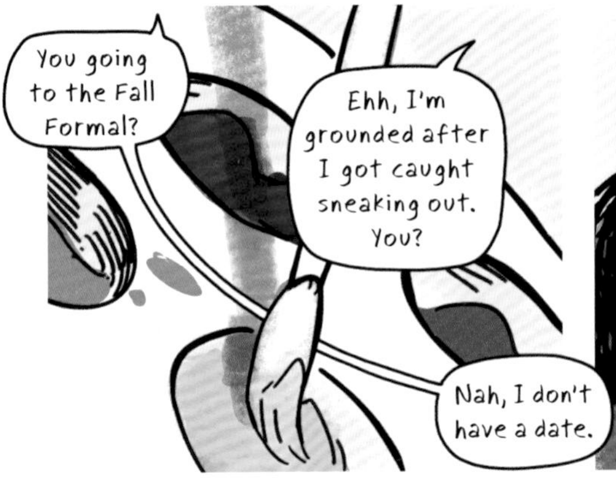
You going to the Fall Formal?
Ehh, I'm grounded after I got caught sneaking out. You?
Nah, I don't have a date.

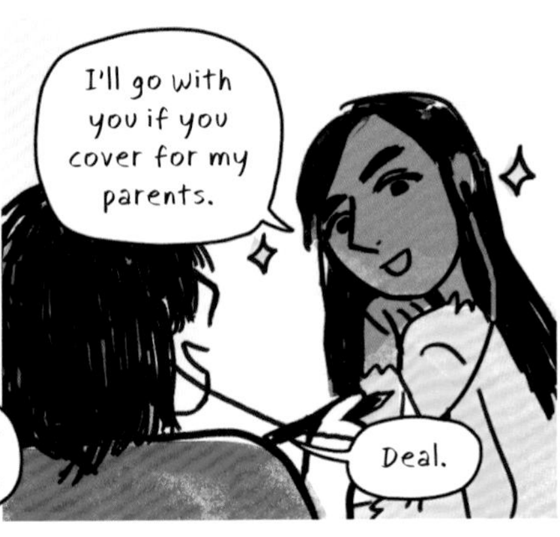
I'll go with you if you cover for my parents.
Deal.

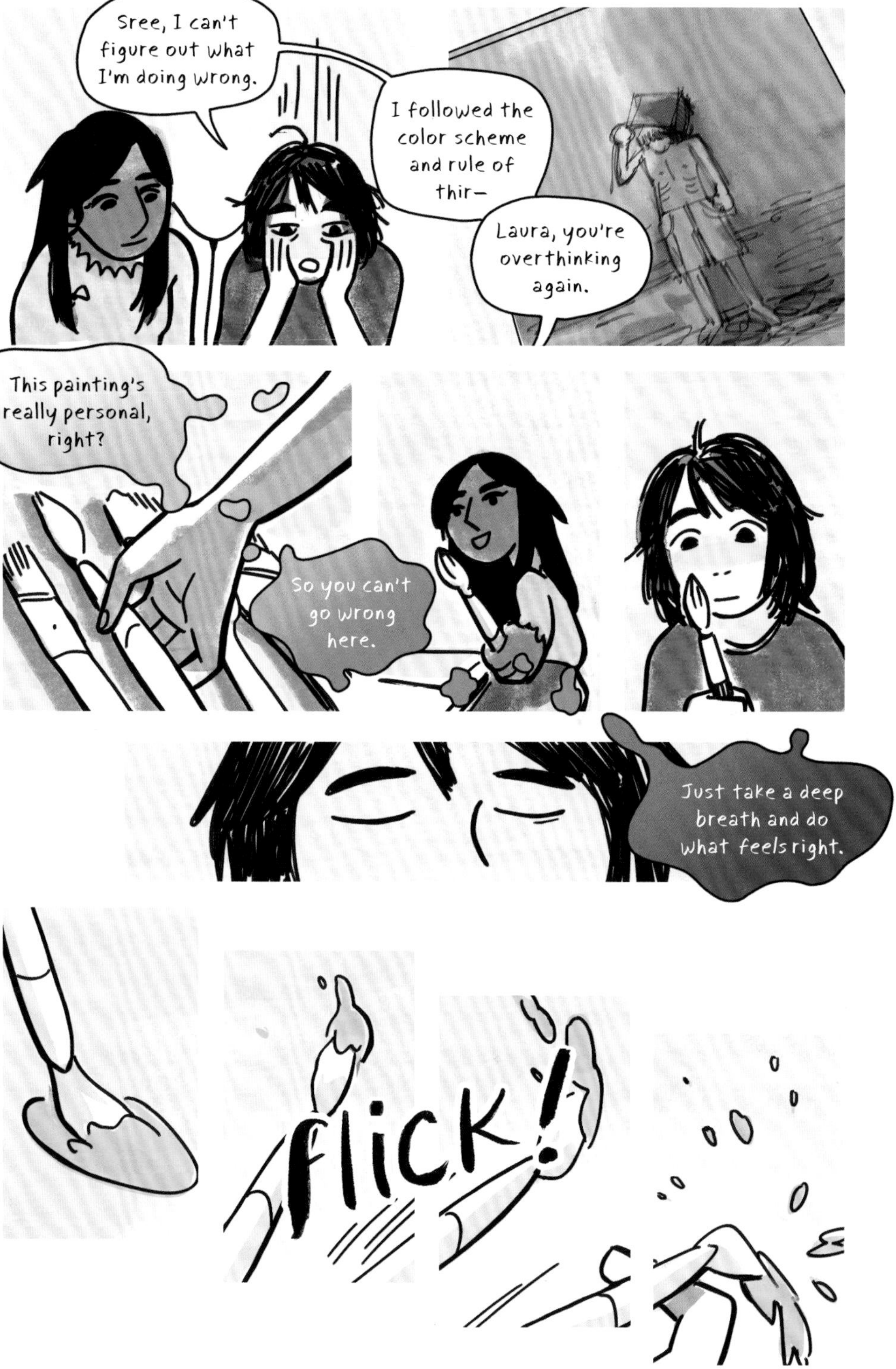
Sree, I can't figure out what I'm doing wrong.
I followed the color scheme and rule of thir—
Laura, you're overthinking again.
This painting's really personal, right?
So you can't go wrong here.
Just take a deep breath and do what feels right.
flick!

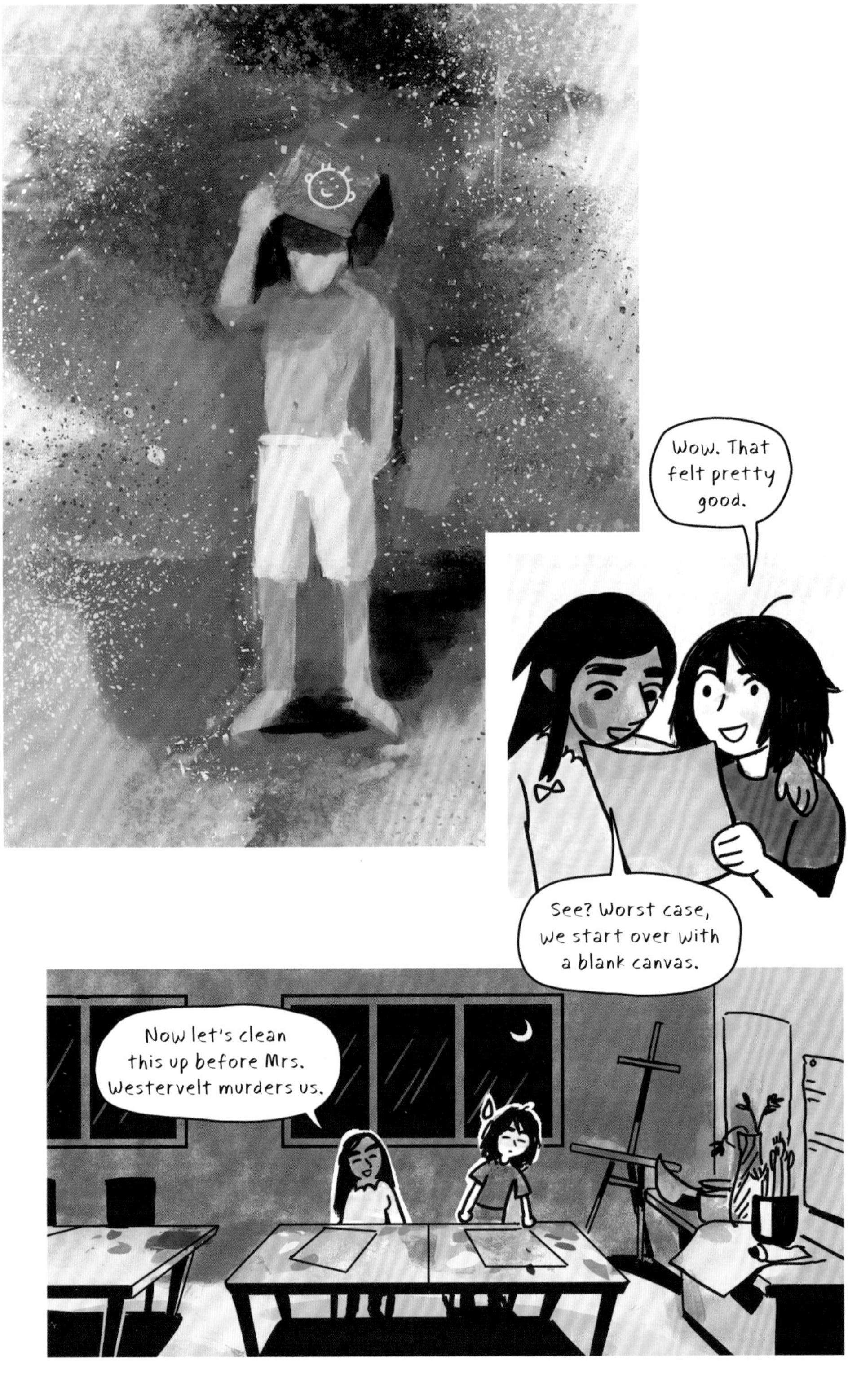
Wow. That felt pretty good.
See? Worst case, we start over with a blank canvas.
Now let's clean this up before Mrs. Westervelt murders us.

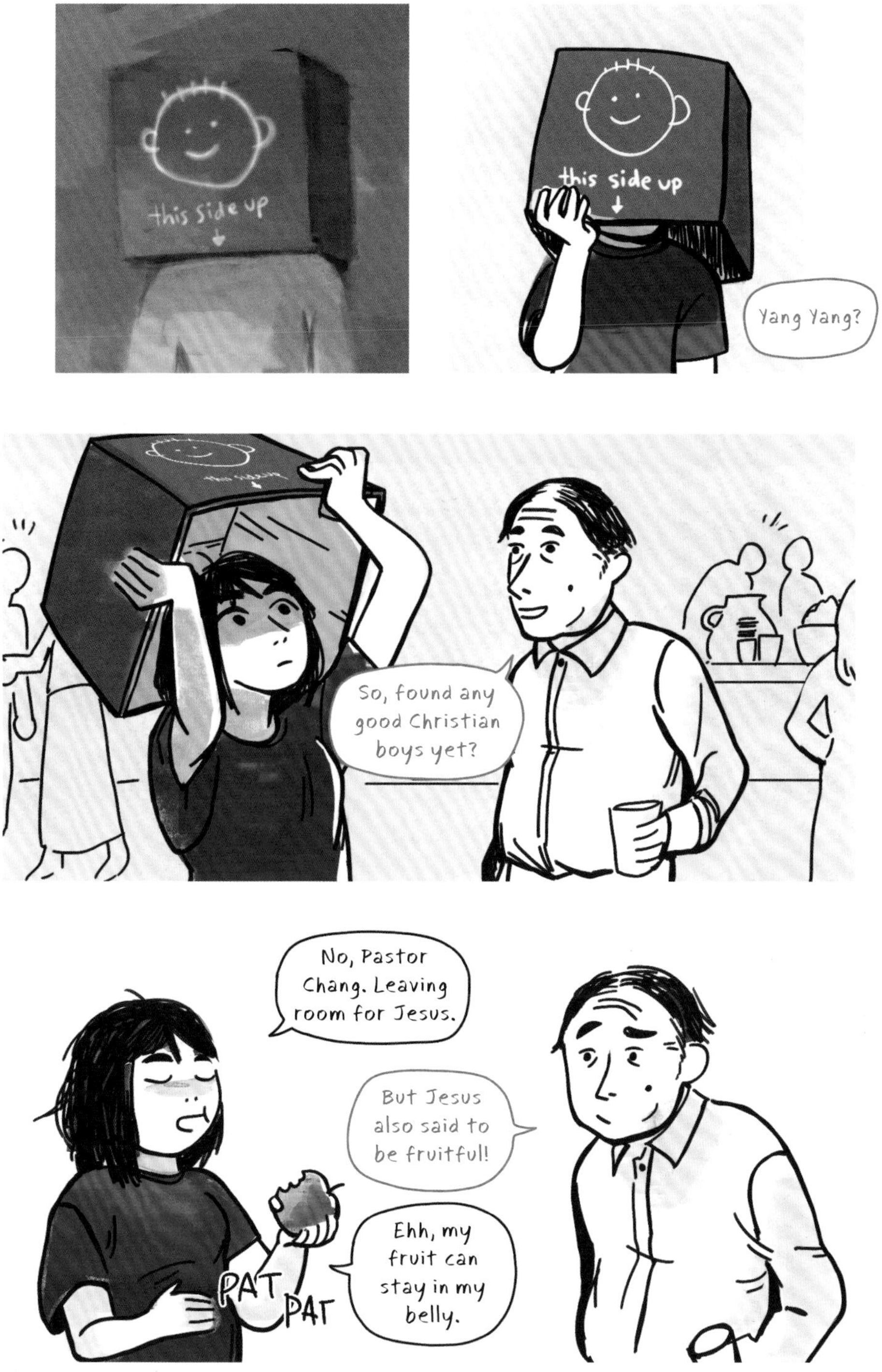
this side up
this side up
Yang Yang?
So, found any good Christian boys yet?
No, Pastor Chang. Leaving room for Jesus.
But Jesus also said to be fruitful!
Ehh, my fruit can stay in my belly.
PAT PAT

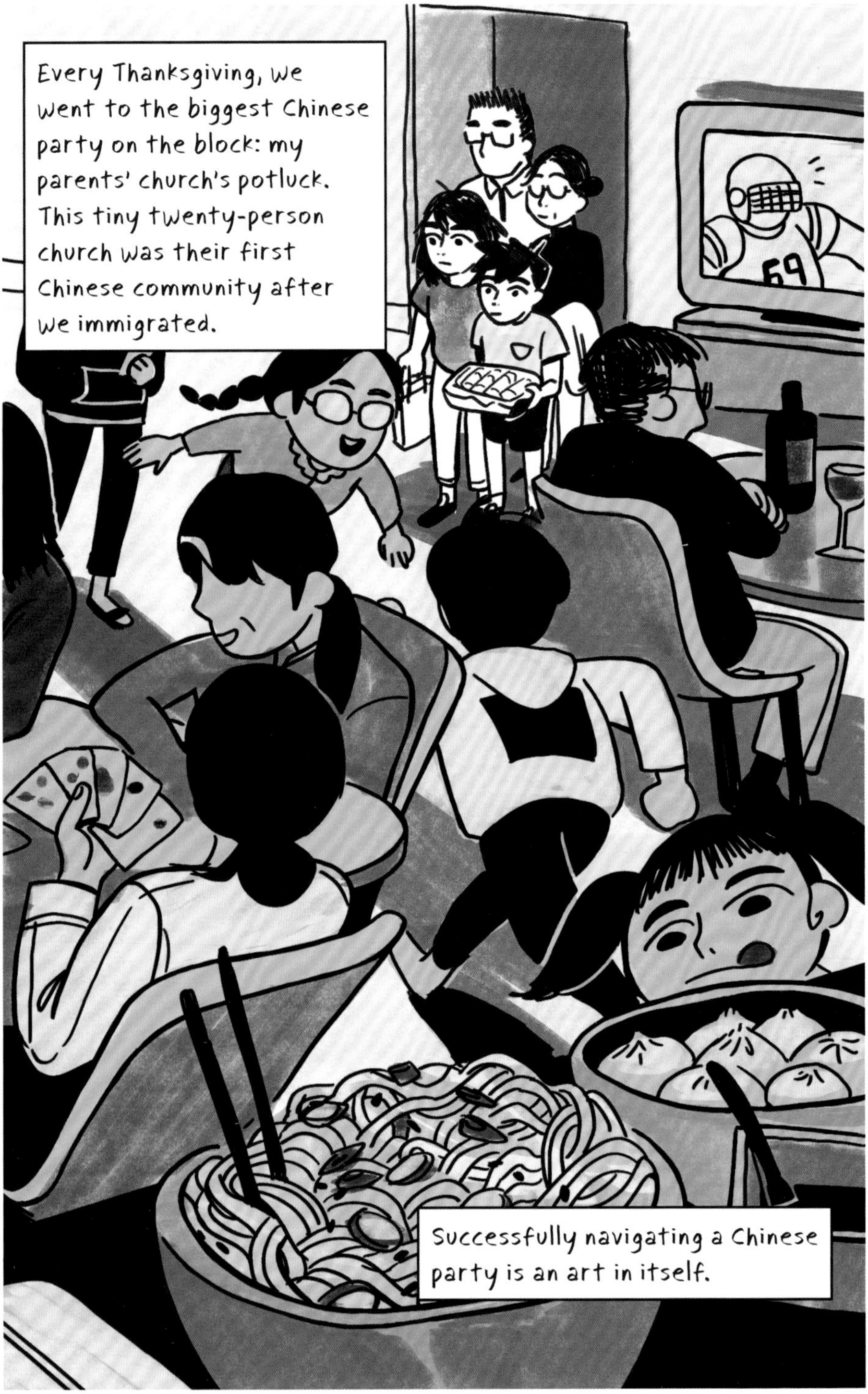
Every Thanksgiving, we went to the biggest Chinese party on the block: my parents' church's potluck. This tiny twenty-person church was their first Chinese community after we immigrated.
69
Successfully navigating a Chinese party is an art in itself.

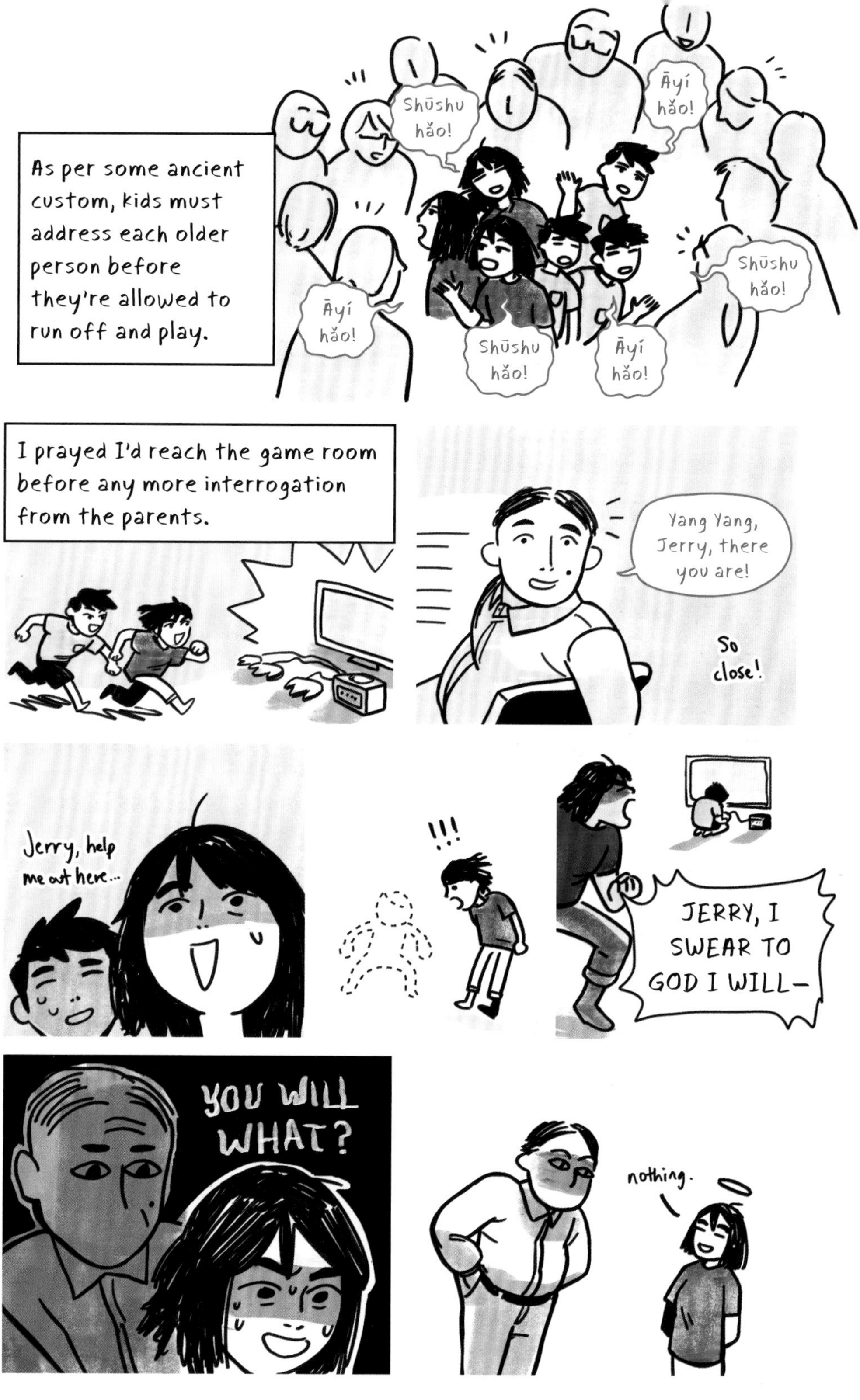
As per some ancient custom, kids must address each older person before they're allowed to run off and play.
Shūshu hǎo!
Āyí hǎo!
Āyí hǎo!
Shūshu hǎo!
Shūshu hǎo!
Āyí hǎo!
I prayed I'd reach the game room before any more interrogation from the parents.
Yang Yang, Jerry, there you are!
So close!
Jerry, help me out here...
!!!
JERRY, I SWEAR TO GOD I WILL—
YOU WILL WHAT?
nothing.

I started off going to my parents' church before switching to Jessie's American one. I thought I'd connect better with the sermons if they were in English.

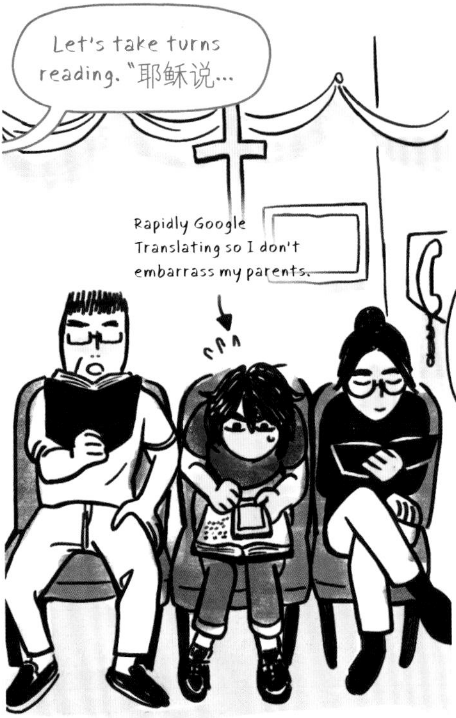

Let's take turns reading. "耶稣说...
Rapidly Google Translating so I don't embarrass my parents.

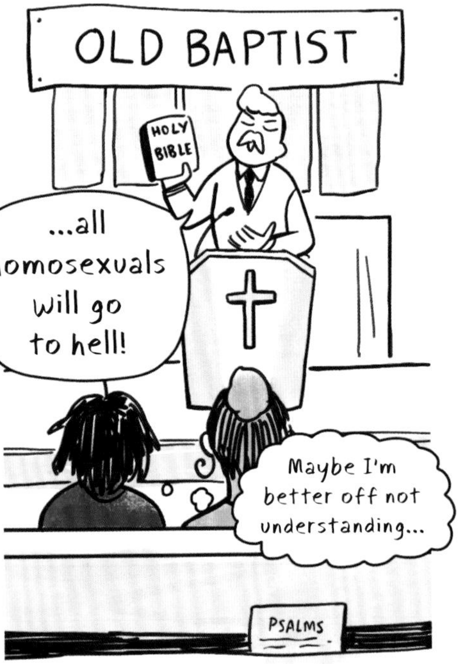

OLD BAPTIST
HOLY BIBLE
...all homosexuals will go to hell!
Maybe I'm better off not understanding...
PSALMS

It seemed like everyone else had it figured out except me.

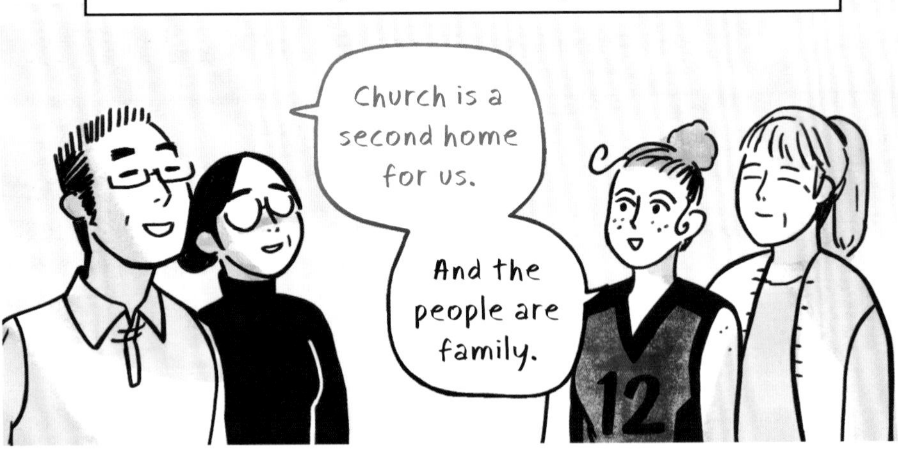

Church is a second home for us.
And the people are family.
12

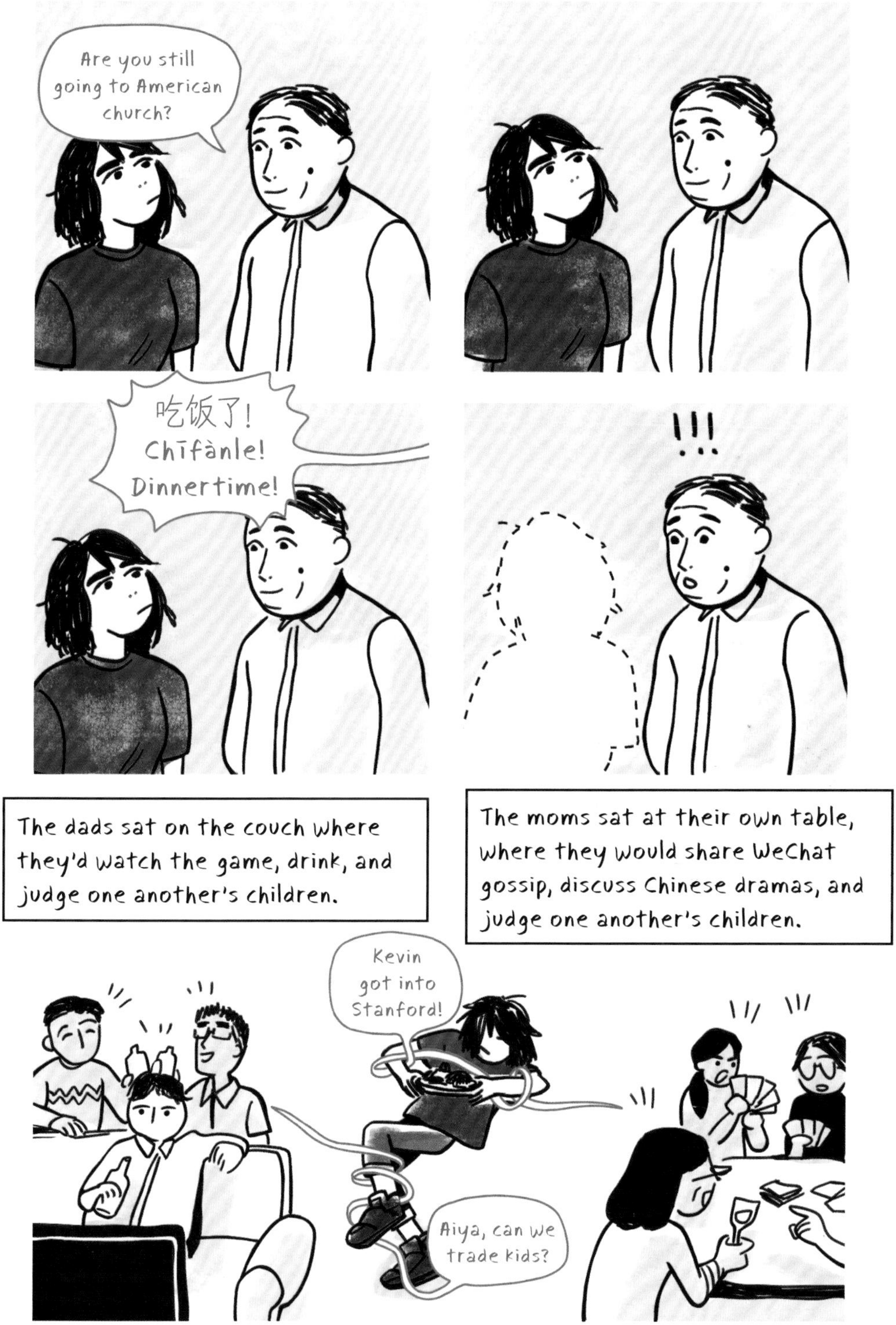
Are you still going to American church?
吃饭了!
Chīfànle!
Dinnertime!
!!!
...
The dads sat on the couch where they'd watch the game, drink, and judge one another's children.
The moms sat at their own table, where they would share WeChat gossip, discuss Chinese dramas, and judge one another's children.
Kevin got into Stanford!
Aiya, can we trade kids?

The kids sat in the game room, where we squeezed in Super Smash Bros. fights between bites. It didn't matter if you were two or twenty-two, you never aged out of the kids' table.

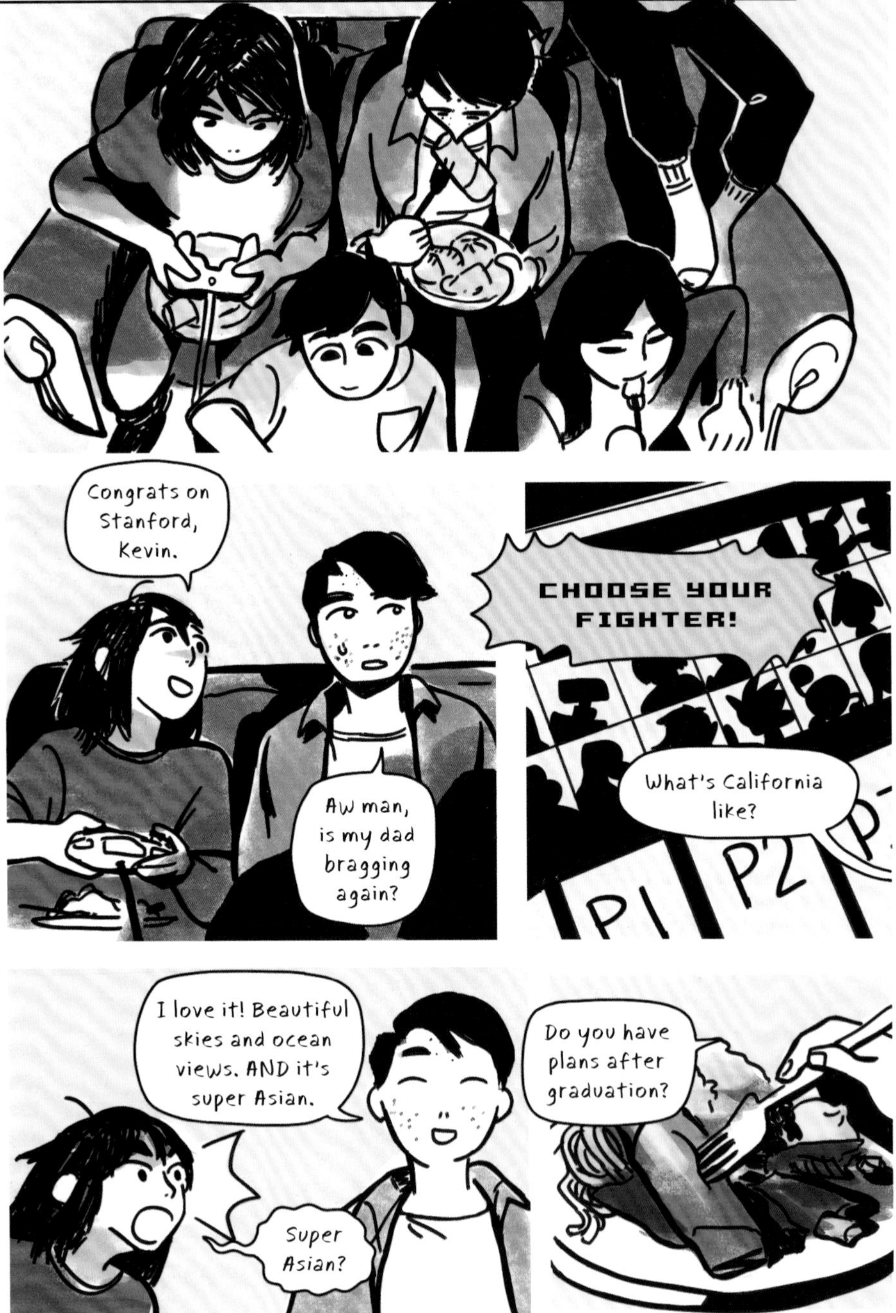

Congrats on Stanford, Kevin.
Aw man, is my dad bragging again?
CHOOSE YOUR FIGHTER!
What's California like?
P1
P2
I love it! Beautiful skies and ocean views. AND it's super Asian.
Super Asian?
Do you have plans after graduation?

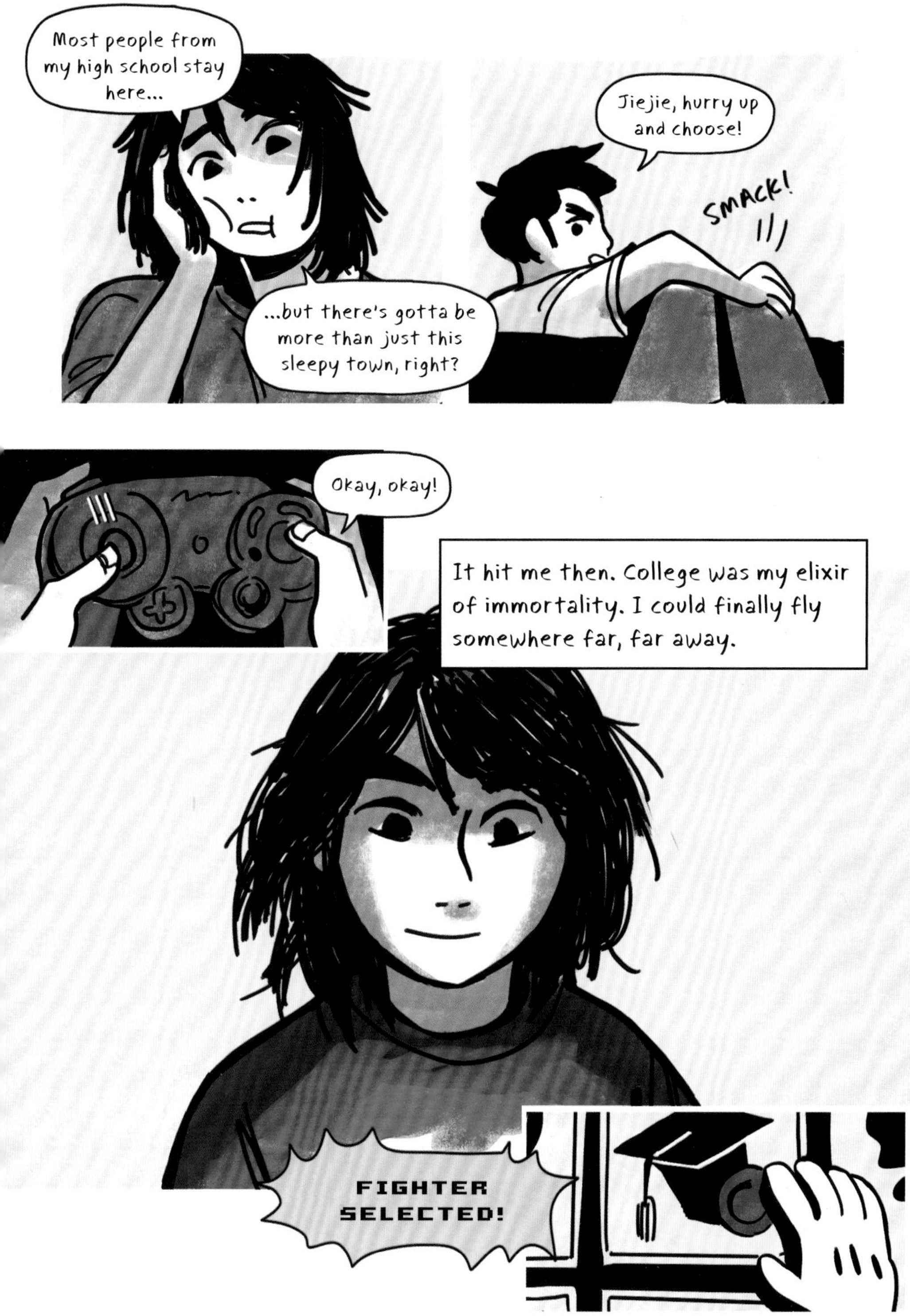
Most people from my high school stay here...
...but there's gotta be more than just this sleepy town, right?
Jiejie, hurry up and choose!
SMACK!
Okay, okay!
It hit me then. College was my elixir of immortality. I could finally fly somewhere far, far away.
FIGHTER SELECTED!

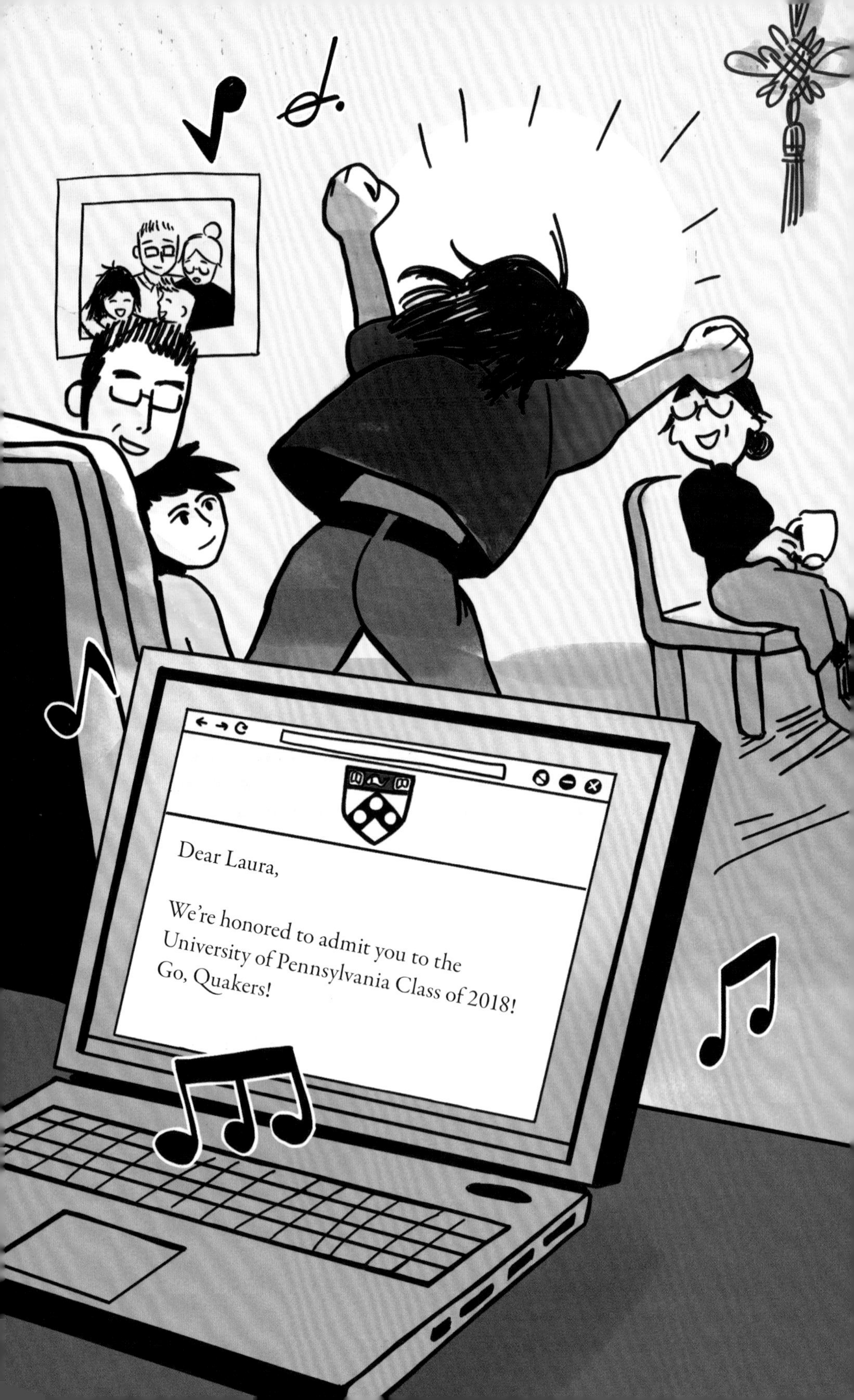
Dear Laura,
We're honored to admit you to the University of Pennsylvania Class of 2018! Go, Quakers!

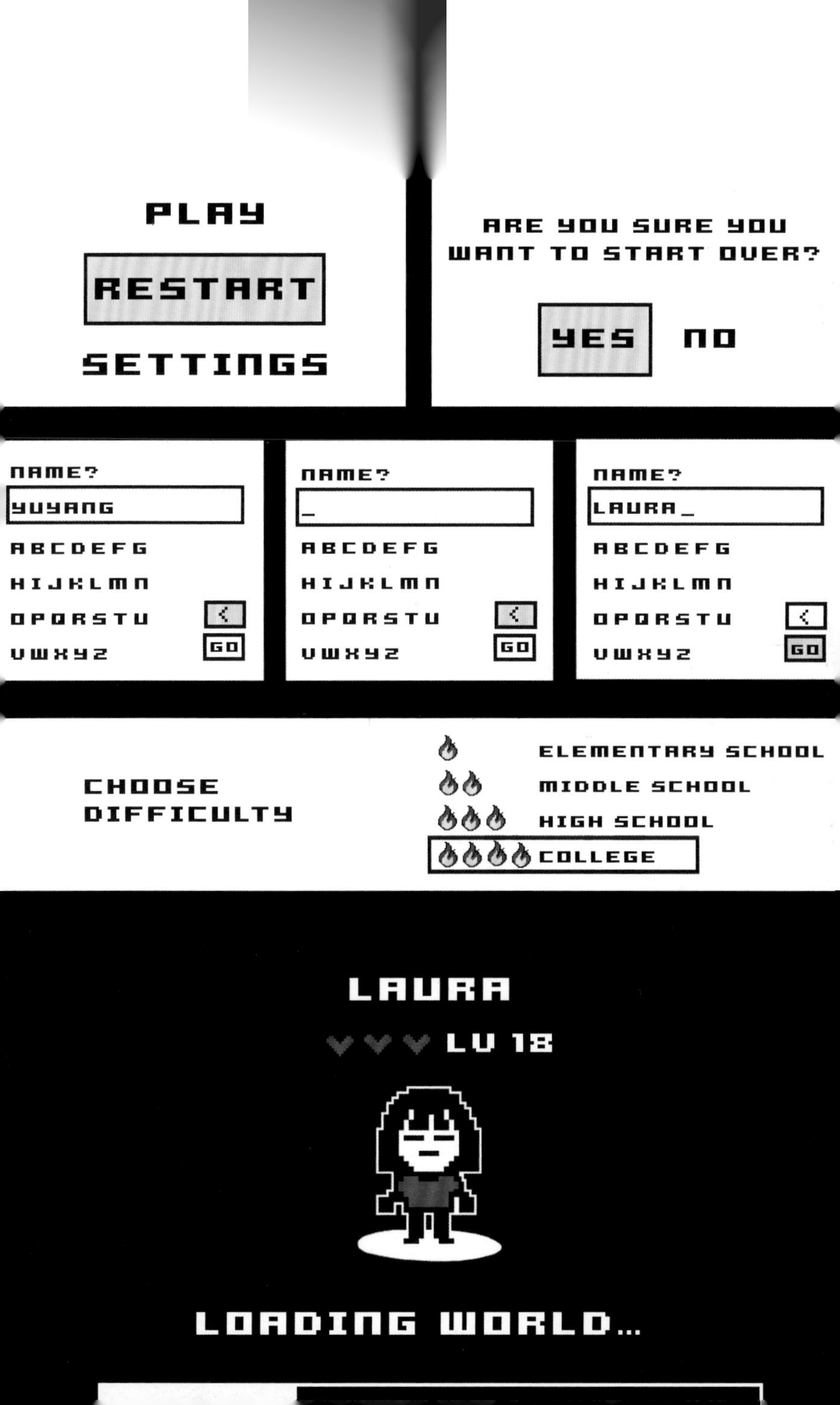
PLAY
RESTART
SETTINGS
ARE YOU SURE YOU WANT TO START OVER?
YES
NO
NAME?
YUYANG
ABCDEFG
HIJKLMN
OPQRSTU
VWXYZ
GO
NAME?
ABCDEFG
HIJKLMN
OPQRSTU
VWXYZ
GO
NAME?
LAURA
ABCDEFG
HIJKLMN
OPQRSTU
VWXYZ
GO
CHOOSE DIFFICULTY
ELEMENTARY SCHOOL
MIDDLE SCHOOL
HIGH SCHOOL
COLLEGE
LAURA
LV 18
LOADING WORLD...

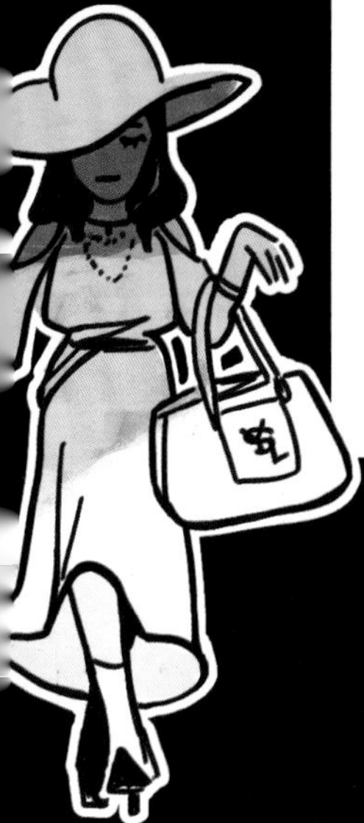

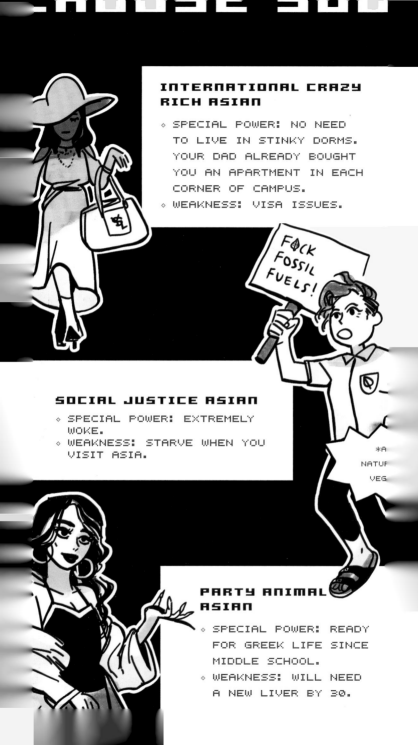

INTERNATIONAL CRAZY RICH ASIAN

- SPECIAL POWER: NO NEED TO LIVE IN STINKY DORMS. YOUR DAD ALREADY BOUGHT YOU AN APARTMENT IN EACH CORNER OF CAMPUS.
- WEAKNESS: VISA ISSUES.

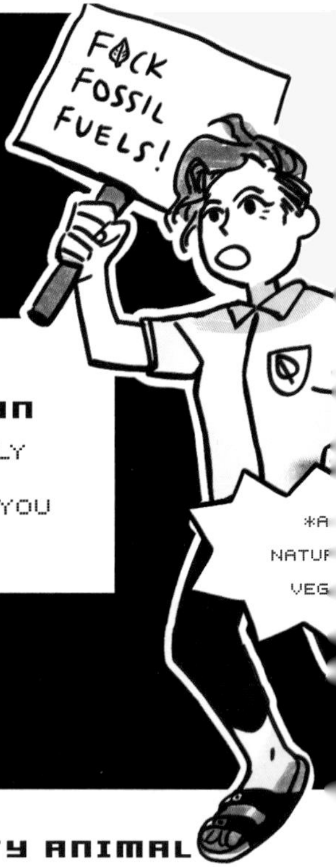
FOSSIL
FUELS!

SOCIAL JUSTICE ASIAN

- SPECIAL POWER: EXTREMELY WOKE.
- WEAKNESS: STARVE WHEN YOU VISIT ASIA.

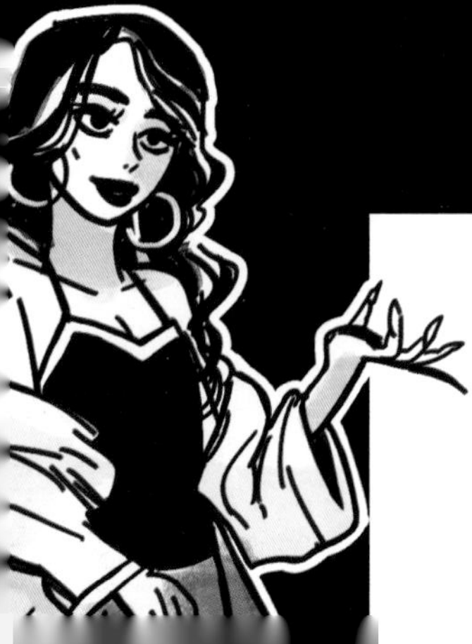

PARTY ANIMAL ASIAN

- SPECIAL POWER: READY FOR GREEK LIFE SINCE MIDDLE SCHOOL.
- WEAKNESS: WILL NEED A NEW LIVER BY 30.

FIGHTER!

TRIPLE MAJOR DOCTOR/ENGINEER/BANKER ASIAN

- SPECIAL POWER: CELEBRITY AT ASIAN PARTIES.
- WEAKNESS: HAS NOT SLEPT SINCE MIDDLE SCHOOL.

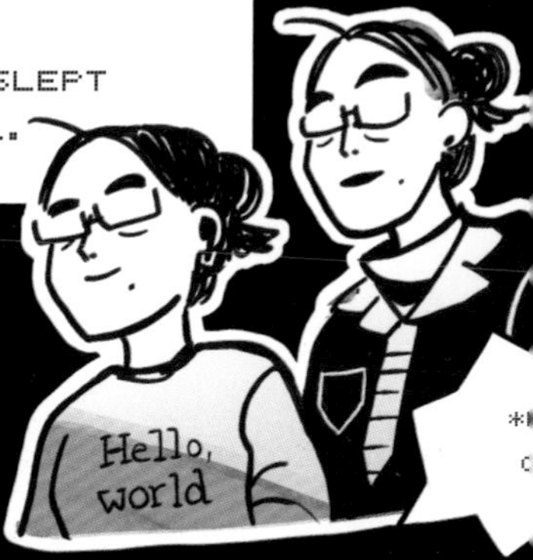
Hello, world

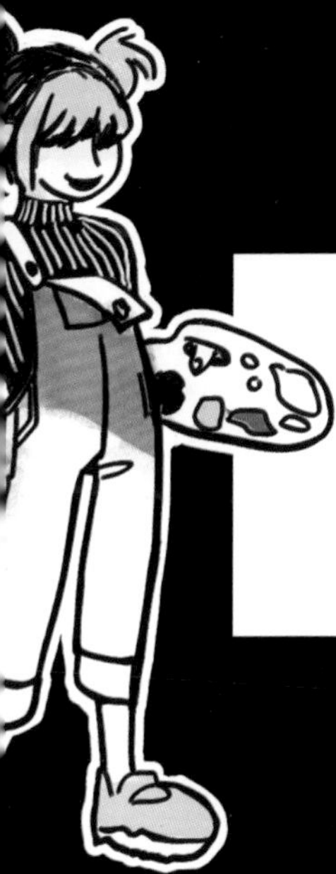

HIPSTER ARTSY ASIAN

- SPECIAL POWER: TRENDIEST AESTHETIC.
- WEAKNESS: EVERYONE WANTS YOU TO TAKE THEIR PROFILE PHOTOS.

[???] ×LOCKED×

- SPECIAL POWER: FIT IN WITH THE MAJORITY.
- WEAKNESS: ???

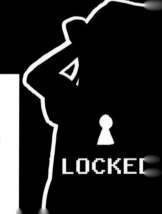

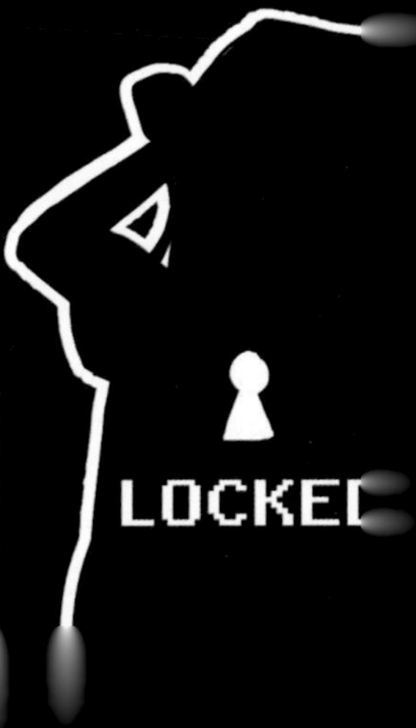
LOCKED

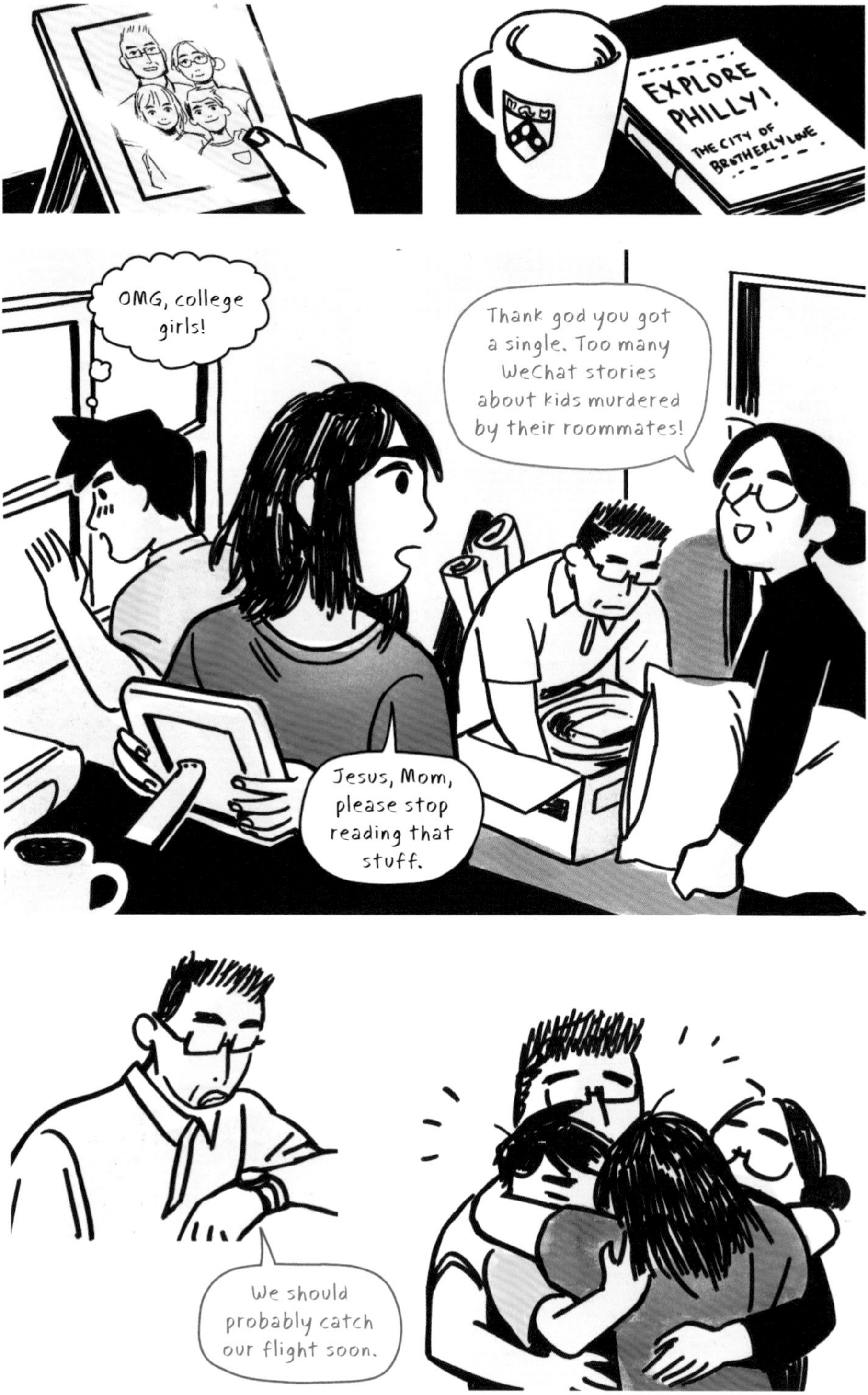
EXPLORE PHILLY! THE CITY OF BROTHERLY LOVE
OMG, college girls!
Thank god you got a single. Too many WeChat stories about kids murdered by their roommates!
Jesus, Mom, please stop reading that stuff.
We should probably catch our flight soon.

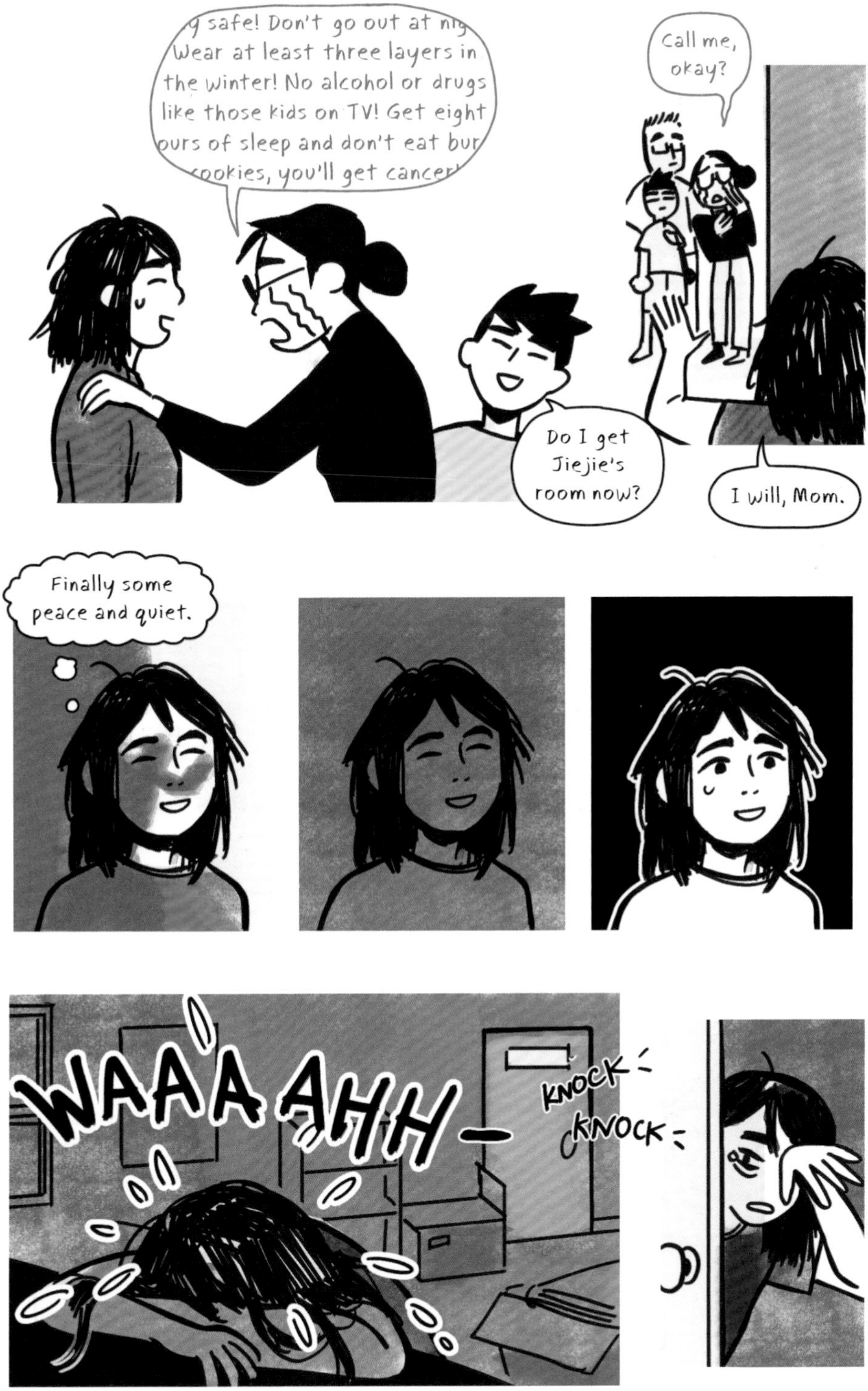
safe! Don't go out at nig Wear at least three layers in the winter! No alcohol or drugs like those kids on TV! Get eight ours of sleep and don't eat bur cookies, you'll get cancer
Do I get Jiejie's room now?
Call me, okay?
I will, Mom.
Finally some peace and quiet.
WAAAAHH—
KNOCK KNOCK

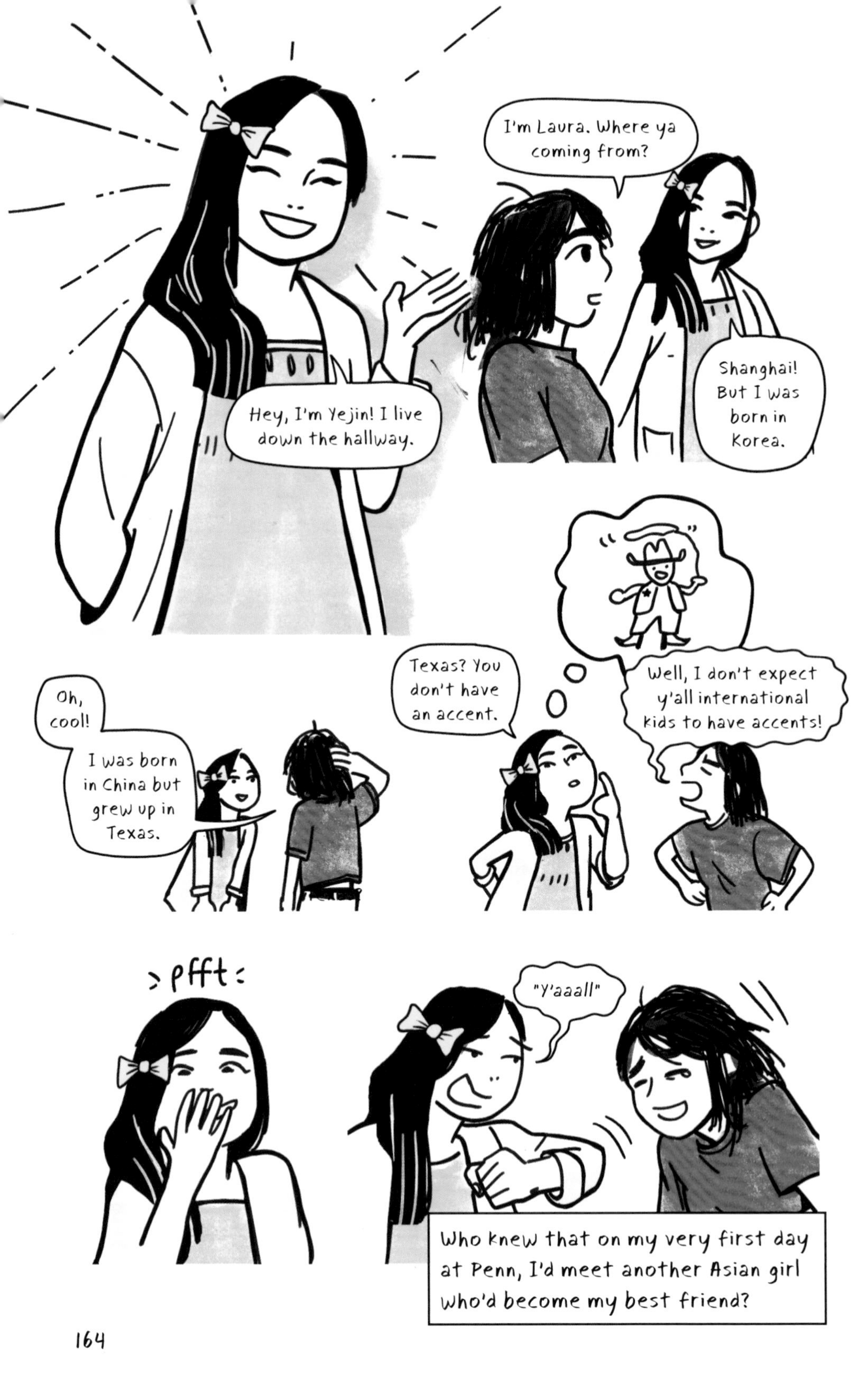
Hey, I'm Yejin! I live down the hallway.
I'm Laura. Where ya coming from?
Shanghai! But I was born in Korea.
Oh, cool!
I was born in China but grew up in Texas.
Texas? You don't have an accent.
Well, I don't expect y'all international kids to have accents!
pfft
"Y'aaall"
Who knew that on my very first day at Penn, I'd meet another Asian girl who'd become my best friend?

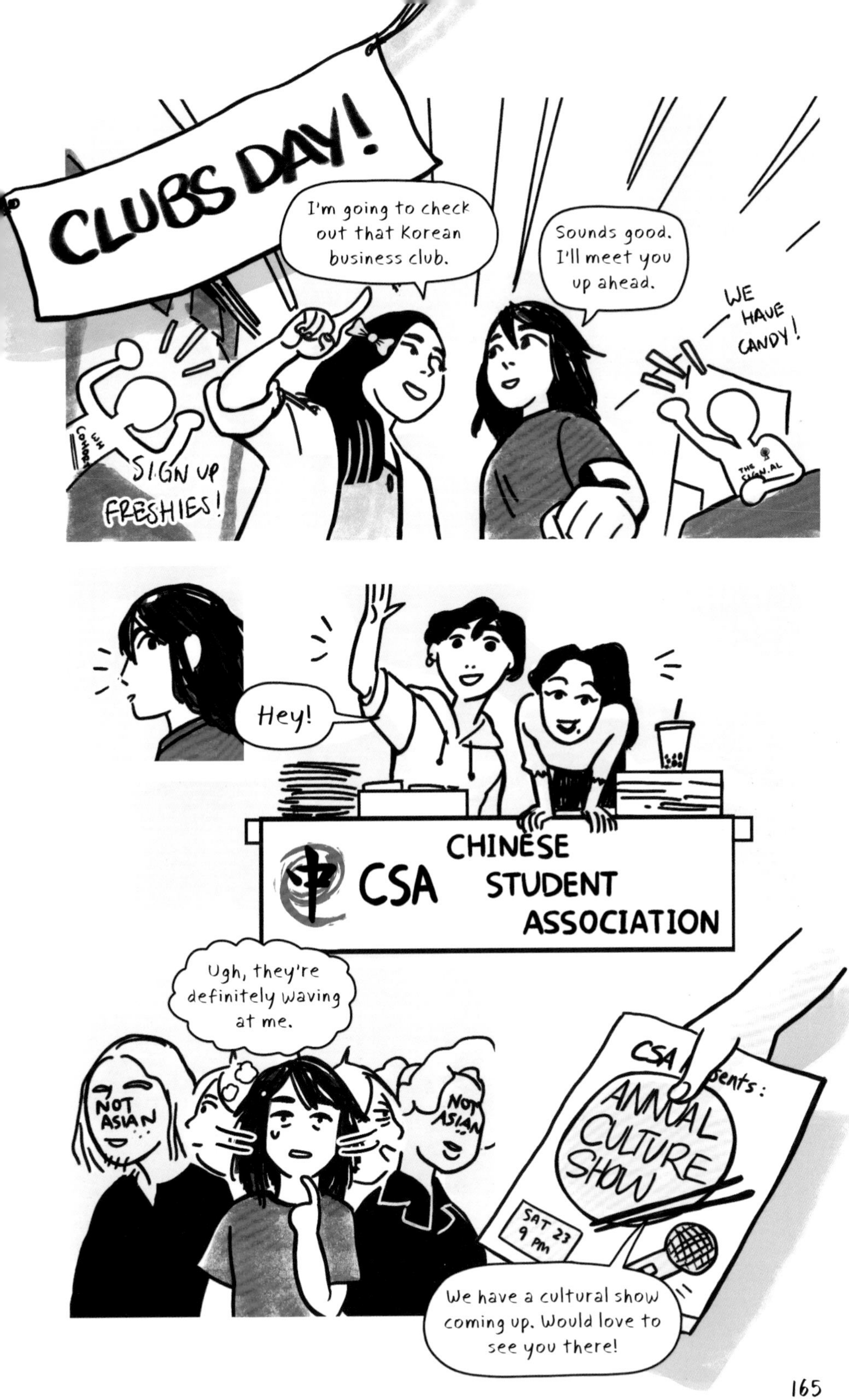
CLUBS DAY!
I'm going to check out that Korean business club.
Sounds good. I'll meet you up ahead.
WE HAVE CANDY!
SIGN UP FRESHIES!
Hey!
CSA CHINESE STUDENT ASSOCIATION
Ugh, they're definitely waving at me.
NOT ASIAN
NOT ASIAN
CSA Presents: ANNUAL CULTURE SHOW
SAT 23 9 PM
We have a cultural show coming up. Would love to see you there!

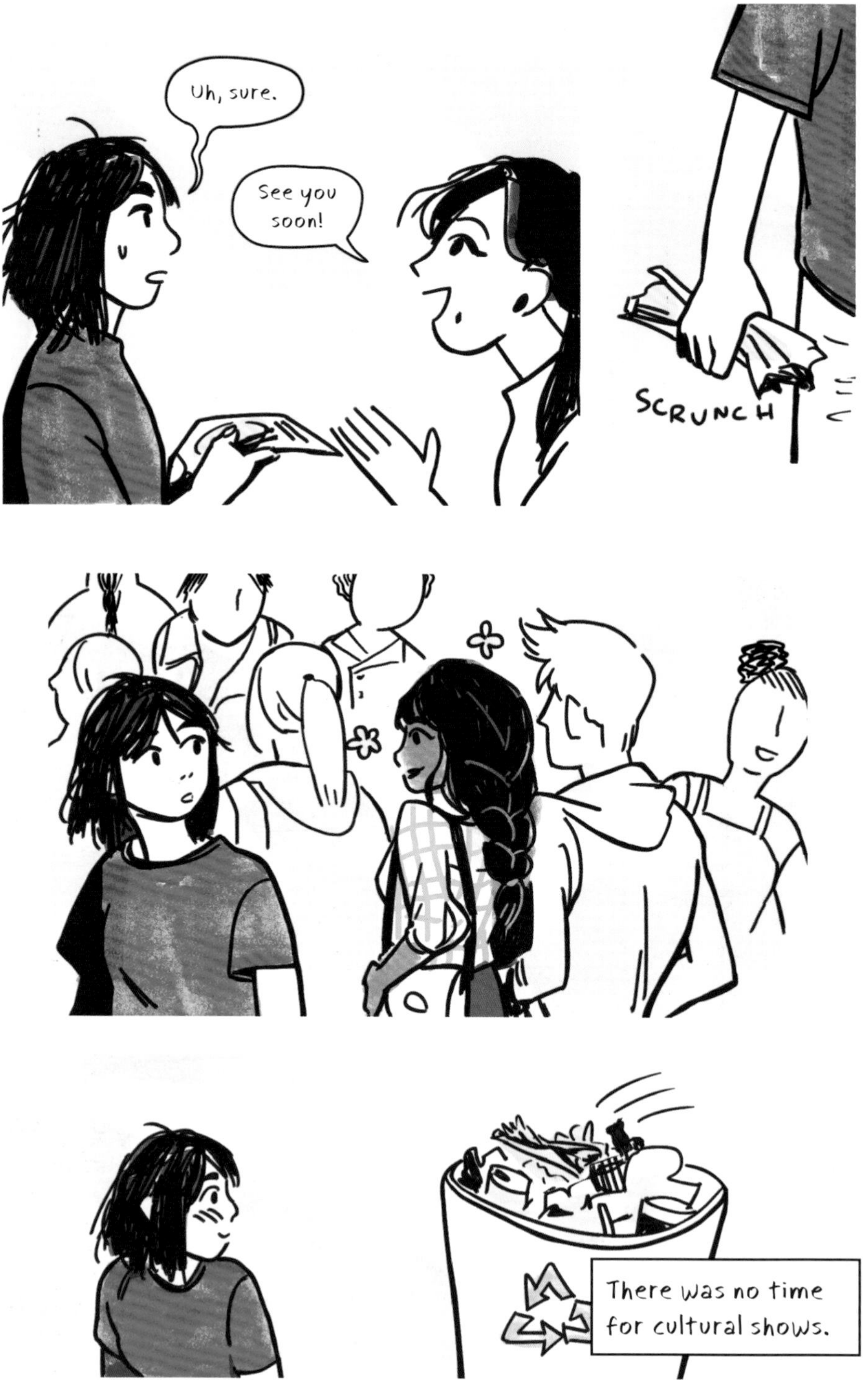
Uh, sure.
See you soon!
SCRUNCH
There was no time for cultural shows.

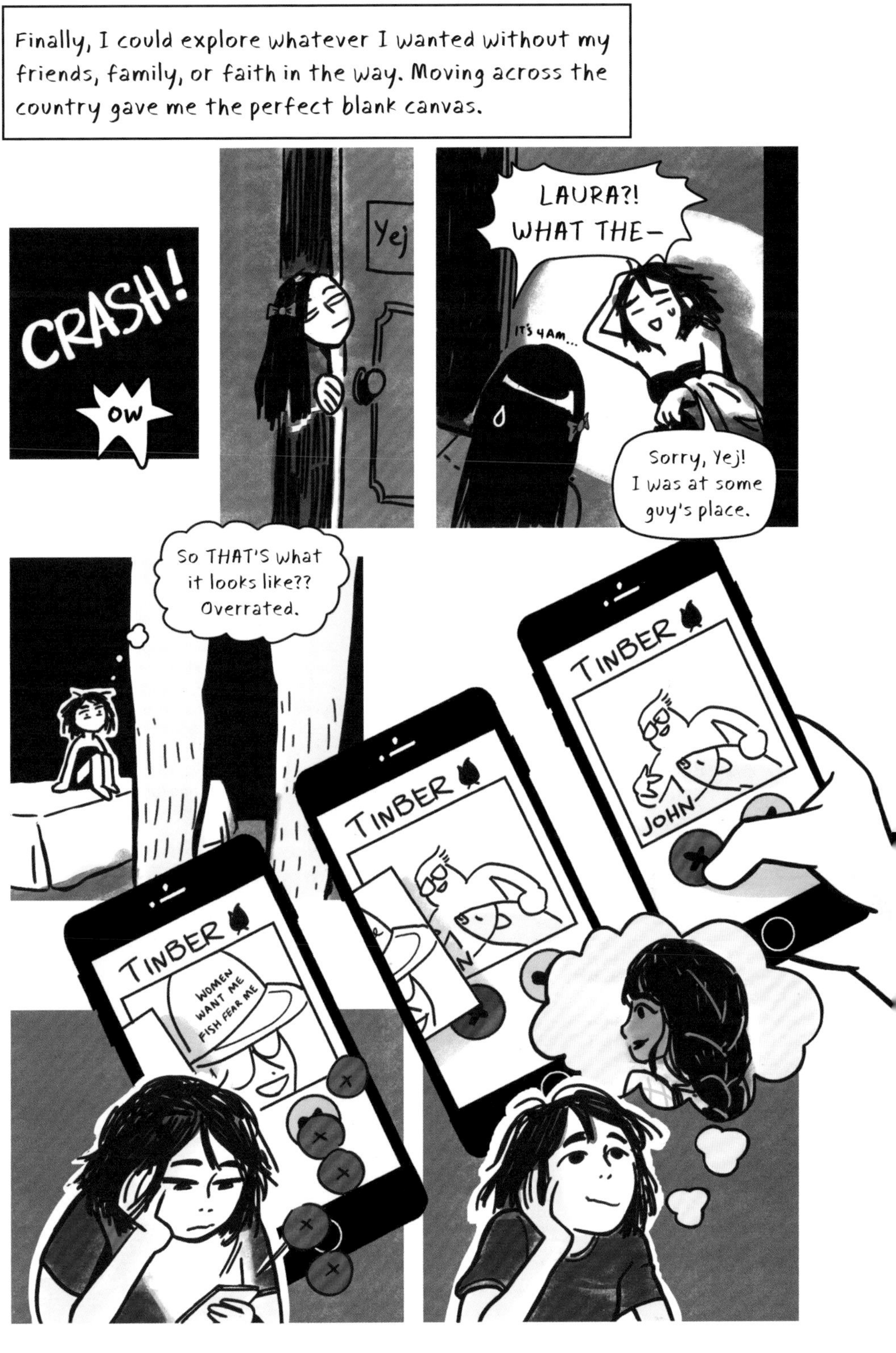
Finally, I could explore whatever I wanted without my friends, family, or faith in the way. Moving across the country gave me the perfect blank canvas.
CRASH!
OW
Yej
LAURA?! WHAT THE—
IT'S 4AM...
Sorry, Yej! I was at some guy's place.
So THAT'S what it looks like?? Overrated.
TINBER
JOHN
TINBER
TINBER
WOMEN WANT ME FISH FEAR ME

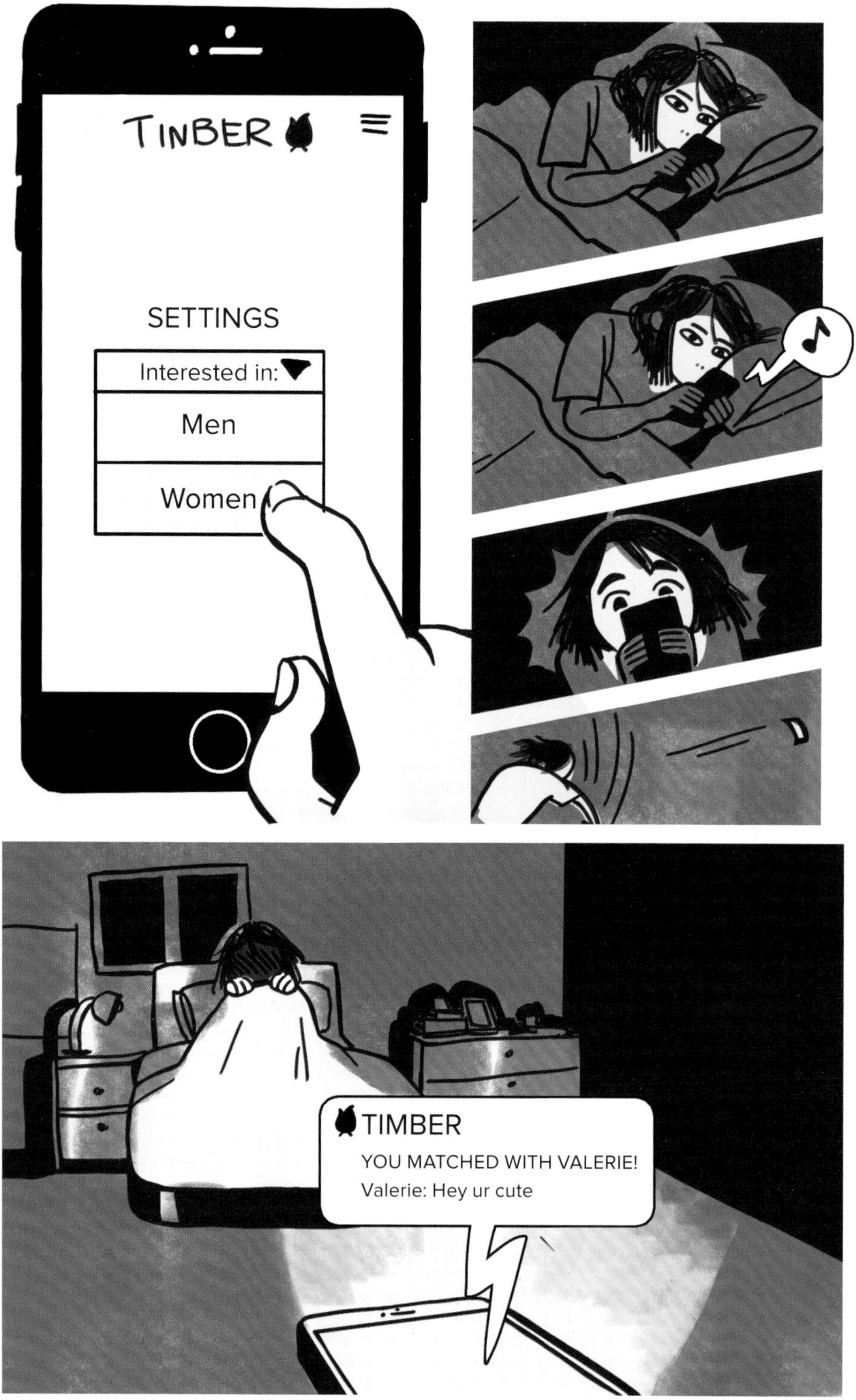

TINBER
SETTINGS
Interested in:
Men
Women
TIMBER
YOU MATCHED WITH VALERIE!
Valerie: Hey ur cute

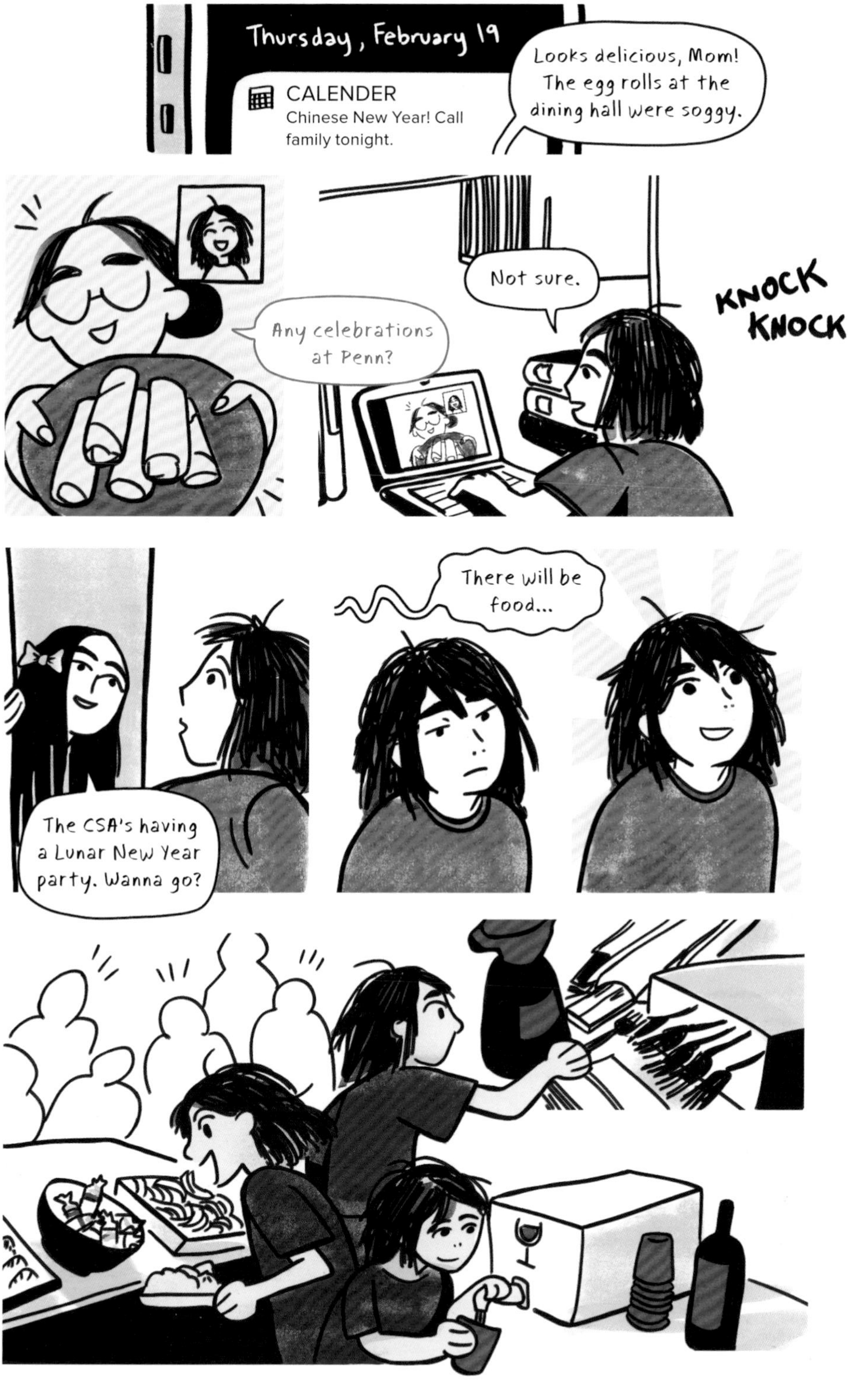
Thursday, February 19
CALENDER
Chinese New Year! Call family tonight.
Looks delicious, Mom! The egg rolls at the dining hall were soggy.
Any celebrations at Penn?
Not sure.
KNOCK KNOCK
The CSA's having a Lunar New Year party. Wanna go?
There will be food...

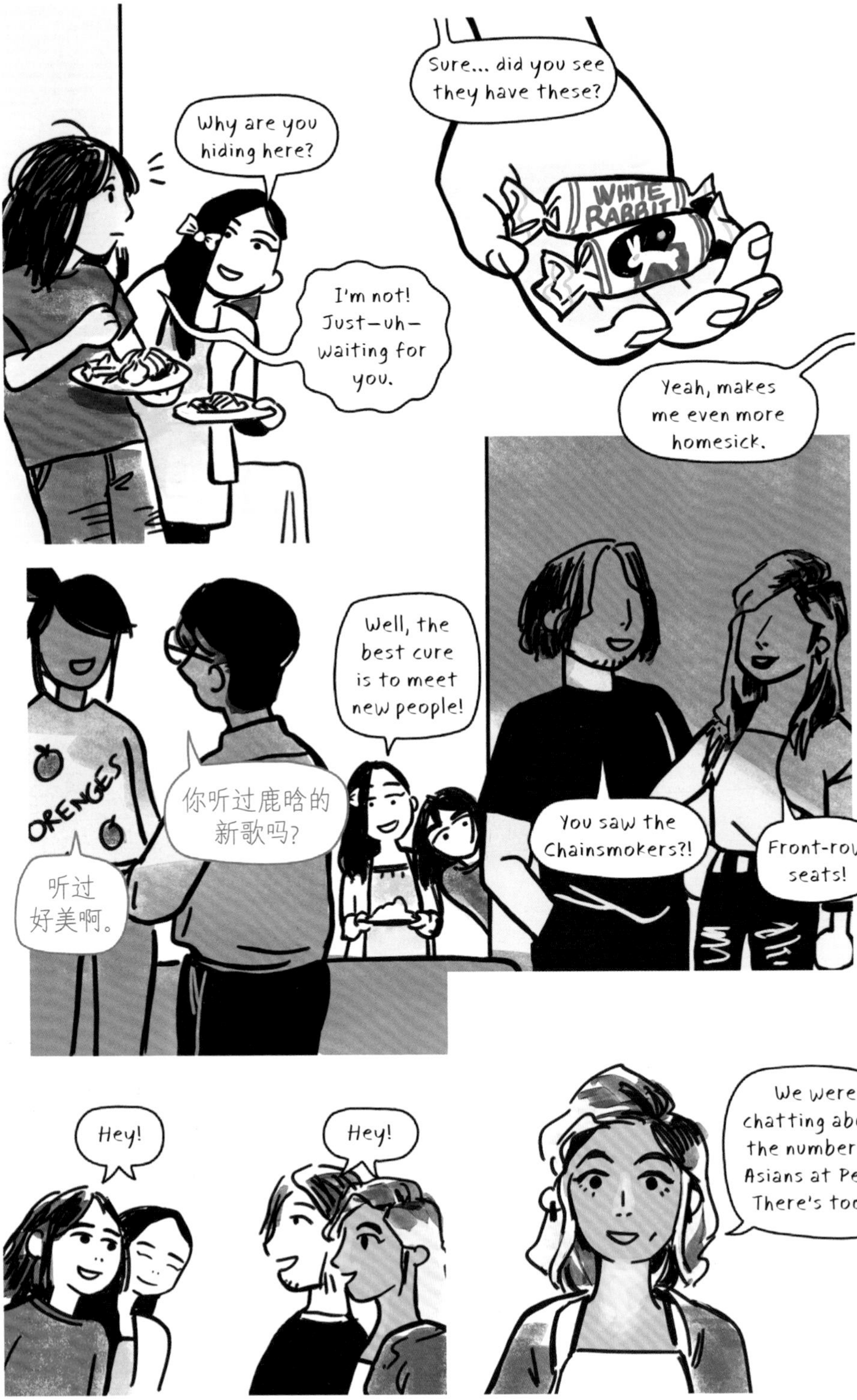
Why are you hiding here?
I'm not! Just—uh—waiting for you.
Sure... did you see they have these?
WHITE RABBIT
Yeah, makes me even more homesick.
ORENGES
你听过鹿晗的新歌吗?
听过好美啊。
Well, the best cure is to meet new people!
You saw the Chainsmokers?!
Front-row seats!
Hey!
Hey!
We were chatting about the number of Asians at Penn. There's too—

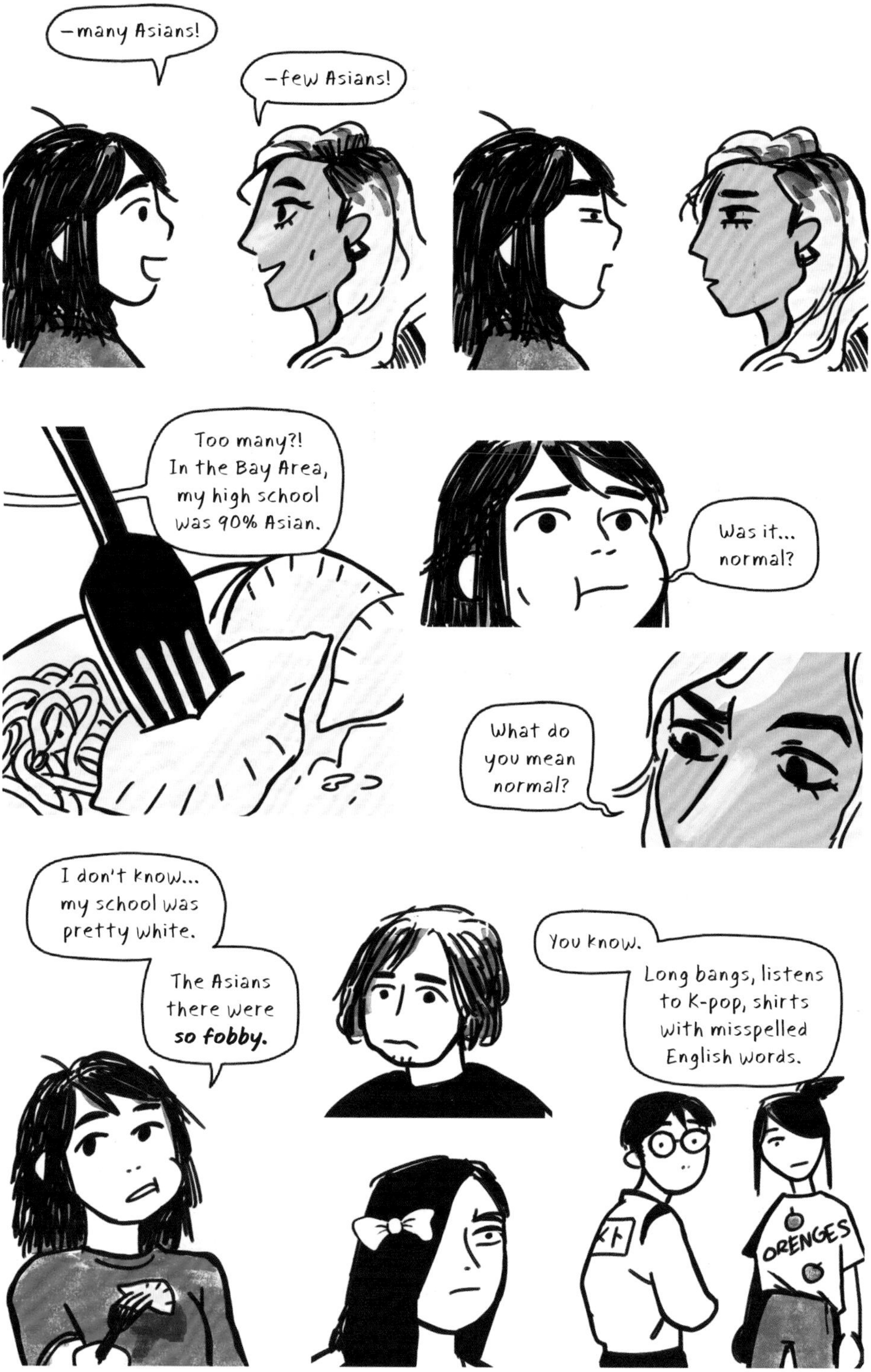

—many Asians!
—few Asians!
Too many?! In the Bay Area, my high school was 90% Asian.
Was it... normal?
What do you mean normal?
I don't know... my school was pretty white.
The Asians there were **so fobby.**
You know.
Long bangs, listens to K-pop, shirts with misspelled English words.
사
ORENGES

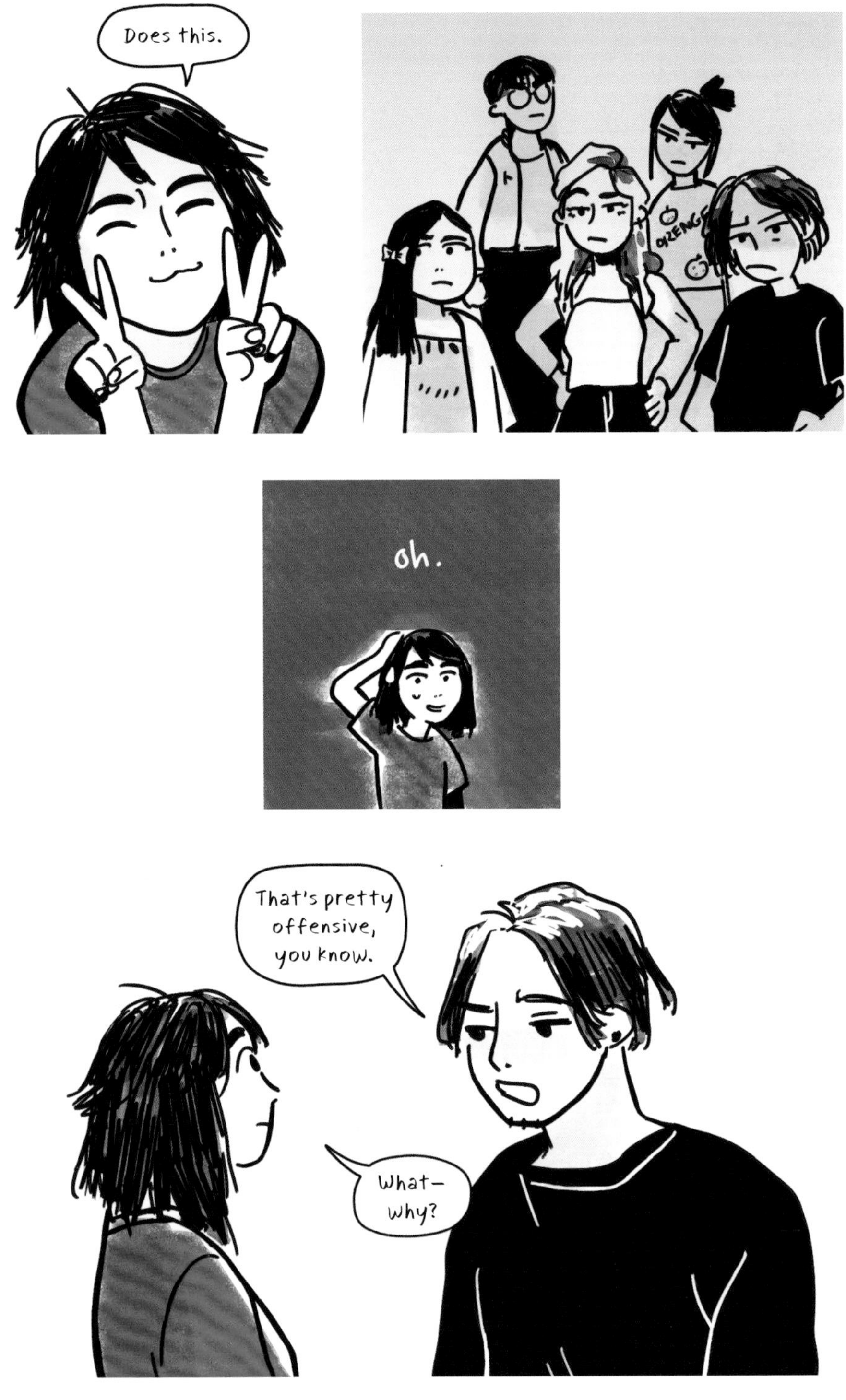
Does this.
oh.
That's pretty offensive, you know.
What—why?

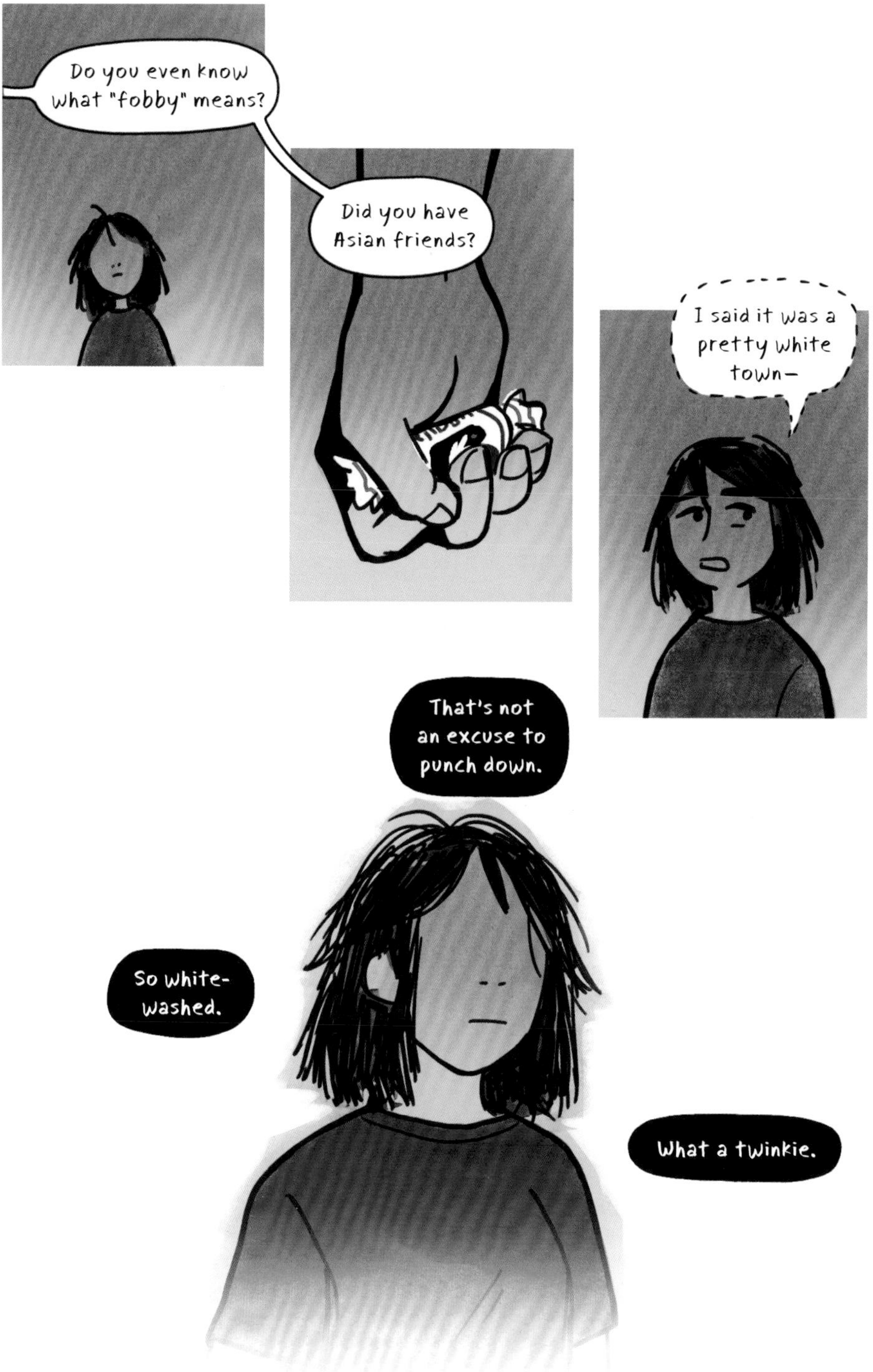
Do you even know what "fobby" means?
Did you have Asian friends?
I said it was a pretty white town—
That's not an excuse to punch down.
So white-washed.
What a twinkie.

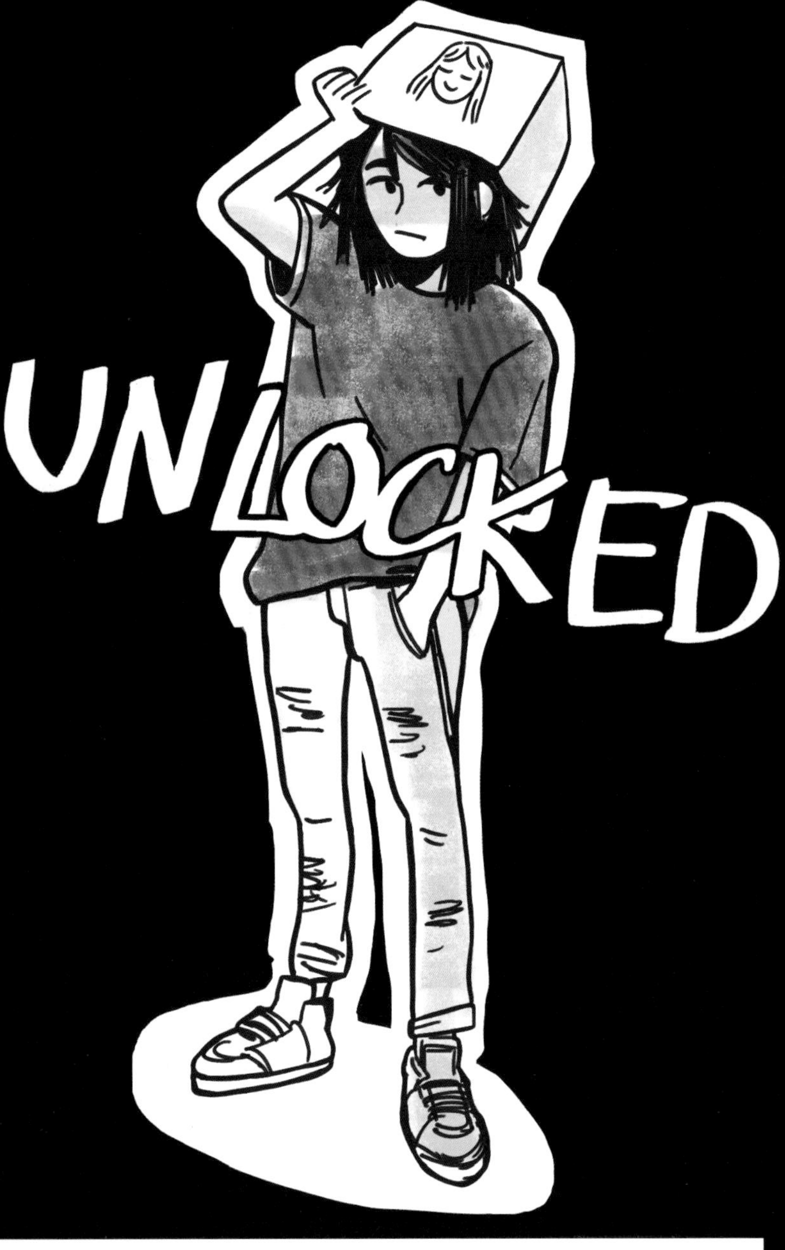
UNLOCKED

WHITE-WASHED "TWINKIE" ASIAN

- SPECIAL POWER: FITS IN WITH THE MAJORITY.
- WEAKNESS: HAS MAJOR IDENTITY ISSUES.

CHAPTER 12
White Rabbit Candy

A QUICK WHITE RABBIT CANDY HISTORY LESSON

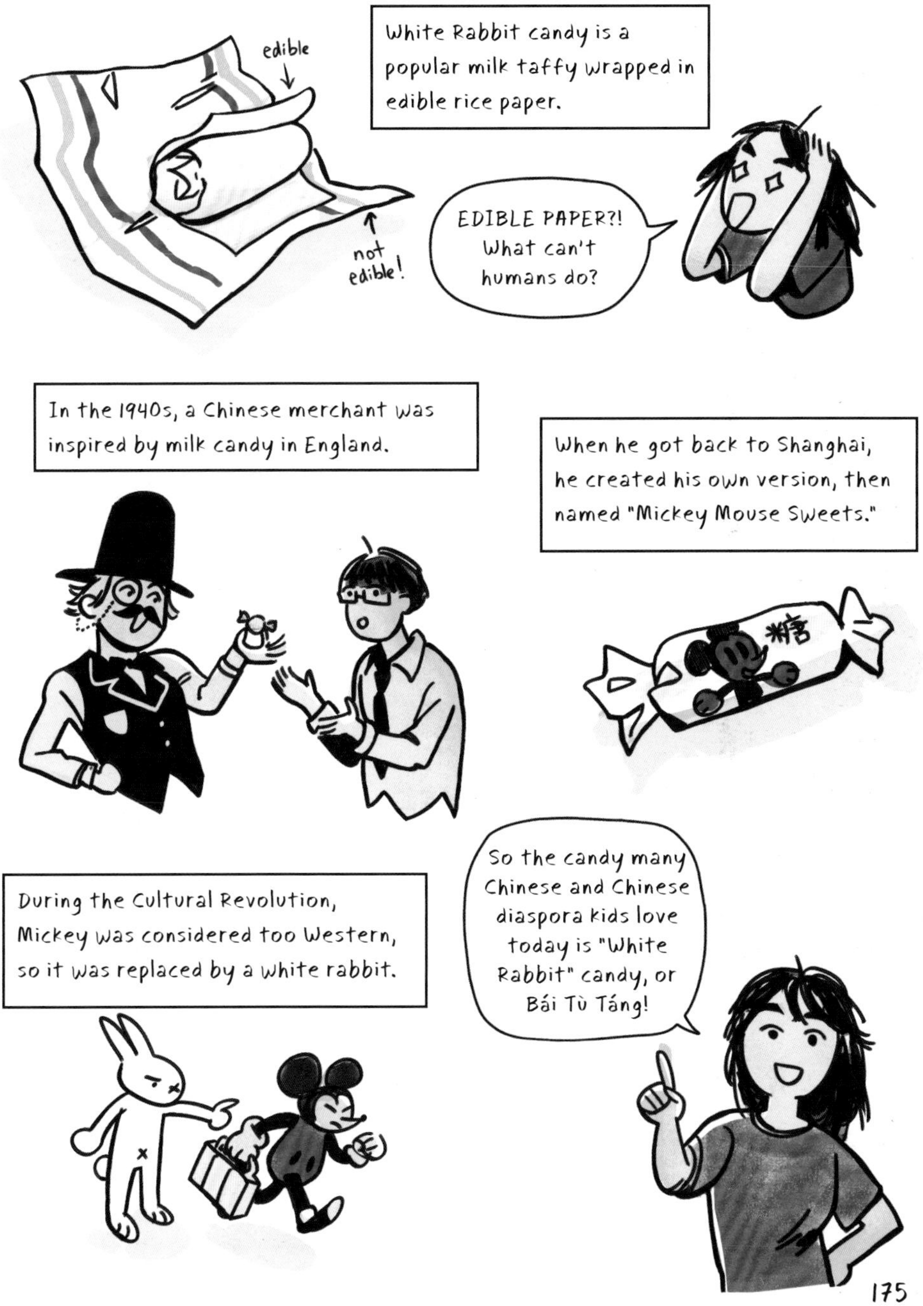

White Rabbit candy is a popular milk taffy wrapped in edible rice paper.
edible
not edible!
EDIBLE PAPER?! What can't humans do?
In the 1940s, a Chinese merchant was inspired by milk candy in England.
When he got back to Shanghai, he created his own version, then named "Mickey Mouse Sweets."
糖
During the Cultural Revolution, Mickey was considered too Western, so it was replaced by a white rabbit.
So the candy many Chinese and Chinese diaspora kids love today is "White Rabbit" candy, or Bái Tù Táng!

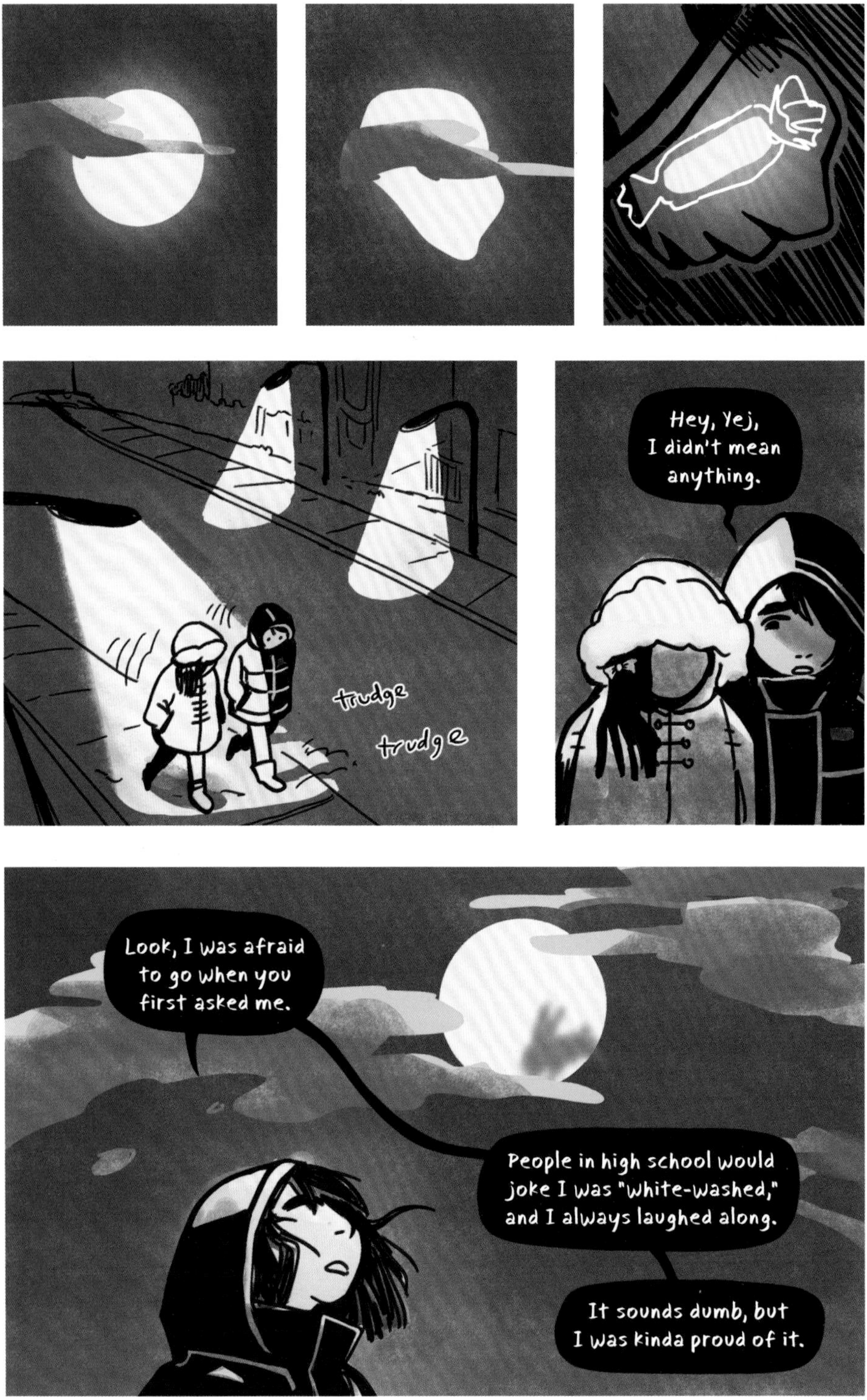
trudge
trudge
Hey, Yej, I didn't mean anything.
Look, I was afraid to go when you first asked me.
People in high school would joke I was "white-washed," and I always laughed along.
It sounds dumb, but I was kinda proud of it.

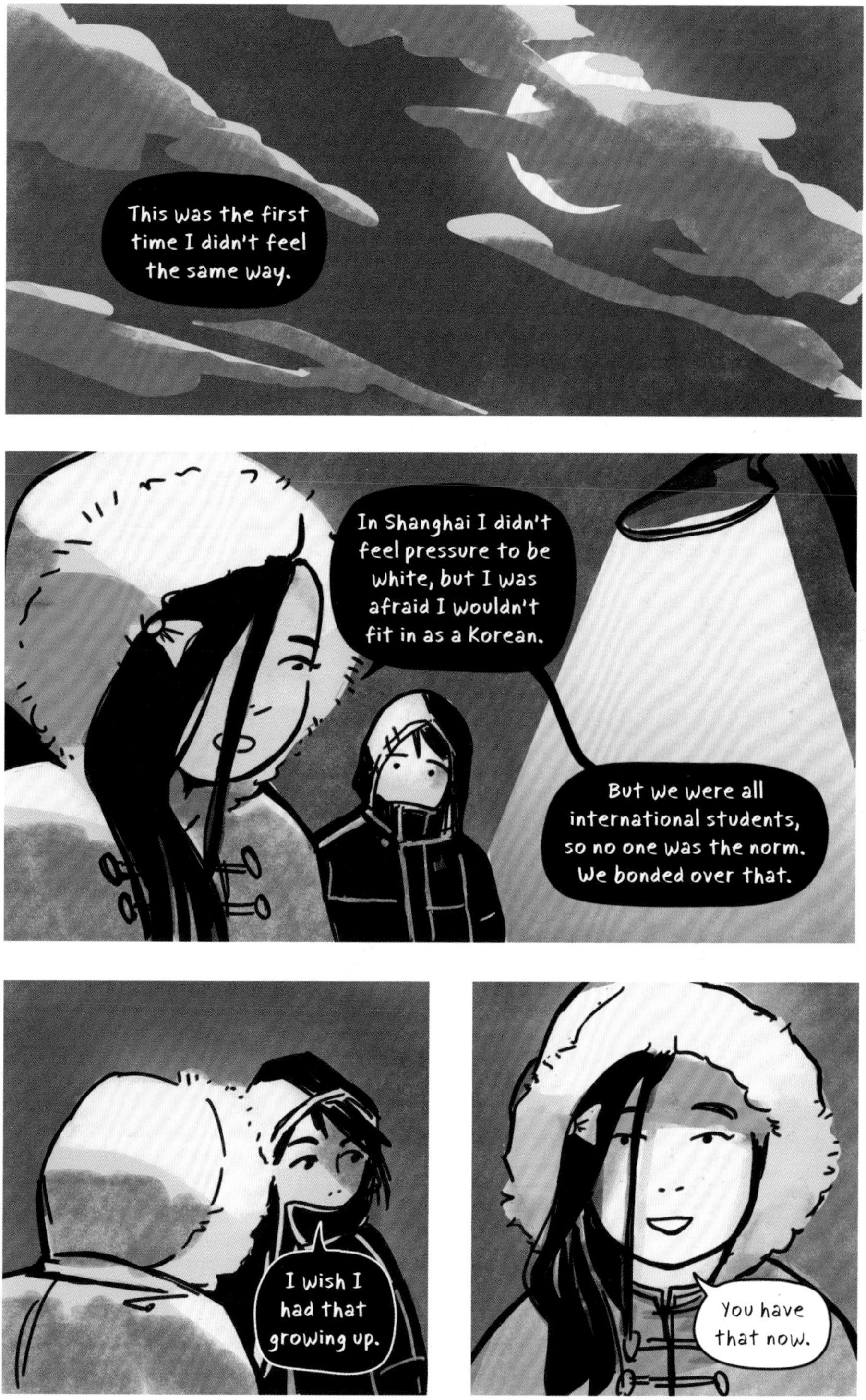
This was the first time I didn't feel the same way.
In Shanghai I didn't feel pressure to be white, but I was afraid I wouldn't fit in as a Korean.
But we were all international students, so no one was the norm. We bonded over that.
I wish I had that growing up.
You have that now.

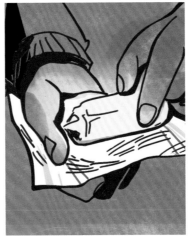

Yeah, you're right.

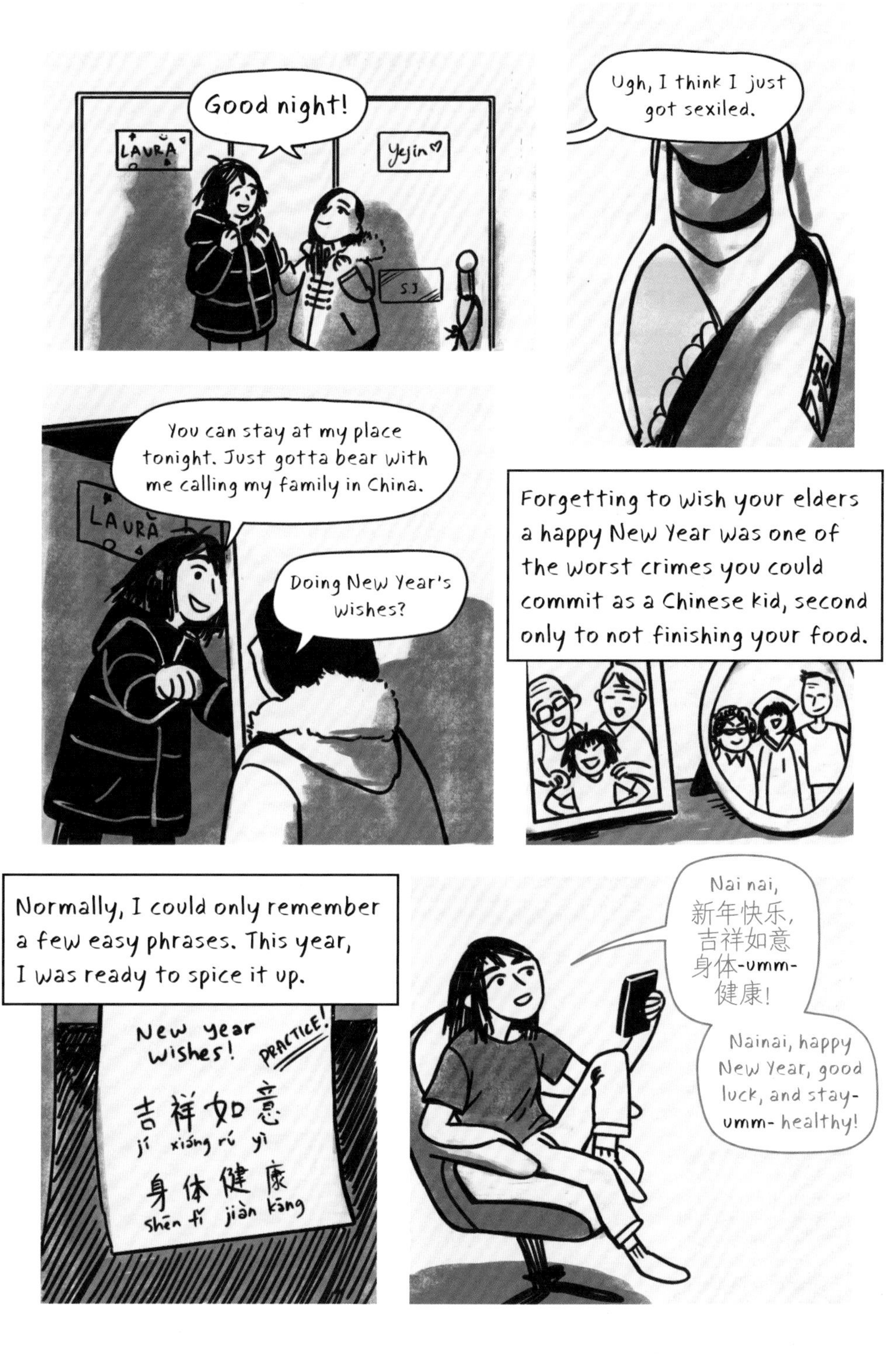
LAURA
Yejin
Good night!
S.J.
Ugh, I think I just got sexiled.
LAURA
You can stay at my place tonight. Just gotta bear with me calling my family in China.
Doing New Year's wishes?
Forgetting to wish your elders a happy New Year was one of the worst crimes you could commit as a Chinese kid, second only to not finishing your food.
Normally, I could only remember a few easy phrases. This year, I was ready to spice it up.
New year wishes!
PRACTICE!
吉祥如意
jí xiáng rú yì
身体健康
shēn tǐ jiàn kāng
Nai nai, 新年快乐, 吉祥如意 身体-umm-健康!
Nainai, happy New Year, good luck, and stay-umm- healthy!

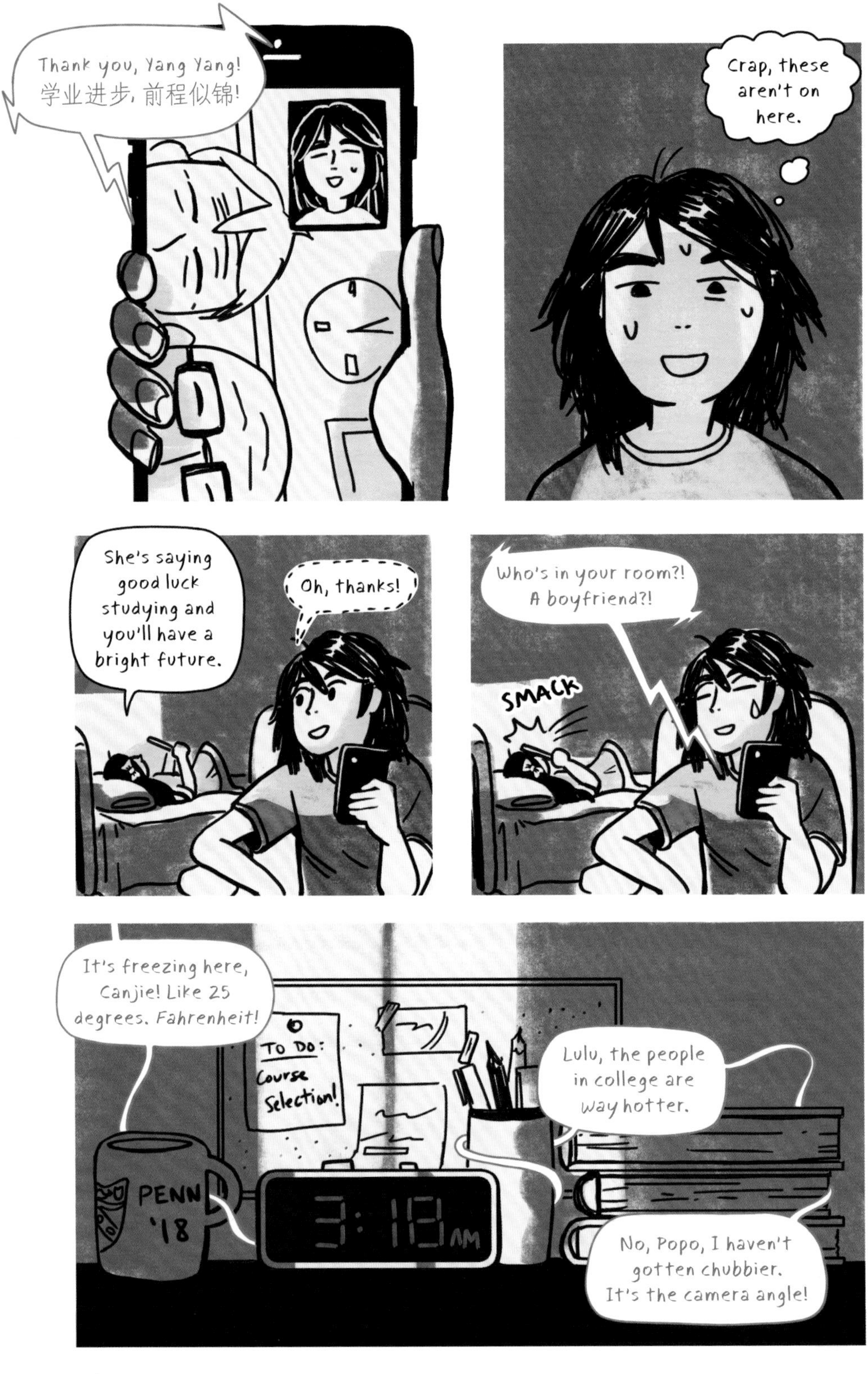
Thank you, Yang Yang!
学业进步，前程似锦!
Crap, these aren't on here.
She's saying good luck studying and you'll have a bright future.
Oh, thanks!
Who's in your room?! A boyfriend?!
SMACK
It's freezing here, Canjie! Like 25 degrees. Fahrenheit!
TO DO: Course Selection!
PENN '18
3:18 AM
Lulu, the people in college are way hotter.
No, Popo, I haven't gotten chubbier. It's the camera angle!

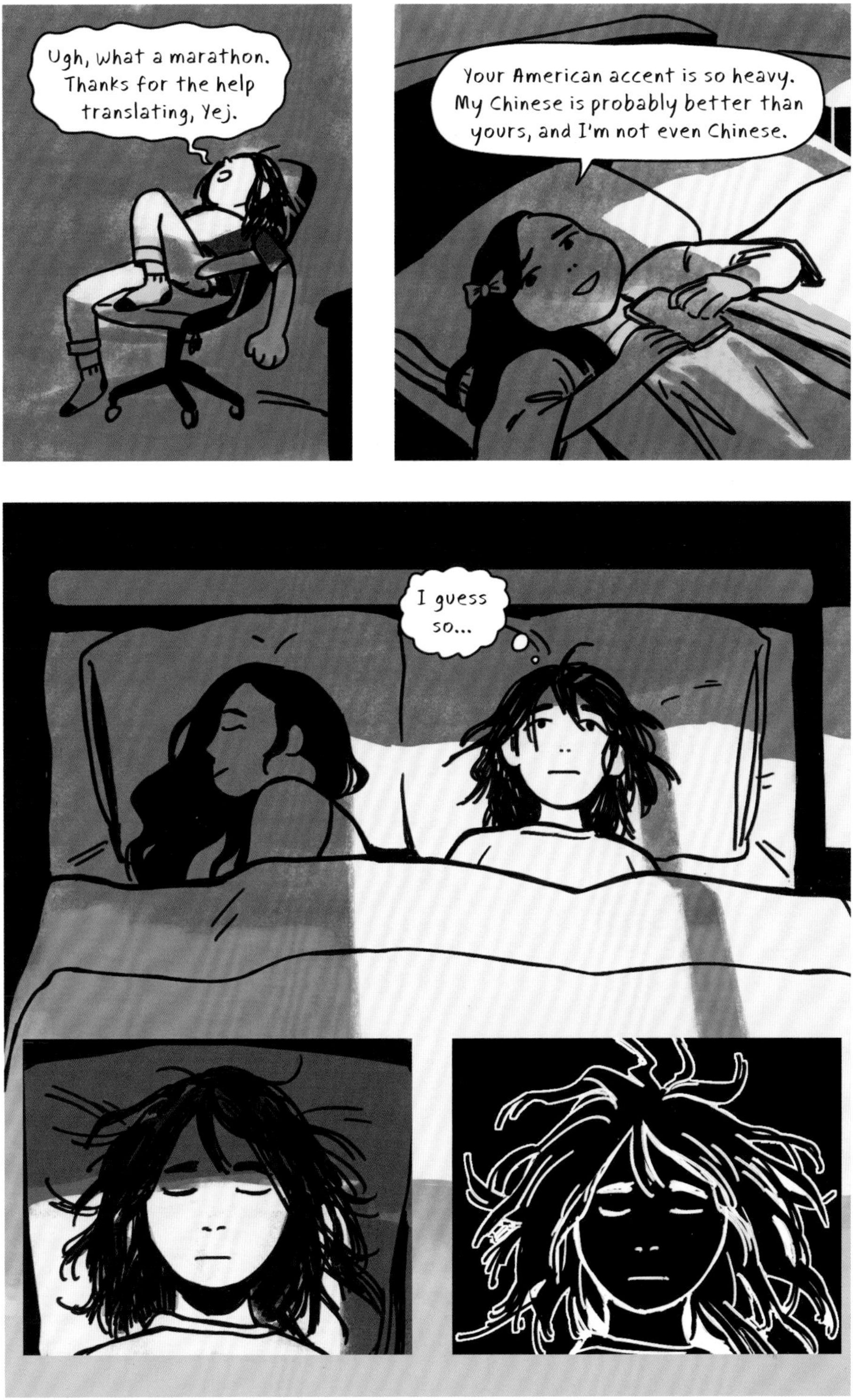

Ugh, what a marathon. Thanks for the help translating, Yej.
Your American accent is so heavy. My Chinese is probably better than yours, and I'm not even Chinese.
I guess so...

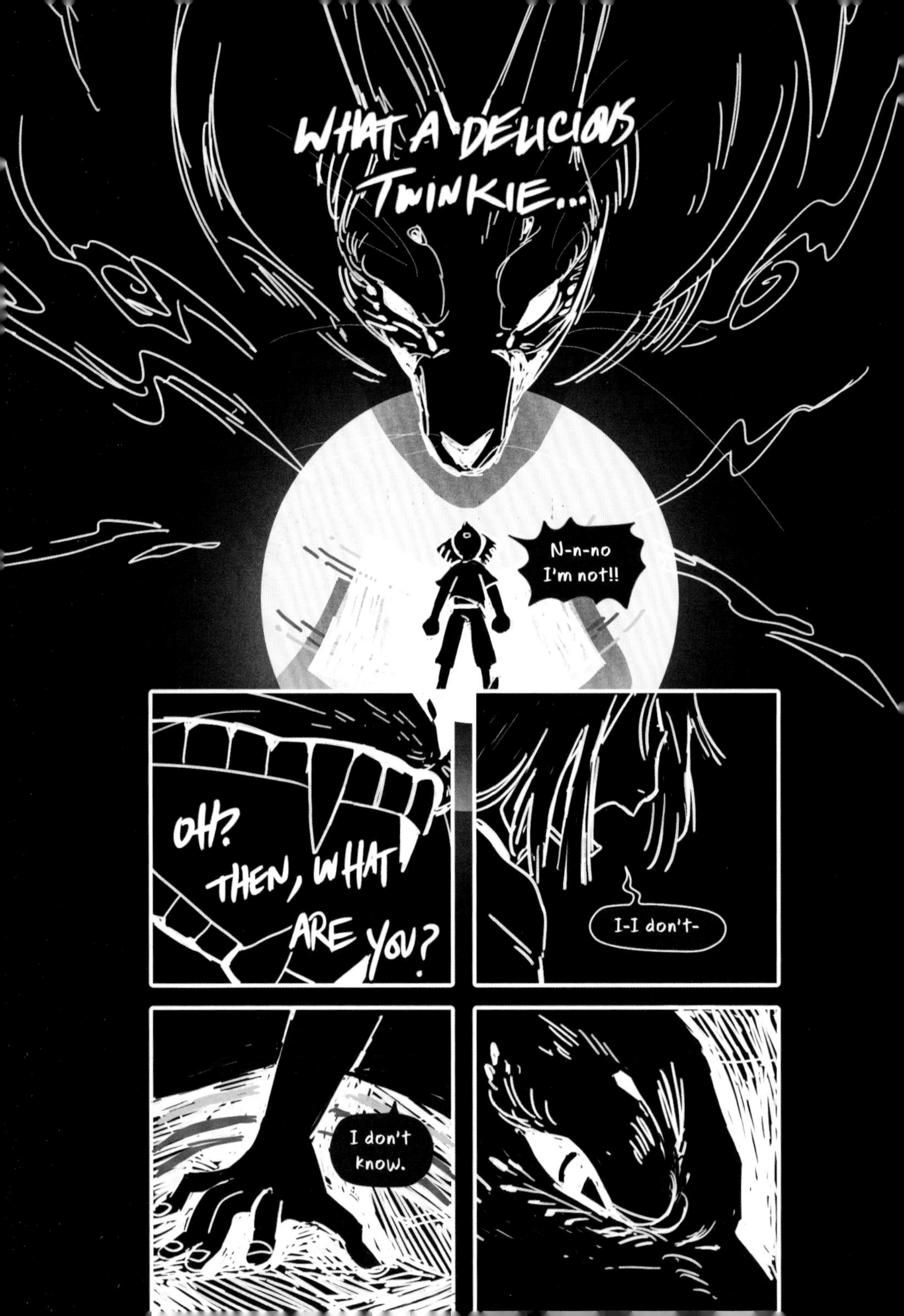
WHAT A DELICIOUS TWINKIE...
N-n-no I'm not!!
OH? THEN, WHAT ARE YOU?
I-I don't-
I don't know.

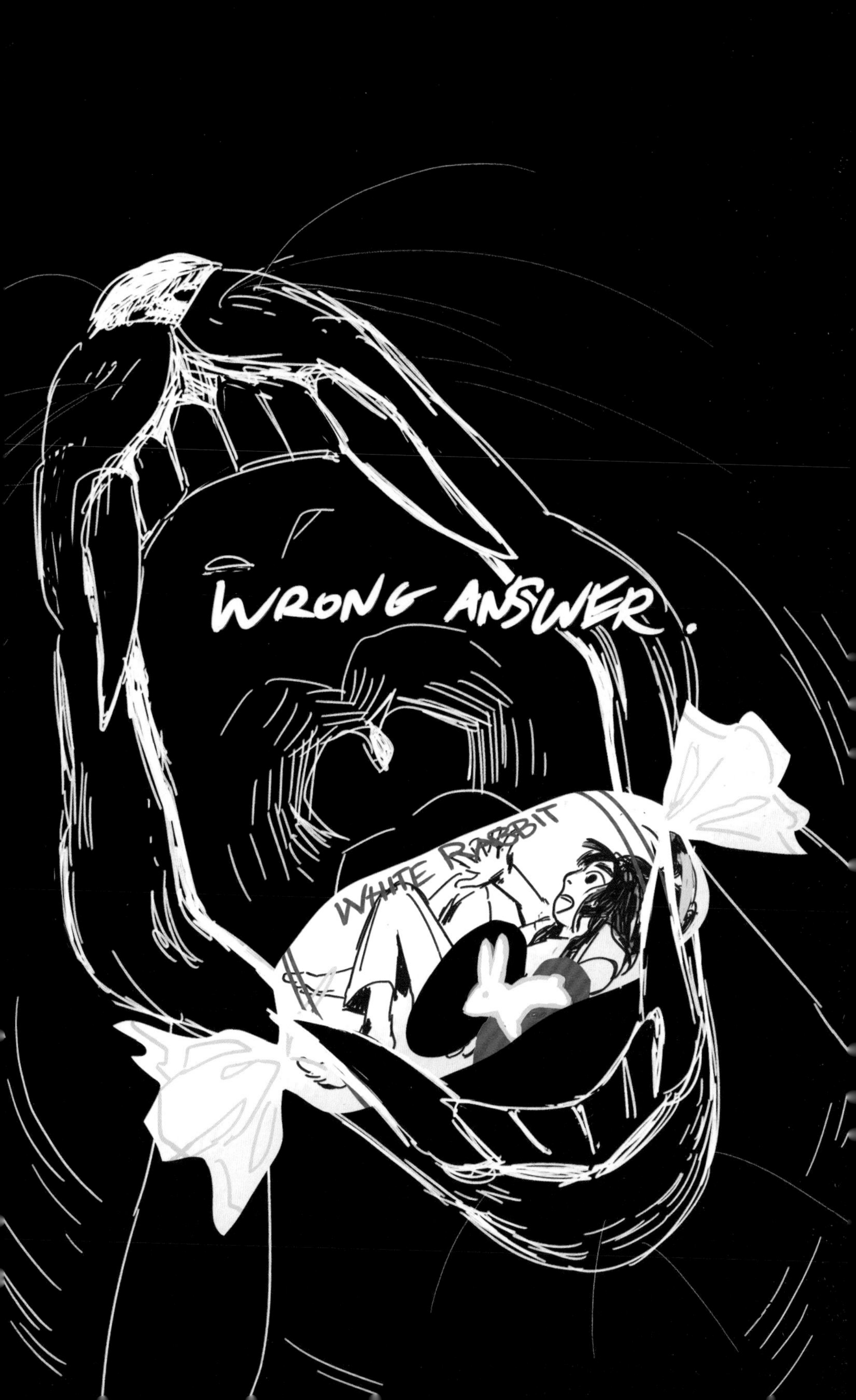

WRONG ANSWER.
WHITE RABBIT

Course Selection

Search for a course below.

CHINESE | ENTER

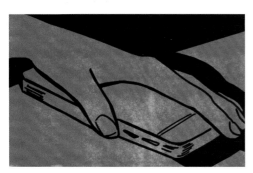

CHIN031
CHINESE LANG & CULTURE I

ADD

CHAPTER 13
Q&A

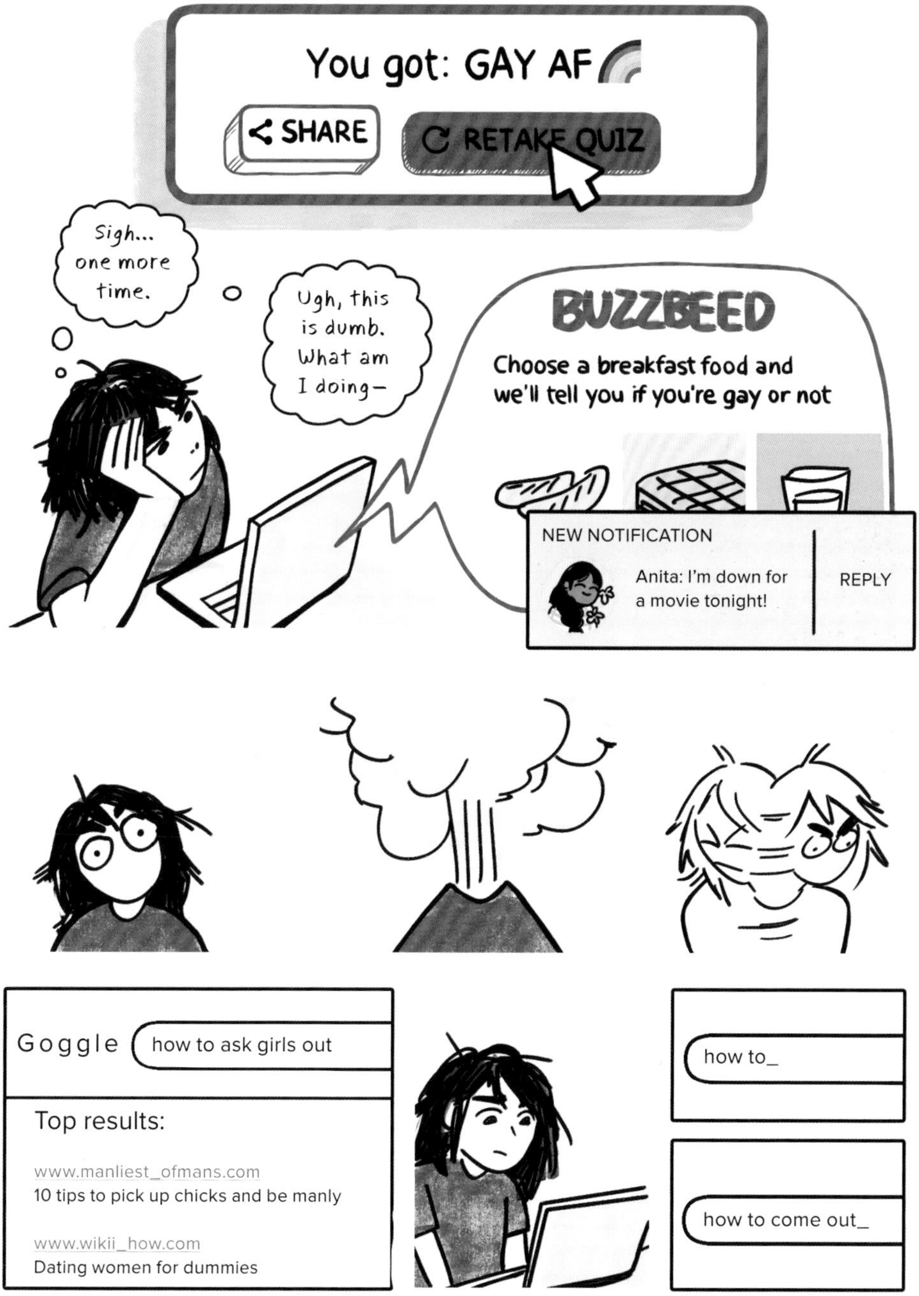
You got: GAY AF
SHARE
RETAKE QUIZ
Sigh... one more time.
Ugh, this is dumb. What am I doing—
BUZZBEED
Choose a breakfast food and we'll tell you if you're gay or not
NEW NOTIFICATION
Anita: I'm down for a movie tonight!
REPLY
Goggle
how to ask girls out
Top results:
www.manliest_ofmans.com
10 tips to pick up chicks and be manly
www.wikii_how.com
Dating women for dummies
how to_
how to come out_

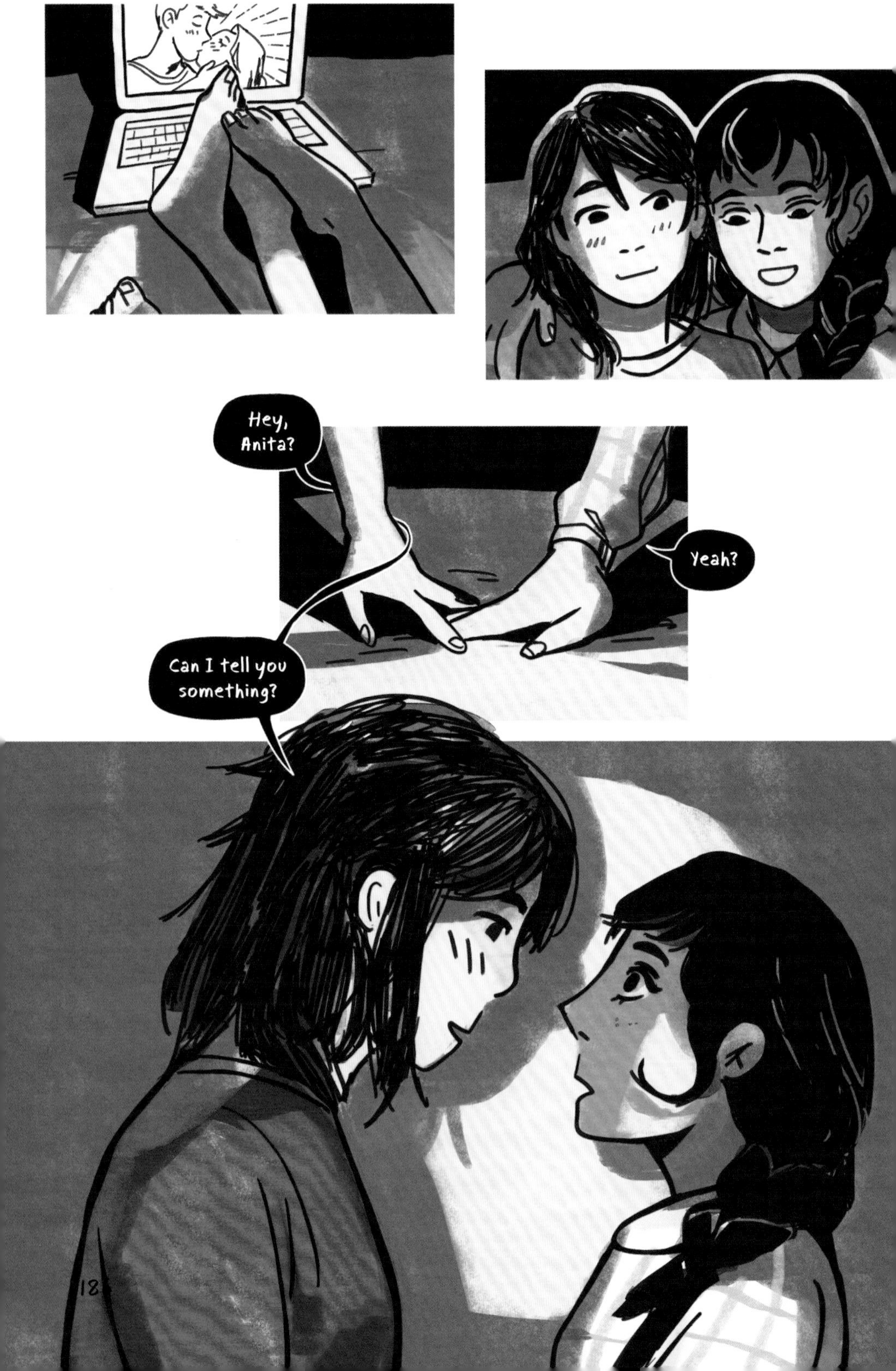
Hey, Anita?
Yeah?
Can I tell you something?

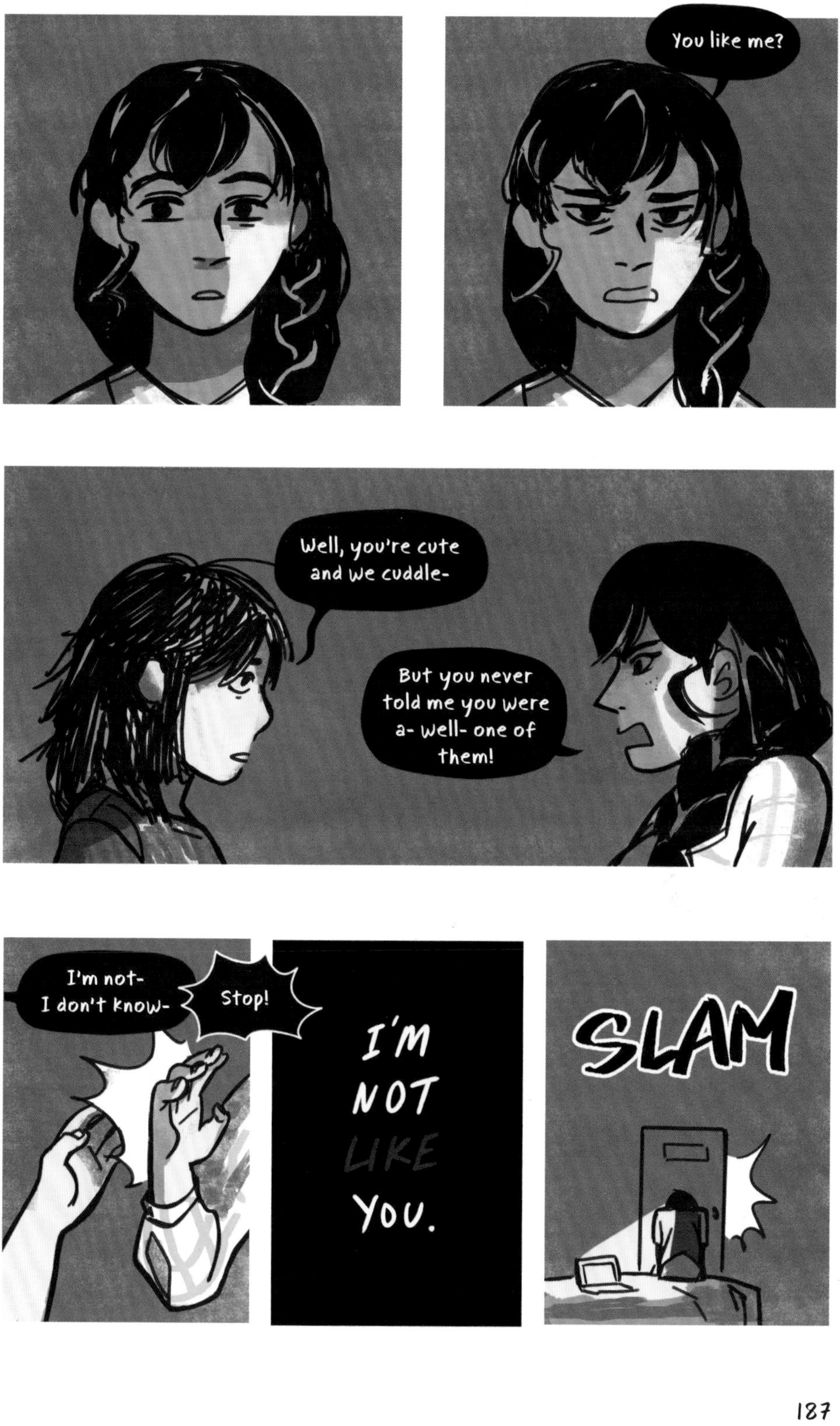
You like me?
Well, you're cute and we cuddle-
But you never told me you were a- well- one of them!
I'm not- I don't know-
Stop!
I'M NOT LIKE YOU.
SLAM

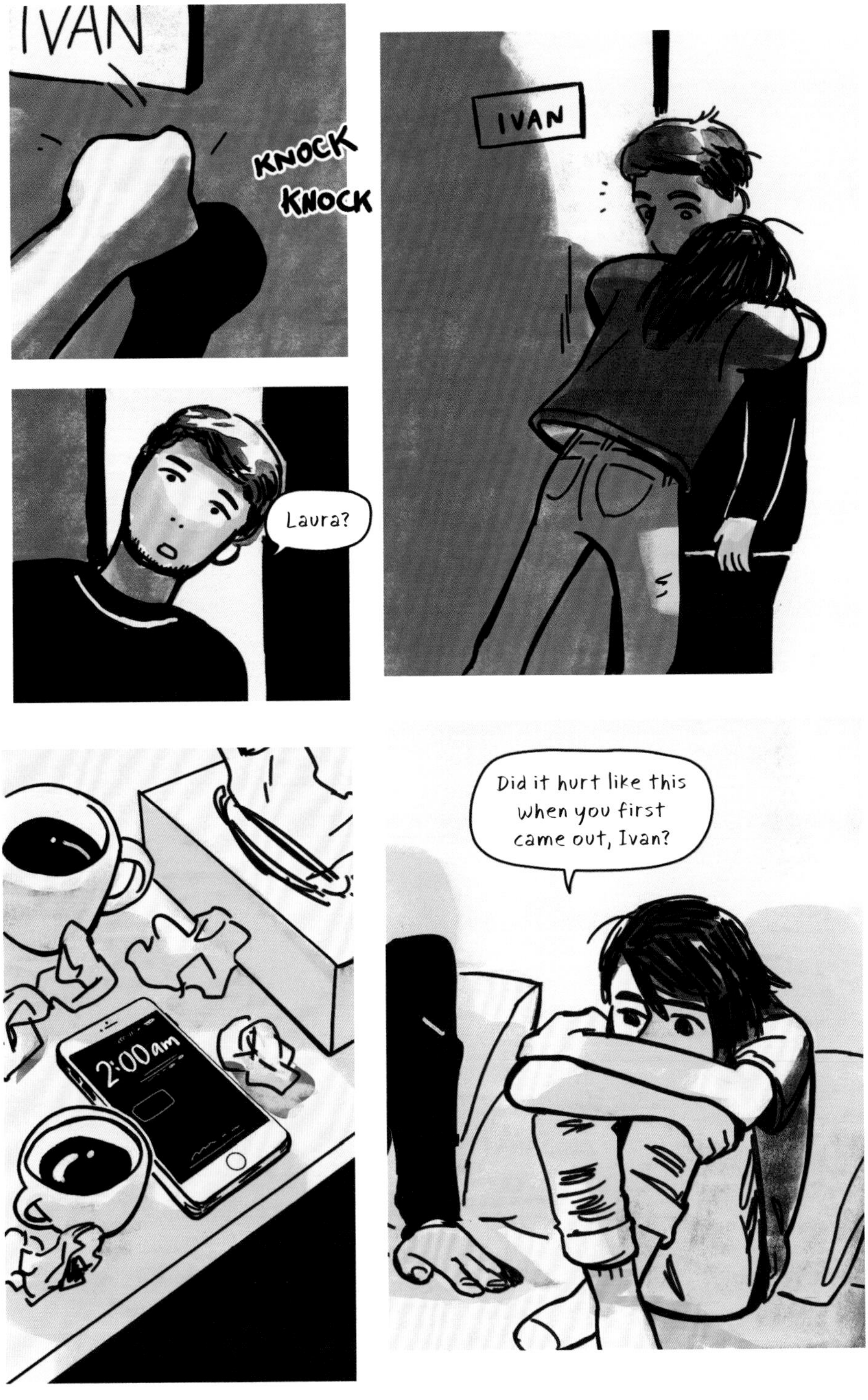
IVAN
KNOCK
KNOCK
Laura?
IVAN
2:00am
Did it hurt like this when you first came out, Ivan?

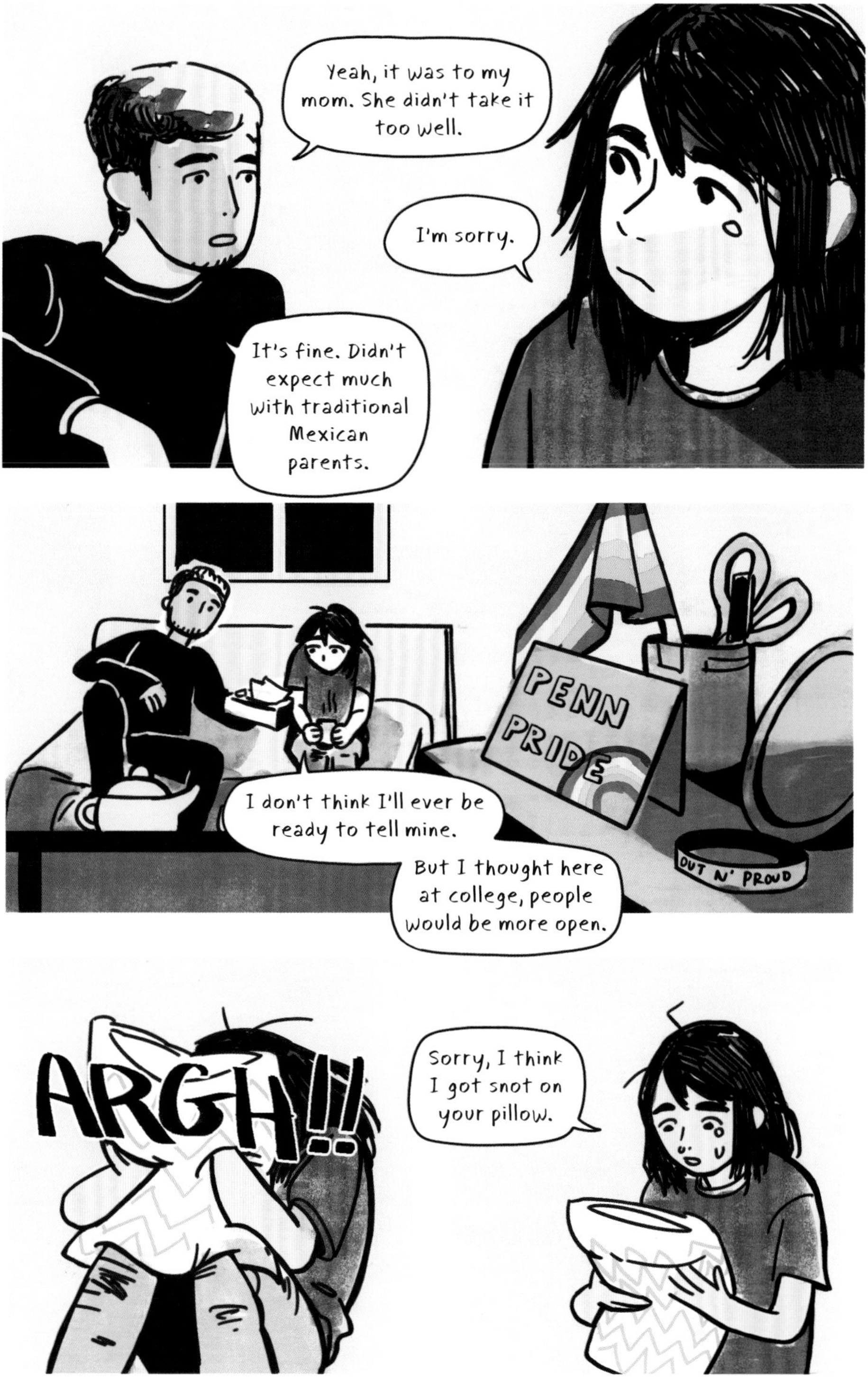
Yeah, it was to my mom. She didn't take it too well.
I'm sorry.
It's fine. Didn't expect much with traditional Mexican parents.
PENN PRIDE
OUT N' PROUD
I don't think I'll ever be ready to tell mine.
But I thought here at college, people would be more open.
ARGH!!!
Sorry, I think I got snot on your pillow.

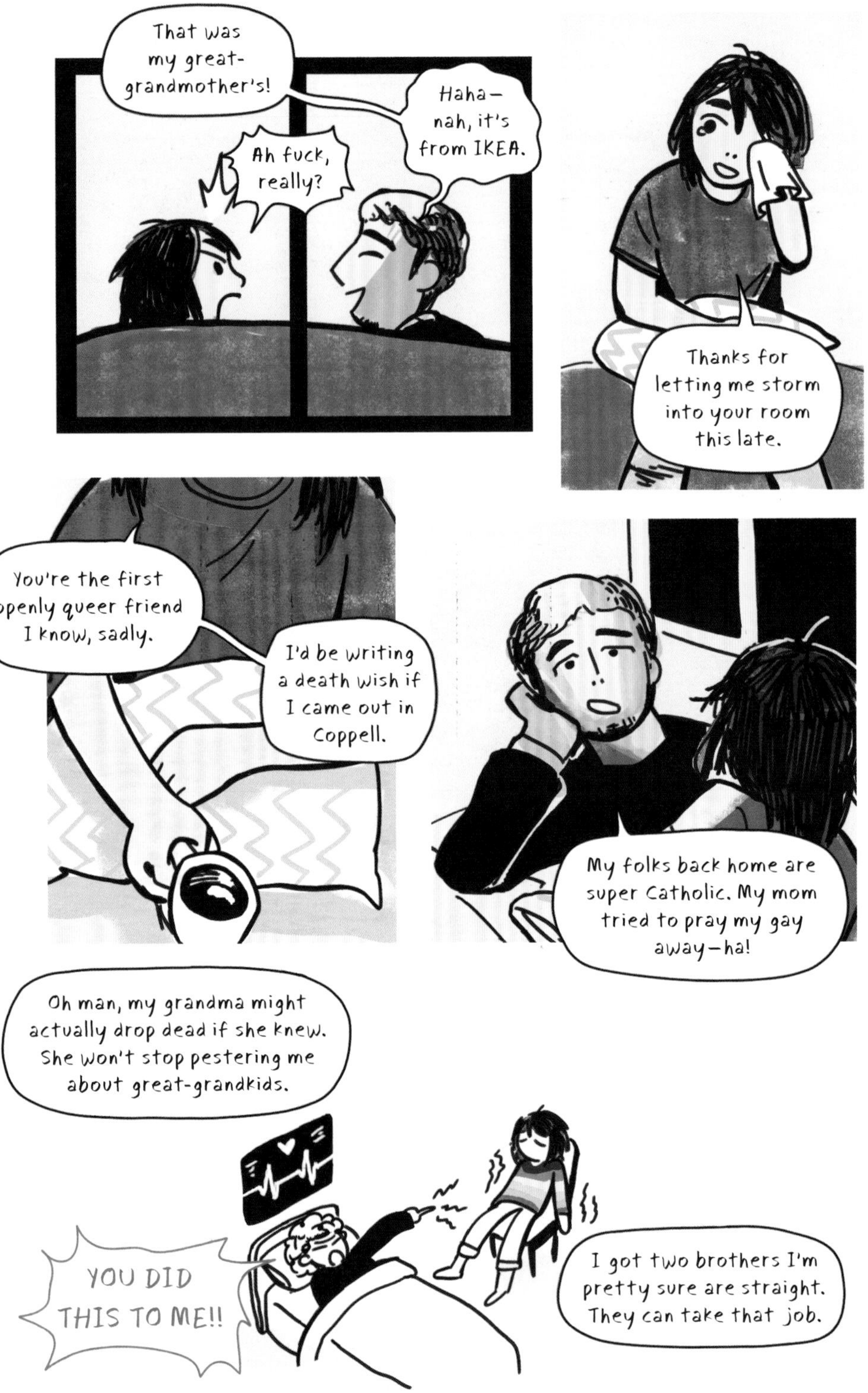
That was my great-grandmother's!
Ah fuck, really?
Haha—nah, it's from IKEA.
Thanks for letting me storm into your room this late.
You're the first openly queer friend I know, sadly.
I'd be writing a death wish if I came out in Coppell.
My folks back home are super Catholic. My mom tried to pray my gay away—ha!
Oh man, my grandma might actually drop dead if she knew. She won't stop pestering me about great-grandkids.
YOU DID THIS TO ME!!
I got two brothers I'm pretty sure are straight. They can take that job.

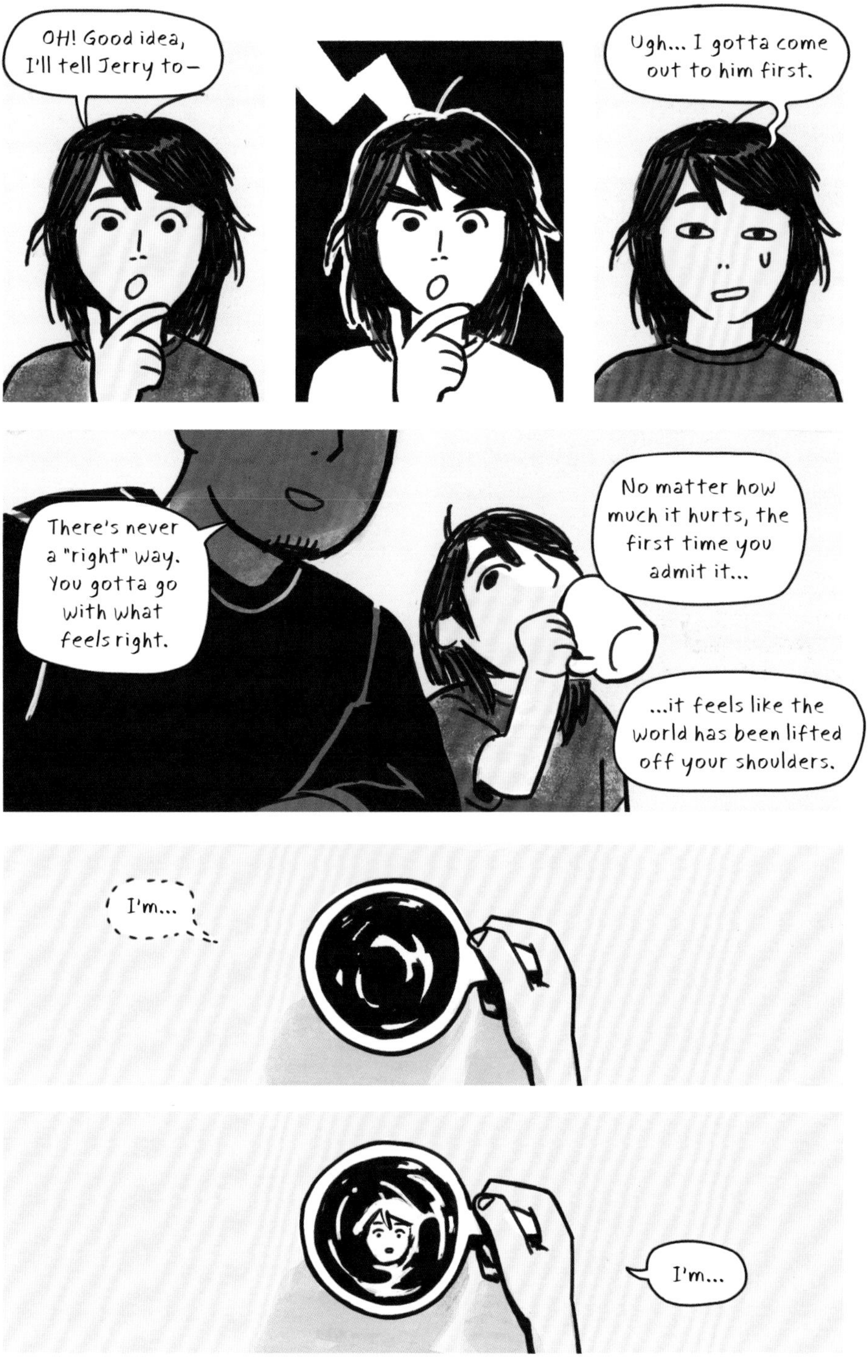
OH! Good idea, I'll tell Jerry to—
Ugh... I gotta come out to him first.
There's never a "right" way. You gotta go with what feels right.
No matter how much it hurts, the first time you admit it...
...it feels like the world has been lifted off your shoulders.
I'm...
I'm...

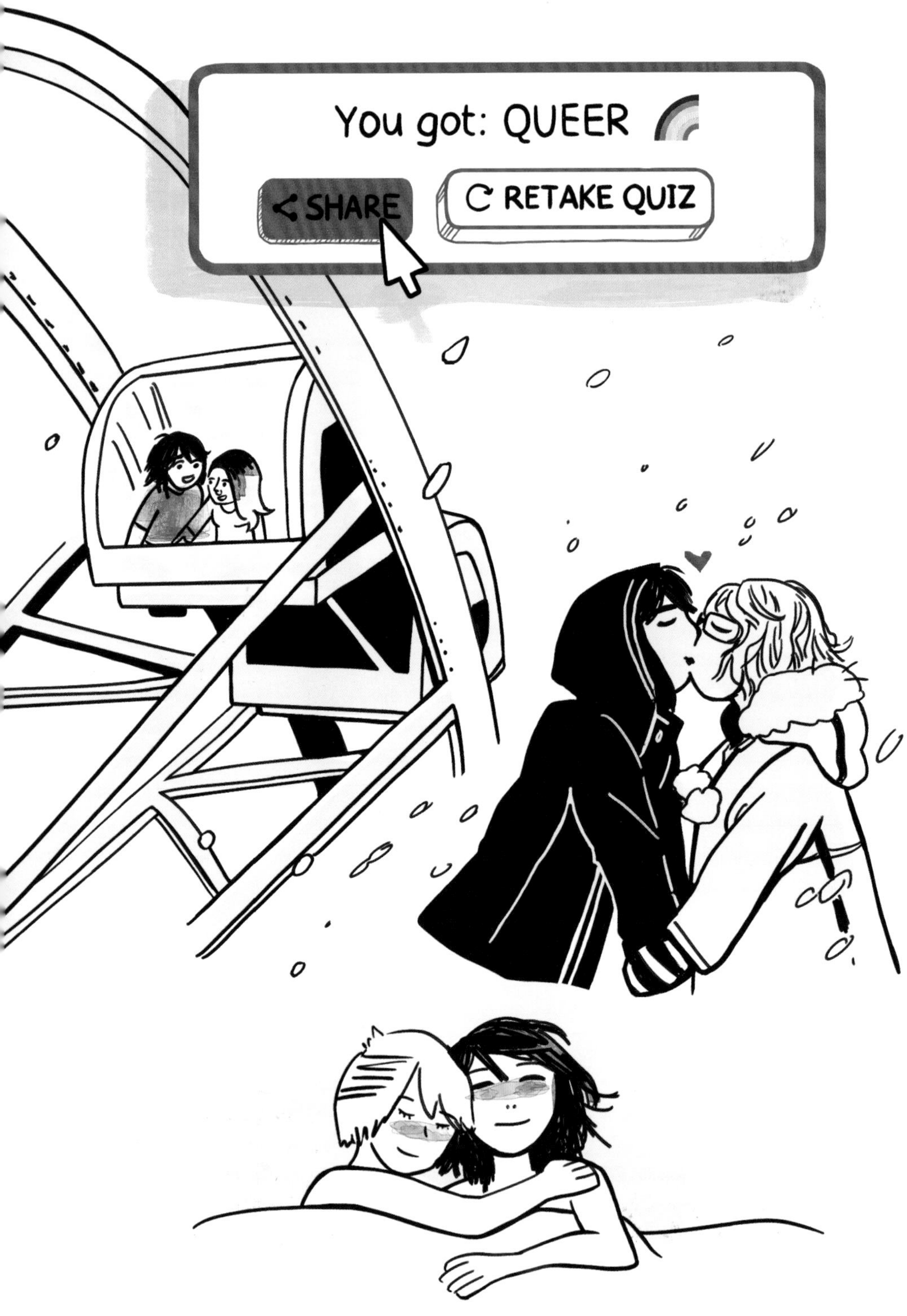
You got: QUEER
SHARE
RETAKE QUIZ

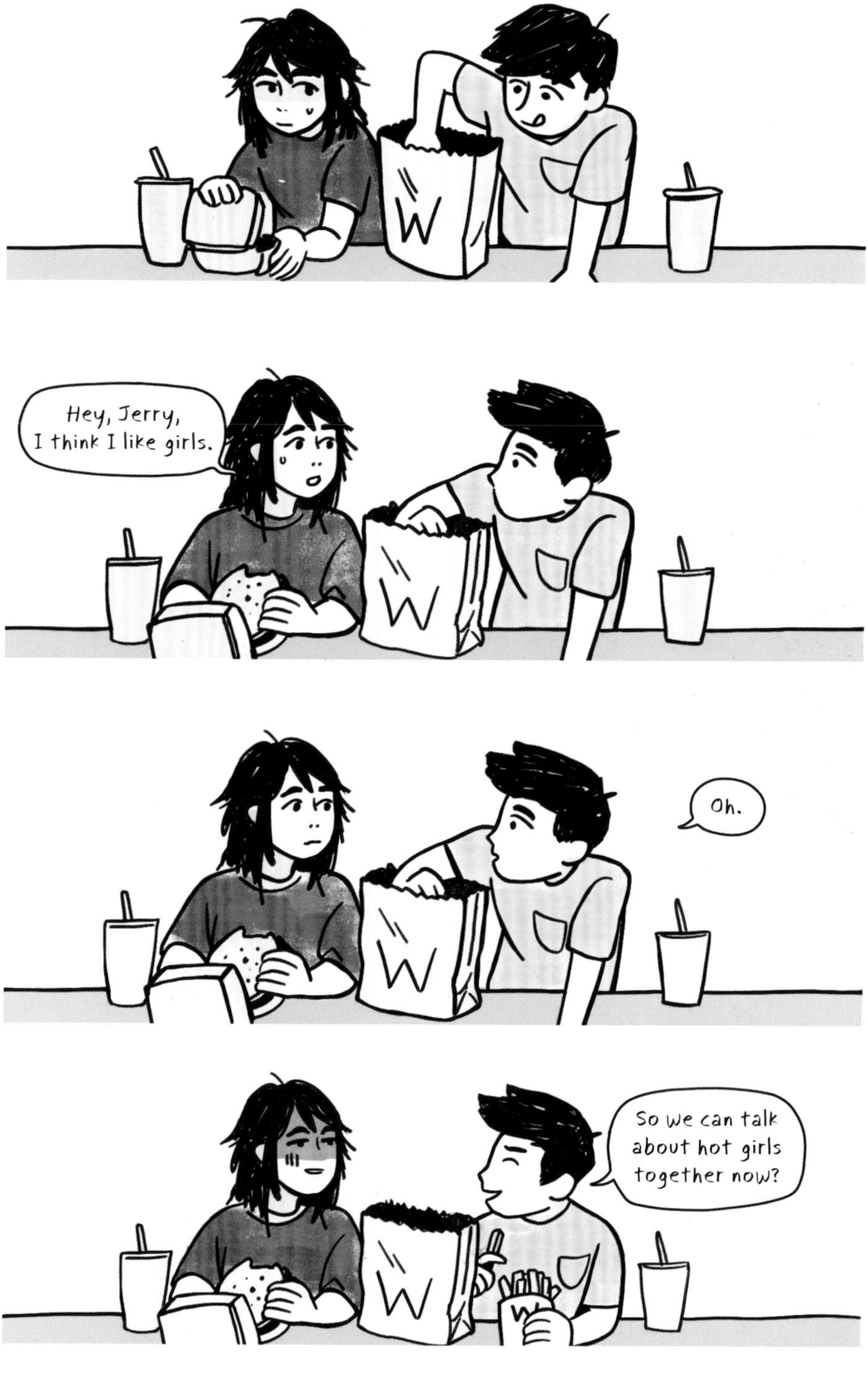
Hey, Jerry, I think I like girls.
Oh.
So we can talk about hot girls together now?

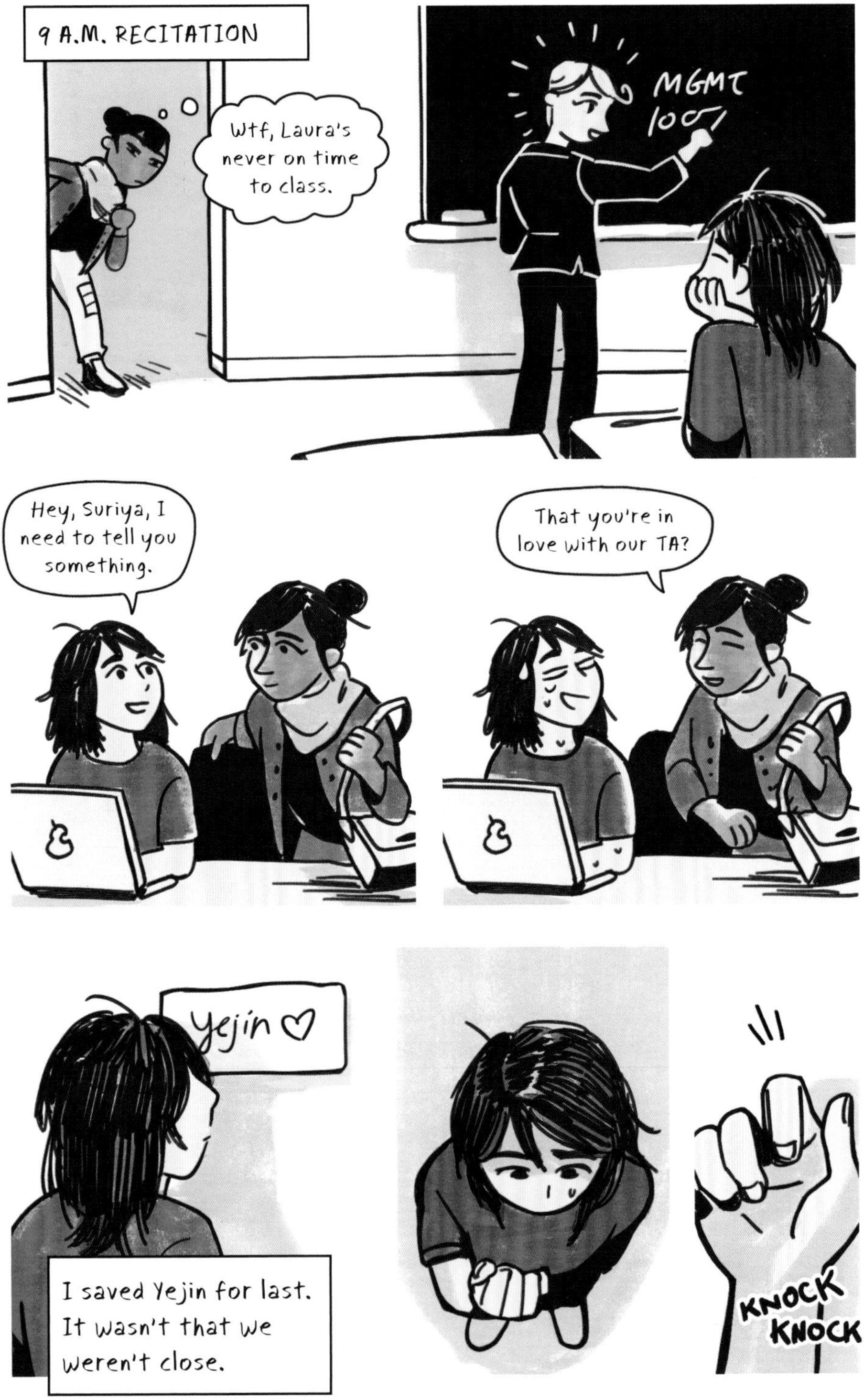
9 A.M. RECITATION
Wtf, Laura's never on time to class.
MGMT 100
Hey, Suriya, I need to tell you something.
That you're in love with our TA?
Yejin ♡
I saved Yejin for last. It wasn't that we weren't close.
KNOCK KNOCK

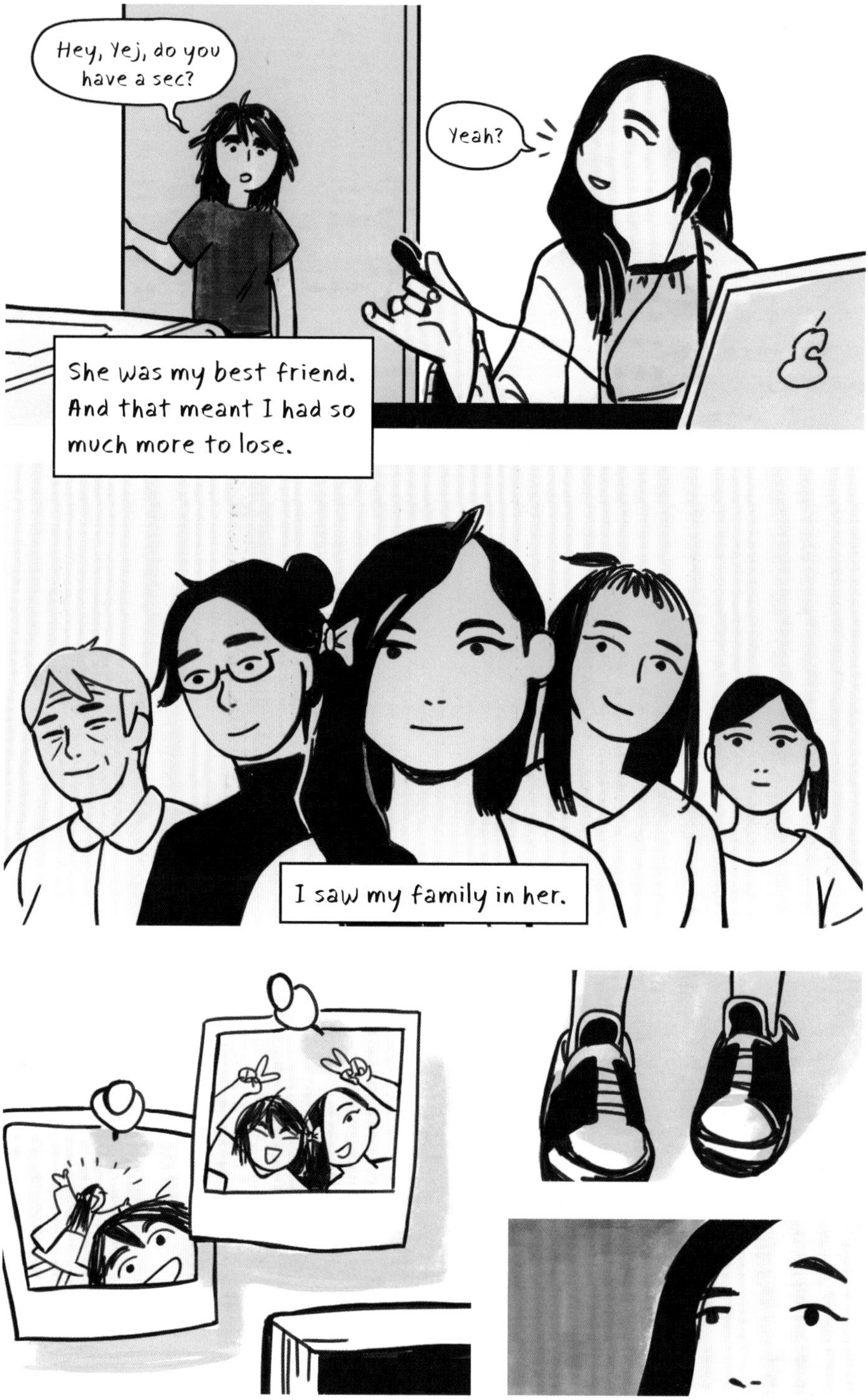
Hey, Yej, do you have a sec?
Yeah?
She was my best friend. And that meant I had so much more to lose.
I saw my family in her.

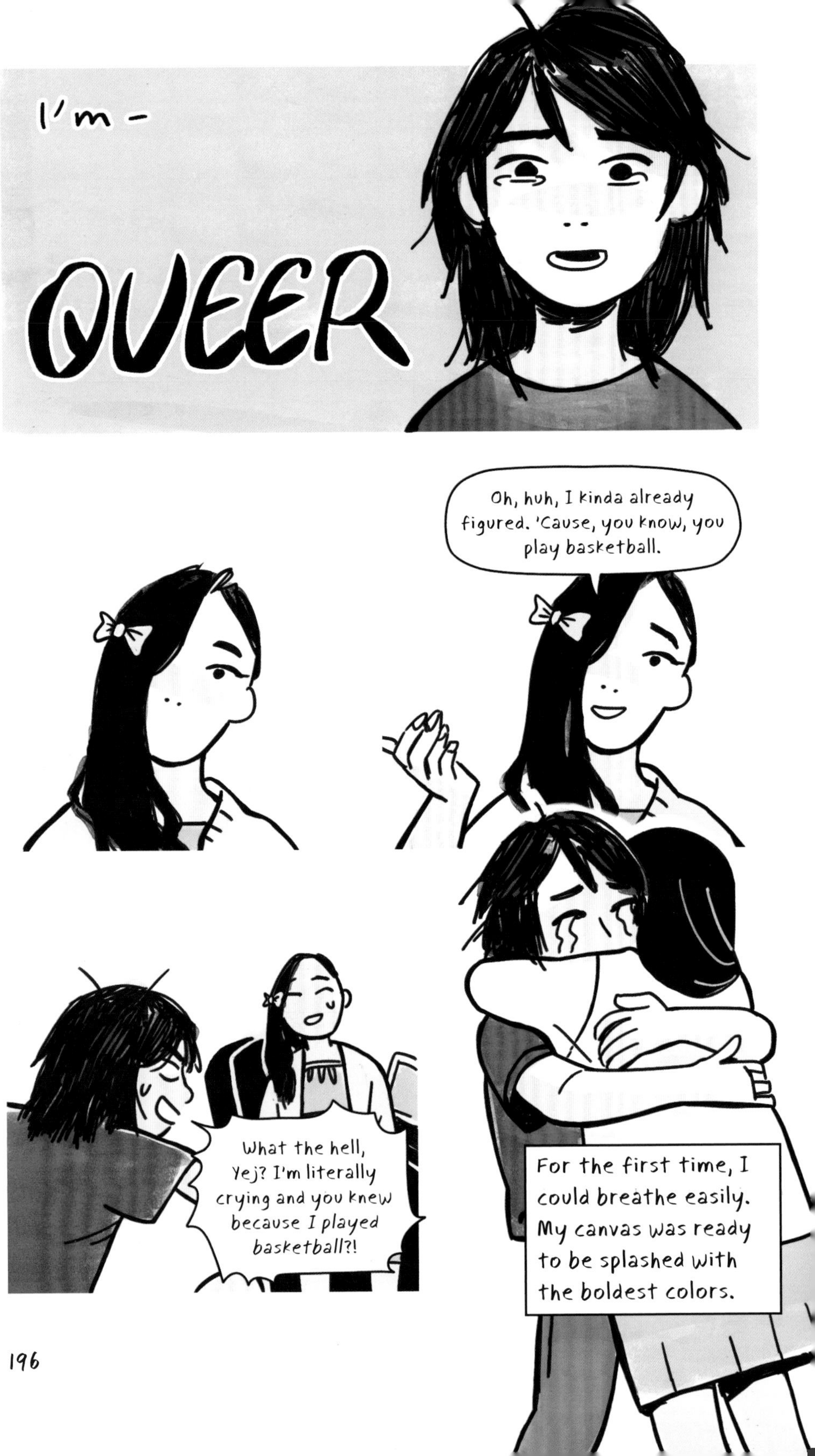
I'm -
QUEER
Oh, huh, I kinda already figured. 'Cause, you know, you play basketball.
What the hell, Yej? I'm literally crying and you knew because I played basketball?!
For the first time, I could breathe easily. My canvas was ready to be splashed with the boldest colors.

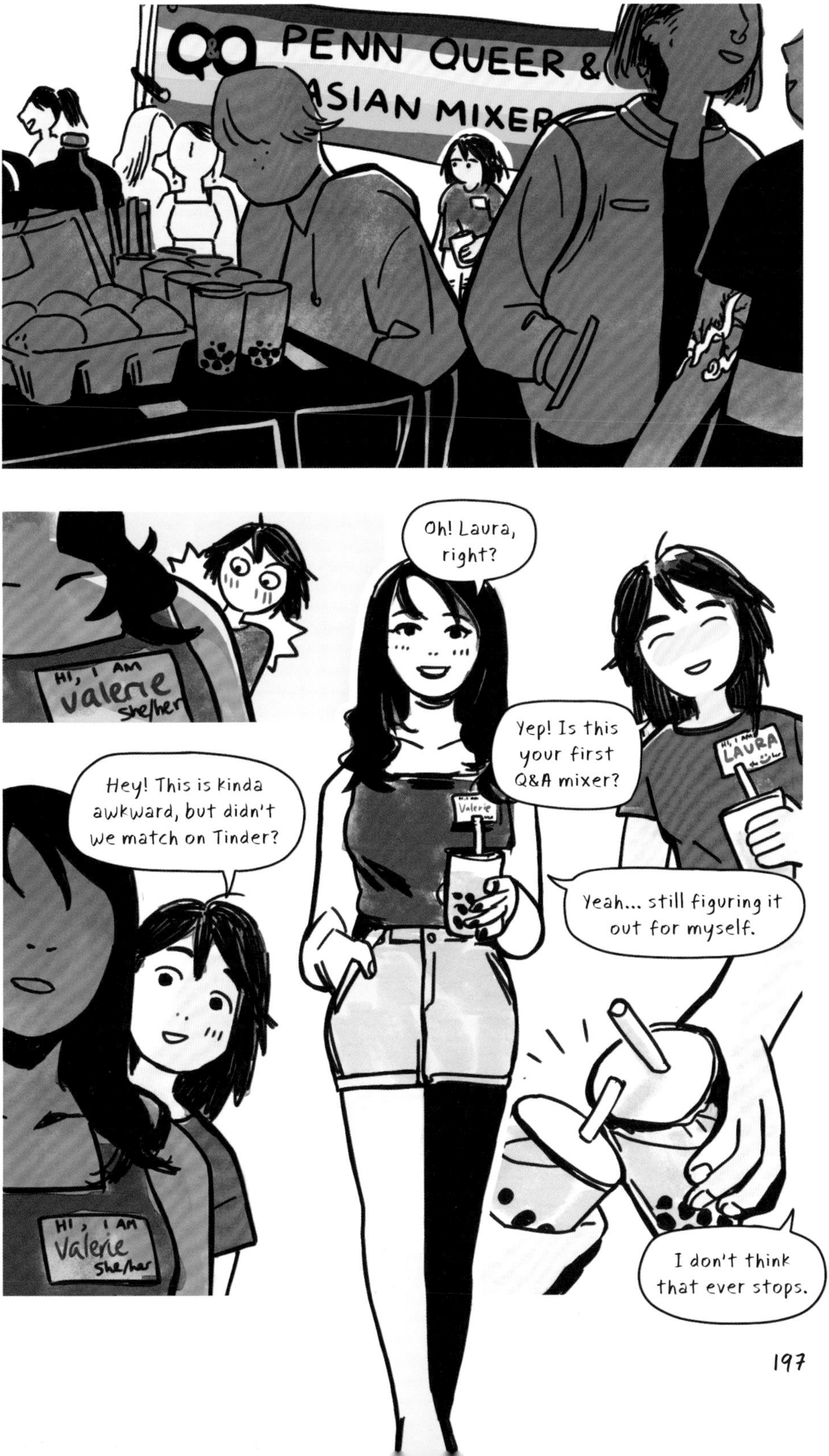
PENN QUEER & ASIAN MIXER
HI, I AM Valerie she/her
Oh! Laura, right?
Yep! Is this your first Q&A mixer?
HI, I AM LAURA
Hey! This is kinda awkward, but didn't we match on Tinder?
Yeah... still figuring it out for myself.
HI, I AM Valerie she/her
I don't think that ever stops.

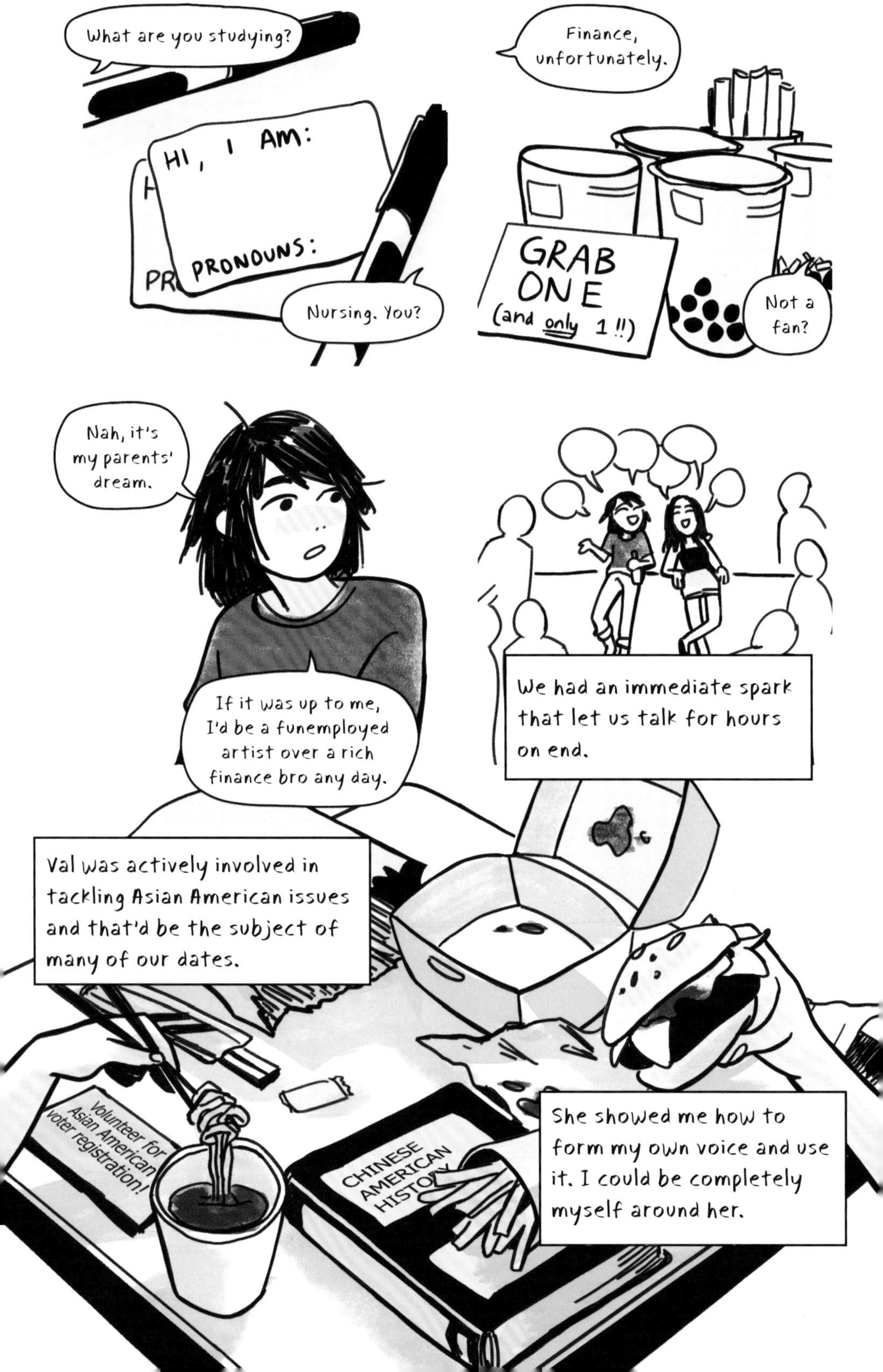
What are you studying?
HI, I AM:
PRONOUNS:
Nursing. You?
Finance, unfortunately.
GRAB ONE (and only 1 !!)
Not a fan?
Nah, it's my parents' dream.
If it was up to me, I'd be a funemployed artist over a rich finance bro any day.
We had an immediate spark that let us talk for hours on end.
Val was actively involved in tackling Asian American issues and that'd be the subject of many of our dates.
Volunteer for Asian American voter registration!
CHINESE AMERICAN HISTORY
She showed me how to form my own voice and use it. I could be completely myself around her.

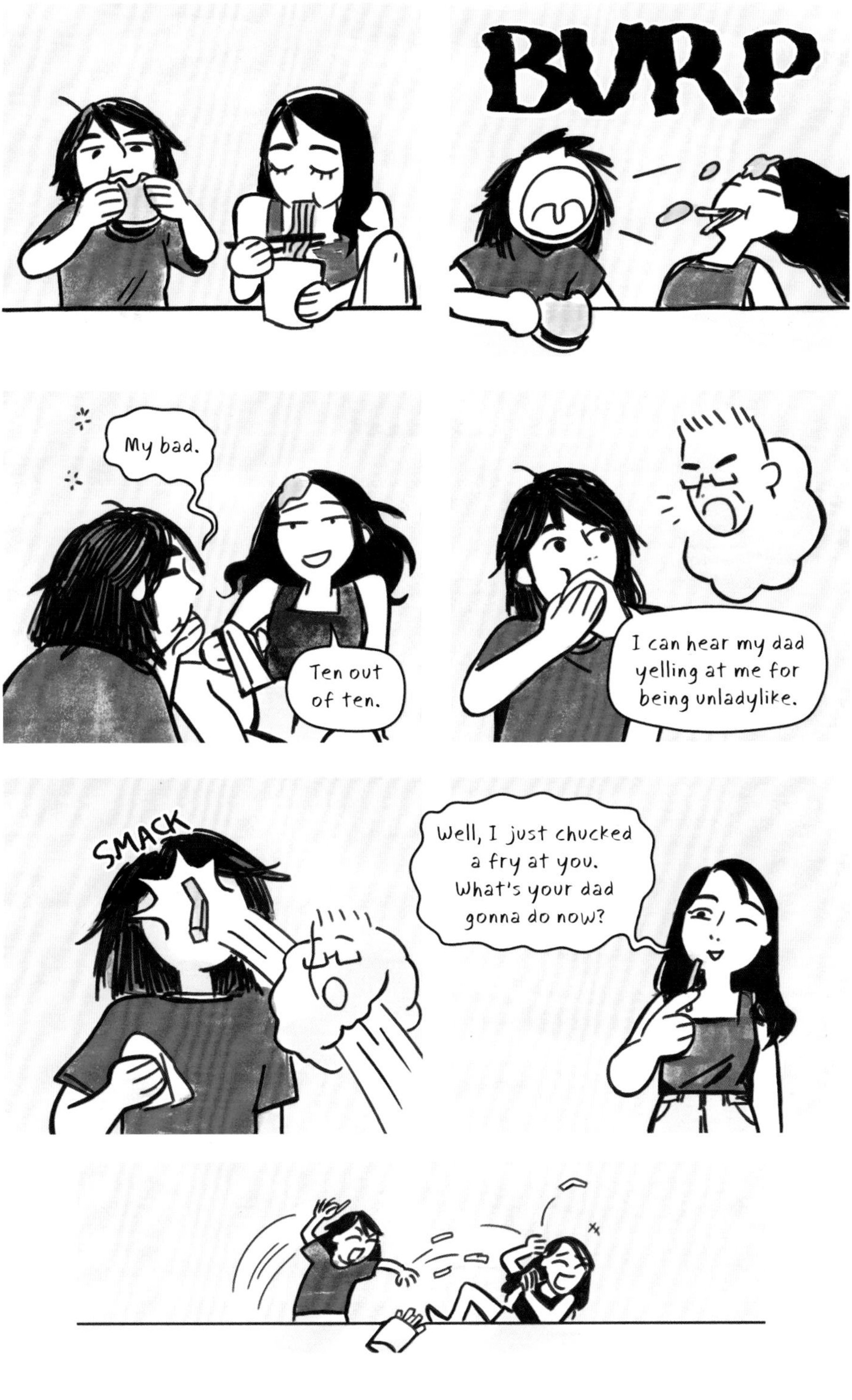
BURP
My bad.
Ten out of ten.
I can hear my dad yelling at me for being unladylike.
SMACK
Well, I just chucked a fry at you. What's your dad gonna do now?

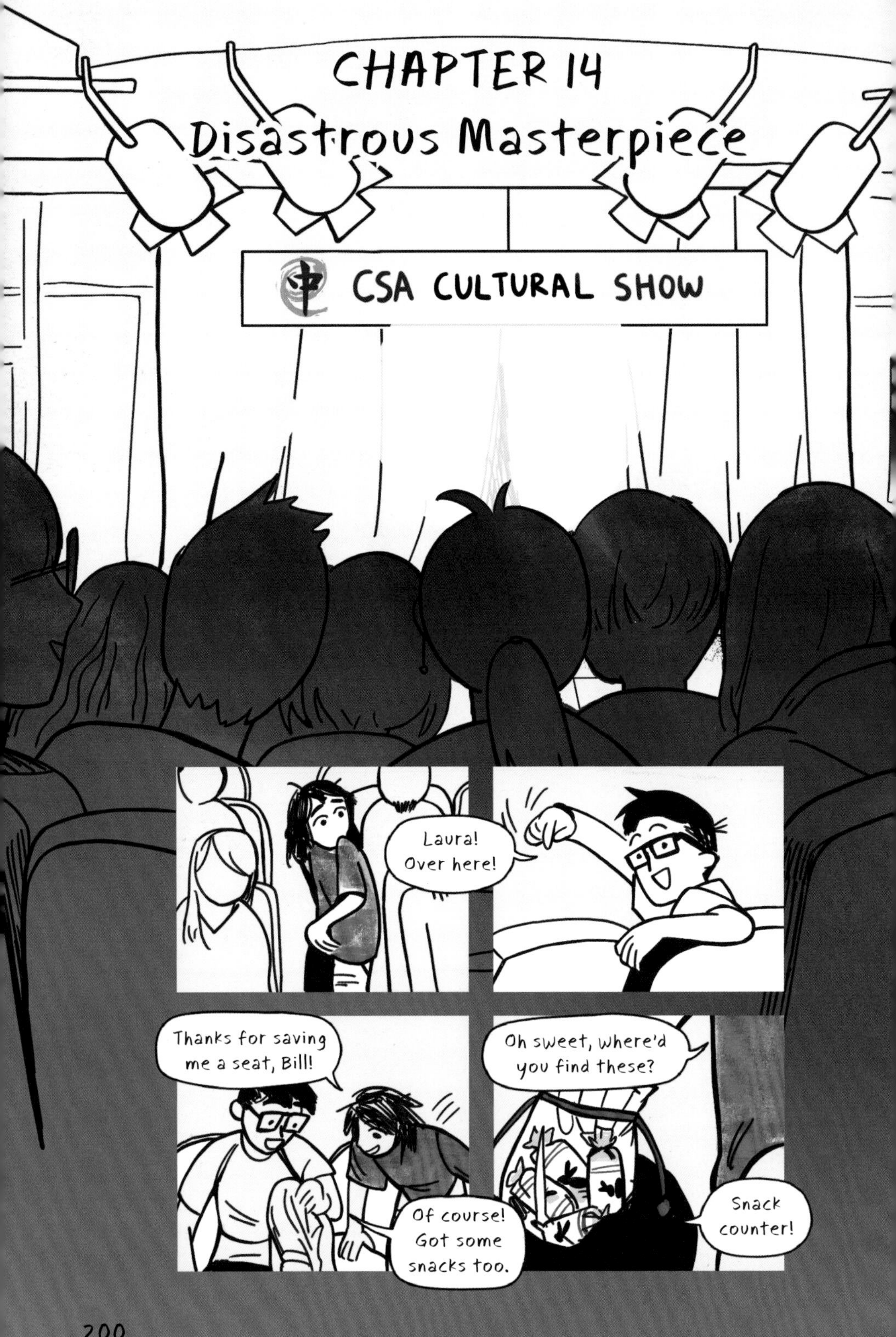
CHAPTER 14
Disastrous Masterpiece
CSA CULTURAL SHOW
Laura! Over here!
Thanks for saving me a seat, Bill!
Of course! Got some snacks too.
Oh sweet, where'd you find these?
Snack counter!

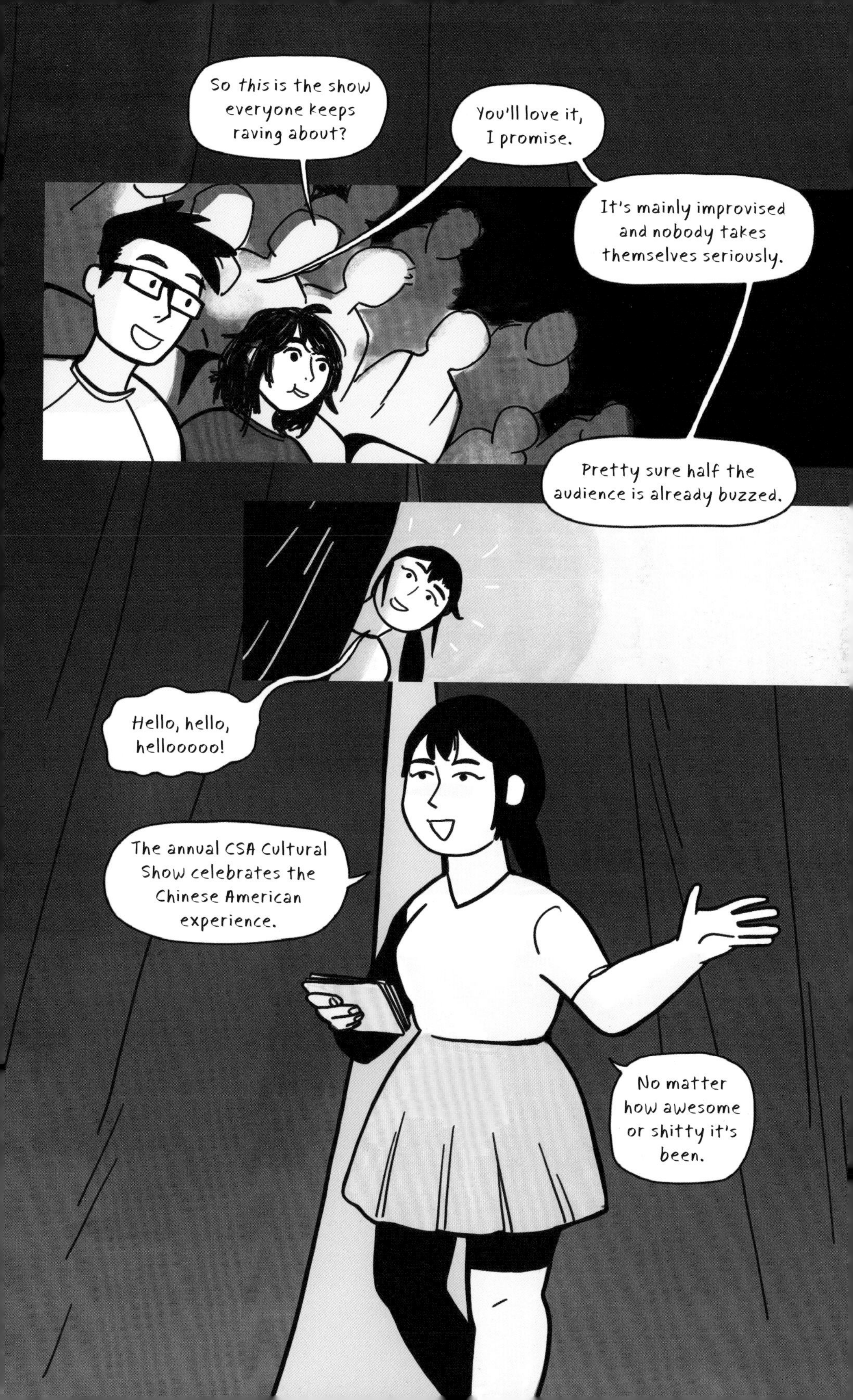
So *this* is the show everyone keeps raving about?
You'll love it, I promise.
It's mainly improvised and nobody takes themselves seriously.
Pretty sure half the audience is already buzzed.
Hello, hello, hellooooo!
The annual CSA Cultural Show celebrates the Chinese American experience.
No matter how awesome or shitty it's been.

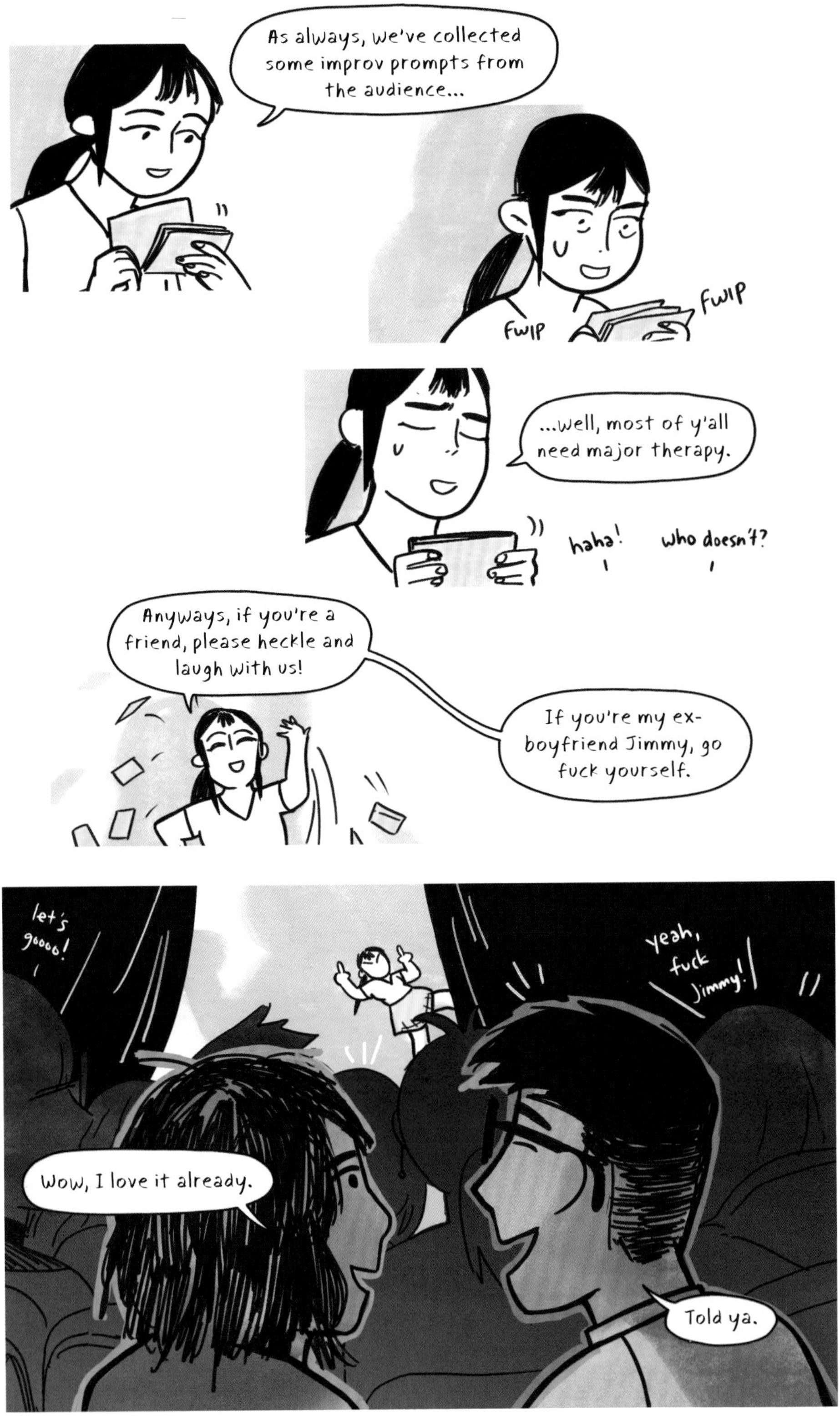

As always, we've collected some improv prompts from the audience...
FWIP
FWIP
...well, most of y'all need major therapy.
haha!
who doesn't?
Anyways, if you're a friend, please heckle and laugh with us!
If you're my ex-boyfriend Jimmy, go fuck yourself.
let's goooo!
yeah, fuck Jimmy!
Wow, I love it already.
Told ya.

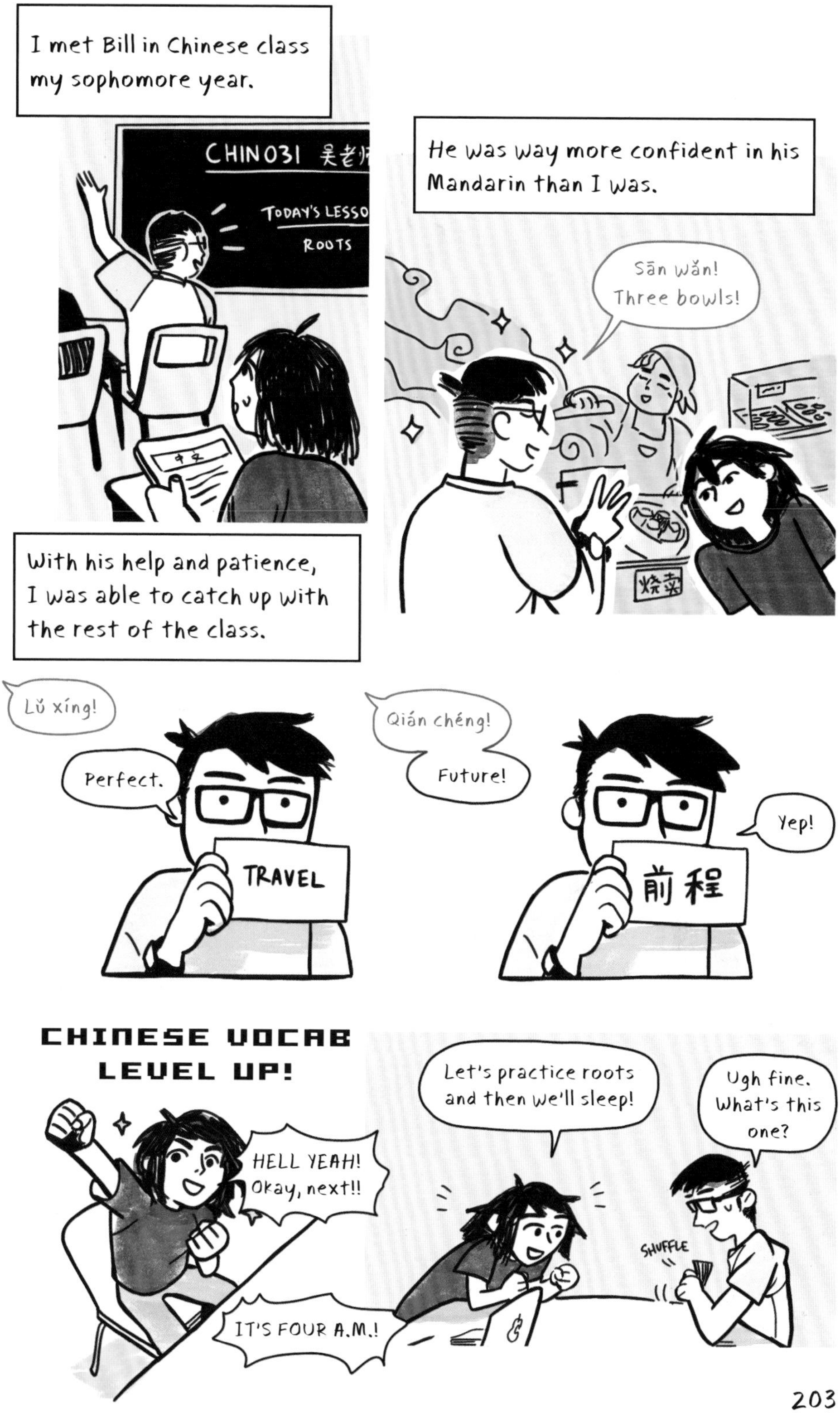
I met Bill in Chinese class my sophomore year.
CHIN031 吴老师
TODAY'S LESSO
ROOTS
中文
He was way more confident in his Mandarin than I was.
Sān wǎn!
Three bowls!
烧菜
With his help and patience, I was able to catch up with the rest of the class.
Lǚ xíng!
Perfect.
TRAVEL
Qián chéng!
Future!
Yep!
前程
CHINESE VOCAB LEVEL UP!
HELL YEAH! Okay, next!!
Let's practice roots and then we'll sleep!
Ugh fine. What's this one?
SHUFFLE
IT'S FOUR A.M.!

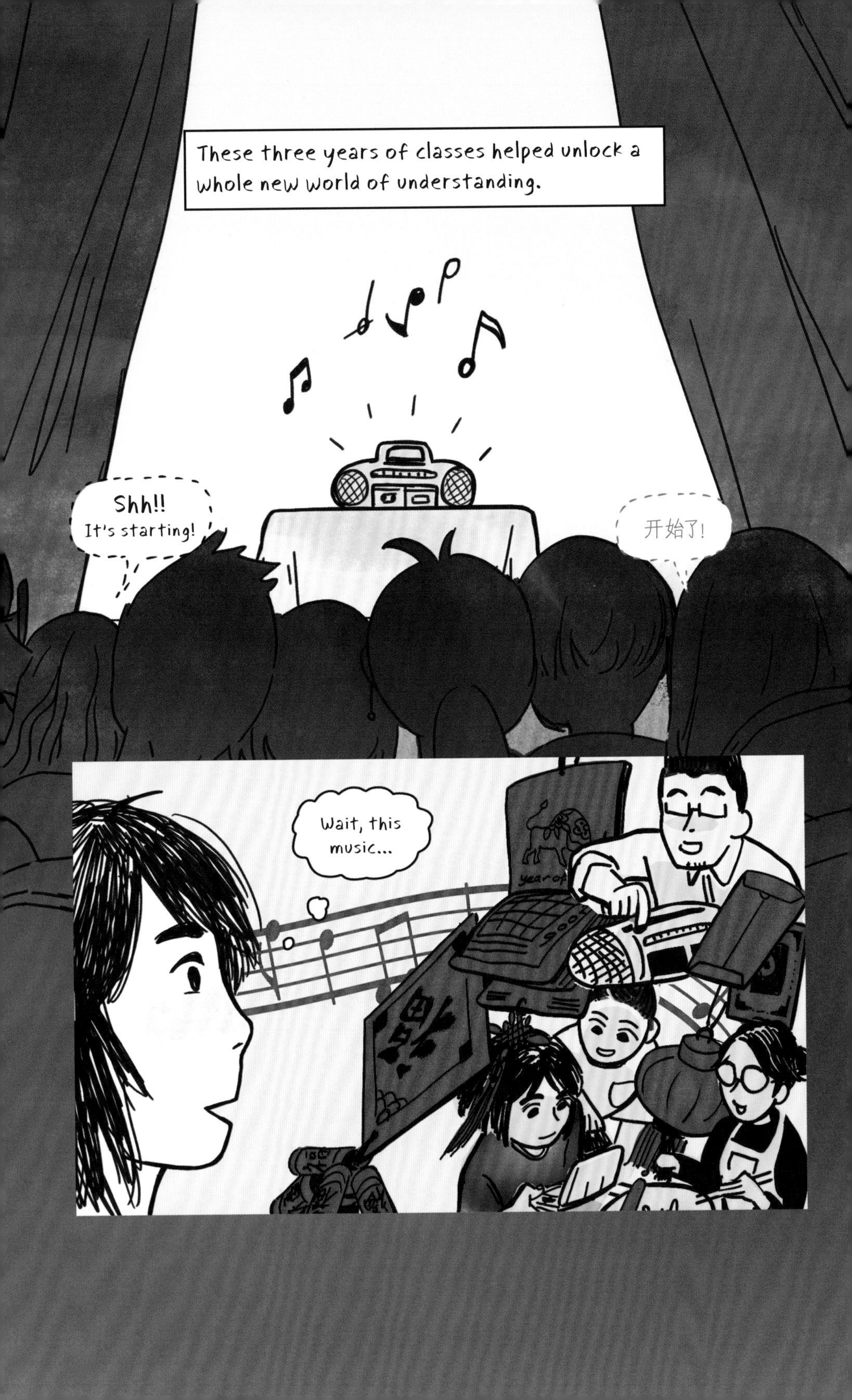
These three years of classes helped unlock a whole new world of understanding.
Shh!! It's starting!
开始了!
Wait, this music...

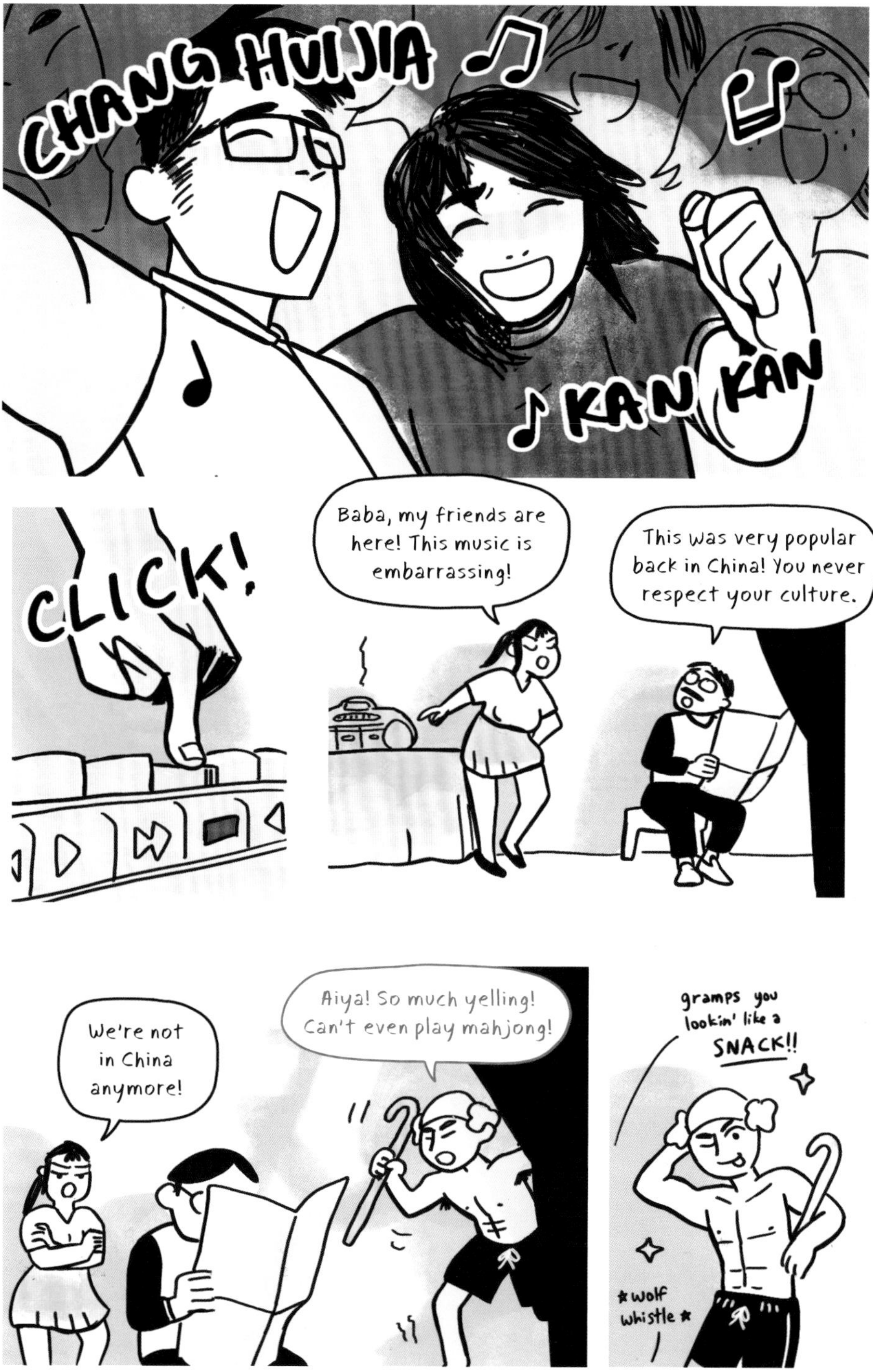
CHANG HUIJIA
KAN KAN
CLICK!
Baba, my friends are here! This music is embarrassing!
This was very popular back in China! You never respect your culture.
We're not in China anymore!
Aiya! So much yelling! Can't even play mahjong!
gramps you lookin' like a SNACK!!
wolf whistle

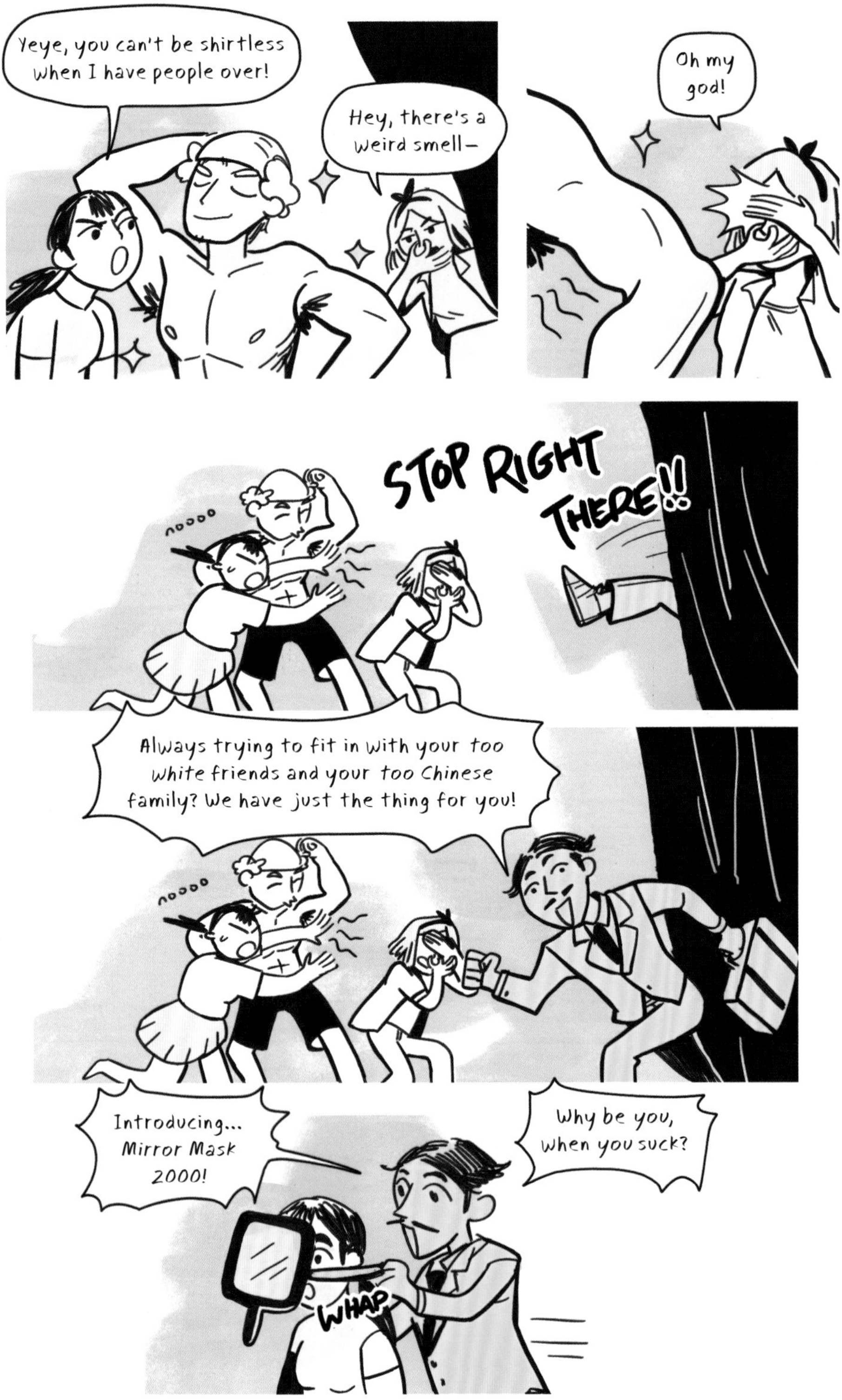

Yeye, you can't be shirtless when I have people over!
Hey, there's a weird smell—
Oh my god!
STOP RIGHT THERE!!
noooo
Always trying to fit in with your too white friends and your too Chinese family? We have just the thing for you!
noooo
Introducing... Mirror Mask 2000!
Why be you, when you suck?
WHAP

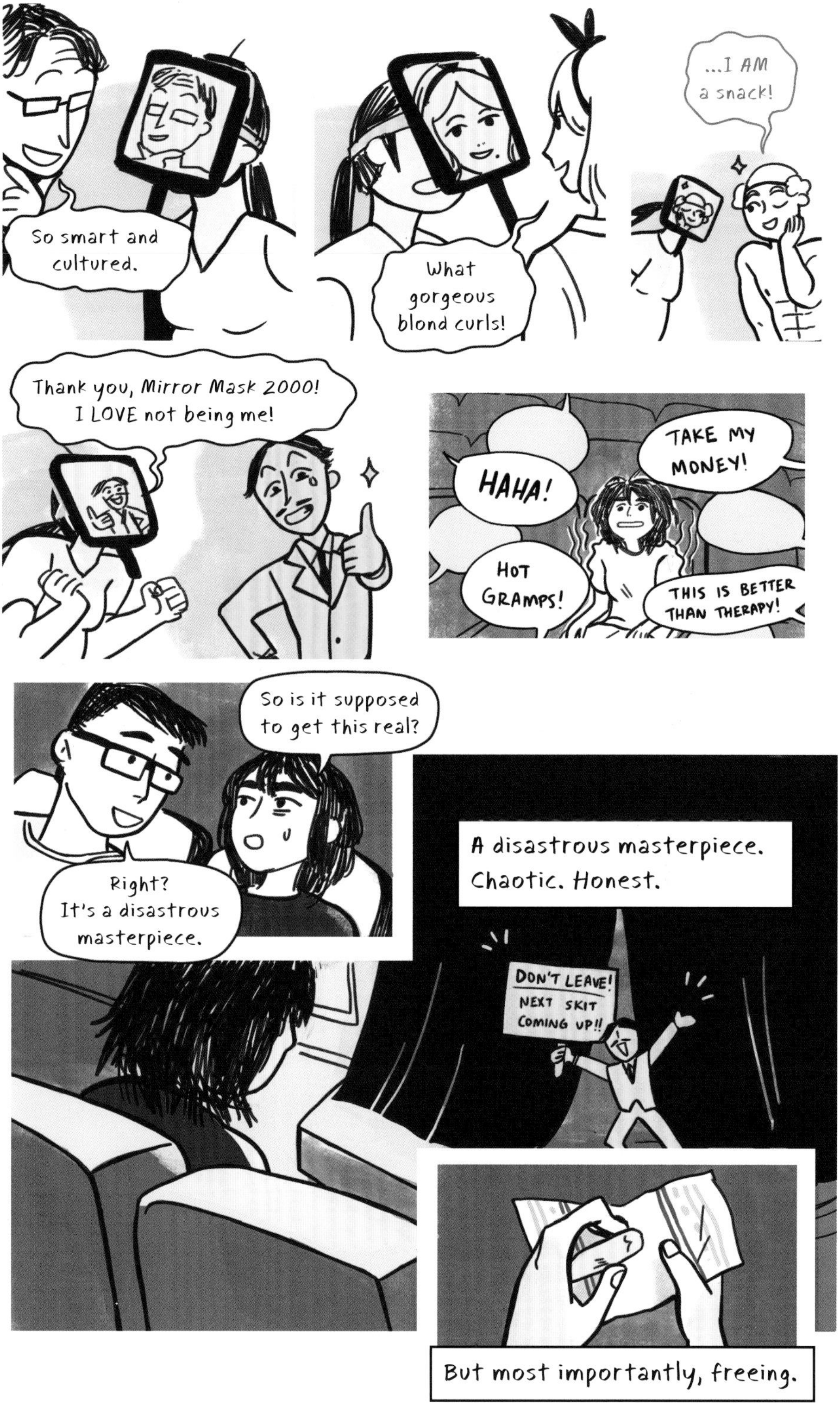

So smart and cultured.
What gorgeous blond curls!
...I AM a snack!
Thank you, Mirror Mask 2000! I LOVE not being me!
HAHA!
TAKE MY MONEY!
HOT GRAMPS!
THIS IS BETTER THAN THERAPY!
So is it supposed to get this real?
Right? It's a disastrous masterpiece.
A disastrous masterpiece. Chaotic. Honest.
DON'T LEAVE! NEXT SKIT COMING UP!!
But most importantly, freeing.

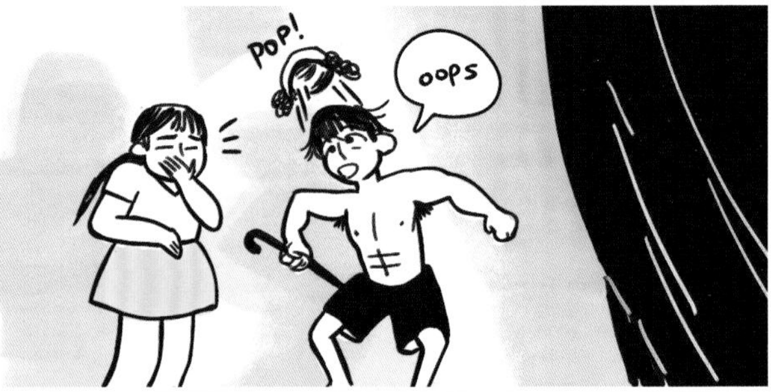
POP!
oops

The show had no structure or script. Botched lines were thrown around as frequently as props and popcorn were.

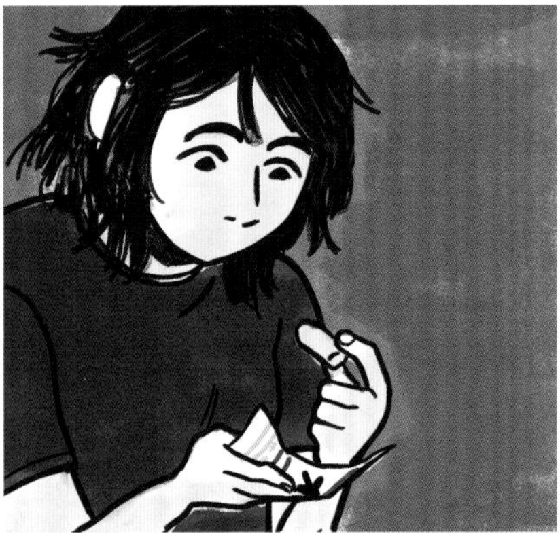

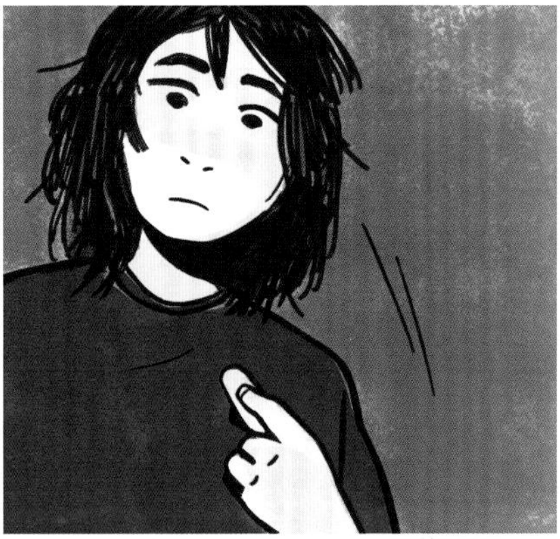

But no matter the amount of cheers or jeers, the performers kept going. Sometimes, they ran with cues from the audience. Other times, they just figured it out as they went.

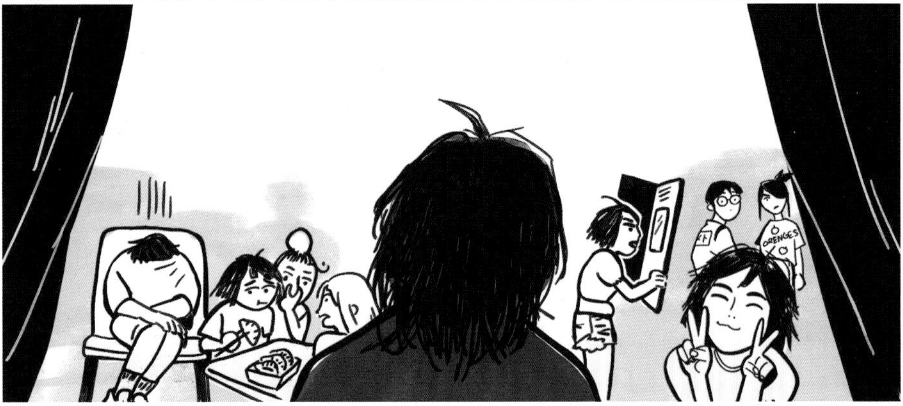
ORENGES

But no matter how much of a formless mess the show felt...

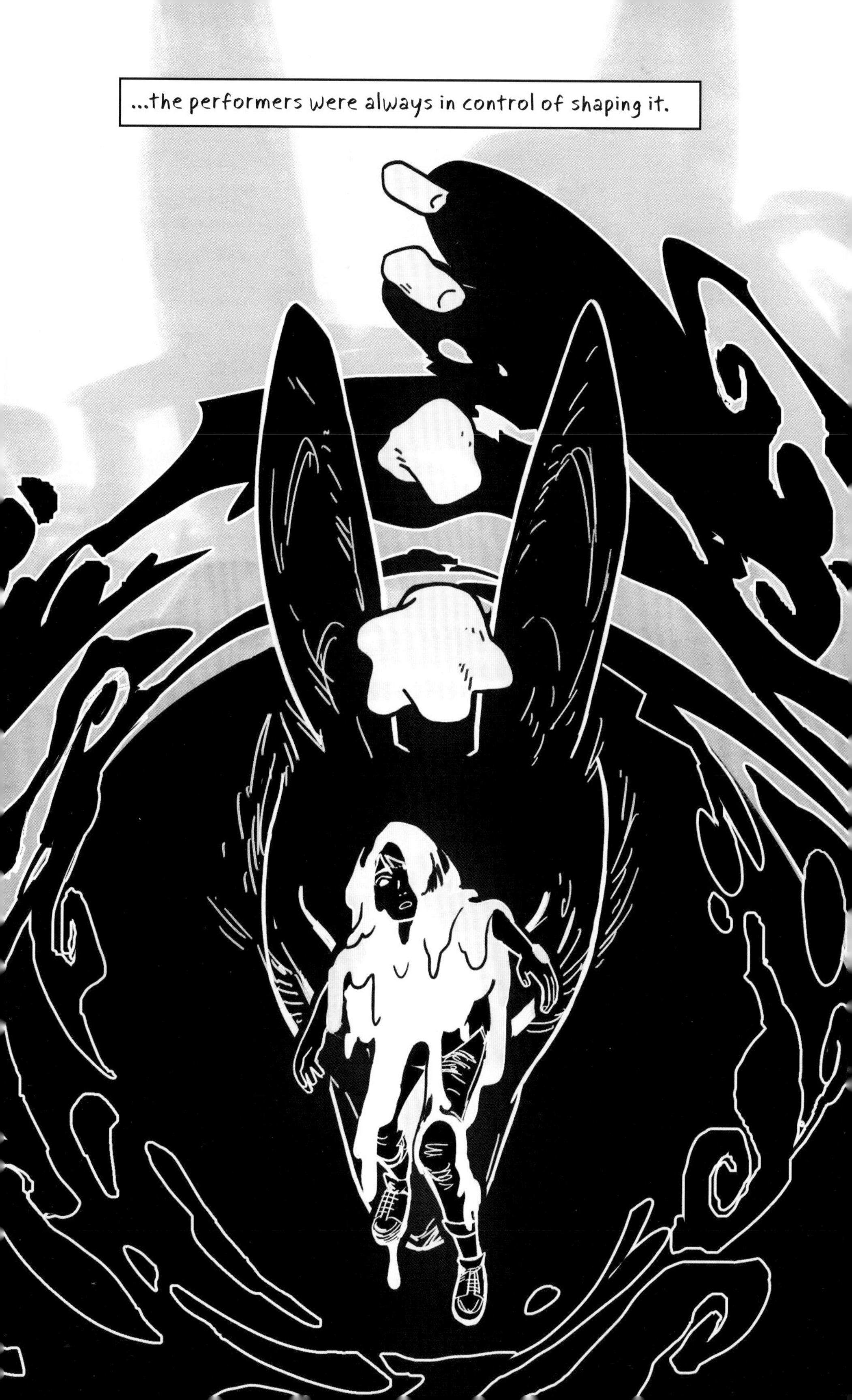
...the performers were always in control of shaping it.

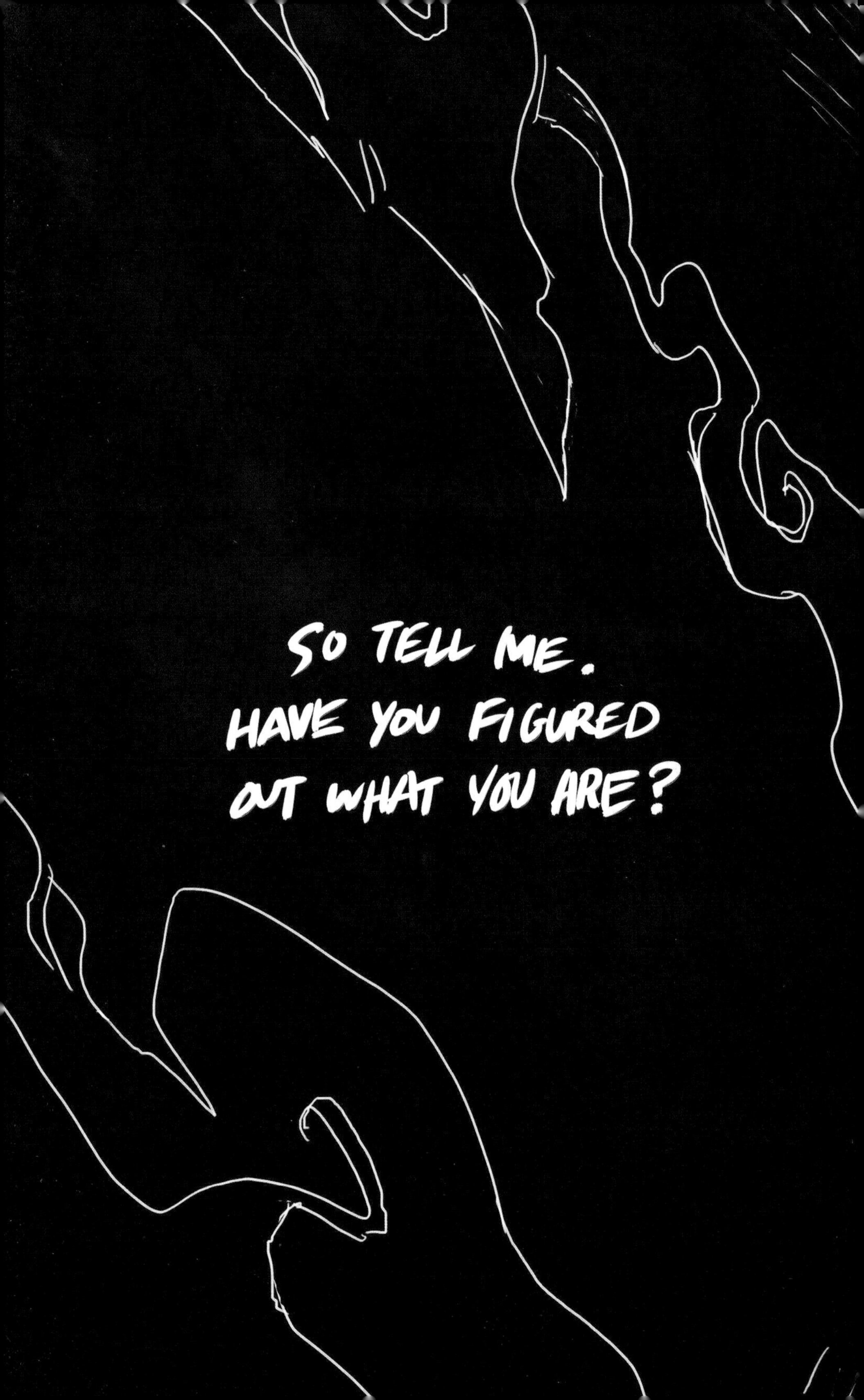
SO TELL ME.
HAVE YOU FIGURED
OUT WHAT YOU ARE?

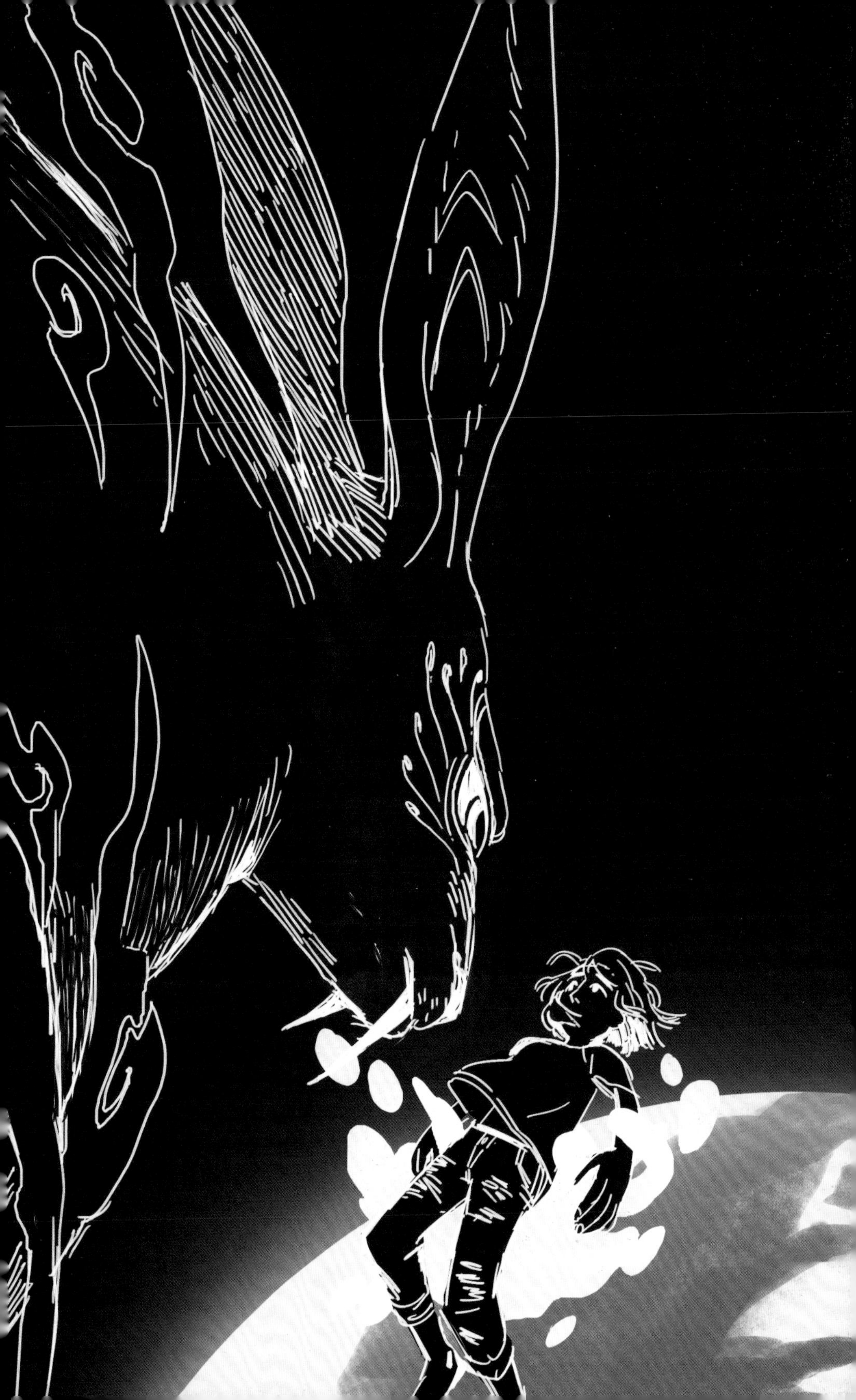

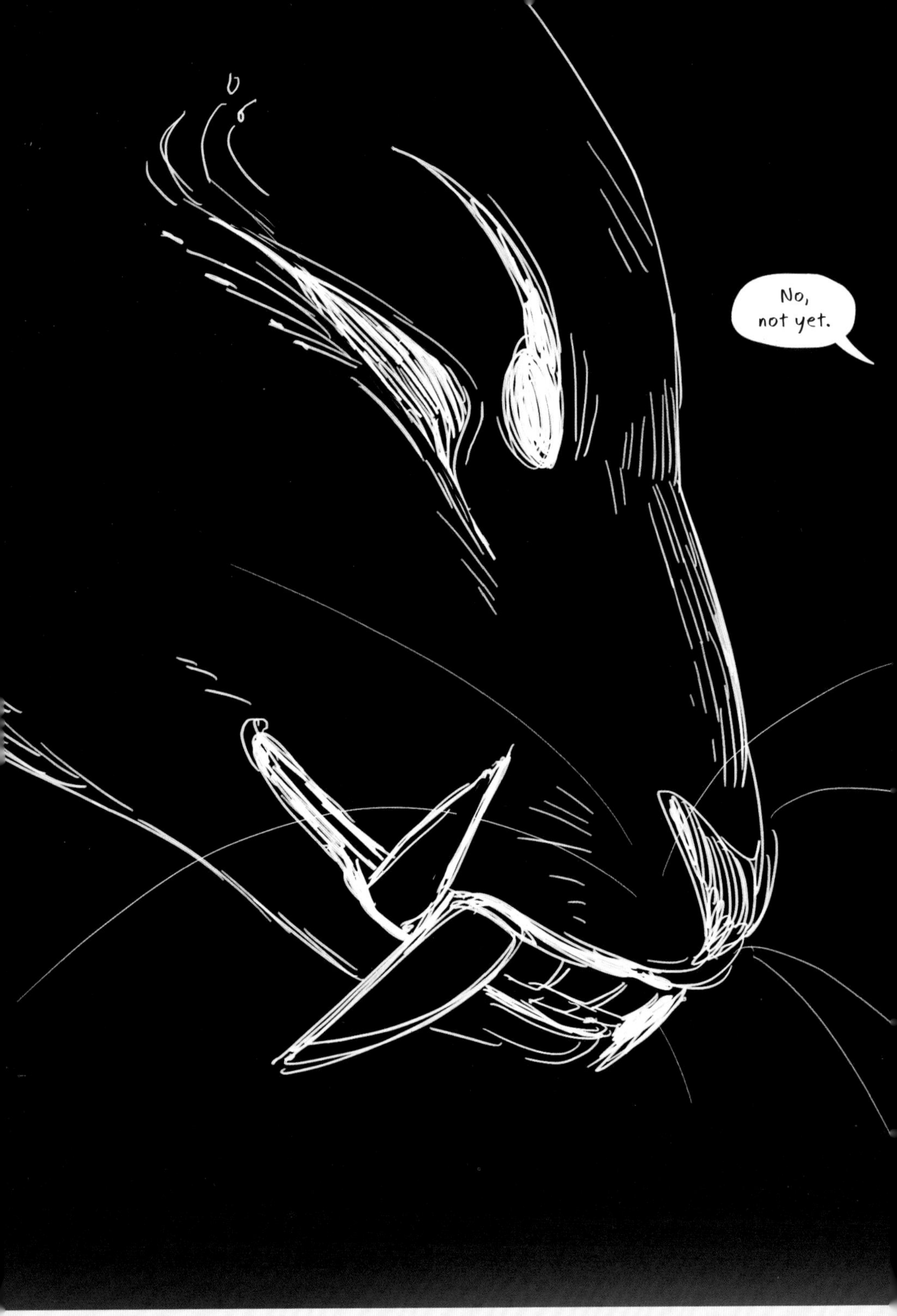
No, not yet.

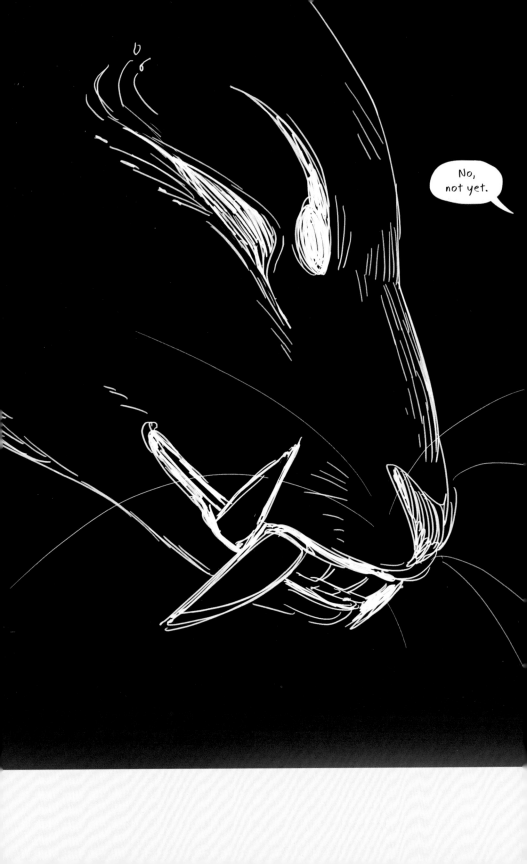

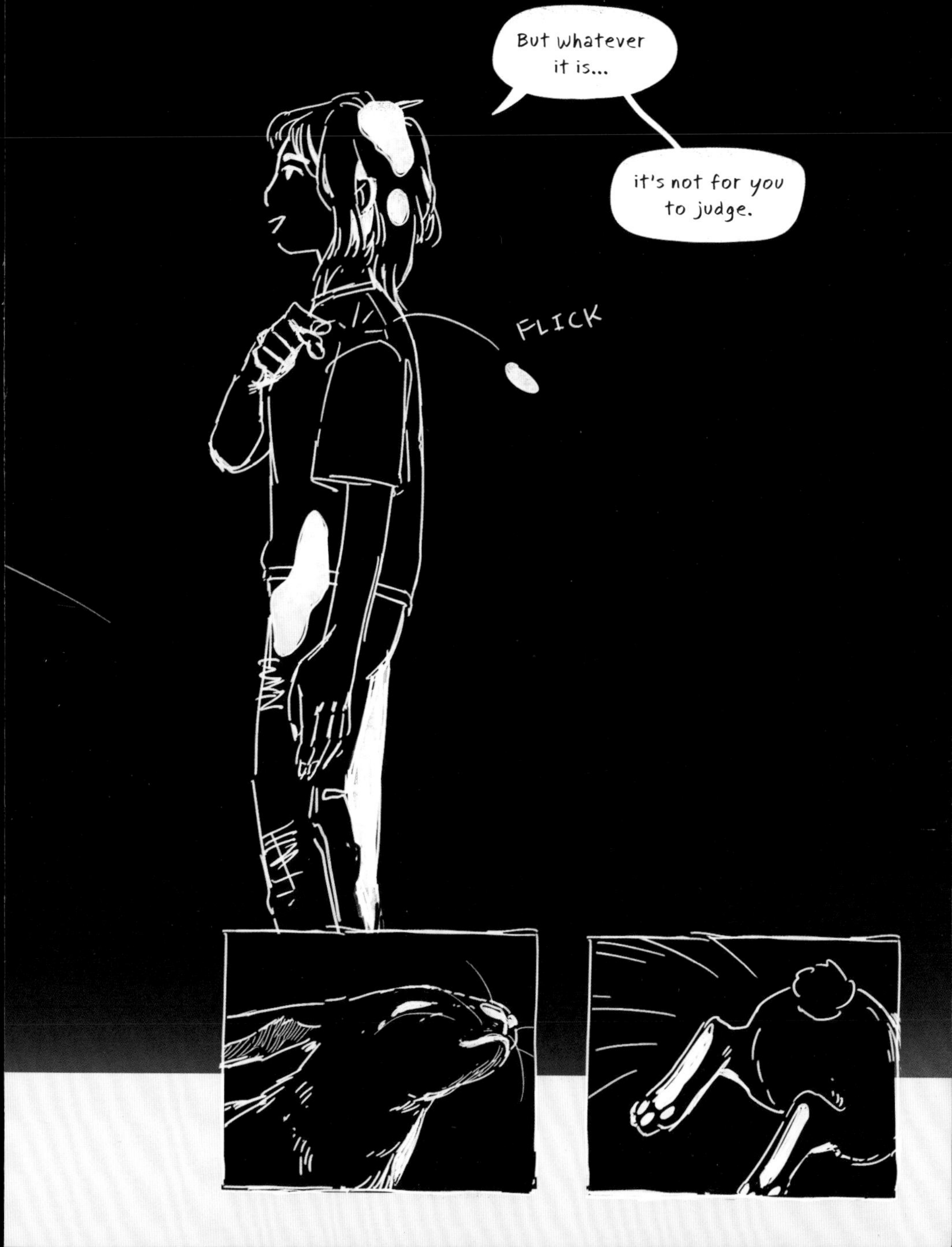
But whatever it is...
it's not for you to judge.
FLICK

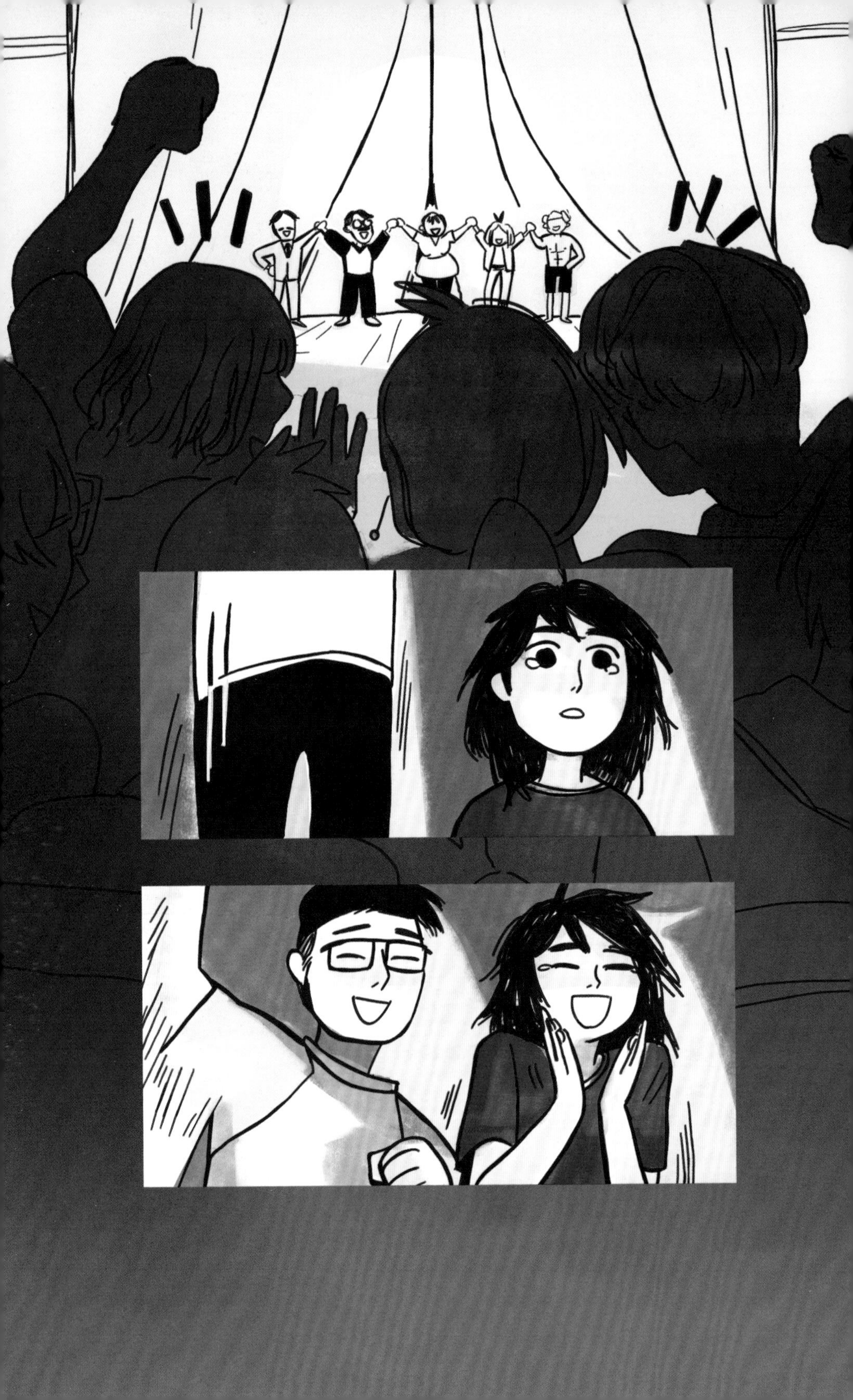

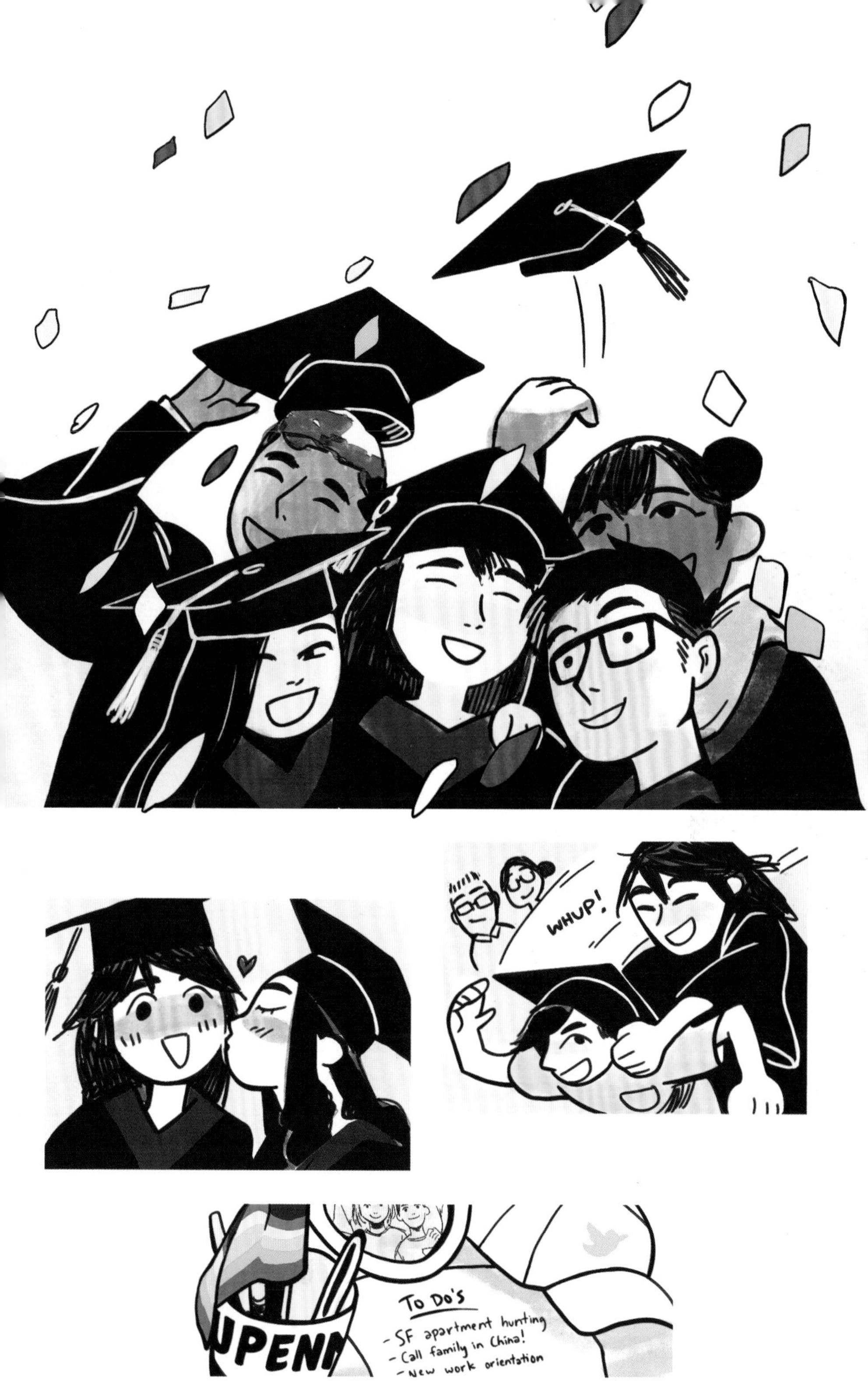
WHUP!
To Do's
- SF apartment hunting
- Call family in China!
- New work orientation
UPENN

CHAPTER 15
Baysian on the Best Coast

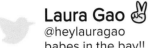

Laura Gao ✌
@heylauragao
babes in the bay!! #westcoastbestcoast

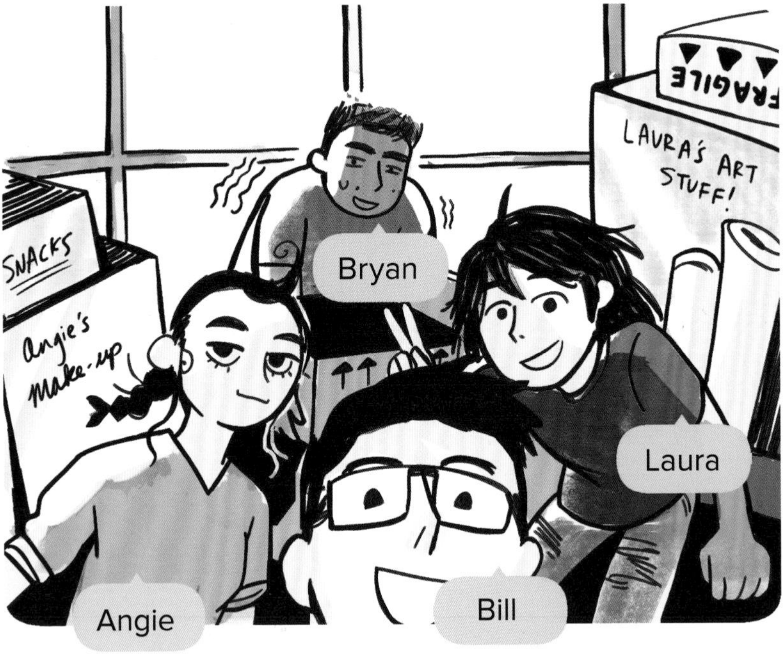
FRAGILE
LAURA'S ART STUFF!
SNACKS
Angie's make-up
Bryan
Laura
Angie
Bill

3 Retweets 24 Likes

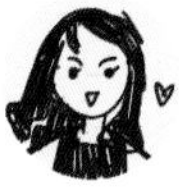

Val @bai-baibai · 1hr
Cuties <33333

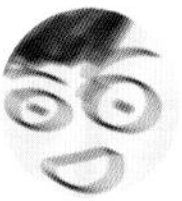

Jerry @the-gaot · 5min
take me with u pls

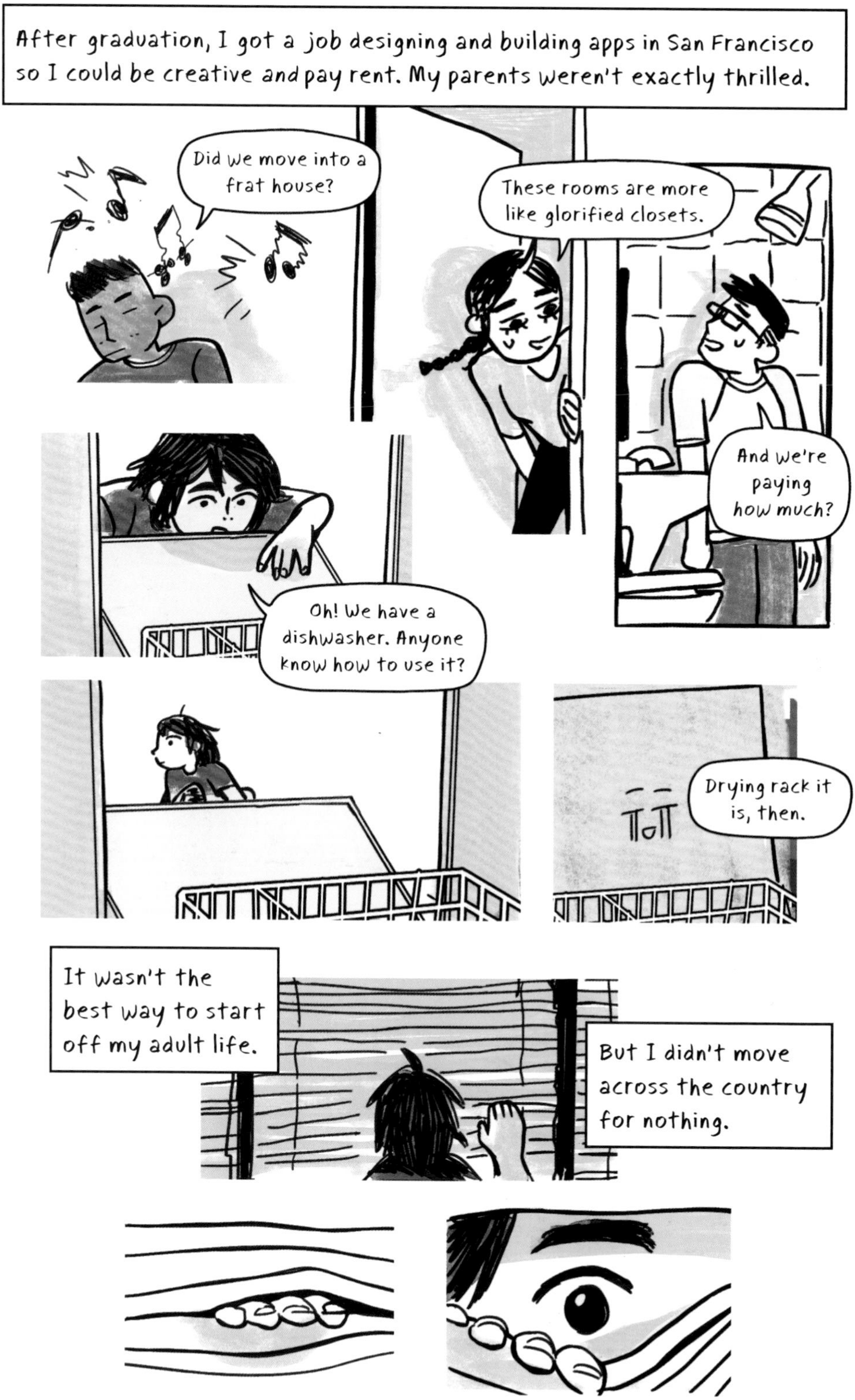
After graduation, I got a job designing and building apps in San Francisco so I could be creative and pay rent. My parents weren't exactly thrilled.
Did we move into a frat house?
These rooms are more like glorified closets.
And we're paying how much?
Oh! We have a dishwasher. Anyone know how to use it?
Drying rack it is, then.
It wasn't the best way to start off my adult life.
But I didn't move across the country for nothing.

I was going to live my life.

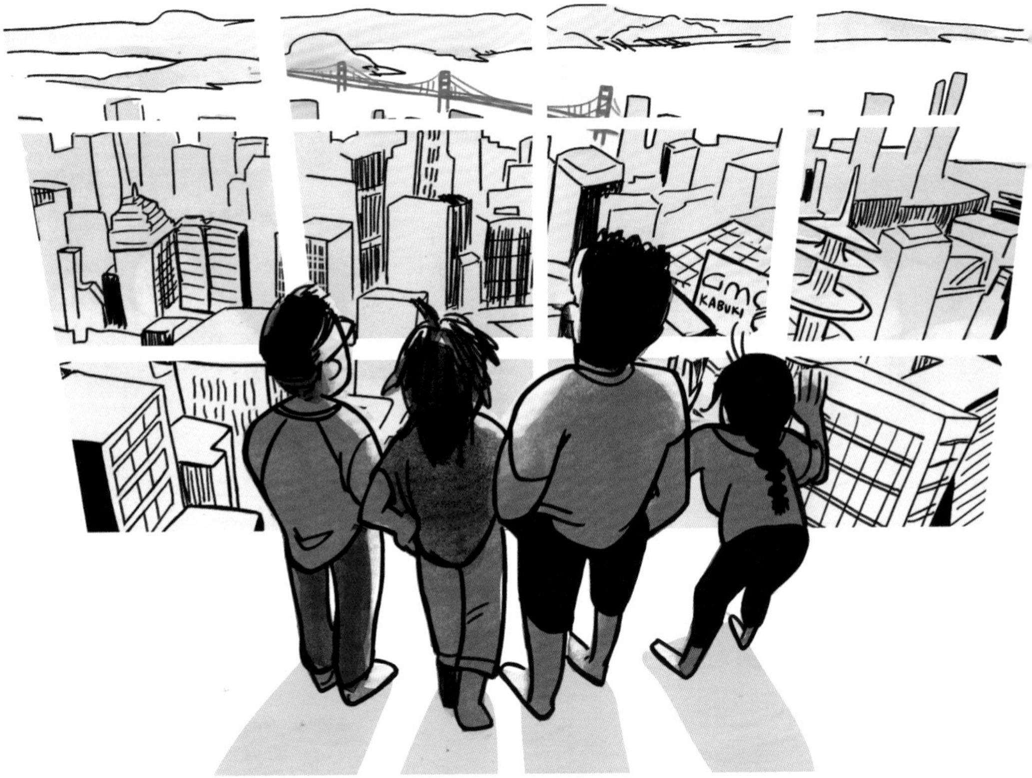
KABUKI

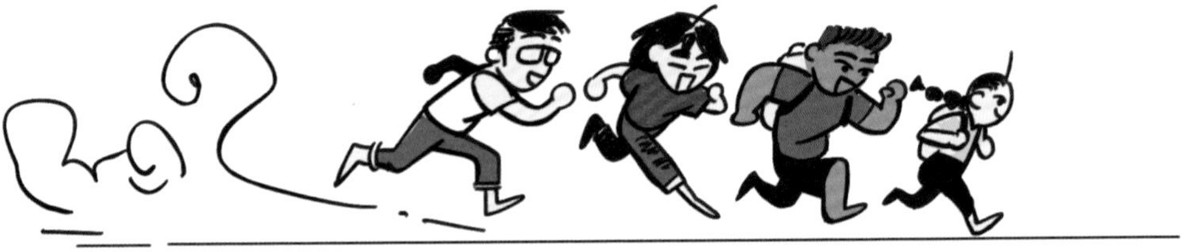

We were all immigrant kids—Angie and I Chinese-American, Bill Chinese-Canadian, and Bryan Mexican-American.

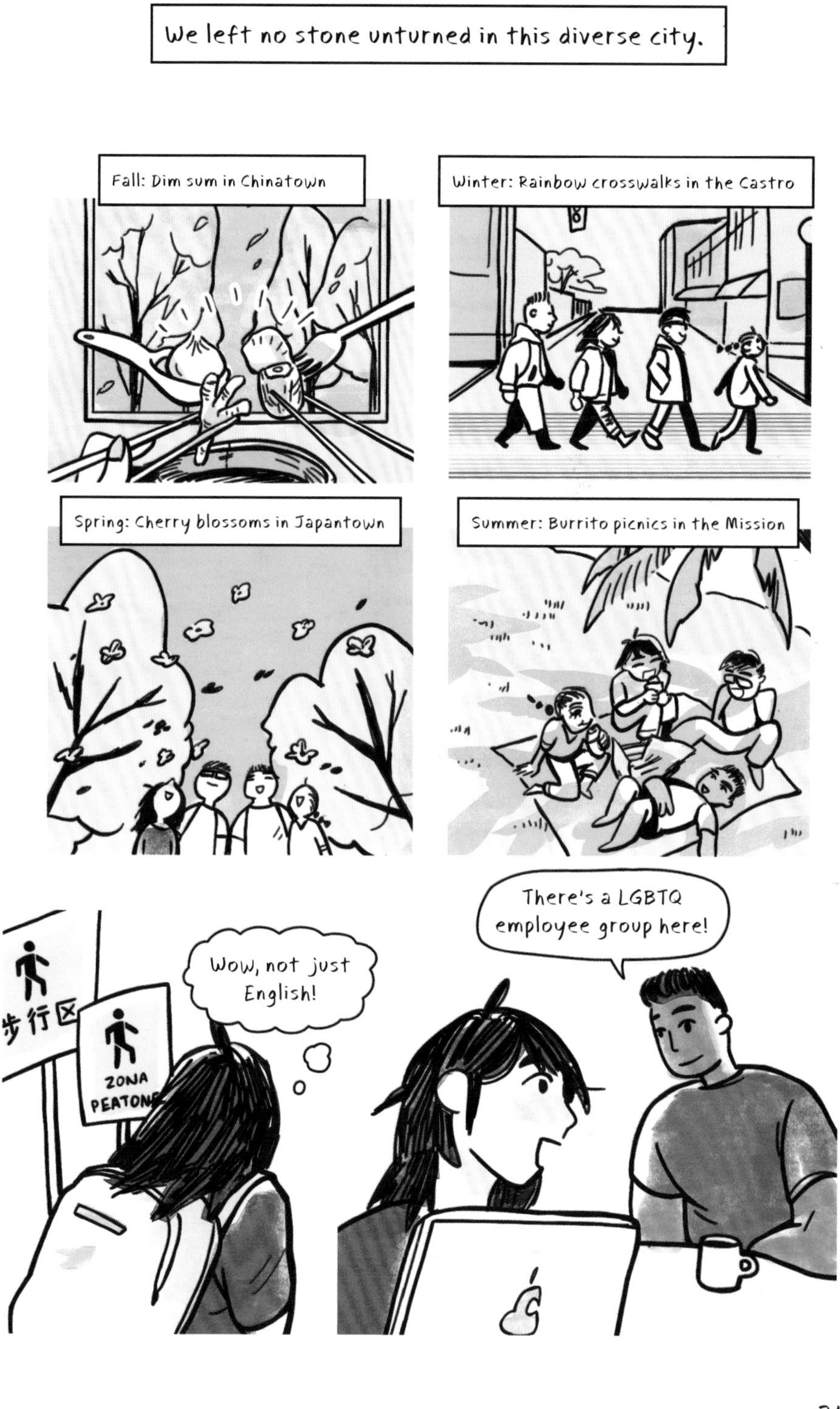
We left no stone unturned in this diverse city.
Fall: Dim sum in Chinatown
Winter: Rainbow crosswalks in the Castro
Spring: Cherry blossoms in Japantown
Summer: Burrito picnics in the Mission
步行区
ZONA PEATON
Wow, not just English!
There's a LGBTQ employee group here!

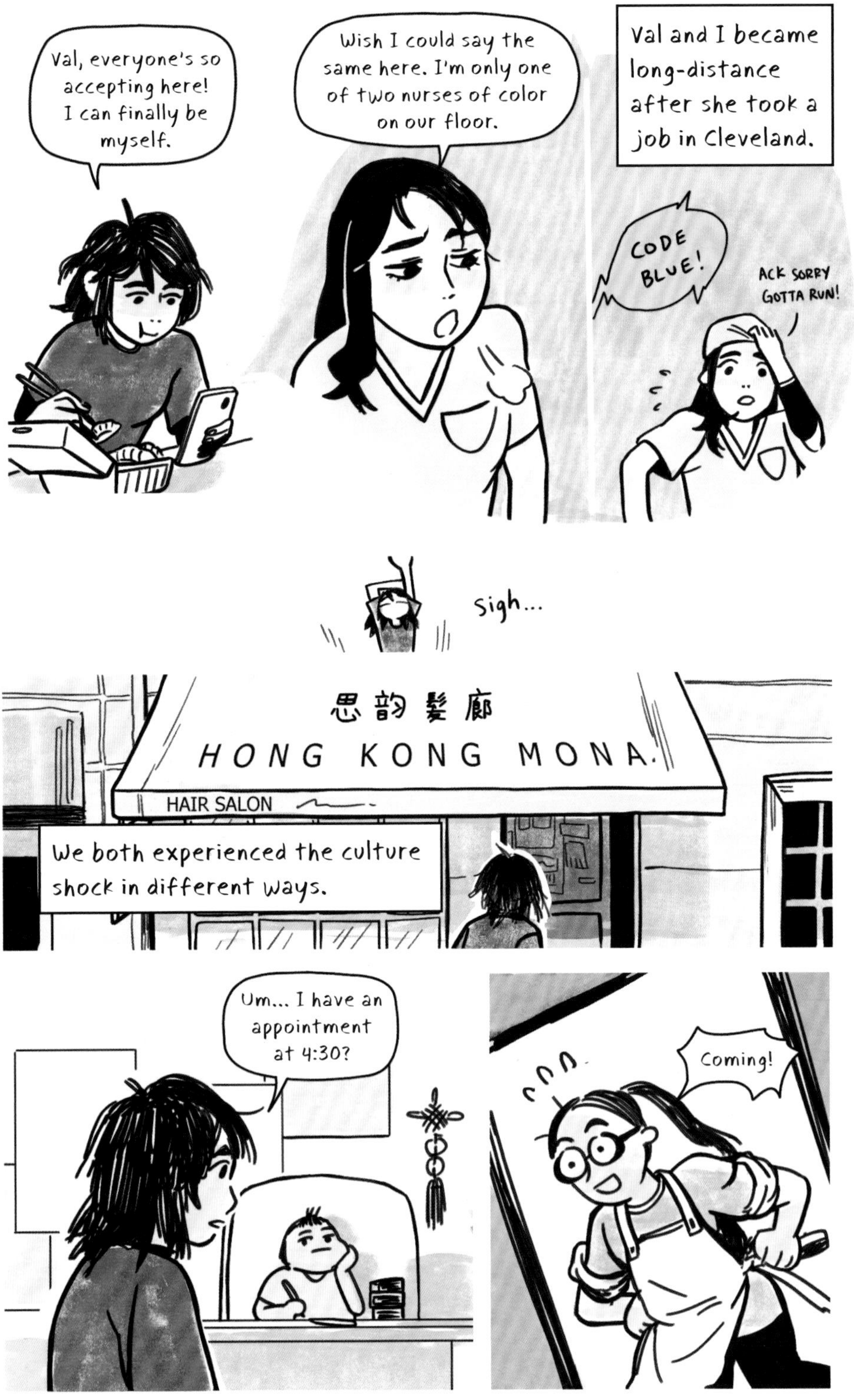
Val, everyone's so accepting here! I can finally be myself.
Wish I could say the same here. I'm only one of two nurses of color on our floor.
Val and I became long-distance after she took a job in Cleveland.
CODE BLUE!
ACK SORRY GOTTA RUN!
Sigh...
思韵髮廊
HONG KONG MONA
HAIR SALON
We both experienced the culture shock in different ways.
Um... I have an appointment at 4:30?
Coming!

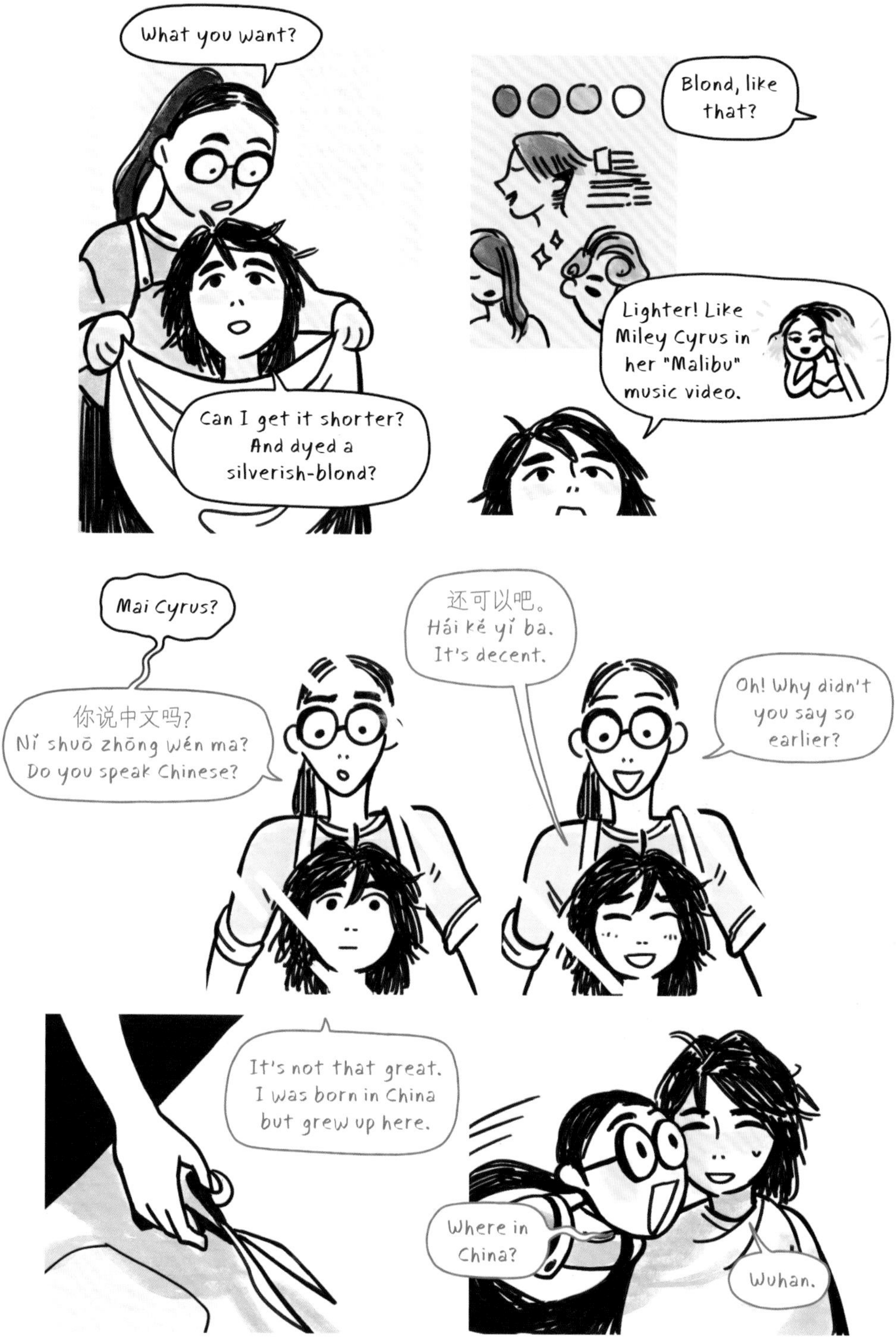
What you want?
Blond, like that?
Can I get it shorter? And dyed a silverish-blond?
Lighter! Like Miley Cyrus in her "Malibu" music video.
Mai Cyrus?
你说中文吗?
Nǐ shuō zhōng wén ma?
Do you speak Chinese?
还可以吧。
Hái kě yǐ ba.
It's decent.
Oh! Why didn't you say so earlier?
It's not that great. I was born in China but grew up here.
Where in China?
Wuhan.

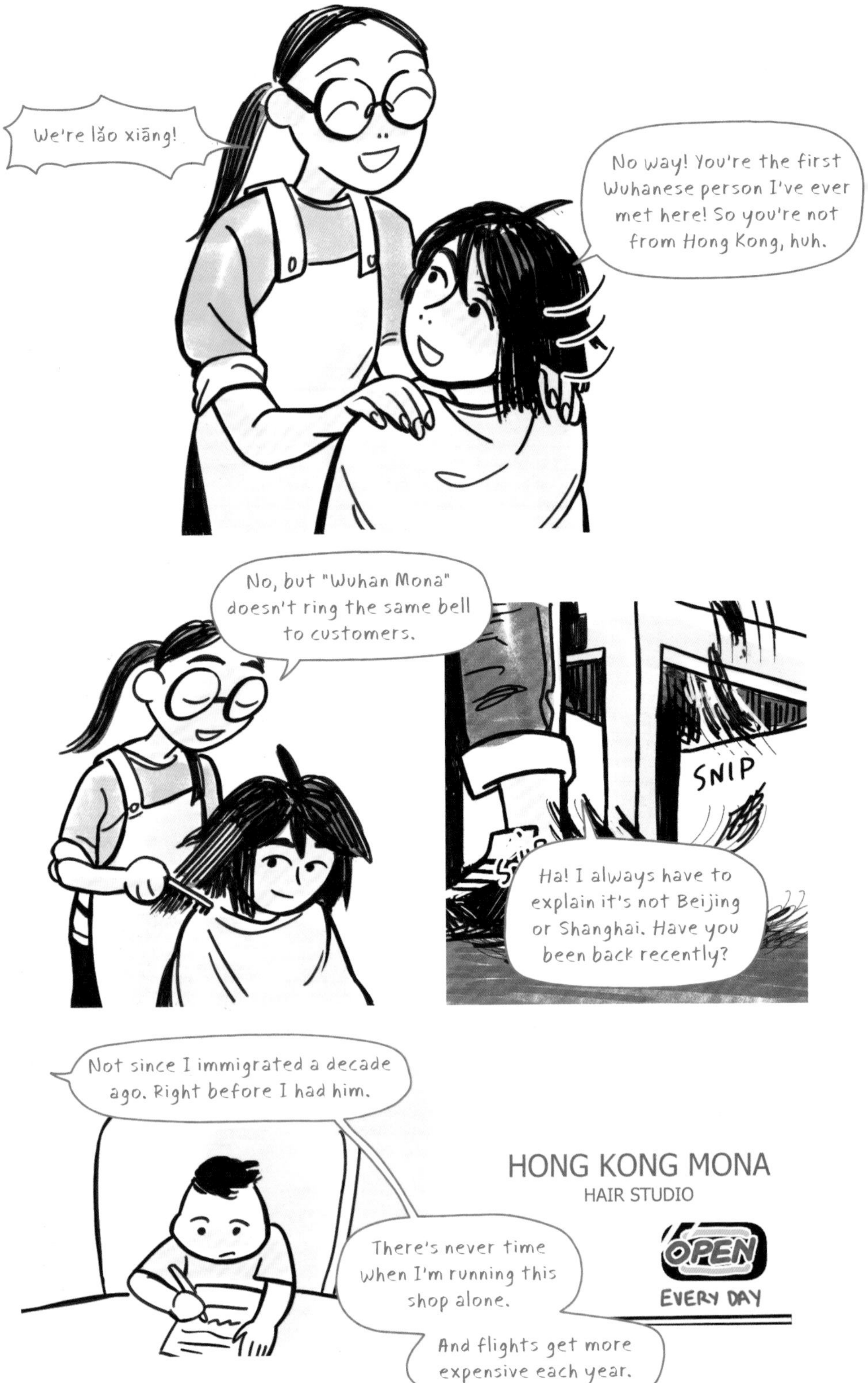
We're lǎo xiāng!
No way! You're the first Wuhanese person I've ever met here! So you're not from Hong Kong, huh.
No, but "Wuhan Mona" doesn't ring the same bell to customers.
SNIP
Ha! I always have to explain it's not Beijing or Shanghai. Have you been back recently?
Not since I immigrated a decade ago. Right before I had him.
HONG KONG MONA
HAIR STUDIO
OPEN
EVERY DAY
There's never time when I'm running this shop alone.
And flights get more expensive each year.

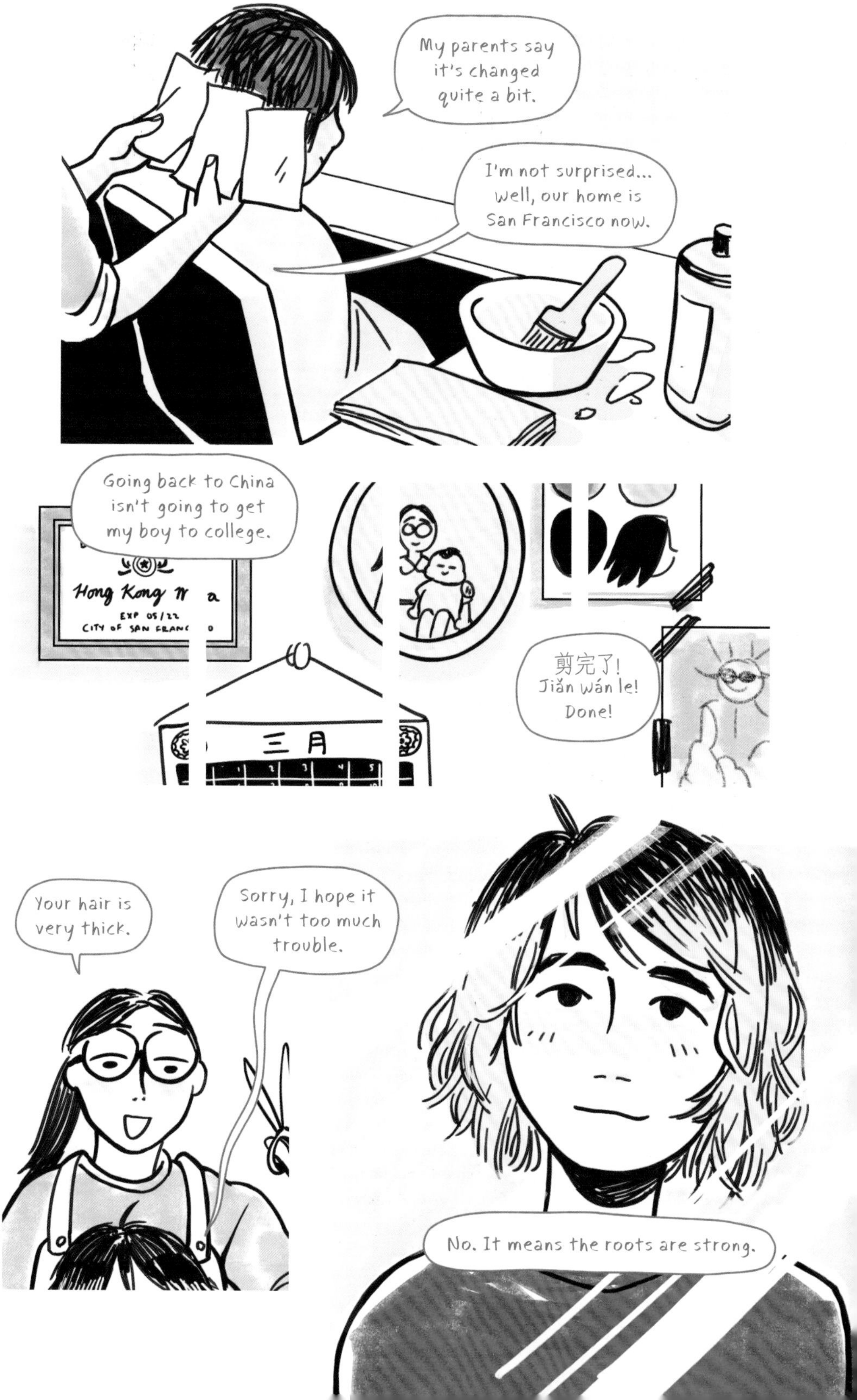
My parents say it's changed quite a bit.
I'm not surprised... well, our home is San Francisco now.
Going back to China isn't going to get my boy to college.
EXP 05/22
三月
剪完了!
Jiǎn wán le!
Done!
Your hair is very thick.
Sorry, I hope it wasn't too much trouble.
No. It means the roots are strong.

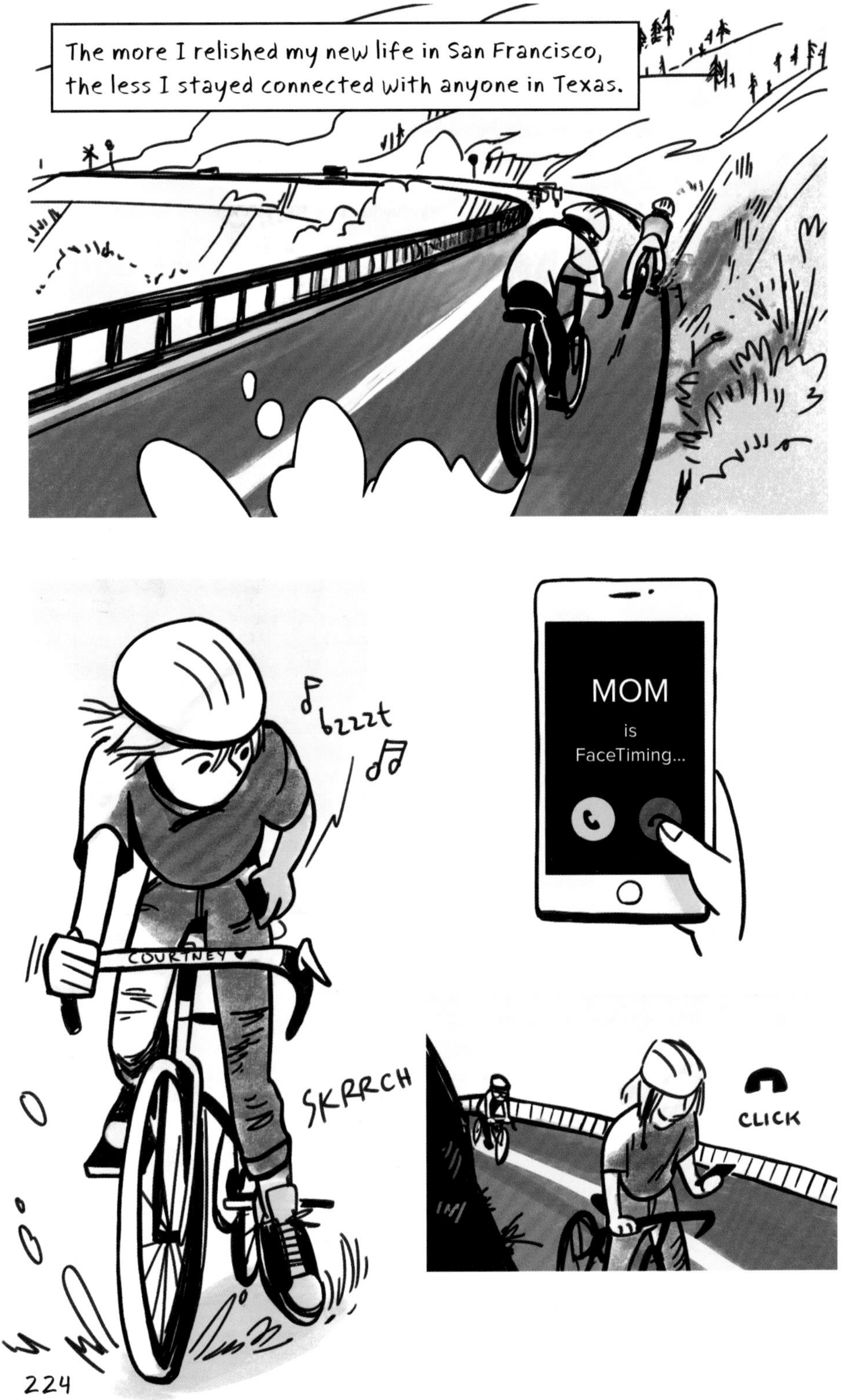
The more I relished my new life in San Francisco, the less I stayed connected with anyone in Texas.
bzzzt
COURTNEY
SKRRCH
MOM
is
FaceTiming...
CLICK

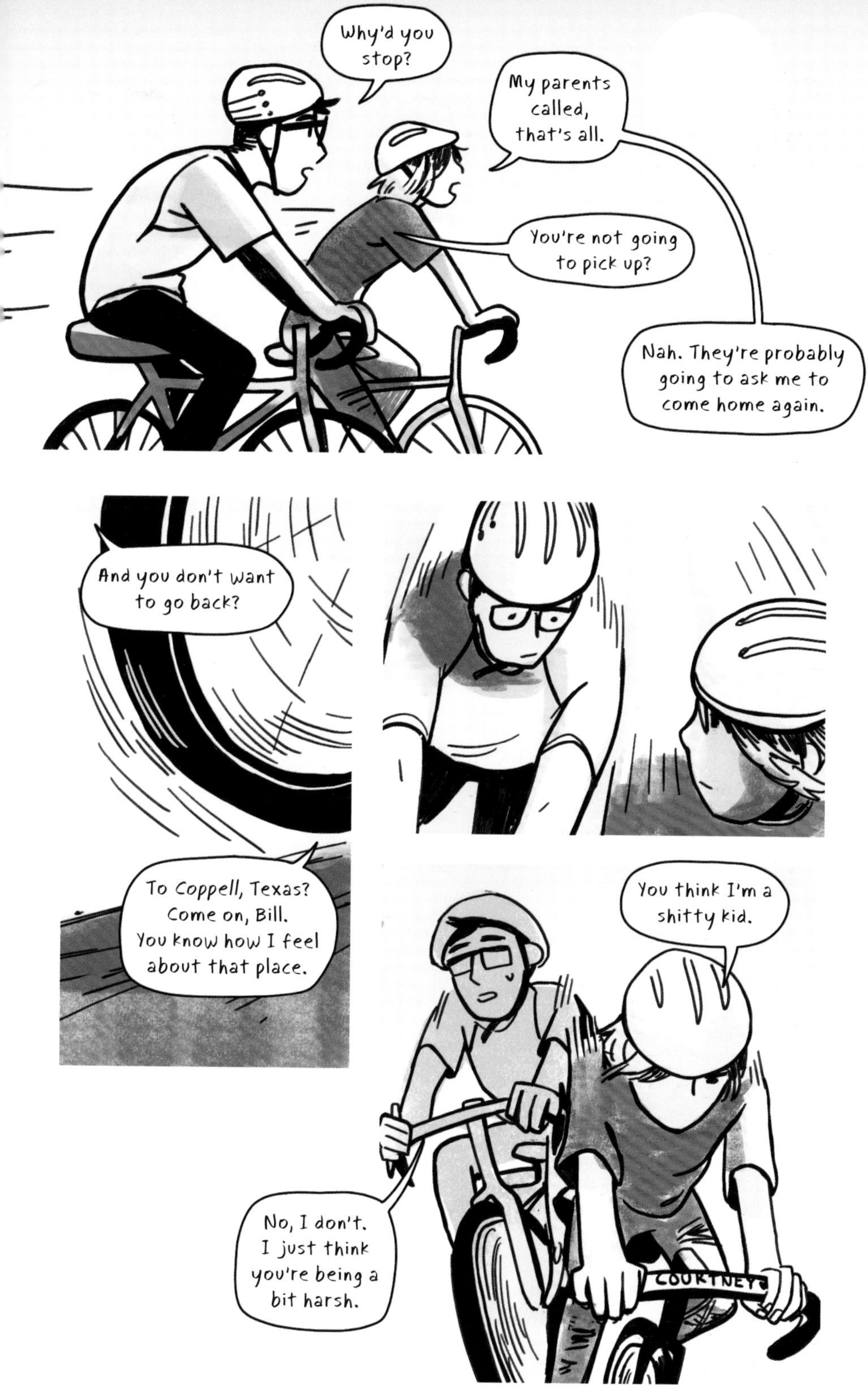
Why'd you stop?
My parents called, that's all.
You're not going to pick up?
Nah. They're probably going to ask me to come home again.
And you don't want to go back?
To Coppell, Texas? Come on, Bill. You know how I feel about that place.
You think I'm a shitty kid.
No, I don't. I just think you're being a bit harsh.
COURTNEY

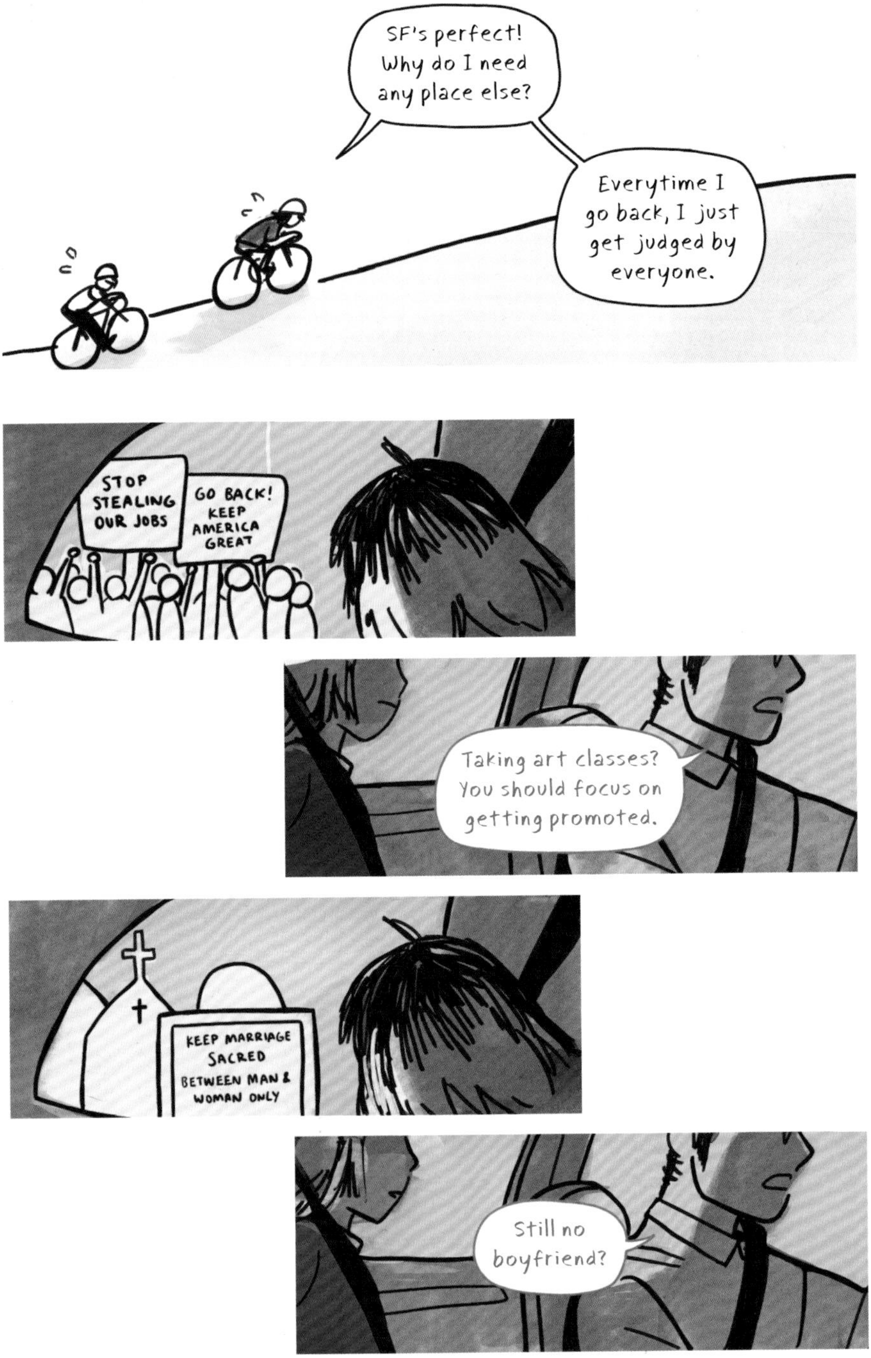
SF's perfect! Why do I need any place else?
Everytime I go back, I just get judged by everyone.
STOP STEALING OUR JOBS
GO BACK! KEEP AMERICA GREAT
Taking art classes? You should focus on getting promoted.
KEEP MARRIAGE SACRED BETWEEN MAN & WOMAN ONLY
Still no boyfriend?

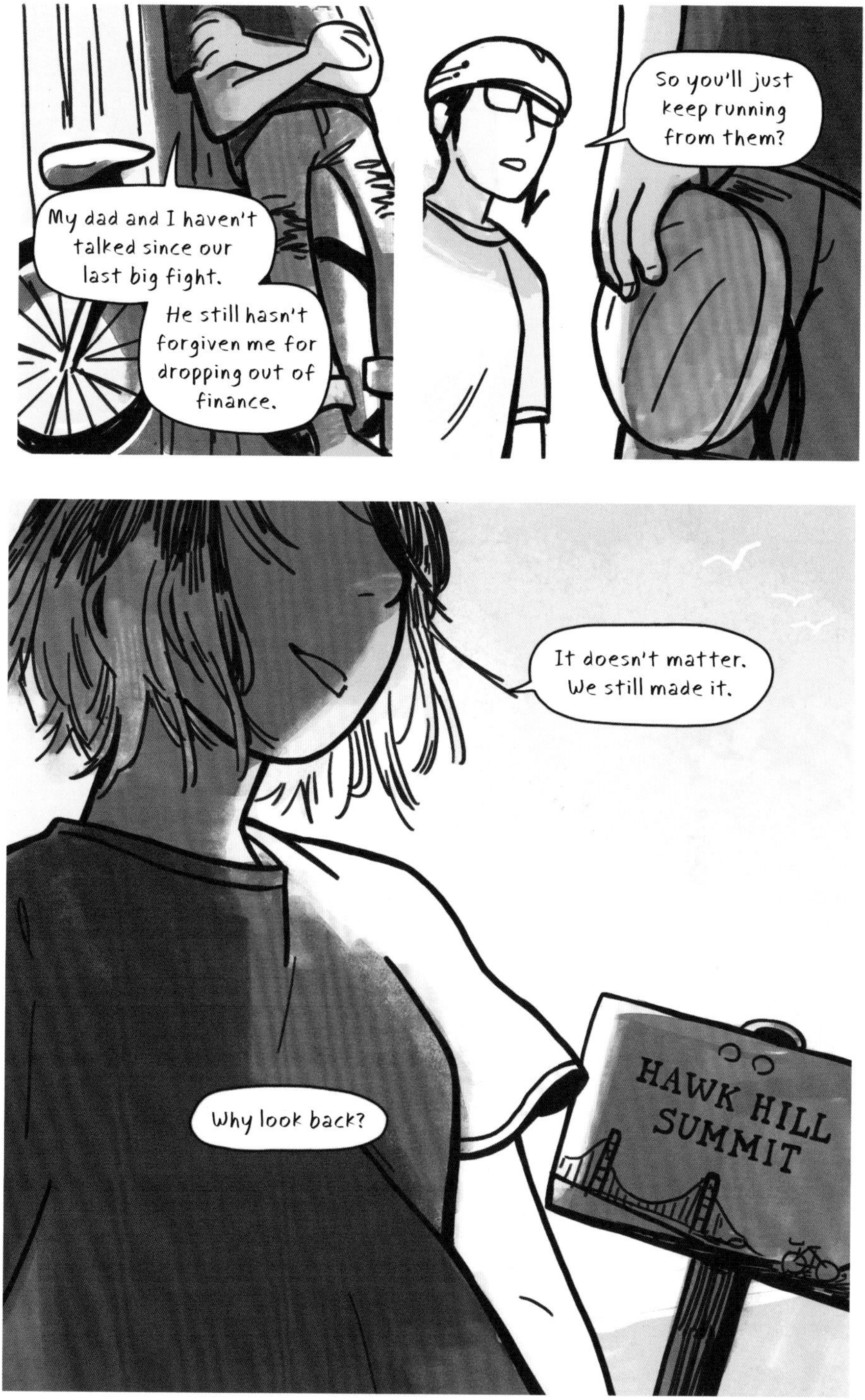
My dad and I haven't talked since our last big fight.
He still hasn't forgiven me for dropping out of finance.
So you'll just keep running from them?
It doesn't matter. We still made it.
Why look back?
HAWK HILL SUMMIT

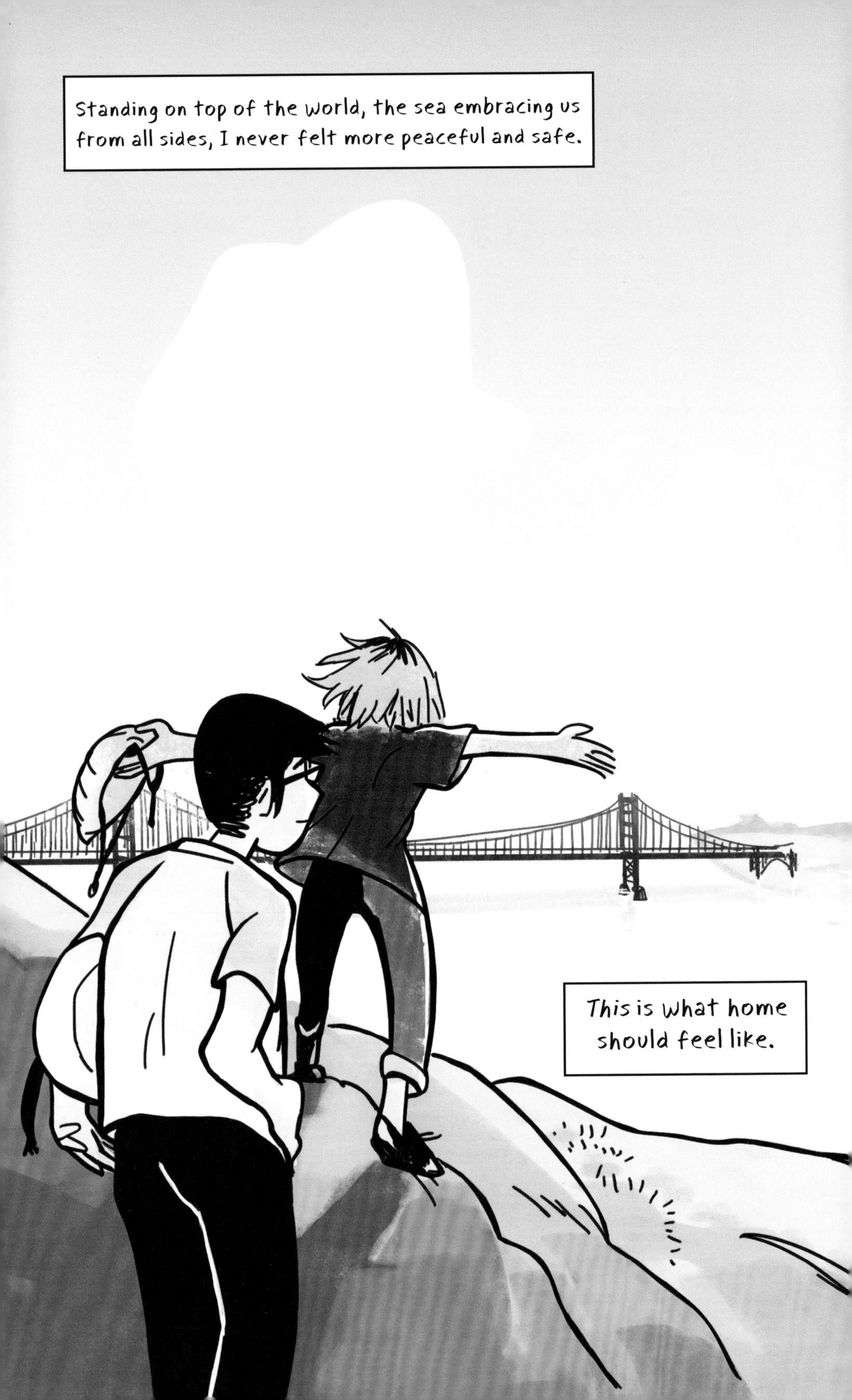
Standing on top of the world, the sea embracing us from all sides, I never felt more peaceful and safe.
This is what home should feel like.

CHAPTER 16
Stranger in My Own Home

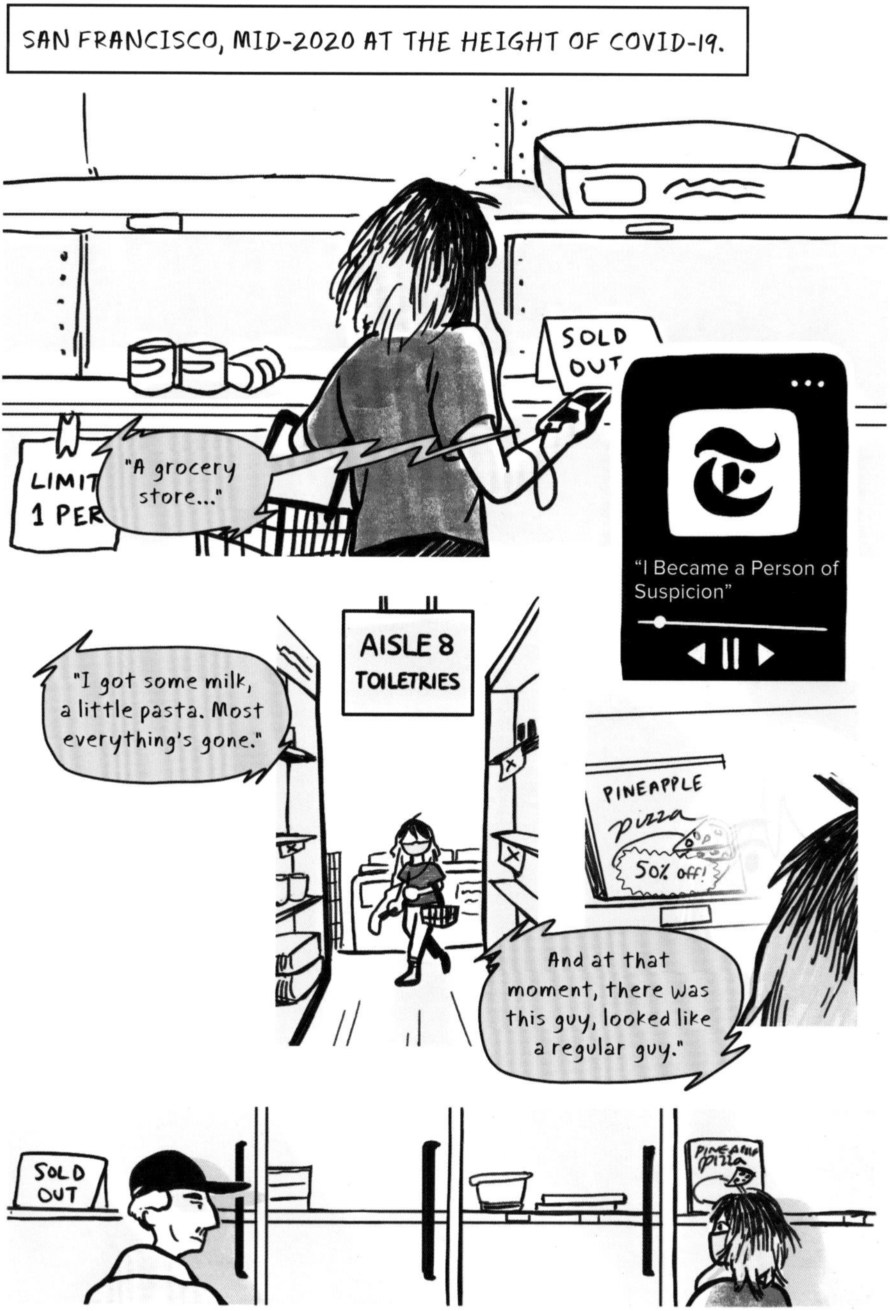
SAN FRANCISCO, MID-2020 AT THE HEIGHT OF COVID-19.
SOLD OUT
LIMIT 1 PER
"A grocery store..."
"I Became a Person of Suspicion"
AISLE 8 TOILETRIES
"I got some milk, a little pasta. Most everything's gone."
PINEAPPLE pizza
50% off!
And at that moment, there was this guy, looked like a regular guy."
SOLD OUT

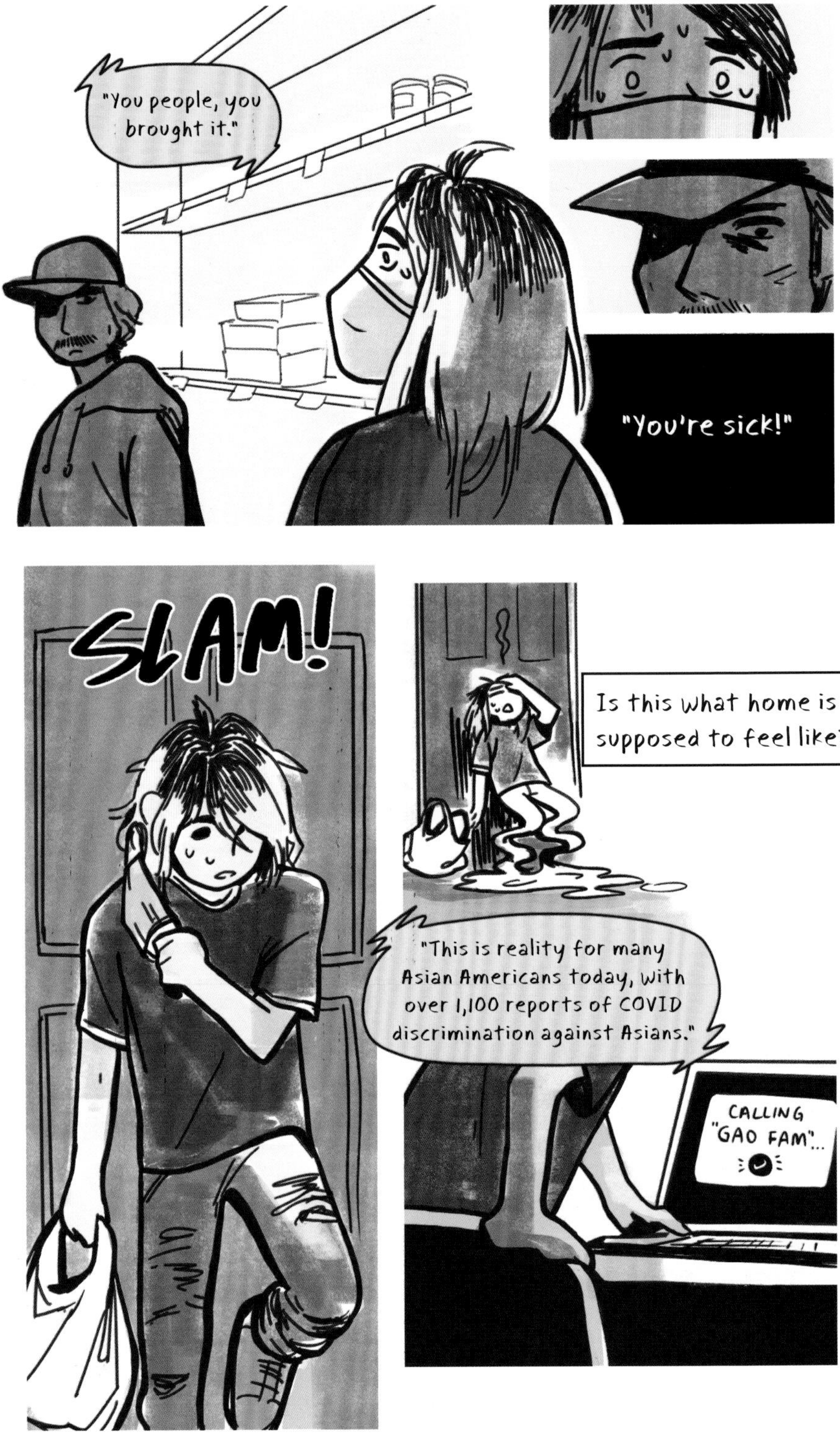
"You people, you brought it."
"You're sick!"
SLAM!
Is this what home is supposed to feel like?
"This is reality for many Asian Americans today, with over 1,100 reports of COVID discrimination against Asians."
CALLING "GAO FAM"...

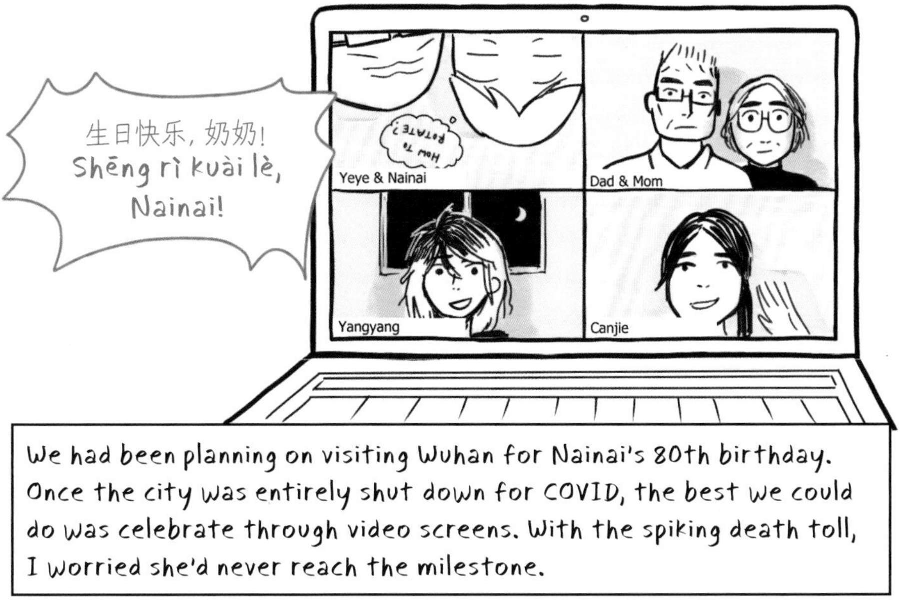
生日快乐，奶奶！
Shēng rì kuài lè, Nainai!
How to ROTATE?
Yeye & Nainai
Dad & Mom
Yangyang
Canjie
We had been planning on visiting Wuhan for Nainai's 80th birthday. Once the city was entirely shut down for COVID, the best we could do was celebrate through video screens. With the spiking death toll, I worried she'd never reach the milestone.

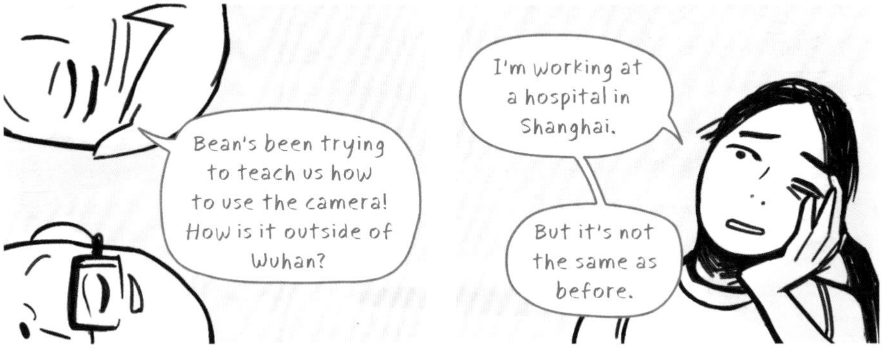
Bean's been trying to teach us how to use the camera! How is it outside of Wuhan?
I'm working at a hospital in Shanghai.
But it's not the same as before.

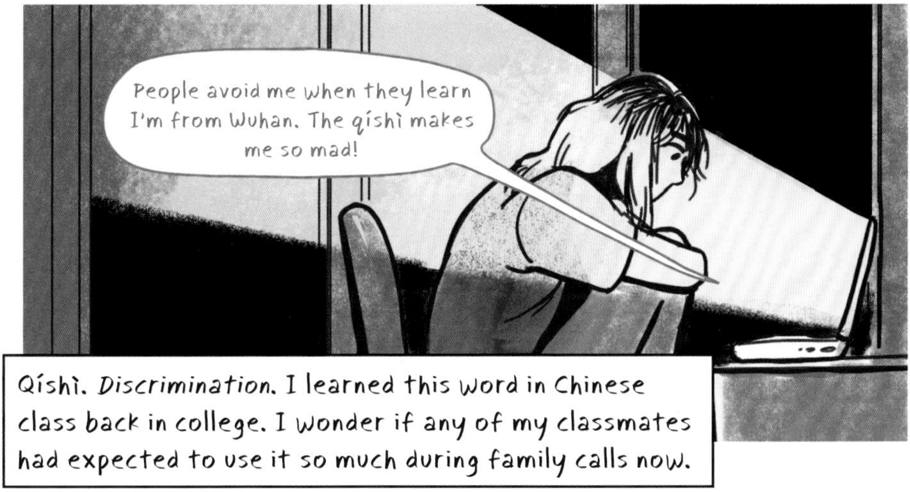
People avoid me when they learn I'm from Wuhan. The qíshì makes me so mad!
Qíshì. *Discrimination.* I learned this word in Chinese class back in college. I wonder if any of my classmates had expected to use it so much during family calls now.

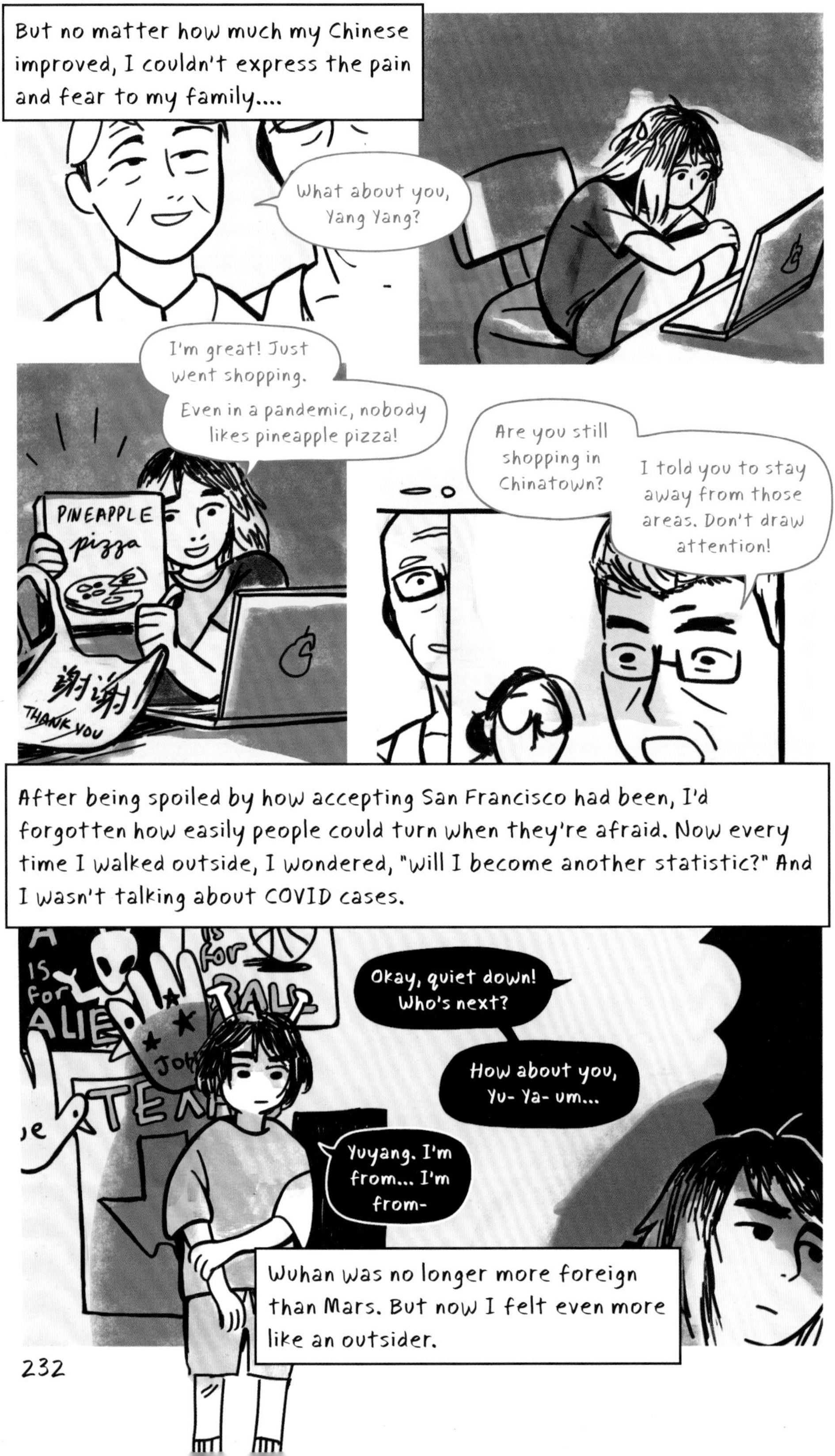
But no matter how much my Chinese improved, I couldn't express the pain and fear to my family....
What about you, Yang Yang?
I'm great! Just went shopping.
Even in a pandemic, nobody likes pineapple pizza!
PINEAPPLE pizza
谢谢
THANK YOU
Are you still shopping in Chinatown?
I told you to stay away from those areas. Don't draw attention!
After being spoiled by how accepting San Francisco had been, I'd forgotten how easily people could turn when they're afraid. Now every time I walked outside, I wondered, "will I become another statistic?" And I wasn't talking about COVID cases.
Okay, quiet down! Who's next?
How about you, Yu- Ya- um...
Yuyang. I'm from... I'm from-
Wuhan was no longer more foreign than Mars. But now I felt even more like an outsider.

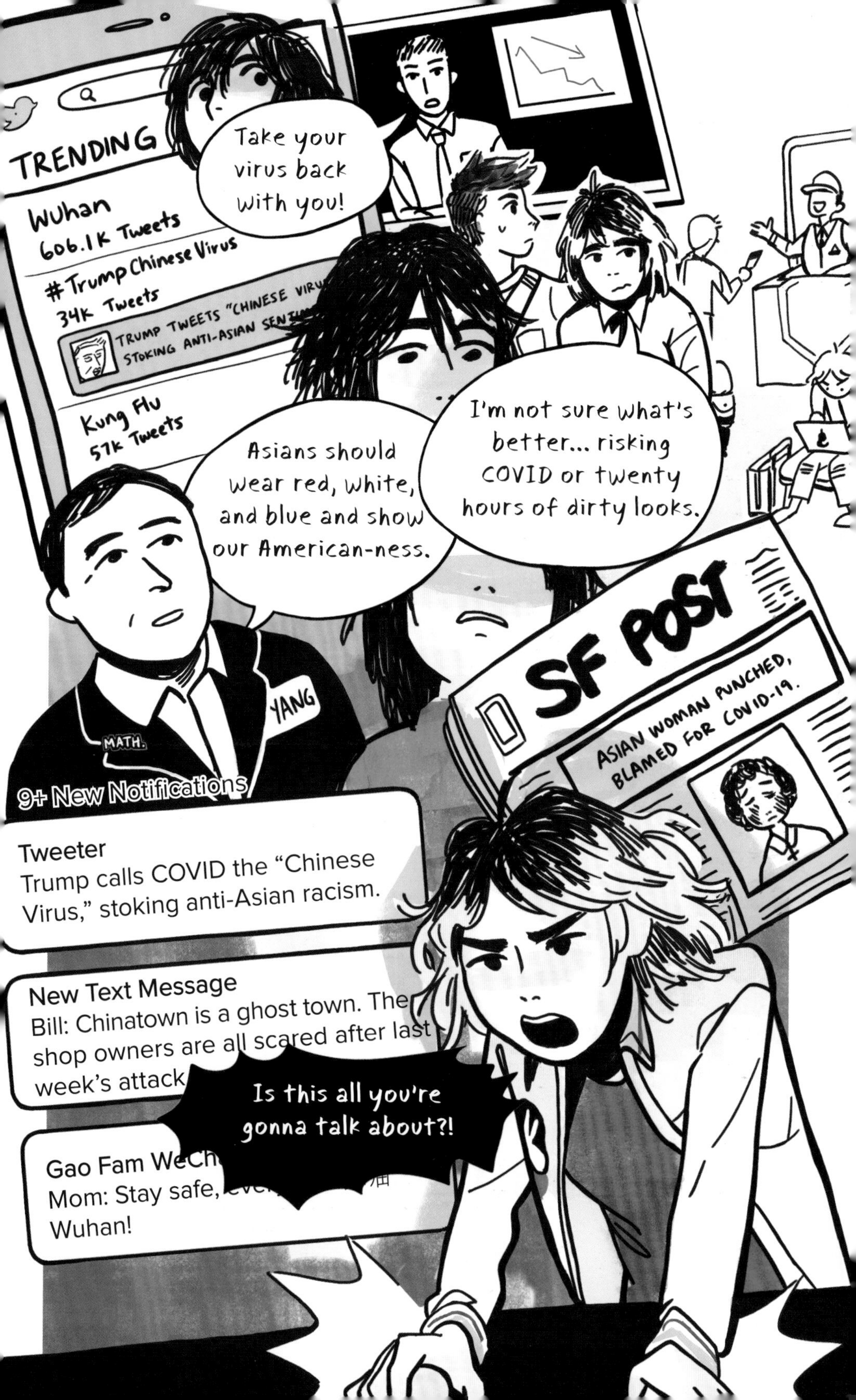

TRENDING
Wuhan
606.1K Tweets
#Trump Chinese Virus
34K Tweets
TRUMP TWEETS
STOKING ANTI-ASIAN
Kung Flu
57K Tweets
Take your virus back with you!
I'm not sure what's better... risking COVID or twenty hours of dirty looks.
Asians should wear red, white, and blue and show our American-ness.
YANG
MATH.
SF POST
ASIAN WOMAN PUNCHED, BLAMED FOR COVID-19.
9+ New Notifications
Tweeter
Trump calls COVID the "Chinese Virus," stoking anti-Asian racism.
New Text Message
Bill: Chinatown is a ghost town. The shop owners are all scared after last week's attack
Is this all you're gonna talk about?!
Gao Fam
Mom: Stay safe,
Wuhan!

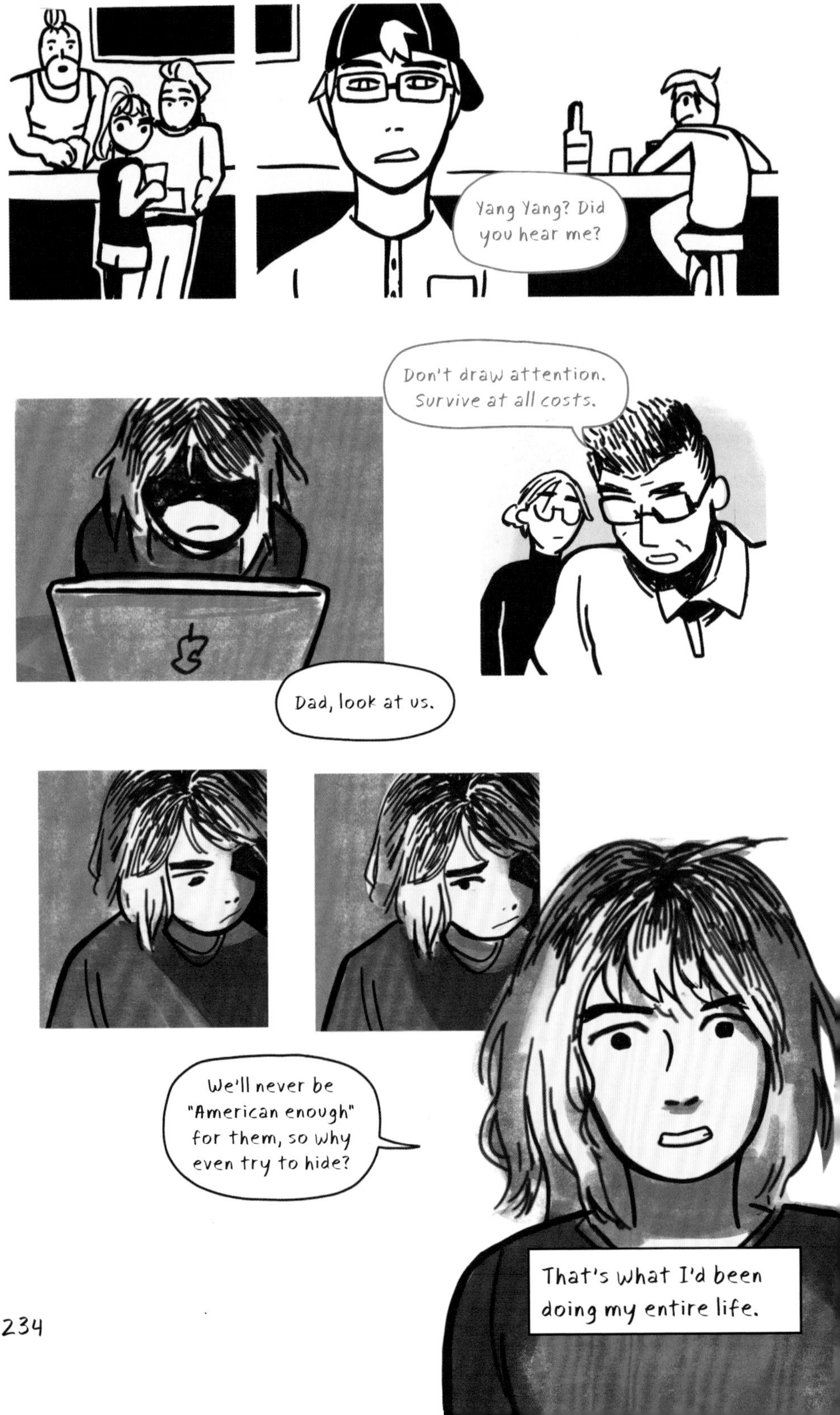

Yang Yang? Did you hear me?
Don't draw attention. Survive at all costs.
Dad, look at us.
We'll never be "American enough" for them, so why even try to hide?
That's what I'd been doing my entire life.

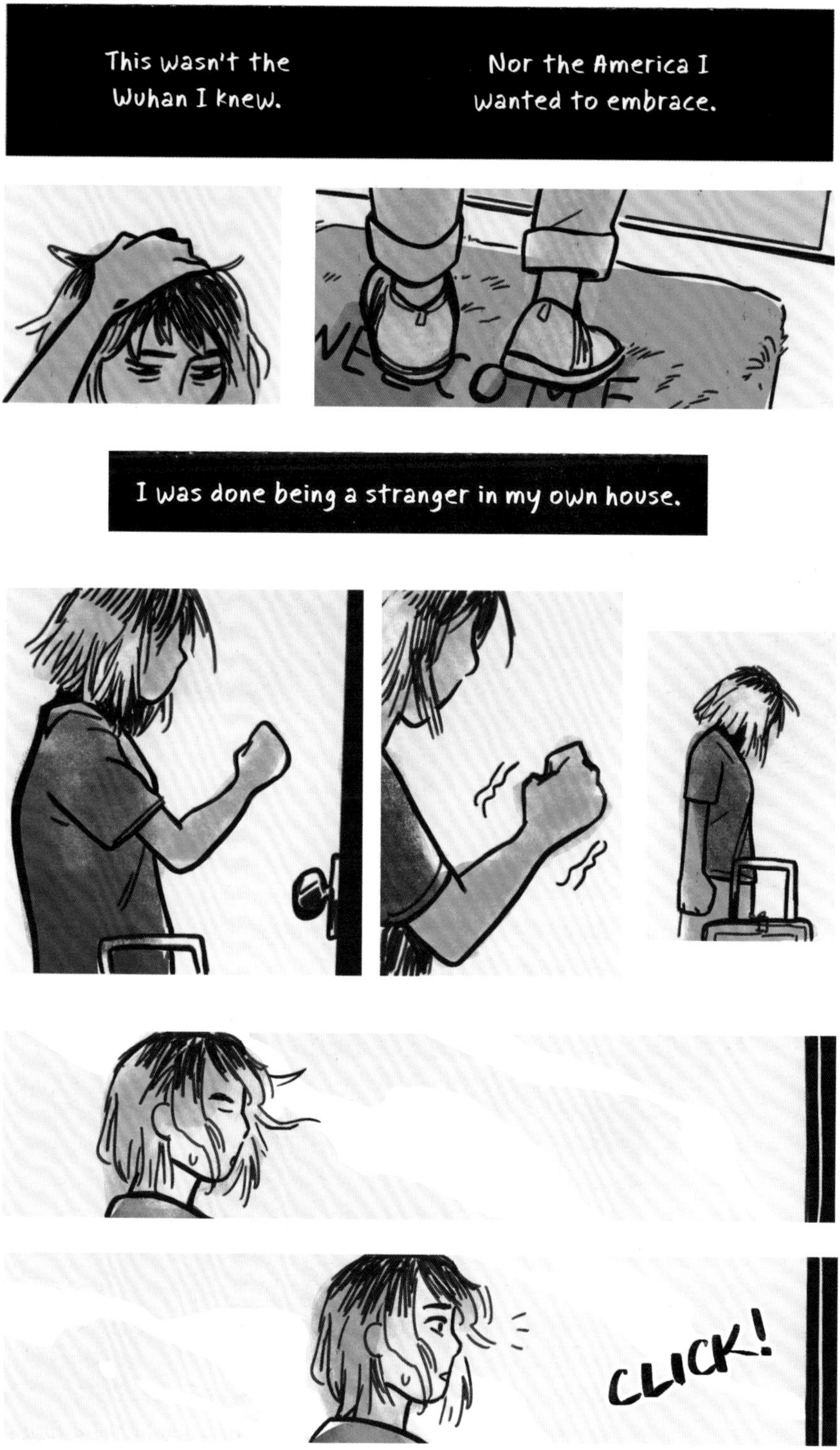

This wasn't the Wuhan I knew.
Nor the America I wanted to embrace.
WE COME
I was done being a stranger in my own house.
CLICK!

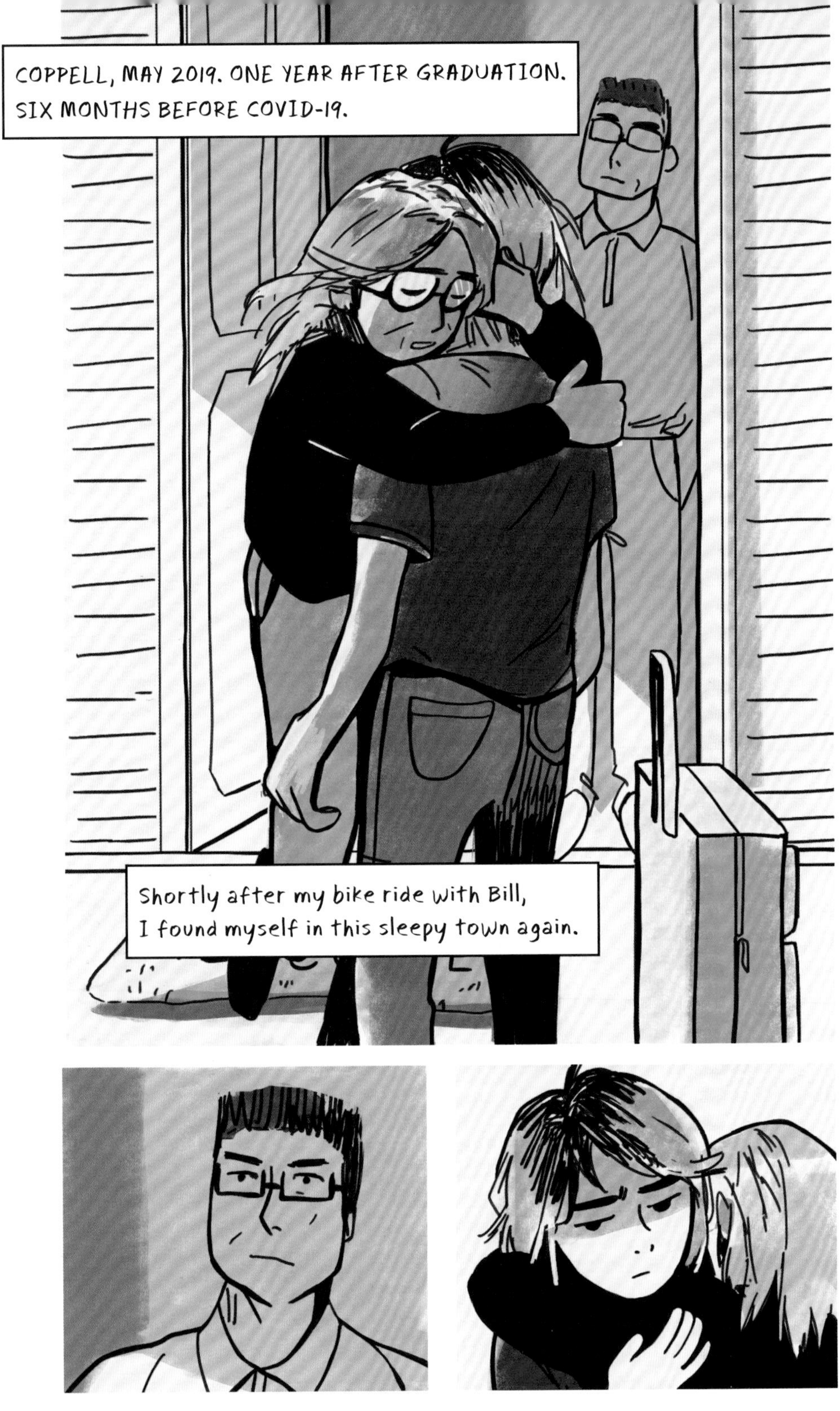
COPPELL, MAY 2019. ONE YEAR AFTER GRADUATION. SIX MONTHS BEFORE COVID-19.
Shortly after my bike ride with Bill, I found myself in this sleepy town again.

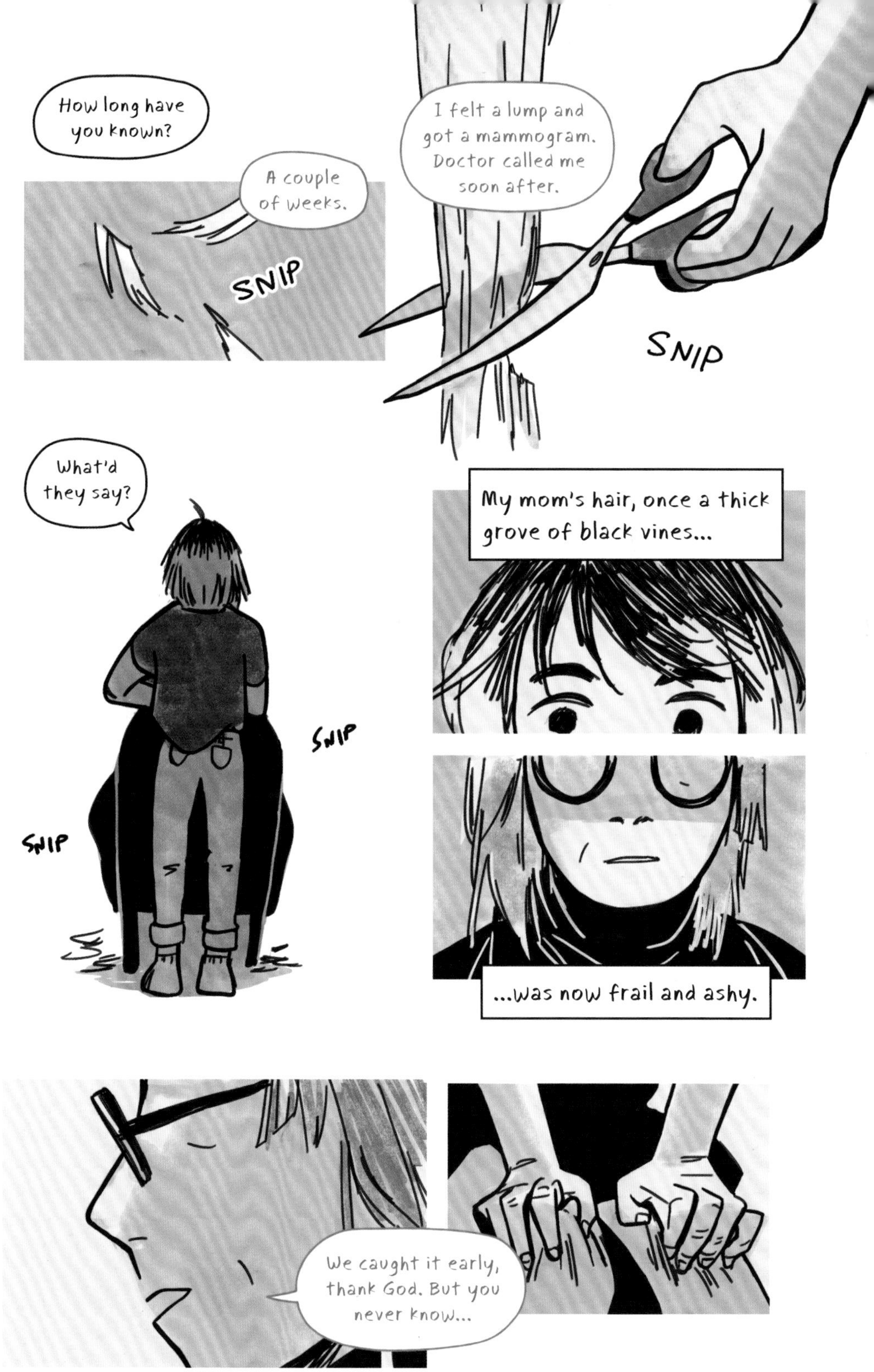
How long have you known?
A couple of weeks.
SNIP
I felt a lump and got a mammogram. Doctor called me soon after.
SNIP
What'd they say?
SNIP
SNIP
My mom's hair, once a thick grove of black vines...
...was now frail and ashy.
We caught it early, thank God. But you never know...

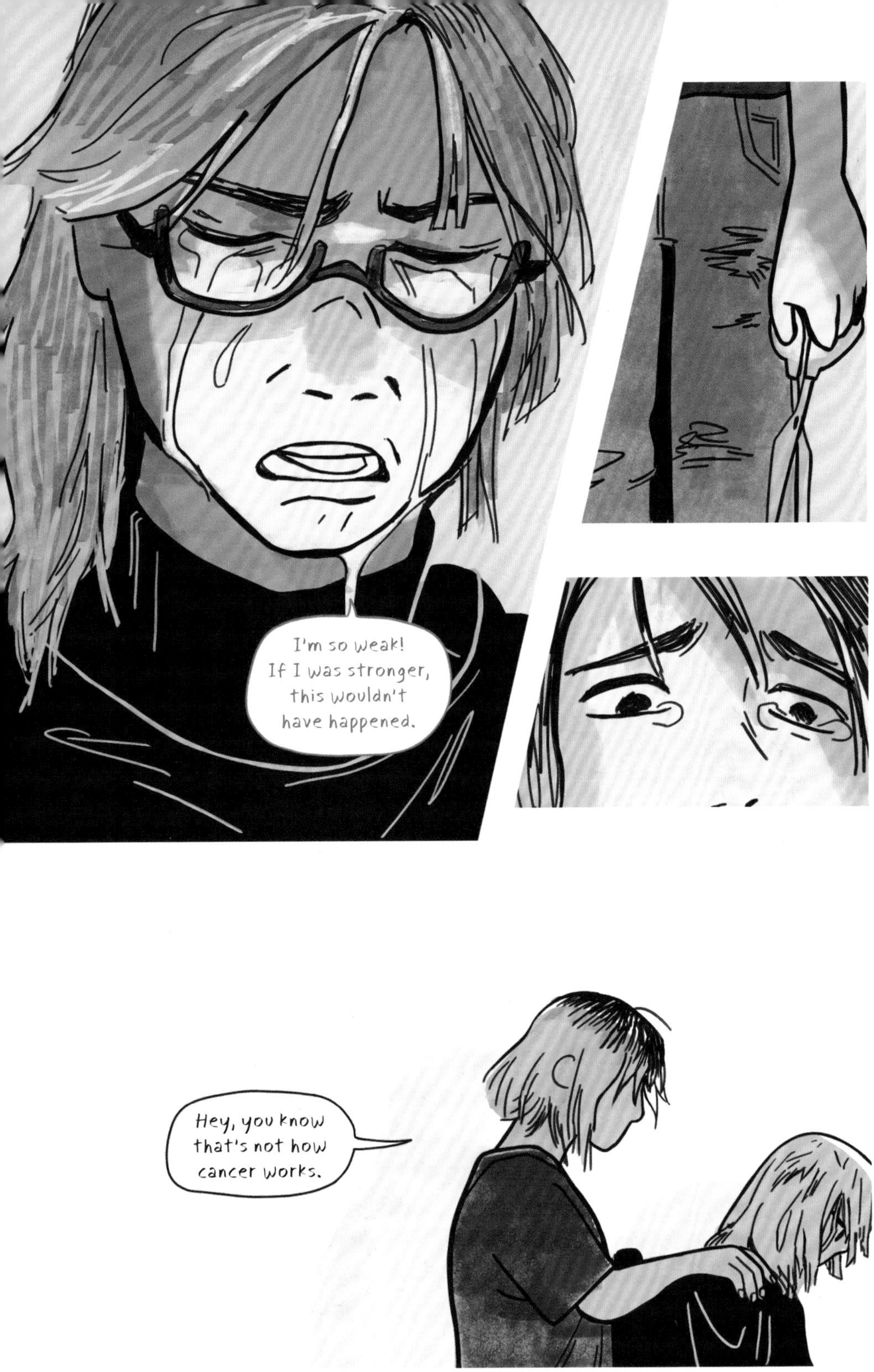
I'm so weak! If I was stronger, this wouldn't have happened.
Hey, you know that's not how cancer works.

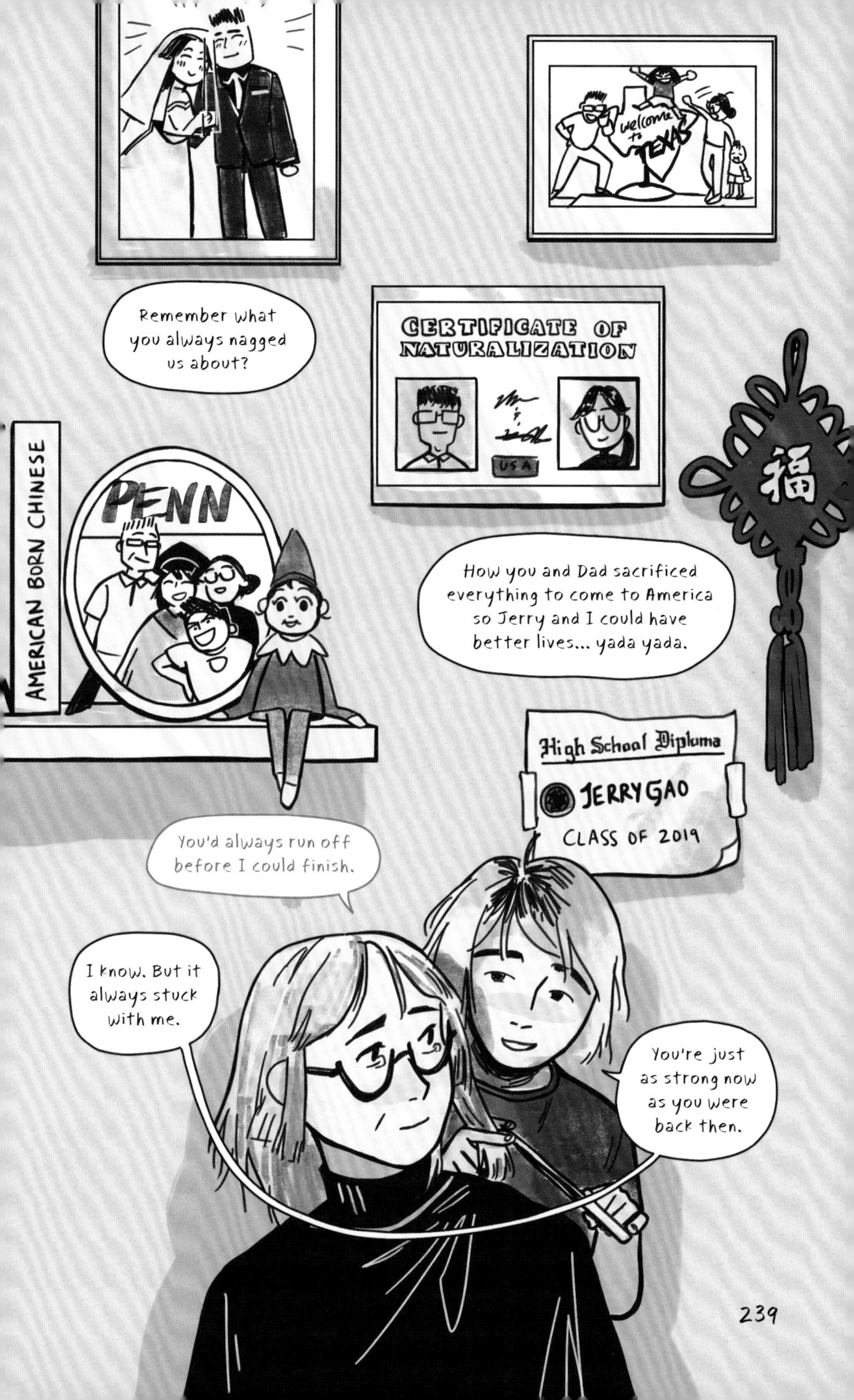
welcome to TEXAS
Remember what you always nagged us about?
CERTIFICATE OF NATURALIZATION
USA
AMERICAN BORN CHINESE
PENN
福
How you and Dad sacrificed everything to come to America so Jerry and I could have better lives... yada yada.
High School Diploma
JERRY GAO
CLASS OF 2019
You'd always run off before I could finish.
I know. But it always stuck with me.
You're just as strong now as you were back then.

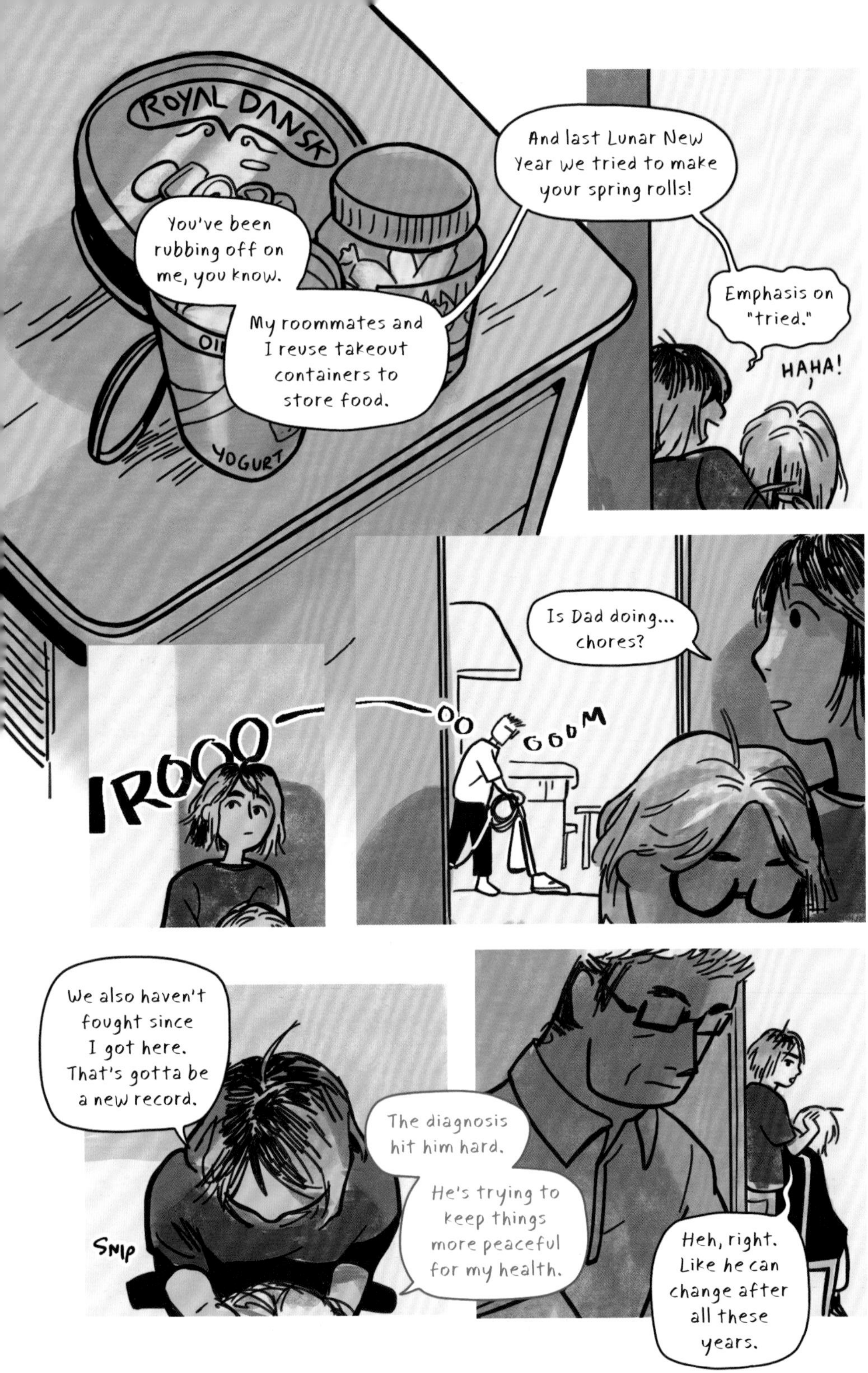
ROYAL DANSK
You've been rubbing off on me, you know.
My roommates and I reuse takeout containers to store food.
OIL
YOGURT
And last Lunar New Year we tried to make your spring rolls!
Emphasis on "tried."
HAHA!
Is Dad doing... chores?
IROOO——OO GOOM
We also haven't fought since I got here. That's gotta be a new record.
SNIP
The diagnosis hit him hard.
He's trying to keep things more peaceful for my health.
Heh, right. Like he can change after all these years.

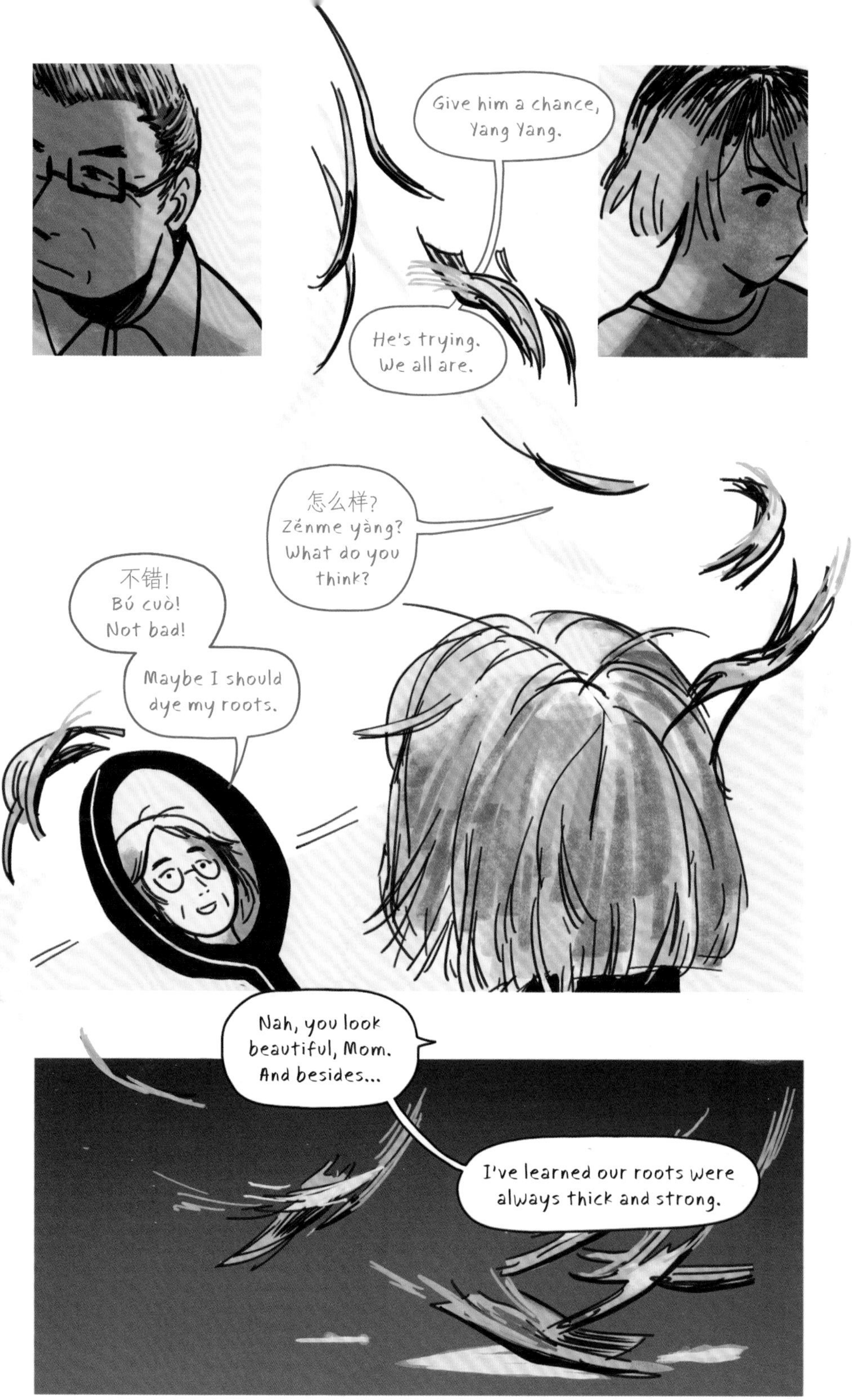

Give him a chance, Yang Yang.
He's trying. We all are.
怎么样? Zénme yàng? What do you think?
不错! Bú cuò! Not bad!
Maybe I should dye my roots.
Nah, you look beautiful, Mom. And besides...
I've learned our roots were always thick and strong.

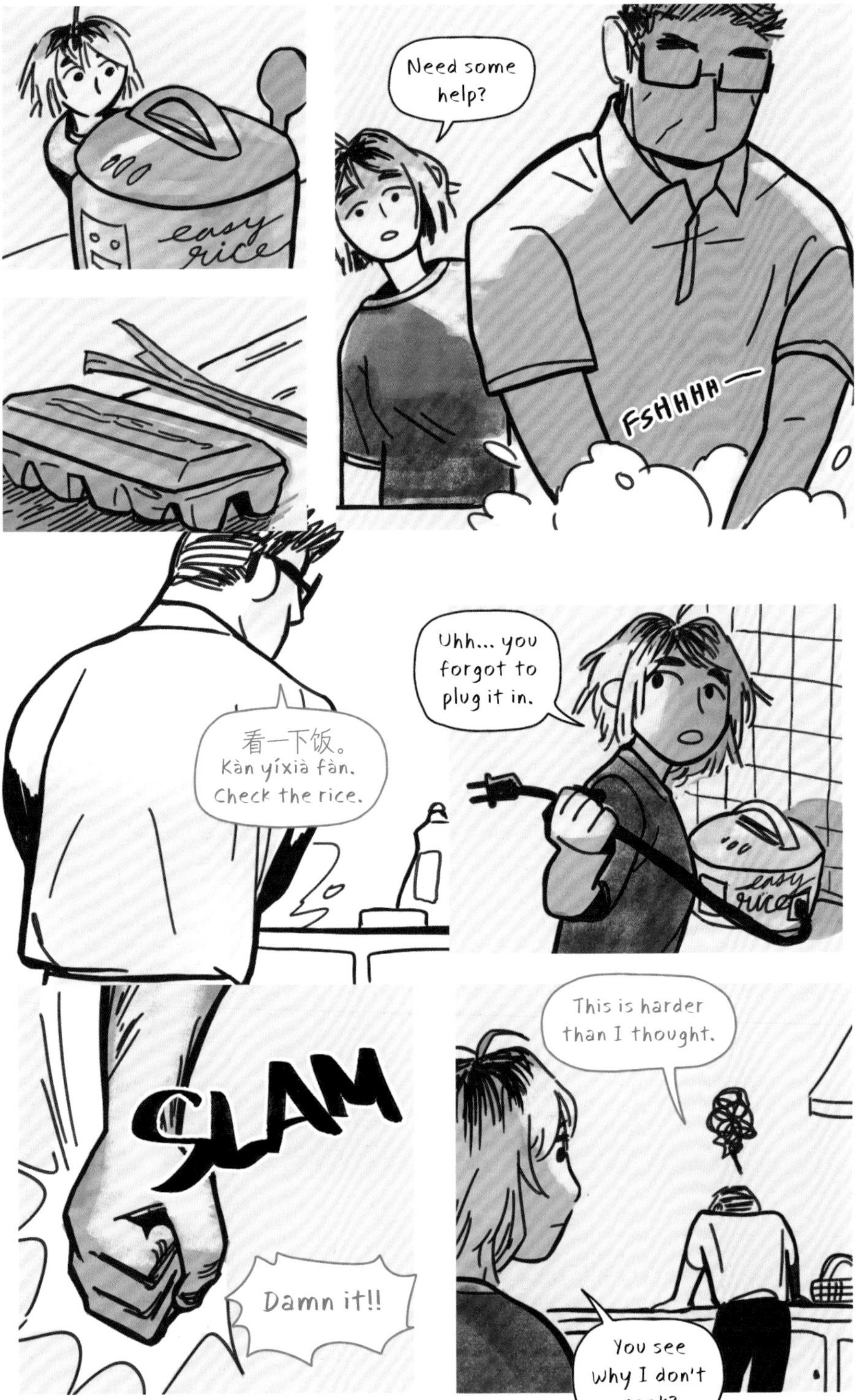
Need some help?
FSHHHH—
Uhh... you forgot to plug it in.
看一下饭。
Kàn yíxià fàn.
Check the rice.
SLAM
Damn it!!
This is harder than I thought.
You see why I don't cook?

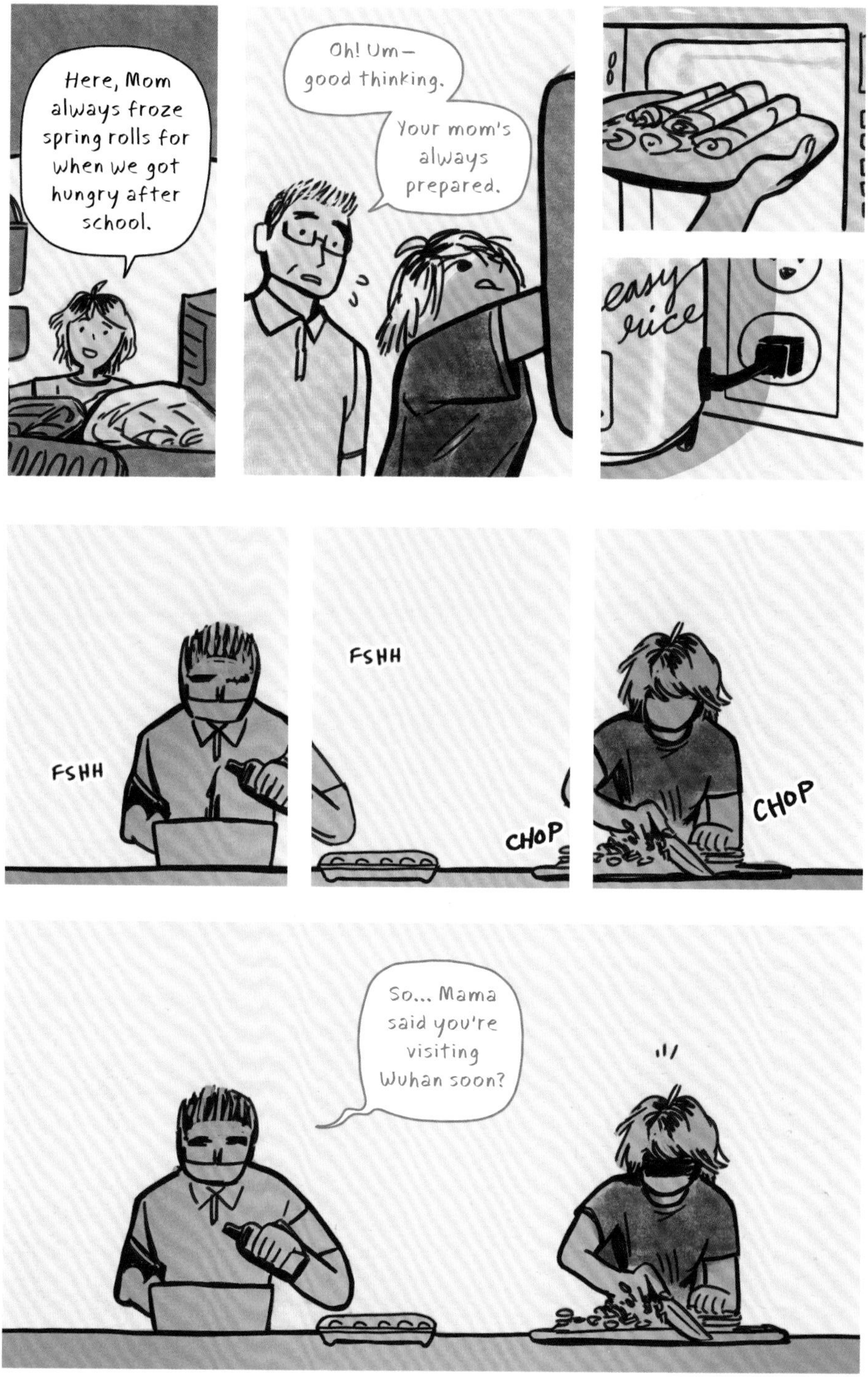
Here, Mom always froze spring rolls for when we got hungry after school.
Oh! Um— good thinking.
Your mom's always prepared.
easy rice
FSHH
FSHH
CHOP
CHOP
So... Mama said you're visiting Wuhan soon?

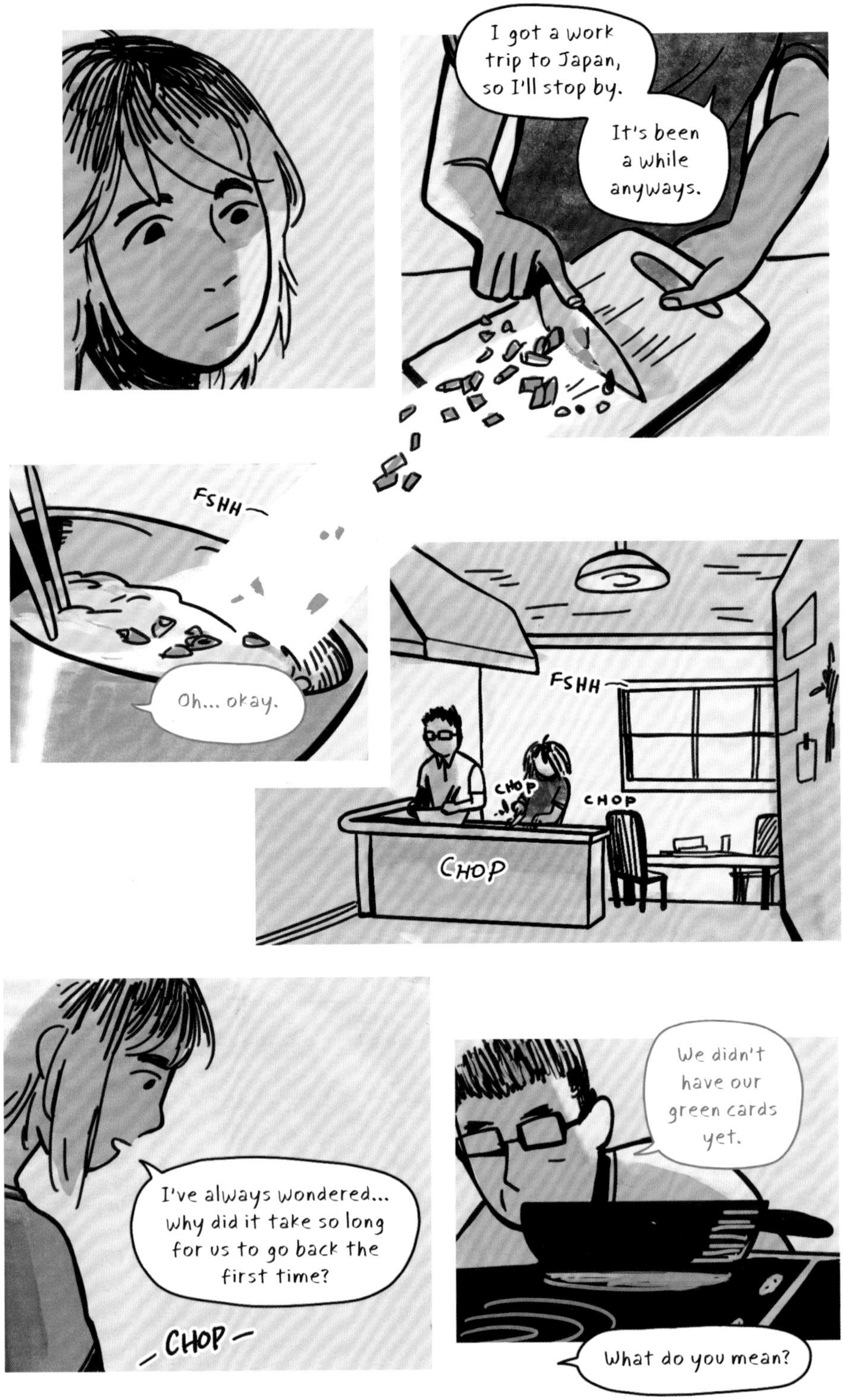
I got a work trip to Japan, so I'll stop by.
It's been a while anyways.
FSHH—
Oh... okay.
FSHH—
CHOP
CHOP
CHOP
I've always wondered... why did it take so long for us to go back the first time?
—CHOP—
We didn't have our green cards yet.
What do you mean?

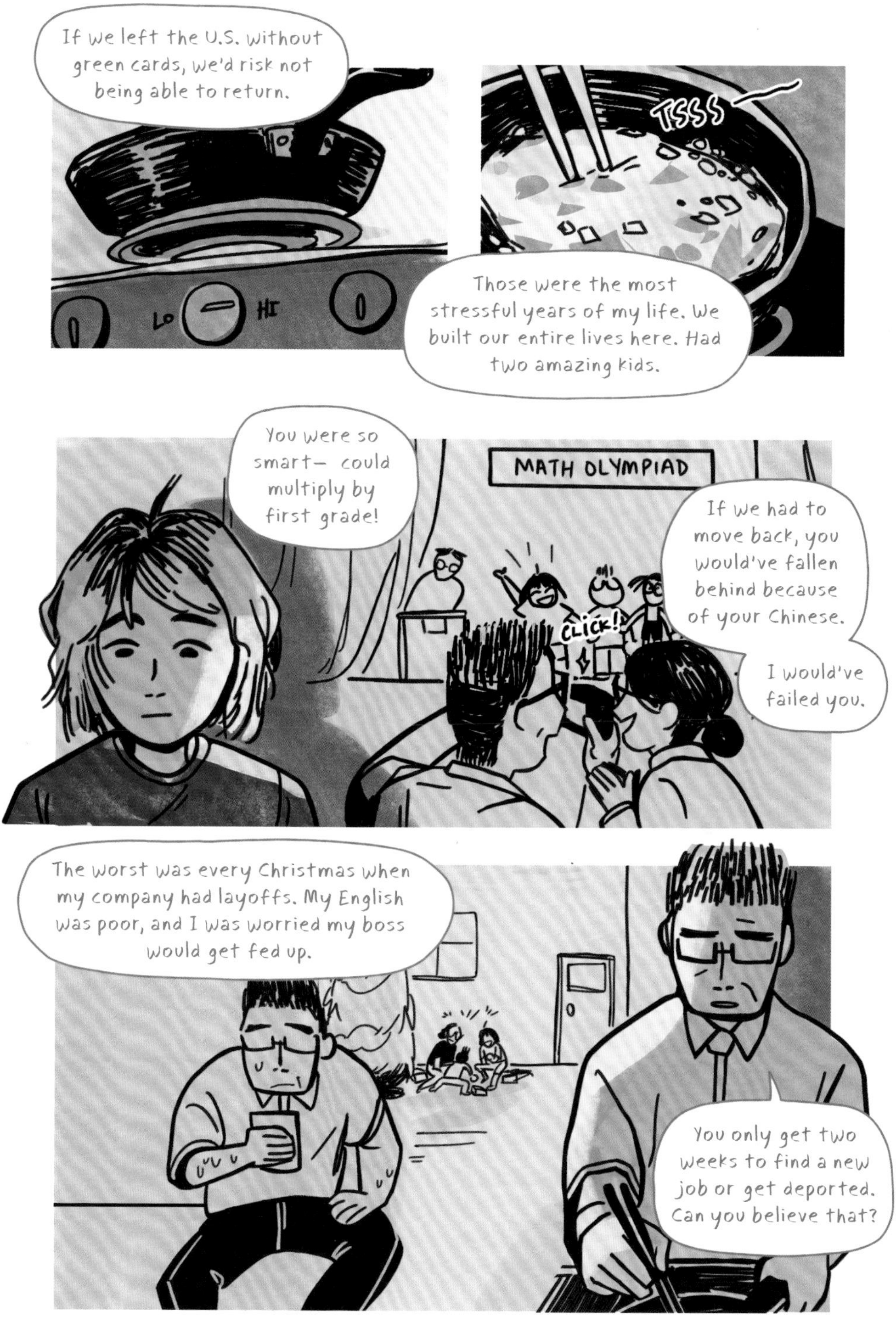

If we left the U.S. without green cards, we'd risk not being able to return.
LO
HI
TSSS
Those were the most stressful years of my life. We built our entire lives here. Had two amazing kids.
You were so smart— could multiply by first grade!
MATH OLYMPIAD
If we had to move back, you would've fallen behind because of your Chinese.
CLICK!
I would've failed you.
The worst was every Christmas when my company had layoffs. My English was poor, and I was worried my boss would get fed up.
You only get two weeks to find a new job or get deported. Can you believe that?

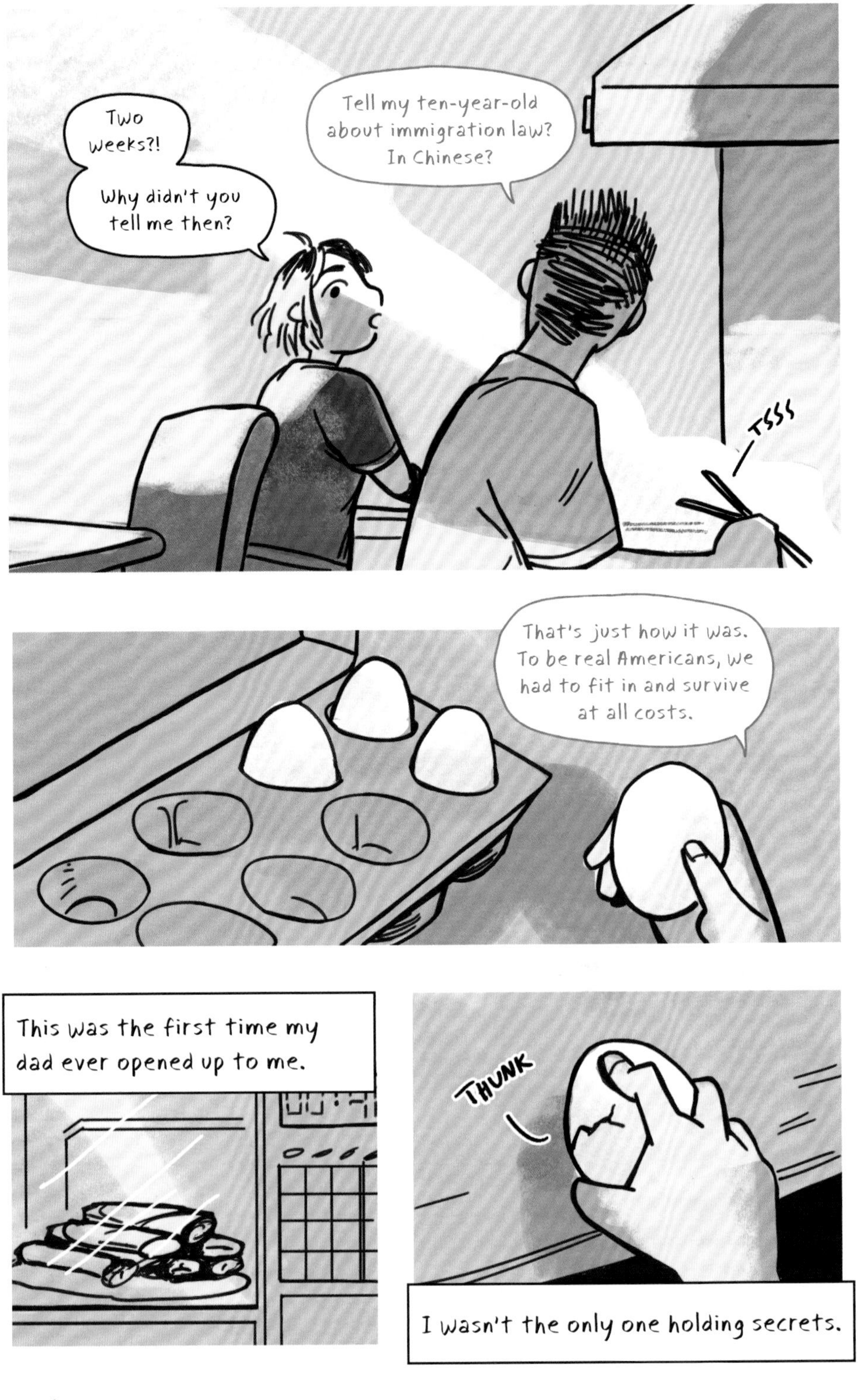
Two weeks?!
Why didn't you tell me then?
Tell my ten-year-old about immigration law? In Chinese?
TSSS
That's just how it was. To be real Americans, we had to fit in and survive at all costs.
This was the first time my dad ever opened up to me.
THUNK
I wasn't the only one holding secrets.

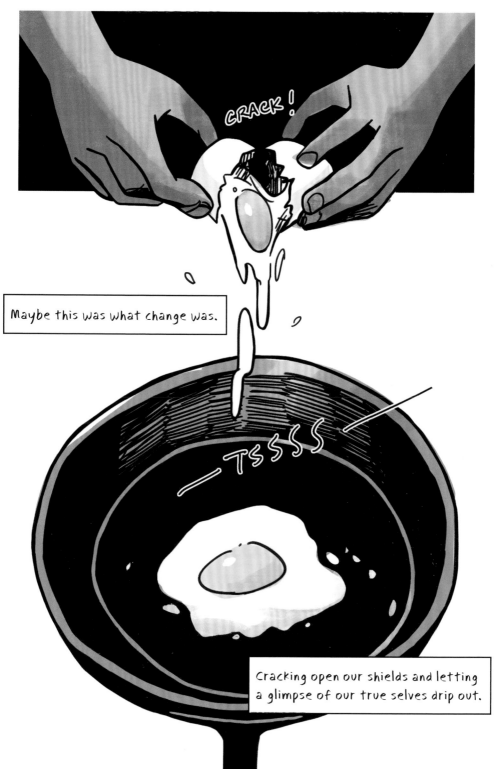

CRACK!

Maybe this was what change was.

TSSSS

Cracking open our shields and letting a glimpse of our true selves drip out.

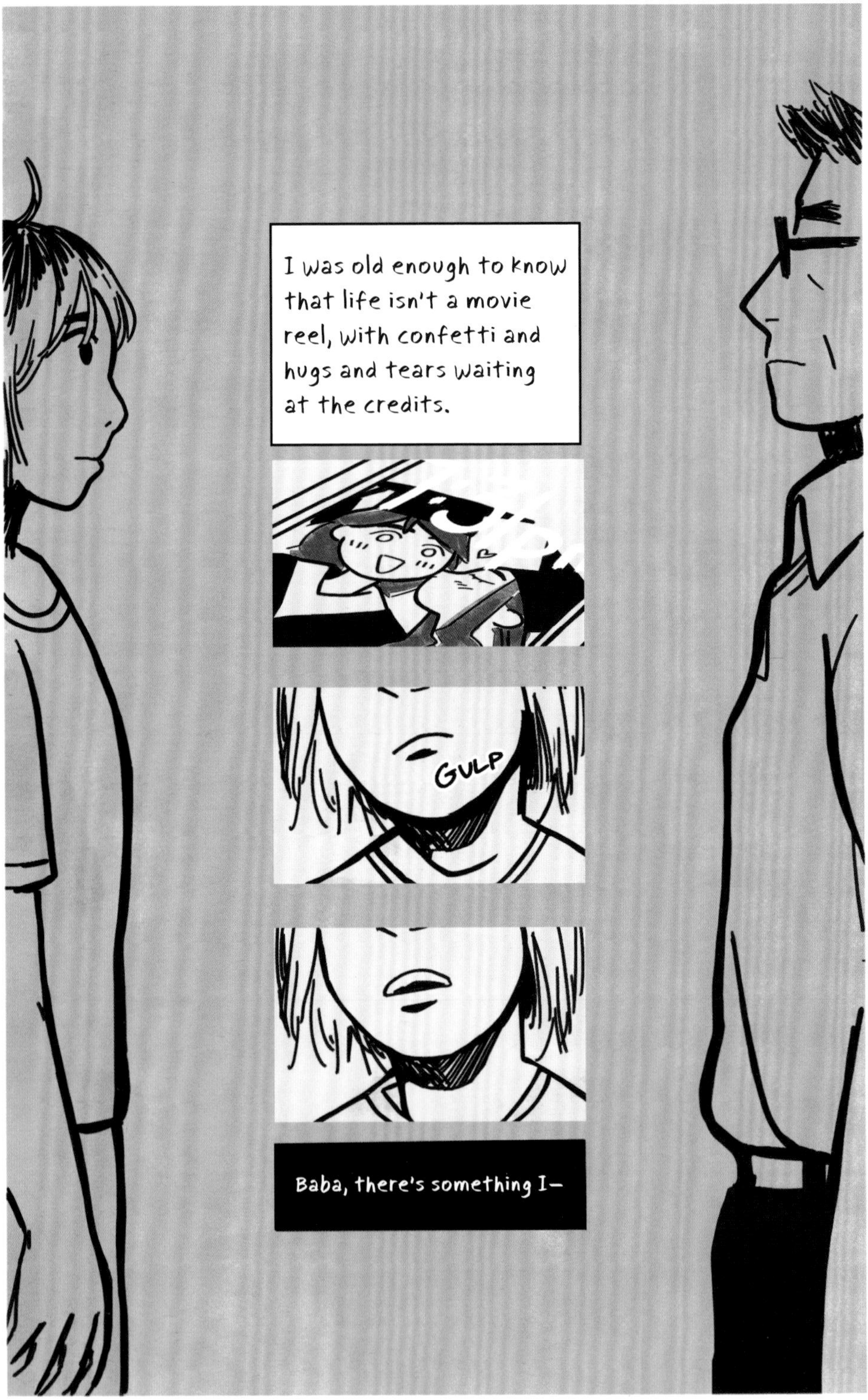
I was old enough to know that life isn't a movie reel, with confetti and hugs and tears waiting at the credits.
GULP
Baba, there's something I–

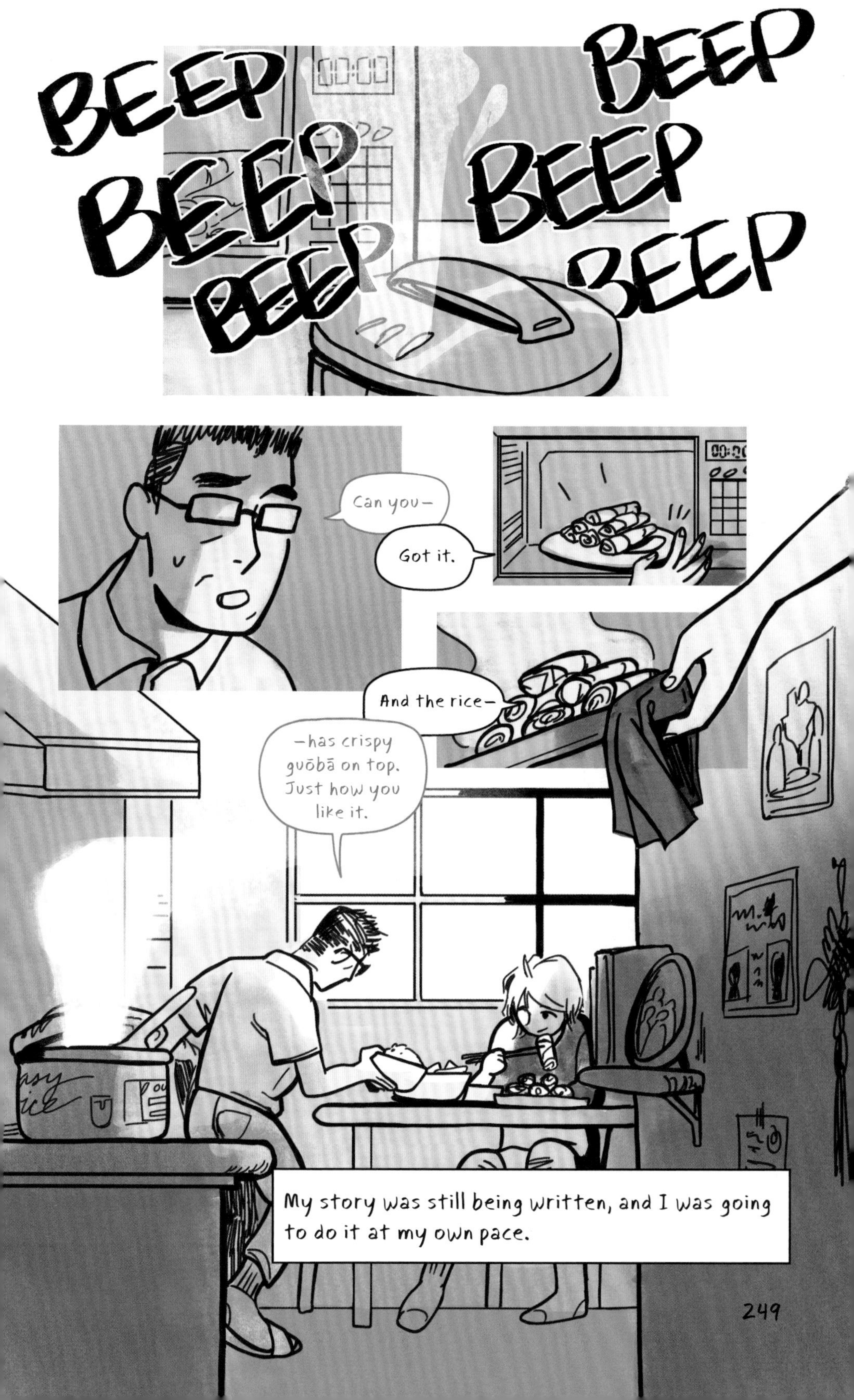
BEEP
BEEP
BEEP
BEEP
BEEP
BEEP
Can you—
Got it.
And the rice—
—has crispy guōbā on top. Just how you like it.
My story was still being written, and I was going to do it at my own pace.

CHAPTER 17
The Wuhan I Love

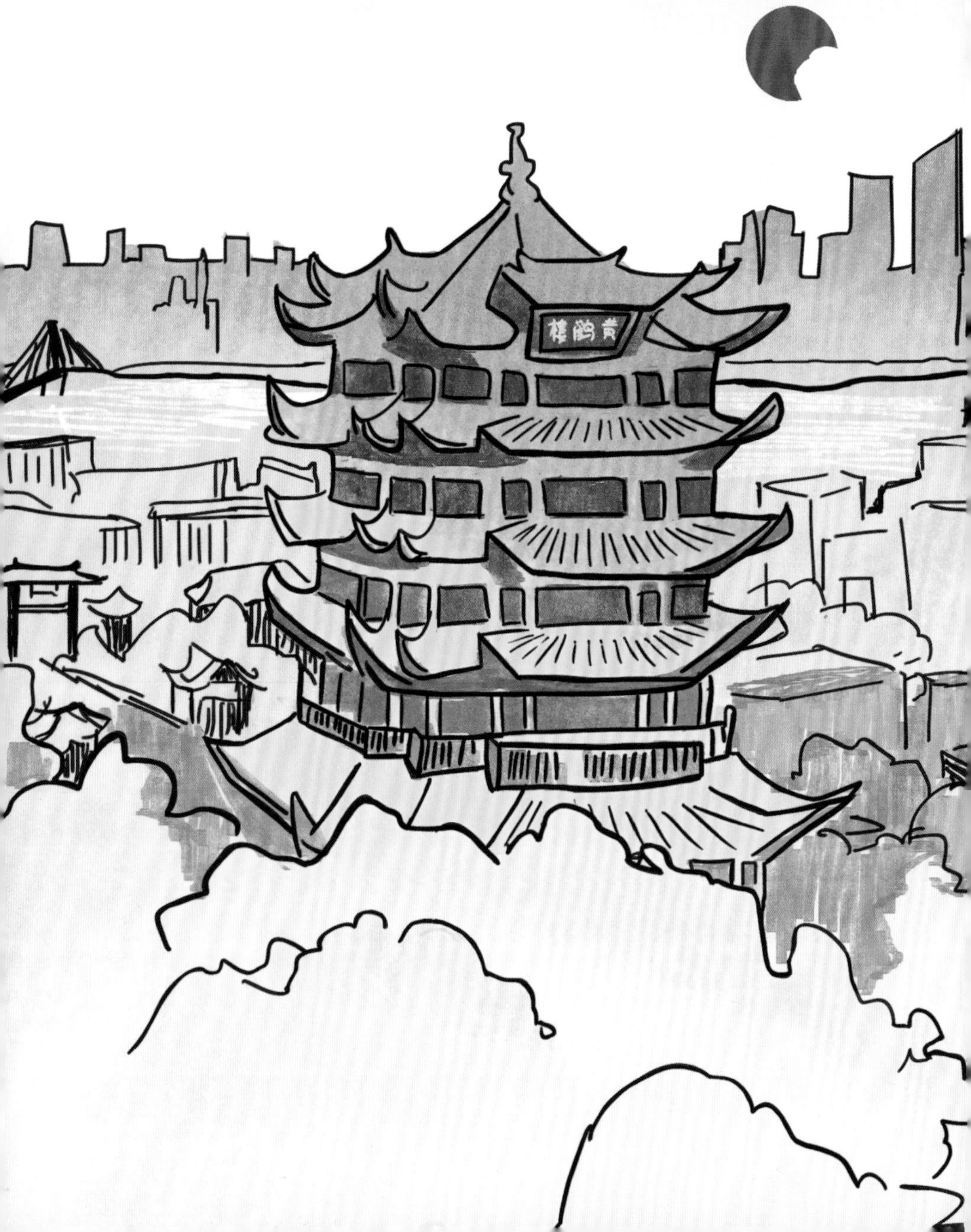
黄鹤楼

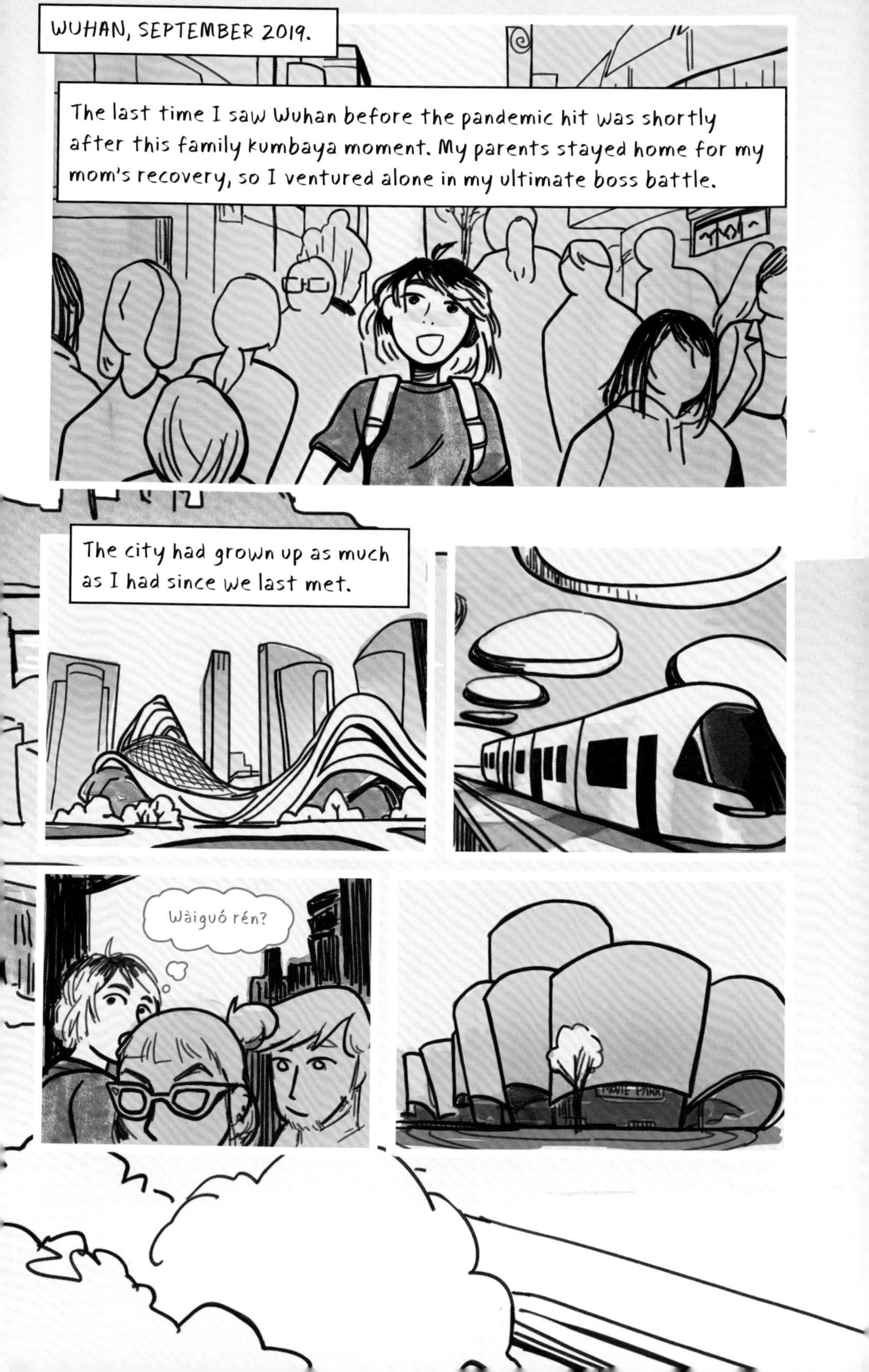
WUHAN, SEPTEMBER 2019.
The last time I saw Wuhan before the pandemic hit was shortly after this family kumbaya moment. My parents stayed home for my mom's recovery, so I ventured alone in my ultimate boss battle.
The city had grown up as much as I had since we last met.
Wàiguó rén?

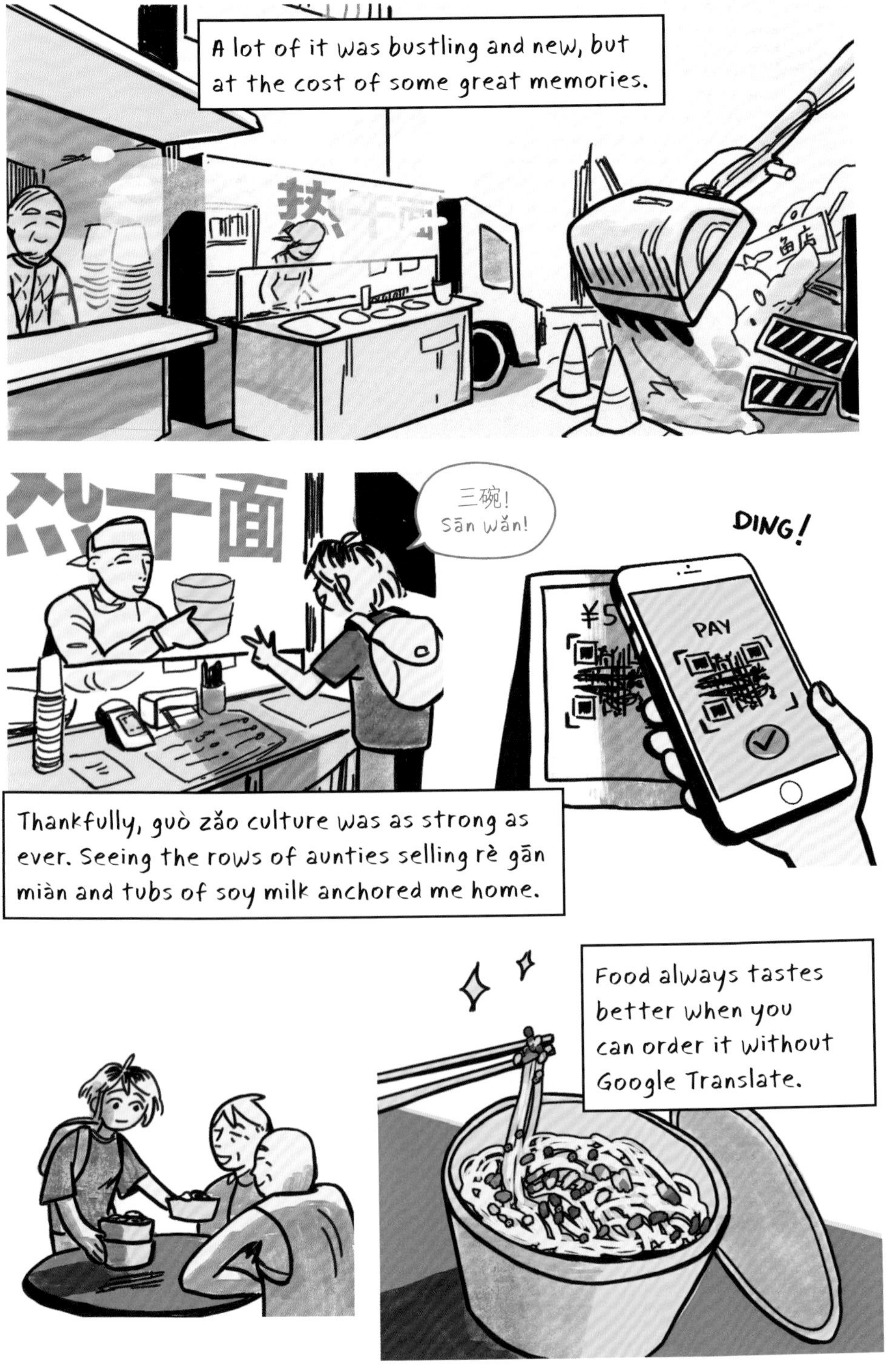
A lot of it was bustling and new, but at the cost of some great memories.
三碗!
Sān wǎn!
DING!
¥5
PAY
Thankfully, guò zǎo culture was as strong as ever. Seeing the rows of aunties selling rè gān miàn and tubs of soy milk anchored me home.
Food always tastes better when you can order it without Google Translate.

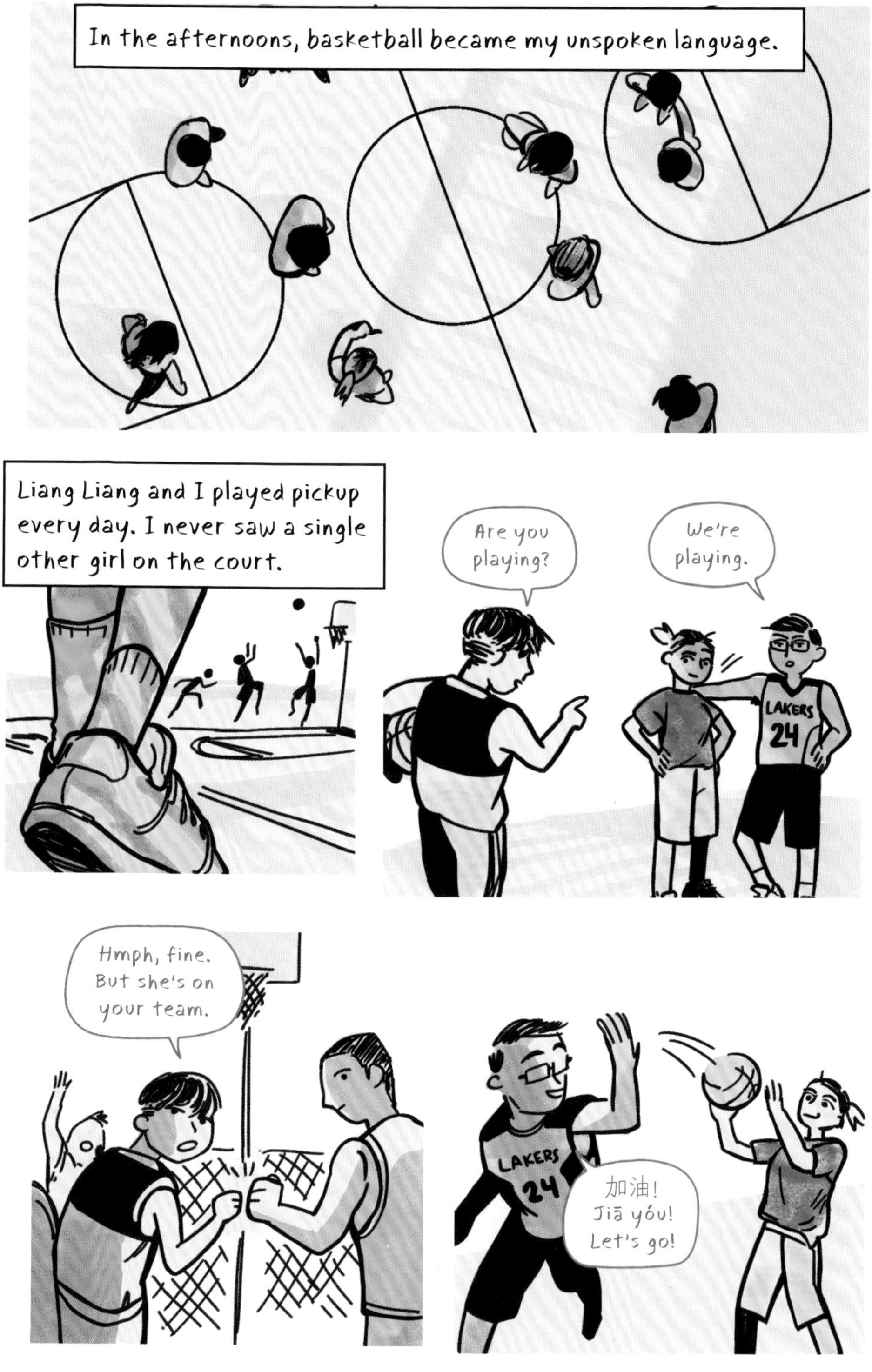
In the afternoons, basketball became my unspoken language.
Liang Liang and I played pickup every day. I never saw a single other girl on the court.
Are you playing?
We're playing.
Hmph, fine. But she's on your team.
LAKERS 24
加油! Jiā yóu! Let's go!

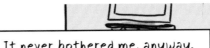
It never bothered me, anyway.

WHOOSH

It was refreshing, feeling the leather grip on my fingers again.

The clink of the chain net when a ball dropped cleanly through.

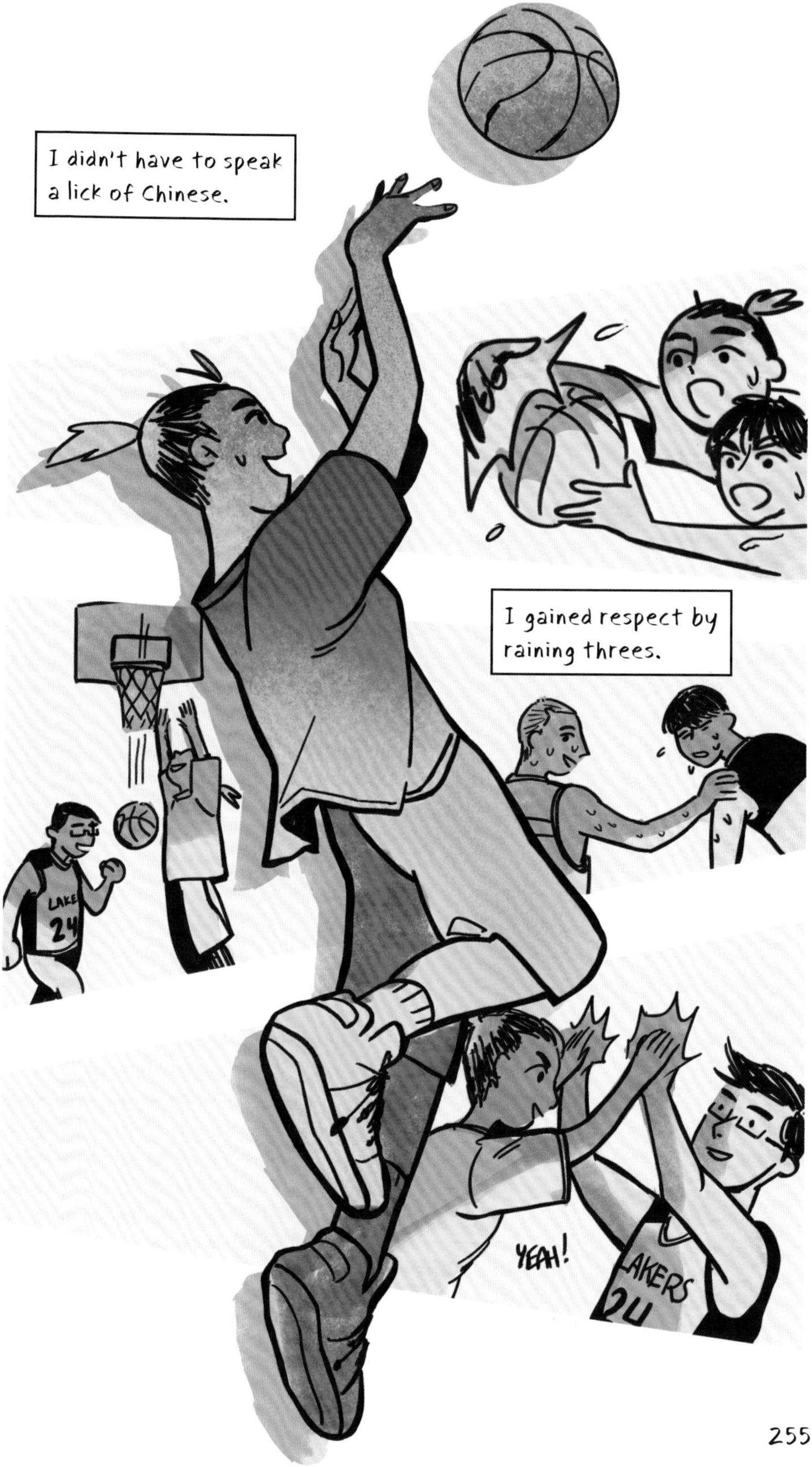
I didn't have to speak a lick of Chinese.
I gained respect by raining threes.
LAKE 24
YEAH!
LAKERS 24

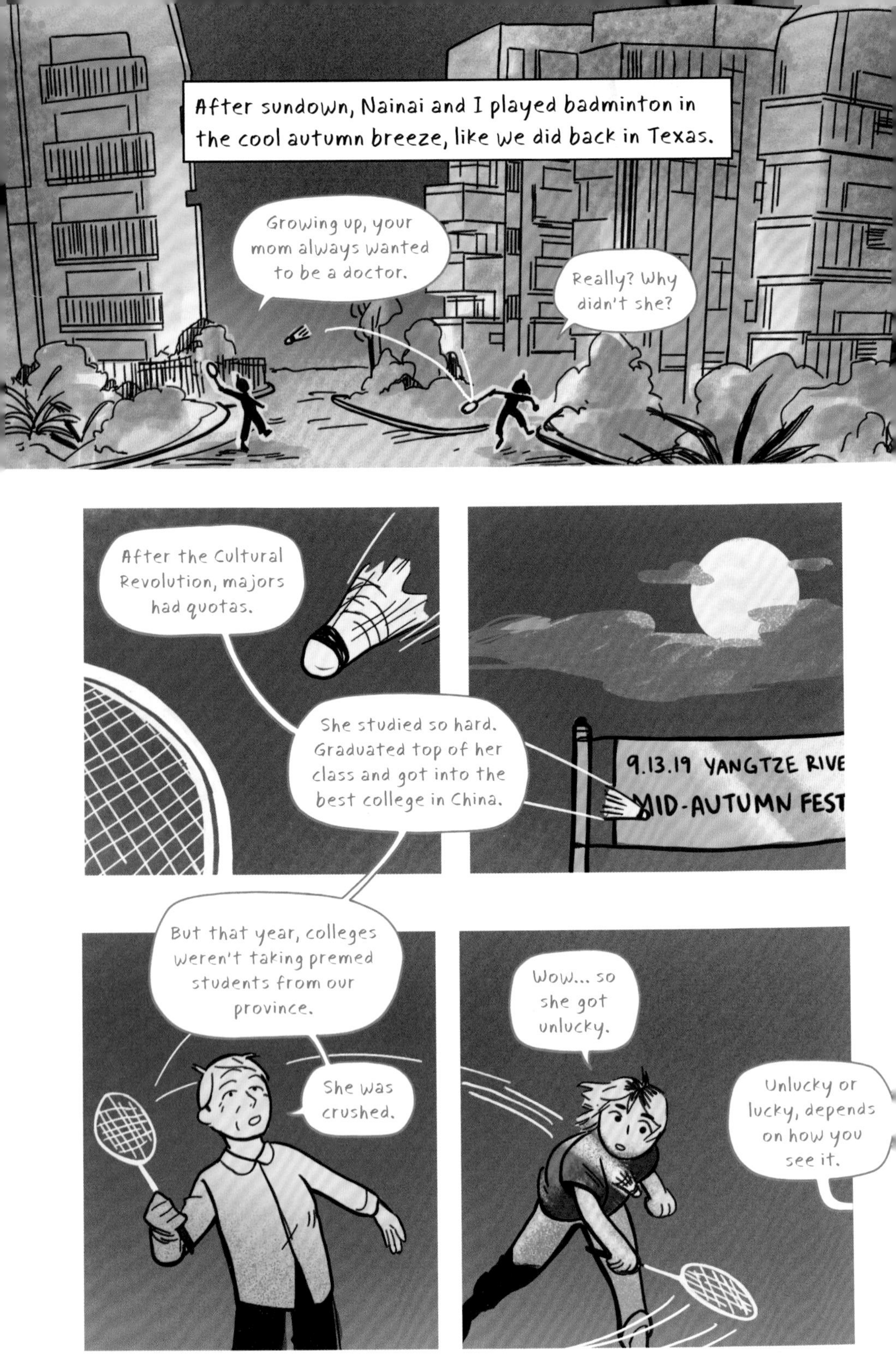
After sundown, Nainai and I played badminton in the cool autumn breeze, like we did back in Texas.
Growing up, your mom always wanted to be a doctor.
Really? Why didn't she?
After the Cultural Revolution, majors had quotas.
She studied so hard. Graduated top of her class and got into the best college in China.
9.13.19 YANGTZE RIVE
MID-AUTUMN FEST
But that year, colleges weren't taking premed students from our province.
She was crushed.
Wow... so she got unlucky.
Unlucky or lucky, depends on how you see it.

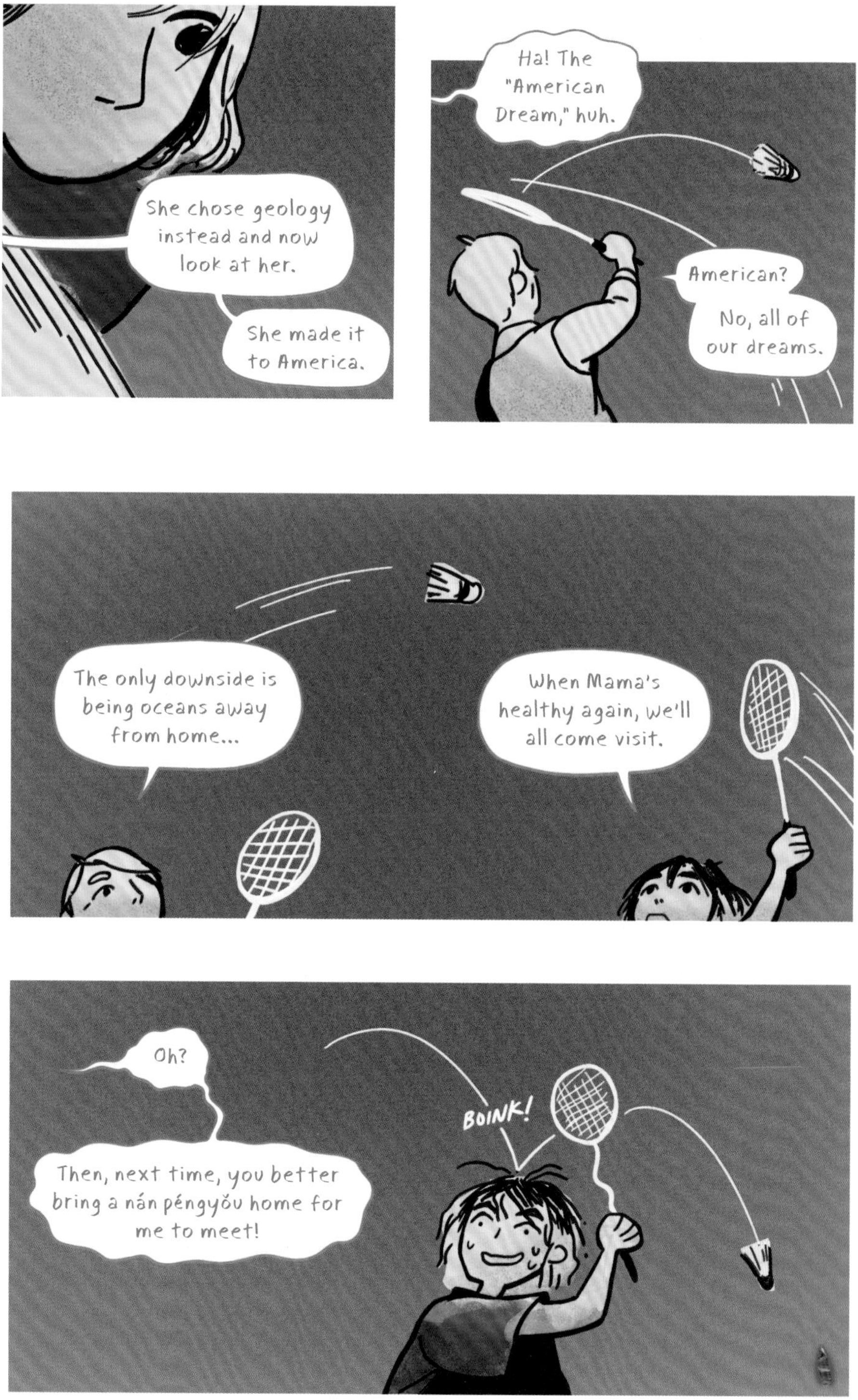
She chose geology instead and now look at her.
She made it to America.
Ha! The "American Dream," huh.
American?
No, all of our dreams.
The only downside is being oceans away from home...
When Mama's healthy again, we'll all come visit.
Oh?
Then, next time, you better bring a nán péngyǒu home for me to meet!
BOINK!

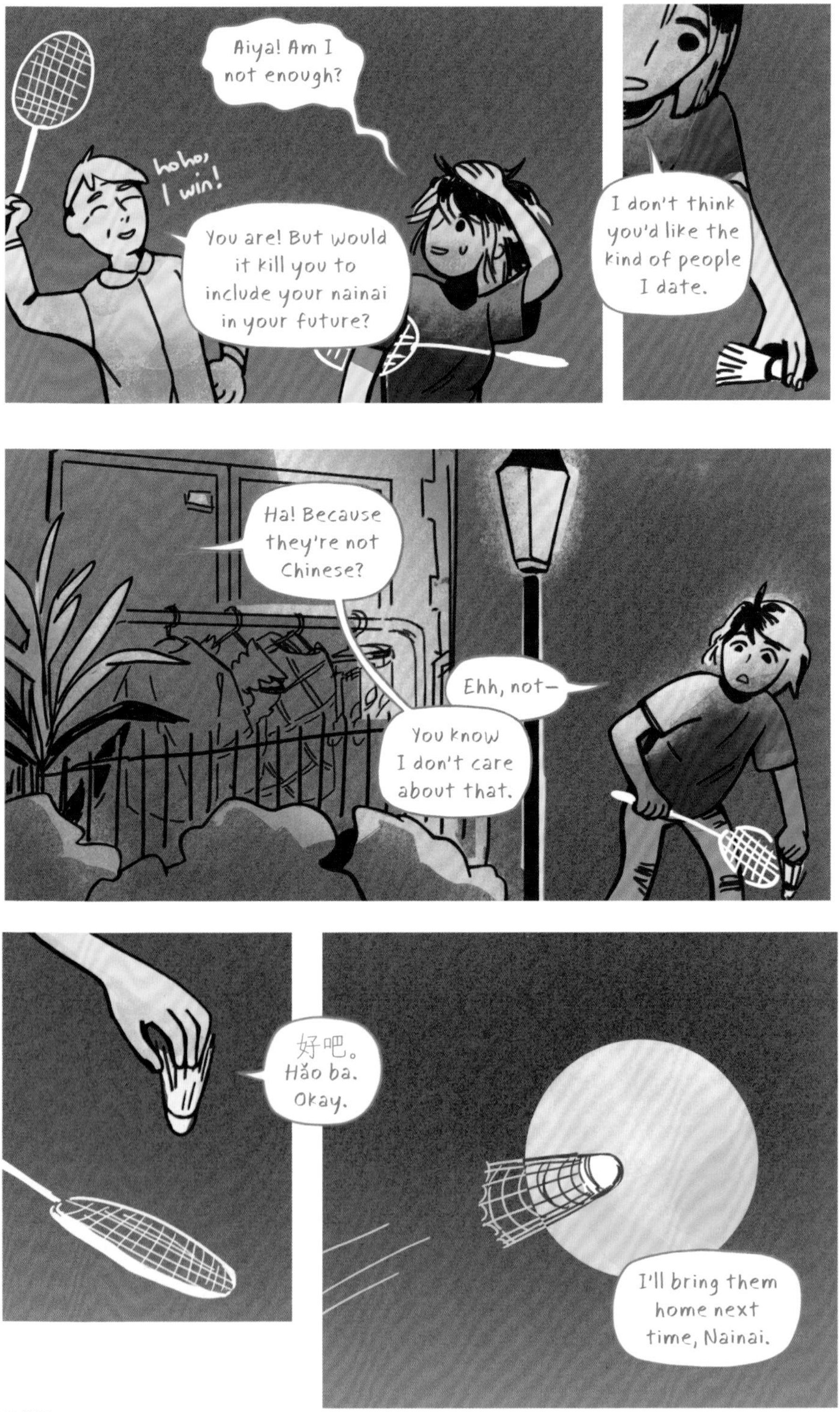
Aiya! Am I not enough?
ho ho, I win!
You are! But would it kill you to include your nainai in your future?
I don't think you'd like the kind of people I date.
Ha! Because they're not Chinese?
Ehh, not—
You know I don't care about that.
好吧。
Hǎo ba.
Okay.
I'll bring them home next time, Nainai.

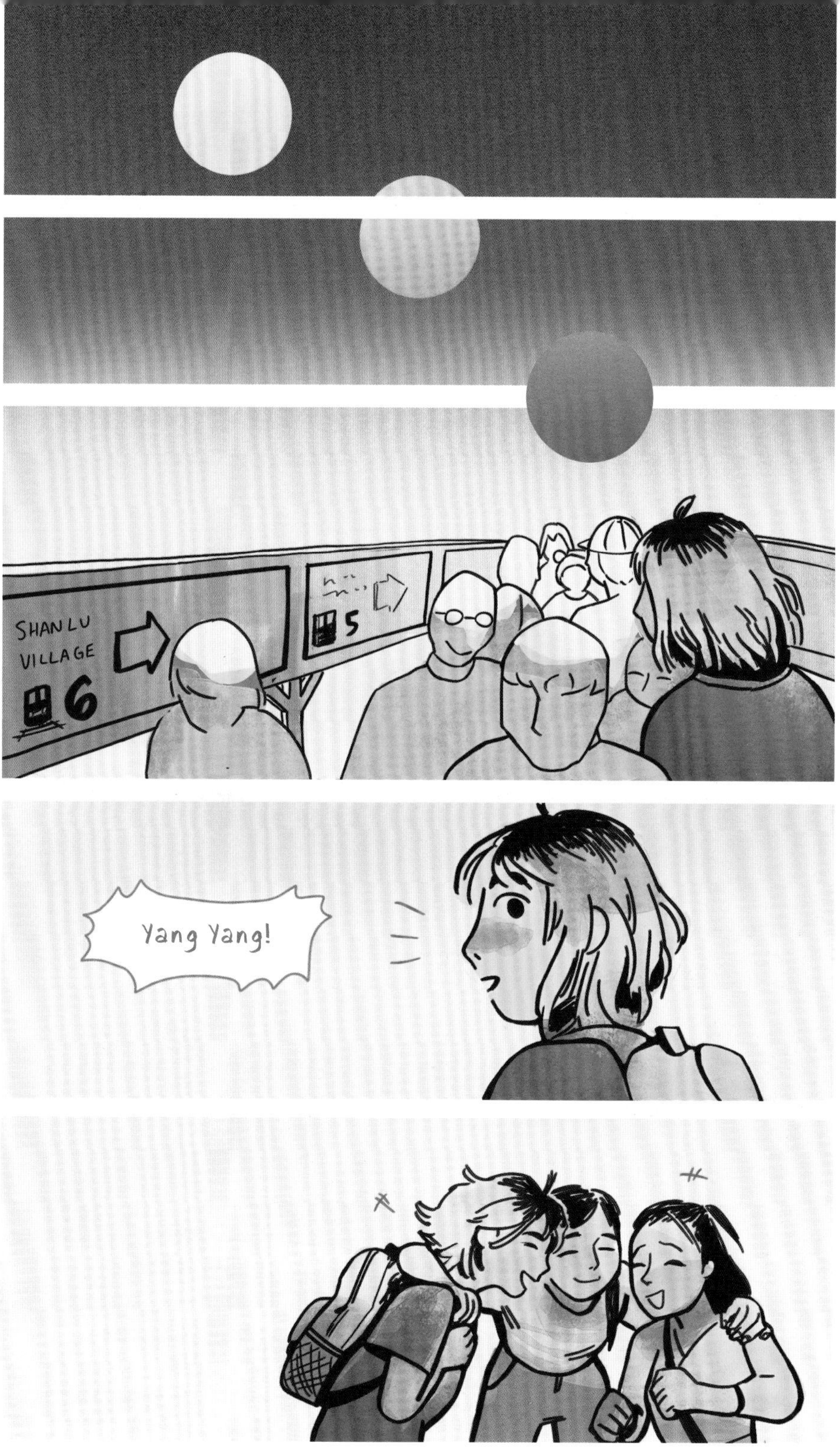
SHANLU VILLAGE
6
5
Yang Yang!

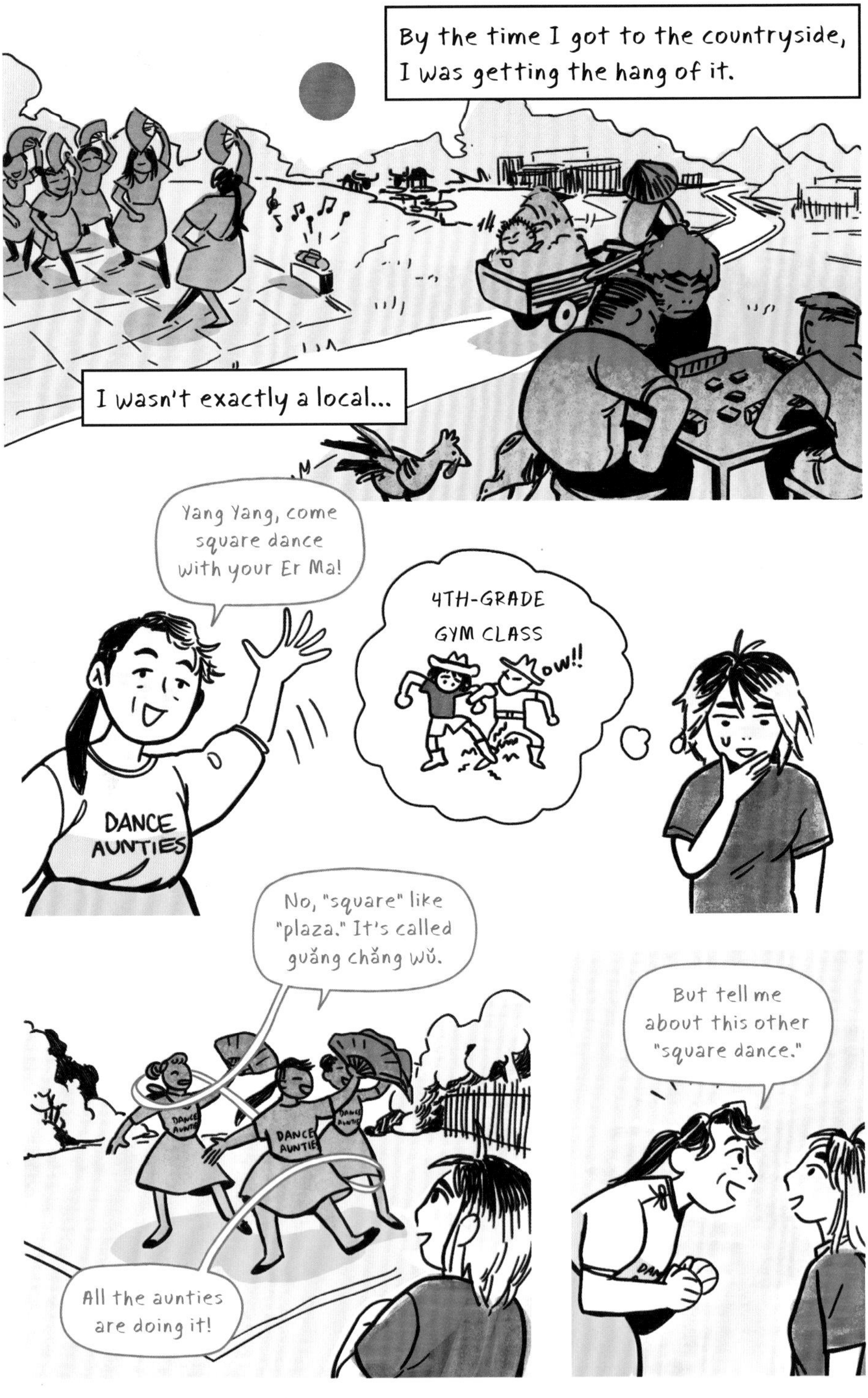
By the time I got to the countryside, I was getting the hang of it.
I wasn't exactly a local...
Yang Yang, come square dance with your Er Ma!
DANCE AUNTIES
4TH-GRADE GYM CLASS
OW!!
No, "square" like "plaza." It's called guǎng chǎng wǔ.
DANCE AUNTIES
All the aunties are doing it!
But tell me about this other "square dance."

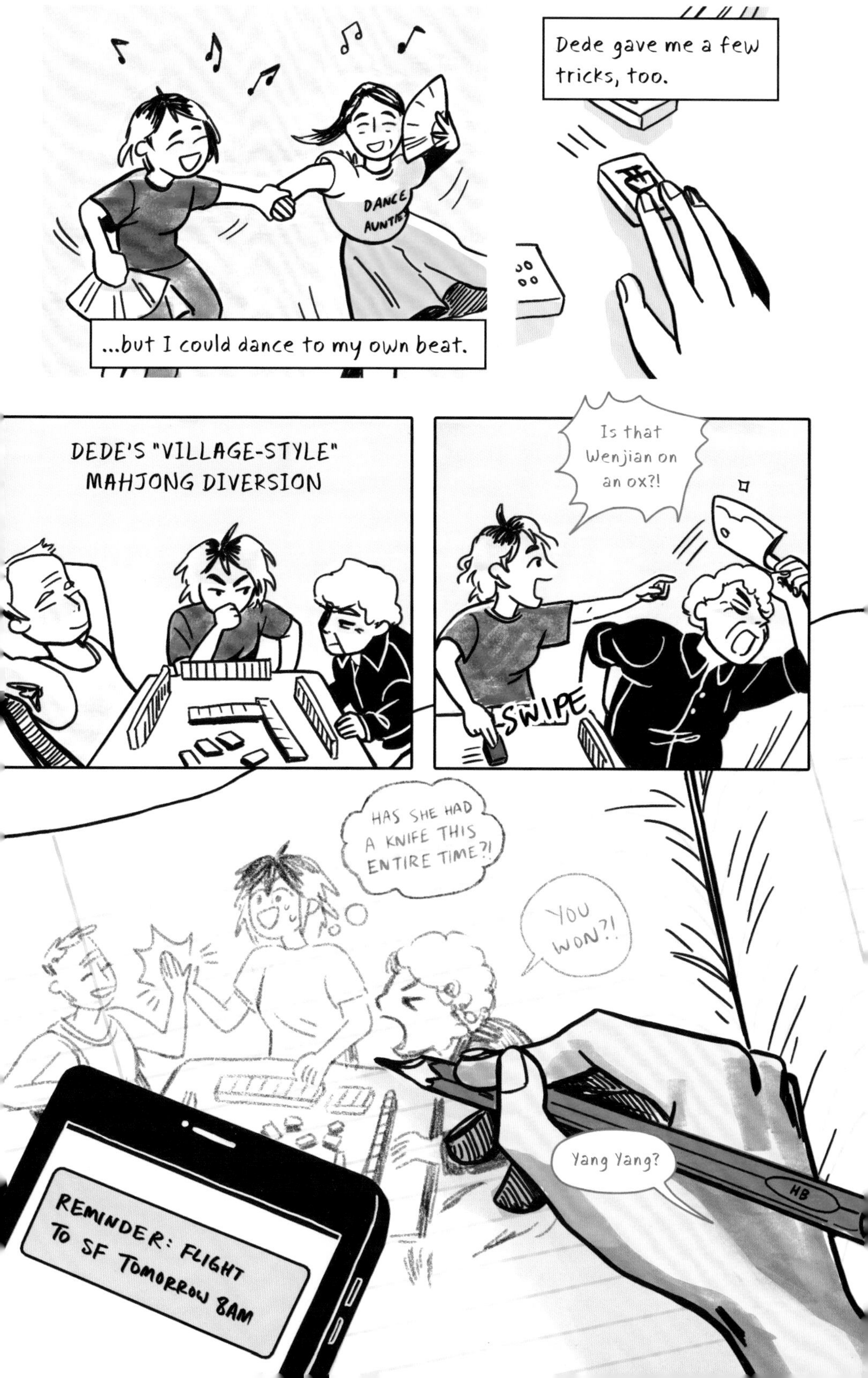
...but I could dance to my own beat.
DANCE AUNTIES
Dede gave me a few tricks, too.
DEDE'S "VILLAGE-STYLE" MAHJONG DIVERSION
Is that Wenjian on an ox?!
SWIPE
HAS SHE HAD A KNIFE THIS ENTIRE TIME?!
YOU WON?!
Yang Yang?
HB
REMINDER: FLIGHT TO SF TOMORROW 8AM

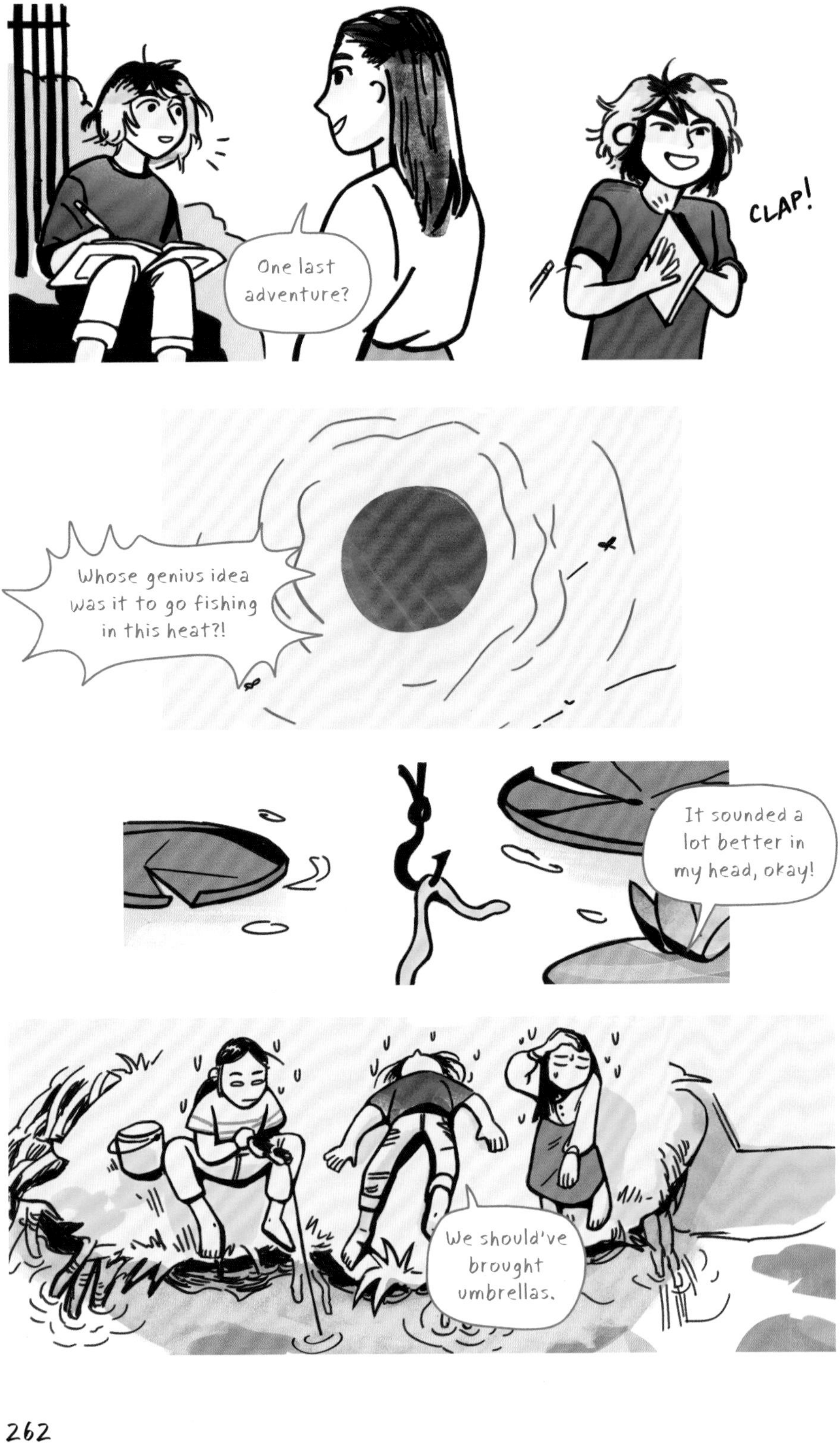
One last adventure?
CLAP!
Whose genius idea was it to go fishing in this heat?!
It sounded a lot better in my head, okay!
We should've brought umbrellas.

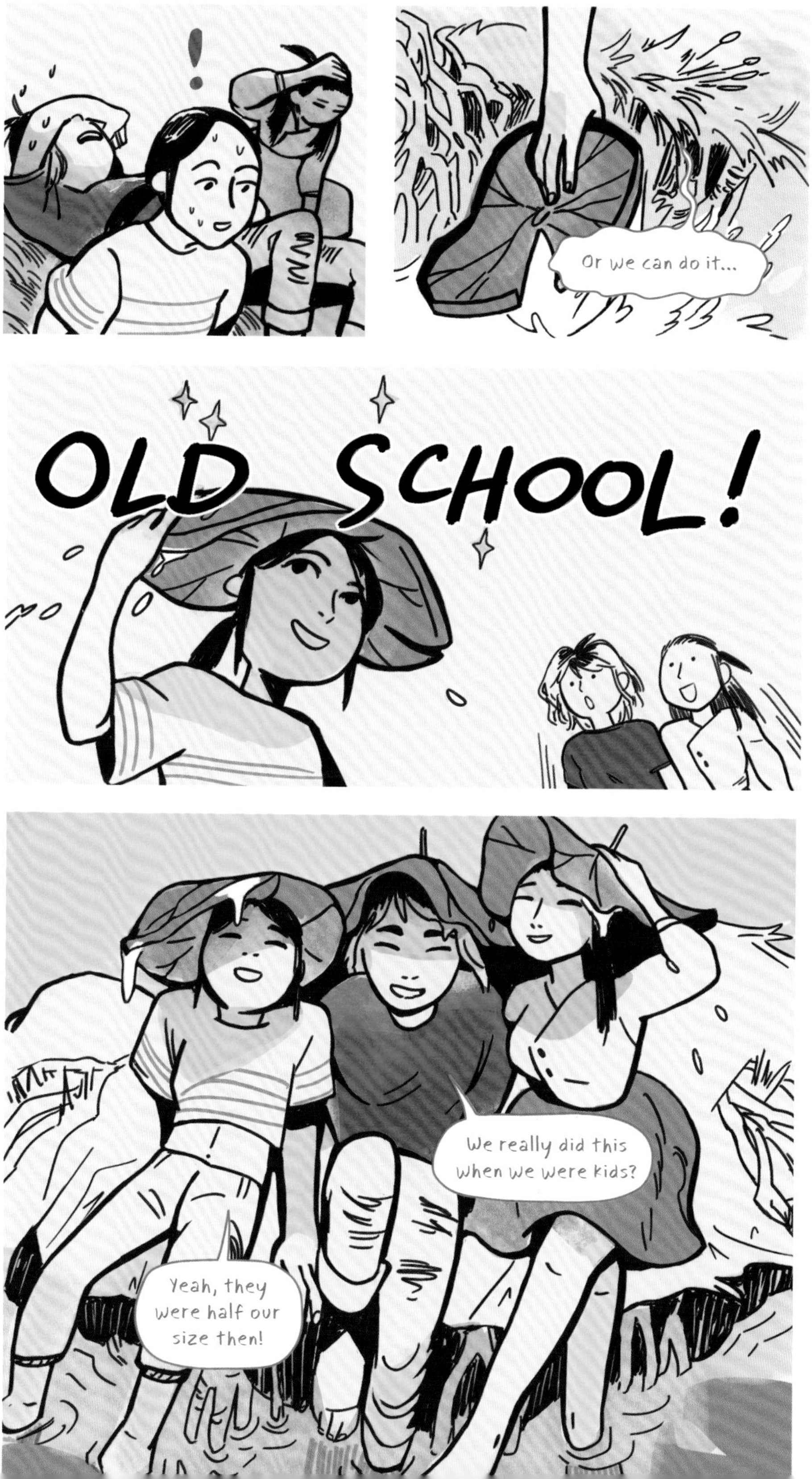
!
Or we can do it...
OLD SCHOOL!
We really did this when we were kids?
Yeah, they were half our size then!

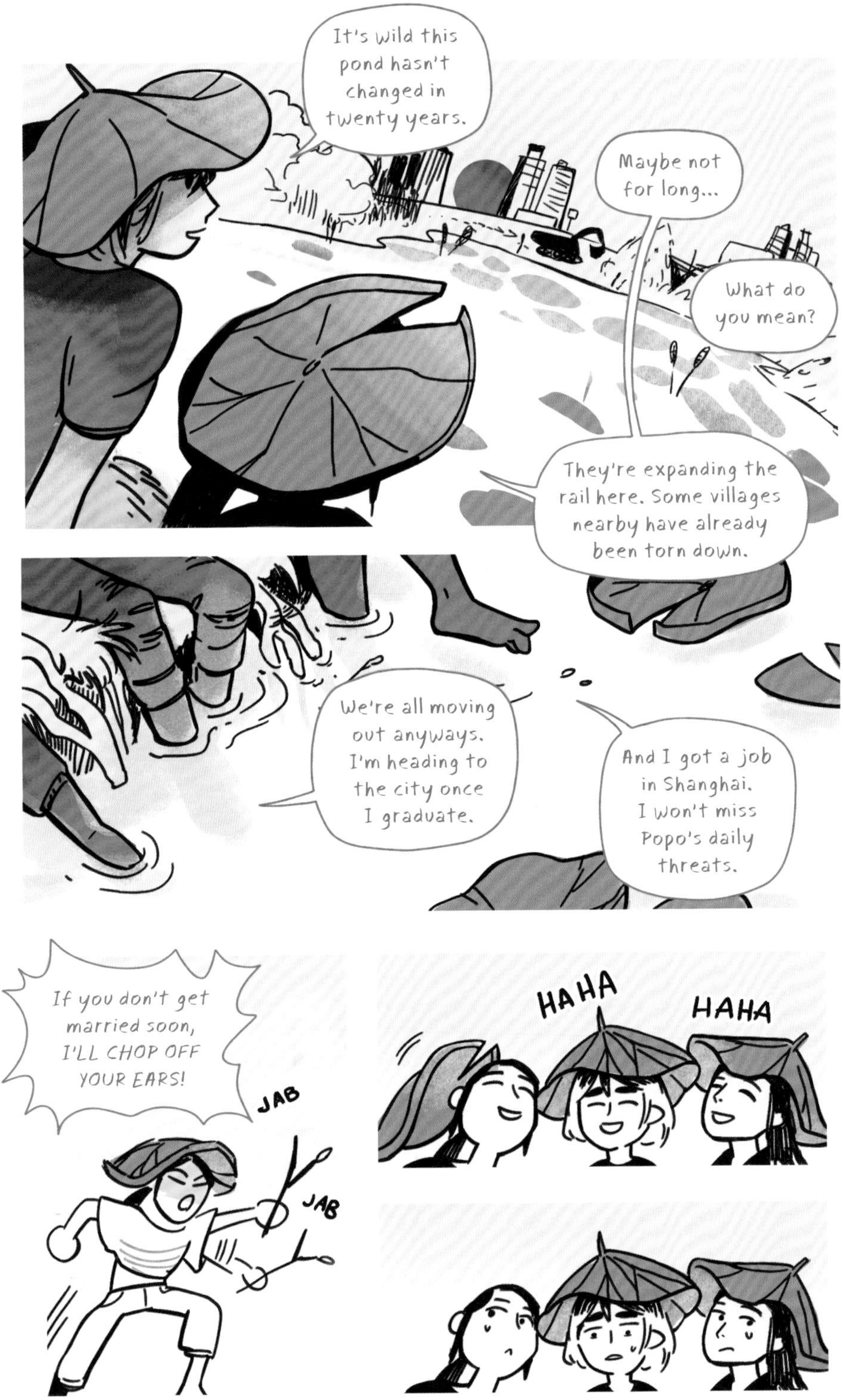
It's wild this pond hasn't changed in twenty years.
Maybe not for long...
What do you mean?
They're expanding the rail here. Some villages nearby have already been torn down.
We're all moving out anyways. I'm heading to the city once I graduate.
And I got a job in Shanghai. I won't miss Popo's daily threats.
If you don't get married soon, I'LL CHOP OFF YOUR EARS!
JAB
JAB
HAHA
HAHA

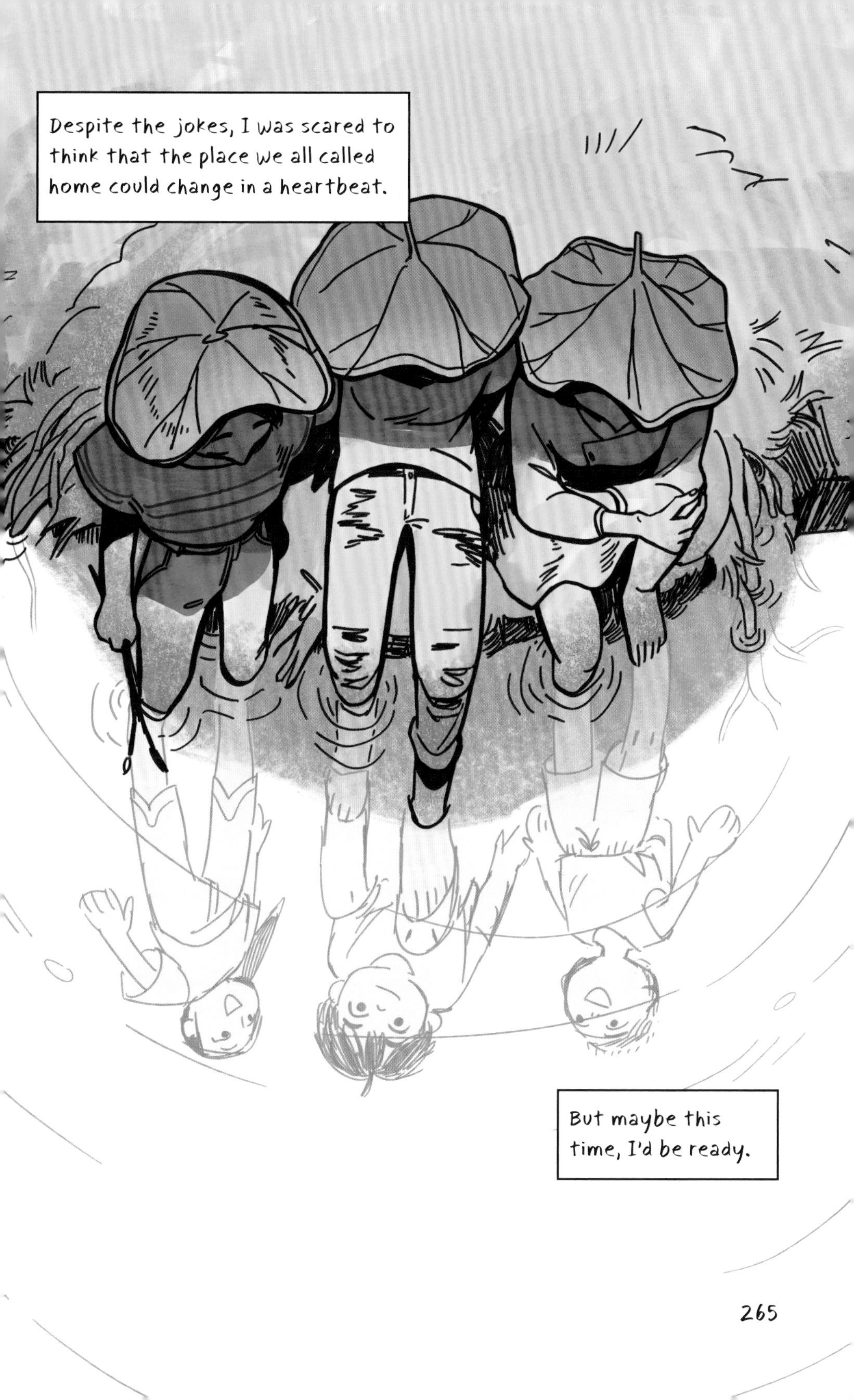
Despite the jokes, I was scared to think that the place we all called home could change in a heartbeat.
But maybe this time, I'd be ready.

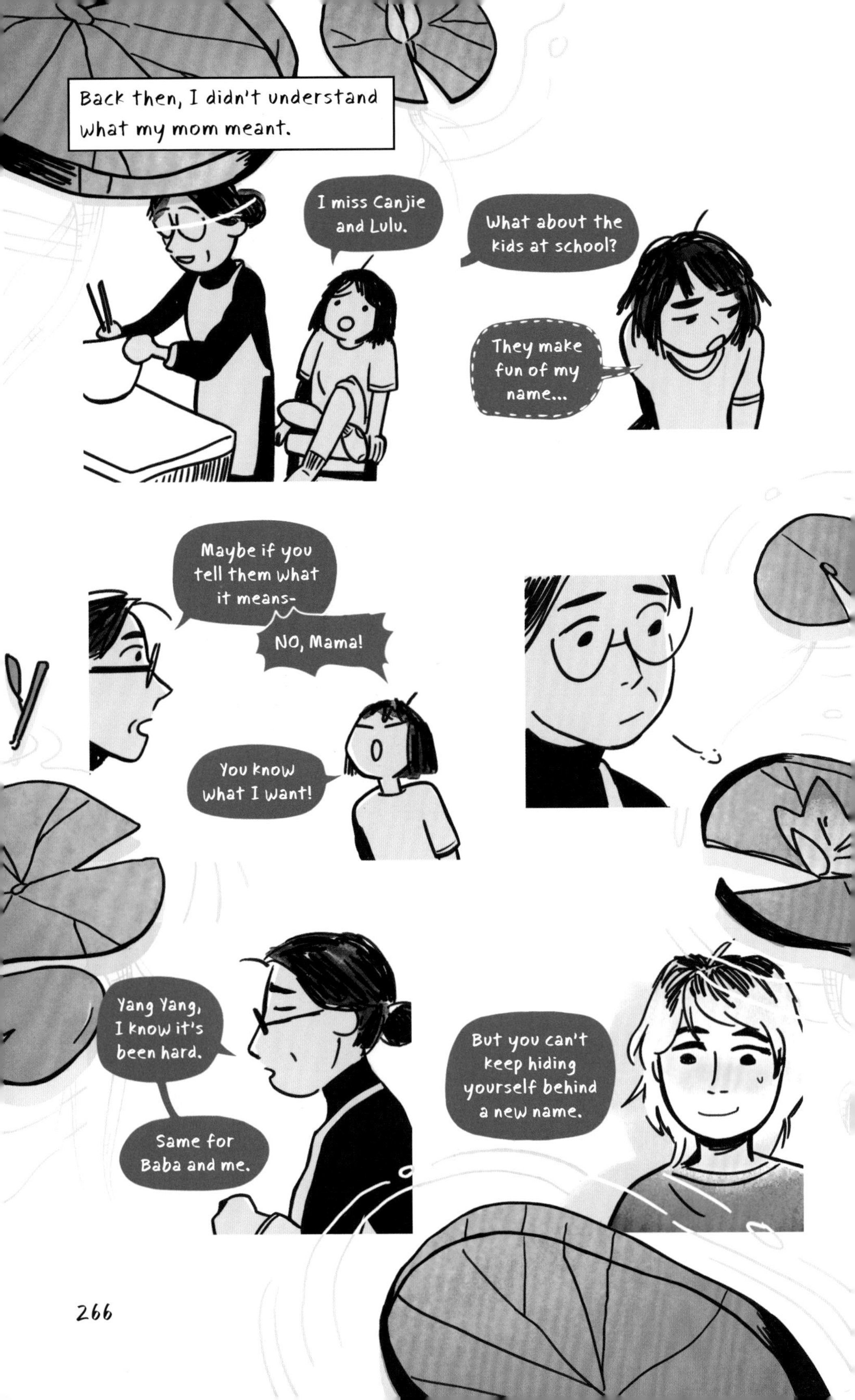
Back then, I didn't understand what my mom meant.
I miss Canjie and Lulu.
What about the kids at school?
They make fun of my name...
Maybe if you tell them what it means-
NO, Mama!
You know what I want!
Yang Yang, I know it's been hard.
Same for Baba and me.
But you can't keep hiding yourself behind a new name.

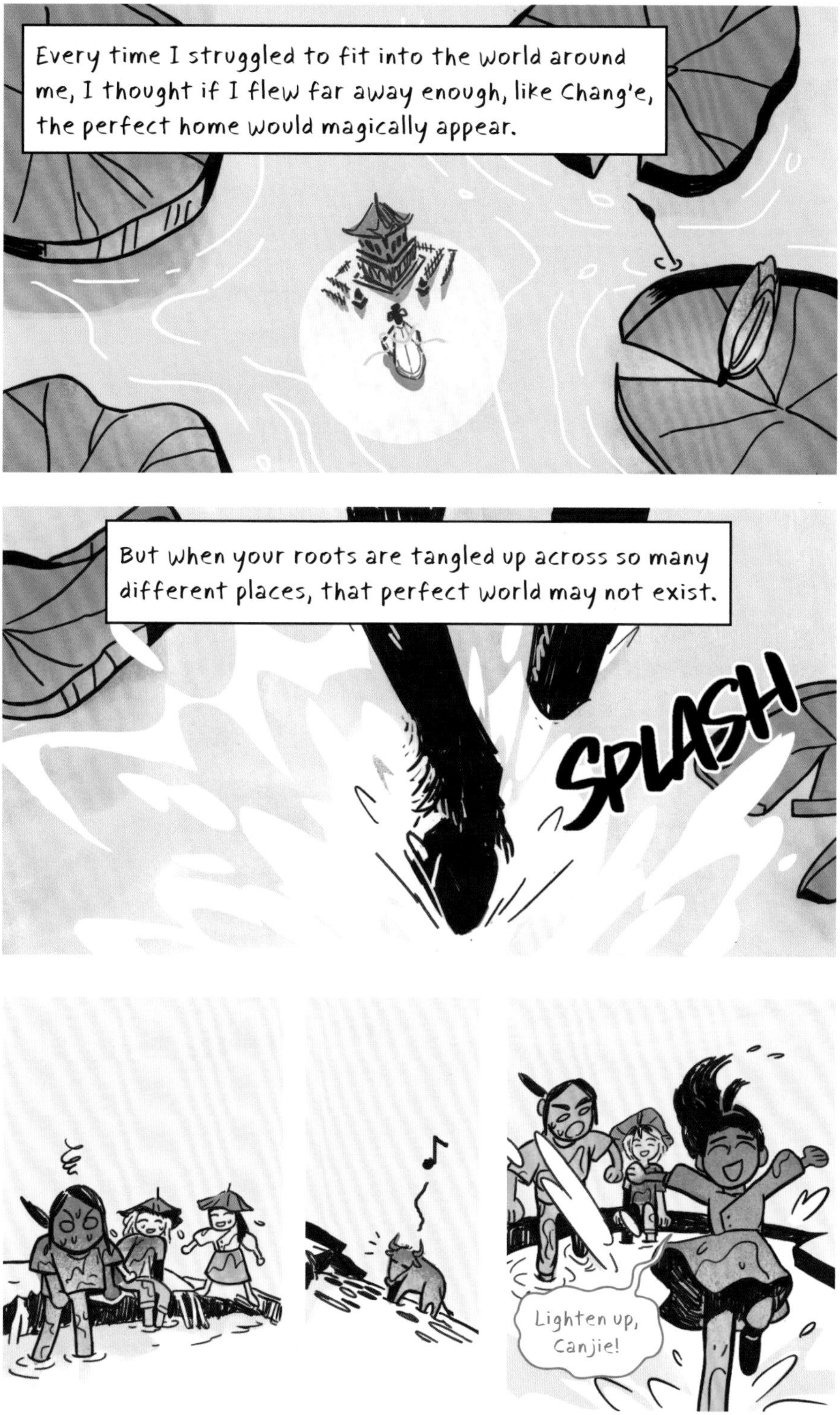
Every time I struggled to fit into the world around me, I thought if I flew far away enough, like Chang'e, the perfect home would magically appear.
But when your roots are tangled up across so many different places, that perfect world may not exist.
SPLASH
Lighten up, Canjie!

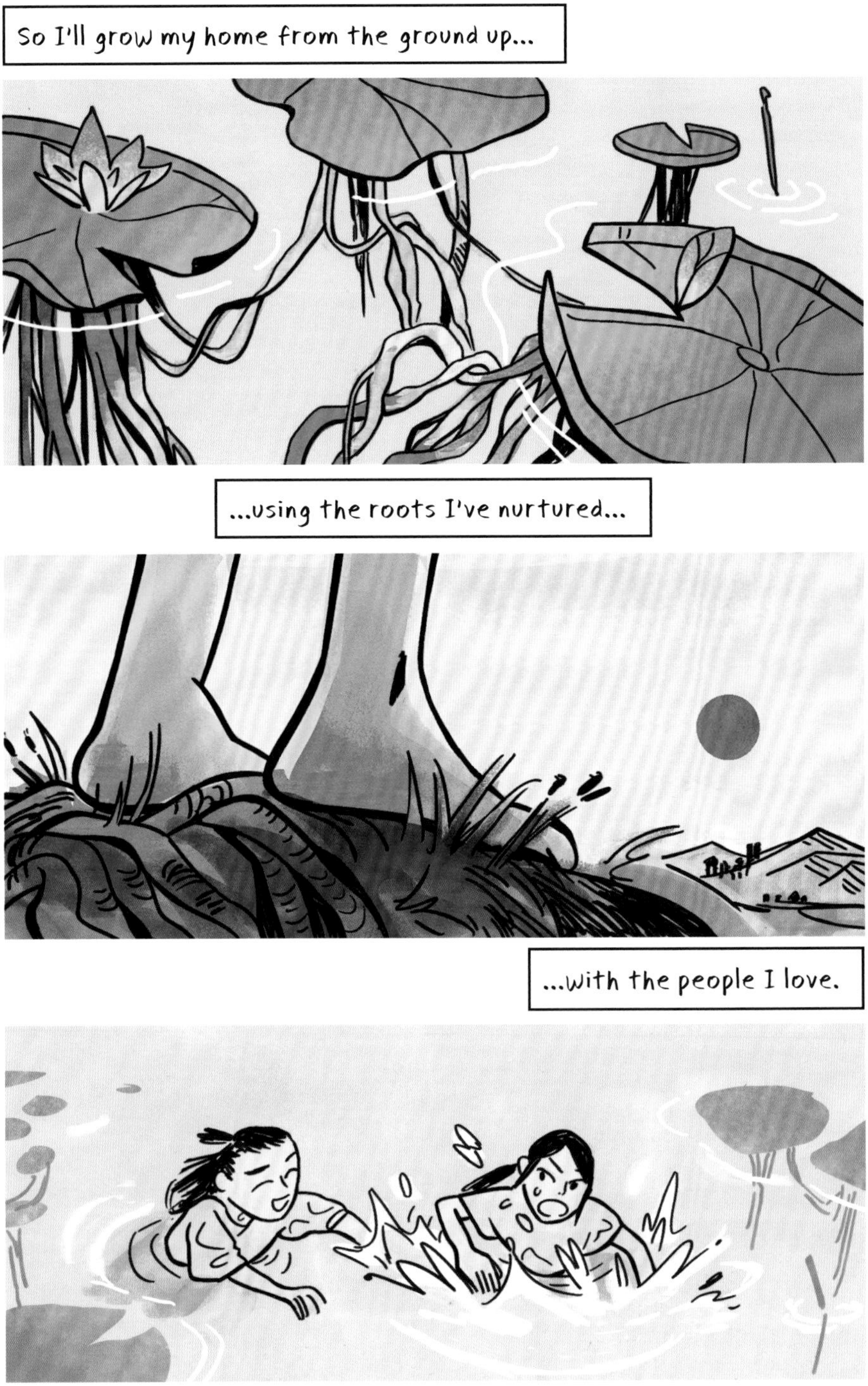
So I'll grow my home from the ground up...
...using the roots I've nurtured...
...with the people I love.

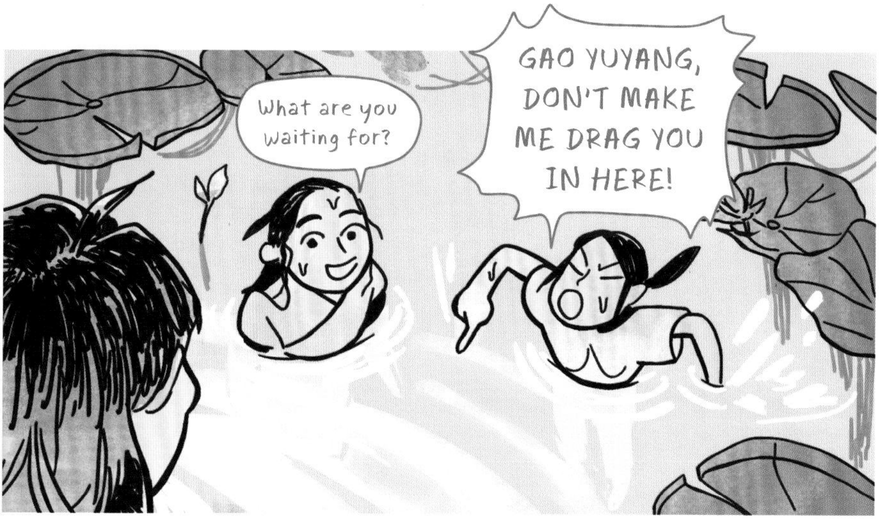
What are you waiting for?
GAO YUYANG, DON'T MAKE ME DRAG YOU IN HERE!

There's still so much about myself I've yet to explore.

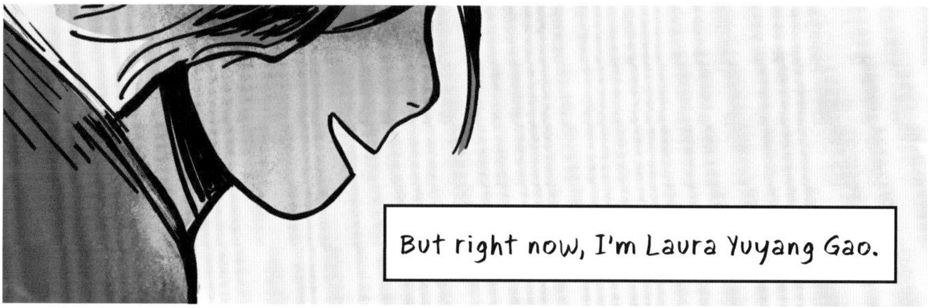
But right now, I'm Laura Yuyang Gao.

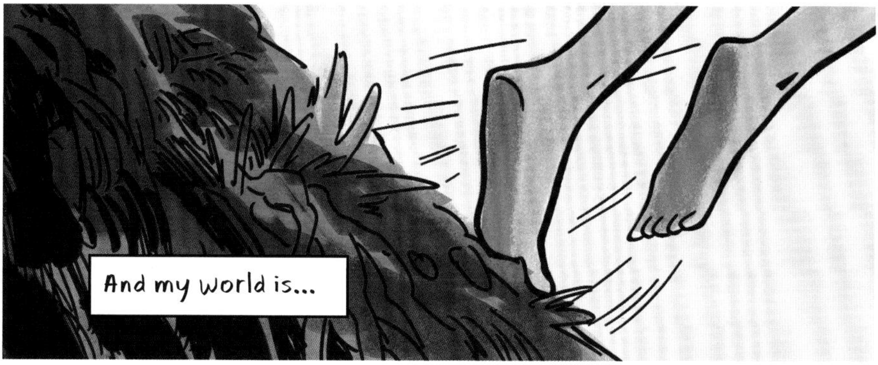
And my world is...

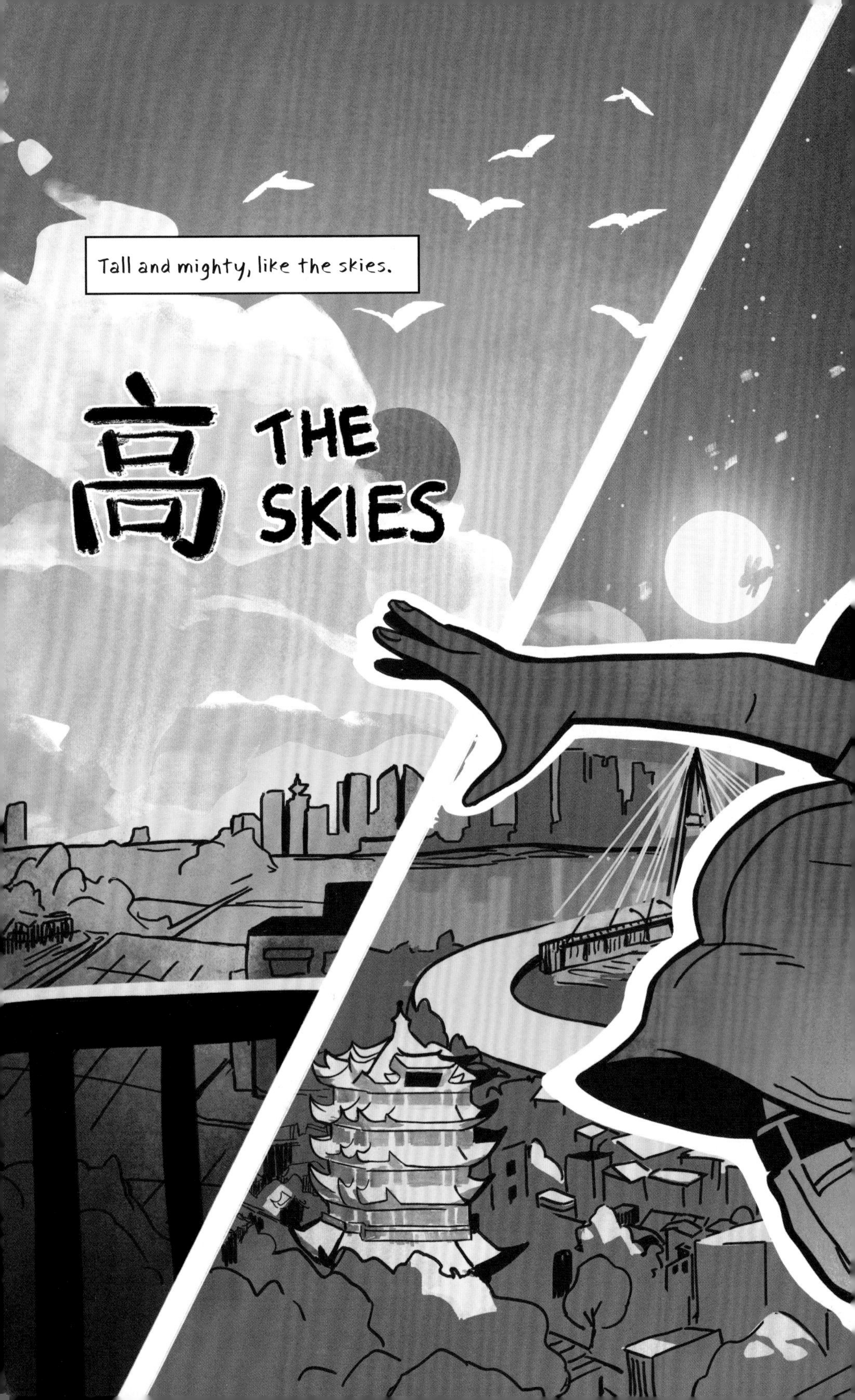

Tall and mighty, like the skies.
高 THE SKIES

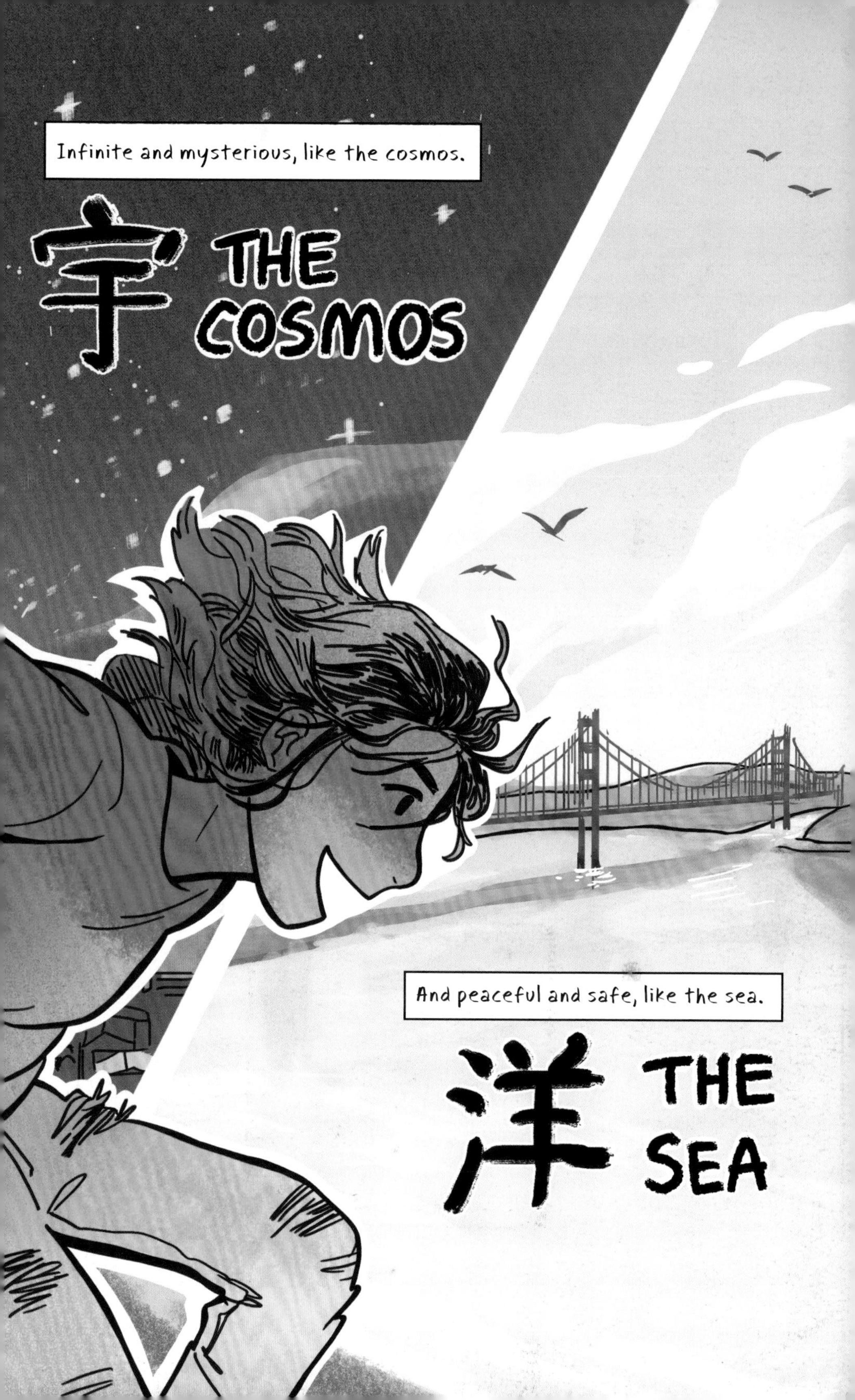
Infinite and mysterious, like the cosmos.
宇 THE COSMOS
And peaceful and safe, like the sea.
洋 THE SEA

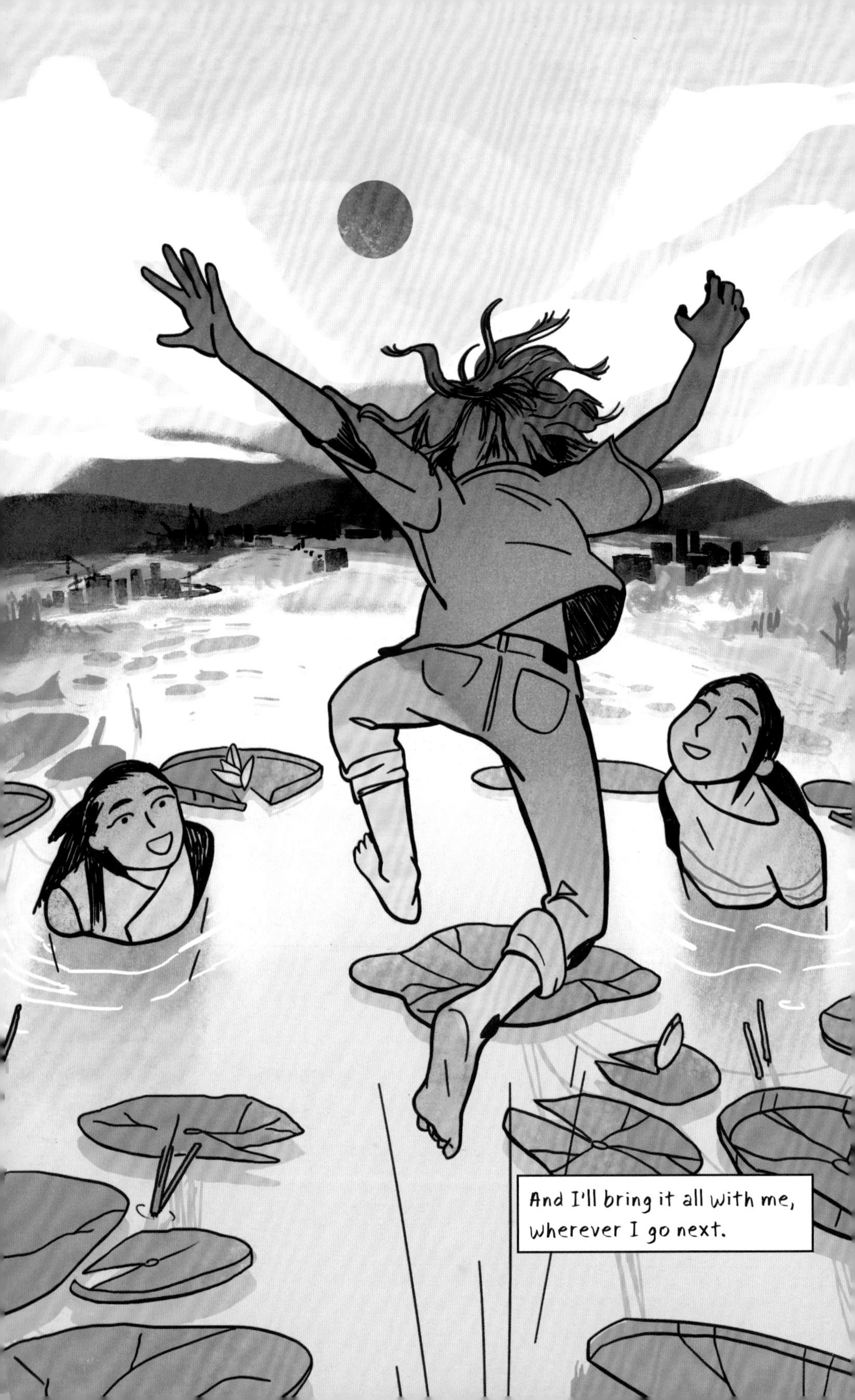
And I'll bring it all with me, wherever I go next.